Original Idea
Amélie Fléchais & Jonathan Garnier

Written by
Jonathan Garnier

Art by
Amélie Fléchais

Original Idea AMÉLIE FLÉCHAIS & JONATHAN GARNIER
Written by JONATHAN GARNIER
Art by AMÉLIE FLÉCHAIS
Translation by IVANKA HAHNENBERGER
Letters by VIBRANT STUDIOS

Special thanks to Julia Skorcz and Ivanka Hahnenberger.

FOR ABLAZE

managing editor RICH YOUNG
editor KEVIN KETNER
associate editor AMY JACKSON
designers JULIA STEZOVSKY & RODOLFO MURAGUCHI

Shepherdess Warriors Volume 1
Bergères guerrières – Tome 01: La Relève & Bergères guerrières T02 : La Menace © Editions Glénat
2017-2018 by J. Garnier & A. Fléchais – ALL RIGHTS RESERVED. ABLAZE TM & © 2024 ABLAZE
LLC. All rights reserved. All name, characters, events, and locales in this publication are entirely
fictional. Any resemblance to actual persons (living or dead), events or places, without satiric intent
is coincidental. No portion of this book may be reproduced by any means (digital or print) without the
written permission of Ablaze Publishing except for review purposes. Printed in China. This book may
be purchased for educational, business, or promotional use in bulk. For sales information, advertising
opportunities or licensing, email: info@ablazepublishing.com

Publisher's Cataloging-in-Publication data

Names: Amélie Fléchais, Cover. Jonathan Garnier, Writer. Amélie Fléchais, Artist.
Title: Shepherdess Warriors 1 and 2
Description: Portland, OR: Ablaze Publishing, 2024.
Identifiers: ISBN: 978-1-68497-169-5
Subjects: LCSH Horror–Comic books, strips, etc. | Graphic novels. | BISAC COMICS & GRAPHIC NOVELS /
Fantasy, Action/Adventure
Classification: LCC PN6790.J33 .N5613 G36 2023 | DDC 741.5–dc23

ablazepub @AblazePub @AblazePub

www.ablaze.net

To find a comics shop in your area go to:
www.comicshoplocator.com

We would like to thank:

Our families and friends for their support.

Our first readers --Marietta, Harald, Mathias, Mona, Marius and Pablo-- for their constructive feedback.

Our friend Klapstok for lending us his name.

Jean-Claude Camano for his enthusiasm in discovering the project.
Nicolas Forsans and the Glenat team for their professionalism and sympathy.

Amelie created Les Bergeres Guerrieres during her participation in the "Cavalry" illustration revival initiated and published by Tarmasz.
We would therefore like to thank her in particular for having offered Amelie the fertile ground for the creation of these proud fighters!
To discover Tarmasz's superb work, it's here: http://tarmasz.tumblr.com/

Amelie & Jonathan

Part 1 - Succession

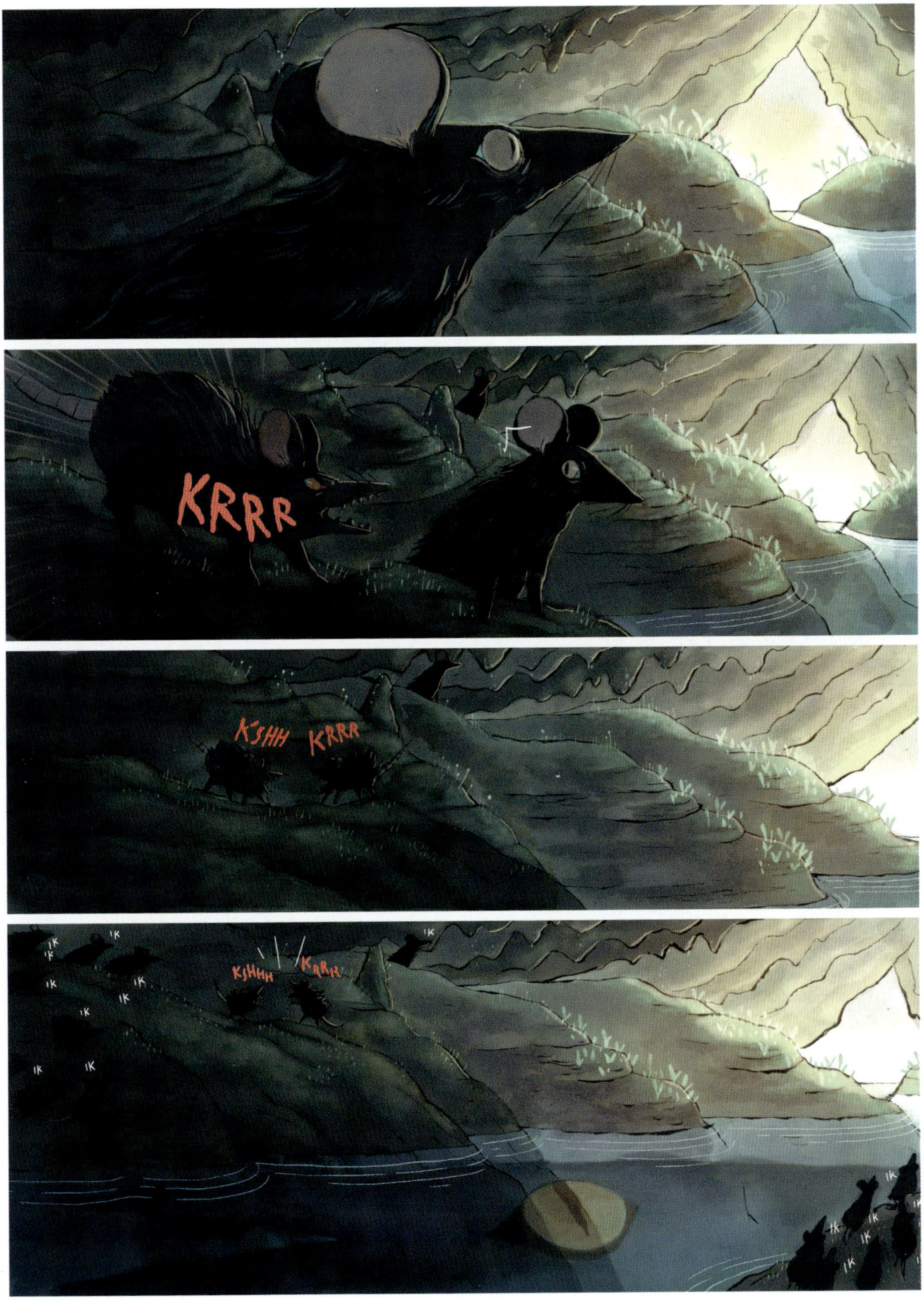
KRRR
K'SHH
KRRR
IK
IK
IK
IK
IK
IK
IK
IK
KSHHH
KRRH
IK
IK
IK
IK
IK
IK

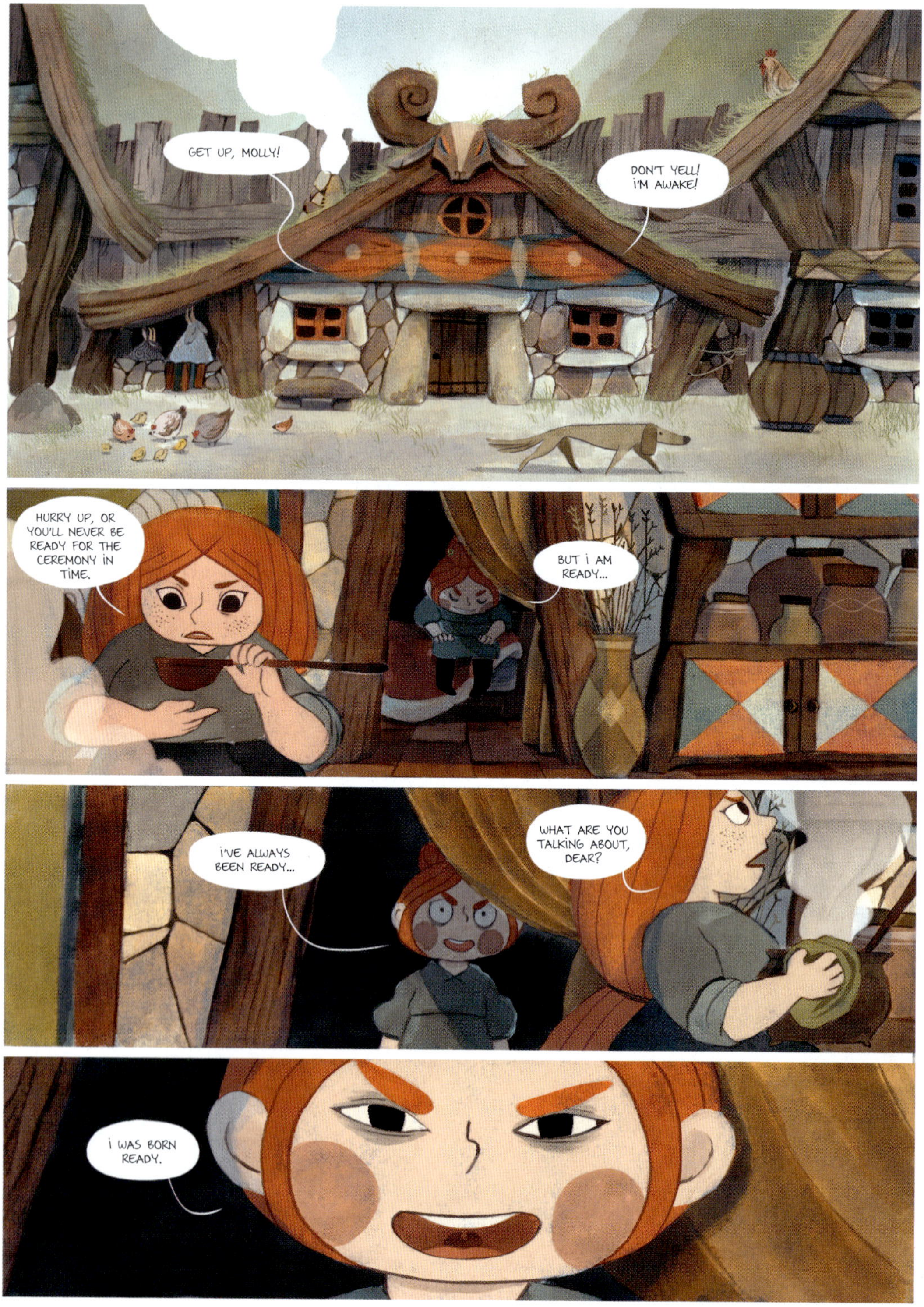
GET UP, MOLLY!
DON'T YELL! I'M AWAKE!
HURRY UP, OR YOU'LL NEVER BE READY FOR THE CEREMONY IN TIME.
BUT I AM READY...
I'VE ALWAYS BEEN READY...
WHAT ARE YOU TALKING ABOUT, DEAR?
I WAS BORN READY.

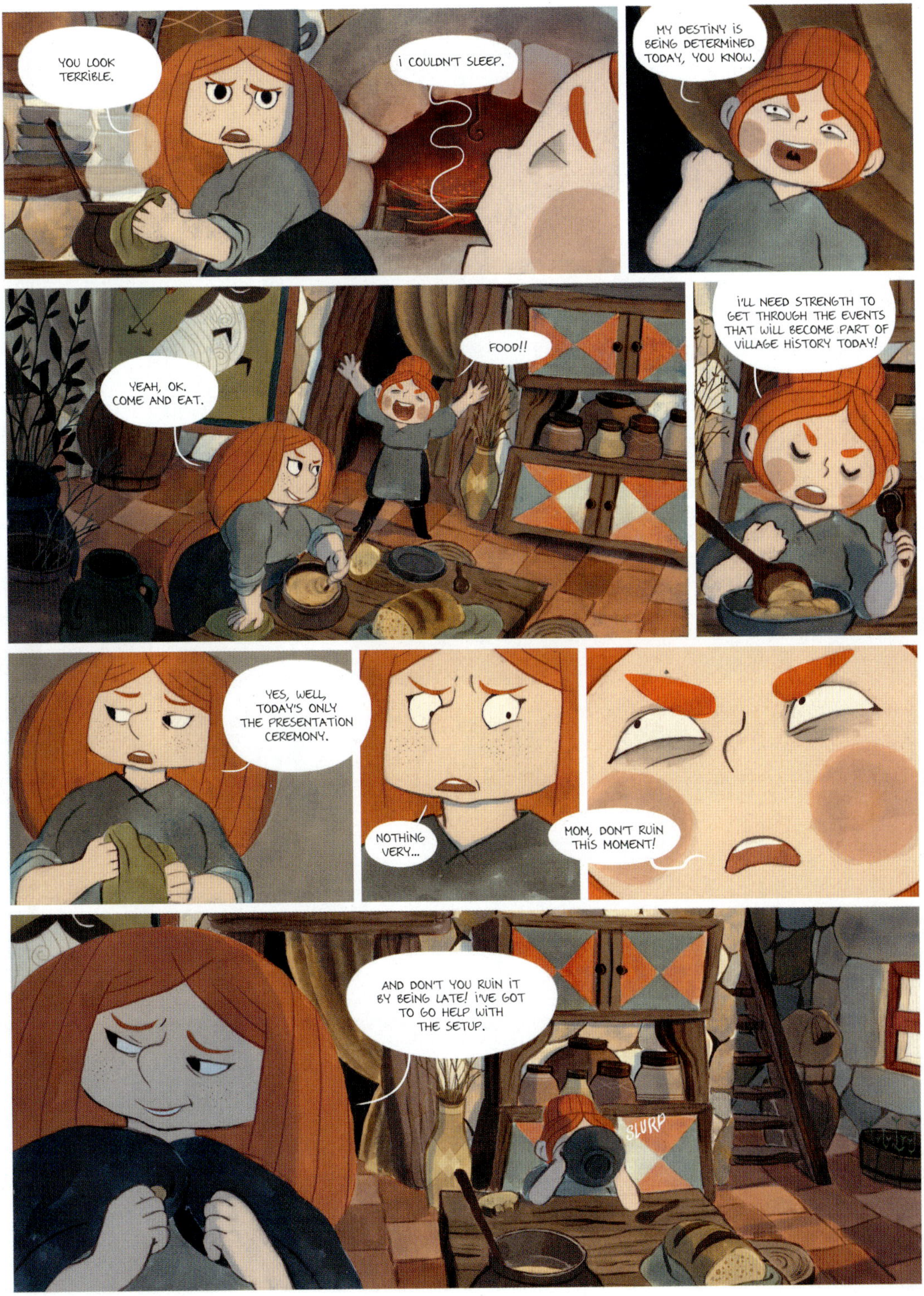

YOU LOOK TERRIBLE.
I COULDN'T SLEEP.
MY DESTINY IS BEING DETERMINED TODAY, YOU KNOW.
YEAH, OK. COME AND EAT.
FOOD!!
I'LL NEED STRENGTH TO GET THROUGH THE EVENTS THAT WILL BECOME PART OF VILLAGE HISTORY TODAY!
YES, WELL, TODAY'S ONLY THE PRESENTATION CEREMONY.
NOTHING VERY...
MOM, DON'T RUIN THIS MOMENT!
AND DON'T YOU RUIN IT BY BEING LATE! I'VE GOT TO GO HELP WITH THE SETUP.
SLURP

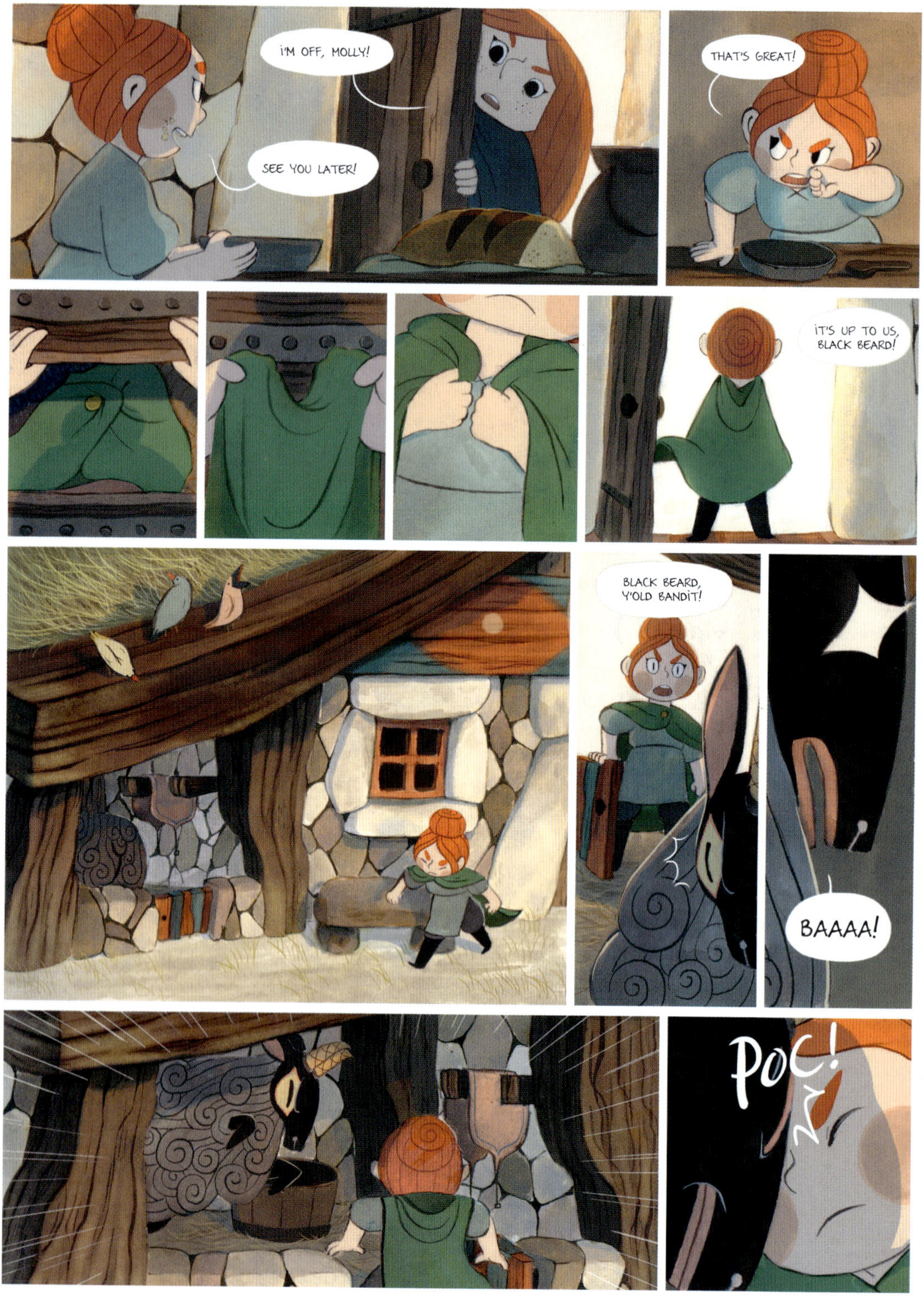
I'M OFF, MOLLY!
SEE YOU LATER!
THAT'S GREAT!
IT'S UP TO US, BLACK BEARD!
BLACK BEARD, Y'OLD BANDIT!
BAAAA!
POC!

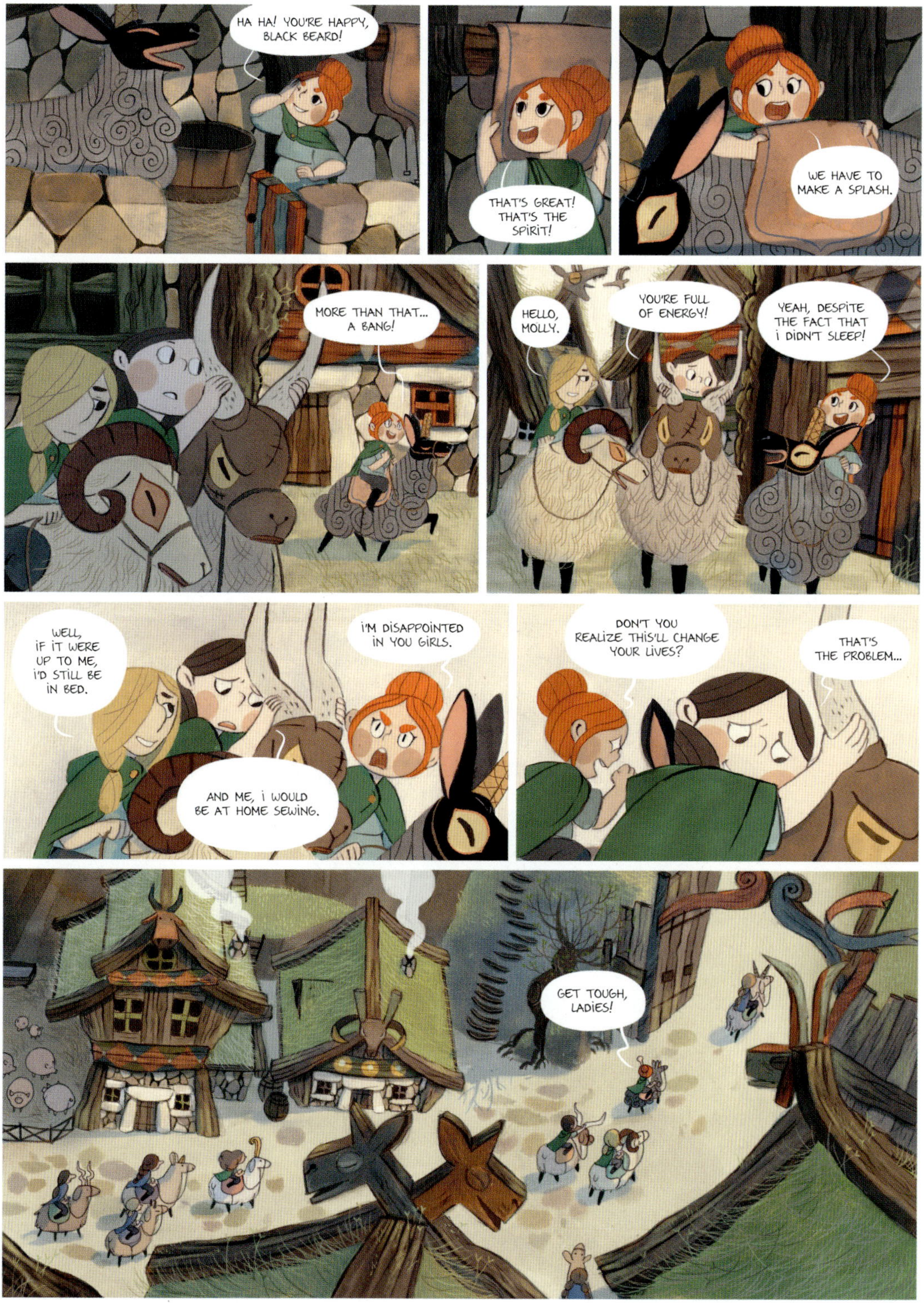
HA HA! YOU'RE HAPPY, BLACK BEARD!
THAT'S GREAT! THAT'S THE SPIRIT!
WE HAVE TO MAKE A SPLASH.
MORE THAN THAT... A BANG!
HELLO, MOLLY.
YOU'RE FULL OF ENERGY!
YEAH, DESPITE THE FACT THAT I DIDN'T SLEEP!
WELL, IF IT WERE UP TO ME, I'D STILL BE IN BED.
AND ME, I WOULD BE AT HOME SEWING.
I'M DISAPPOINTED IN YOU GIRLS.
DON'T YOU REALIZE THIS'LL CHANGE YOUR LIVES?
THAT'S THE PROBLEM...
GET TOUGH, LADIES!

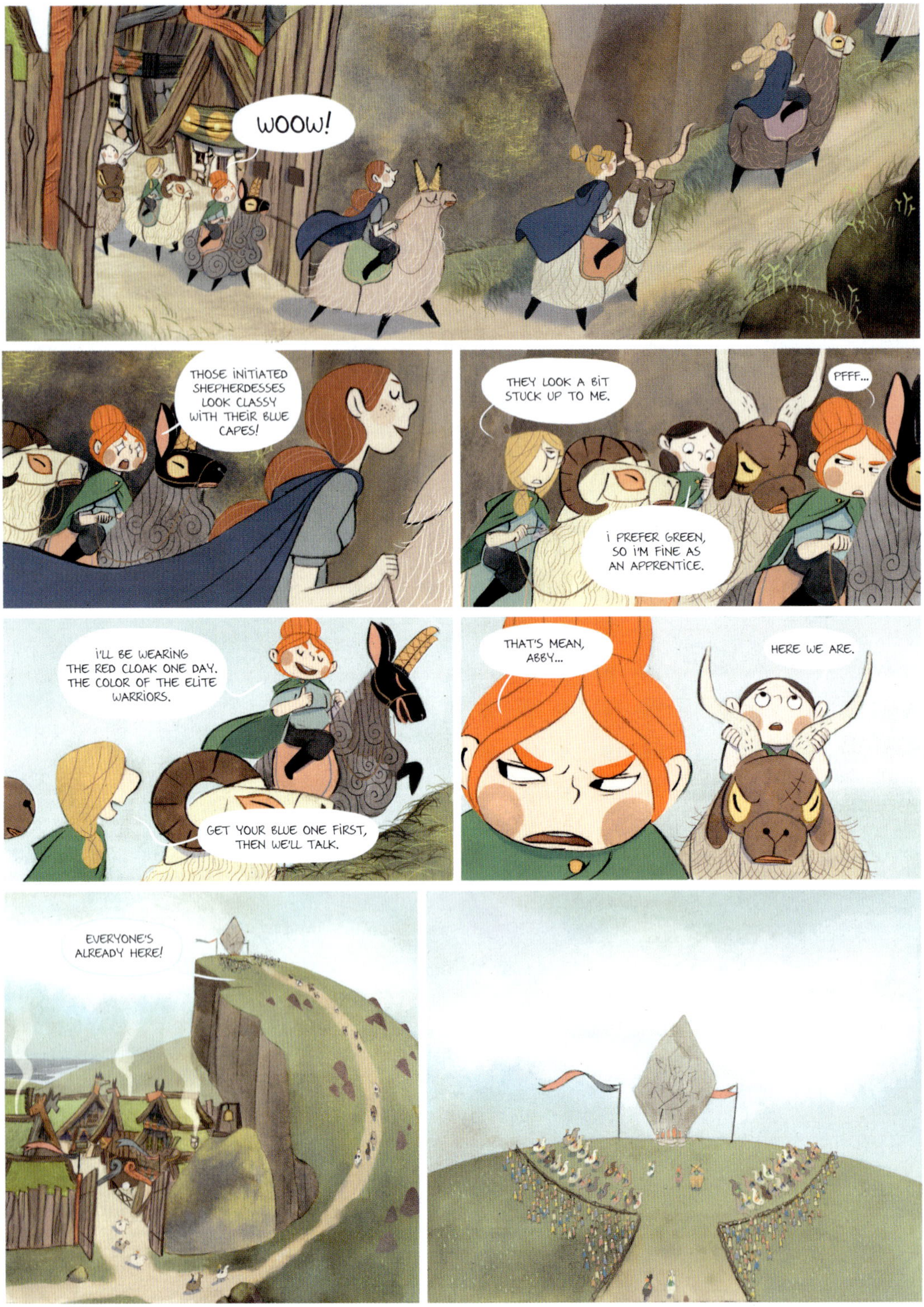
WOOW!
THOSE INITIATED SHEPHERDESSES LOOK CLASSY WITH THEIR BLUE CAPES!
THEY LOOK A BIT STUCK UP TO ME.
PFFF...
I PREFER GREEN, SO I'M FINE AS AN APPRENTICE.
I'LL BE WEARING THE RED CLOAK ONE DAY. THE COLOR OF THE ELITE WARRIORS.
GET YOUR BLUE ONE FIRST, THEN WE'LL TALK.
THAT'S MEAN, ABBY...
HERE WE ARE.
EVERYONE'S ALREADY HERE!

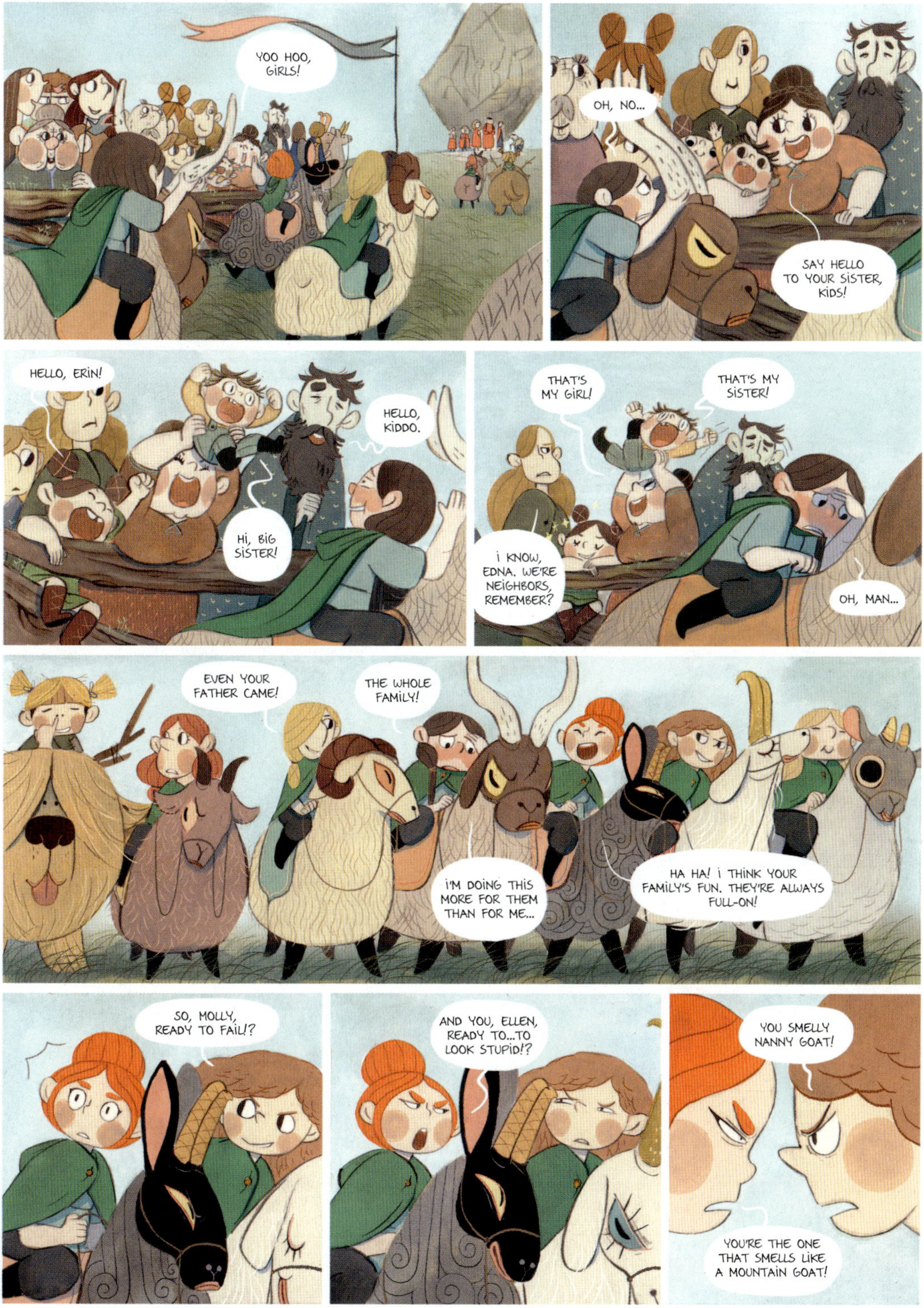
YOO HOO, GIRLS!
OH, NO...
SAY HELLO TO YOUR SISTER, KIDS!
HELLO, ERIN!
HELLO, KIDDO.
HI, BIG SISTER!
THAT'S MY GIRL!
THAT'S MY SISTER!
I KNOW, EDNA. WE'RE NEIGHBORS, REMEMBER?
OH, MAN...
EVEN YOUR FATHER CAME!
THE WHOLE FAMILY!
I'M DOING THIS MORE FOR THEM THAN FOR ME...
HA HA! I THINK YOUR FAMILY'S FUN. THEY'RE ALWAYS FULL-ON!
SO, MOLLY, READY TO FAIL!?
AND YOU, ELLEN, READY TO...TO LOOK STUPID!?
YOU SMELLY NANNY GOAT!
YOU'RE THE ONE THAT SMELLS LIKE A MOUNTAIN GOAT!

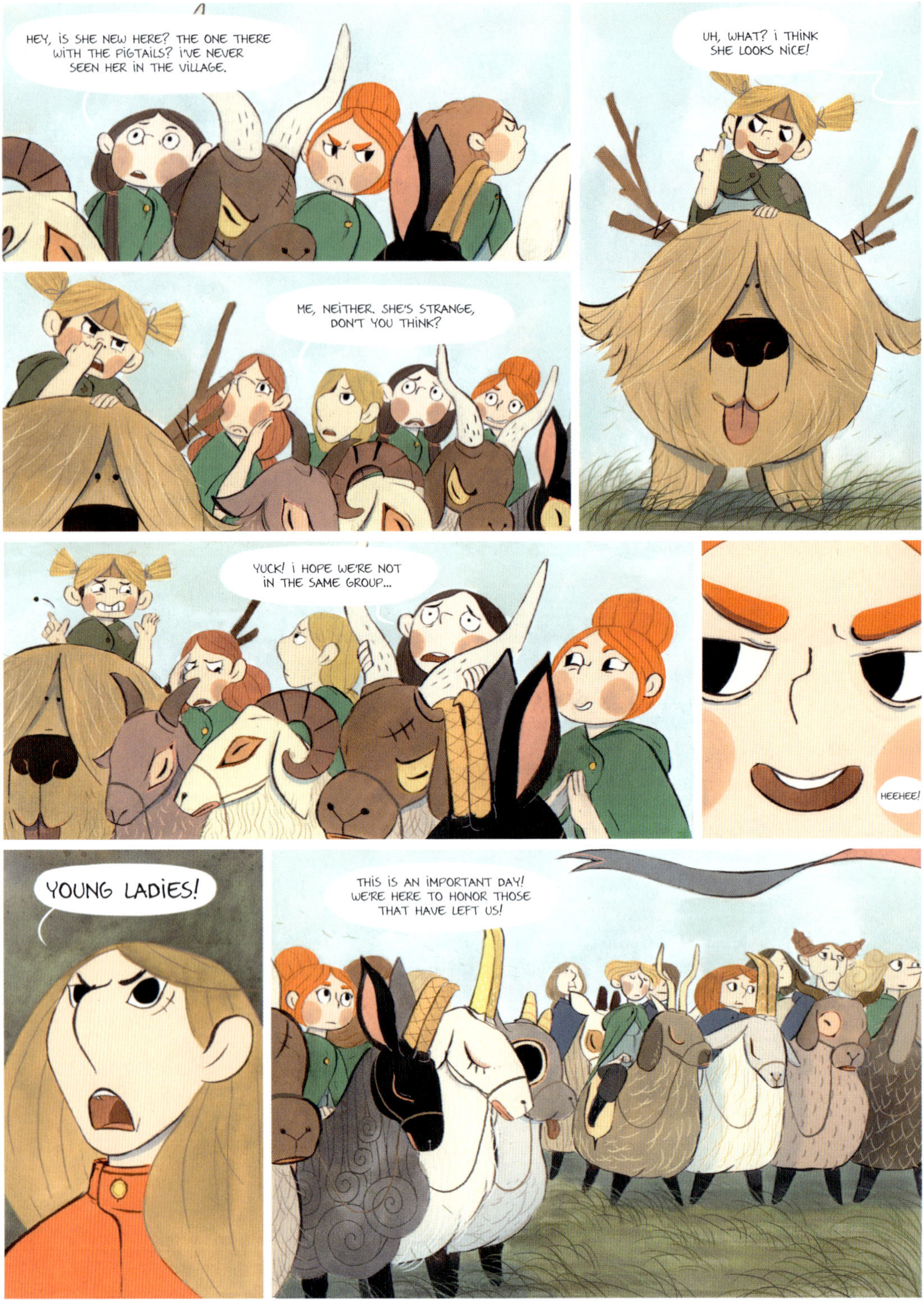
HEY, IS SHE NEW HERE? THE ONE THERE WITH THE PIGTAILS? I'VE NEVER SEEN HER IN THE VILLAGE.
UH, WHAT? I THINK SHE LOOKS NICE!
ME, NEITHER. SHE'S STRANGE, DON'T YOU THINK?
YUCK! I HOPE WE'RE NOT IN THE SAME GROUP...
HEEHEE!
YOUNG LADIES!
THIS IS AN IMPORTANT DAY! WE'RE HERE TO HONOR THOSE THAT HAVE LEFT US!

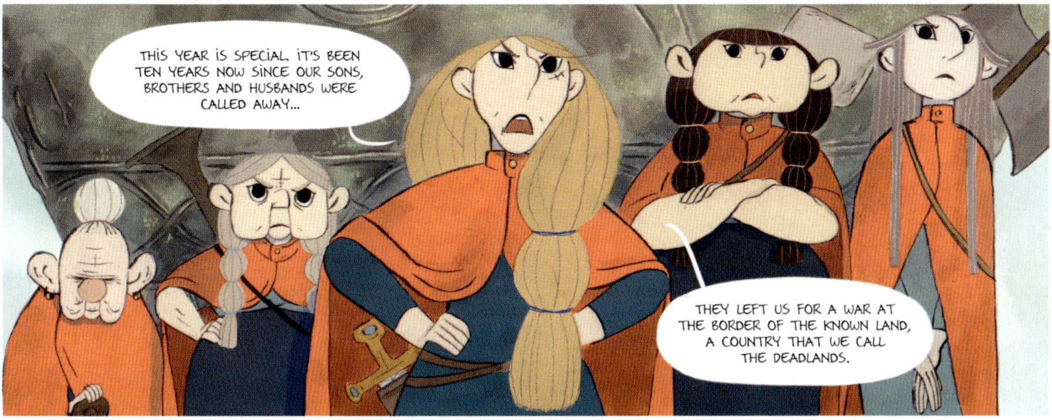
THIS YEAR IS SPECIAL. IT'S BEEN TEN YEARS NOW SINCE OUR SONS, BROTHERS AND HUSBANDS WERE CALLED AWAY...
THEY LEFT US FOR A WAR AT THE BORDER OF THE KNOWN LAND, A COUNTRY THAT WE CALL THE DEADLANDS.

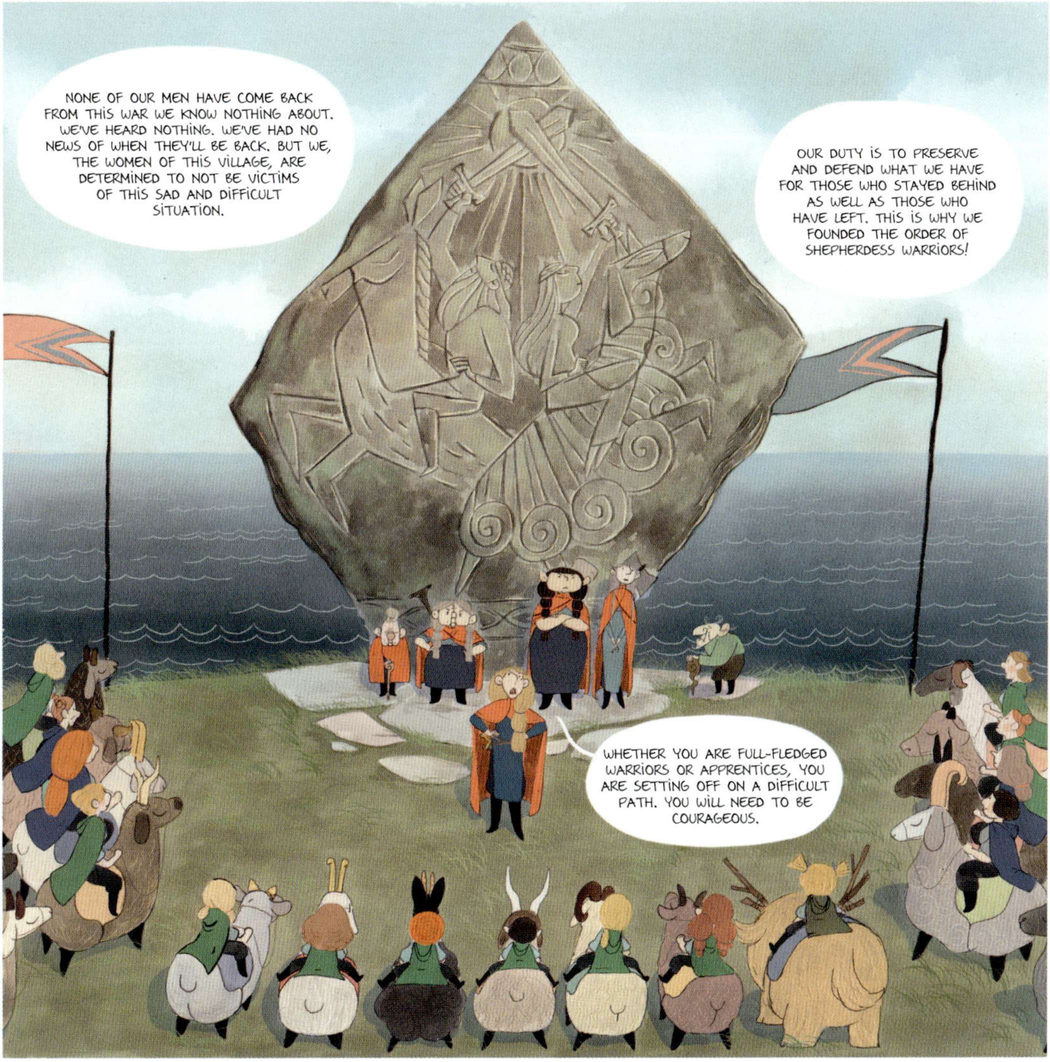
NONE OF OUR MEN HAVE COME BACK FROM THIS WAR WE KNOW NOTHING ABOUT. WE'VE HEARD NOTHING. WE'VE HAD NO NEWS OF WHEN THEY'LL BE BACK. BUT WE, THE WOMEN OF THIS VILLAGE, ARE DETERMINED TO NOT BE VICTIMS OF THIS SAD AND DIFFICULT SITUATION.
OUR DUTY IS TO PRESERVE AND DEFEND WHAT WE HAVE FOR THOSE WHO STAYED BEHIND AS WELL AS THOSE WHO HAVE LEFT. THIS IS WHY WE FOUNDED THE ORDER OF SHEPHERDESS WARRIORS!
WHETHER YOU ARE FULL-FLEDGED WARRIORS OR APPRENTICES, YOU ARE SETTING OFF ON A DIFFICULT PATH. YOU WILL NEED TO BE COURAGEOUS.

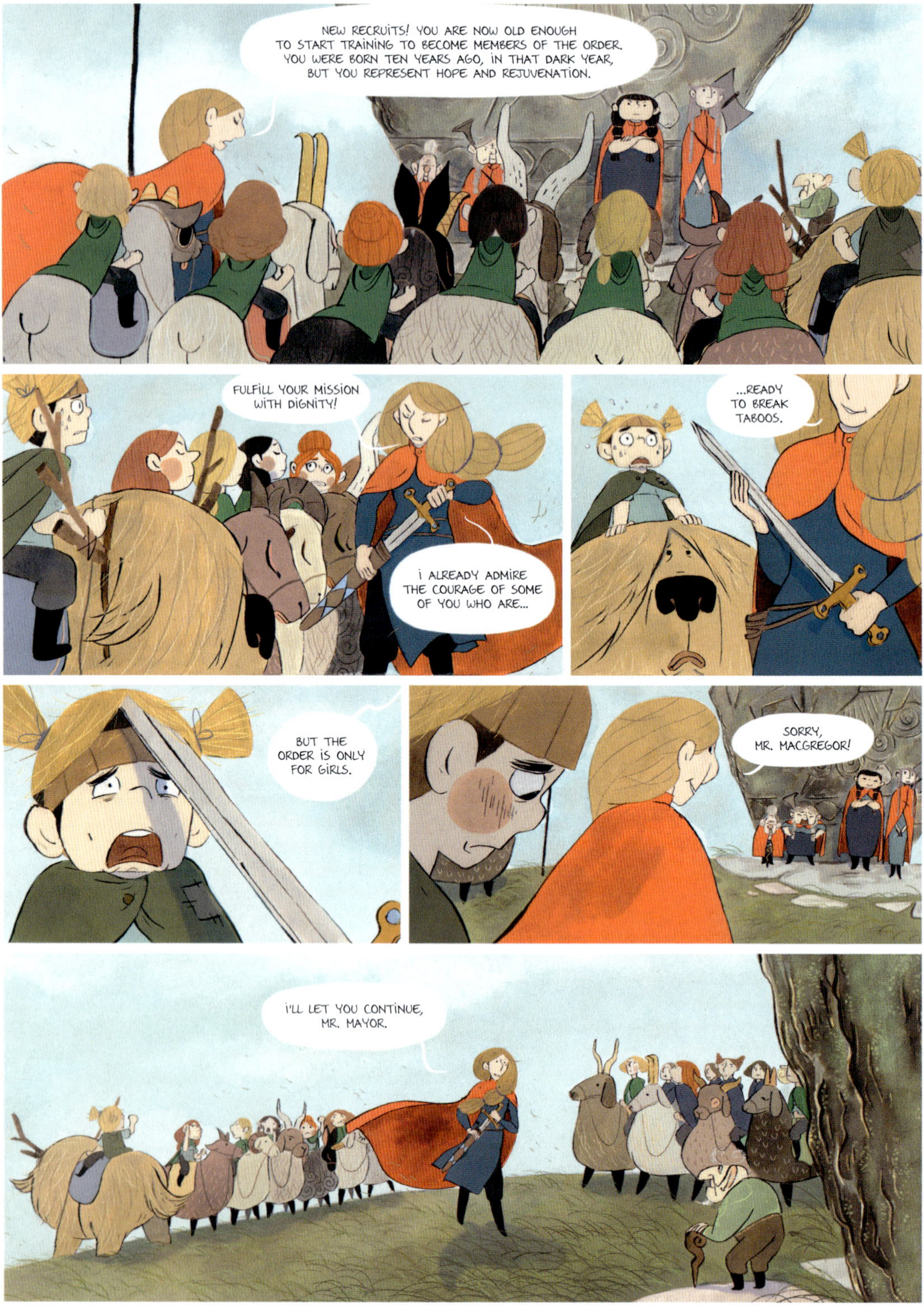
NEW RECRUITS! YOU ARE NOW OLD ENOUGH TO START TRAINING TO BECOME MEMBERS OF THE ORDER. YOU WERE BORN TEN YEARS AGO, IN THAT DARK YEAR, BUT YOU REPRESENT HOPE AND REJUVENATION.
FULFILL YOUR MISSION WITH DIGNITY!
I ALREADY ADMIRE THE COURAGE OF SOME OF YOU WHO ARE...
...READY TO BREAK TABOOS.
BUT THE ORDER IS ONLY FOR GIRLS.
SORRY, MR. MACGREGOR!
I'LL LET YOU CONTINUE, MR. MAYOR.

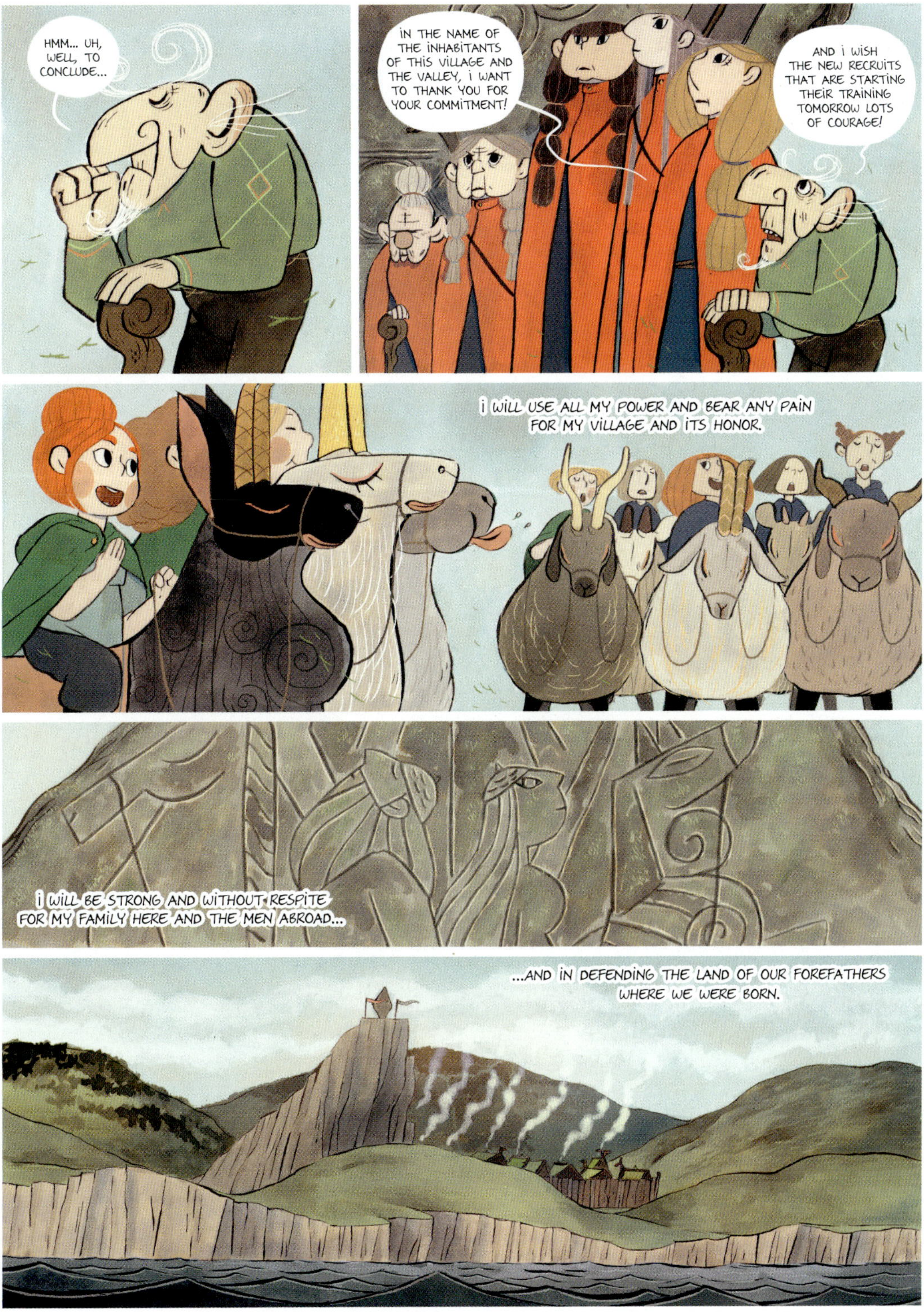
HMM... UH, WELL, TO CONCLUDE...
IN THE NAME OF THE INHABITANTS OF THIS VILLAGE AND THE VALLEY, I WANT TO THANK YOU FOR YOUR COMMITMENT!
AND I WISH THE NEW RECRUITS THAT ARE STARTING THEIR TRAINING TOMORROW LOTS OF COURAGE!
I WILL USE ALL MY POWER AND BEAR ANY PAIN FOR MY VILLAGE AND ITS HONOR.
I WILL BE STRONG AND WITHOUT RESPITE FOR MY FAMILY HERE AND THE MEN ABROAD...
...AND IN DEFENDING THE LAND OF OUR FOREFATHERS WHERE WE WERE BORN.

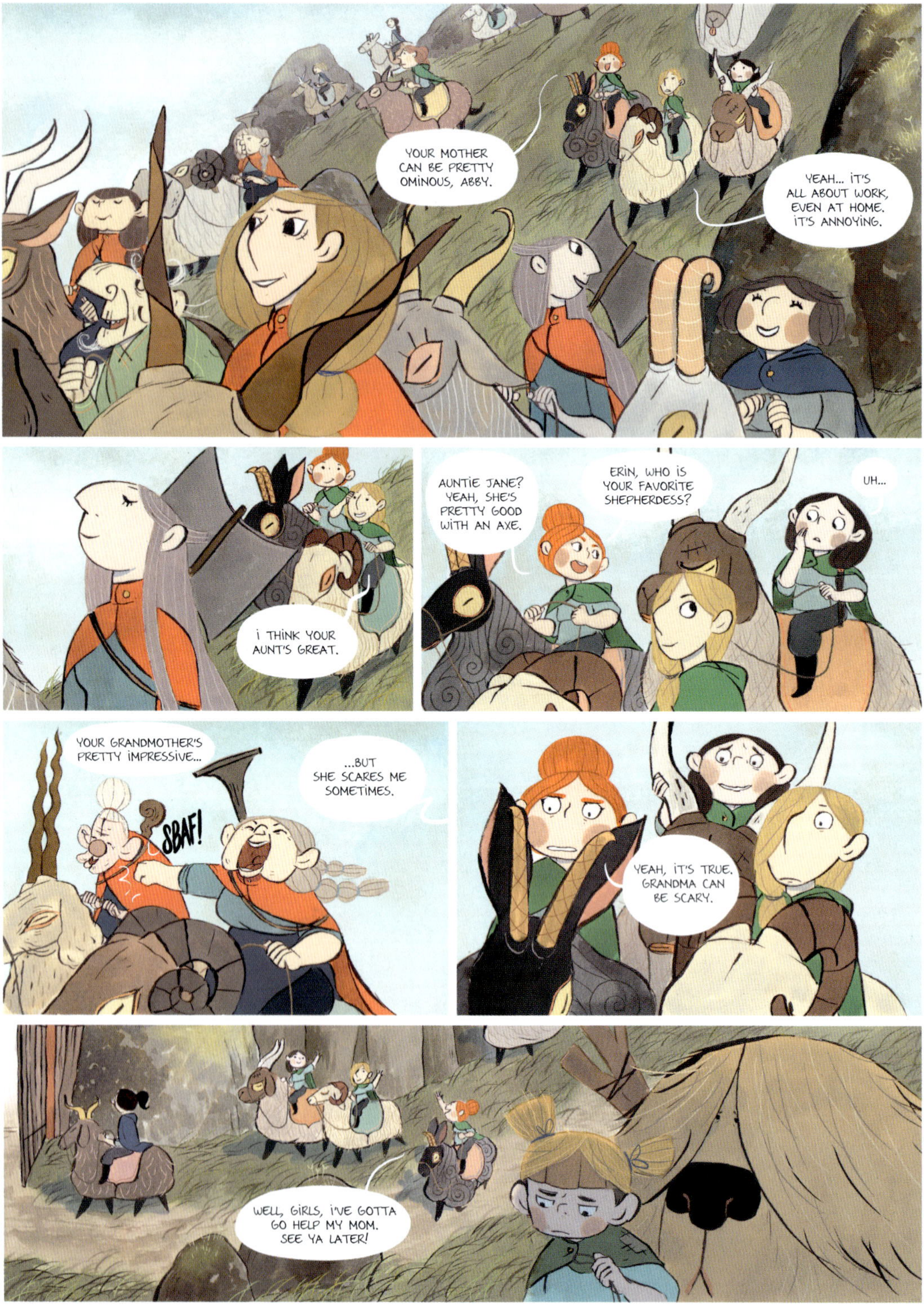
YOUR MOTHER CAN BE PRETTY OMINOUS, ABBY.
YEAH... IT'S ALL ABOUT WORK, EVEN AT HOME. IT'S ANNOYING.
I THINK YOUR AUNT'S GREAT.
AUNTIE JANE? YEAH, SHE'S PRETTY GOOD WITH AN AXE.
ERIN, WHO IS YOUR FAVORITE SHEPHERDESS?
UH...
YOUR GRANDMOTHER'S PRETTY IMPRESSIVE...
SBAF!
...BUT SHE SCARES ME SOMETIMES.
YEAH, IT'S TRUE. GRANDMA CAN BE SCARY.
WELL, GIRLS, I'VE GOTTA GO HELP MY MOM. SEE YA LATER!

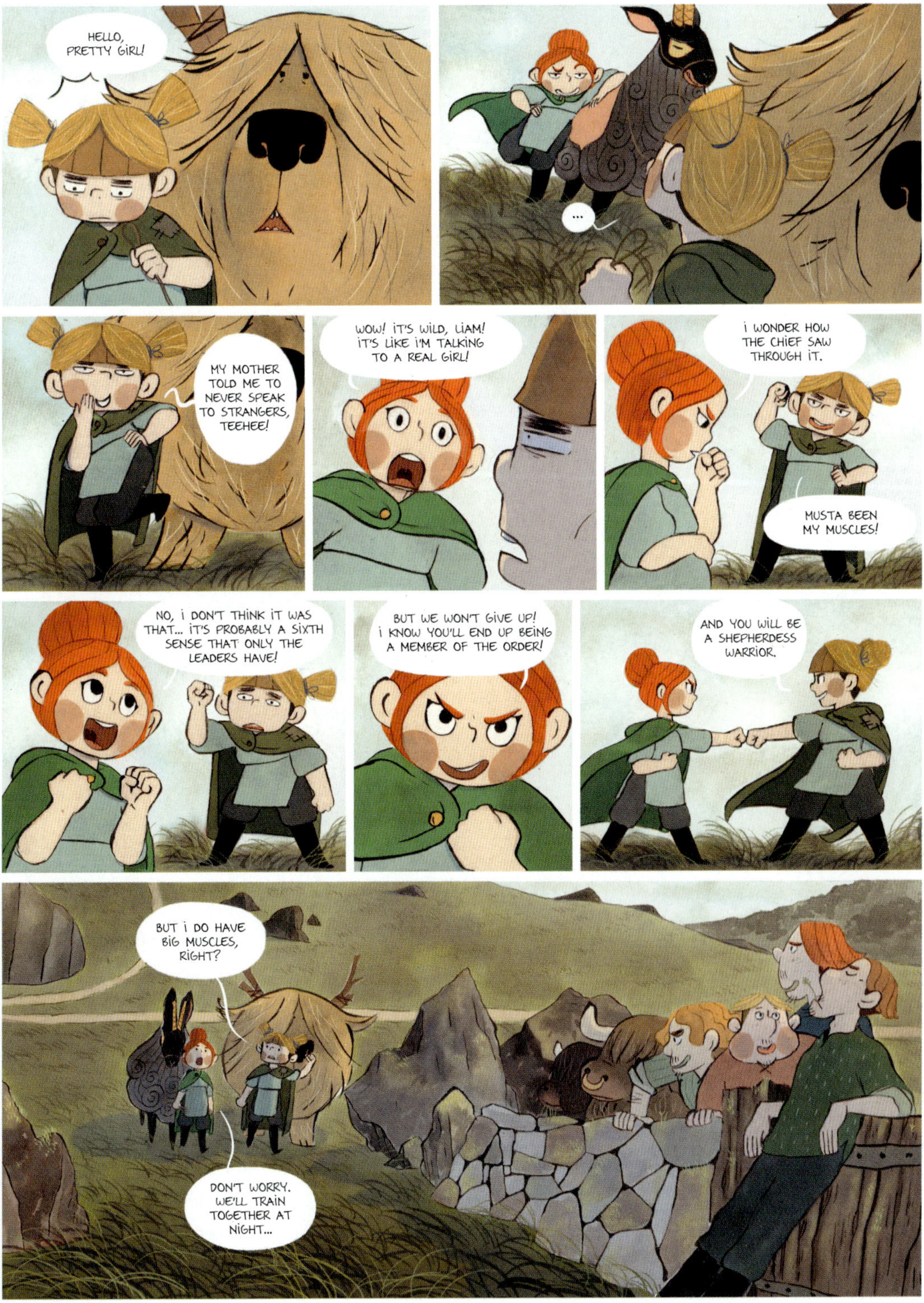
HELLO, PRETTY GIRL!
...
MY MOTHER TOLD ME TO NEVER SPEAK TO STRANGERS, TEEHEE!
WOW! IT'S WILD, LIAM! IT'S LIKE I'M TALKING TO A REAL GIRL!
I WONDER HOW THE CHIEF SAW THROUGH IT.
MUSTA BEEN MY MUSCLES!
NO, I DON'T THINK IT WAS THAT... IT'S PROBABLY A SIXTH SENSE THAT ONLY THE LEADERS HAVE!
BUT WE WON'T GIVE UP! I KNOW YOU'LL END UP BEING A MEMBER OF THE ORDER!
AND YOU WILL BE A SHEPHERDESS WARRIOR.
BUT I DO HAVE BIG MUSCLES, RIGHT?
DON'T WORRY. WE'LL TRAIN TOGETHER AT NIGHT...

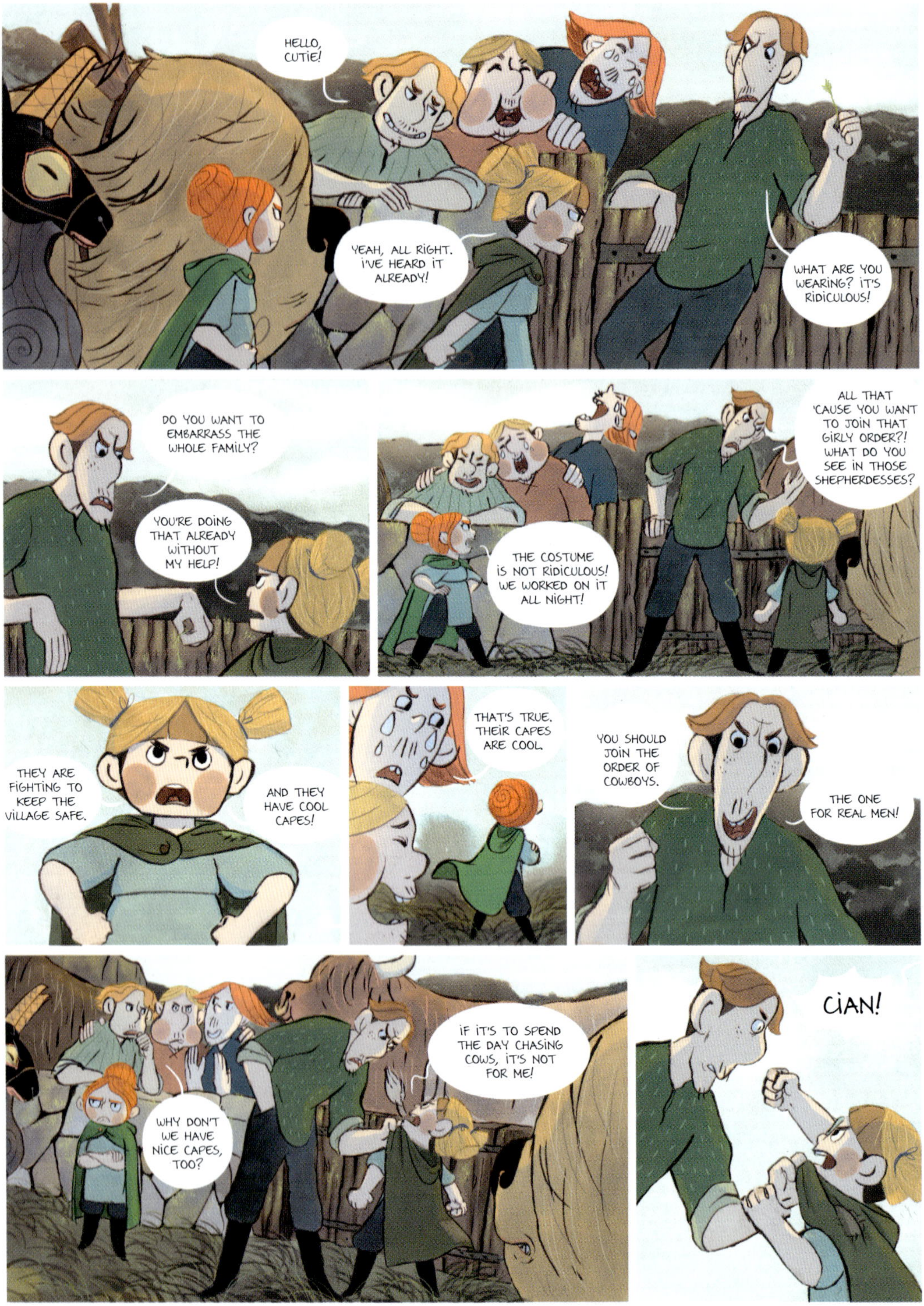
HELLO, CUTIE!
YEAH, ALL RIGHT. I'VE HEARD IT ALREADY!
WHAT ARE YOU WEARING? IT'S RIDICULOUS!
DO YOU WANT TO EMBARRASS THE WHOLE FAMILY?
YOU'RE DOING THAT ALREADY WITHOUT MY HELP!
THE COSTUME IS NOT RIDICULOUS! WE WORKED ON IT ALL NIGHT!
ALL THAT 'CAUSE YOU WANT TO JOIN THAT GIRLY ORDER?! WHAT DO YOU SEE IN THOSE SHEPHERDESSES?
THEY ARE FIGHTING TO KEEP THE VILLAGE SAFE.
AND THEY HAVE COOL CAPES!
THAT'S TRUE. THEIR CAPES ARE COOL.
YOU SHOULD JOIN THE ORDER OF COWBOYS.
THE ONE FOR REAL MEN!
WHY DON'T WE HAVE NICE CAPES, TOO?
IF IT'S TO SPEND THE DAY CHASING COWS, IT'S NOT FOR ME!
CIAN!

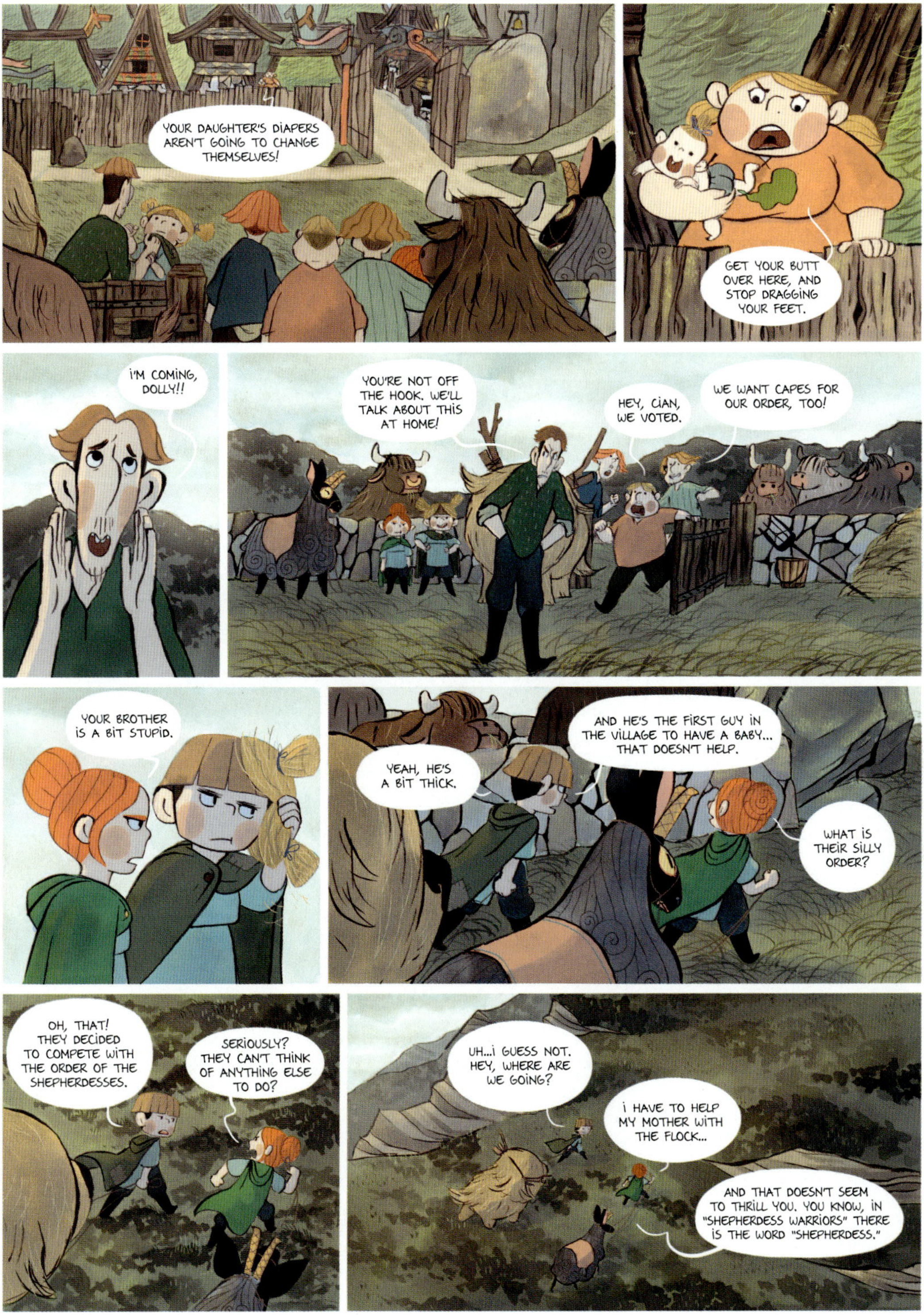
YOUR DAUGHTER'S DIAPERS AREN'T GOING TO CHANGE THEMSELVES!
GET YOUR BUTT OVER HERE, AND STOP DRAGGING YOUR FEET.
I'M COMING, DOLLY!!
YOU'RE NOT OFF THE HOOK. WE'LL TALK ABOUT THIS AT HOME!
HEY, CIAN, WE VOTED.
WE WANT CAPES FOR OUR ORDER, TOO!
YOUR BROTHER IS A BIT STUPID.
YEAH, HE'S A BIT THICK.
AND HE'S THE FIRST GUY IN THE VILLAGE TO HAVE A BABY... THAT DOESN'T HELP.
WHAT IS THEIR SILLY ORDER?
OH, THAT! THEY DECIDED TO COMPETE WITH THE ORDER OF THE SHEPHERDESSES.
SERIOUSLY? THEY CAN'T THINK OF ANYTHING ELSE TO DO?
UH...I GUESS NOT. HEY, WHERE ARE WE GOING?
I HAVE TO HELP MY MOTHER WITH THE FLOCK...
AND THAT DOESN'T SEEM TO THRILL YOU. YOU KNOW, IN "SHEPHERDESS WARRIORS" THERE IS THE WORD "SHEPHERDESS."

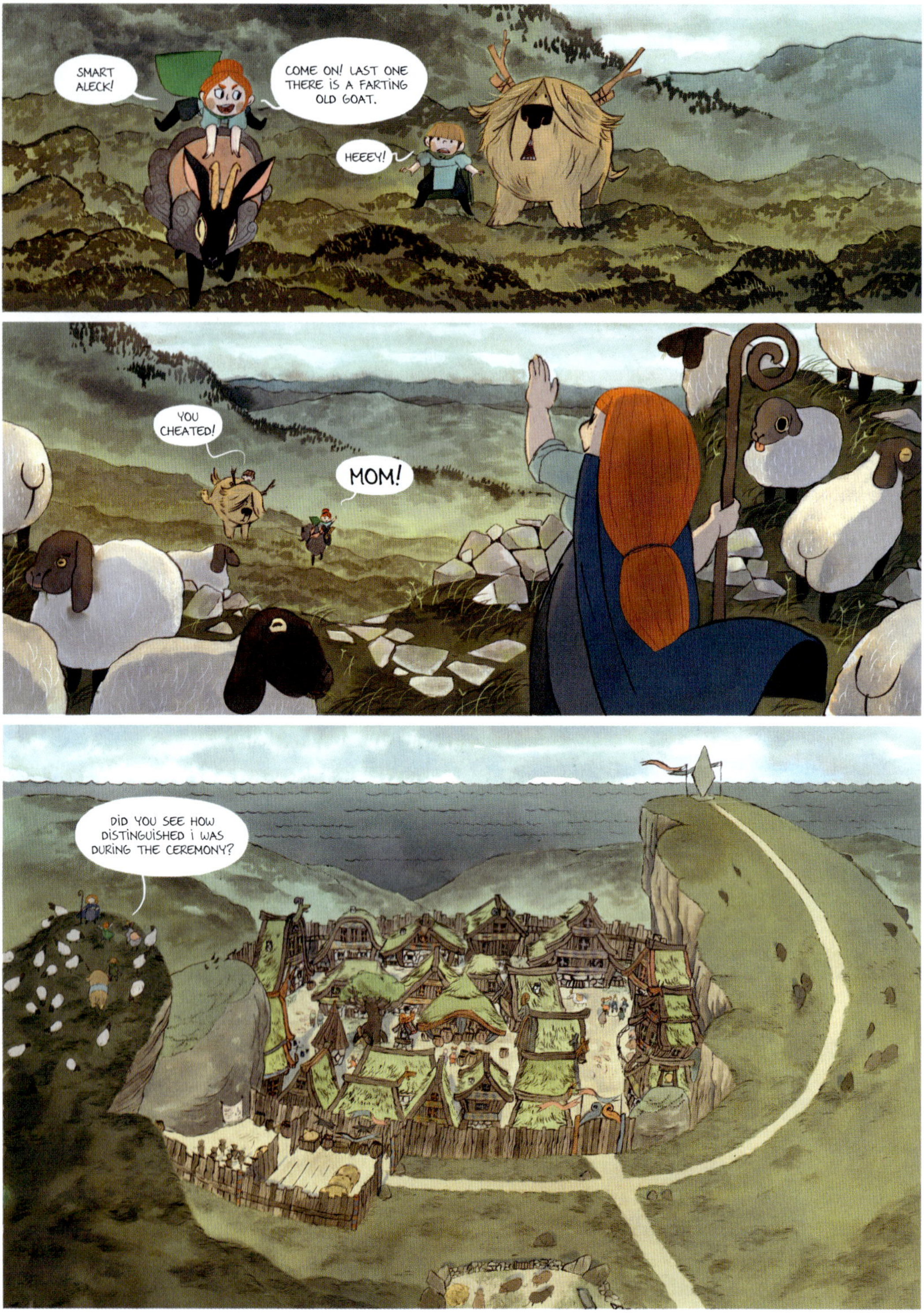
SMART ALECK!
COME ON! LAST ONE THERE IS A FARTING OLD GOAT.
HEEEY!
YOU CHEATED!
MOM!
DID YOU SEE HOW DISTINGUISHED I WAS DURING THE CEREMONY?

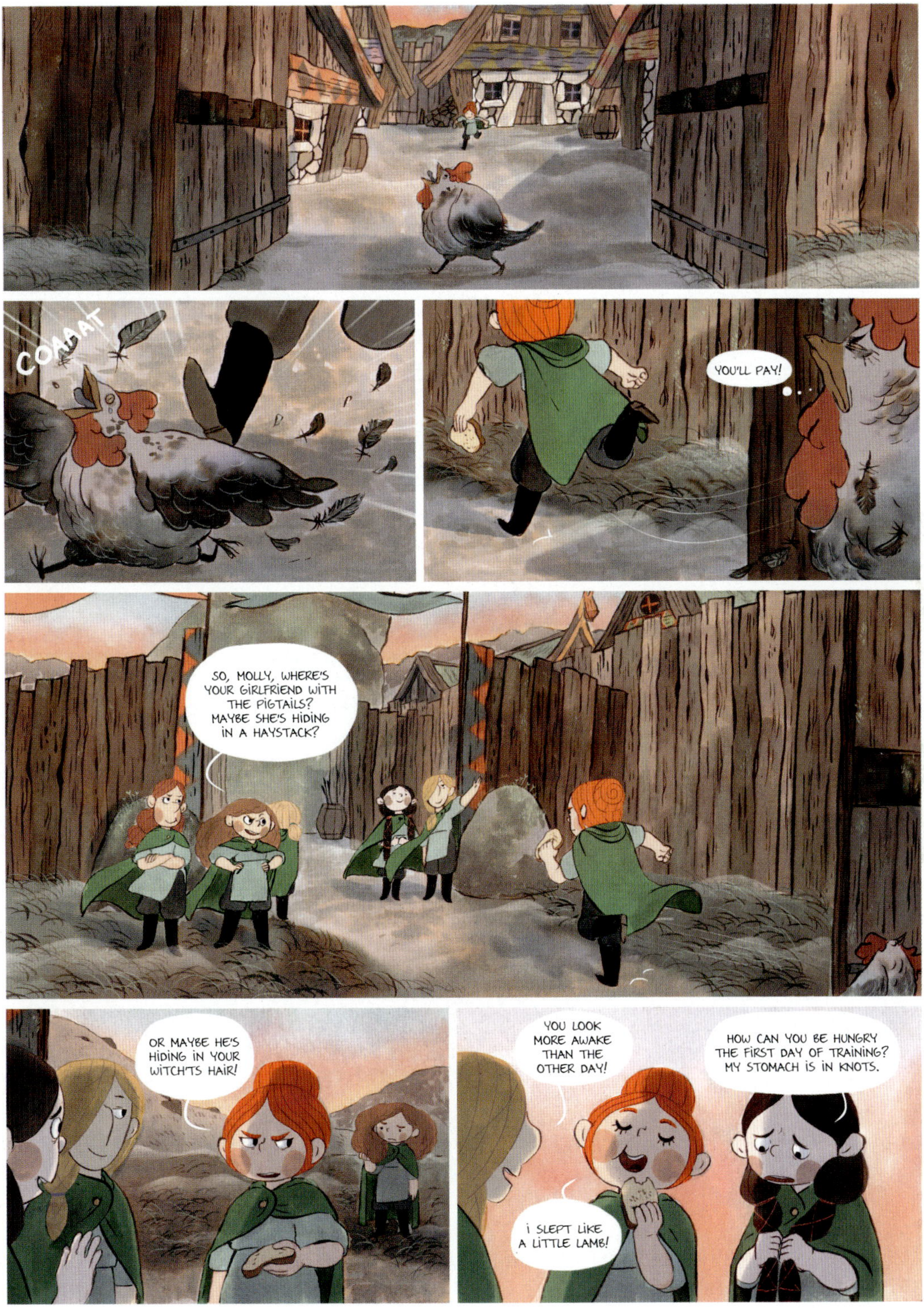
COAAAT
YOU'LL PAY!
SO, MOLLY, WHERE'S YOUR GIRLFRIEND WITH THE PIGTAILS? MAYBE SHE'S HIDING IN A HAYSTACK?
OR MAYBE HE'S HIDING IN YOUR WITCH'TS HAIR!
YOU LOOK MORE AWAKE THAN THE OTHER DAY!
I SLEPT LIKE A LITTLE LAMB!
HOW CAN YOU BE HUNGRY THE FIRST DAY OF TRAINING? MY STOMACH IS IN KNOTS.

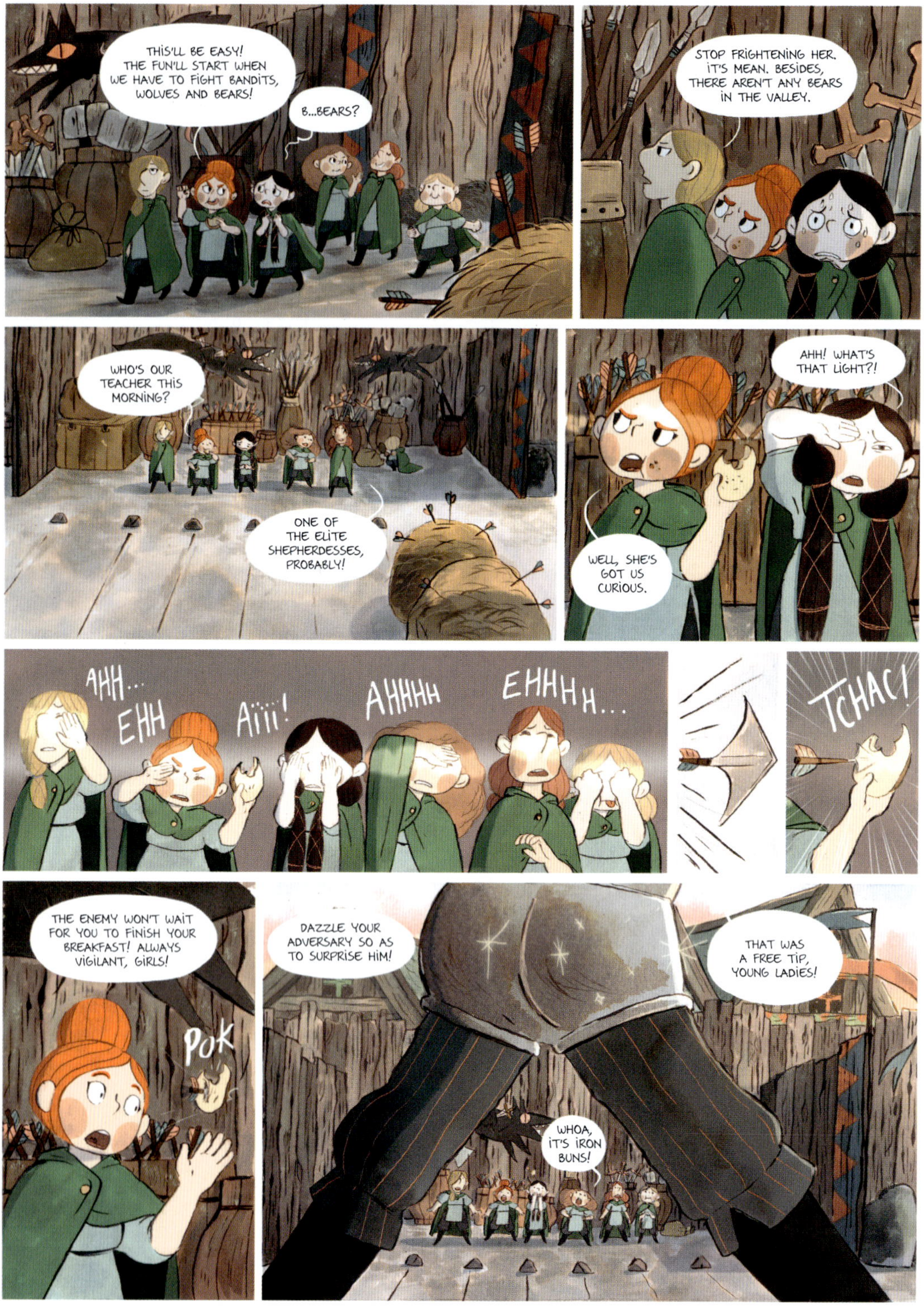
THIS'LL BE EASY! THE FUN'LL START WHEN WE HAVE TO FIGHT BANDITS, WOLVES AND BEARS!
B...BEARS?
STOP FRIGHTENING HER. IT'S MEAN. BESIDES, THERE AREN'T ANY BEARS IN THE VALLEY.
WHO'S OUR TEACHER THIS MORNING?
ONE OF THE ELITE SHEPHERDESSES, PROBABLY!
AHH! WHAT'S THAT LIGHT?!
WELL, SHE'S GOT US CURIOUS.
AHH...
EHH
AÏÏÏ!
AHHHH
EHHHH...
TCHAC!
THE ENEMY WON'T WAIT FOR YOU TO FINISH YOUR BREAKFAST! ALWAYS VIGILANT, GIRLS!
POK
DAZZLE YOUR ADVERSARY SO AS TO SURPRISE HIM!
THAT WAS A FREE TIP, YOUNG LADIES!
WHOA, IT'S IRON BUNS!

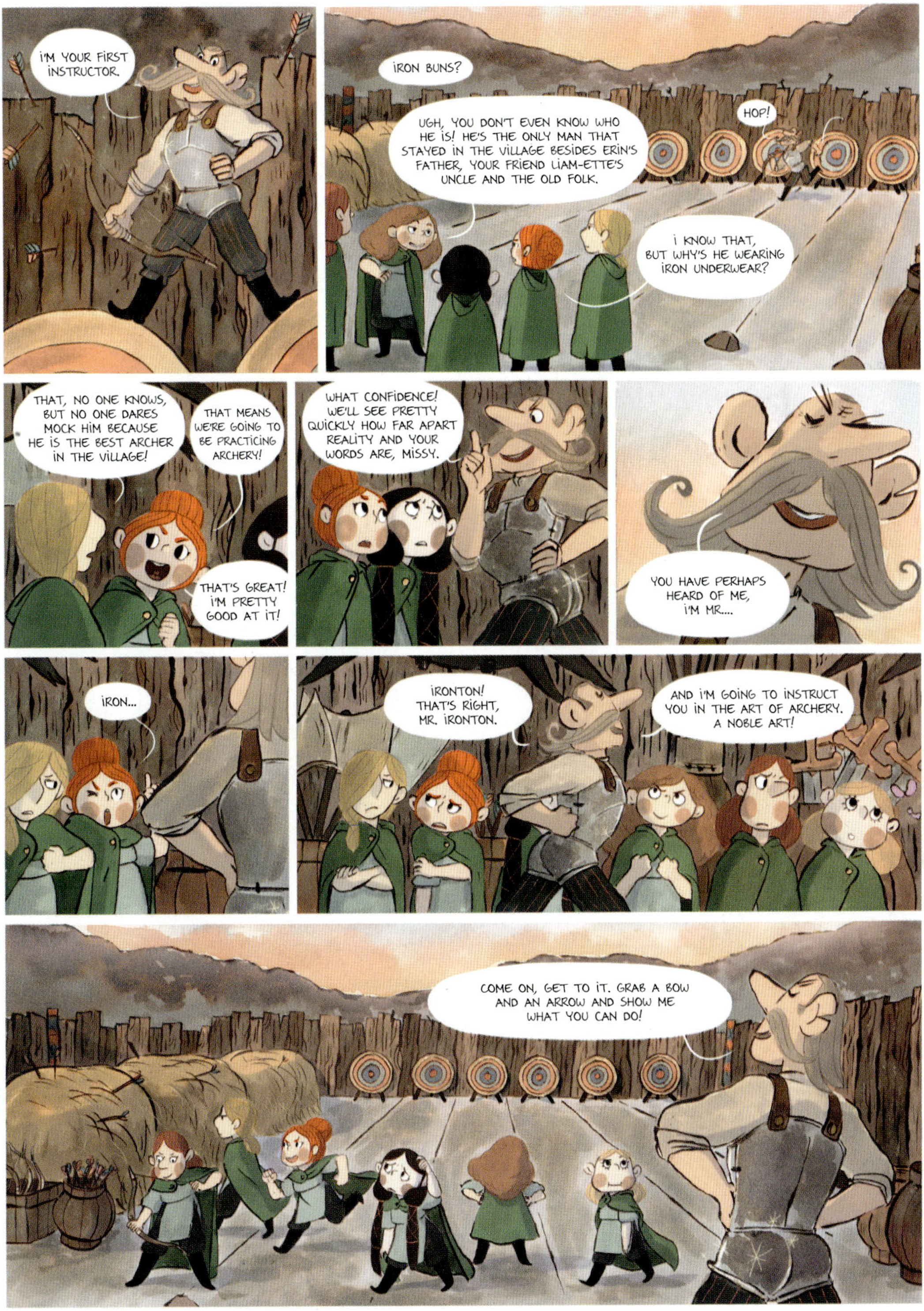
I'M YOUR FIRST INSTRUCTOR.
IRON BUNS?
UGH, YOU DON'T EVEN KNOW WHO HE IS! HE'S THE ONLY MAN THAT STAYED IN THE VILLAGE BESIDES ERIN'S FATHER, YOUR FRIEND LIAM-ETTE'S UNCLE AND THE OLD FOLK.
HOP!
I KNOW THAT, BUT WHY'S HE WEARING IRON UNDERWEAR?
THAT, NO ONE KNOWS, BUT NO ONE DARES MOCK HIM BECAUSE HE IS THE BEST ARCHER IN THE VILLAGE!
THAT MEANS WE'RE GOING TO BE PRACTICING ARCHERY!
THAT'S GREAT! I'M PRETTY GOOD AT IT!
WHAT CONFIDENCE! WE'LL SEE PRETTY QUICKLY HOW FAR APART REALITY AND YOUR WORDS ARE, MISSY.
YOU HAVE PERHAPS HEARD OF ME, I'M MR....
IRON...
IRONTON! THAT'S RIGHT, MR. IRONTON.
AND I'M GOING TO INSTRUCT YOU IN THE ART OF ARCHERY. A NOBLE ART!
COME ON, GET TO IT. GRAB A BOW AND AN ARROW AND SHOW ME WHAT YOU CAN DO!

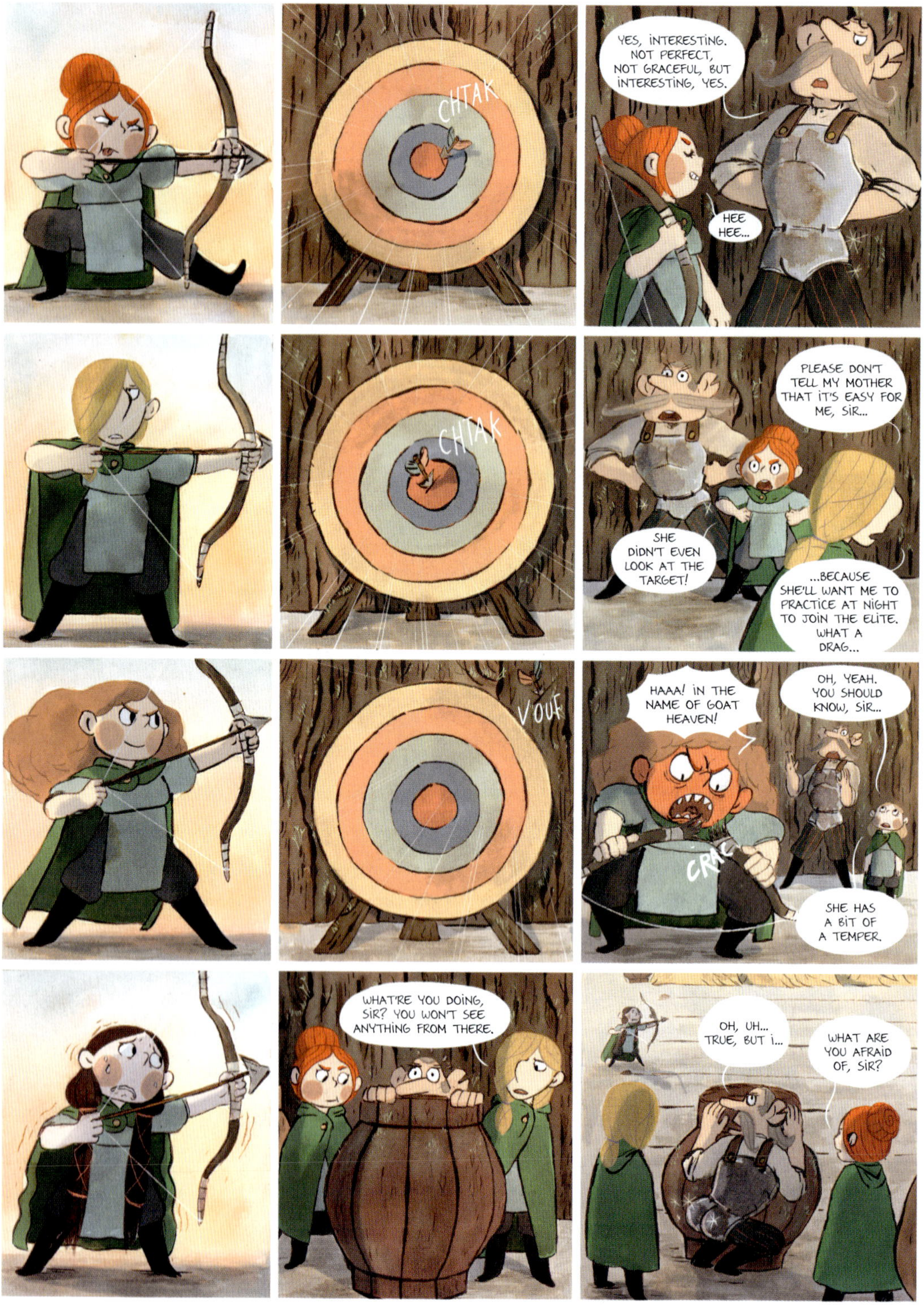
CHTAK
YES, INTERESTING. NOT PERFECT, NOT GRACEFUL, BUT INTERESTING, YES.
HEE HEE...
CHTAK
PLEASE DON'T TELL MY MOTHER THAT IT'S EASY FOR ME, SIR...
SHE DIDN'T EVEN LOOK AT THE TARGET!
...BECAUSE SHE'LL WANT ME TO PRACTICE AT NIGHT TO JOIN THE ELITE. WHAT A DRAG...
VOUF
HAAA! IN THE NAME OF GOAT HEAVEN!
OH, YEAH. YOU SHOULD KNOW, SIR...
CRAC
SHE HAS A BIT OF A TEMPER.
WHAT'RE YOU DOING, SIR? YOU WON'T SEE ANYTHING FROM THERE.
OH, UH... TRUE, BUT I...
WHAT ARE YOU AFRAID OF, SIR?

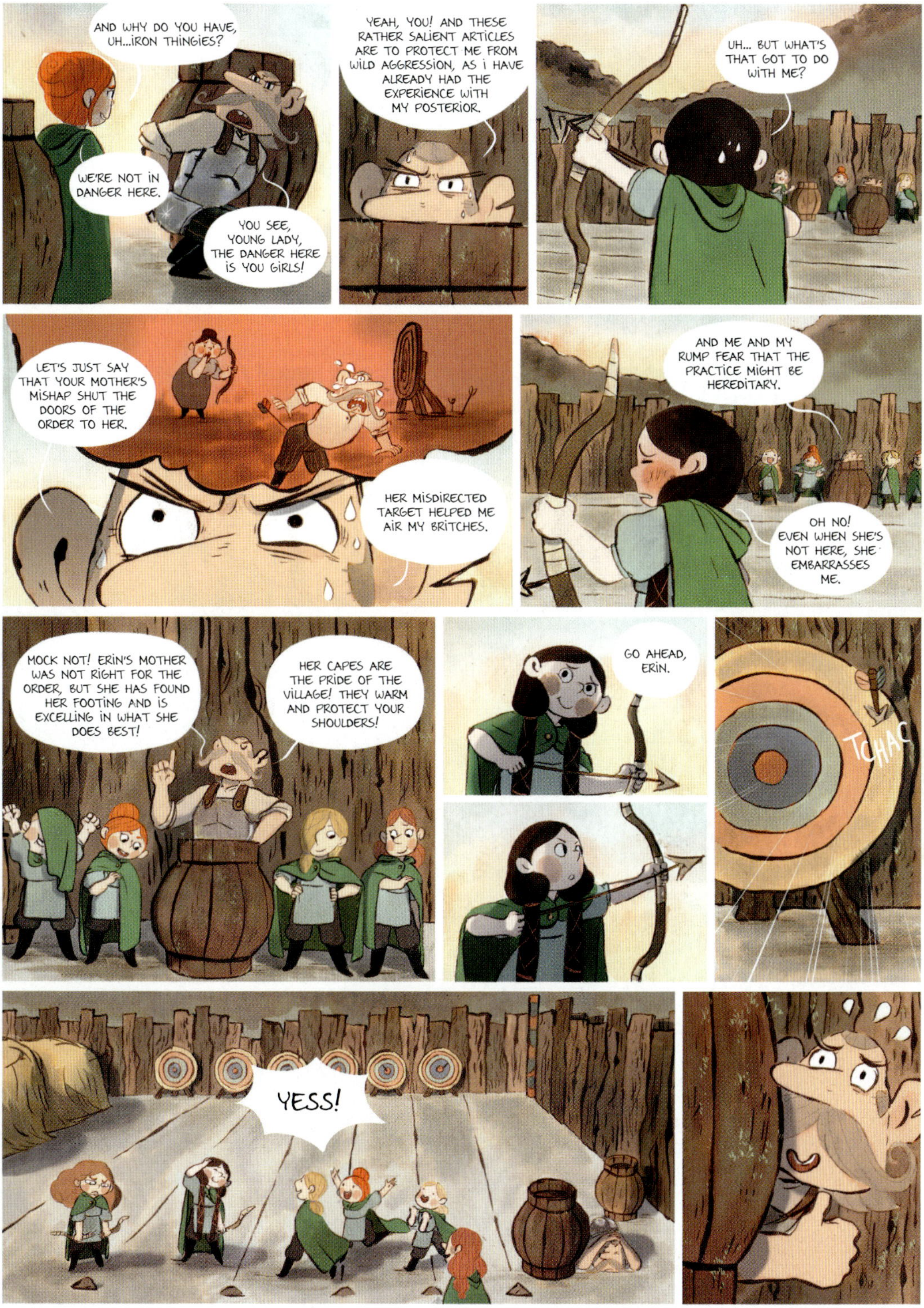
AND WHY DO YOU HAVE, UH...IRON THINGIES?
WE'RE NOT IN DANGER HERE.
YOU SEE, YOUNG LADY, THE DANGER HERE IS YOU GIRLS!
YEAH, YOU! AND THESE RATHER SALIENT ARTICLES ARE TO PROTECT ME FROM WILD AGGRESSION, AS I HAVE ALREADY HAD THE EXPERIENCE WITH MY POSTERIOR.
UH... BUT WHAT'S THAT GOT TO DO WITH ME?
LET'S JUST SAY THAT YOUR MOTHER'S MISHAP SHUT THE DOORS OF THE ORDER TO HER.
HER MISDIRECTED TARGET HELPED ME AIR MY BRITCHES.
AND ME AND MY RUMP FEAR THAT THE PRACTICE MIGHT BE HEREDITARY.
OH NO! EVEN WHEN SHE'S NOT HERE, SHE EMBARRASSES ME.
MOCK NOT! ERIN'S MOTHER WAS NOT RIGHT FOR THE ORDER, BUT SHE HAS FOUND HER FOOTING AND IS EXCELLING IN WHAT SHE DOES BEST!
HER CAPES ARE THE PRIDE OF THE VILLAGE! THEY WARM AND PROTECT YOUR SHOULDERS!
GO AHEAD, ERIN.
TCHAC
YESS!

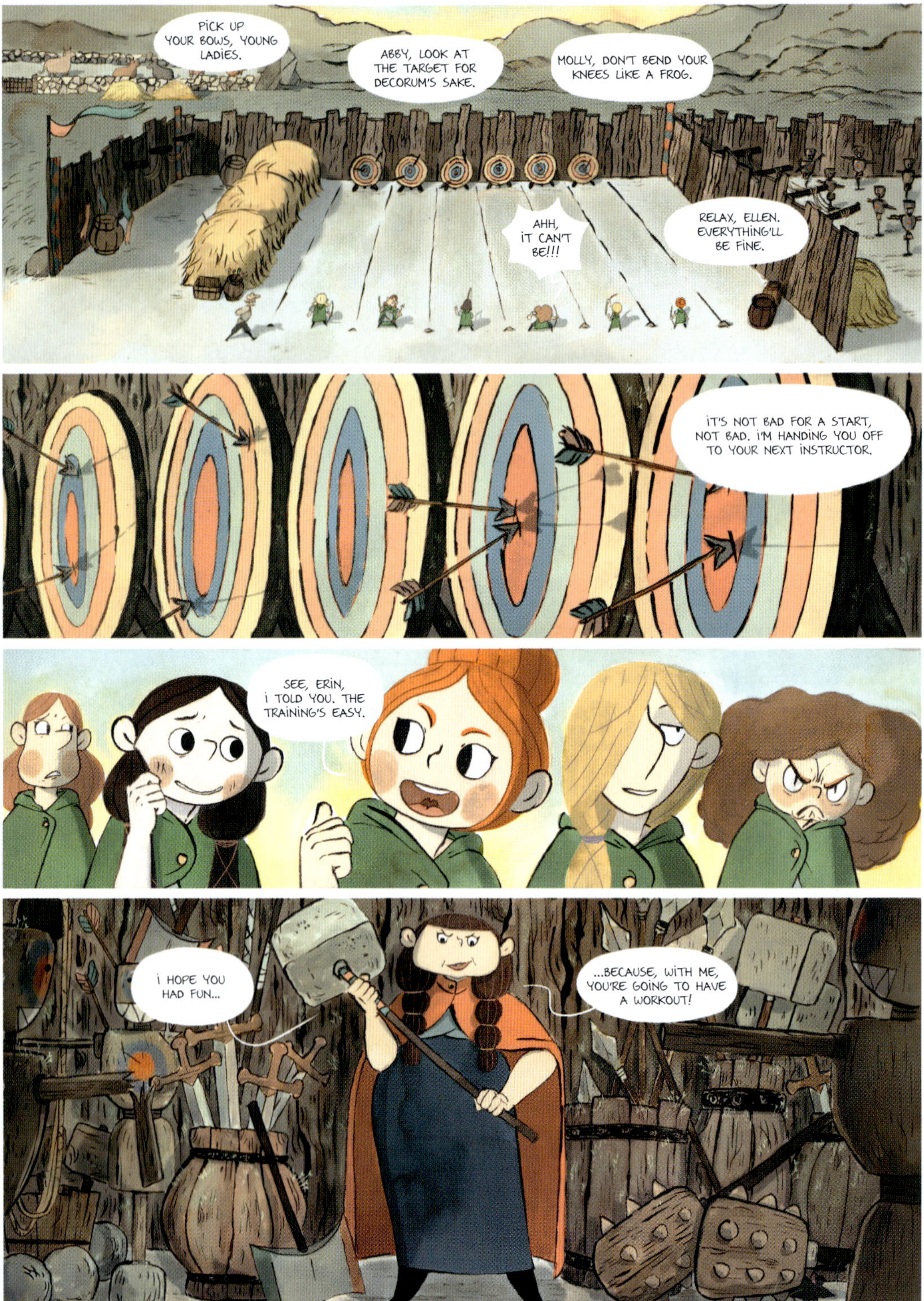
PICK UP YOUR BOWS, YOUNG LADIES.
ABBY, LOOK AT THE TARGET FOR DECORUM'S SAKE.
MOLLY, DON'T BEND YOUR KNEES LIKE A FROG.
AHH, IT CAN'T BE!!!
RELAX, ELLEN. EVERYTHING'LL BE FINE.
IT'S NOT BAD FOR A START, NOT BAD. I'M HANDING YOU OFF TO YOUR NEXT INSTRUCTOR.
SEE, ERIN, I TOLD YOU. THE TRAINING'S EASY.
I HOPE YOU HAD FUN...
...BECAUSE, WITH ME, YOU'RE GOING TO HAVE A WORKOUT!

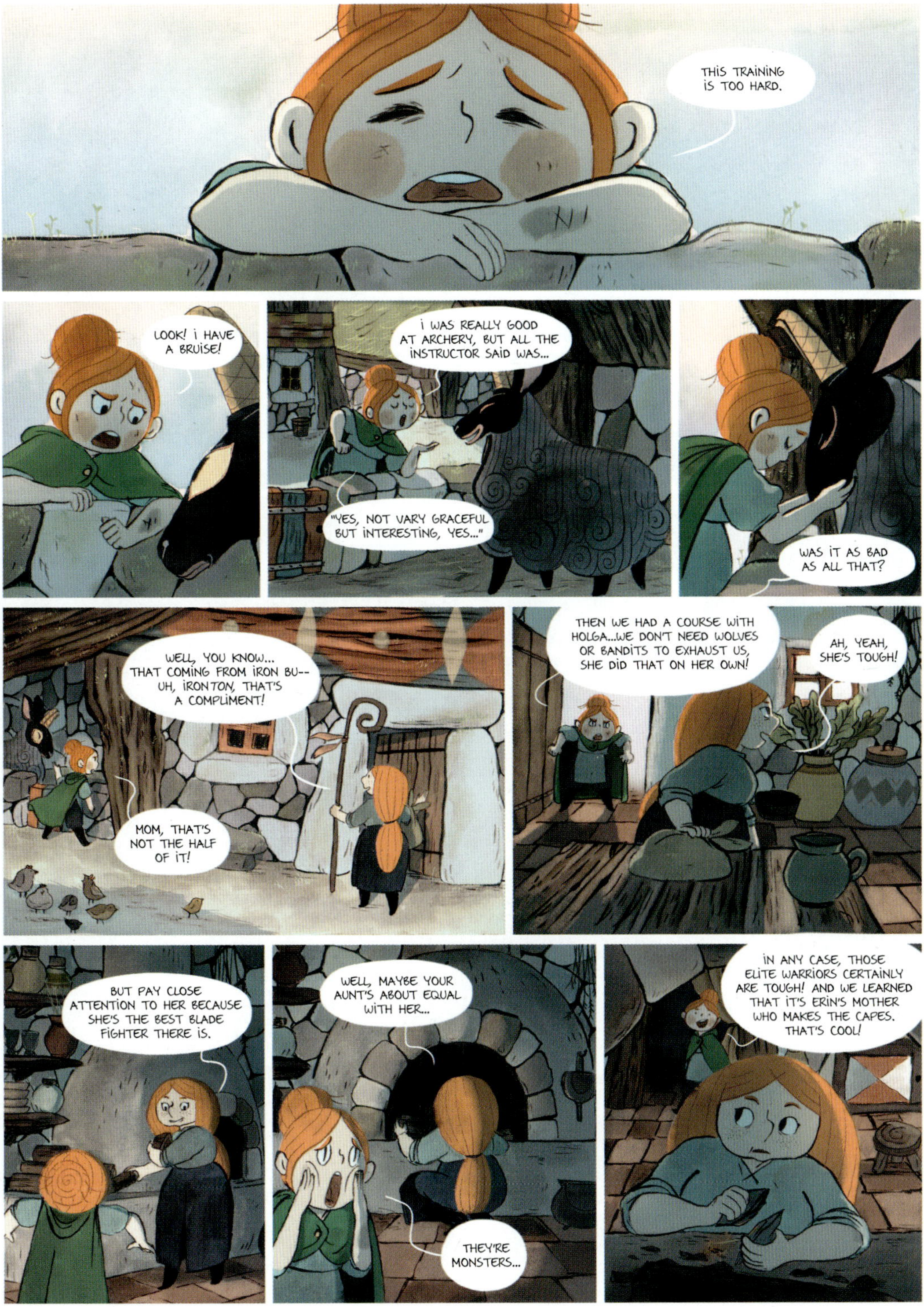
THIS TRAINING IS TOO HARD.
LOOK! I HAVE A BRUISE!
I WAS REALLY GOOD AT ARCHERY, BUT ALL THE INSTRUCTOR SAID WAS...
"YES, NOT VARY GRACEFUL BUT INTERESTING, YES..."
WAS IT AS BAD AS ALL THAT?
WELL, YOU KNOW... THAT COMING FROM IRON BU-- UH, IRONTON, THAT'S A COMPLIMENT!
MOM, THAT'S NOT THE HALF OF IT!
THEN WE HAD A COURSE WITH HOLGA...WE DON'T NEED WOLVES OR BANDITS TO EXHAUST US, SHE DID THAT ON HER OWN!
AH, YEAH, SHE'S TOUGH!
BUT PAY CLOSE ATTENTION TO HER BECAUSE SHE'S THE BEST BLADE FIGHTER THERE IS.
WELL, MAYBE YOUR AUNT'S ABOUT EQUAL WITH HER...
THEY'RE MONSTERS...
IN ANY CASE, THOSE ELITE WARRIORS CERTAINLY ARE TOUGH! AND WE LEARNED THAT IT'S ERIN'S MOTHER WHO MAKES THE CAPES. THAT'S COOL!

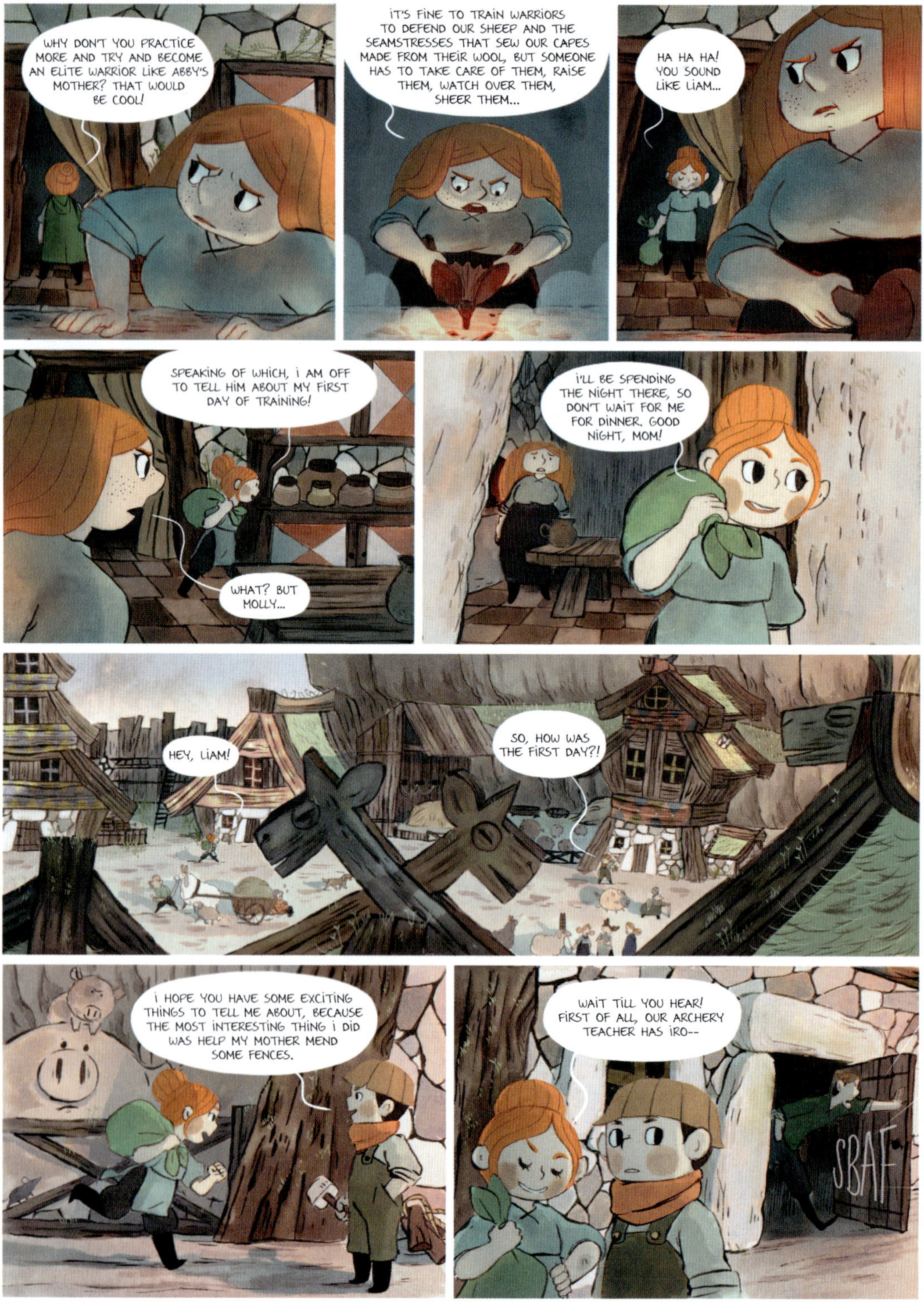
WHY DON'T YOU PRACTICE MORE AND TRY AND BECOME AN ELITE WARRIOR LIKE ABBY'S MOTHER? THAT WOULD BE COOL!
IT'S FINE TO TRAIN WARRIORS TO DEFEND OUR SHEEP AND THE SEAMSTRESSES THAT SEW OUR CAPES MADE FROM THEIR WOOL, BUT SOMEONE HAS TO TAKE CARE OF THEM, RAISE THEM, WATCH OVER THEM, SHEER THEM...
HA HA HA! YOU SOUND LIKE LIAM...
SPEAKING OF WHICH, I AM OFF TO TELL HIM ABOUT MY FIRST DAY OF TRAINING!
WHAT? BUT MOLLY...
I'LL BE SPENDING THE NIGHT THERE, SO DON'T WAIT FOR ME FOR DINNER. GOOD NIGHT, MOM!
HEY, LIAM!
SO, HOW WAS THE FIRST DAY?!
I HOPE YOU HAVE SOME EXCITING THINGS TO TELL ME ABOUT, BECAUSE THE MOST INTERESTING THING I DID WAS HELP MY MOTHER MEND SOME FENCES.
WAIT TILL YOU HEAR! FIRST OF ALL, OUR ARCHERY TEACHER HAS IRO--
SBAF

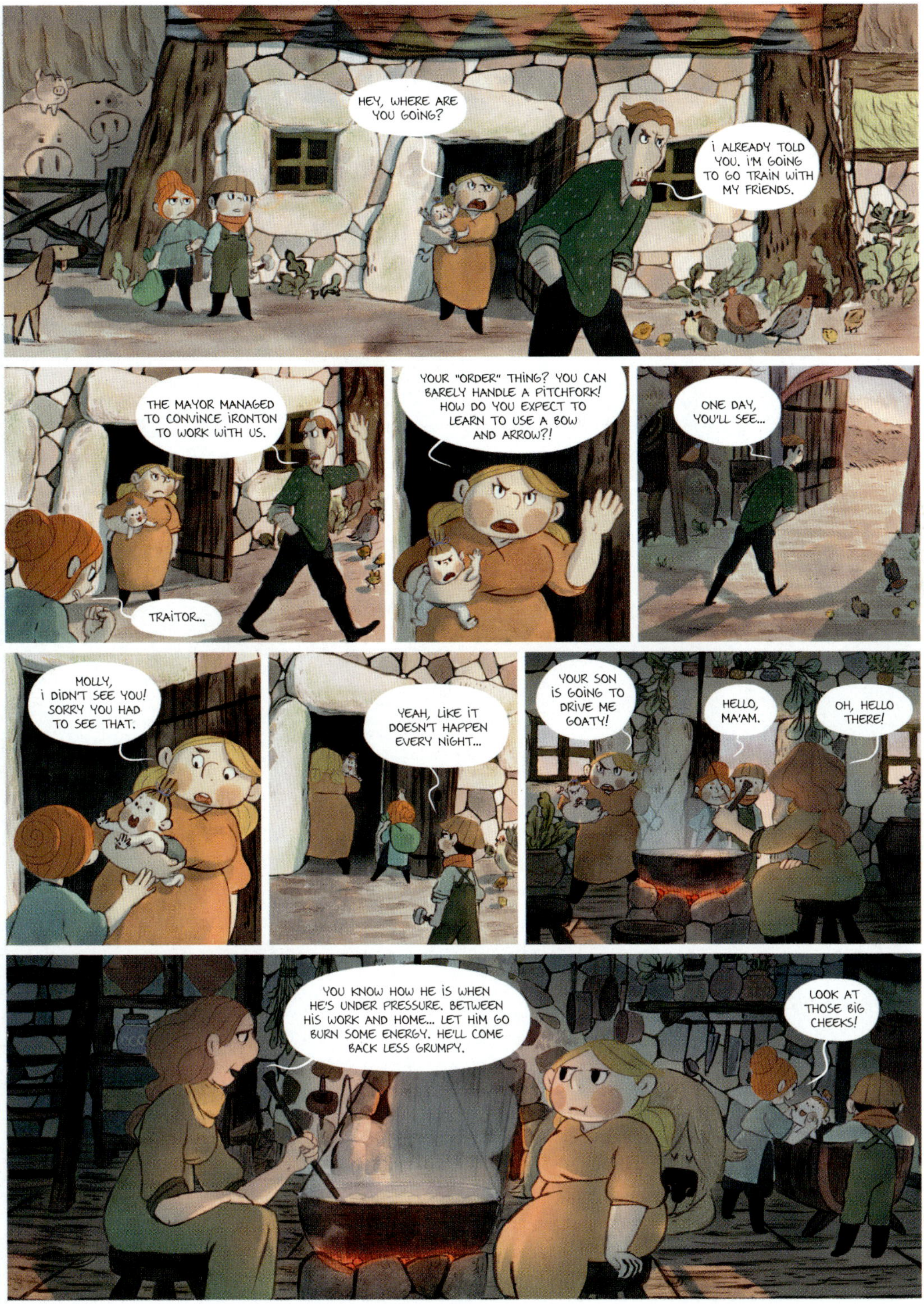
HEY, WHERE ARE YOU GOING?
I ALREADY TOLD YOU. I'M GOING TO GO TRAIN WITH MY FRIENDS.
THE MAYOR MANAGED TO CONVINCE IRONTON TO WORK WITH US.
TRAITOR...
YOUR "ORDER" THING? YOU CAN BARELY HANDLE A PITCHFORK! HOW DO YOU EXPECT TO LEARN TO USE A BOW AND ARROW?!
ONE DAY, YOU'LL SEE...
MOLLY, I DIDN'T SEE YOU! SORRY YOU HAD TO SEE THAT.
YEAH, LIKE IT DOESN'T HAPPEN EVERY NIGHT...
YOUR SON IS GOING TO DRIVE ME GOATY!
HELLO, MA'AM.
OH, HELLO THERE!
YOU KNOW HOW HE IS WHEN HE'S UNDER PRESSURE. BETWEEN HIS WORK AND HOME... LET HIM GO BURN SOME ENERGY. HE'LL COME BACK LESS GRUMPY.
LOOK AT THOSE BIG CHEEKS!

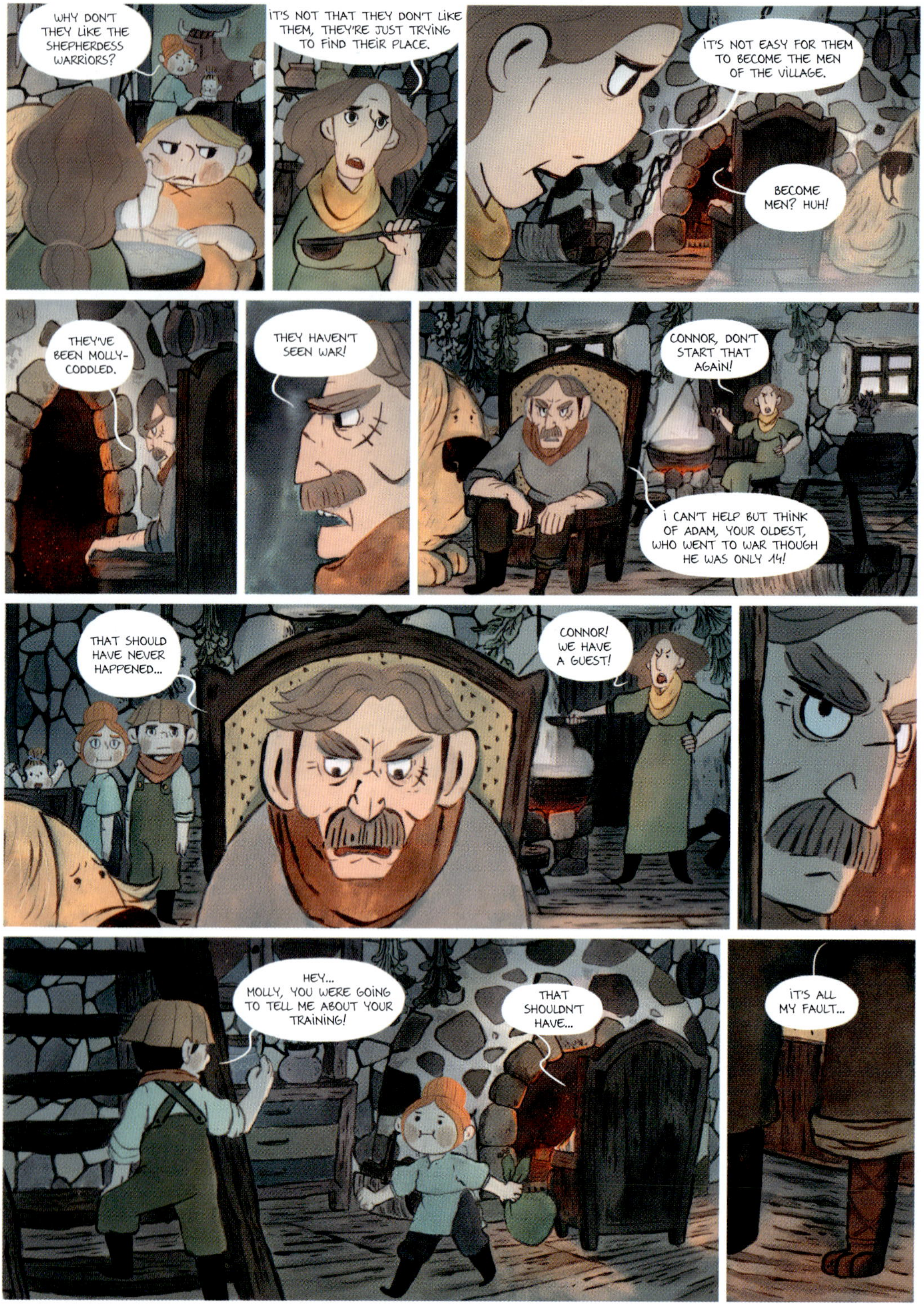
WHY DON'T THEY LIKE THE SHEPHERDESS WARRIORS?
IT'S NOT THAT THEY DON'T LIKE THEM, THEY'RE JUST TRYING TO FIND THEIR PLACE.
IT'S NOT EASY FOR THEM TO BECOME THE MEN OF THE VILLAGE.
BECOME MEN? HUH!
THEY'VE BEEN MOLLY-CODDLED.
THEY HAVEN'T SEEN WAR!
CONNOR, DON'T START THAT AGAIN!
I CAN'T HELP BUT THINK OF ADAM, YOUR OLDEST, WHO WENT TO WAR THOUGH HE WAS ONLY 14!
THAT SHOULD HAVE NEVER HAPPENED...
CONNOR! WE HAVE A GUEST!
HEY... MOLLY, YOU WERE GOING TO TELL ME ABOUT YOUR TRAINING!
THAT SHOULDN'T HAVE...
IT'S ALL MY FAULT...

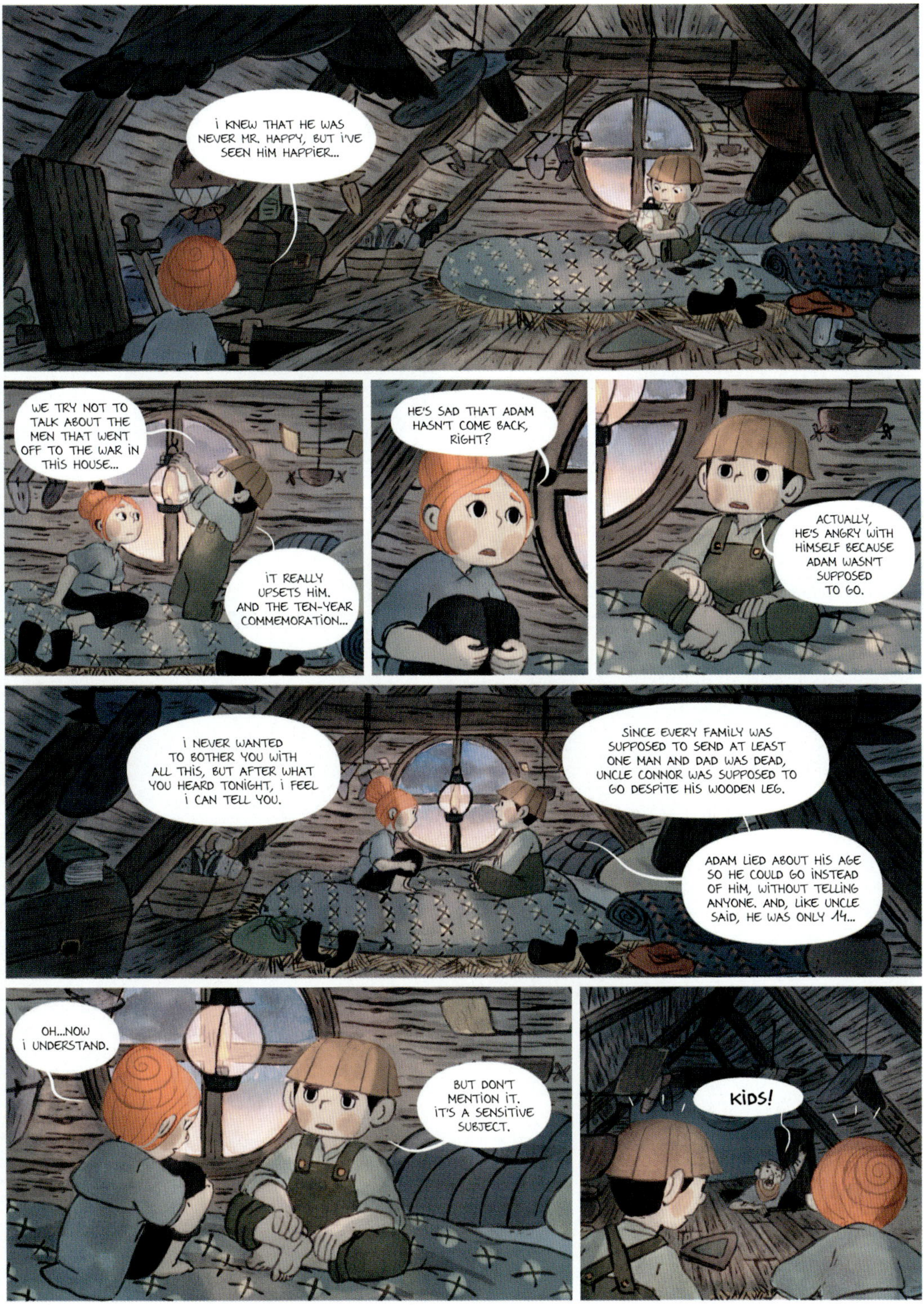
I KNEW THAT HE WAS NEVER MR. HAPPY, BUT I'VE SEEN HIM HAPPIER...
WE TRY NOT TO TALK ABOUT THE MEN THAT WENT OFF TO THE WAR IN THIS HOUSE...
IT REALLY UPSETS HIM. AND THE TEN-YEAR COMMEMORATION...
HE'S SAD THAT ADAM HASN'T COME BACK, RIGHT?
ACTUALLY, HE'S ANGRY WITH HIMSELF BECAUSE ADAM WASN'T SUPPOSED TO GO.
I NEVER WANTED TO BOTHER YOU WITH ALL THIS, BUT AFTER WHAT YOU HEARD TONIGHT, I FEEL I CAN TELL YOU.
SINCE EVERY FAMILY WAS SUPPOSED TO SEND AT LEAST ONE MAN AND DAD WAS DEAD, UNCLE CONNOR WAS SUPPOSED TO GO DESPITE HIS WOODEN LEG.
ADAM LIED ABOUT HIS AGE SO HE COULD GO INSTEAD OF HIM, WITHOUT TELLING ANYONE. AND, LIKE UNCLE SAID, HE WAS ONLY 14...
OH...NOW I UNDERSTAND.
BUT DON'T MENTION IT. IT'S A SENSITIVE SUBJECT.
KIDS!

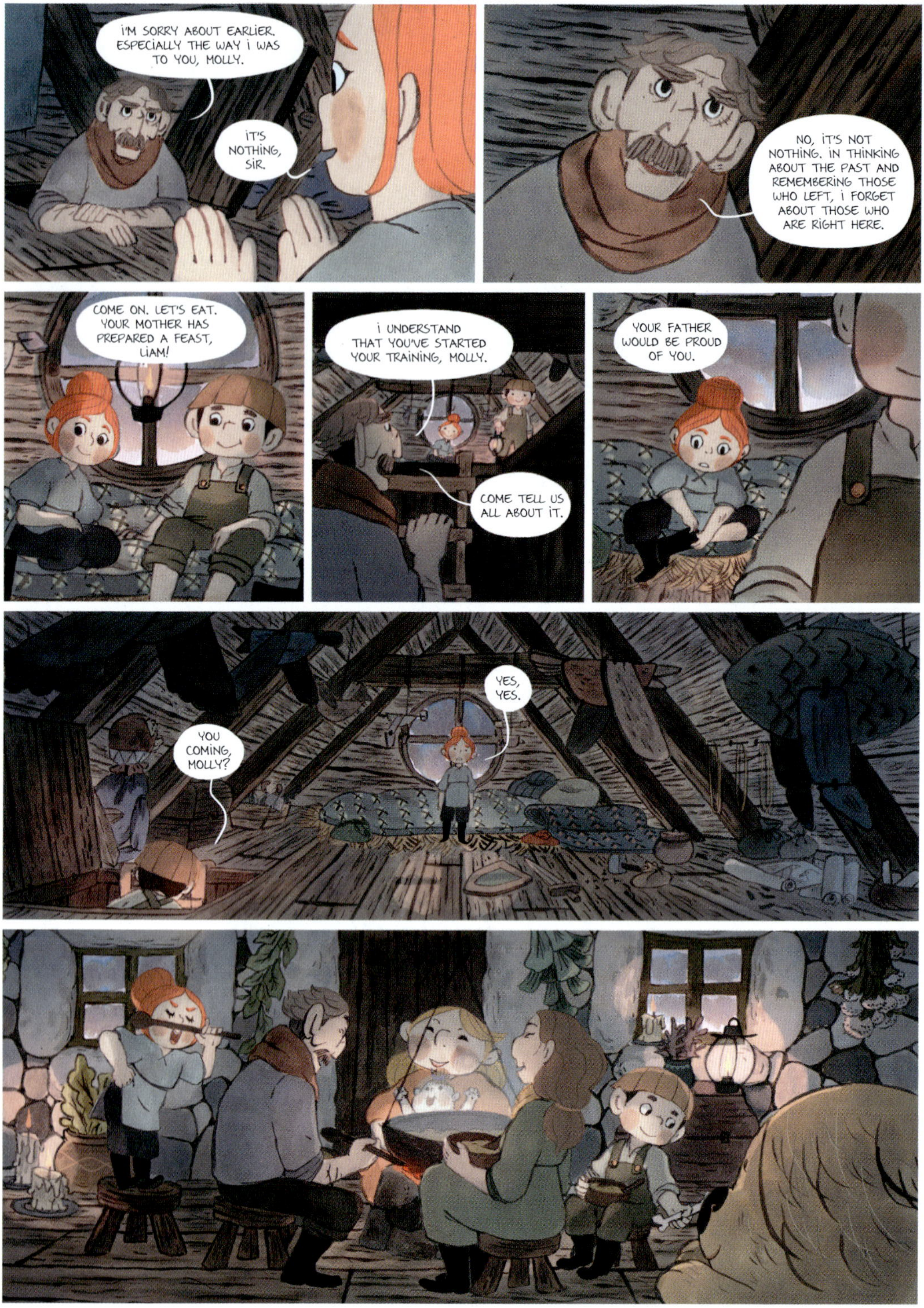
I'M SORRY ABOUT EARLIER. ESPECIALLY THE WAY I WAS TO YOU, MOLLY.
IT'S NOTHING, SIR.
NO, IT'S NOT NOTHING. IN THINKING ABOUT THE PAST AND REMEMBERING THOSE WHO LEFT, I FORGET ABOUT THOSE WHO ARE RIGHT HERE.
COME ON. LET'S EAT. YOUR MOTHER HAS PREPARED A FEAST, LIAM!
I UNDERSTAND THAT YOU'VE STARTED YOUR TRAINING, MOLLY.
COME TELL US ALL ABOUT IT.
YOUR FATHER WOULD BE PROUD OF YOU.
YES, YES.
YOU COMING, MOLLY?

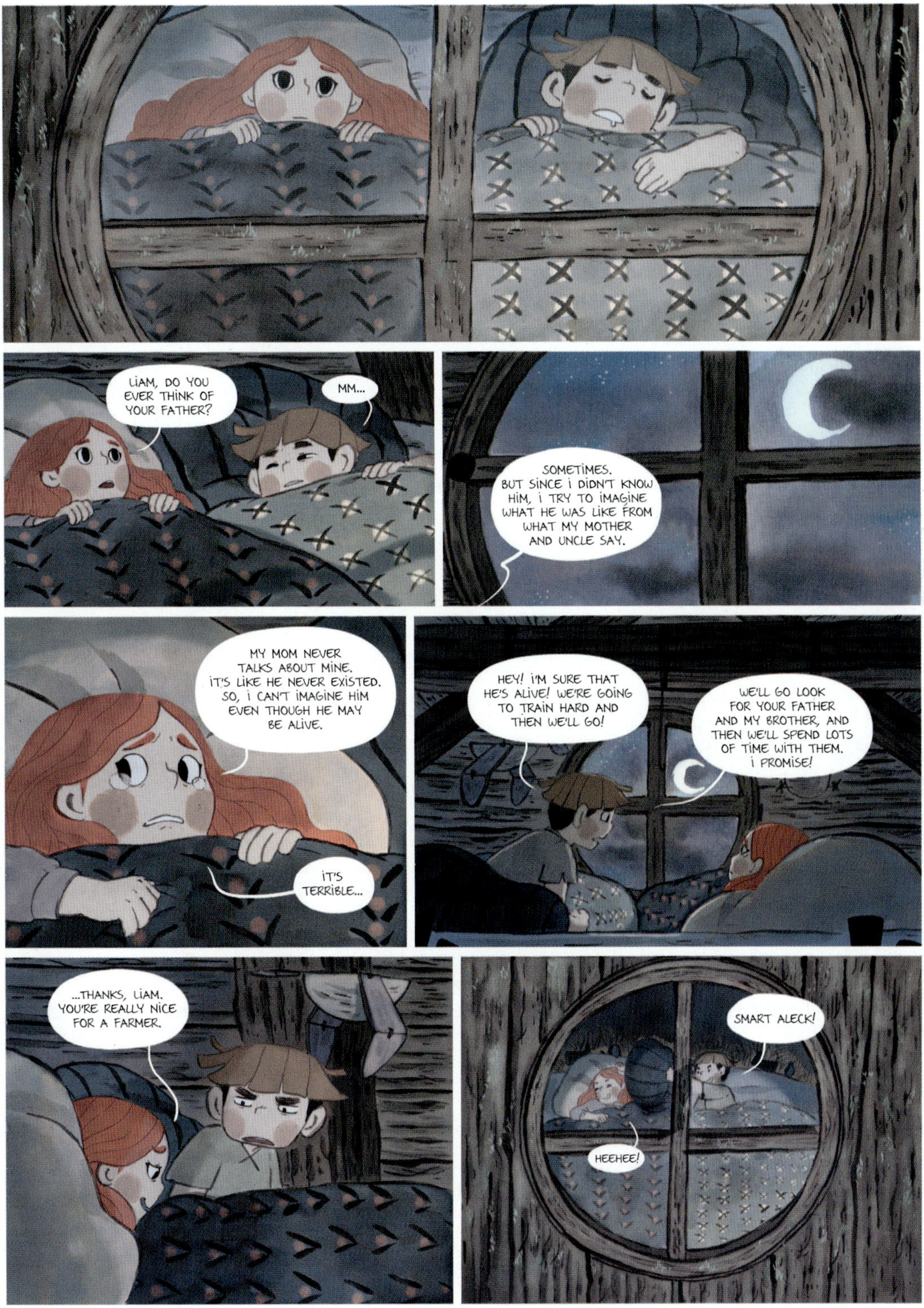
LIAM, DO YOU EVER THINK OF YOUR FATHER?
MM...
SOMETIMES. BUT SINCE I DIDN'T KNOW HIM, I TRY TO IMAGINE WHAT HE WAS LIKE FROM WHAT MY MOTHER AND UNCLE SAY.
MY MOM NEVER TALKS ABOUT MINE. IT'S LIKE HE NEVER EXISTED. SO, I CAN'T IMAGINE HIM EVEN THOUGH HE MAY BE ALIVE.
IT'S TERRIBLE...
HEY! I'M SURE THAT HE'S ALIVE! WE'RE GOING TO TRAIN HARD AND THEN WE'LL GO!
WE'LL GO LOOK FOR YOUR FATHER AND MY BROTHER, AND THEN WE'LL SPEND LOTS OF TIME WITH THEM. I PROMISE!
...THANKS, LIAM. YOU'RE REALLY NICE FOR A FARMER.
SMART ALECK!
HEEHEE!

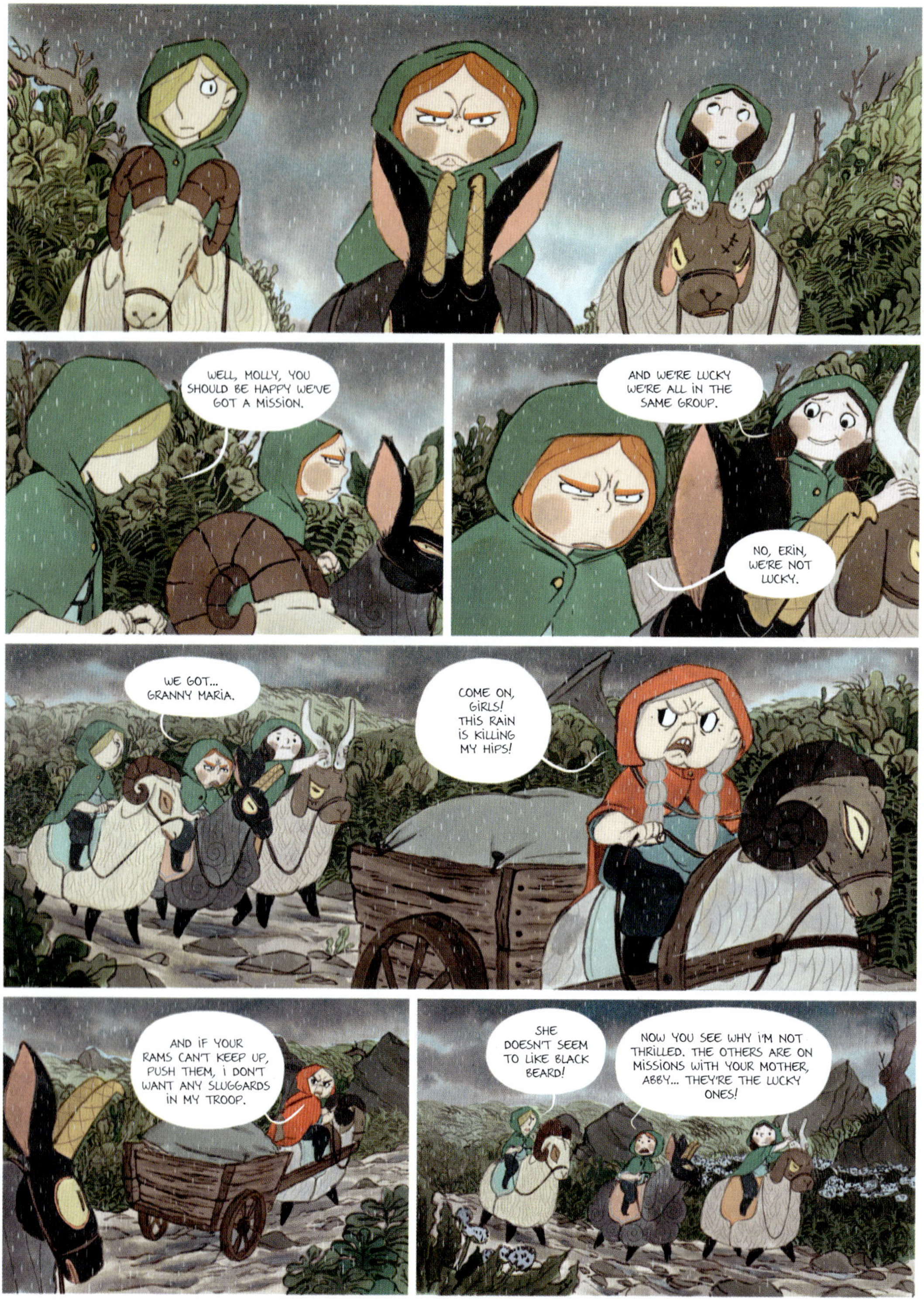
WELL, MOLLY, YOU SHOULD BE HAPPY WE'VE GOT A MISSION.
AND WE'RE LUCKY WE'RE ALL IN THE SAME GROUP.
NO, ERIN, WE'RE NOT LUCKY.
WE GOT... GRANNY MARIA.
COME ON, GIRLS! THIS RAIN IS KILLING MY HIPS!
AND IF YOUR RAMS CAN'T KEEP UP, PUSH THEM, I DON'T WANT ANY SLUGGARDS IN MY TROOP.
SHE DOESN'T SEEM TO LIKE BLACK BEARD!
NOW YOU SEE WHY I'M NOT THRILLED. THE OTHERS ARE ON MISSIONS WITH YOUR MOTHER, ABBY... THEY'RE THE LUCKY ONES!

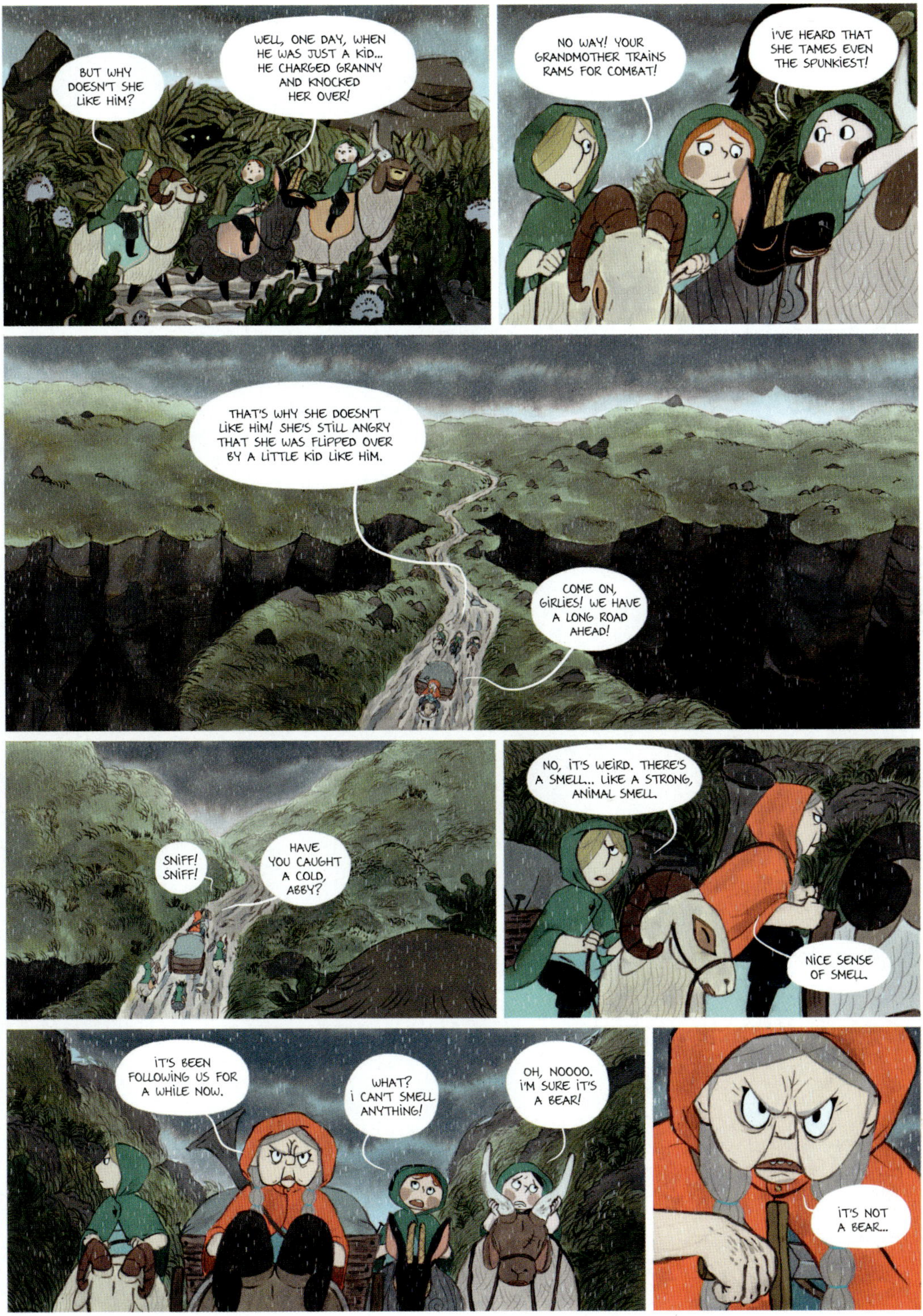

BUT WHY DOESN'T SHE LIKE HIM?
WELL, ONE DAY, WHEN HE WAS JUST A KID... HE CHARGED GRANNY AND KNOCKED HER OVER!
NO WAY! YOUR GRANDMOTHER TRAINS RAMS FOR COMBAT!
I'VE HEARD THAT SHE TAMES EVEN THE SPUNKIEST!
THAT'S WHY SHE DOESN'T LIKE HIM! SHE'S STILL ANGRY THAT SHE WAS FLIPPED OVER BY A LITTLE KID LIKE HIM.
COME ON, GIRLIES! WE HAVE A LONG ROAD AHEAD!
SNIFF! SNIFF!
HAVE YOU CAUGHT A COLD, ABBY?
NO, IT'S WEIRD. THERE'S A SMELL... LIKE A STRONG, ANIMAL SMELL.
NICE SENSE OF SMELL.
IT'S BEEN FOLLOWING US FOR A WHILE NOW.
WHAT? I CAN'T SMELL ANYTHING!
OH, NOOOO. I'M SURE IT'S A BEAR!
IT'S NOT A BEAR...

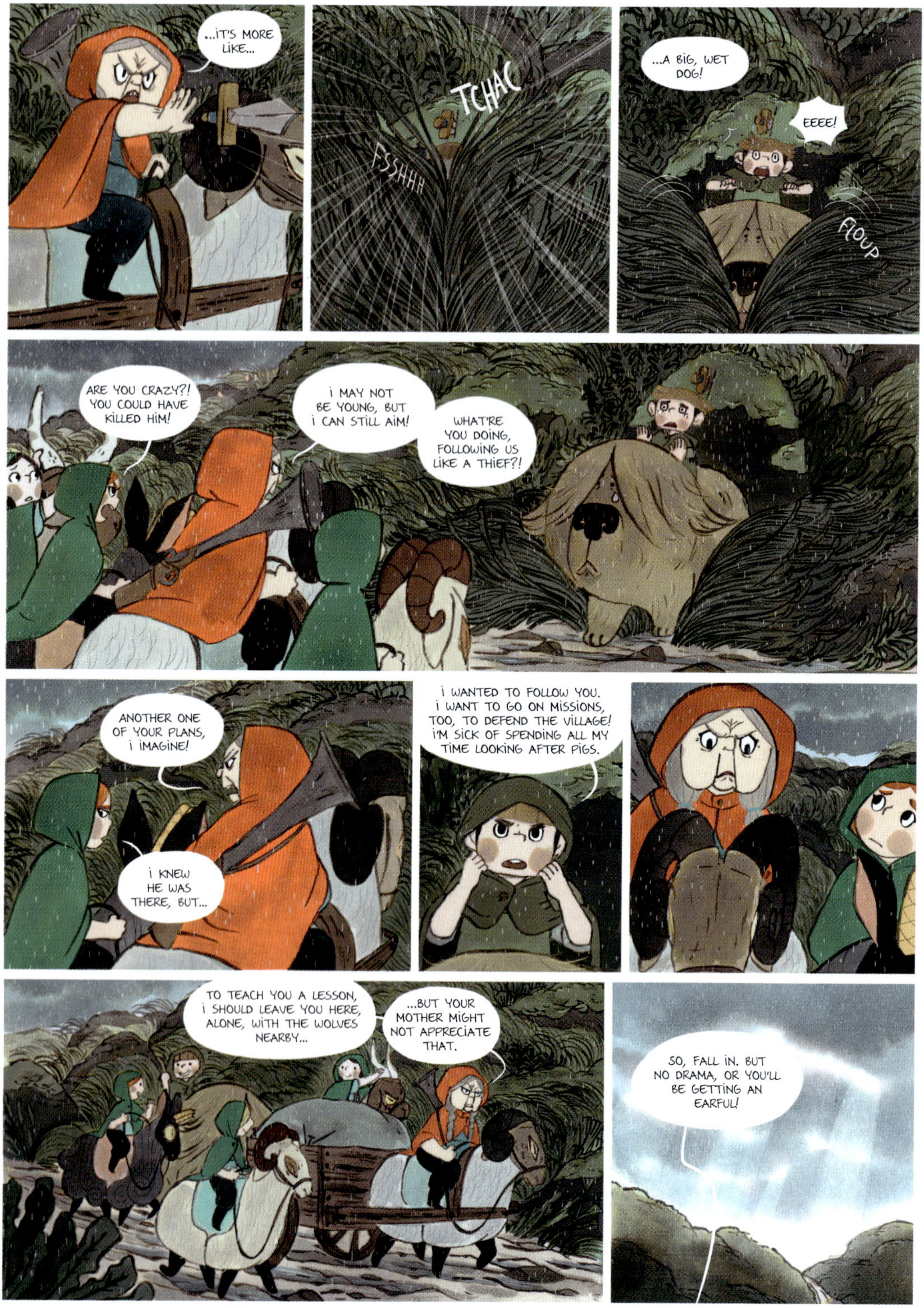
...IT'S MORE LIKE...
TCHAC
FSSHHH
...A BIG, WET DOG!
EEEE!
FLOUP
ARE YOU CRAZY?! YOU COULD HAVE KILLED HIM!
I MAY NOT BE YOUNG, BUT I CAN STILL AIM!
WHAT'RE YOU DOING, FOLLOWING US LIKE A THIEF?!
ANOTHER ONE OF YOUR PLANS, I IMAGINE!
I KNEW HE WAS THERE, BUT...
I WANTED TO FOLLOW YOU. I WANT TO GO ON MISSIONS, TOO, TO DEFEND THE VILLAGE! I'M SICK OF SPENDING ALL MY TIME LOOKING AFTER PIGS.
TO TEACH YOU A LESSON, I SHOULD LEAVE YOU HERE, ALONE, WITH THE WOLVES NEARBY...
...BUT YOUR MOTHER MIGHT NOT APPRECIATE THAT.
SO, FALL IN. BUT NO DRAMA, OR YOU'LL BE GETTING AN EARFUL!

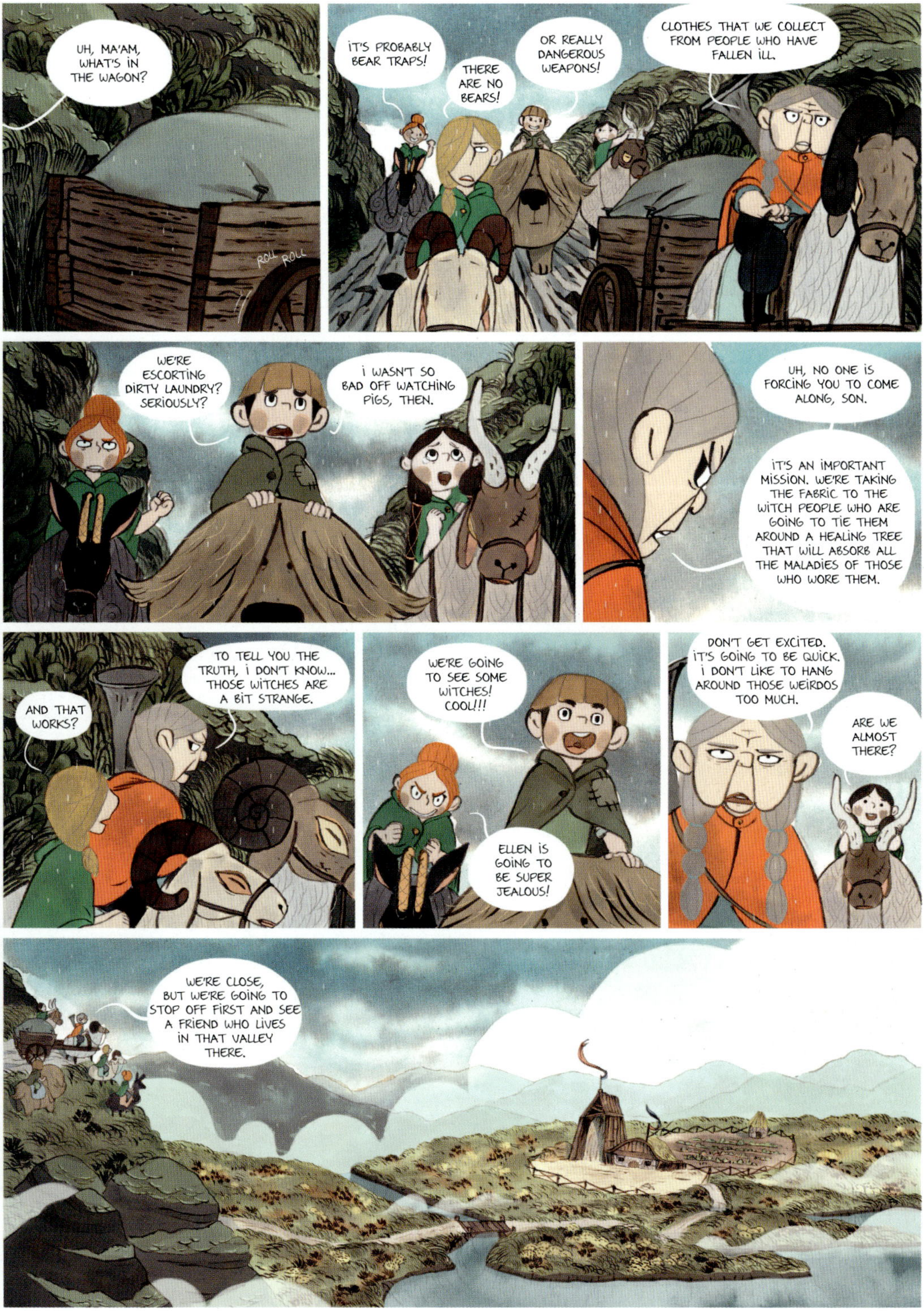

UH, MA'AM, WHAT'S IN THE WAGON?
ROLL ROLL
IT'S PROBABLY BEAR TRAPS!
THERE ARE NO BEARS!
OR REALLY DANGEROUS WEAPONS!
CLOTHES THAT WE COLLECT FROM PEOPLE WHO HAVE FALLEN ILL.
WE'RE ESCORTING DIRTY LAUNDRY? SERIOUSLY?
I WASN'T SO BAD OFF WATCHING PIGS, THEN.
UH, NO ONE IS FORCING YOU TO COME ALONG, SON.
IT'S AN IMPORTANT MISSION. WE'RE TAKING THE FABRIC TO THE WITCH PEOPLE WHO ARE GOING TO TIE THEM AROUND A HEALING TREE THAT WILL ABSORB ALL THE MALADIES OF THOSE WHO WORE THEM.
AND THAT WORKS?
TO TELL YOU THE TRUTH, I DON'T KNOW... THOSE WITCHES ARE A BIT STRANGE.
WE'RE GOING TO SEE SOME WITCHES! COOL!!!
ELLEN IS GOING TO BE SUPER JEALOUS!
DON'T GET EXCITED. IT'S GOING TO BE QUICK. I DON'T LIKE TO HANG AROUND THOSE WEIRDOS TOO MUCH.
ARE WE ALMOST THERE?
WE'RE CLOSE, BUT WE'RE GOING TO STOP OFF FIRST AND SEE A FRIEND WHO LIVES IN THAT VALLEY THERE.

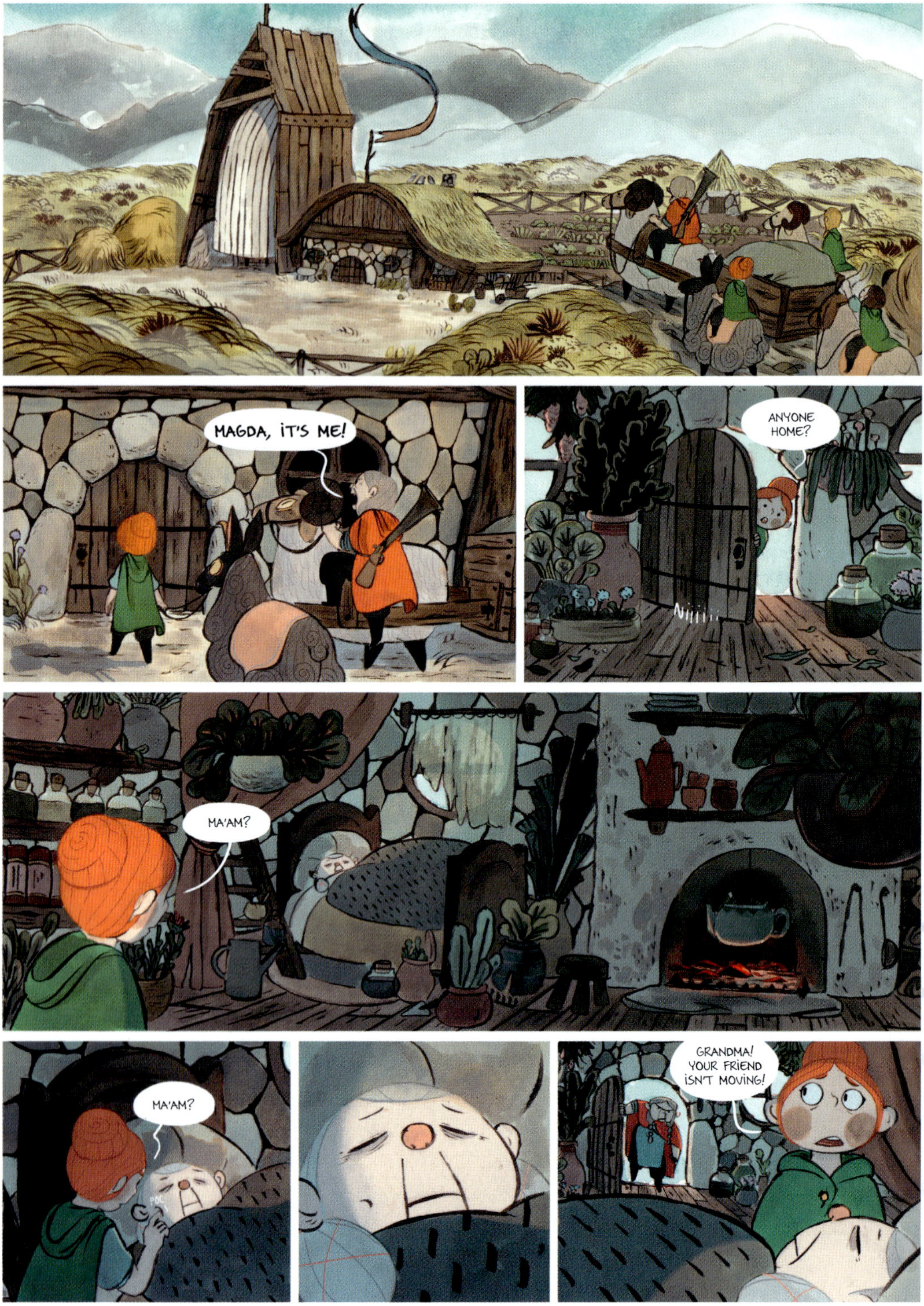
MAGDA, IT'S ME!
ANYONE HOME?
Niiiii
MA'AM?
MA'AM?
POC
GRANDMA! YOUR FRIEND ISN'T MOVING!

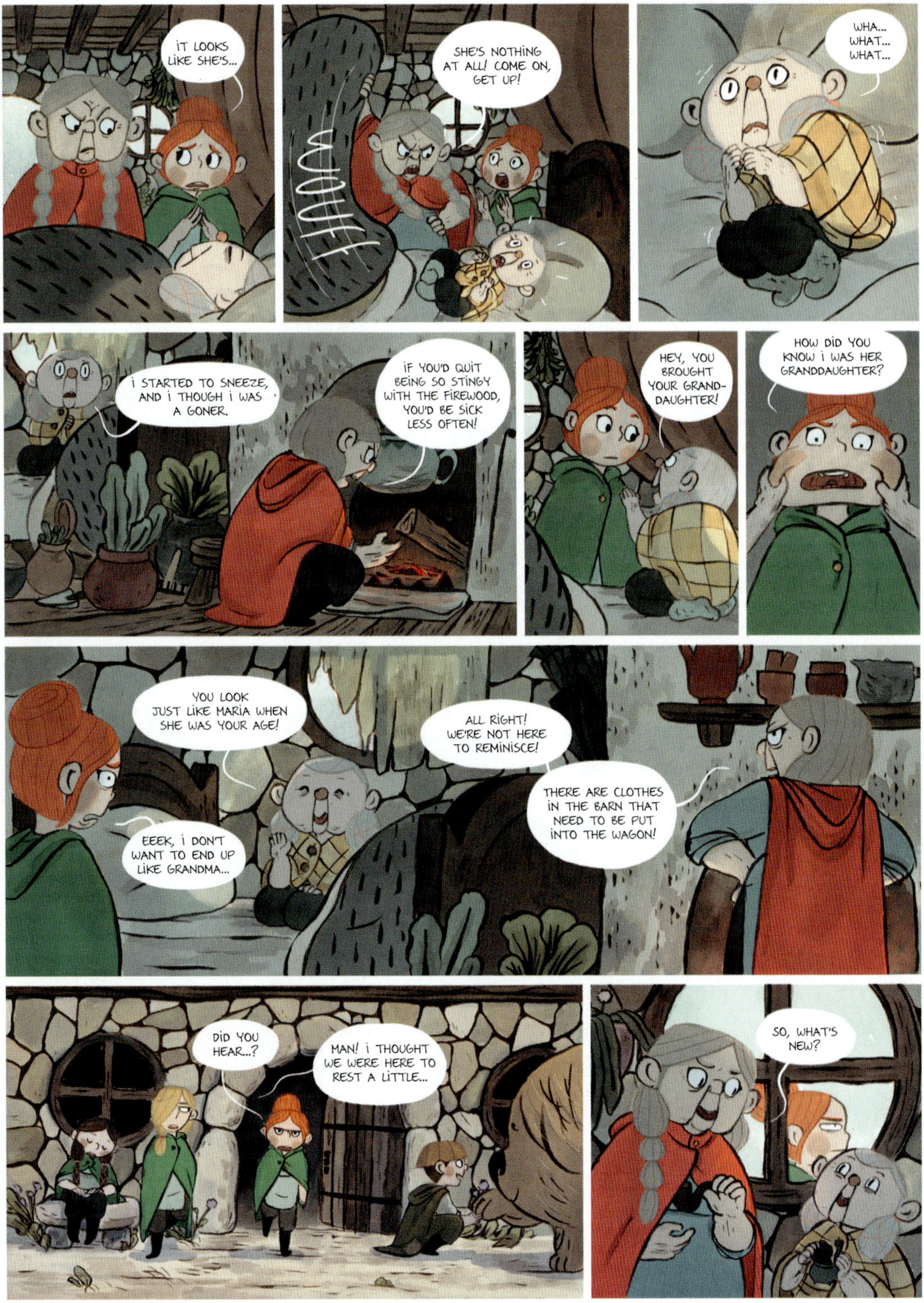
IT LOOKS LIKE SHE'S...
SHE'S NOTHING AT ALL! COME ON, GET UP!
WOUFF
WHA... WHAT... WHAT...
I STARTED TO SNEEZE, AND I THOUGH I WAS A GONER.
IF YOU'D QUIT BEING SO STINGY WITH THE FIREWOOD, YOU'D BE SICK LESS OFTEN!
HEY, YOU BROUGHT YOUR GRAND-DAUGHTER!
HOW DID YOU KNOW I WAS HER GRANDDAUGHTER?
YOU LOOK JUST LIKE MARIA WHEN SHE WAS YOUR AGE!
EEEK, I DON'T WANT TO END UP LIKE GRANDMA...
ALL RIGHT! WE'RE NOT HERE TO REMINISCE!
THERE ARE CLOTHES IN THE BARN THAT NEED TO BE PUT INTO THE WAGON!
DID YOU HEAR...?
MAN! I THOUGHT WE WERE HERE TO REST A LITTLE...
SO, WHAT'S NEW?

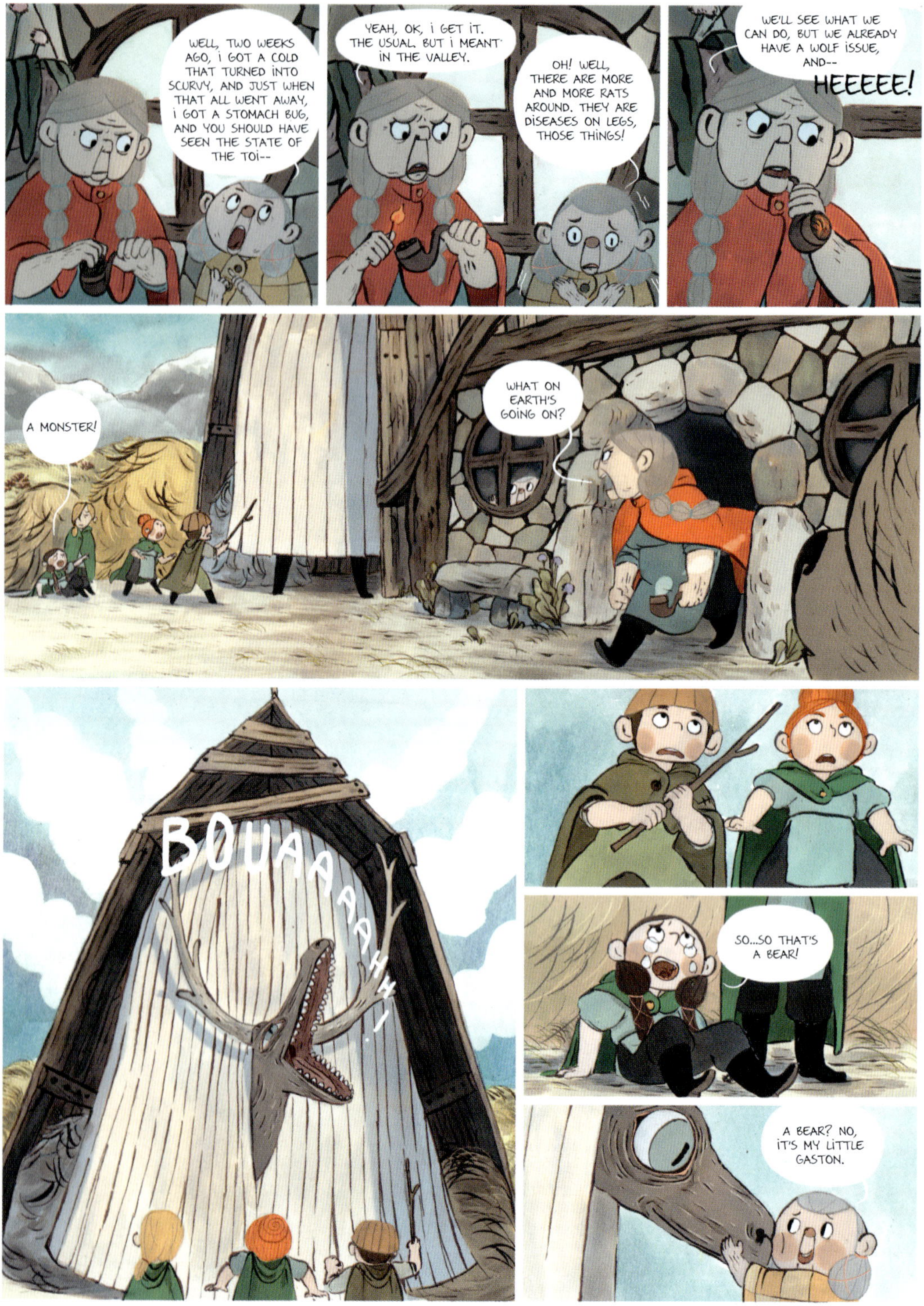
WELL, TWO WEEKS AGO, i GOT A COLD THAT TURNED iNTO SCURVY, AND JUST WHEN THAT ALL WENT AWAY, i GOT A STOMACH BUG, AND YOU SHOULD HAVE SEEN THE STATE OF THE TOi--
YEAH, OK, i GET iT. THE USUAL. BUT i MEANT iN THE VALLEY.
OH! WELL, THERE ARE MORE AND MORE RATS AROUND. THEY ARE DiSEASES ON LEGS, THOSE THiNGS!
WE'LL SEE WHAT WE CAN DO, BUT WE ALREADY HAVE A WOLF iSSUE, AND--
HEEEEEE!
A MONSTER!
WHAT ON EARTH'S GOiNG ON?
BOUAAAAAHH!
SO...SO THAT'S A BEAR!
A BEAR? NO, iT'S MY LiTTLE GASTON.

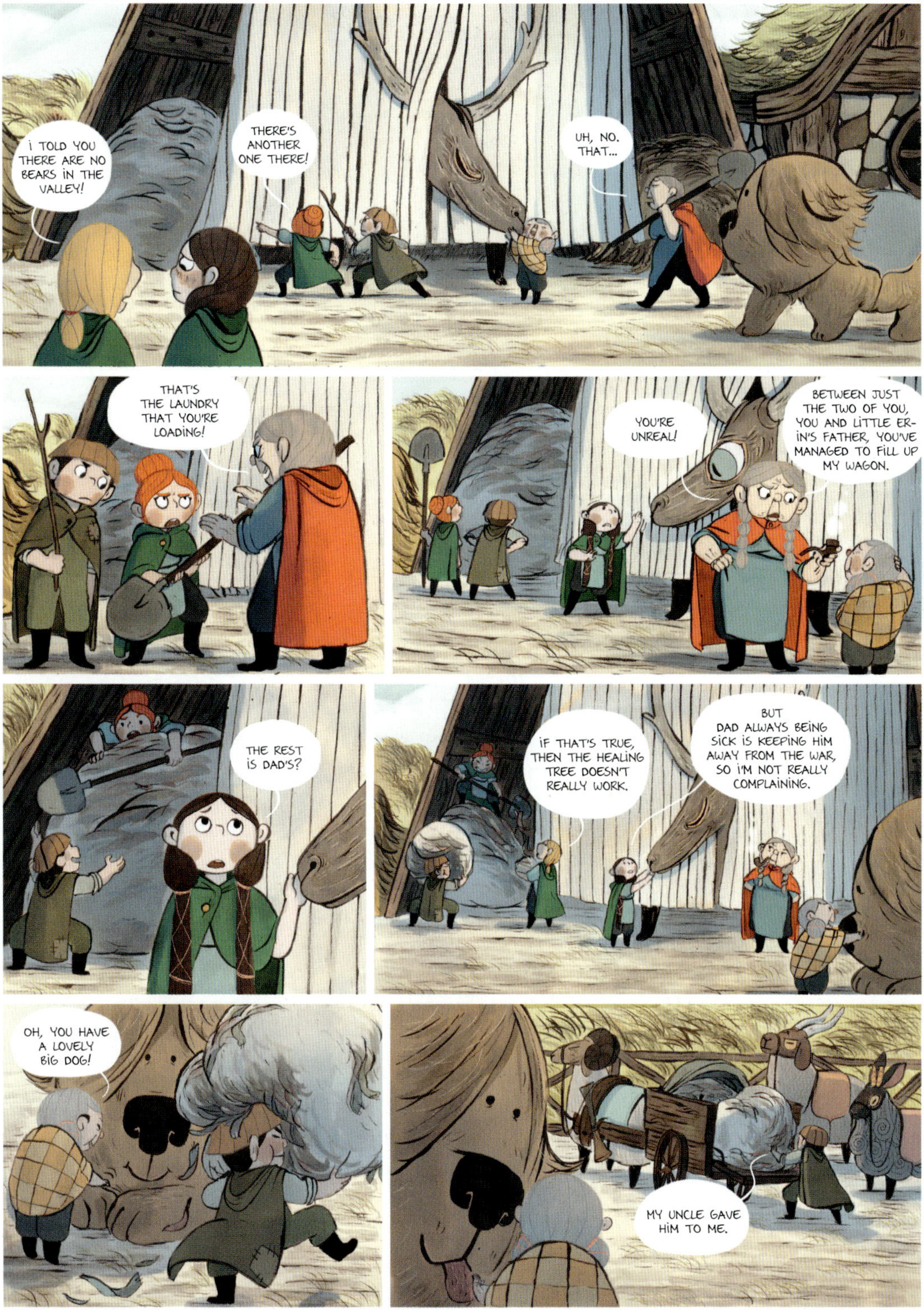

I TOLD YOU THERE ARE NO BEARS IN THE VALLEY!
THERE'S ANOTHER ONE THERE!
UH, NO. THAT...
THAT'S THE LAUNDRY THAT YOU'RE LOADING!
YOU'RE UNREAL!
BETWEEN JUST THE TWO OF YOU, YOU AND LITTLE ERIN'S FATHER, YOU'VE MANAGED TO FILL UP MY WAGON.
THE REST IS DAD'S?
IF THAT'S TRUE, THEN THE HEALING TREE DOESN'T REALLY WORK.
BUT DAD ALWAYS BEING SICK IS KEEPING HIM AWAY FROM THE WAR, SO I'M NOT REALLY COMPLAINING.
OH, YOU HAVE A LOVELY BIG DOG!
MY UNCLE GAVE HIM TO ME.

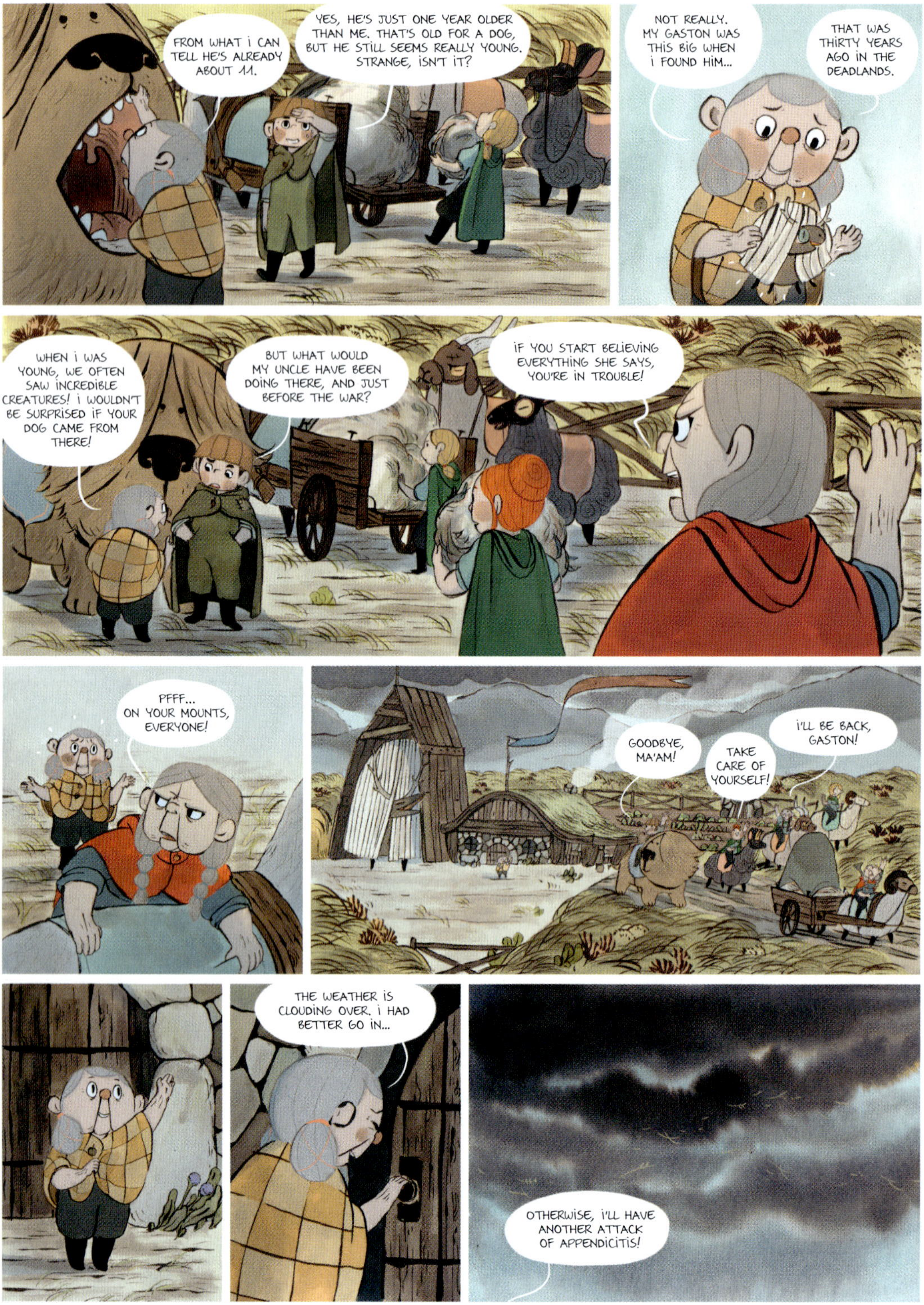
FROM WHAT I CAN TELL HE'S ALREADY ABOUT 11.
YES, HE'S JUST ONE YEAR OLDER THAN ME. THAT'S OLD FOR A DOG, BUT HE STILL SEEMS REALLY YOUNG. STRANGE, ISN'T IT?
NOT REALLY. MY GASTON WAS THIS BIG WHEN I FOUND HIM...
THAT WAS THIRTY YEARS AGO IN THE DEADLANDS.
WHEN I WAS YOUNG, WE OFTEN SAW INCREDIBLE CREATURES! I WOULDN'T BE SURPRISED IF YOUR DOG CAME FROM THERE!
BUT WHAT WOULD MY UNCLE HAVE BEEN DOING THERE, AND JUST BEFORE THE WAR?
IF YOU START BELIEVING EVERYTHING SHE SAYS, YOU'RE IN TROUBLE!
PFFF... ON YOUR MOUNTS, EVERYONE!
GOODBYE, MA'AM!
TAKE CARE OF YOURSELF!
I'LL BE BACK, GASTON!
THE WEATHER IS CLOUDING OVER. I HAD BETTER GO IN...
OTHERWISE, I'LL HAVE ANOTHER ATTACK OF APPENDICITIS!

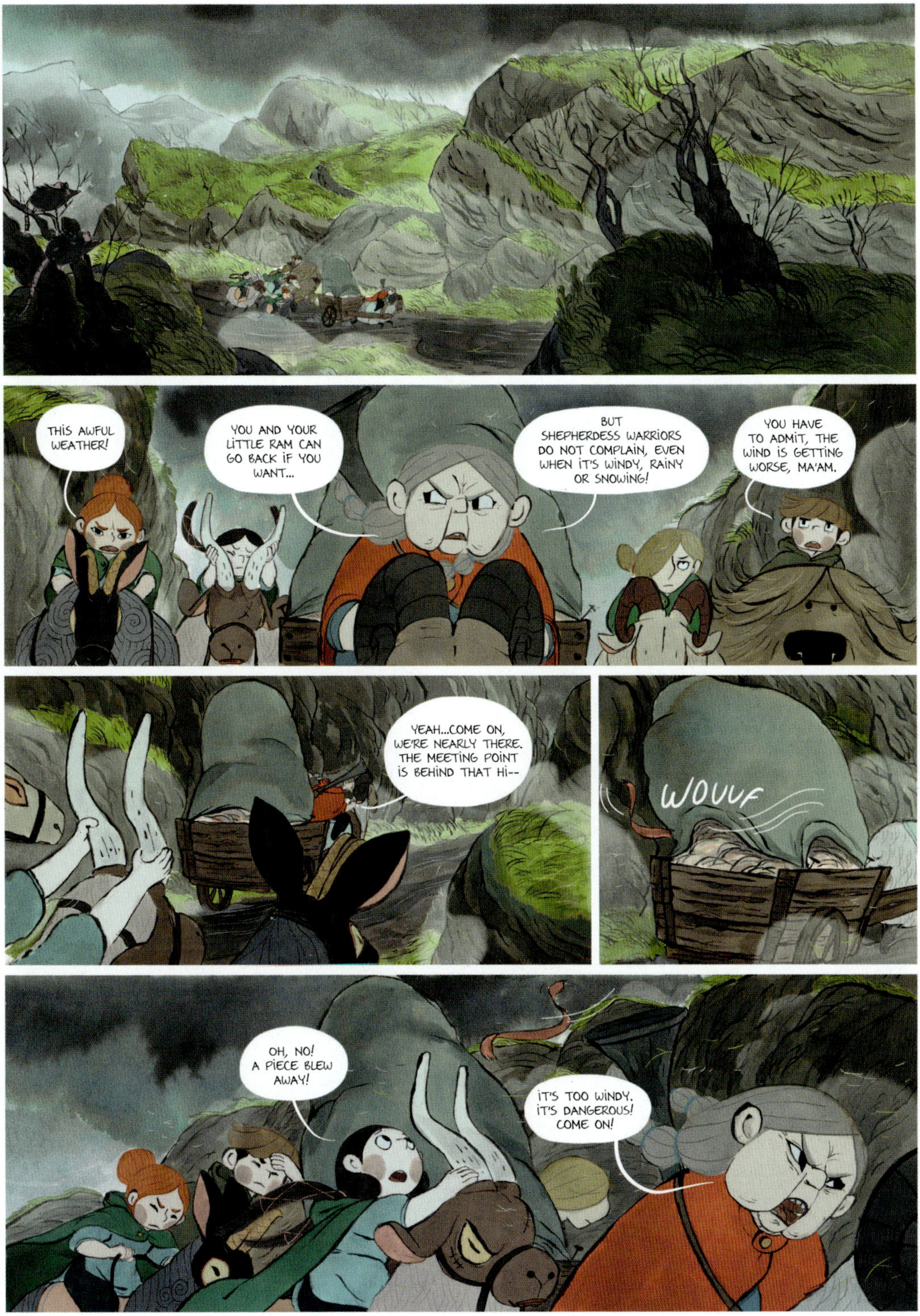
THIS AWFUL WEATHER!
YOU AND YOUR LITTLE RAM CAN GO BACK IF YOU WANT...
BUT SHEPHERDESS WARRIORS DO NOT COMPLAIN, EVEN WHEN IT'S WINDY, RAINY OR SNOWING!
YOU HAVE TO ADMIT, THE WIND IS GETTING WORSE, MA'AM.
YEAH...COME ON, WE'RE NEARLY THERE. THE MEETING POINT IS BEHIND THAT HI--
WOUUF
OH, NO! A PIECE BLEW AWAY!
IT'S TOO WINDY. IT'S DANGEROUS! COME ON!

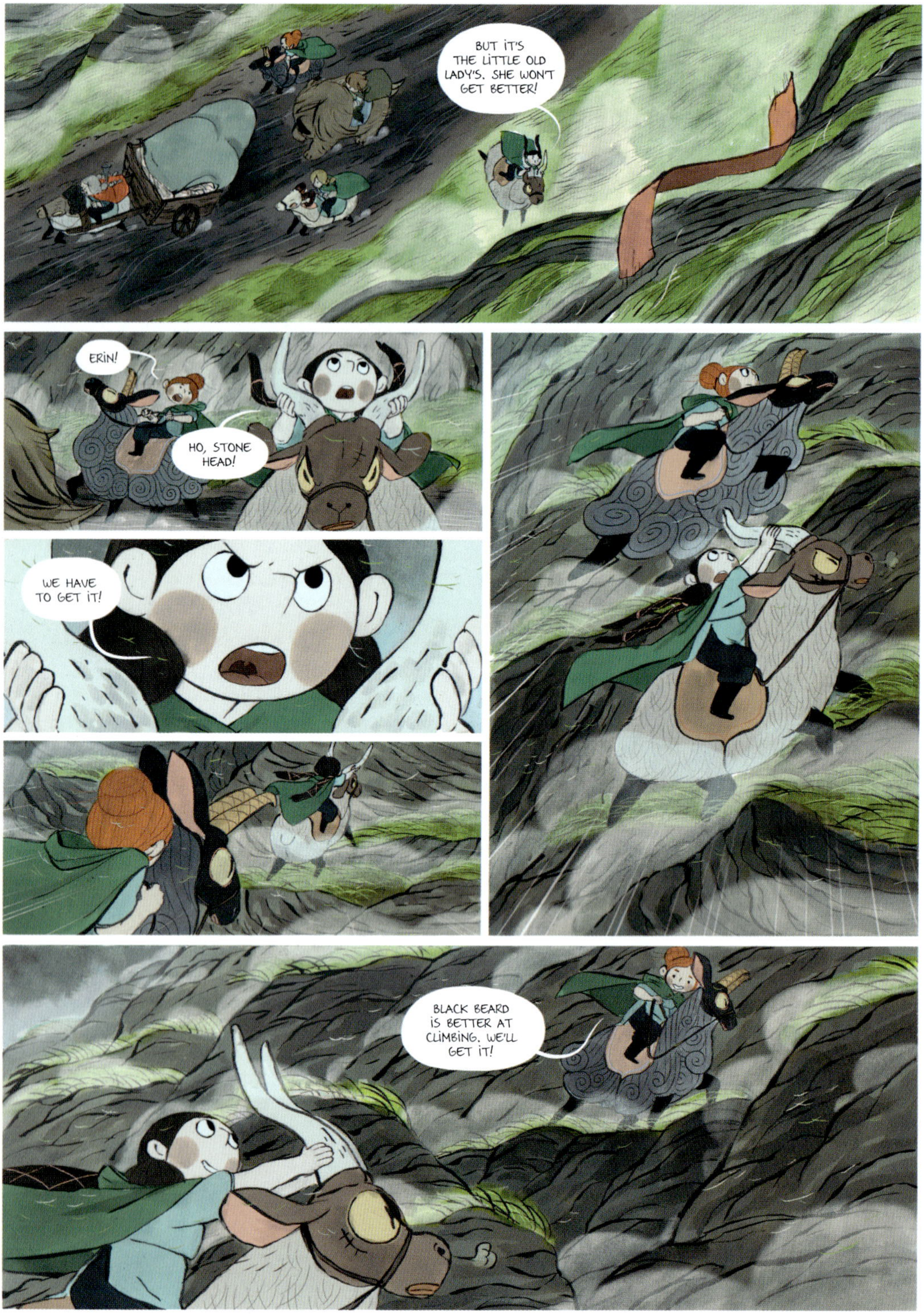
BUT IT'S THE LITTLE OLD LADY'S. SHE WON'T GET BETTER!
ERIN!
HO, STONE HEAD!
WE HAVE TO GET IT!
BLACK BEARD IS BETTER AT CLIMBING. WE'LL GET IT!

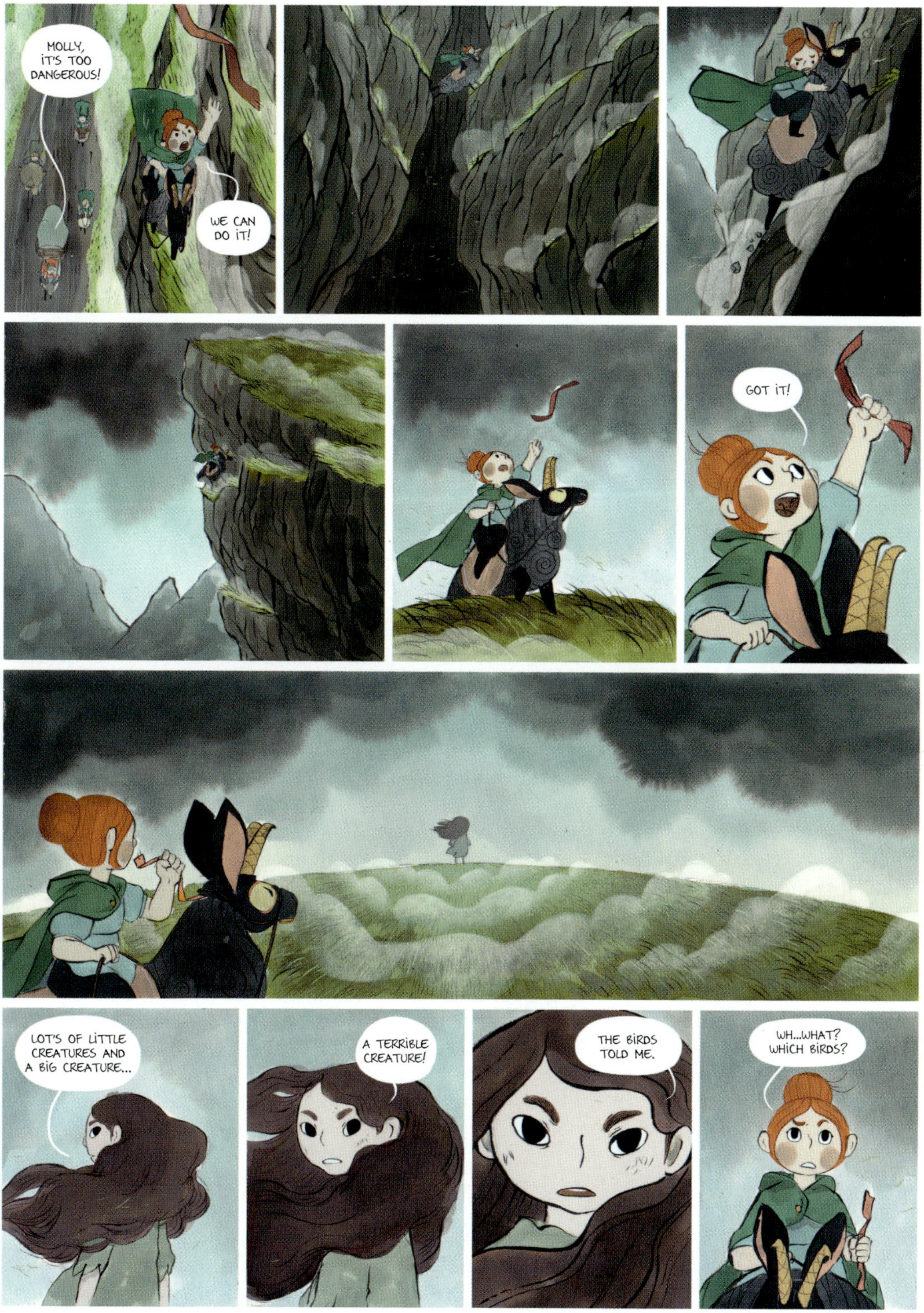
MOLLY, IT'S TOO DANGEROUS!
WE CAN DO IT!
GOT IT!
LOT'S OF LITTLE CREATURES AND A BIG CREATURE...
A TERRIBLE CREATURE!
THE BIRDS TOLD ME.
WH...WHAT? WHICH BIRDS?

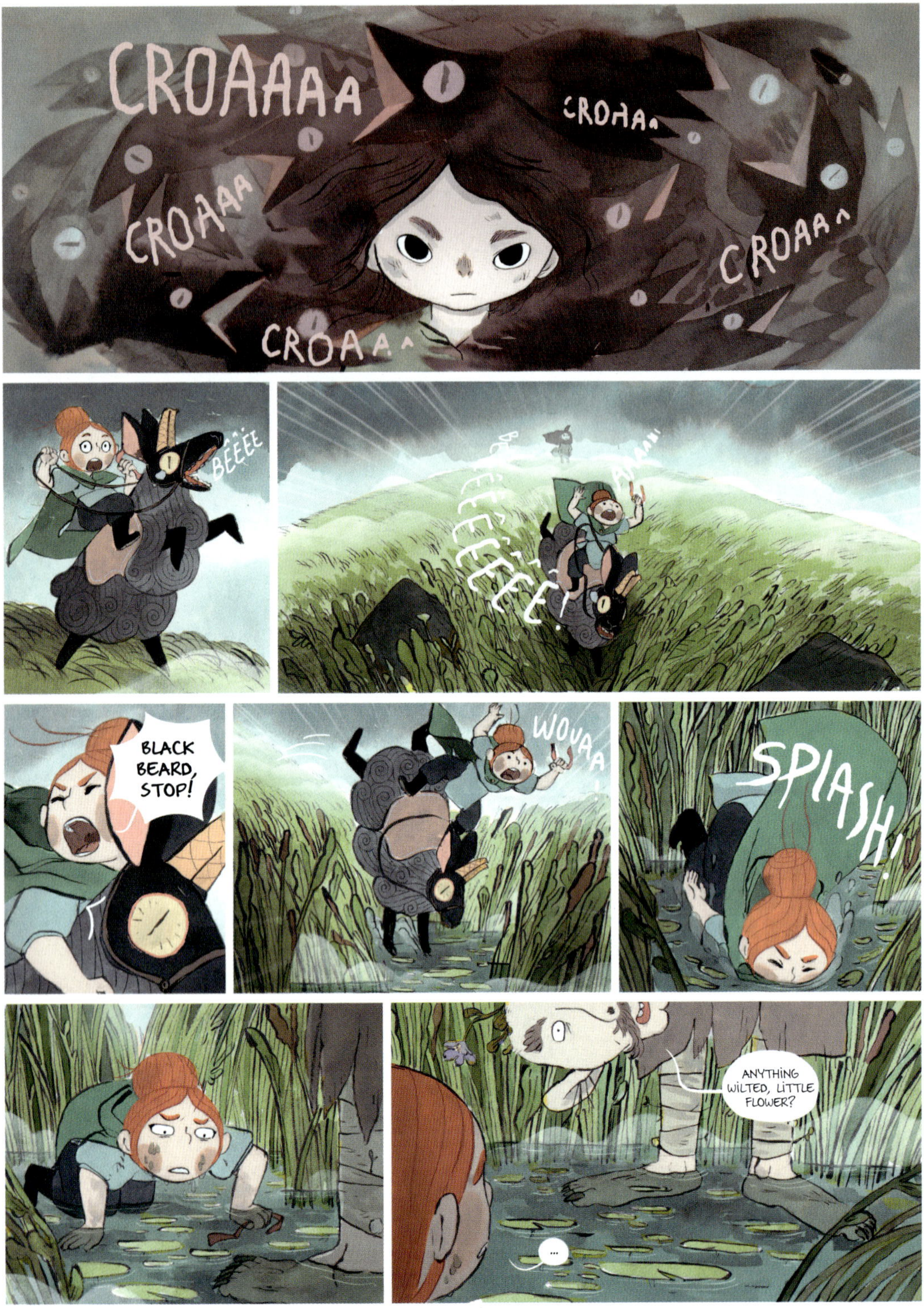
CROAAAAA
CROAA
CROAAA
CROAA
CROAA
BEEEE
BEEEEEEE!
BLACK BEARD, STOP!
WOUAA!
SPLASH!
ANYTHING WILTED, LITTLE FLOWER?
...

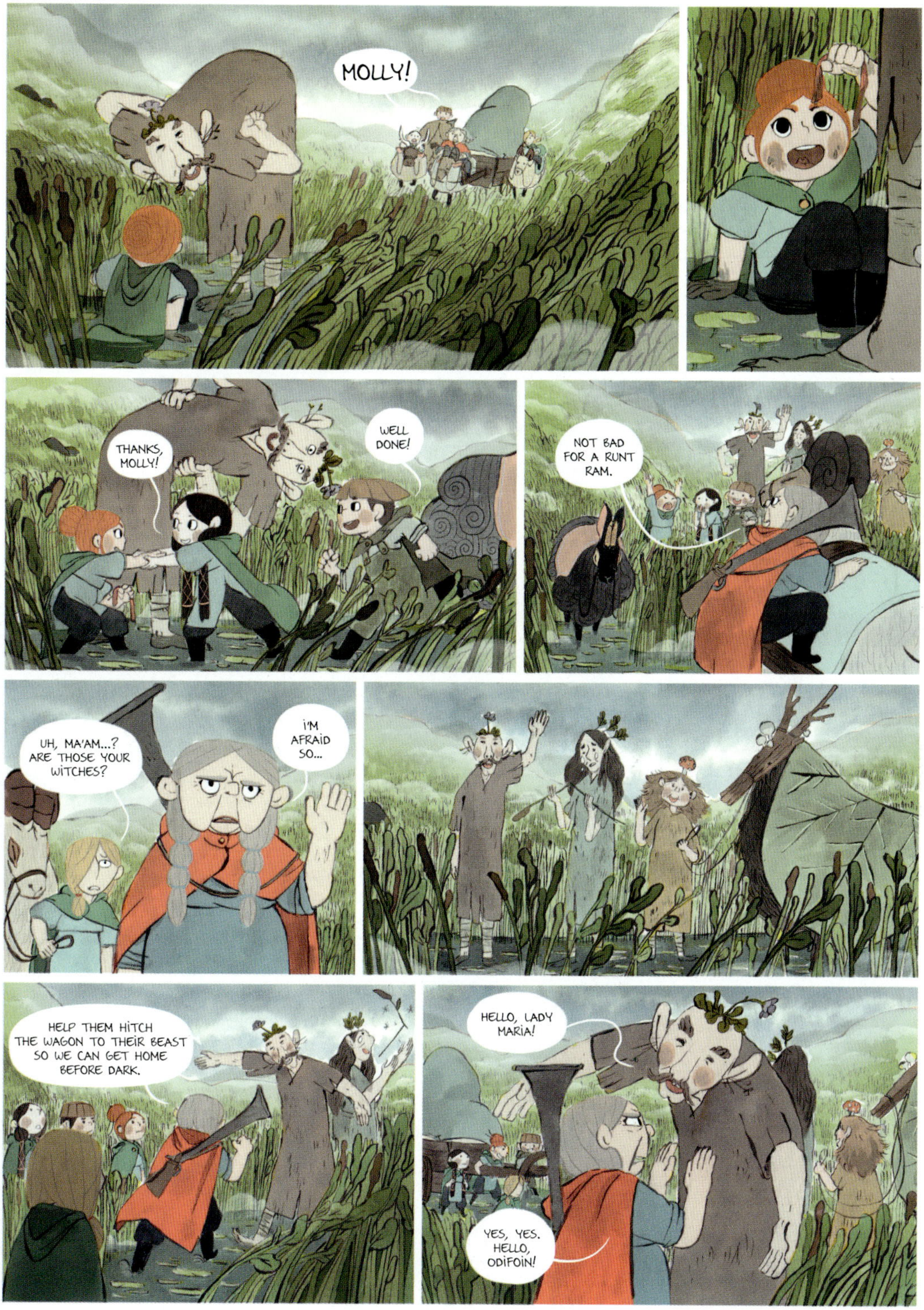
MOLLY!
THANKS, MOLLY!
WELL DONE!
NOT BAD FOR A RUNT RAM.
UH, MA'AM...? ARE THOSE YOUR WITCHES?
I'M AFRAID SO...
HELP THEM HITCH THE WAGON TO THEIR BEAST SO WE CAN GET HOME BEFORE DARK.
HELLO, LADY MARIA!
YES, YES. HELLO, ODIFOIN!

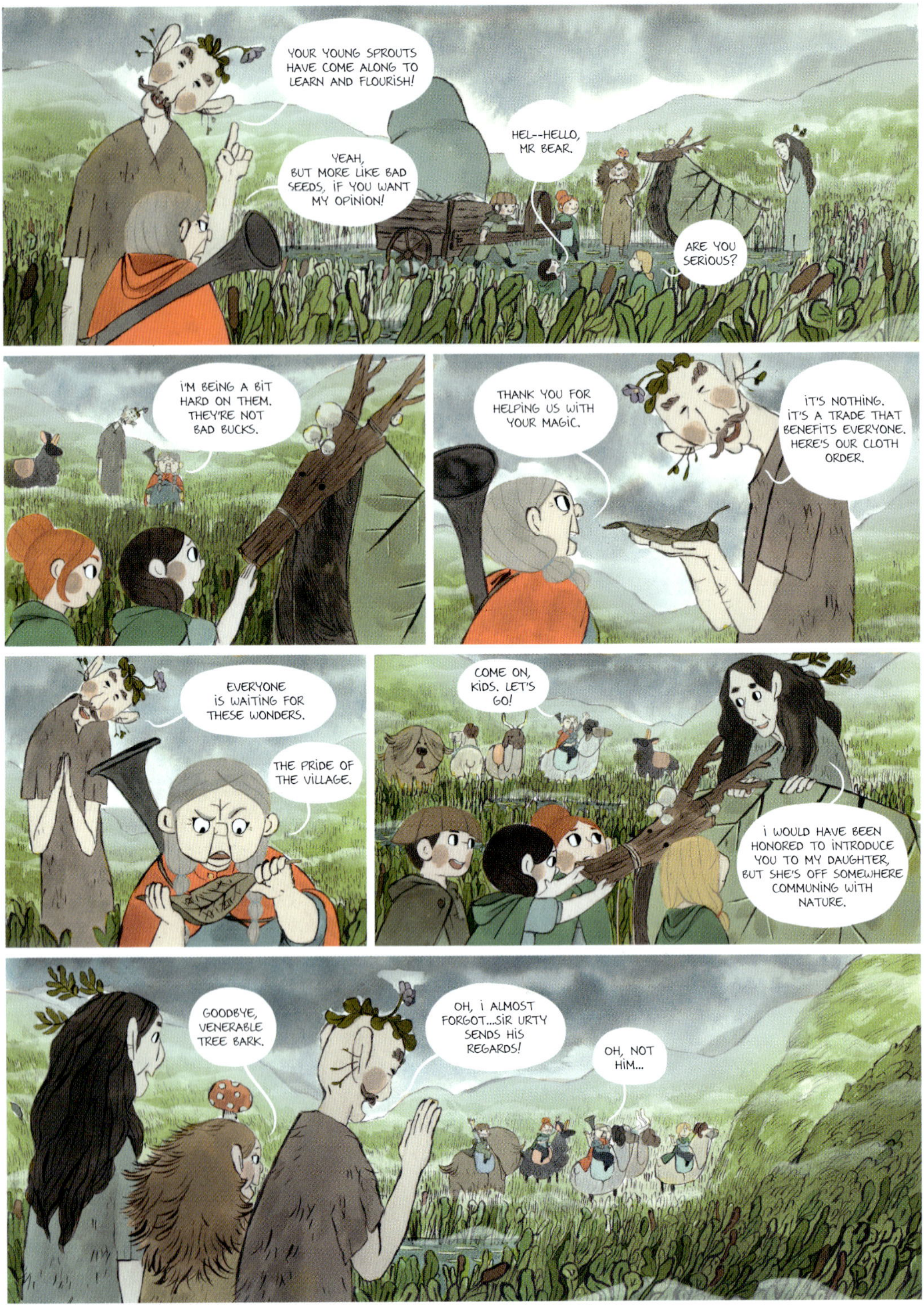
YOUR YOUNG SPROUTS HAVE COME ALONG TO LEARN AND FLOURISH!
YEAH, BUT MORE LIKE BAD SEEDS, IF YOU WANT MY OPINION!
HEL--HELLO, MR BEAR.
ARE YOU SERIOUS?
I'M BEING A BIT HARD ON THEM. THEY'RE NOT BAD BUCKS.
THANK YOU FOR HELPING US WITH YOUR MAGIC.
IT'S NOTHING. IT'S A TRADE THAT BENEFITS EVERYONE. HERE'S OUR CLOTH ORDER.
EVERYONE IS WAITING FOR THESE WONDERS.
THE PRIDE OF THE VILLAGE.
COME ON, KIDS. LET'S GO!
I WOULD HAVE BEEN HONORED TO INTRODUCE YOU TO MY DAUGHTER, BUT SHE'S OFF SOMEWHERE COMMUNING WITH NATURE.
GOODBYE, VENERABLE TREE BARK.
OH, I ALMOST FORGOT...SIR URTY SENDS HIS REGARDS!
OH, NOT HIM...

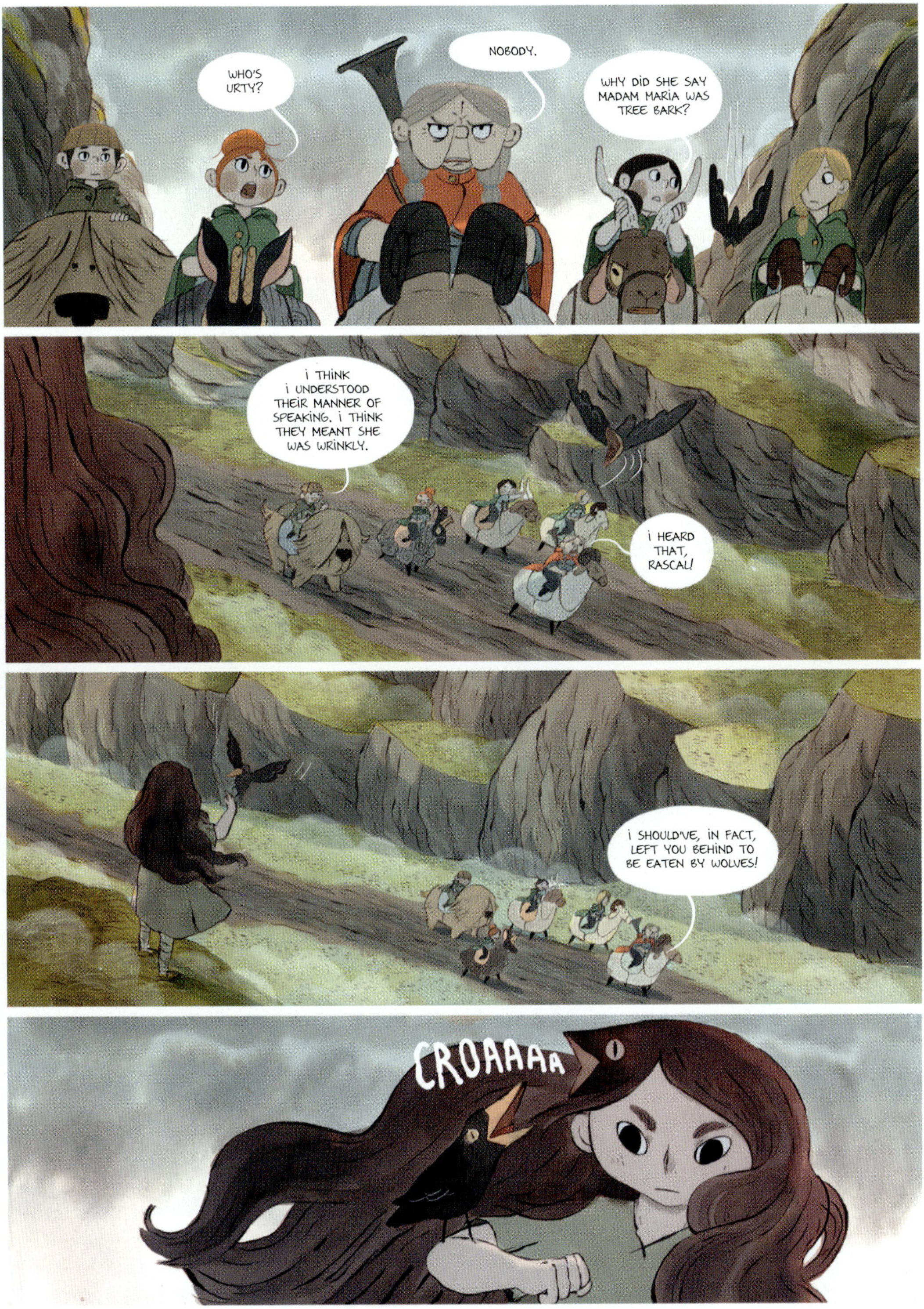
WHO'S URTY?
NOBODY.
WHY DID SHE SAY MADAM MARIA WAS TREE BARK?
I THINK I UNDERSTOOD THEIR MANNER OF SPEAKING. I THINK THEY MEANT SHE WAS WRINKLY.
I HEARD THAT, RASCAL!
I SHOULD'VE, IN FACT, LEFT YOU BEHIND TO BE EATEN BY WOLVES!
CROAAAA

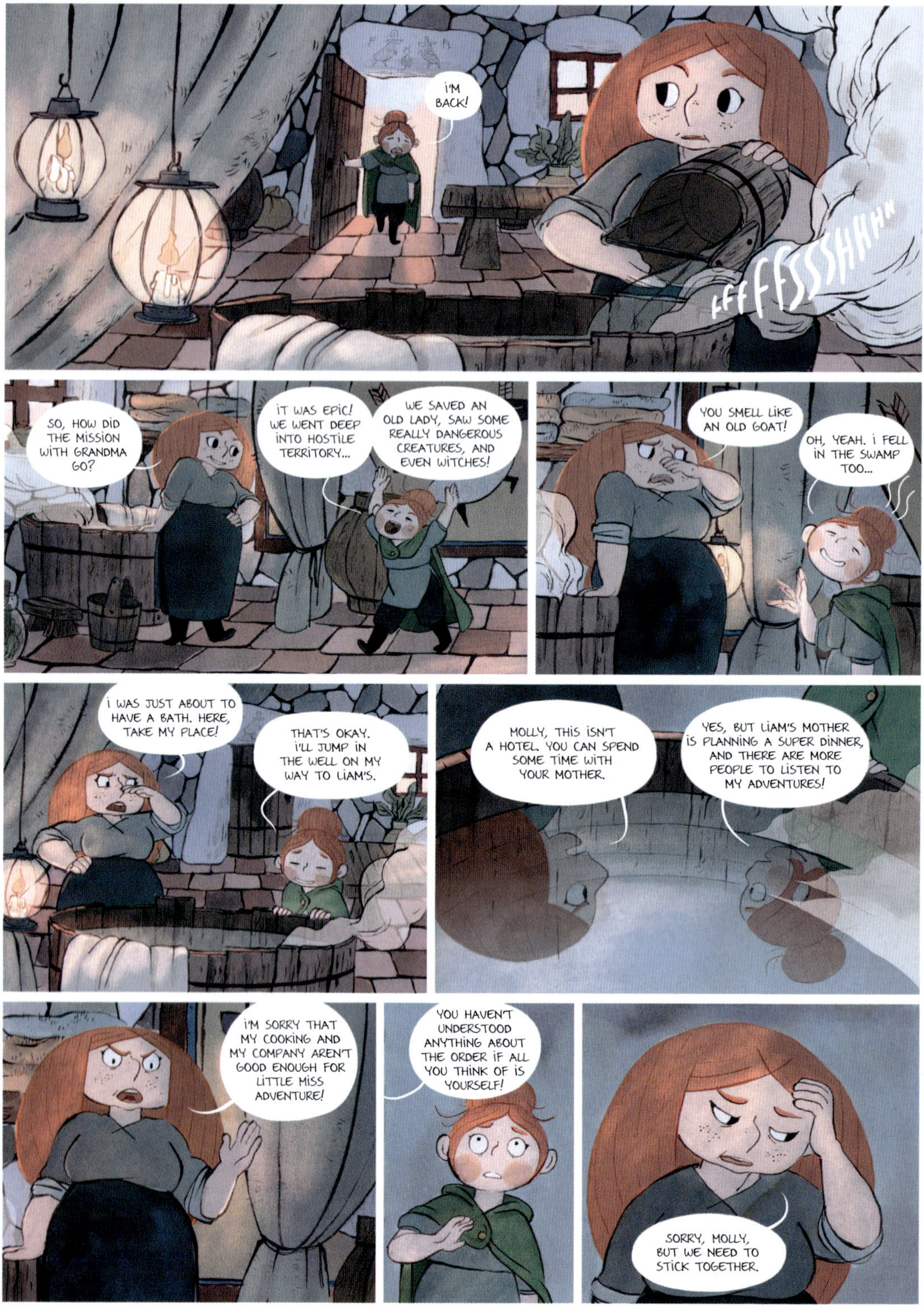
I'M BACK!
FFFFSSSHHHH
SO, HOW DID THE MISSION WITH GRANDMA GO?
IT WAS EPIC! WE WENT DEEP INTO HOSTILE TERRITORY...
WE SAVED AN OLD LADY, SAW SOME REALLY DANGEROUS CREATURES, AND EVEN WITCHES!
YOU SMELL LIKE AN OLD GOAT!
OH, YEAH. I FELL IN THE SWAMP TOO...
I WAS JUST ABOUT TO HAVE A BATH. HERE, TAKE MY PLACE!
THAT'S OKAY. I'LL JUMP IN THE WELL ON MY WAY TO LIAM'S.
MOLLY, THIS ISN'T A HOTEL. YOU CAN SPEND SOME TIME WITH YOUR MOTHER.
YES, BUT LIAM'S MOTHER IS PLANNING A SUPER DINNER, AND THERE ARE MORE PEOPLE TO LISTEN TO MY ADVENTURES!
I'M SORRY THAT MY COOKING AND MY COMPANY AREN'T GOOD ENOUGH FOR LITTLE MISS ADVENTURE!
YOU HAVEN'T UNDERSTOOD ANYTHING ABOUT THE ORDER IF ALL YOU THINK OF IS YOURSELF!
SORRY, MOLLY, BUT WE NEED TO STICK TOGETHER.

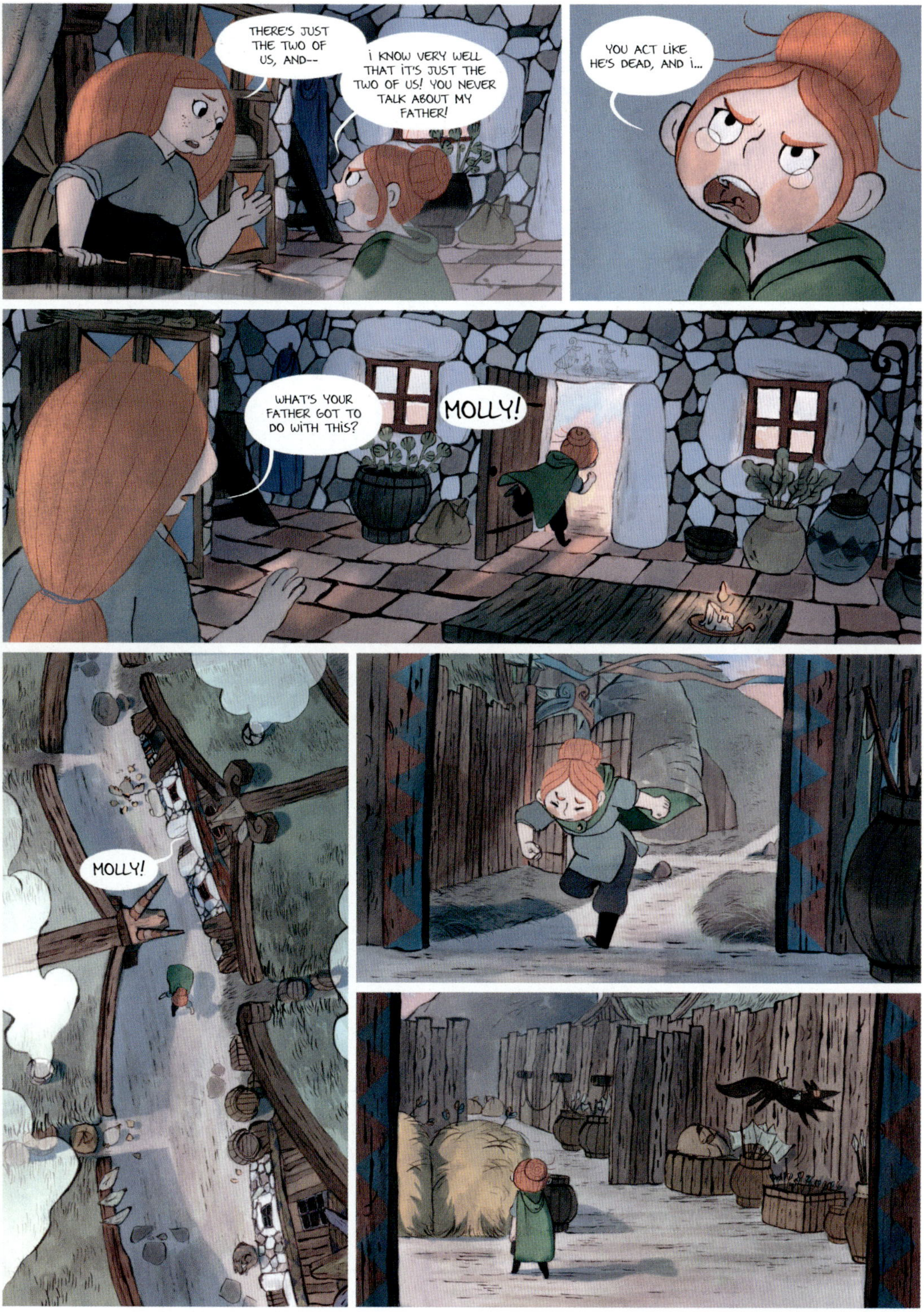
THERE'S JUST THE TWO OF US, AND--
I KNOW VERY WELL THAT IT'S JUST THE TWO OF US! YOU NEVER TALK ABOUT MY FATHER!
YOU ACT LIKE HE'S DEAD, AND I...
WHAT'S YOUR FATHER GOT TO DO WITH THIS?
MOLLY!
MOLLY!

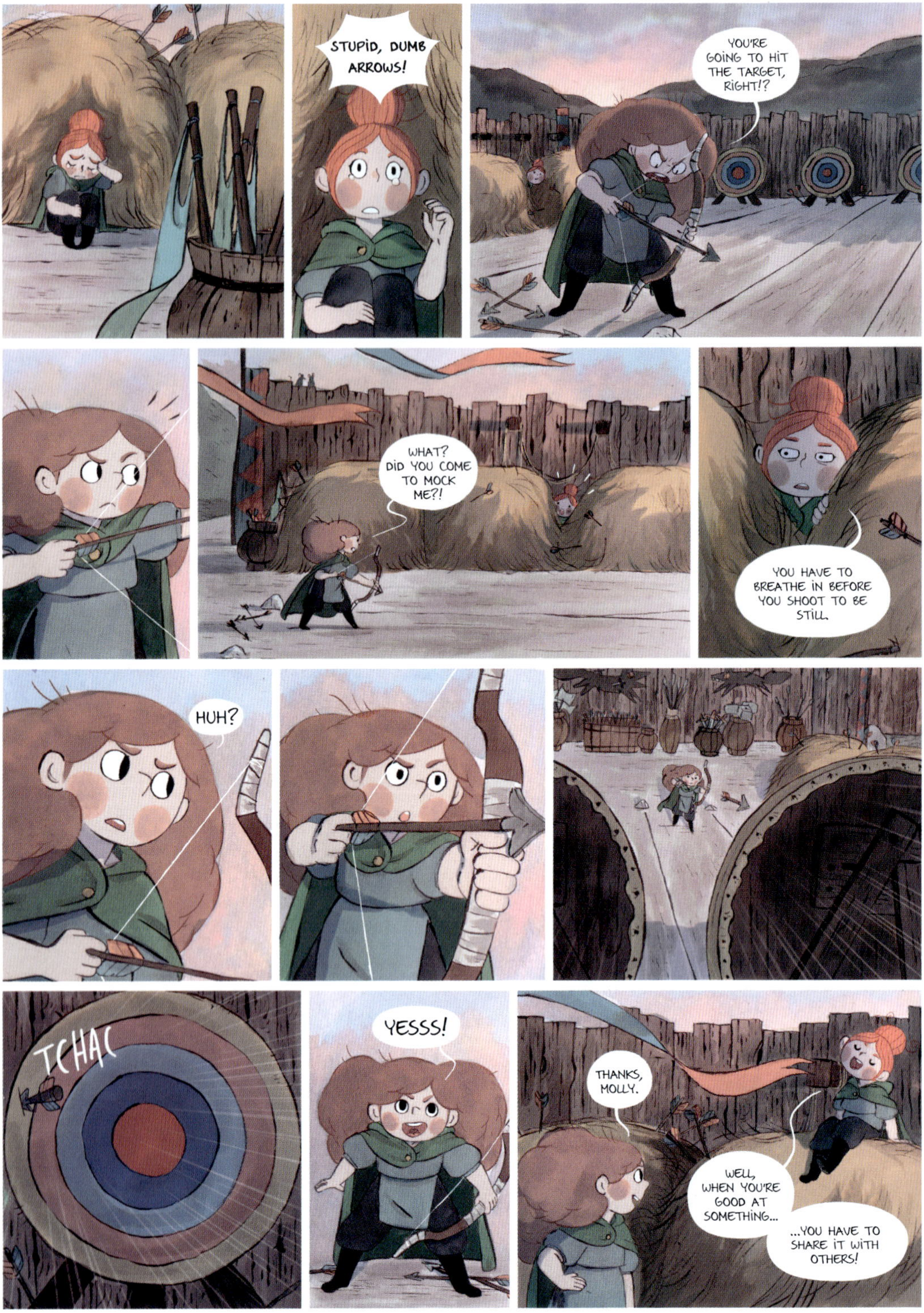
STUPID, DUMB ARROWS!
YOU'RE GOING TO HIT THE TARGET, RIGHT!?
WHAT? DID YOU COME TO MOCK ME?!
YOU HAVE TO BREATHE IN BEFORE YOU SHOOT TO BE STILL.
HUH?
TCHAC
YESSS!
THANKS, MOLLY.
WELL, WHEN YOU'RE GOOD AT SOMETHING...
...YOU HAVE TO SHARE IT WITH OTHERS!

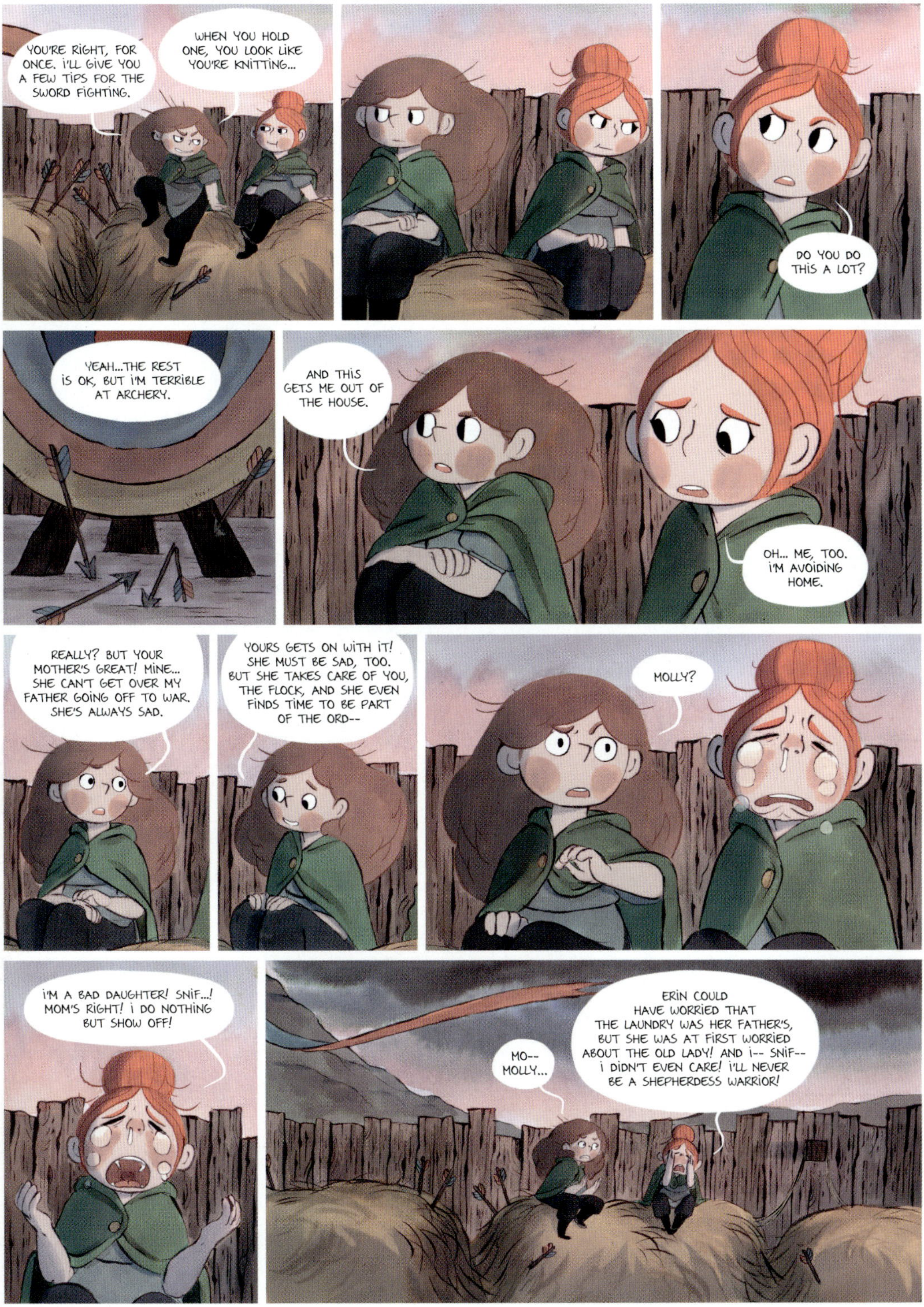
YOU'RE RIGHT, FOR ONCE. I'LL GIVE YOU A FEW TIPS FOR THE SWORD FIGHTING.
WHEN YOU HOLD ONE, YOU LOOK LIKE YOU'RE KNITTING...
DO YOU DO THIS A LOT?
YEAH...THE REST IS OK, BUT I'M TERRIBLE AT ARCHERY.
AND THIS GETS ME OUT OF THE HOUSE.
OH... ME, TOO. I'M AVOIDING HOME.
REALLY? BUT YOUR MOTHER'S GREAT! MINE... SHE CAN'T GET OVER MY FATHER GOING OFF TO WAR. SHE'S ALWAYS SAD.
YOURS GETS ON WITH IT! SHE MUST BE SAD, TOO. BUT SHE TAKES CARE OF YOU, THE FLOCK, AND SHE EVEN FINDS TIME TO BE PART OF THE ORD--
MOLLY?
I'M A BAD DAUGHTER! SNIF...! MOM'S RIGHT! I DO NOTHING BUT SHOW OFF!
MO-- MOLLY...
ERIN COULD HAVE WORRIED THAT THE LAUNDRY WAS HER FATHER'S, BUT SHE WAS AT FIRST WORRIED ABOUT THE OLD LADY! AND I-- SNIF-- I DIDN'T EVEN CARE! I'LL NEVER BE A SHEPHERDESS WARRIOR!

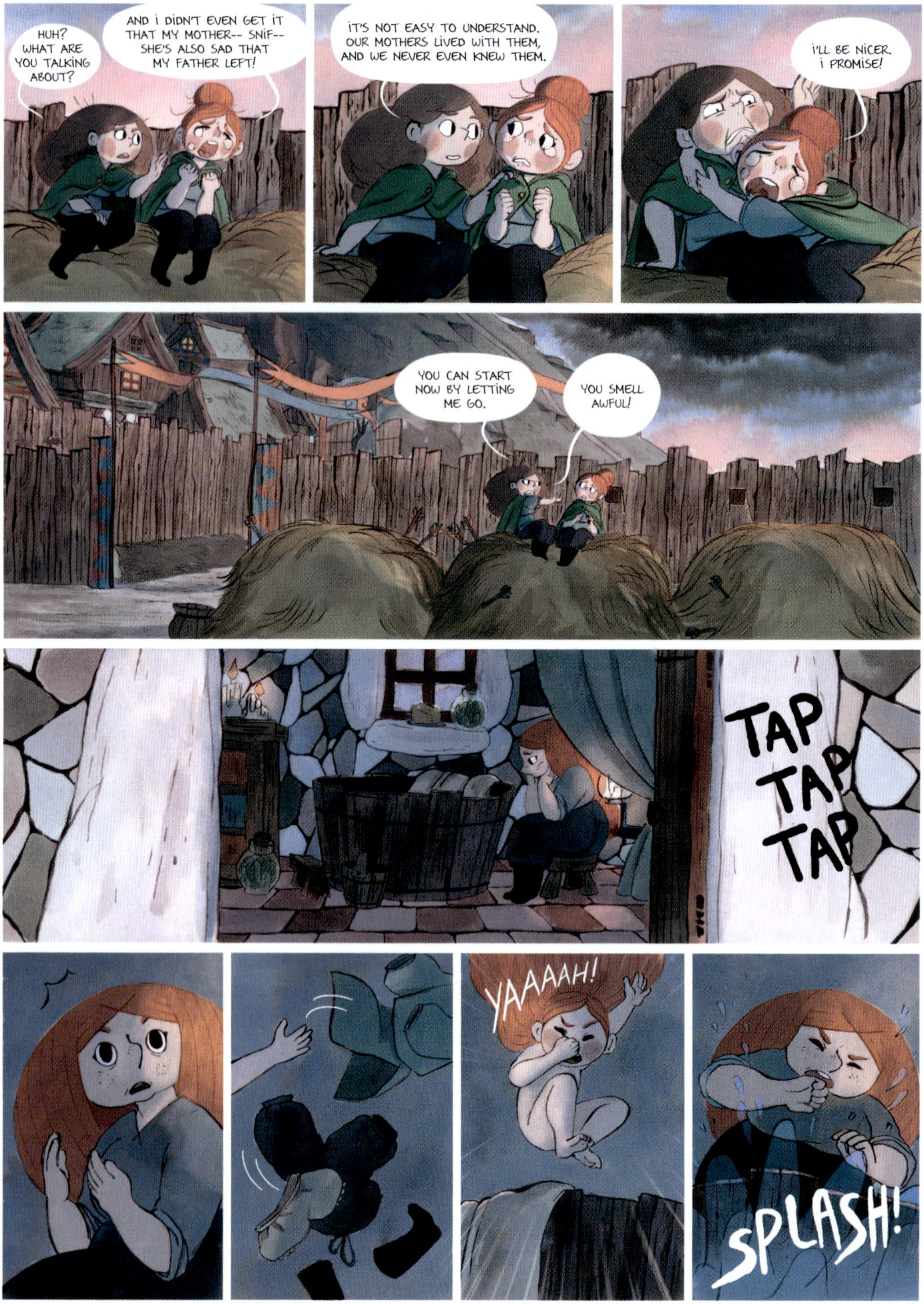
HUH? WHAT ARE YOU TALKING ABOUT?
AND i DiDN'T EVEN GET iT THAT MY MOTHER-- SNiF-- SHE'S ALSO SAD THAT MY FATHER LEFT!
iT'S NOT EASY TO UNDERSTAND. OUR MOTHERS LiVED WiTH THEM, AND WE NEVER EVEN KNEW THEM.
i'LL BE NiCER. i PROMiSE!
YOU CAN START NOW BY LETTiNG ME GO.
YOU SMELL AWFUL!
TAP TAP TAP
YAAAAH!
SPLASH!

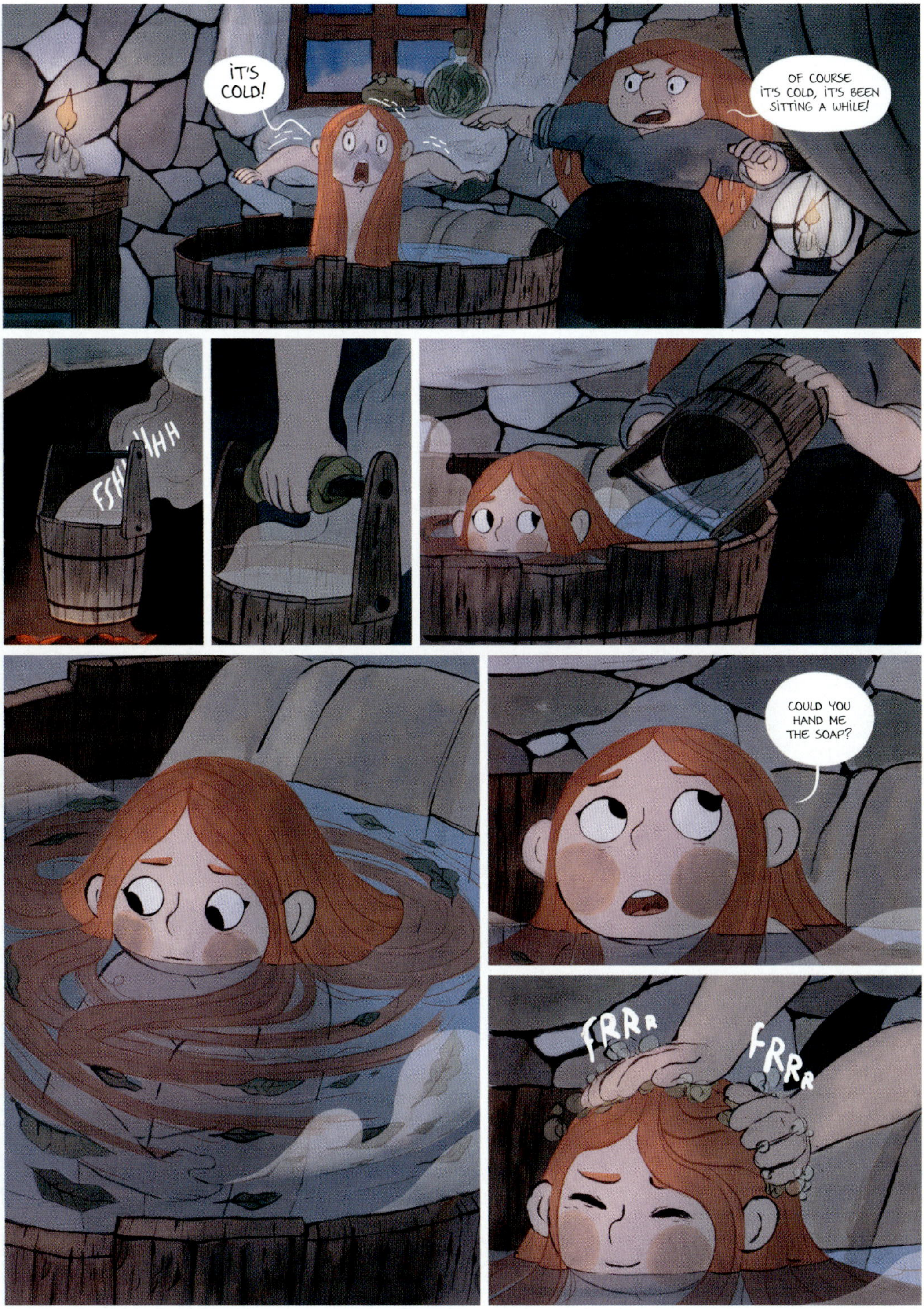
IT'S COLD!
OF COURSE IT'S COLD, IT'S BEEN SITTING A WHILE!
FSHHHH
COULD YOU HAND ME THE SOAP?
FRRR
FRRR

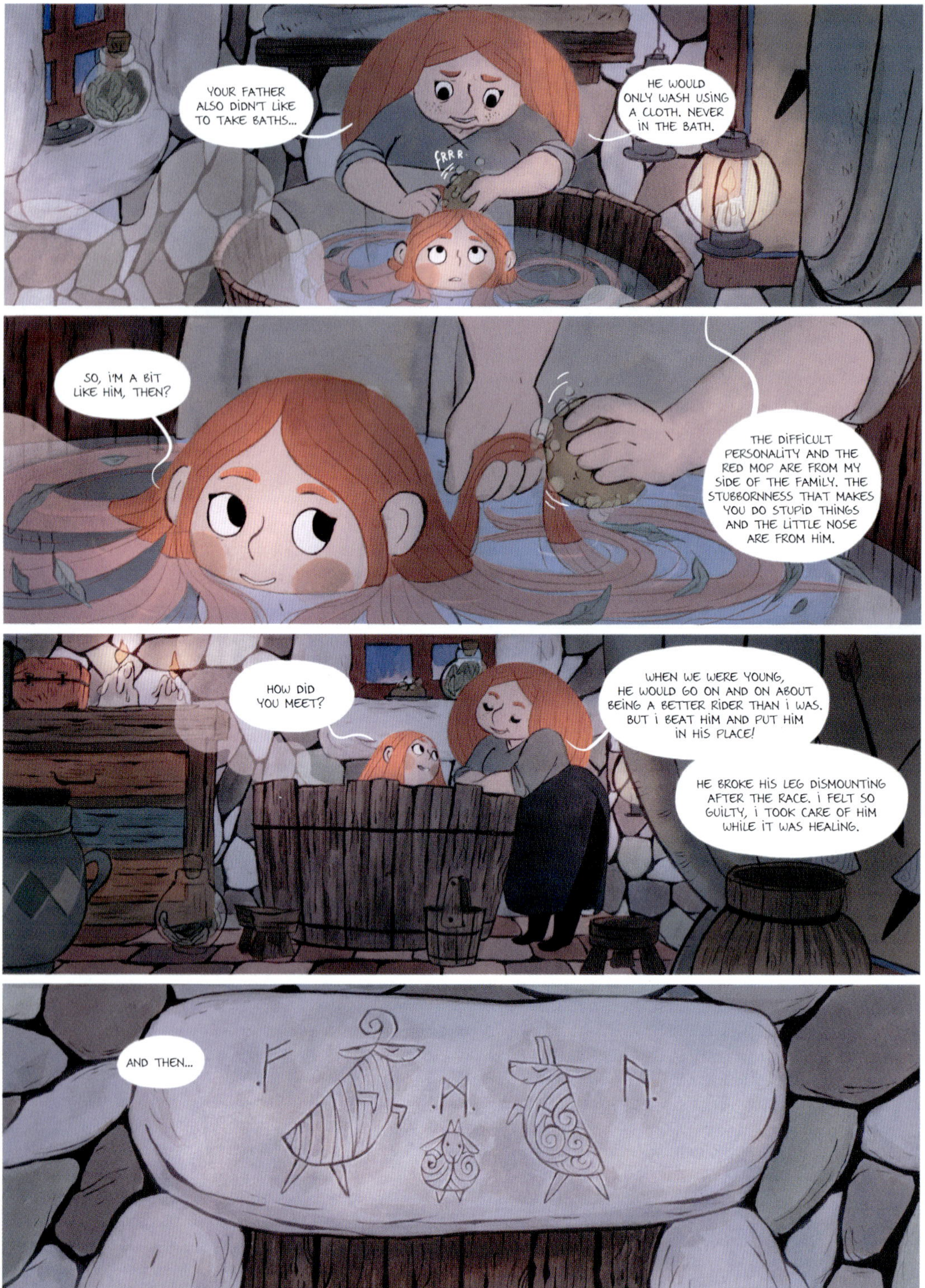
YOUR FATHER ALSO DIDN'T LIKE TO TAKE BATHS...
HE WOULD ONLY WASH USING A CLOTH. NEVER IN THE BATH.
FRRR
SO, I'M A BIT LIKE HIM, THEN?
THE DIFFICULT PERSONALITY AND THE RED MOP ARE FROM MY SIDE OF THE FAMILY. THE STUBBORNNESS THAT MAKES YOU DO STUPID THINGS AND THE LITTLE NOSE ARE FROM HIM.
HOW DID YOU MEET?
WHEN WE WERE YOUNG, HE WOULD GO ON AND ON ABOUT BEING A BETTER RIDER THAN I WAS. BUT I BEAT HIM AND PUT HIM IN HIS PLACE!
HE BROKE HIS LEG DISMOUNTING AFTER THE RACE. I FELT SO GUILTY, I TOOK CARE OF HIM WHILE IT WAS HEALING.
AND THEN...

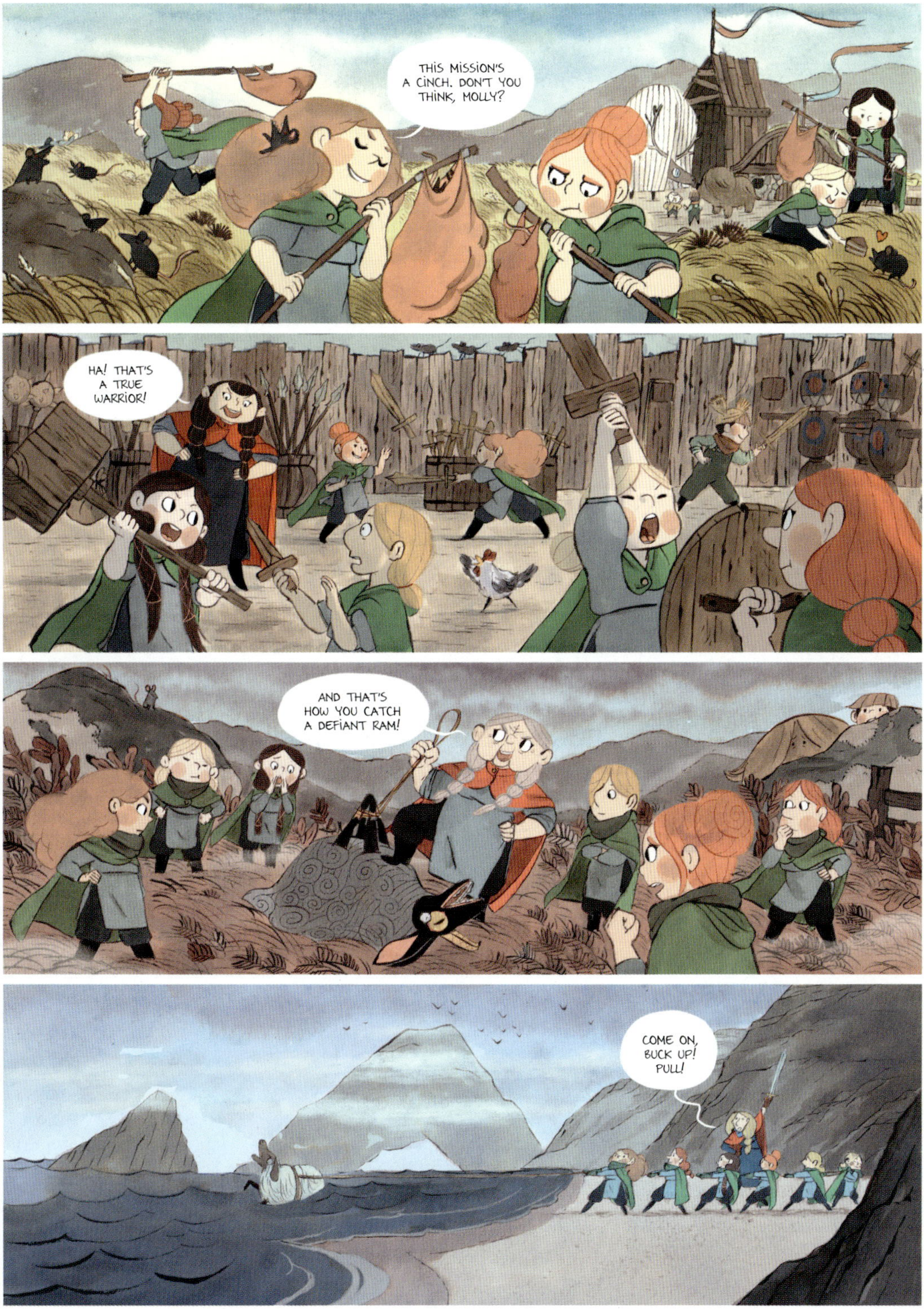
THIS MISSION'S A CINCH. DON'T YOU THINK, MOLLY?
HA! THAT'S A TRUE WARRIOR!
AND THAT'S HOW YOU CATCH A DEFIANT RAM!
COME ON, BUCK UP! PULL!

7ᵀᴴ CLASS OF SHEPHERDESS WARRIOR APPRENTICES.

The order was started 3 years after our fathers left.
Since we were the last to be born before they left, there will not be new apprentices for a while.
That's not so easy for the order, so I, Molly, will do everything to be worthy of the title of shepherdess warrior!

-INSTRUCTORS-

HOLGA
As soon as you see her, you get that she's strong!
She's our combat instructor, and she works us hard!
But it's for a good reason. I'm already better with my sword!

THE DEAN
She's so old that you wonder if she wasn't born before the village existed. She teaches us about the laws and the regulations we are to follow... everything that puts me to sleep after 10 minutes! She is grandma's best friend, and they get on like a hau house on fire!

GRANDMA MARIA

NORA
She's the chief, and she's the coolest!
She has a scar (mega cool!). When she talks, everyone shuts up to listen. (Super mega cool!)
One day, I'm going to be an elite Shepherdess Warrior like her!
She doesn't teach any courses, but she does sometimes go on our missions. I would reeeally like to go on a mission with her!
...have I said that she's cool?

AUNT JANE
They say that Auntie is as strong as Holga... that's pretty scary!
She teaches archery sometimes, because, yes, she's really good at archery...
I can understand why Abby admires her so much!

She doesn't need to fight, her face alone'll scare away any wolves or bandits!
She's responsible for raising and training the fighting rams, and teaches us how to take care of them. But she has a tendency to bully Black Beard during the exercises!

IRON BUNS (Mr. Ironton)

Mom says that Mr. Iron Buns has a twin brother.
The two of them decided that Mr. Iron Buns would hide during the mobilization so as to stay behind in the village and let people think that the brother who left was an only child.
Since he was the better archer, he wanted to stay behind and help the women defend themselves by teaching them how to shoot.
He also lost someone. It's sad...

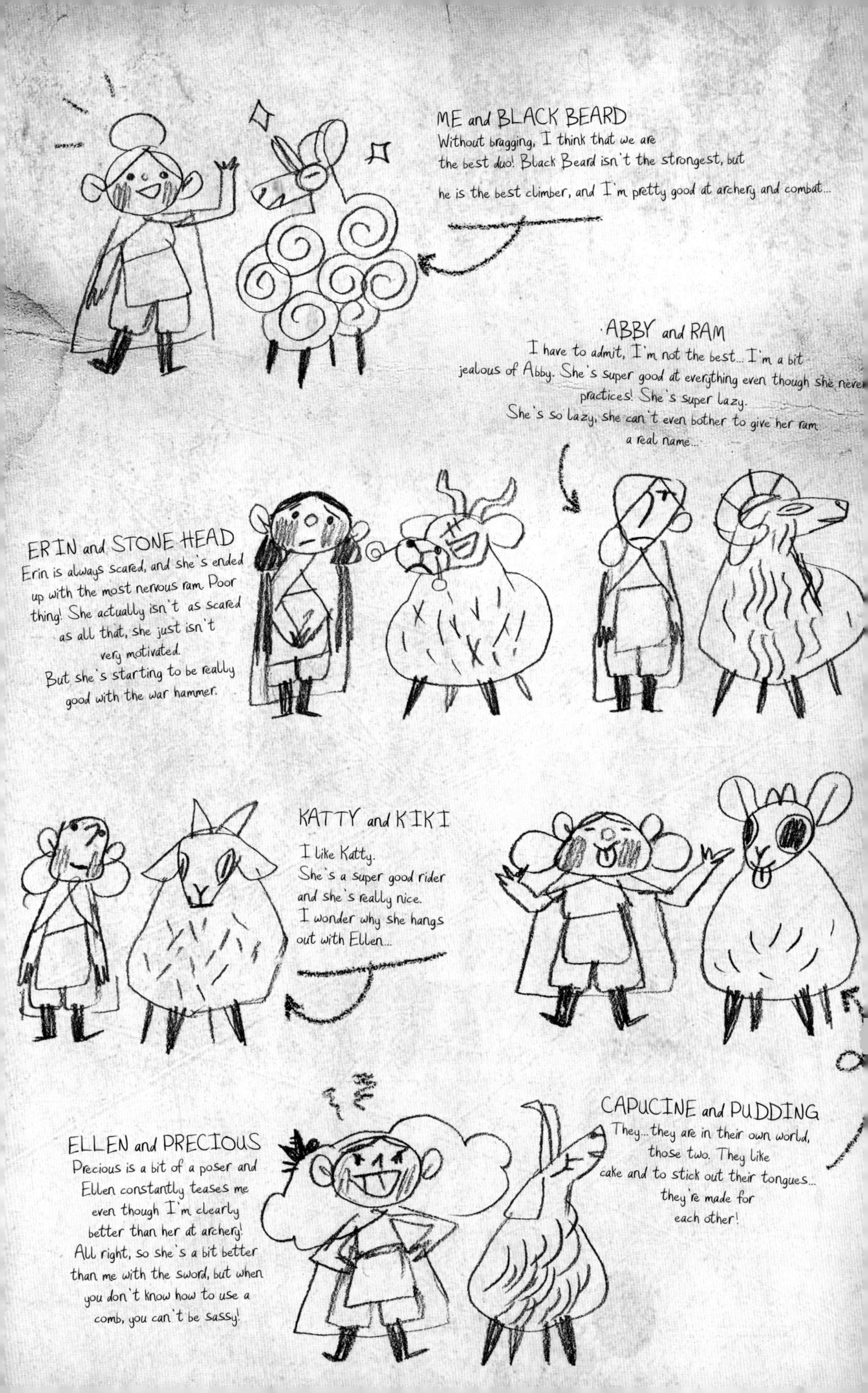
ME and BLACK BEARD
Without bragging, I think that we are
the best duo! Black Beard isn't the strongest, but
he is the best climber, and I'm pretty good at archery and combat...
ABBY and RAM
I have to admit, I'm not the best... I'm a bit
jealous of Abby. She's super good at everything even though she neve
practices! She's super lazy.
She's so lazy, she can't even bother to give her ram
a real name...
ERIN and STONE HEAD
Erin is always scared, and she's ended
up with the most nervous ram. Poor
thing! She actually isn't as scared
as all that, she just isn't
very motivated.
But she's starting to be really
good with the war hammer.
KATTY and KIKI
I like Katty.
She's a super good rider
and she's really nice.
I wonder why she hangs
out with Ellen...
ELLEN and PRECIOUS
Precious is a bit of a poser and
Ellen constantly teases me
even though I'm clearly
better than her at archery!
All right, so she's a bit better
than me with the sword, but when
you don't know how to use a
comb, you can't be sassy!
CAPUCINE and PUDDING
They... they are in their own world,
those two. They like
cake and to stick out their tongues...
they're made for
each other!

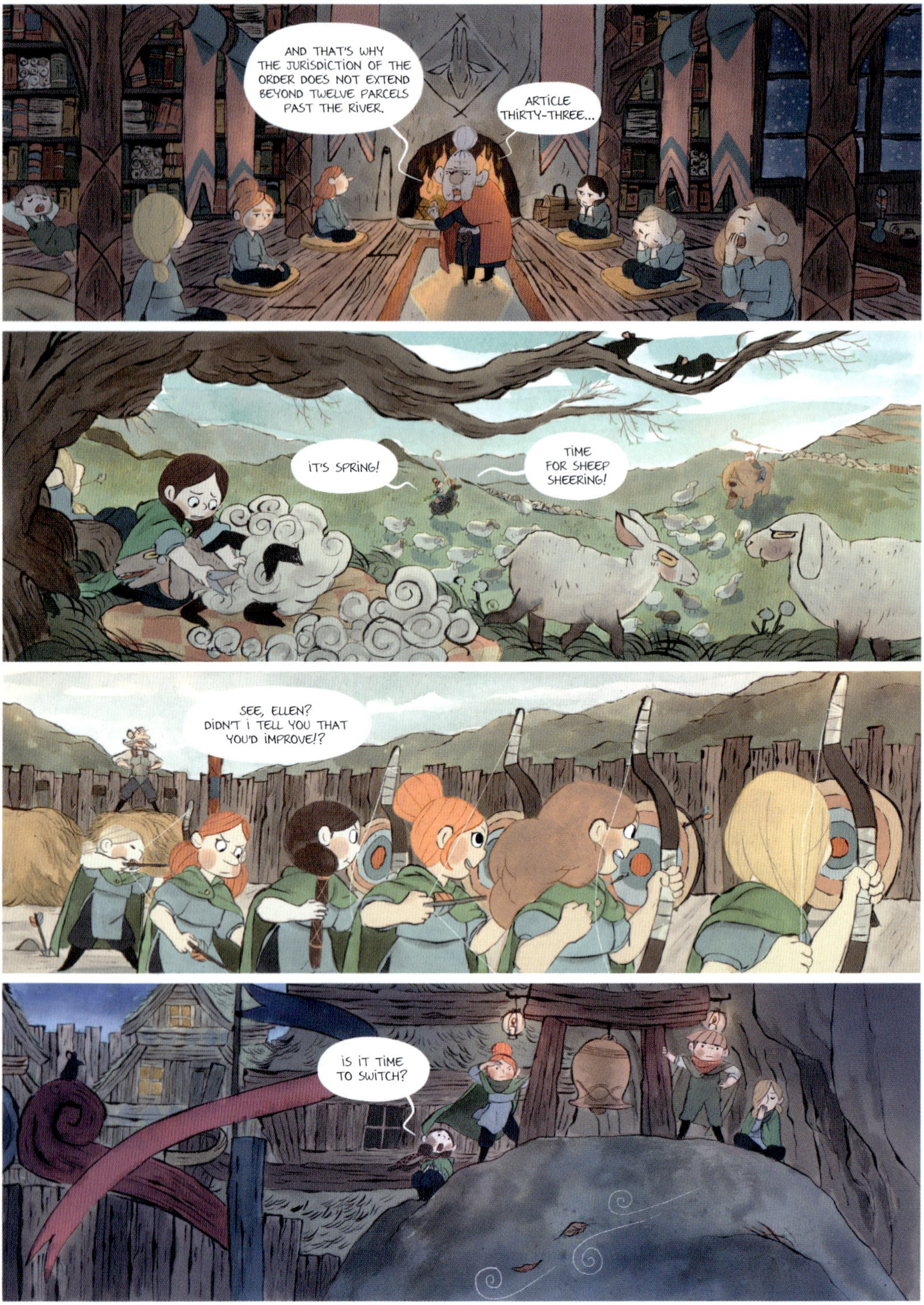
AND THAT'S WHY THE JURISDICTION OF THE ORDER DOES NOT EXTEND BEYOND TWELVE PARCELS PAST THE RIVER.
ARTICLE THIRTY-THREE...
IT'S SPRING!
TIME FOR SHEEP SHEERING!
SEE, ELLEN? DIDN'T I TELL YOU THAT YOU'D IMPROVE!?
IS IT TIME TO SWITCH?

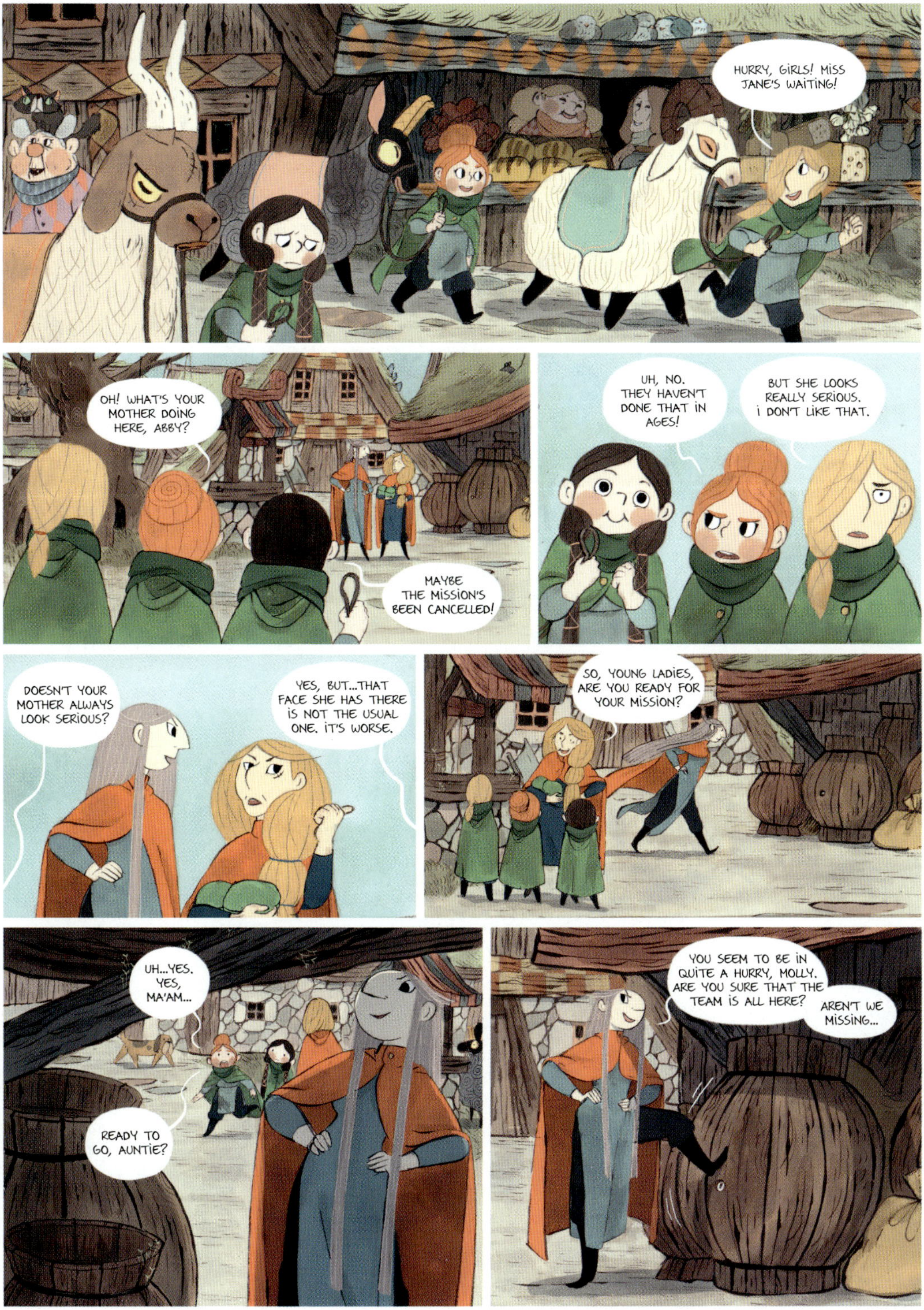
HURRY, GIRLS! MISS JANE'S WAITING!
OH! WHAT'S YOUR MOTHER DOING HERE, ABBY?
MAYBE THE MISSION'S BEEN CANCELLED!
UH, NO. THEY HAVEN'T DONE THAT IN AGES!
BUT SHE LOOKS REALLY SERIOUS. I DON'T LIKE THAT.
DOESN'T YOUR MOTHER ALWAYS LOOK SERIOUS?
YES, BUT...THAT FACE SHE HAS THERE IS NOT THE USUAL ONE. IT'S WORSE.
SO, YOUNG LADIES, ARE YOU READY FOR YOUR MISSION?
UH...YES. YES, MA'AM...
READY TO GO, AUNTIE?
YOU SEEM TO BE IN QUITE A HURRY, MOLLY. ARE YOU SURE THAT THE TEAM IS ALL HERE?
AREN'T WE MISSING...

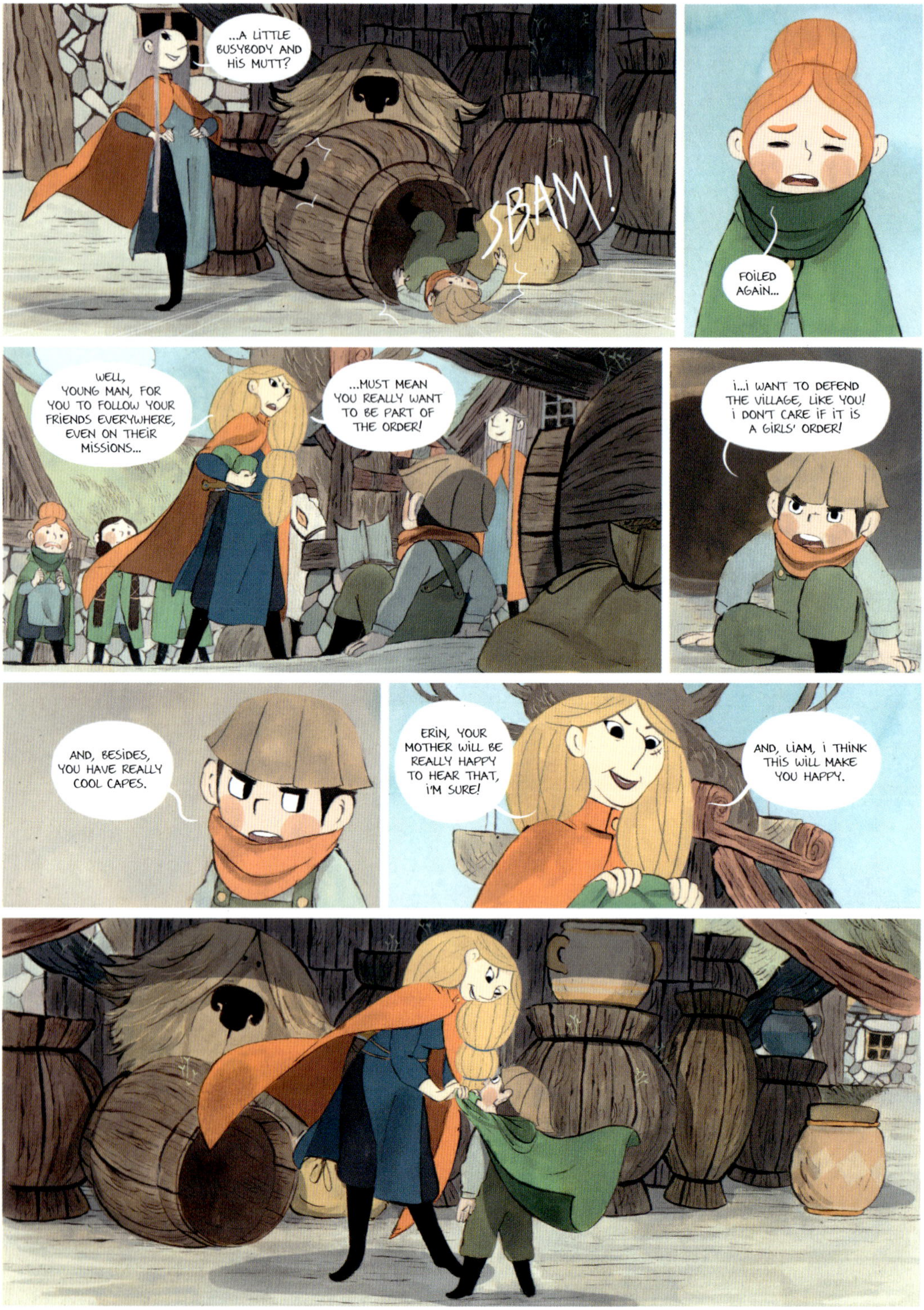
...A LITTLE BUSYBODY AND HIS MUTT?
SBAM!
FOILED AGAIN...
WELL, YOUNG MAN, FOR YOU TO FOLLOW YOUR FRIENDS EVERYWHERE, EVEN ON THEIR MISSIONS...
...MUST MEAN YOU REALLY WANT TO BE PART OF THE ORDER!
I...I WANT TO DEFEND THE VILLAGE, LIKE YOU! I DON'T CARE IF IT IS A GIRLS' ORDER!
AND, BESIDES, YOU HAVE REALLY COOL CAPES.
ERIN, YOUR MOTHER WILL BE REALLY HAPPY TO HEAR THAT, I'M SURE!
AND, LIAM, I THINK THIS WILL MAKE YOU HAPPY.

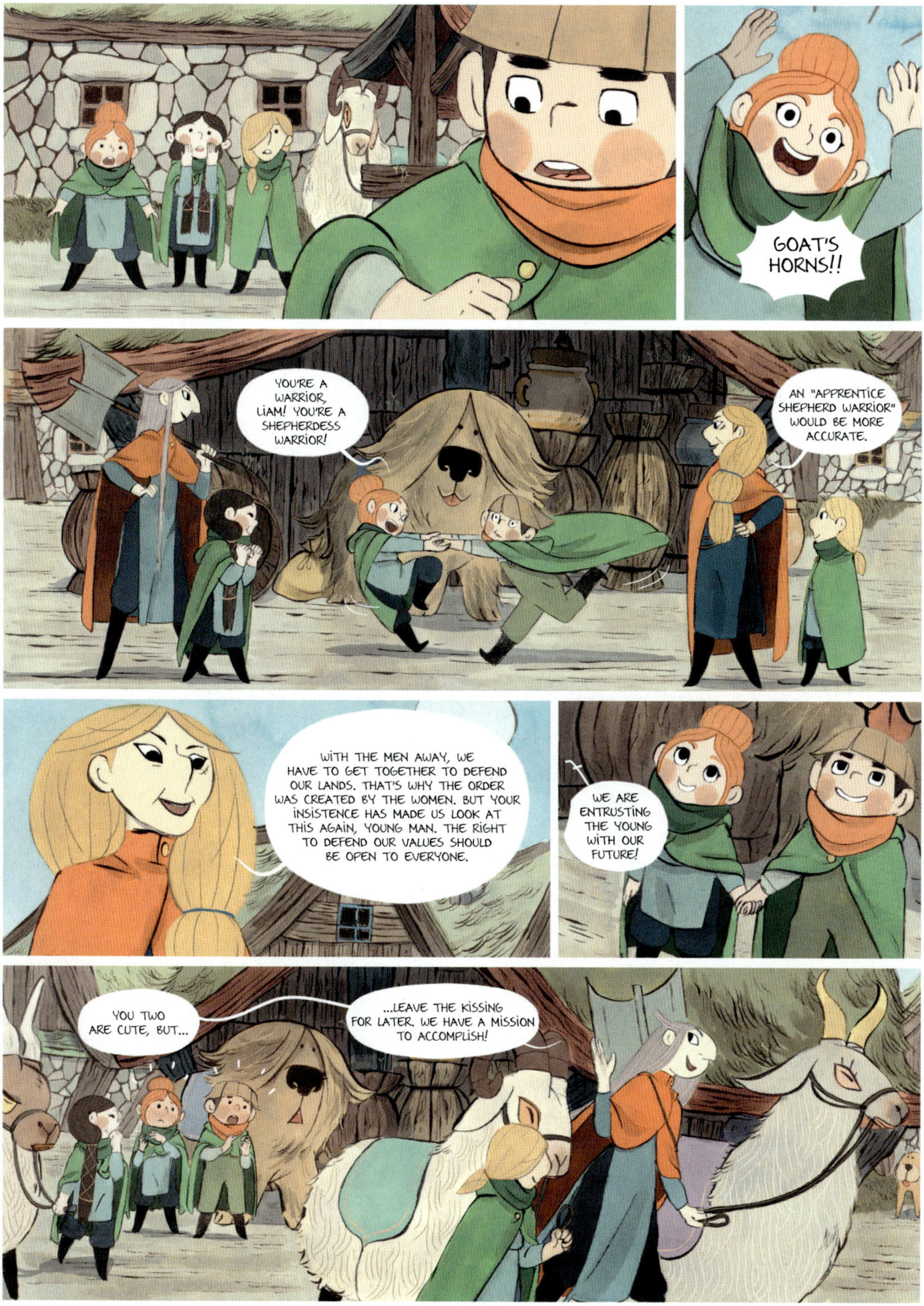
GOAT'S HORNS!!
YOU'RE A WARRIOR, LIAM! YOU'RE A SHEPHERDESS WARRIOR!
AN "APPRENTICE SHEPHERD WARRIOR" WOULD BE MORE ACCURATE.
WITH THE MEN AWAY, WE HAVE TO GET TOGETHER TO DEFEND OUR LANDS. THAT'S WHY THE ORDER WAS CREATED BY THE WOMEN. BUT YOUR INSISTENCE HAS MADE US LOOK AT THIS AGAIN, YOUNG MAN. THE RIGHT TO DEFEND OUR VALUES SHOULD BE OPEN TO EVERYONE.
WE ARE ENTRUSTING THE YOUNG WITH OUR FUTURE!
YOU TWO ARE CUTE, BUT...
...LEAVE THE KISSING FOR LATER. WE HAVE A MISSION TO ACCOMPLISH!

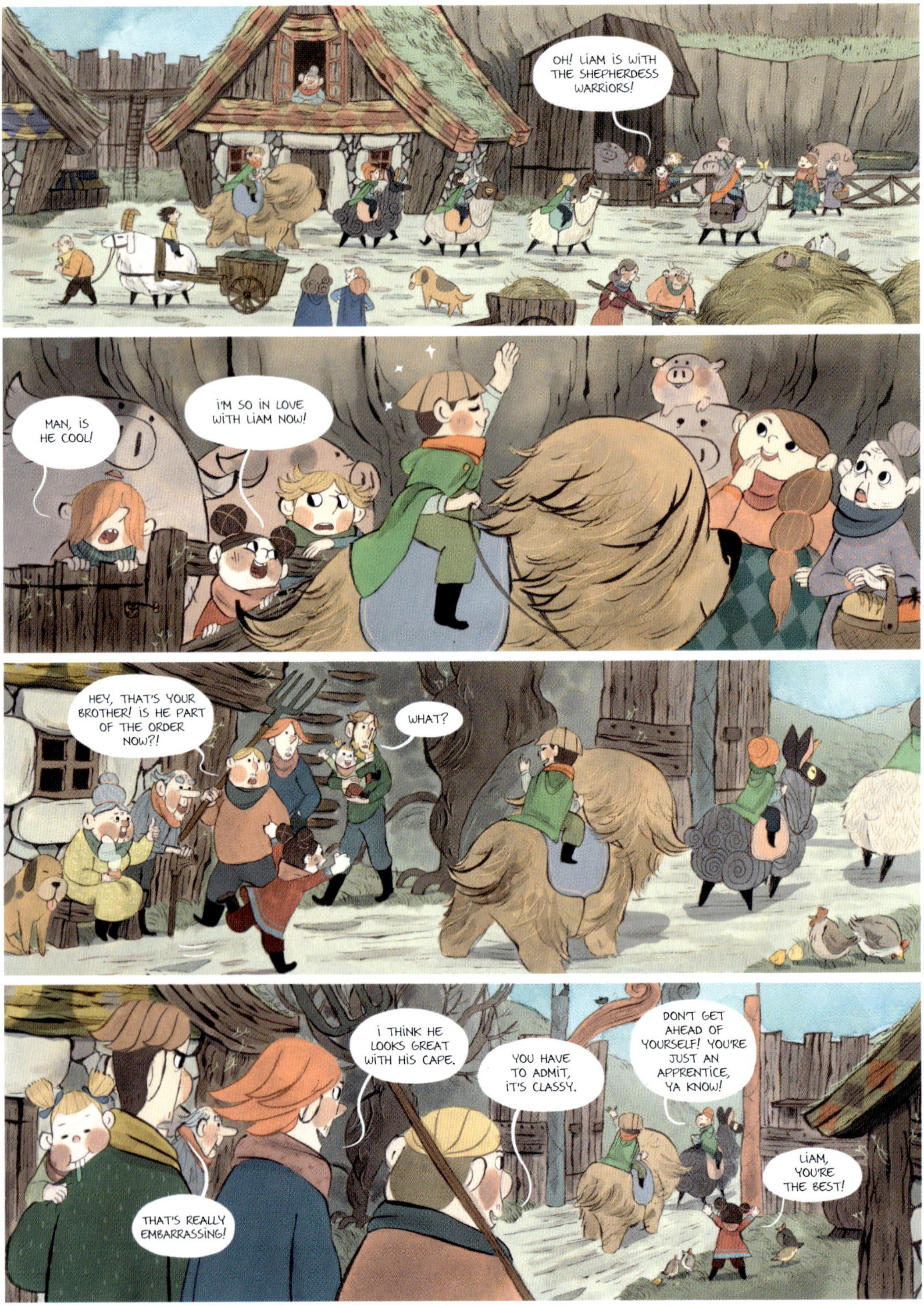
OH! LIAM IS WITH THE SHEPHERDESS WARRIORS!
MAN, IS HE COOL!
I'M SO IN LOVE WITH LIAM NOW!
HEY, THAT'S YOUR BROTHER! IS HE PART OF THE ORDER NOW?!
WHAT?
THAT'S REALLY EMBARRASSING!
I THINK HE LOOKS GREAT WITH HIS CAPE.
YOU HAVE TO ADMIT, IT'S CLASSY.
DON'T GET AHEAD OF YOURSELF! YOU'RE JUST AN APPRENTICE, YA KNOW!
LIAM, YOU'RE THE BEST!

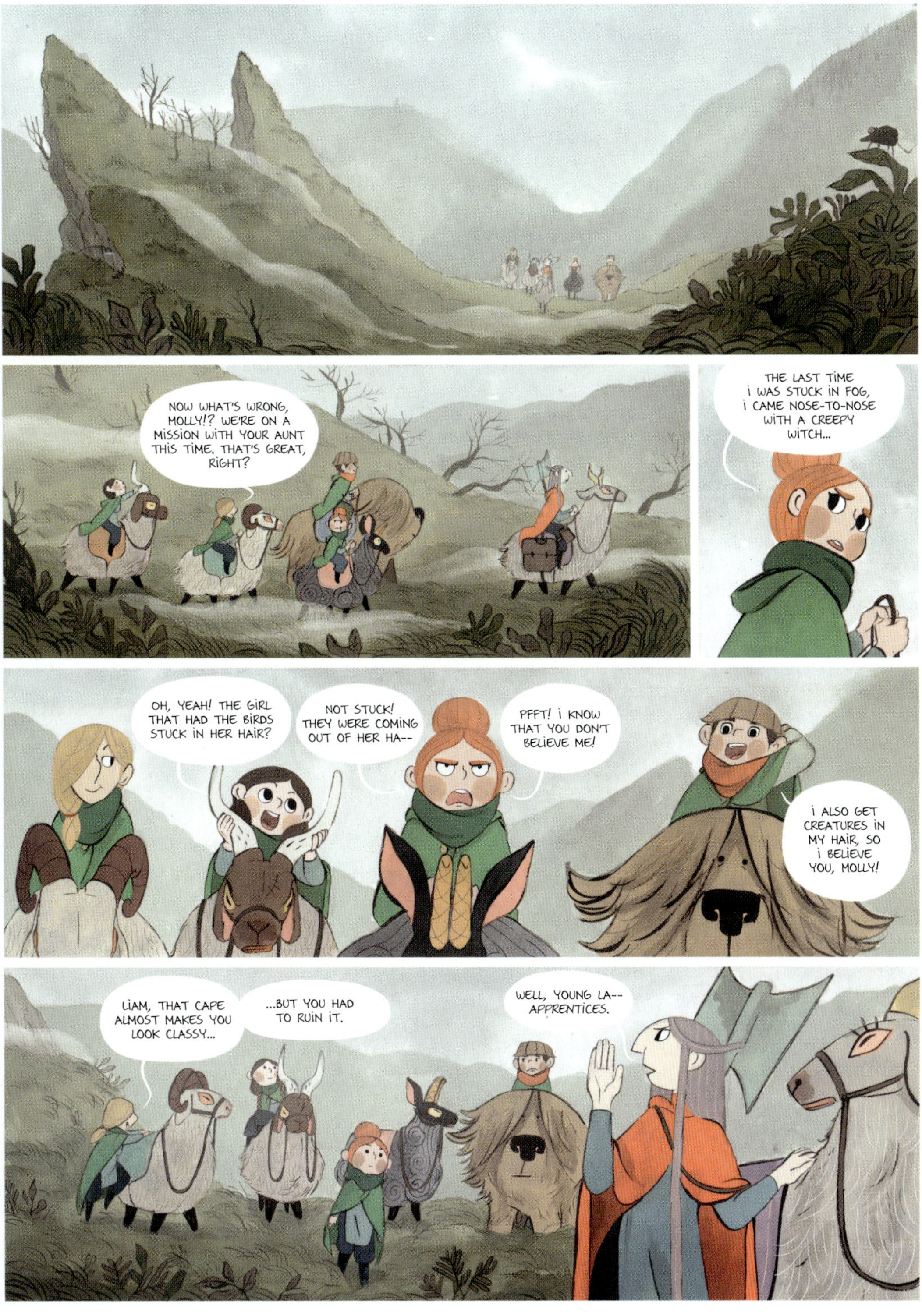
NOW WHAT'S WRONG, MOLLY!? WE'RE ON A MISSION WITH YOUR AUNT THIS TIME. THAT'S GREAT, RIGHT?
THE LAST TIME I WAS STUCK IN FOG, I CAME NOSE-TO-NOSE WITH A CREEPY WITCH...
OH, YEAH! THE GIRL THAT HAD THE BIRDS STUCK IN HER HAIR?
NOT STUCK! THEY WERE COMING OUT OF HER HA--
PFFT! I KNOW THAT YOU DON'T BELIEVE ME!
I ALSO GET CREATURES IN MY HAIR, SO I BELIEVE YOU, MOLLY!
LIAM, THAT CAPE ALMOST MAKES YOU LOOK CLASSY...
...BUT YOU HAD TO RUIN IT.
WELL, YOUNG LA-- APPRENTICES.

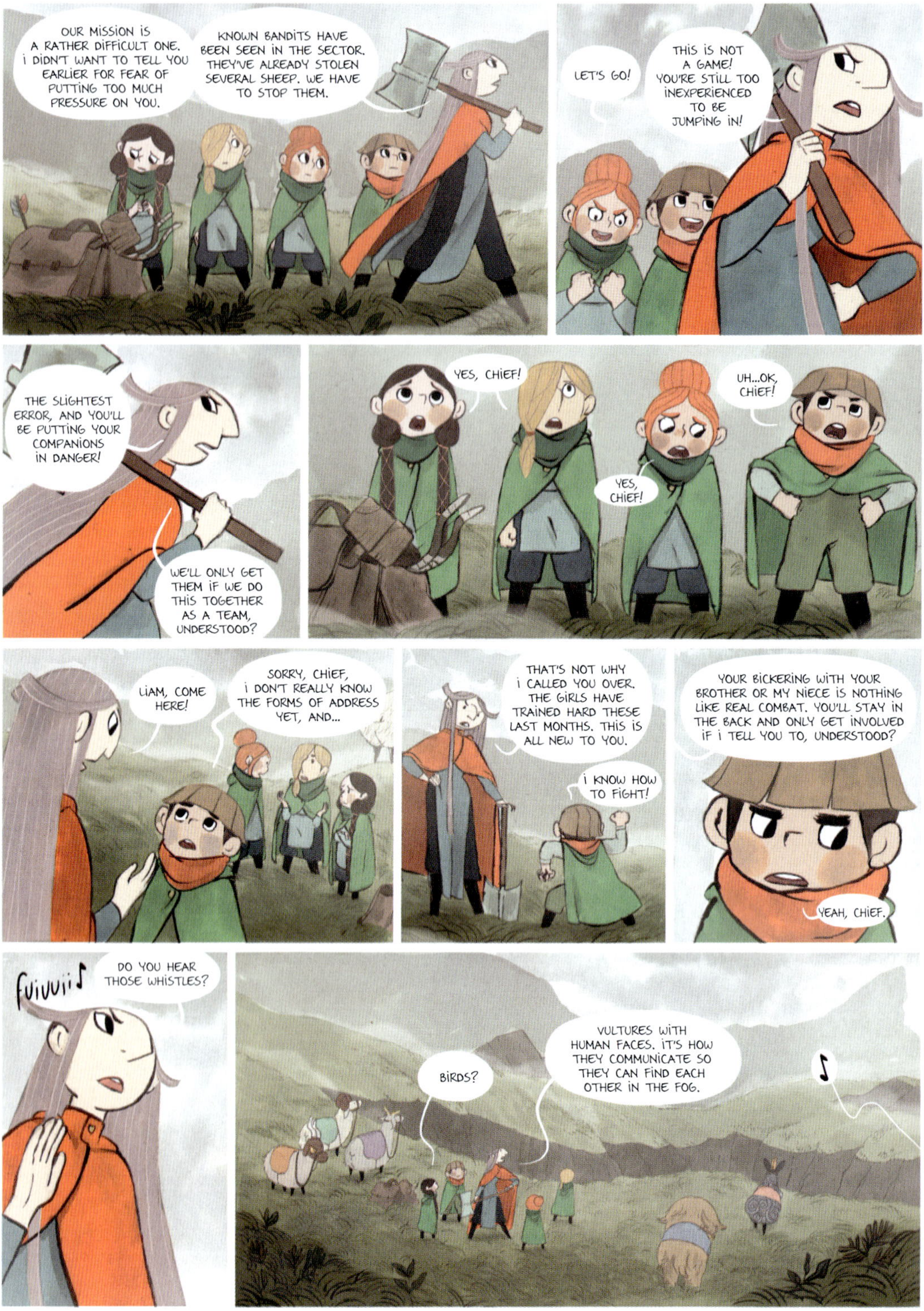

OUR MISSION IS A RATHER DIFFICULT ONE. I DIDN'T WANT TO TELL YOU EARLIER FOR FEAR OF PUTTING TOO MUCH PRESSURE ON YOU.
KNOWN BANDITS HAVE BEEN SEEN IN THE SECTOR. THEY'VE ALREADY STOLEN SEVERAL SHEEP. WE HAVE TO STOP THEM.
LET'S GO!
THIS IS NOT A GAME! YOU'RE STILL TOO INEXPERIENCED TO BE JUMPING IN!
THE SLIGHTEST ERROR, AND YOU'LL BE PUTTING YOUR COMPANIONS IN DANGER!
WE'LL ONLY GET THEM IF WE DO THIS TOGETHER AS A TEAM, UNDERSTOOD?
YES, CHIEF!
YES, CHIEF!
UH...OK, CHIEF!
LIAM, COME HERE!
SORRY, CHIEF, I DON'T REALLY KNOW THE FORMS OF ADDRESS YET, AND...
THAT'S NOT WHY I CALLED YOU OVER. THE GIRLS HAVE TRAINED HARD THESE LAST MONTHS. THIS IS ALL NEW TO YOU.
I KNOW HOW TO FIGHT!
YOUR BICKERING WITH YOUR BROTHER OR MY NIECE IS NOTHING LIKE REAL COMBAT. YOU'LL STAY IN THE BACK AND ONLY GET INVOLVED IF I TELL YOU TO, UNDERSTOOD?
YEAH, CHIEF.
FUIUUII♪
DO YOU HEAR THOSE WHISTLES?
BIRDS?
VULTURES WITH HUMAN FACES. IT'S HOW THEY COMMUNICATE SO THEY CAN FIND EACH OTHER IN THE FOG.
♪

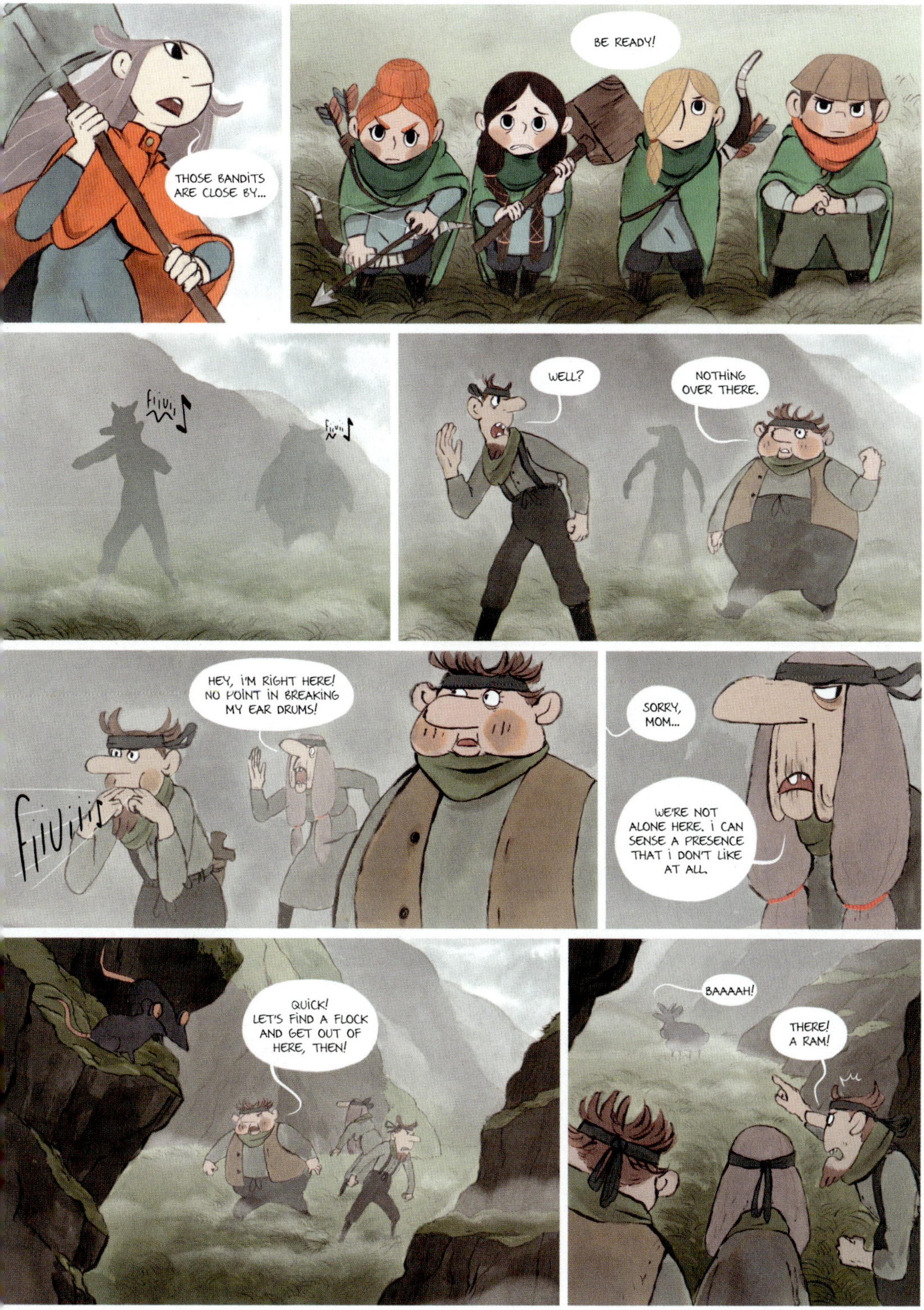
THOSE BANDITS ARE CLOSE BY...
BE READY!
FIIUII
FIIUII
WELL?
NOTHING OVER THERE.
FIIUIII
HEY, I'M RIGHT HERE! NO POINT IN BREAKING MY EAR DRUMS!
SORRY, MOM...
WE'RE NOT ALONE HERE. I CAN SENSE A PRESENCE THAT I DON'T LIKE AT ALL.
QUICK! LET'S FIND A FLOCK AND GET OUT OF HERE, THEN!
BAAAAH!
THERE! A RAM!

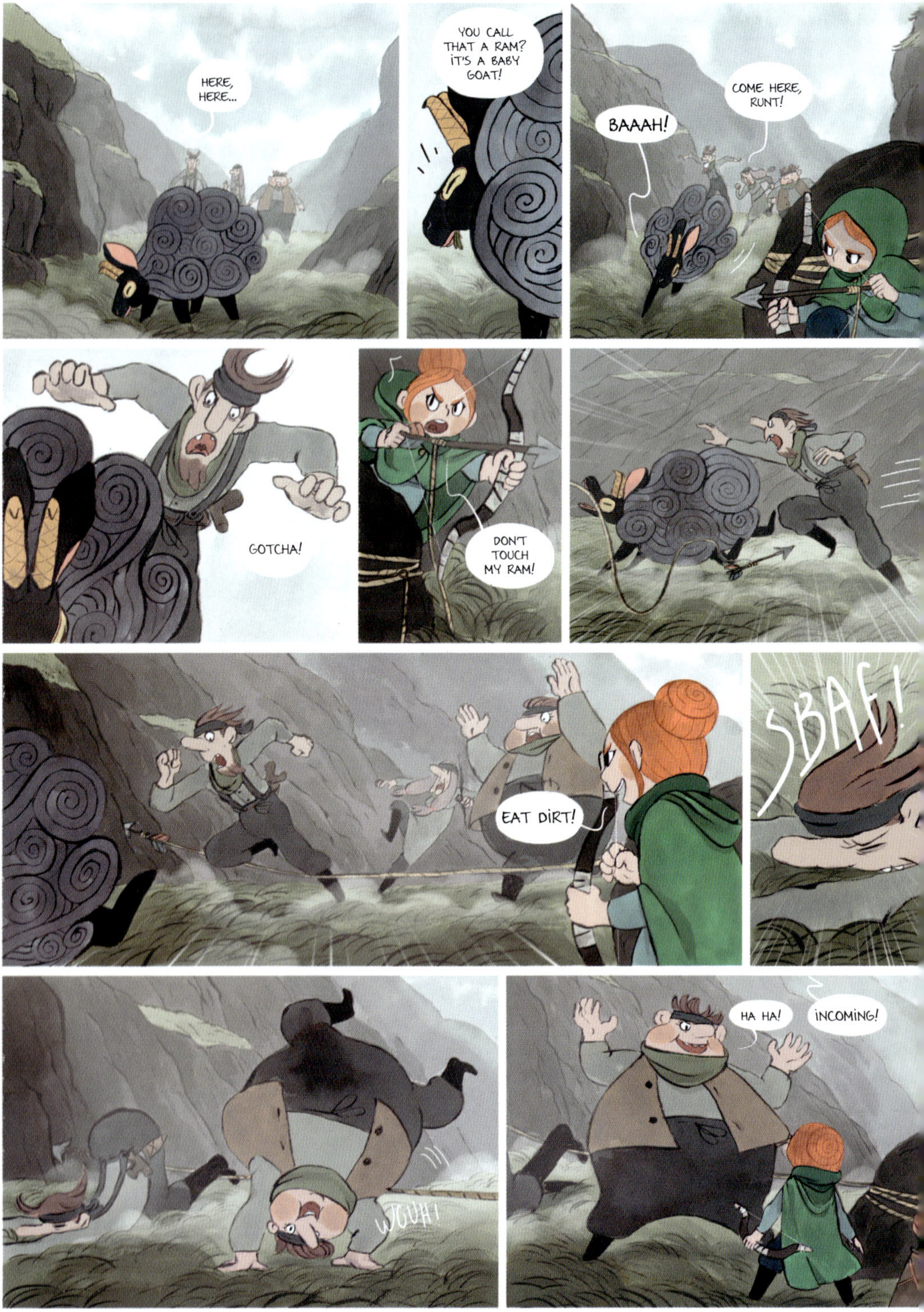
HERE, HERE...
YOU CALL THAT A RAM? IT'S A BABY GOAT!
BAAAH!
COME HERE, RUNT!
GOTCHA!
DON'T TOUCH MY RAM!
EAT DIRT!
SBAF!
WOUH!
HA HA!
INCOMING!

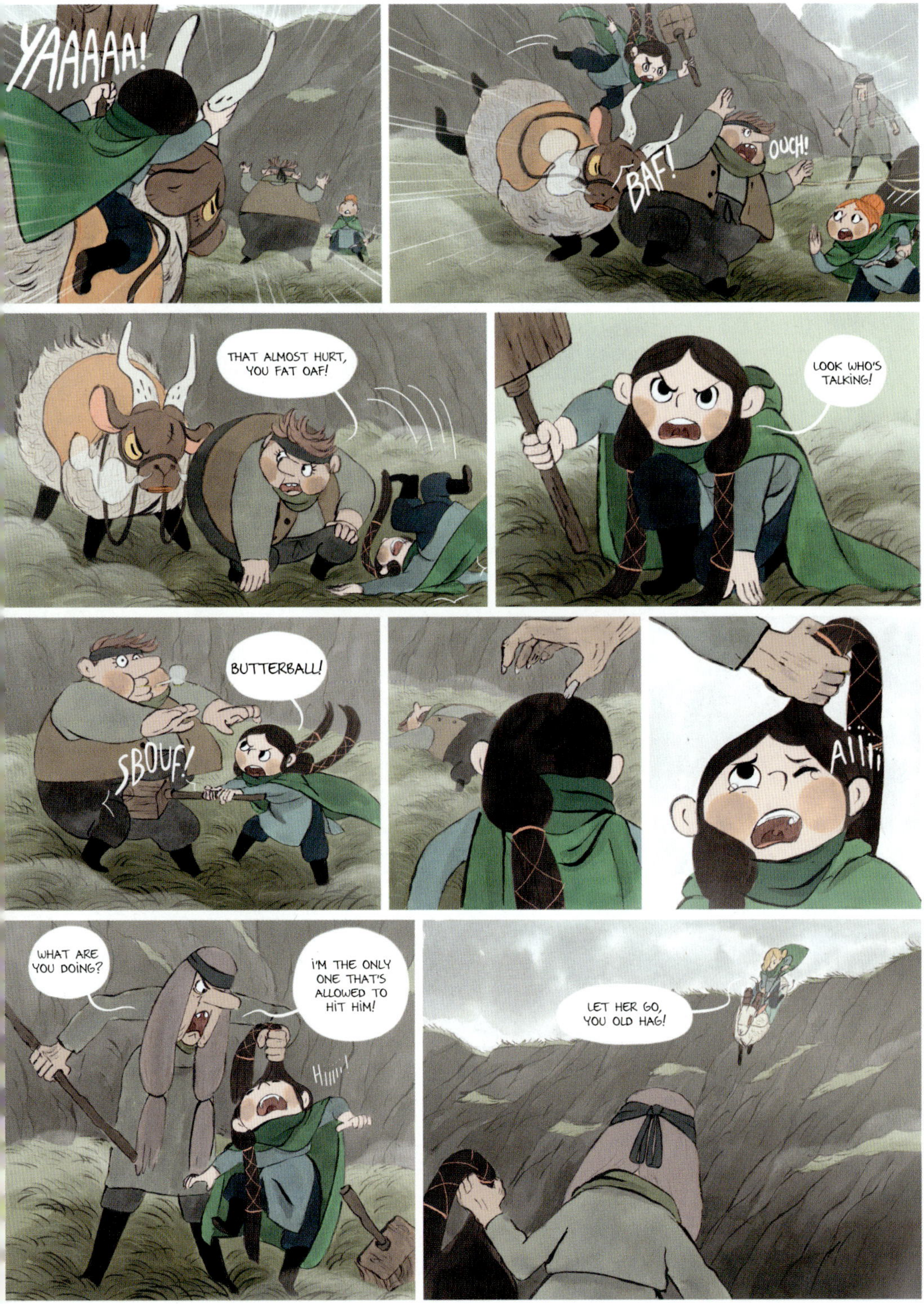
YAAAAA!
BAF!
OUCH!
THAT ALMOST HURT, YOU FAT OAF!
LOOK WHO'S TALKING!
BUTTERBALL!
SBOUF!
AIIII!
WHAT ARE YOU DOING?
I'M THE ONLY ONE THAT'S ALLOWED TO HIT HIM!
LET HER GO, YOU OLD HAG!

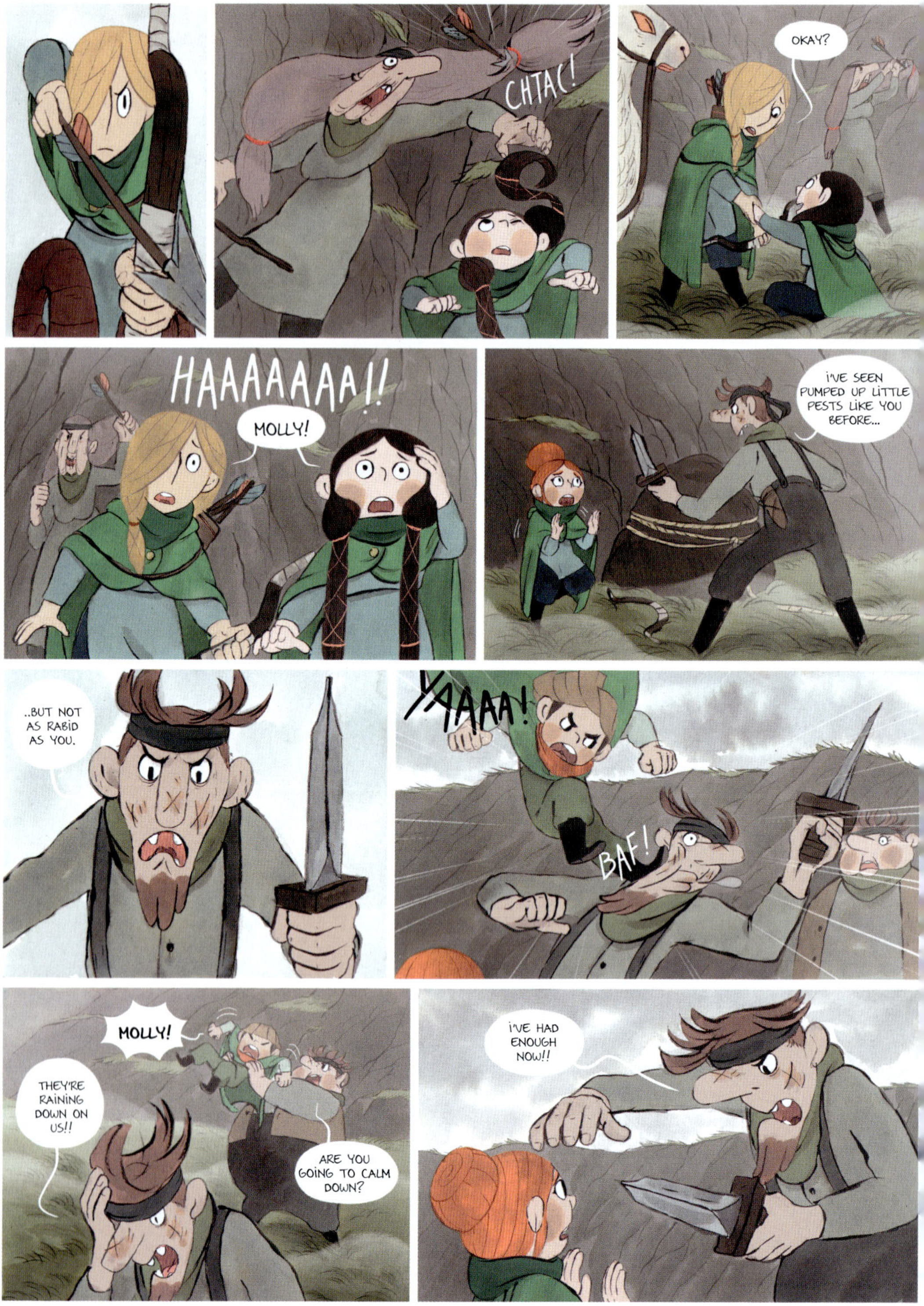
CHTAC!
OKAY?
HAAAAAAA!!
MOLLY!
I'VE SEEN PUMPED UP LITTLE PESTS LIKE YOU BEFORE...
..BUT NOT AS RABID AS YOU.
YAAAA!
BAF!
MOLLY!
THEY'RE RAINING DOWN ON US!!
ARE YOU GOING TO CALM DOWN?
I'VE HAD ENOUGH NOW!!

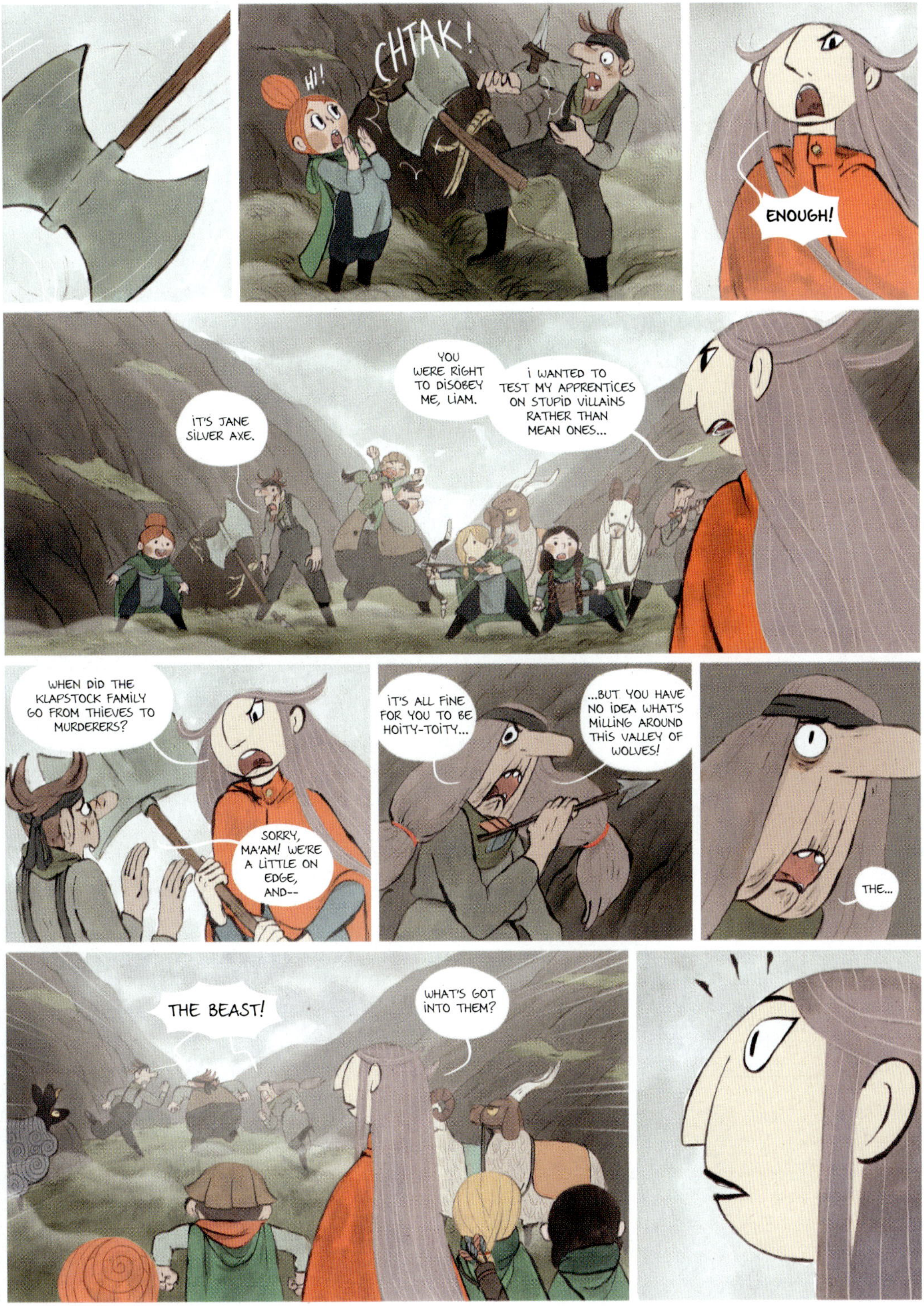
HI!
CHTAK!
ENOUGH!
IT'S JANE SILVER AXE.
YOU WERE RIGHT TO DISOBEY ME, LIAM.
I WANTED TO TEST MY APPRENTICES ON STUPID VILLAINS RATHER THAN MEAN ONES...
WHEN DID THE KLAPSTOCK FAMILY GO FROM THIEVES TO MURDERERS?
SORRY, MA'AM! WE'RE A LITTLE ON EDGE, AND--
IT'S ALL FINE FOR YOU TO BE HOITY-TOITY...
...BUT YOU HAVE NO IDEA WHAT'S MILLING AROUND THIS VALLEY OF WOLVES!
THE...
THE BEAST!
WHAT'S GOT INTO THEM?

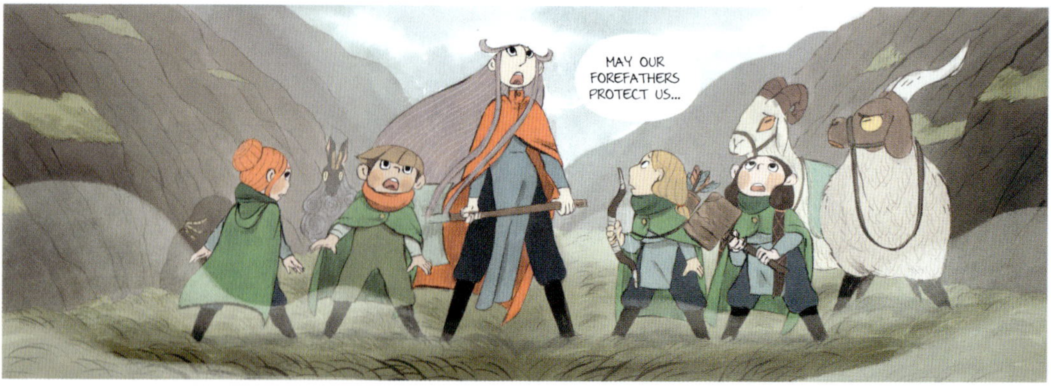
MAY OUR
FOREFATHERS
PROTECT US...

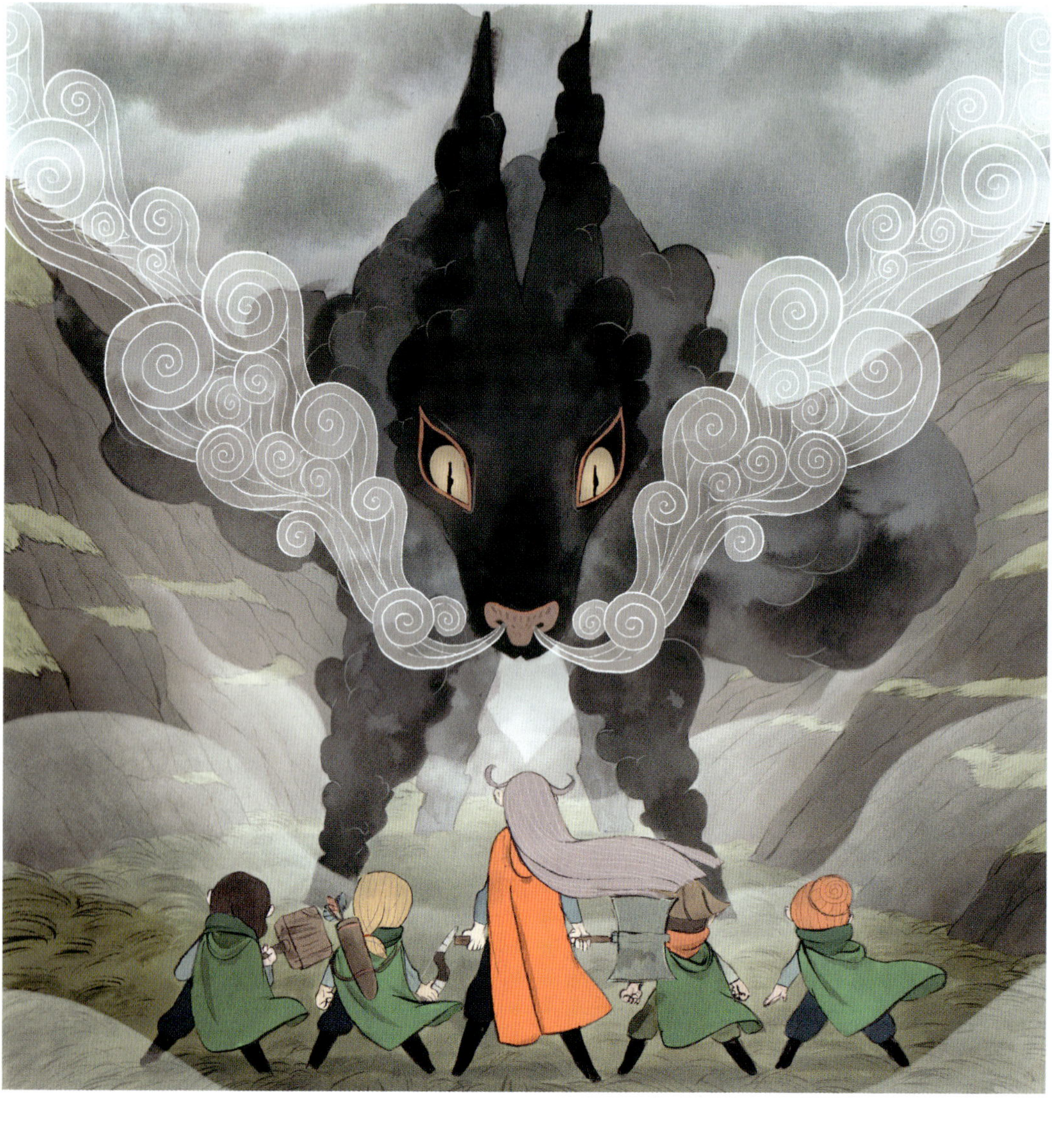

Part 2 - The Threat

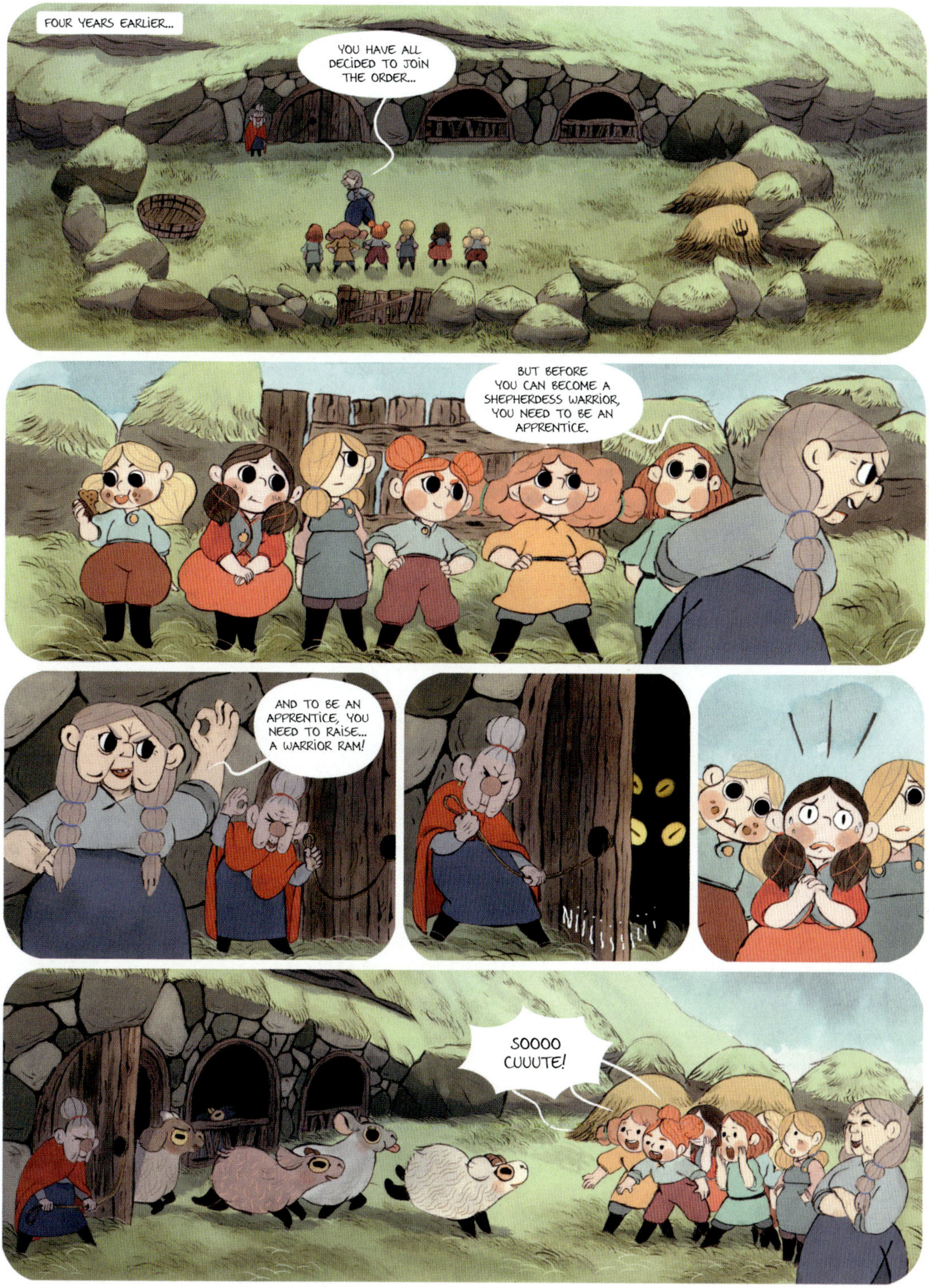
FOUR YEARS EARLIER...
YOU HAVE ALL DECIDED TO JOIN THE ORDER...
BUT BEFORE YOU CAN BECOME A SHEPHERDESS WARRIOR, YOU NEED TO BE AN APPRENTICE.
AND TO BE AN APPRENTICE, YOU NEED TO RAISE... A WARRIOR RAM!
SOOOO CUUUTE!

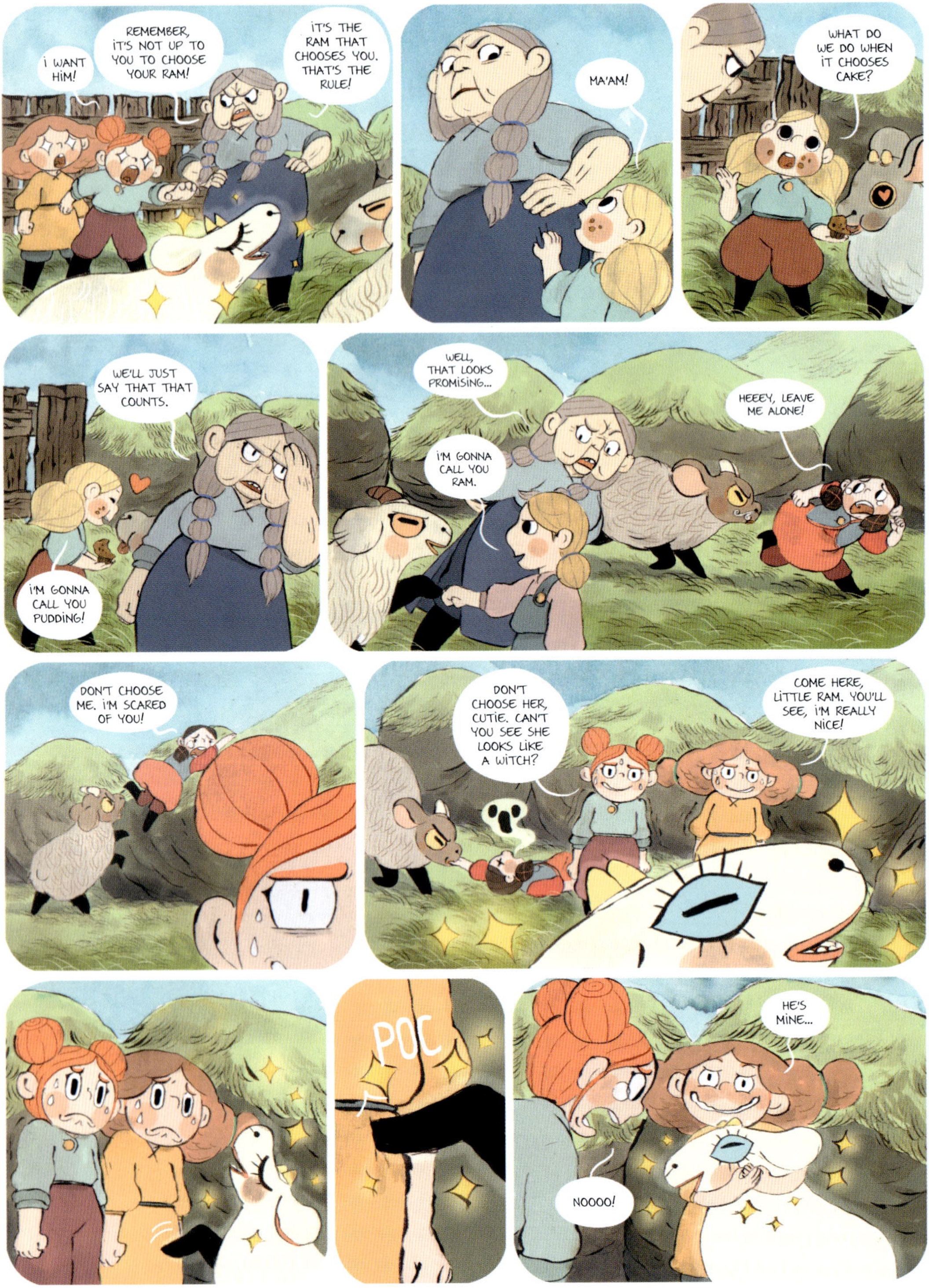
I WANT HIM!
REMEMBER, IT'S NOT UP TO YOU TO CHOOSE YOUR RAM!
IT'S THE RAM THAT CHOOSES YOU. THAT'S THE RULE!
MA'AM!
WHAT DO WE DO WHEN IT CHOOSES CAKE?
WE'LL JUST SAY THAT THAT COUNTS.
I'M GONNA CALL YOU PUDDING!
WELL, THAT LOOKS PROMISING...
I'M GONNA CALL YOU RAM.
HEEEY, LEAVE ME ALONE!
DON'T CHOOSE ME. I'M SCARED OF YOU!
DON'T CHOOSE HER, CUTIE. CAN'T YOU SEE SHE LOOKS LIKE A WITCH?
COME HERE, LITTLE RAM. YOU'LL SEE, I'M REALLY NICE!
POC
HE'S MINE...
NOOOO!

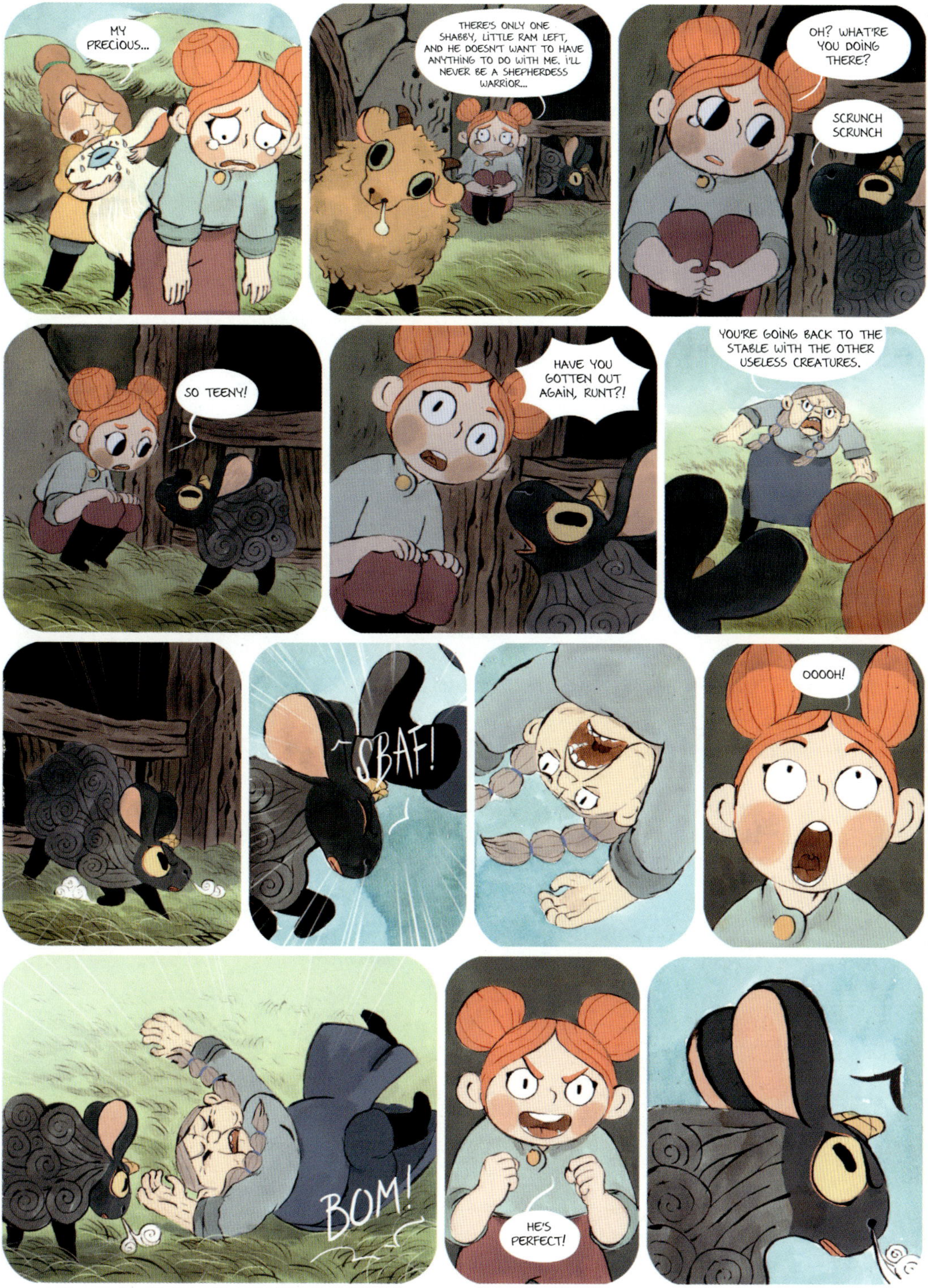
MY PRECIOUS...
THERE'S ONLY ONE SHABBY, LITTLE RAM LEFT, AND HE DOESN'T WANT TO HAVE ANYTHING TO DO WITH ME. I'LL NEVER BE A SHEPHERDESS WARRIOR...
OH? WHAT'RE YOU DOING THERE?
SCRUNCH SCRUNCH
SO TEENY!
HAVE YOU GOTTEN OUT AGAIN, RUNT?!
YOU'RE GOING BACK TO THE STABLE WITH THE OTHER USELESS CREATURES.
SBAF!
OOOOH!
BOM!
HE'S PERFECT!

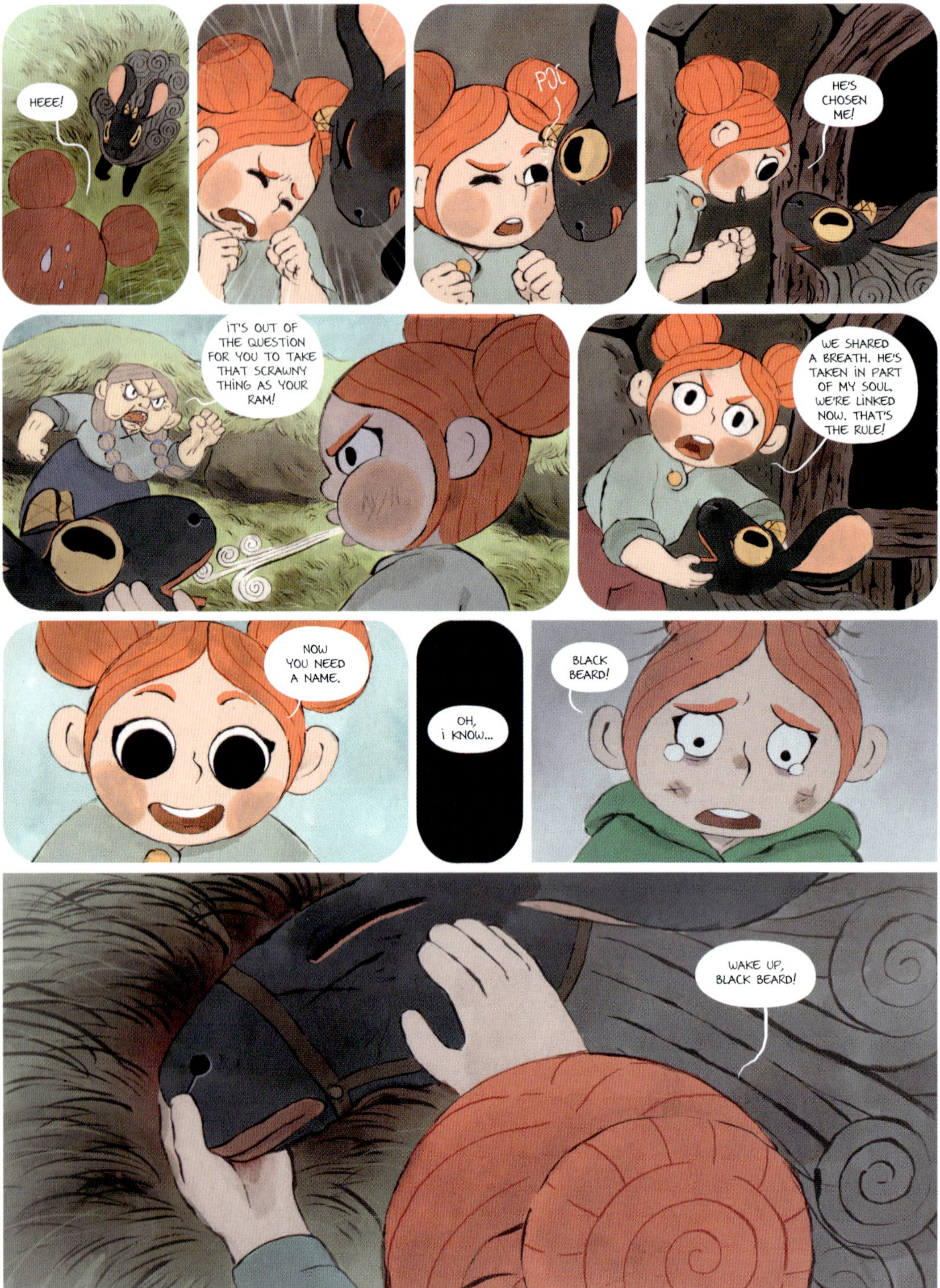
HEEE!
POC
HE'S CHOSEN ME!
IT'S OUT OF THE QUESTION FOR YOU TO TAKE THAT SCRAWNY THING AS YOUR RAM!
WE SHARED A BREATH. HE'S TAKEN IN PART OF MY SOUL. WE'RE LINKED NOW. THAT'S THE RULE!
NOW YOU NEED A NAME.
OH, I KNOW...
BLACK BEARD!
WAKE UP, BLACK BEARD!

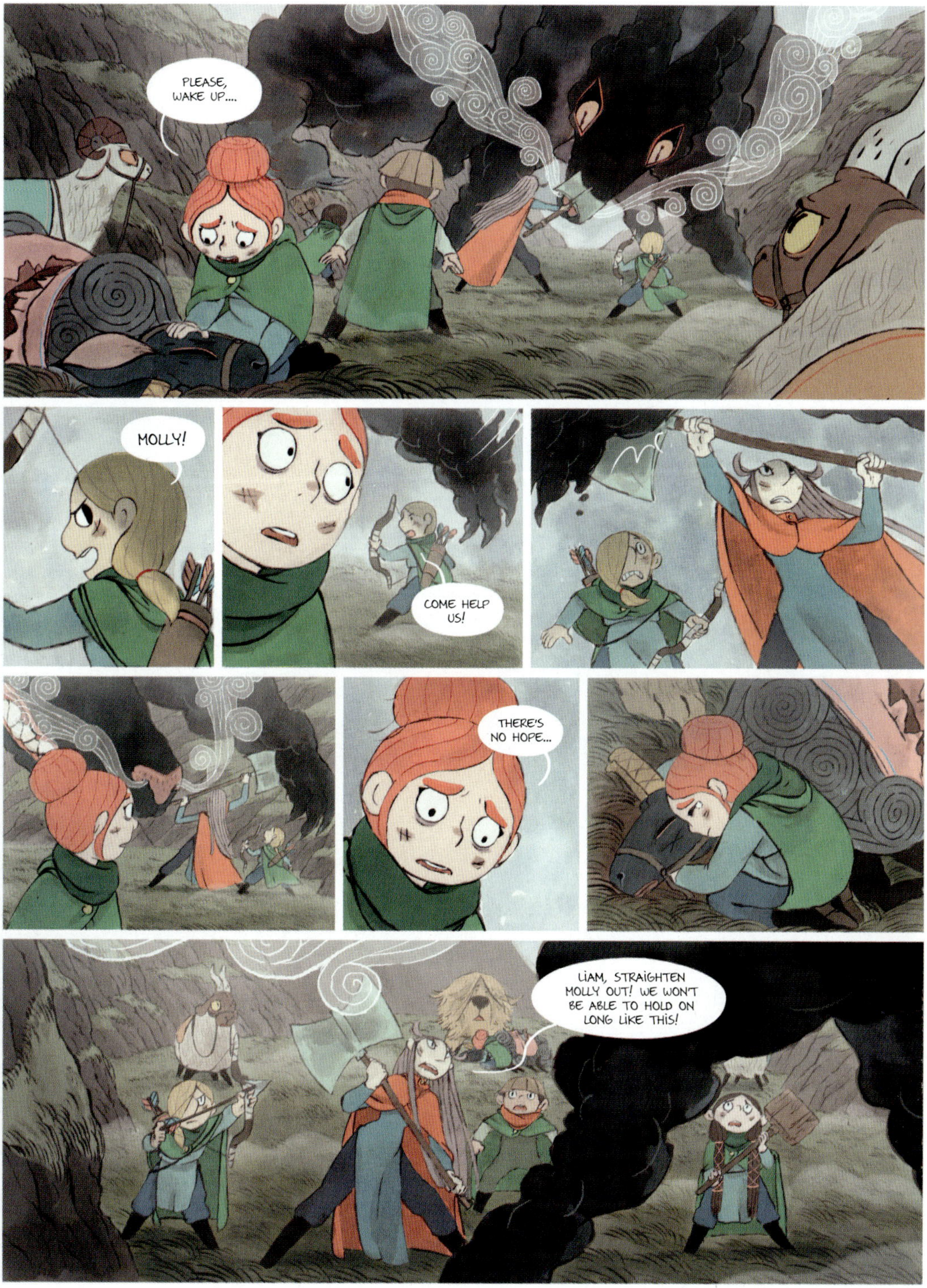
PLEASE, WAKE UP....
MOLLY!
COME HELP US!
THERE'S NO HOPE...
LIAM, STRAIGHTEN MOLLY OUT! WE WON'T BE ABLE TO HOLD ON LONG LIKE THIS!

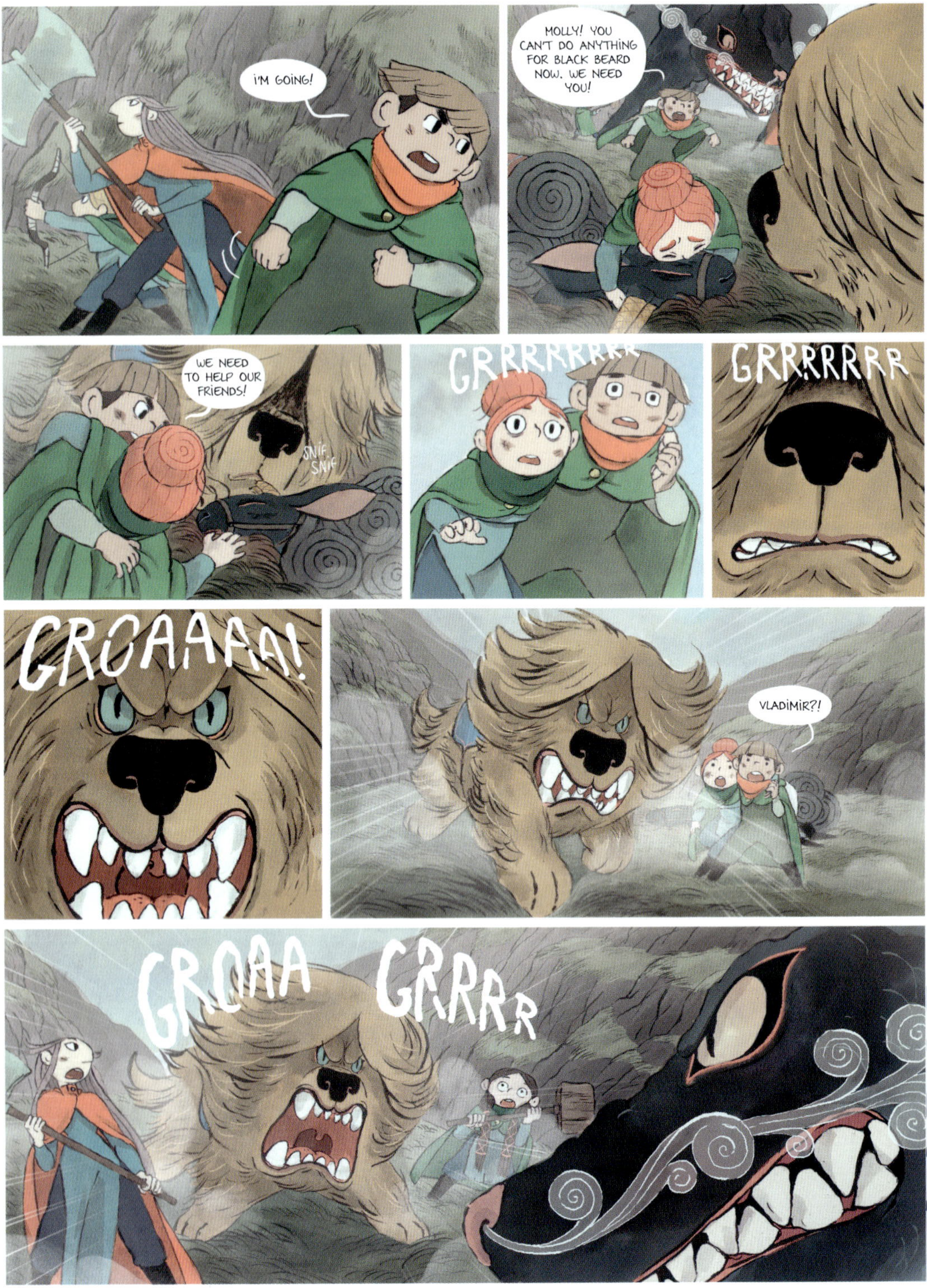
I'M GOING!
MOLLY! YOU CAN'T DO ANYTHING FOR BLACK BEARD NOW. WE NEED YOU!
WE NEED TO HELP OUR FRIENDS!
SNIF SNIF
GRRRRRRRR
GRRRRRRR
GROAAAAA!
VLADIMIR?!
GROAA
GRRRR

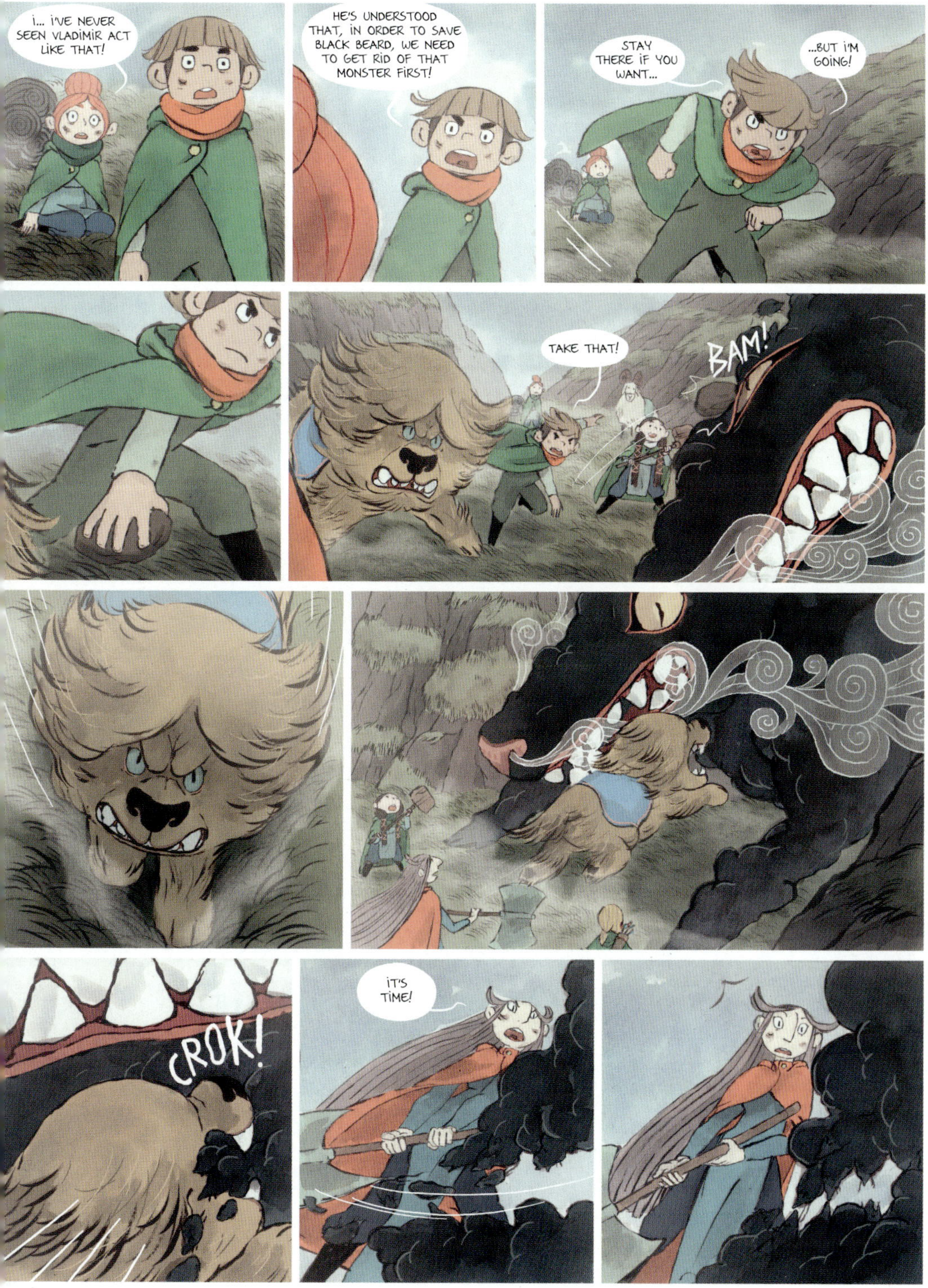
I... I'VE NEVER SEEN VLADIMIR ACT LIKE THAT!
HE'S UNDERSTOOD THAT, IN ORDER TO SAVE BLACK BEARD, WE NEED TO GET RID OF THAT MONSTER FIRST!
STAY THERE IF YOU WANT...
...BUT I'M GOING!
TAKE THAT!
BAM!
CROK!
IT'S TIME!

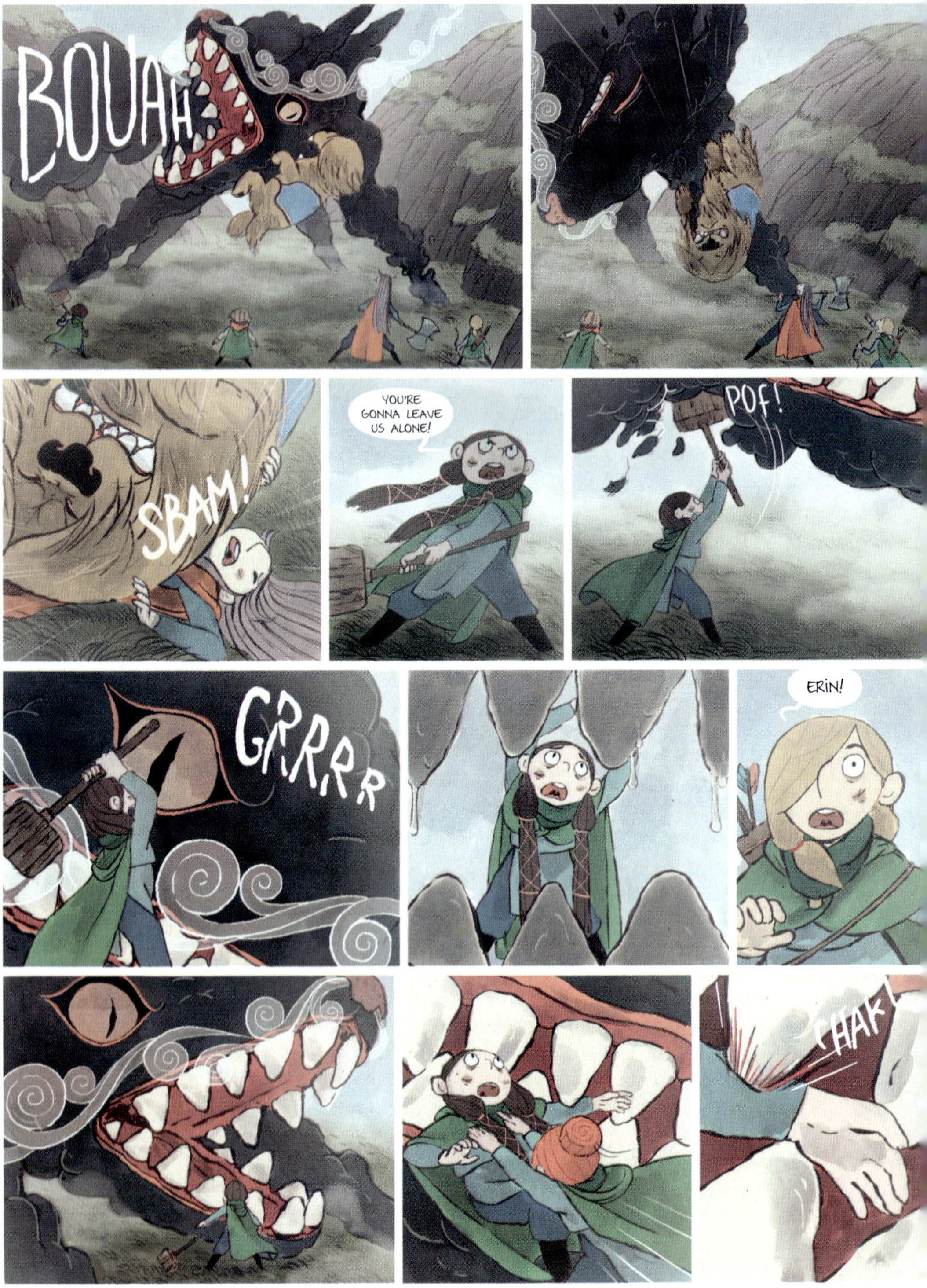
BOUAHH
SBAM!
YOU'RE GONNA LEAVE US ALONE!
POF!
GRRRRR
ERIN!
CHAK!

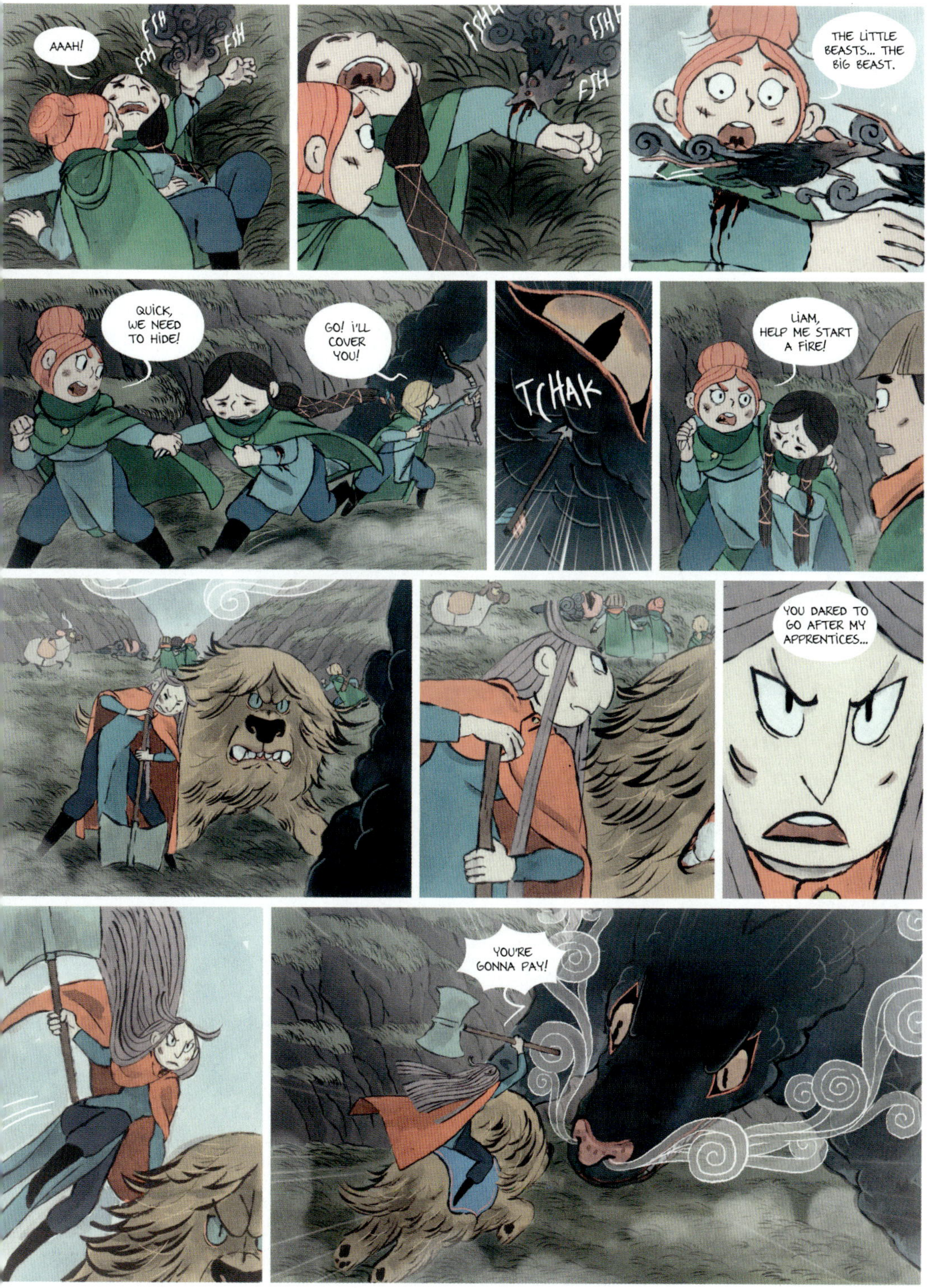
AAAH!
FSH
FSH
FSH
FSH
FSH
THE LITTLE BEASTS... THE BIG BEAST.
QUICK, WE NEED TO HIDE!
GO! I'LL COVER YOU!
TCHAK
LIAM, HELP ME START A FIRE!
YOU DARED TO GO AFTER MY APPRENTICES...
YOU'RE GONNA PAY!

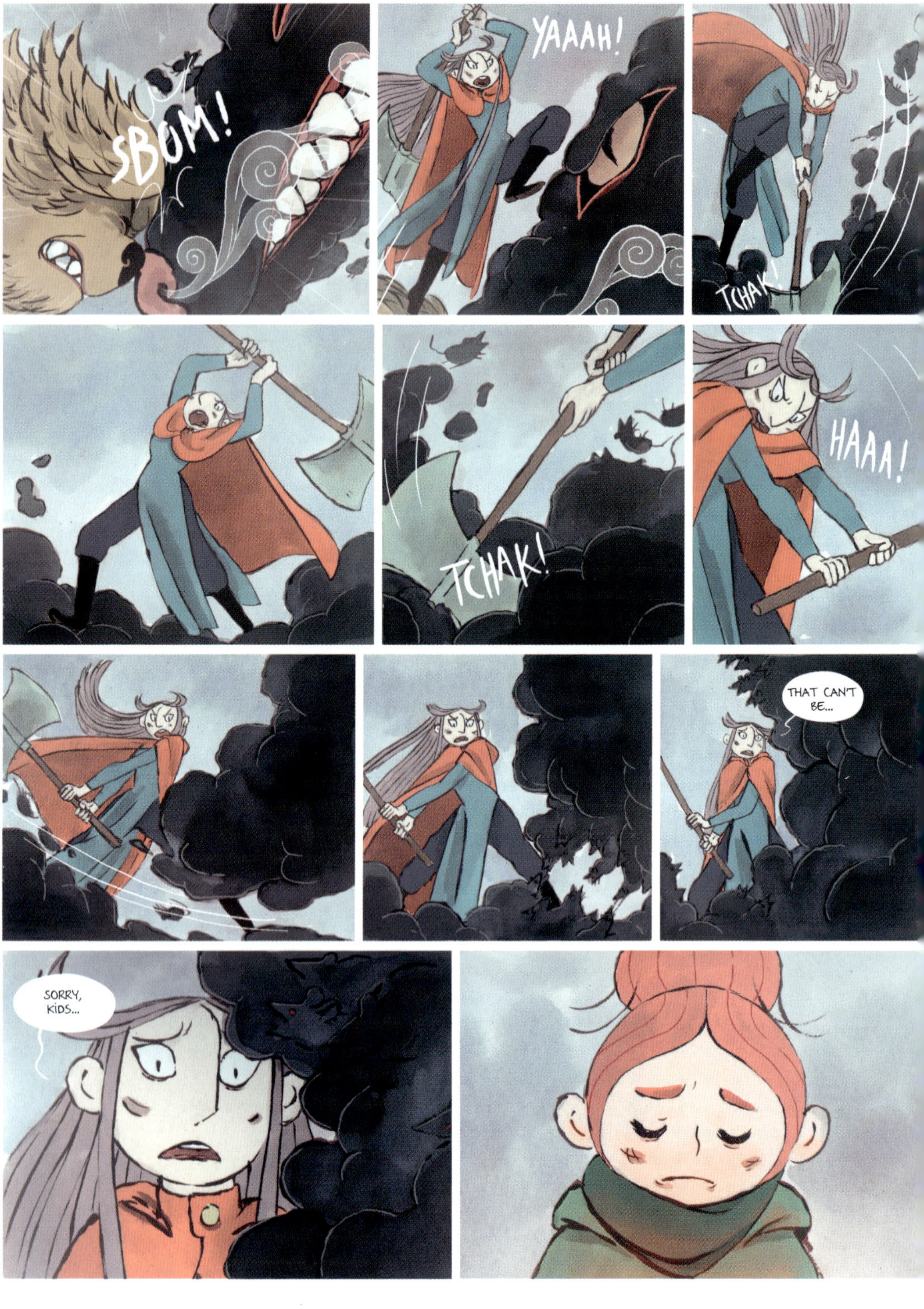
SBOM!
YAAAH!
TCHAK!
TCHAK!
HAAA!
THAT CAN'T BE...
SORRY, KIDS...

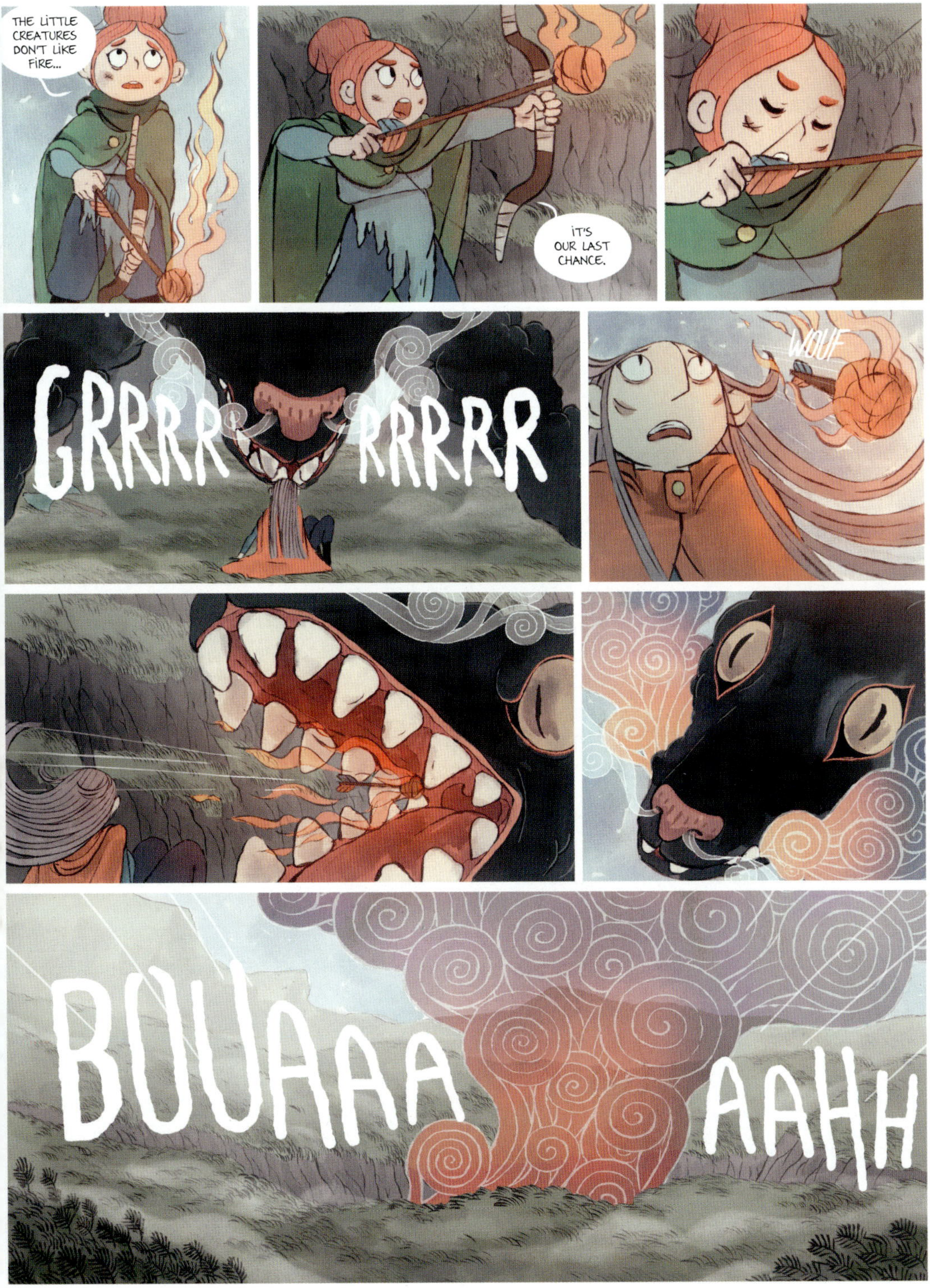
THE LITTLE CREATURES DON'T LIKE FIRE...
IT'S OUR LAST CHANCE.
GRRRR RRRRR
WOUF
BOUAAA AAHH

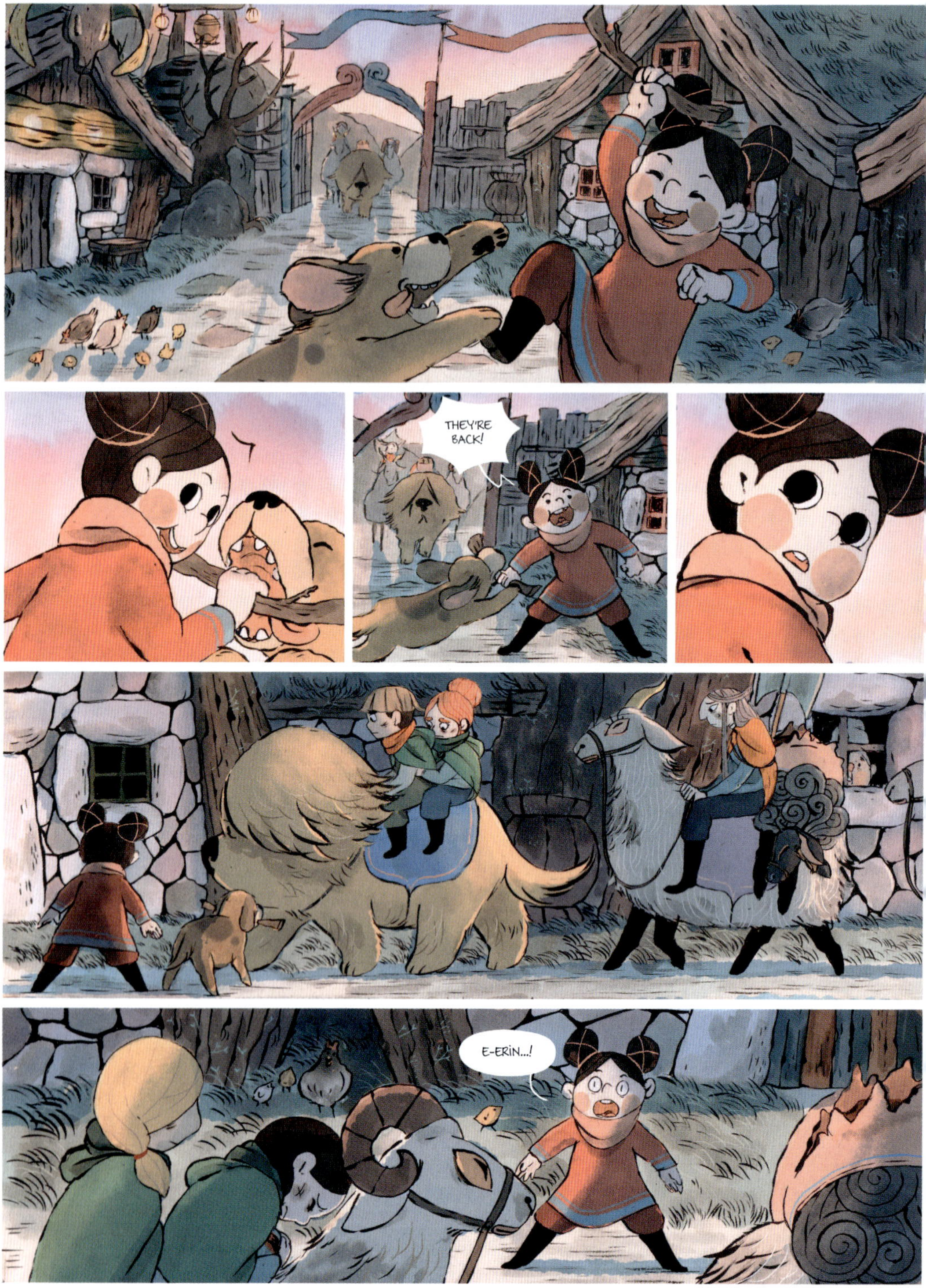
THEY'RE BACK!
E-ERIN...!

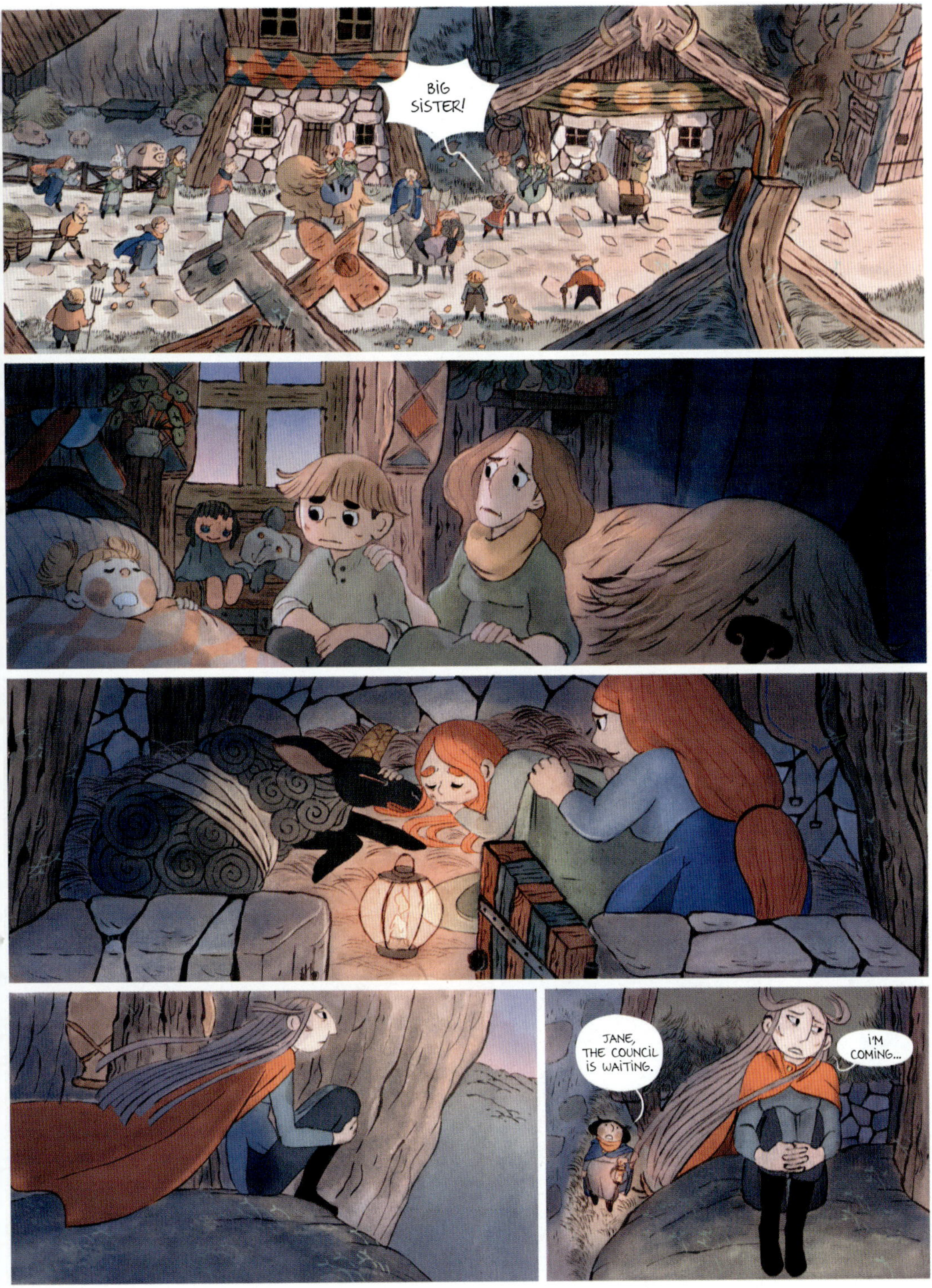
BIG SISTER!
JANE, THE COUNCIL IS WAITING.
I'M COMING...

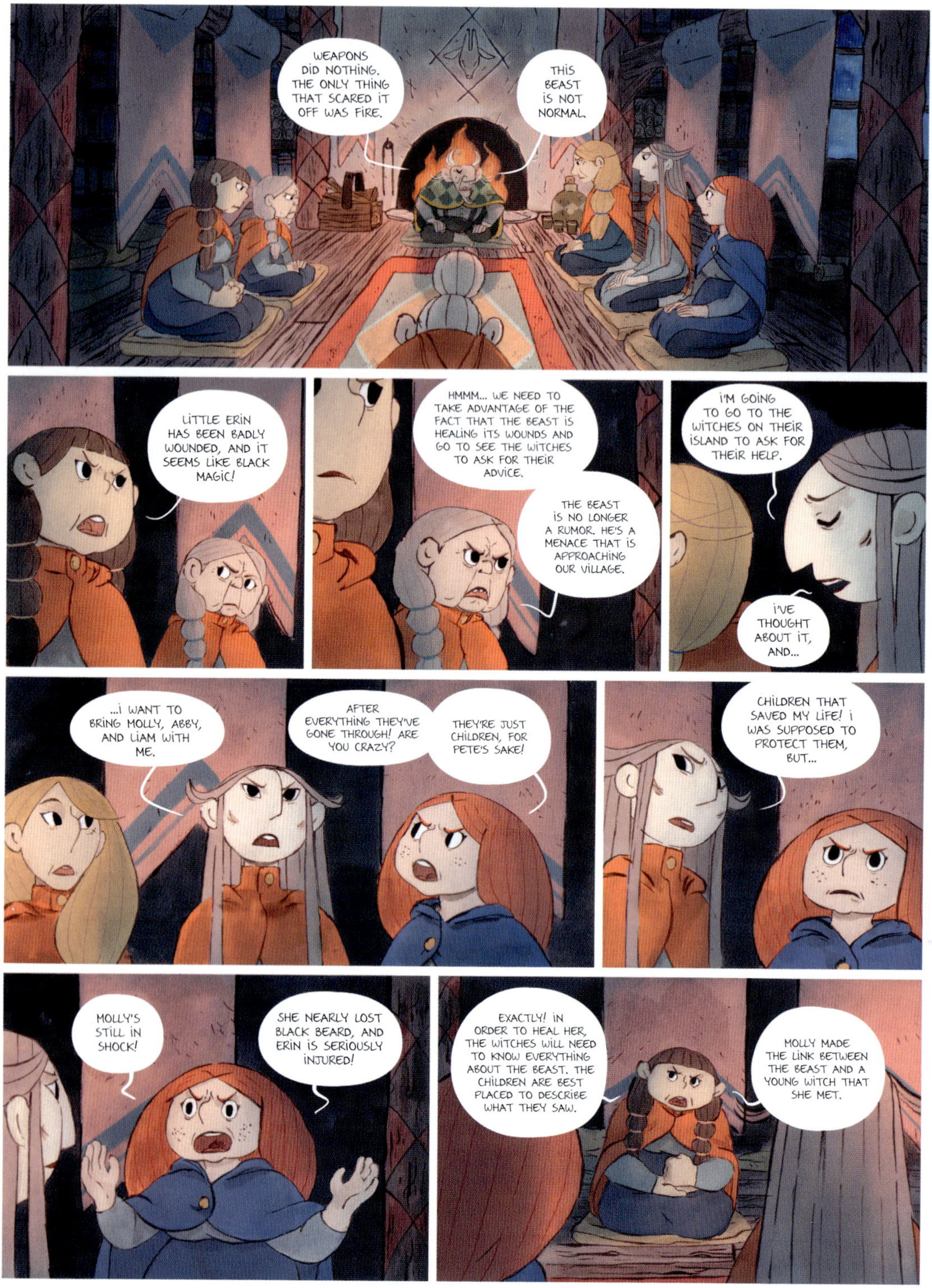
WEAPONS DID NOTHING. THE ONLY THING THAT SCARED IT OFF WAS FIRE.
THIS BEAST IS NOT NORMAL.
LITTLE ERIN HAS BEEN BADLY WOUNDED, AND IT SEEMS LIKE BLACK MAGIC!
HMMM... WE NEED TO TAKE ADVANTAGE OF THE FACT THAT THE BEAST IS HEALING ITS WOUNDS AND GO TO SEE THE WITCHES TO ASK FOR THEIR ADVICE.
THE BEAST IS NO LONGER A RUMOR. HE'S A MENACE THAT IS APPROACHING OUR VILLAGE.
I'M GOING TO GO TO THE WITCHES ON THEIR ISLAND TO ASK FOR THEIR HELP.
I'VE THOUGHT ABOUT IT, AND...
...I WANT TO BRING MOLLY, ABBY, AND LIAM WITH ME.
AFTER EVERYTHING THEY'VE GONE THROUGH! ARE YOU CRAZY?
THEY'RE JUST CHILDREN, FOR PETE'S SAKE!
CHILDREN THAT SAVED MY LIFE! I WAS SUPPOSED TO PROTECT THEM, BUT...
MOLLY'S STILL IN SHOCK!
SHE NEARLY LOST BLACK BEARD, AND ERIN IS SERIOUSLY INJURED!
EXACTLY! IN ORDER TO HEAL HER, THE WITCHES WILL NEED TO KNOW EVERYTHING ABOUT THE BEAST. THE CHILDREN ARE BEST PLACED TO DESCRIBE WHAT THEY SAW.
MOLLY MADE THE LINK BETWEEN THE BEAST AND A YOUNG WITCH THAT SHE MET.

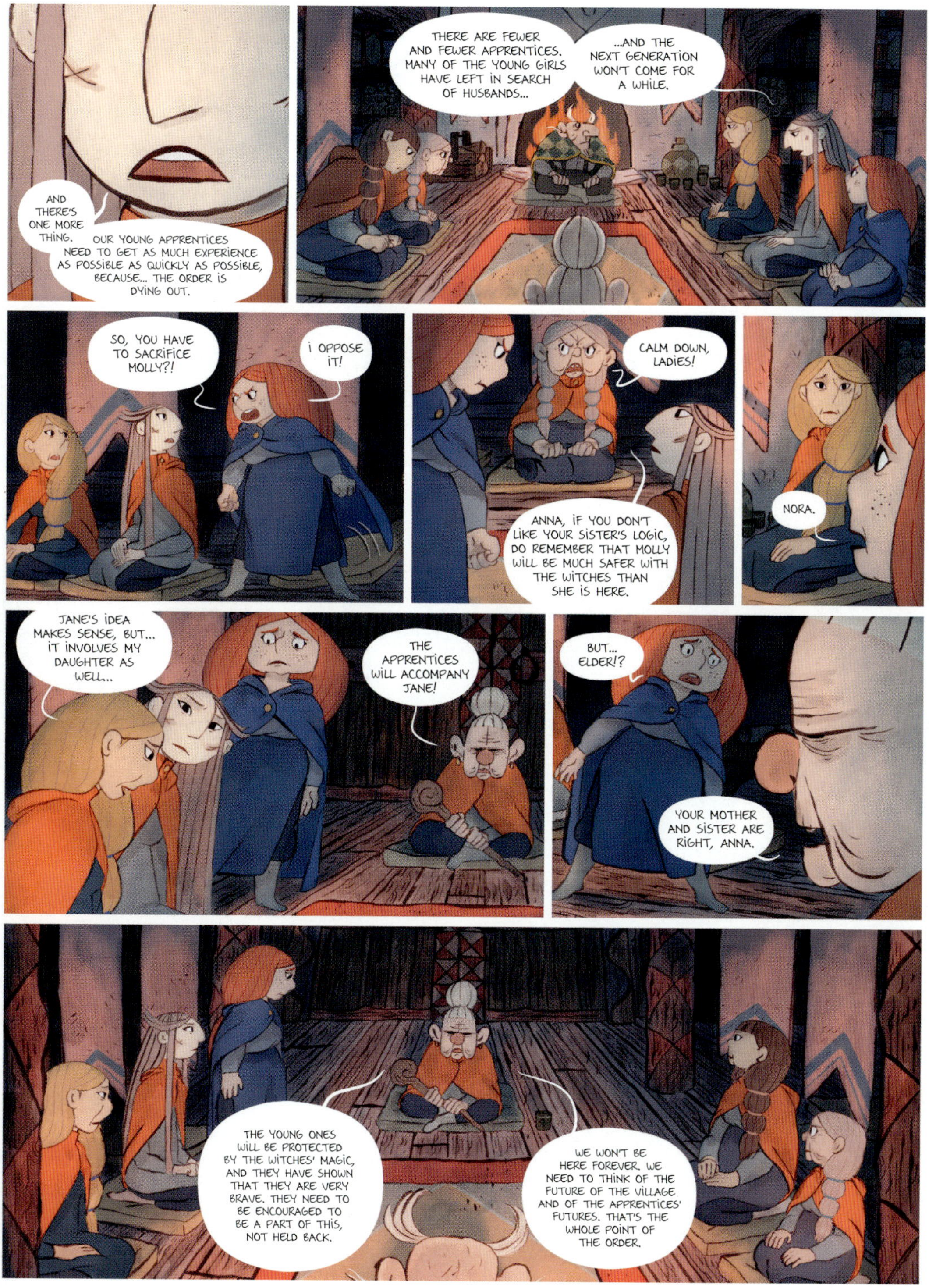
AND THERE'S ONE MORE THING.
OUR YOUNG APPRENTICES NEED TO GET AS MUCH EXPERIENCE AS POSSIBLE AS QUICKLY AS POSSIBLE, BECAUSE... THE ORDER IS DYING OUT.
THERE ARE FEWER AND FEWER APPRENTICES. MANY OF THE YOUNG GIRLS HAVE LEFT IN SEARCH OF HUSBANDS...
...AND THE NEXT GENERATION WON'T COME FOR A WHILE.
SO, YOU HAVE TO SACRIFICE MOLLY?!
I OPPOSE IT!
CALM DOWN, LADIES!
ANNA, IF YOU DON'T LIKE YOUR SISTER'S LOGIC, DO REMEMBER THAT MOLLY WILL BE MUCH SAFER WITH THE WITCHES THAN SHE IS HERE.
NORA.
JANE'S IDEA MAKES SENSE, BUT... IT INVOLVES MY DAUGHTER AS WELL...
THE APPRENTICES WILL ACCOMPANY JANE!
BUT... ELDER!?
YOUR MOTHER AND SISTER ARE RIGHT, ANNA.
THE YOUNG ONES WILL BE PROTECTED BY THE WITCHES' MAGIC, AND THEY HAVE SHOWN THAT THEY ARE VERY BRAVE. THEY NEED TO BE ENCOURAGED TO BE A PART OF THIS, NOT HELD BACK.
WE WON'T BE HERE FOREVER. WE NEED TO THINK OF THE FUTURE OF THE VILLAGE AND OF THE APPRENTICES' FUTURES. THAT'S THE WHOLE POINT OF THE ORDER.

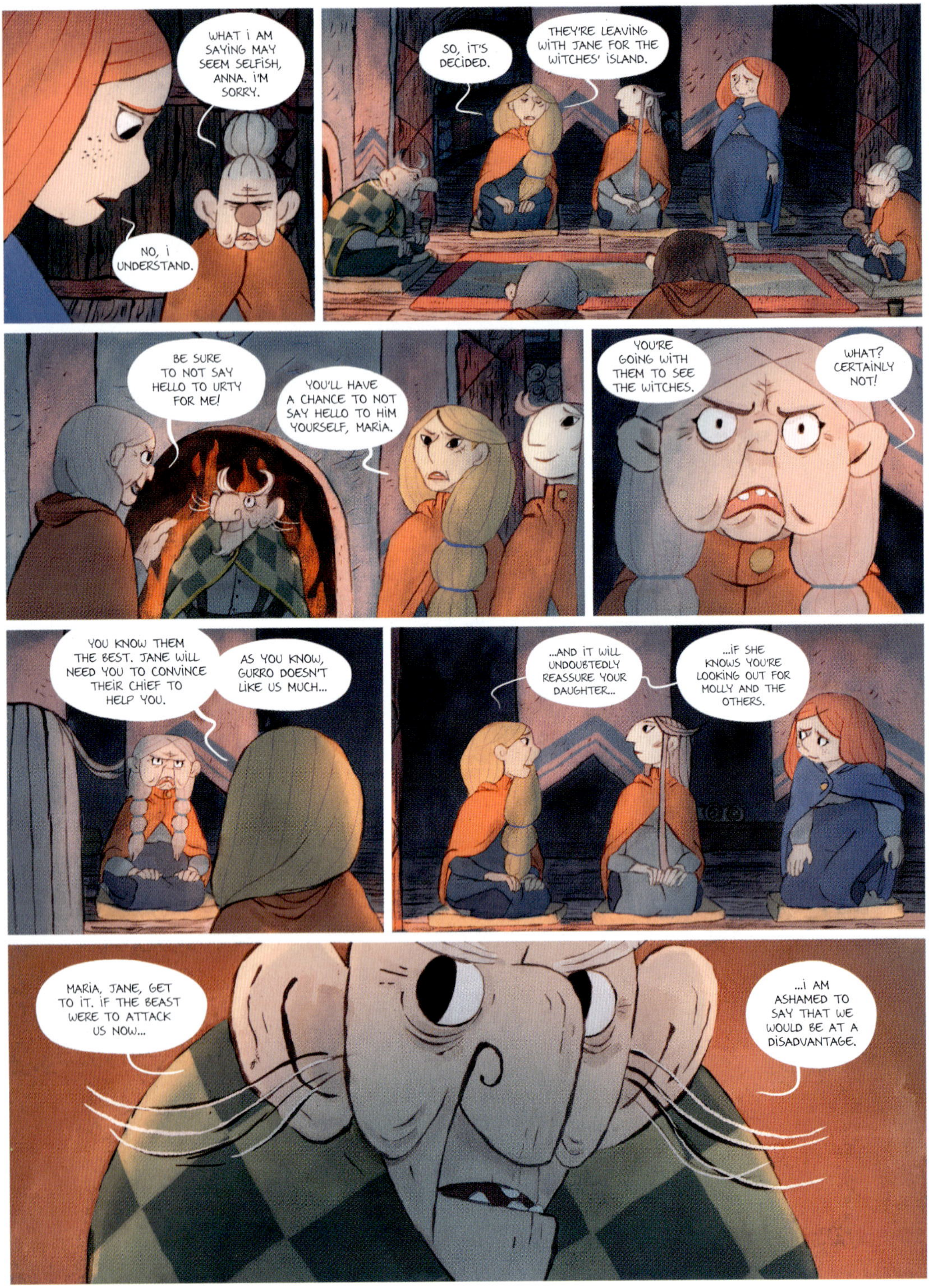
WHAT I AM SAYING MAY SEEM SELFISH, ANNA. I'M SORRY.
NO, I UNDERSTAND.
SO, IT'S DECIDED.
THEY'RE LEAVING WITH JANE FOR THE WITCHES' ISLAND.
BE SURE TO NOT SAY HELLO TO URTY FOR ME!
YOU'LL HAVE A CHANCE TO NOT SAY HELLO TO HIM YOURSELF, MARIA.
YOU'RE GOING WITH THEM TO SEE THE WITCHES.
WHAT? CERTAINLY NOT!
YOU KNOW THEM THE BEST. JANE WILL NEED YOU TO CONVINCE THEIR CHIEF TO HELP YOU.
AS YOU KNOW, GURRO DOESN'T LIKE US MUCH...
...AND IT WILL UNDOUBTEDLY REASSURE YOUR DAUGHTER...
...IF SHE KNOWS YOU'RE LOOKING OUT FOR MOLLY AND THE OTHERS.
MARIA, JANE, GET TO IT. IF THE BEAST WERE TO ATTACK US NOW...
...I AM ASHAMED TO SAY THAT WE WOULD BE AT A DISADVANTAGE.

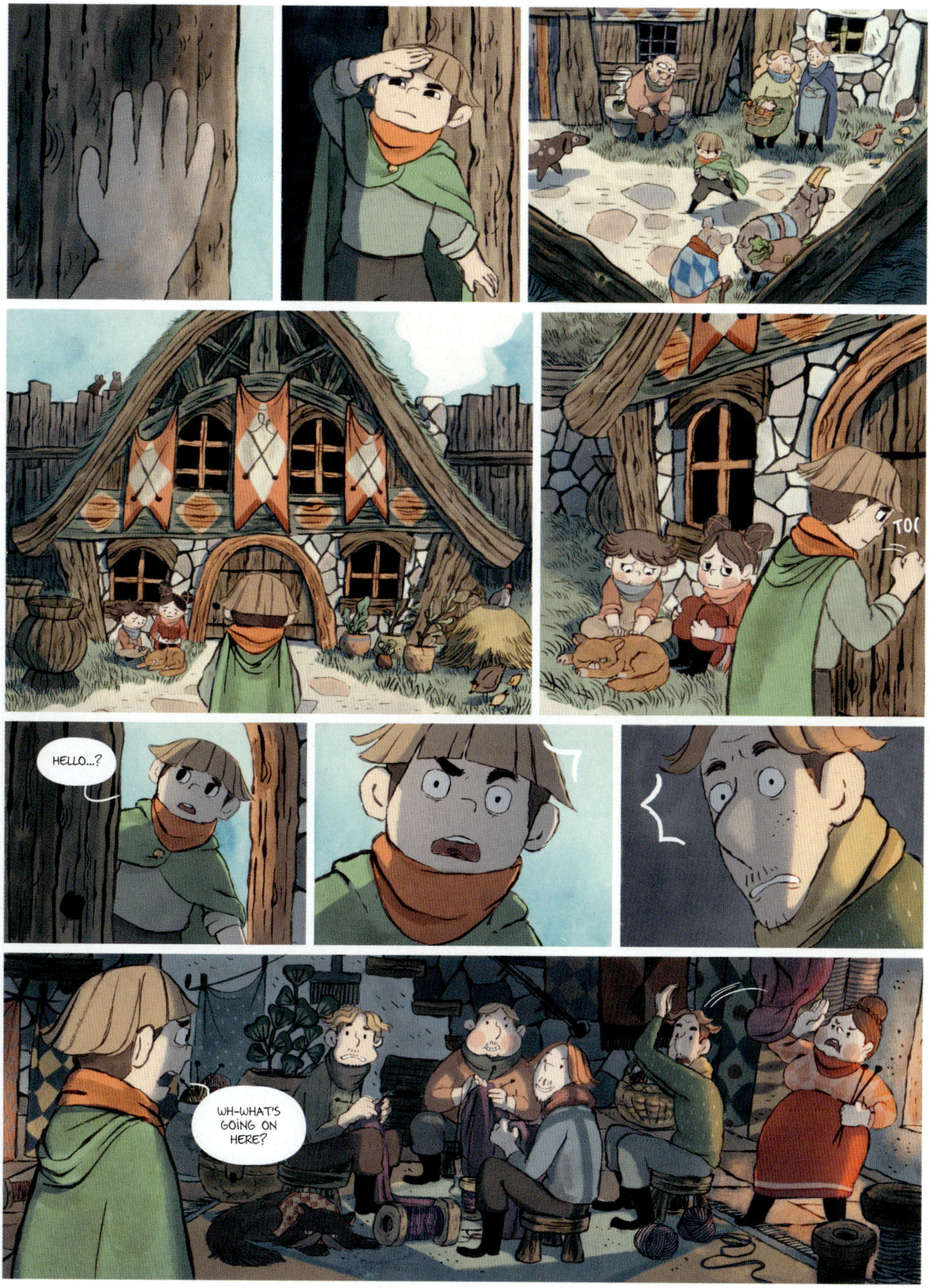
TOC
HELLO...?
WH-WHAT'S GOING ON HERE?

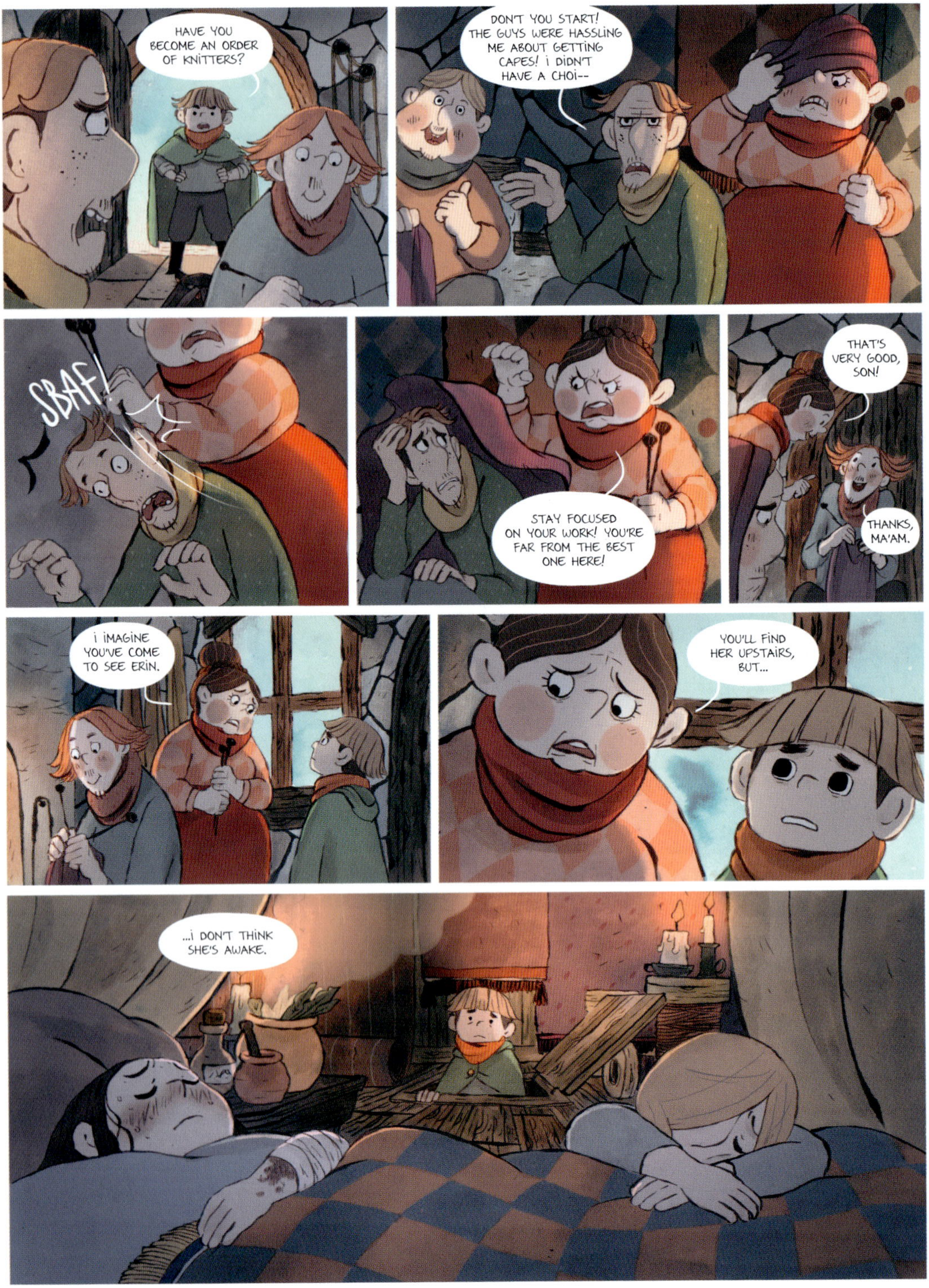
HAVE YOU BECOME AN ORDER OF KNITTERS?
DON'T YOU START! THE GUYS WERE HASSLING ME ABOUT GETTING CAPES! I DIDN'T HAVE A CHOI--
SBAF!
STAY FOCUSED ON YOUR WORK! YOU'RE FAR FROM THE BEST ONE HERE!
THAT'S VERY GOOD, SON!
THANKS, MA'AM.
I IMAGINE YOU'VE COME TO SEE ERIN.
YOU'LL FIND HER UPSTAIRS, BUT...
...I DON'T THINK SHE'S AWAKE.

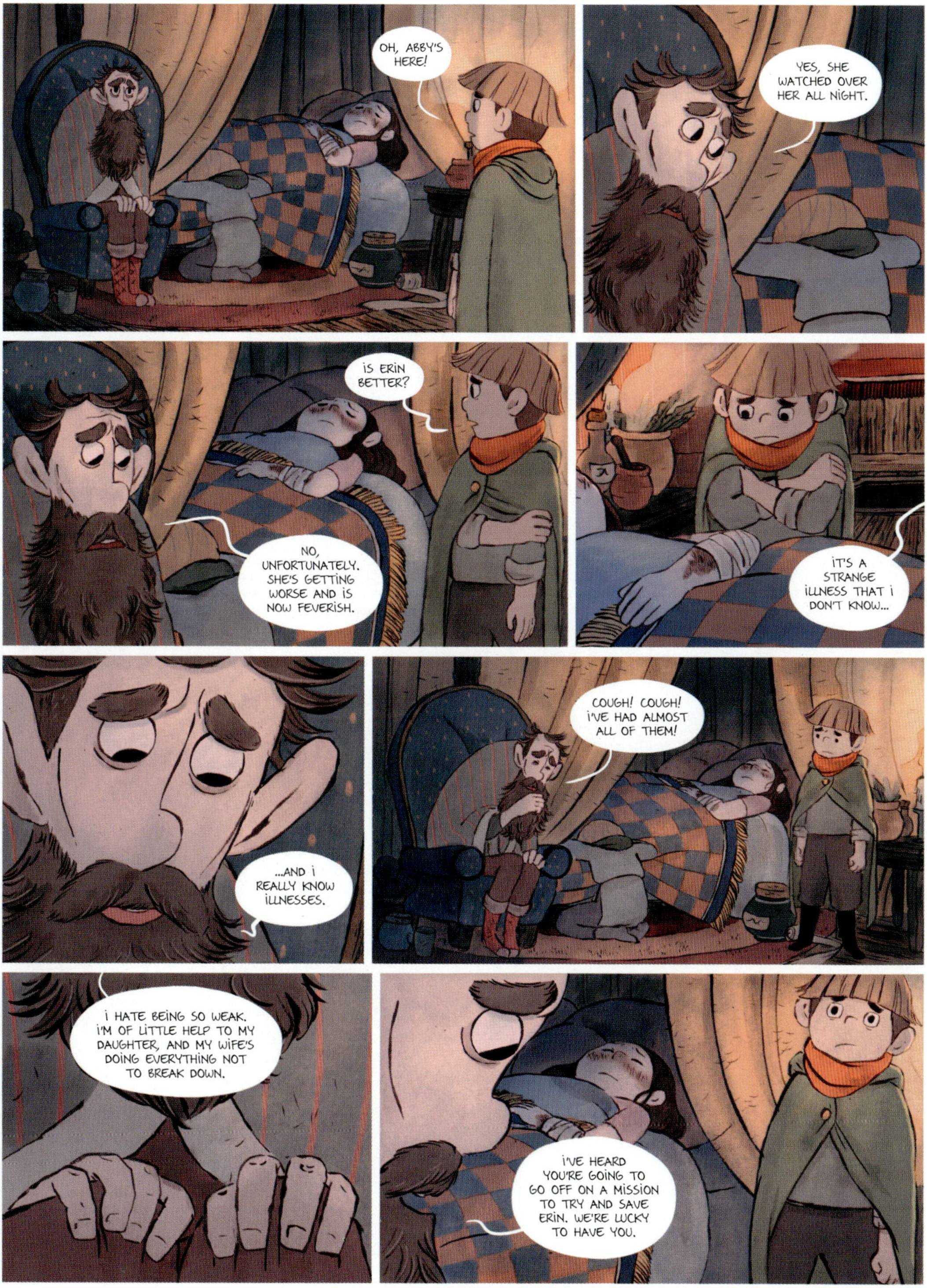
OH, ABBY'S HERE!
YES, SHE WATCHED OVER HER ALL NIGHT.
IS ERIN BETTER?
NO, UNFORTUNATELY. SHE'S GETTING WORSE AND IS NOW FEVERISH.
IT'S A STRANGE ILLNESS THAT I DON'T KNOW...
...AND I REALLY KNOW ILLNESSES.
COUGH! COUGH! I'VE HAD ALMOST ALL OF THEM!
I HATE BEING SO WEAK. I'M OF LITTLE HELP TO MY DAUGHTER, AND MY WIFE'S DOING EVERYTHING NOT TO BREAK DOWN.
I'VE HEARD YOU'RE GOING TO GO OFF ON A MISSION TO TRY AND SAVE ERIN. WE'RE LUCKY TO HAVE YOU.

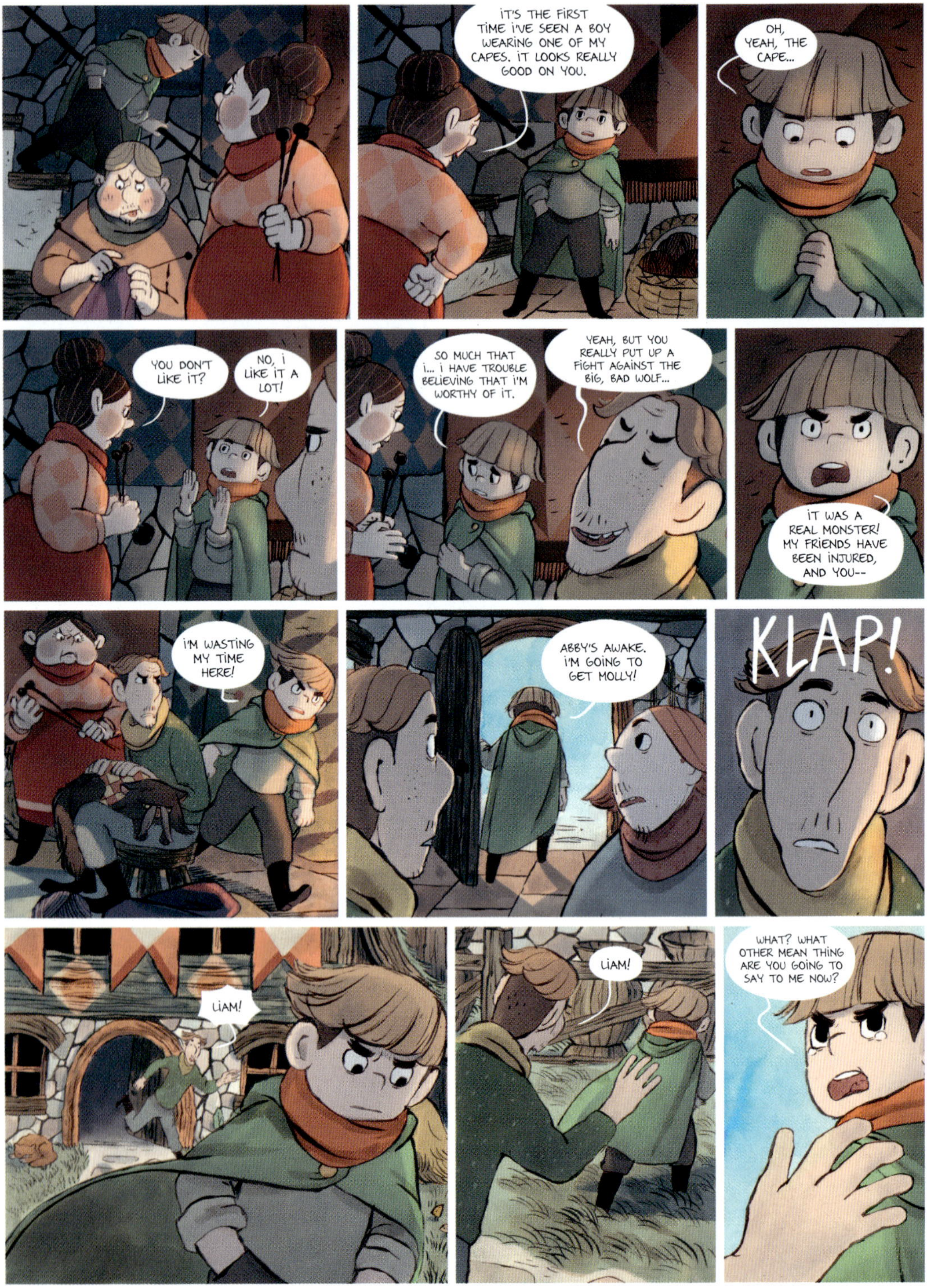
IT'S THE FIRST TIME I'VE SEEN A BOY WEARING ONE OF MY CAPES. IT LOOKS REALLY GOOD ON YOU.
OH, YEAH, THE CAPE...
YOU DON'T LIKE IT?
NO, I LIKE IT A LOT!
SO MUCH THAT I... I HAVE TROUBLE BELIEVING THAT I'M WORTHY OF IT.
YEAH, BUT YOU REALLY PUT UP A FIGHT AGAINST THE BIG, BAD WOLF...
IT WAS A REAL MONSTER! MY FRIENDS HAVE BEEN INJURED, AND YOU--
I'M WASTING MY TIME HERE!
ABBY'S AWAKE. I'M GOING TO GET MOLLY!
KLAP!
LIAM!
LIAM!
WHAT? WHAT OTHER MEAN THING ARE YOU GOING TO SAY TO ME NOW?

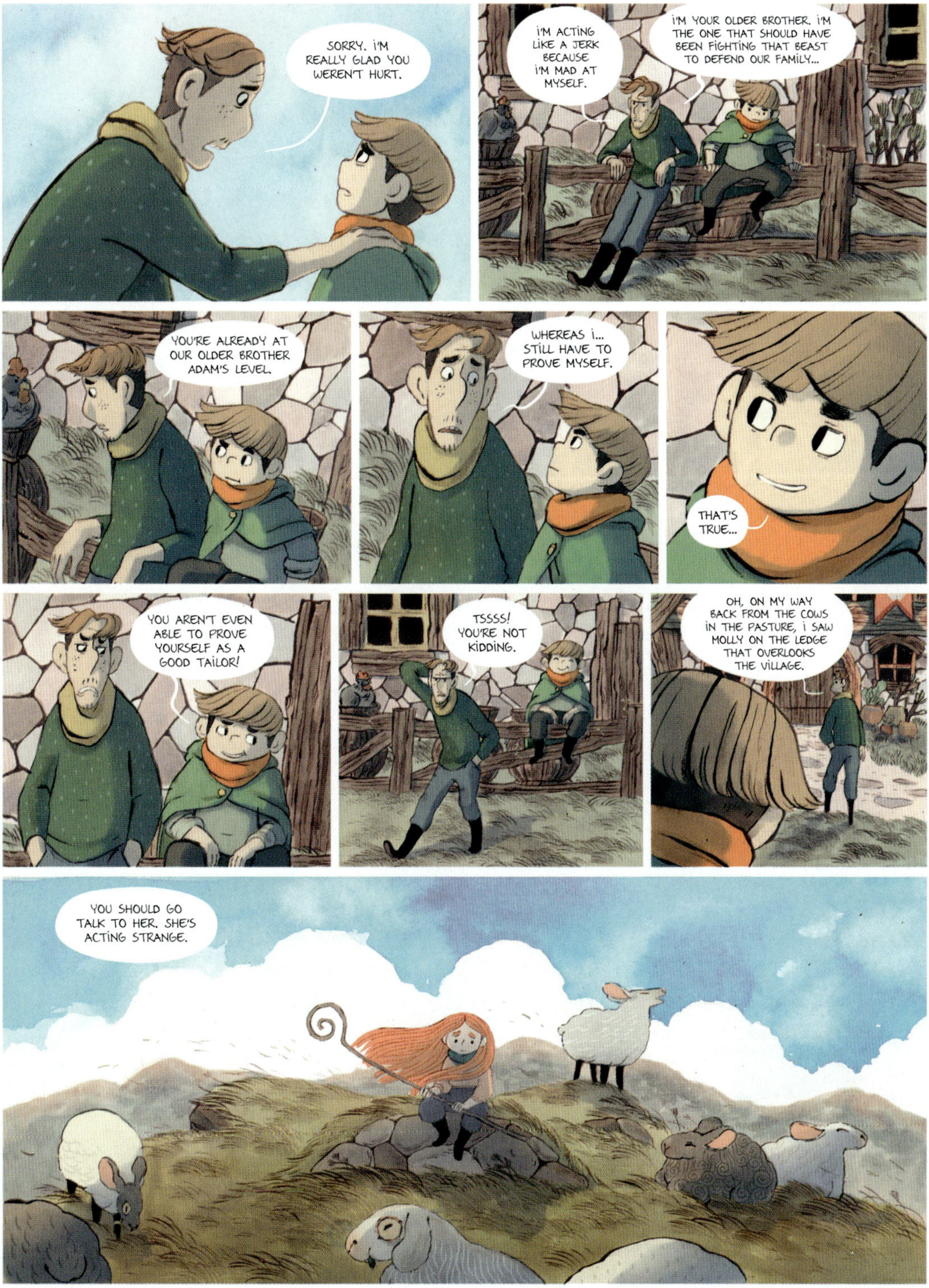
SORRY. I'M REALLY GLAD YOU WEREN'T HURT.
I'M ACTING LIKE A JERK BECAUSE I'M MAD AT MYSELF.
I'M YOUR OLDER BROTHER. I'M THE ONE THAT SHOULD HAVE BEEN FIGHTING THAT BEAST TO DEFEND OUR FAMILY...
YOU'RE ALREADY AT OUR OLDER BROTHER ADAM'S LEVEL.
WHEREAS I... STILL HAVE TO PROVE MYSELF.
THAT'S TRUE...
YOU AREN'T EVEN ABLE TO PROVE YOURSELF AS A GOOD TAILOR!
TSSSS! YOU'RE NOT KIDDING.
OH, ON MY WAY BACK FROM THE COWS IN THE PASTURE, I SAW MOLLY ON THE LEDGE THAT OVERLOOKS THE VILLAGE.
YOU SHOULD GO TALK TO HER. SHE'S ACTING STRANGE.

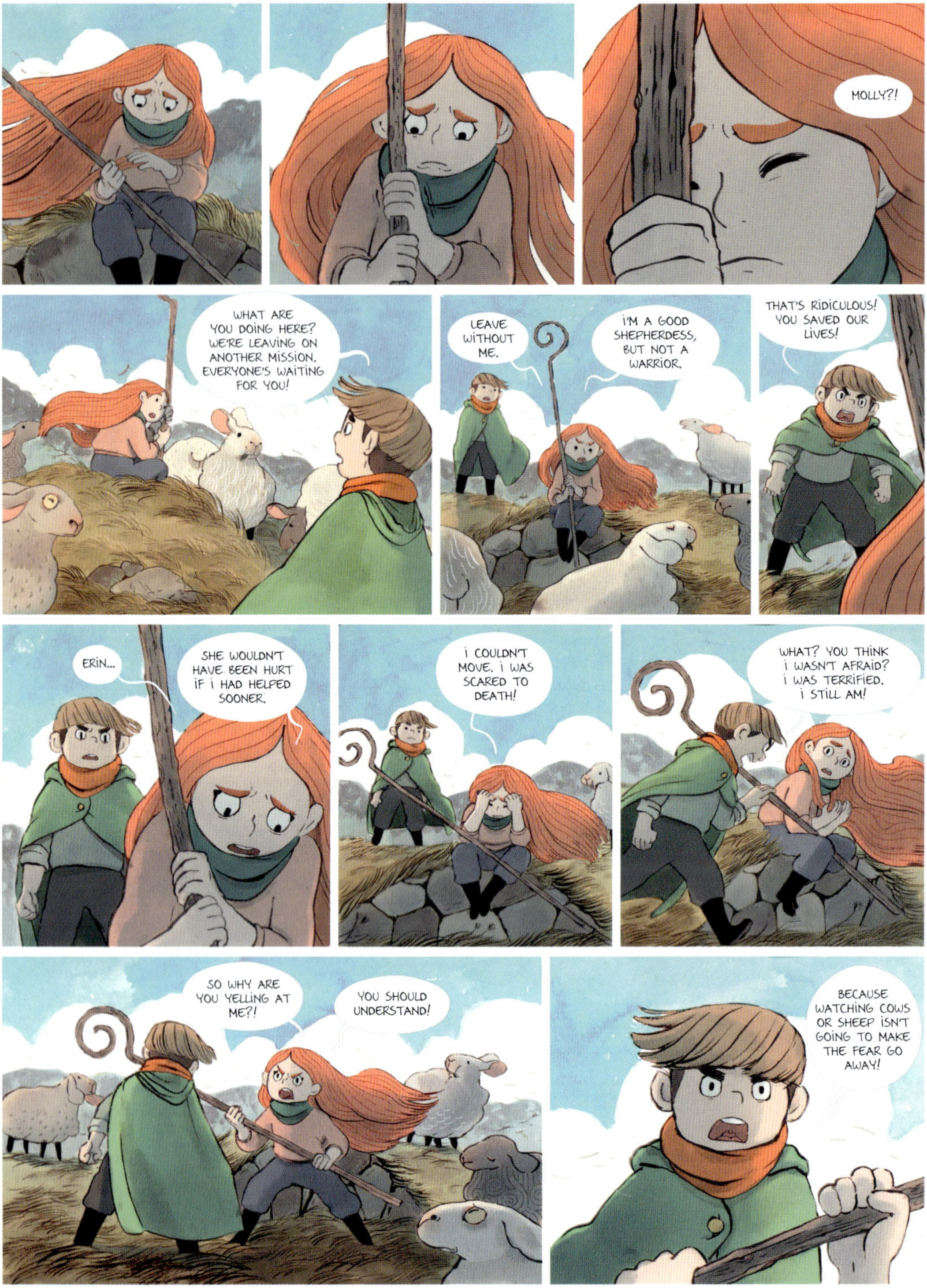
MOLLY?!
WHAT ARE YOU DOING HERE? WE'RE LEAVING ON ANOTHER MISSION. EVERYONE'S WAITING FOR YOU!
LEAVE WITHOUT ME.
I'M A GOOD SHEPHERDESS, BUT NOT A WARRIOR.
THAT'S RIDICULOUS! YOU SAVED OUR LIVES!
ERIN...
SHE WOULDN'T HAVE BEEN HURT IF I HAD HELPED SOONER.
I COULDN'T MOVE. I WAS SCARED TO DEATH!
WHAT? YOU THINK I WASN'T AFRAID? I WAS TERRIFIED. I STILL AM!
SO WHY ARE YOU YELLING AT ME?!
YOU SHOULD UNDERSTAND!
BECAUSE WATCHING COWS OR SHEEP ISN'T GOING TO MAKE THE FEAR GO AWAY!

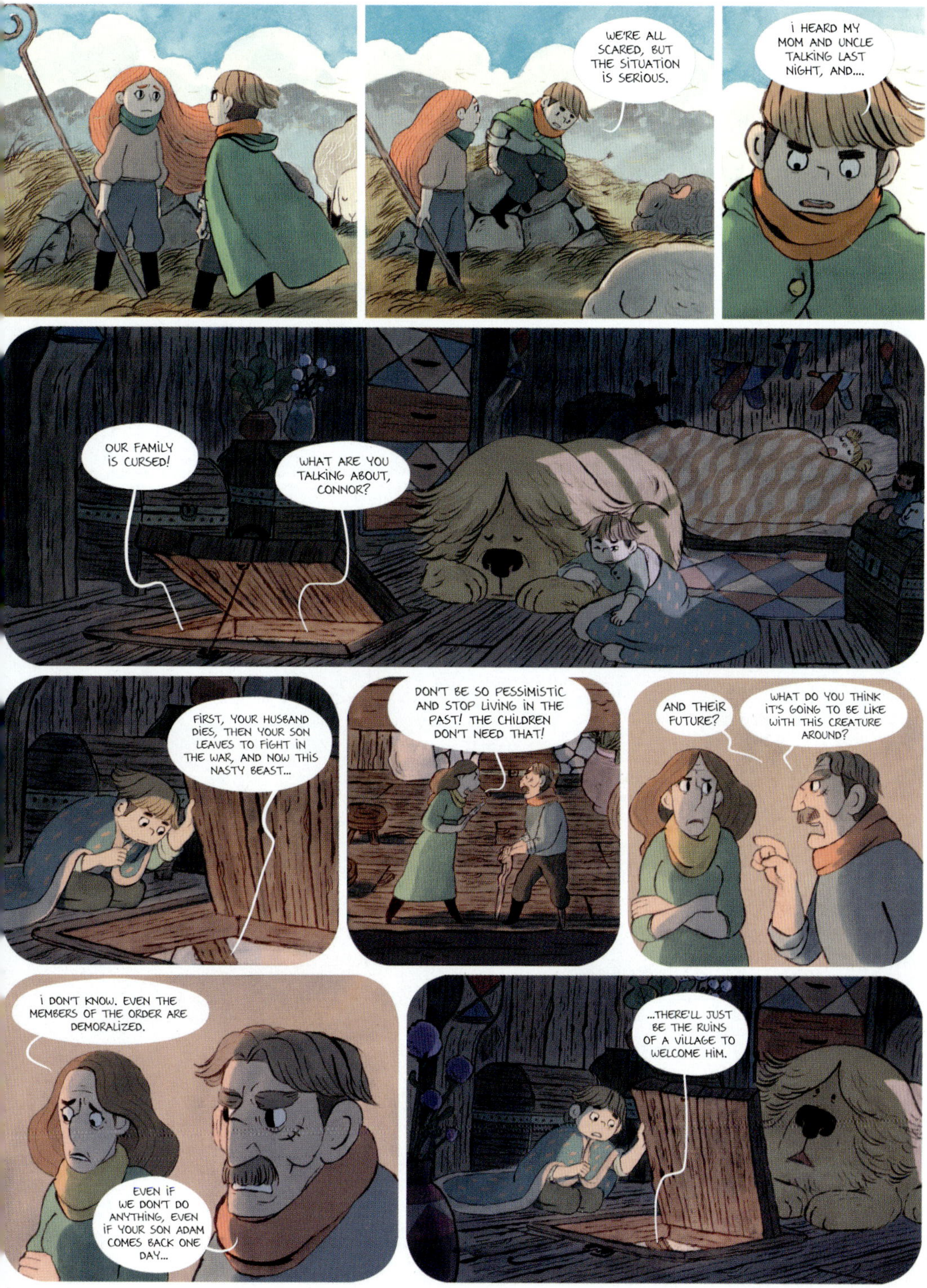
WE'RE ALL SCARED, BUT THE SITUATION IS SERIOUS.
I HEARD MY MOM AND UNCLE TALKING LAST NIGHT, AND....
OUR FAMILY IS CURSED!
WHAT ARE YOU TALKING ABOUT, CONNOR?
FIRST, YOUR HUSBAND DIES, THEN YOUR SON LEAVES TO FIGHT IN THE WAR, AND NOW THIS NASTY BEAST...
DON'T BE SO PESSIMISTIC AND STOP LIVING IN THE PAST! THE CHILDREN DON'T NEED THAT!
AND THEIR FUTURE?
WHAT DO YOU THINK IT'S GOING TO BE LIKE WITH THIS CREATURE AROUND?
I DON'T KNOW. EVEN THE MEMBERS OF THE ORDER ARE DEMORALIZED.
EVEN IF WE DON'T DO ANYTHING, EVEN IF YOUR SON ADAM COMES BACK ONE DAY...
...THERE'LL JUST BE THE RUINS OF A VILLAGE TO WELCOME HIM.

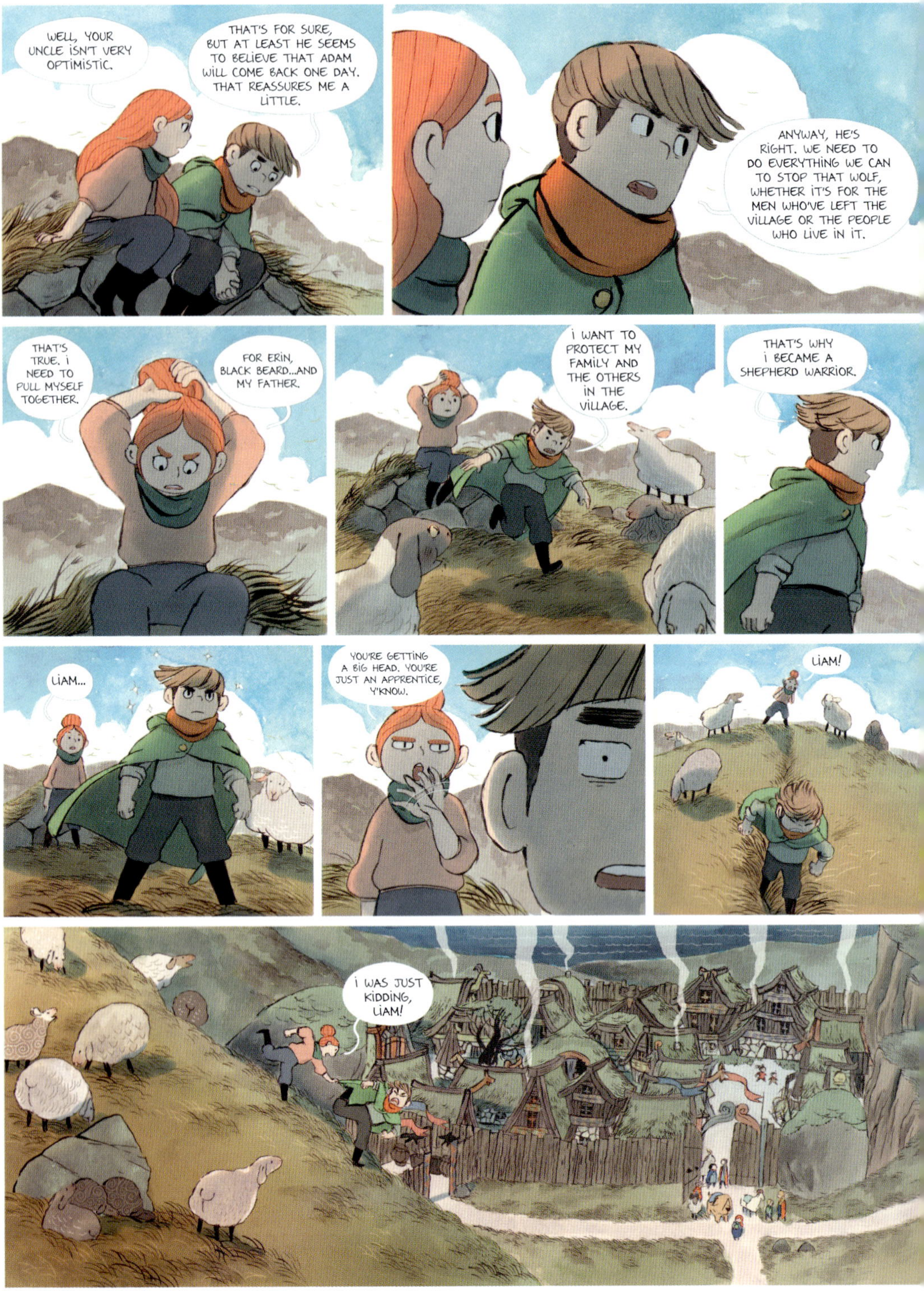
WELL, YOUR UNCLE ISN'T VERY OPTIMISTIC.
THAT'S FOR SURE, BUT AT LEAST HE SEEMS TO BELIEVE THAT ADAM WILL COME BACK ONE DAY. THAT REASSURES ME A LITTLE.
ANYWAY, HE'S RIGHT. WE NEED TO DO EVERYTHING WE CAN TO STOP THAT WOLF, WHETHER IT'S FOR THE MEN WHO'VE LEFT THE VILLAGE OR THE PEOPLE WHO LIVE IN IT.
THAT'S TRUE. I NEED TO PULL MYSELF TOGETHER.
FOR ERIN, BLACK BEARD...AND MY FATHER.
I WANT TO PROTECT MY FAMILY AND THE OTHERS IN THE VILLAGE.
THAT'S WHY I BECAME A SHEPHERD WARRIOR.
LIAM...
YOU'RE GETTING A BIG HEAD. YOU'RE JUST AN APPRENTICE, Y'KNOW.
LIAM!
I WAS JUST KIDDING, LIAM!

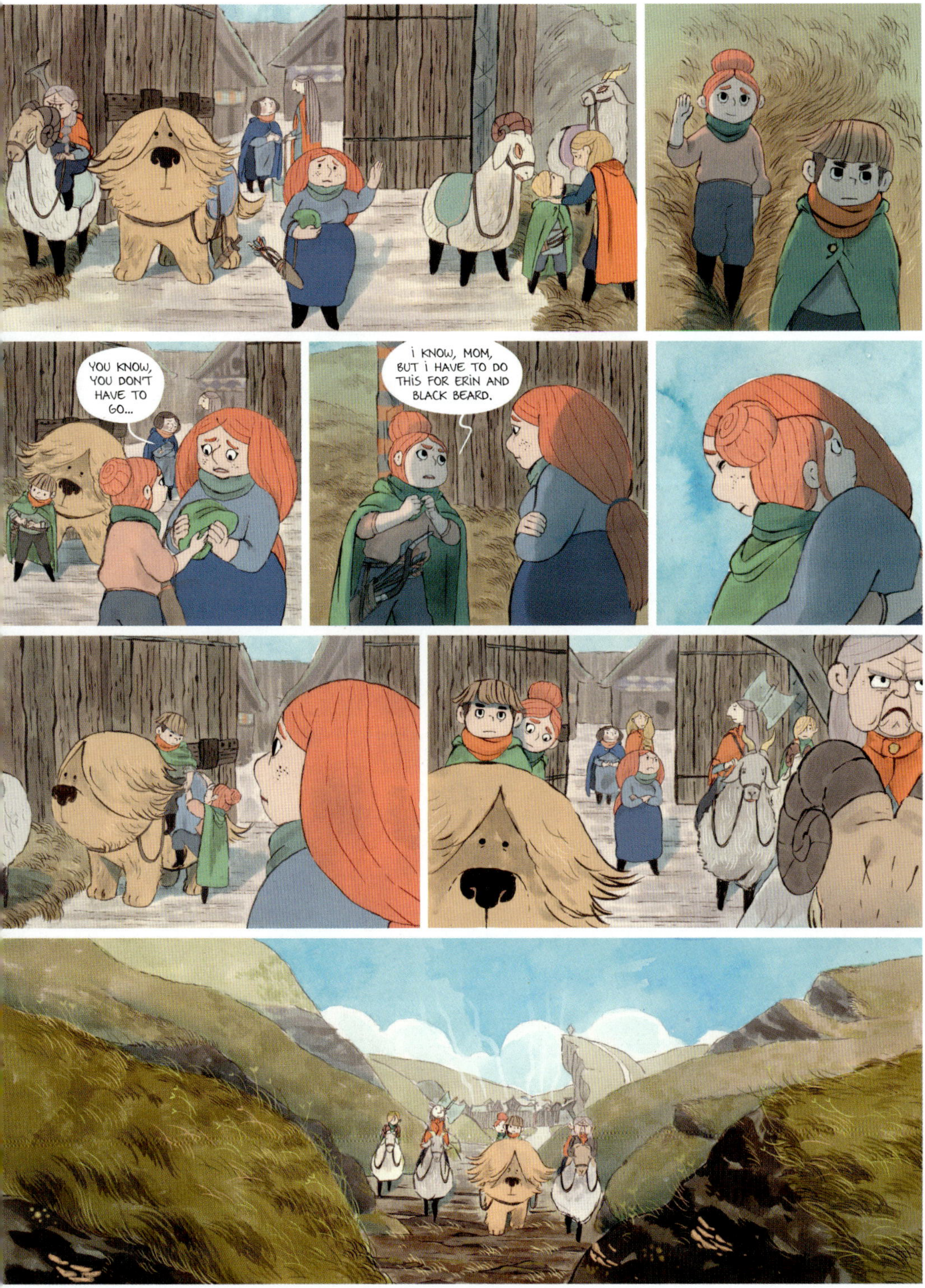
YOU KNOW, YOU DON'T HAVE TO GO...
I KNOW, MOM, BUT I HAVE TO DO THIS FOR ERIN AND BLACK BEARD.

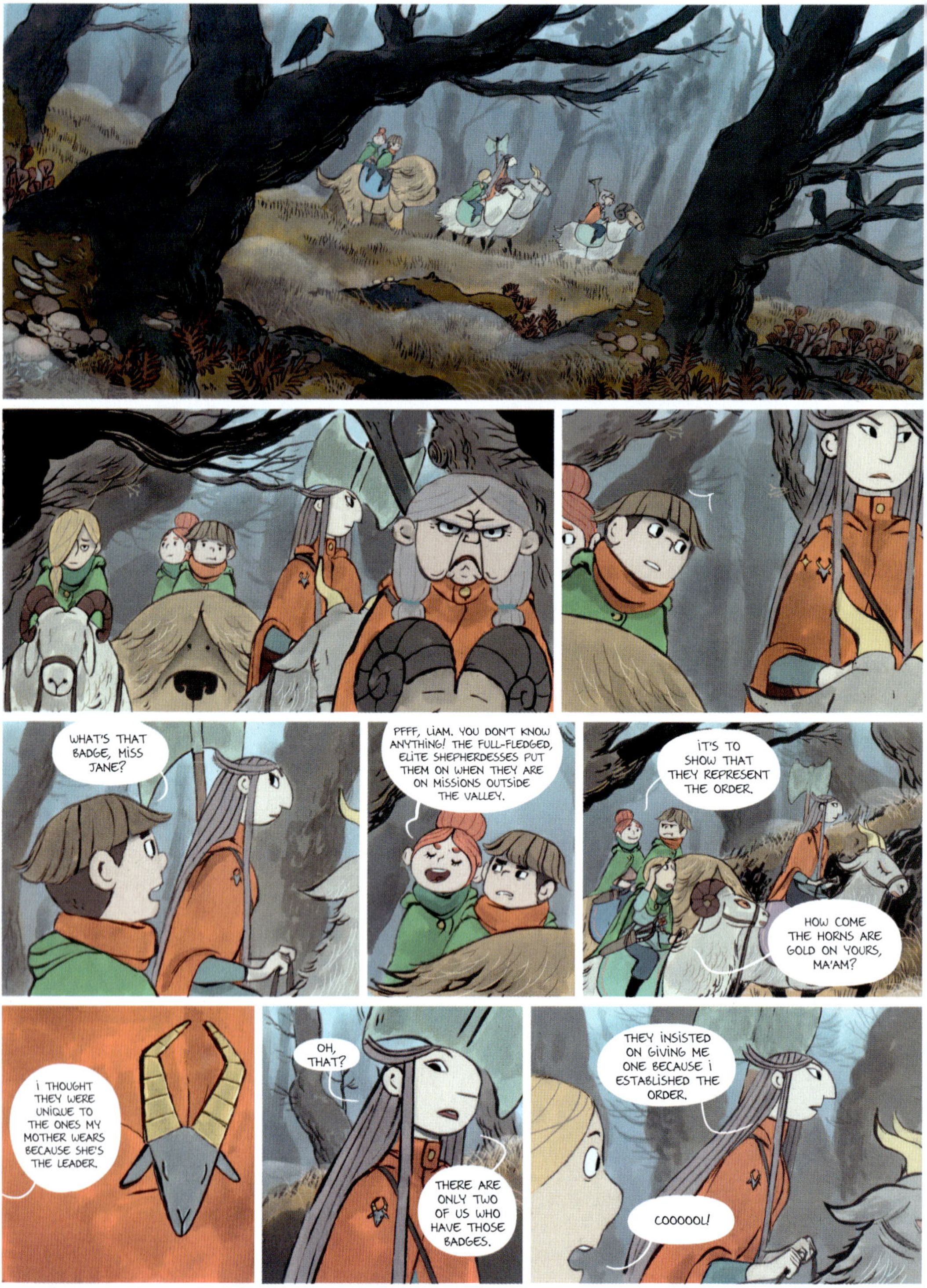
WHAT'S THAT BADGE, MISS JANE?
PFFF, LIAM. YOU DON'T KNOW ANYTHING! THE FULL-FLEDGED, ELITE SHEPHERDESSES PUT THEM ON WHEN THEY ARE ON MISSIONS OUTSIDE THE VALLEY.
IT'S TO SHOW THAT THEY REPRESENT THE ORDER.
HOW COME THE HORNS ARE GOLD ON YOURS, MA'AM?
I THOUGHT THEY WERE UNIQUE TO THE ONES MY MOTHER WEARS BECAUSE SHE'S THE LEADER.
OH, THAT?
THERE ARE ONLY TWO OF US WHO HAVE THOSE BADGES.
THEY INSISTED ON GIVING ME ONE BECAUSE I ESTABLISHED THE ORDER.
COOOOOL!

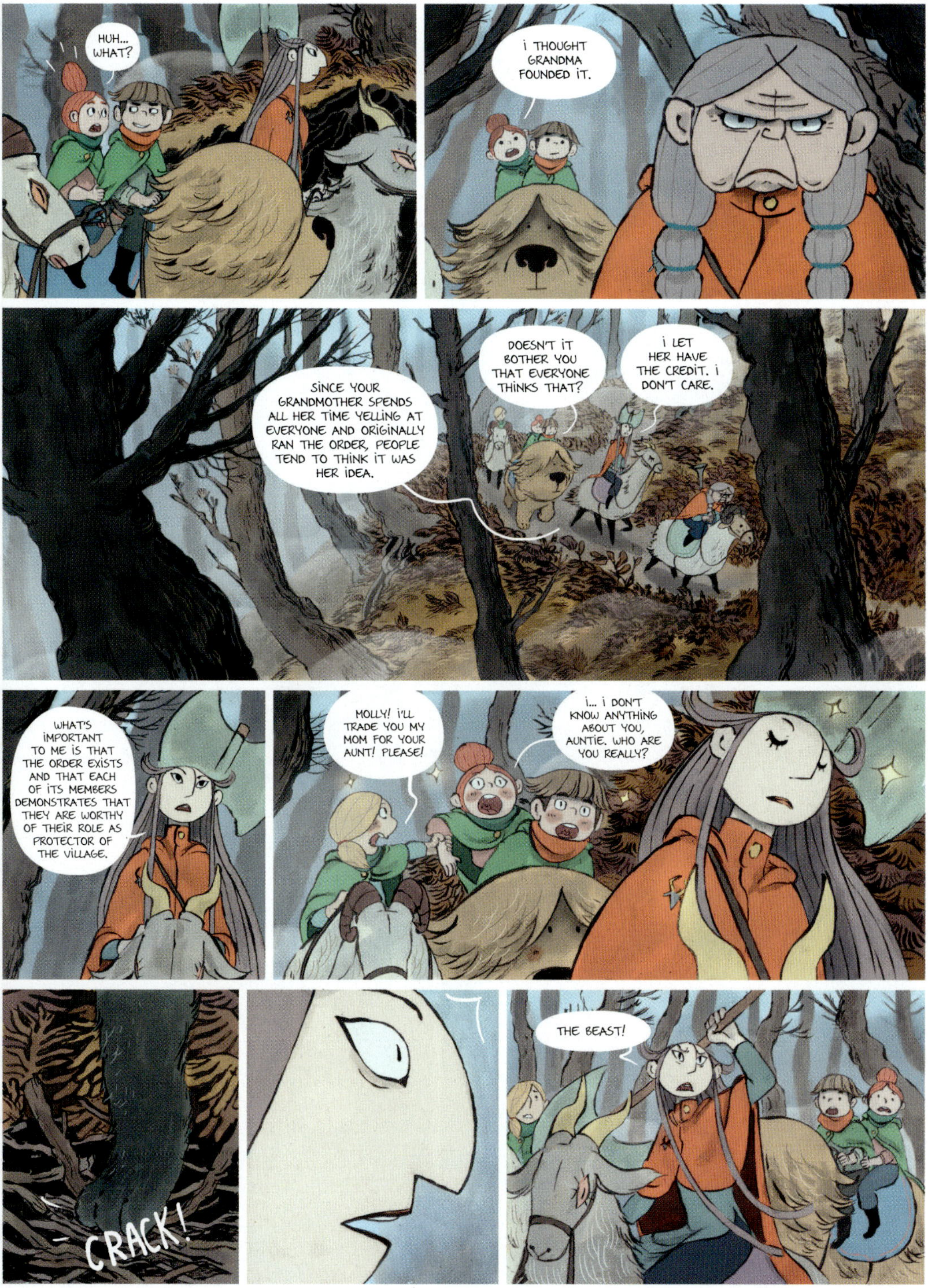
HUH... WHAT?
I THOUGHT GRANDMA FOUNDED IT.
SINCE YOUR GRANDMOTHER SPENDS ALL HER TIME YELLING AT EVERYONE AND ORIGINALLY RAN THE ORDER, PEOPLE TEND TO THINK IT WAS HER IDEA.
DOESN'T IT BOTHER YOU THAT EVERYONE THINKS THAT?
I LET HER HAVE THE CREDIT. I DON'T CARE.
WHAT'S IMPORTANT TO ME IS THAT THE ORDER EXISTS AND THAT EACH OF ITS MEMBERS DEMONSTRATES THAT THEY ARE WORTHY OF THEIR ROLE AS PROTECTOR OF THE VILLAGE.
MOLLY! I'LL TRADE YOU MY MOM FOR YOUR AUNT! PLEASE!
I... I DON'T KNOW ANYTHING ABOUT YOU, AUNTIE. WHO ARE YOU REALLY?
CRACK!
THE BEAST!

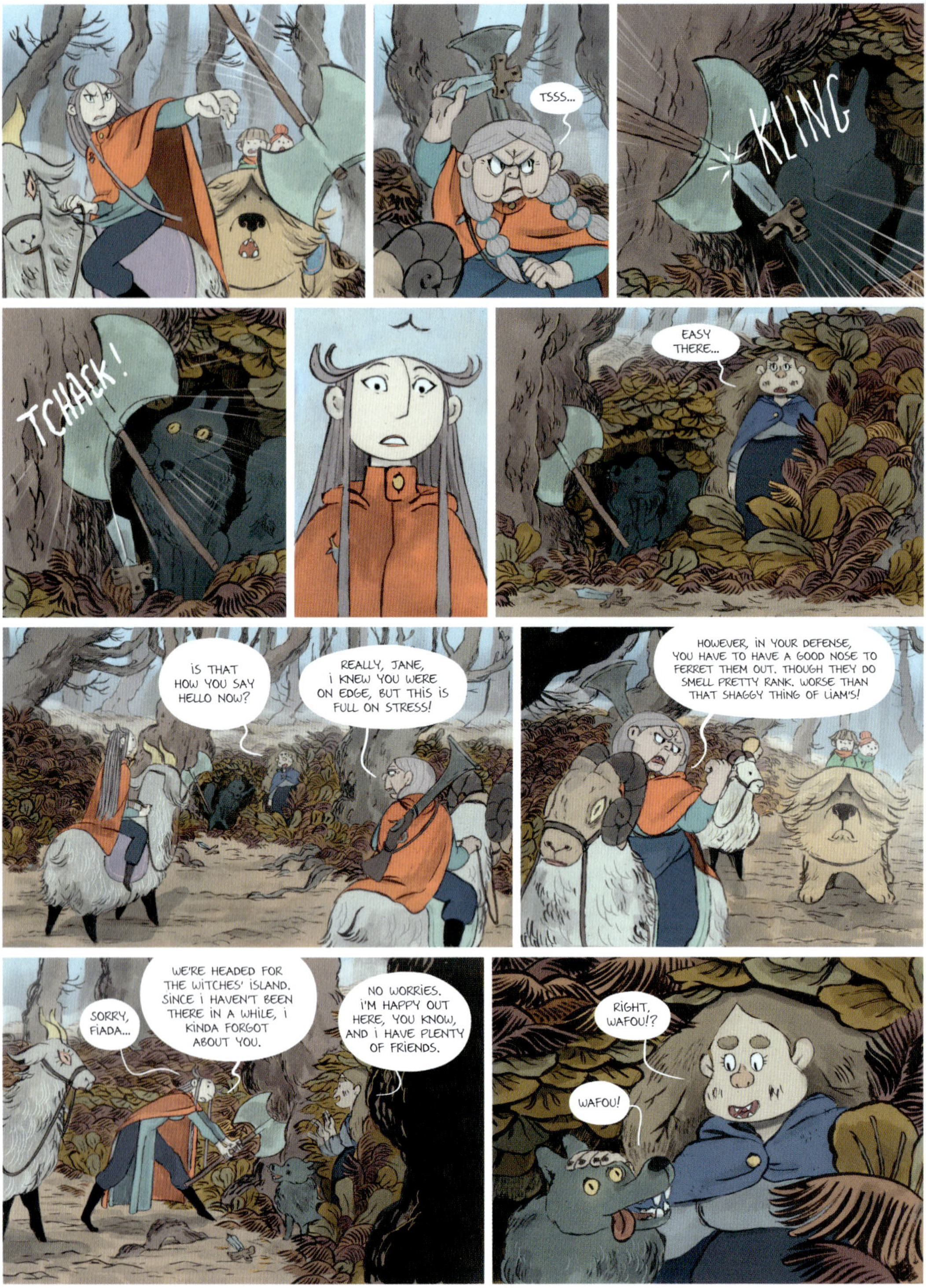
TSSS...
KLING
TCHACK!
EASY THERE...
IS THAT HOW YOU SAY HELLO NOW?
REALLY, JANE, I KNEW YOU WERE ON EDGE, BUT THIS IS FULL ON STRESS!
HOWEVER, IN YOUR DEFENSE, YOU HAVE TO HAVE A GOOD NOSE TO FERRET THEM OUT. THOUGH THEY DO SMELL PRETTY RANK. WORSE THAN THAT SHAGGY THING OF LIAM'S!
SORRY, FIADA...
WE'RE HEADED FOR THE WITCHES' ISLAND. SINCE I HAVEN'T BEEN THERE IN A WHILE, I KINDA FORGOT ABOUT YOU.
NO WORRIES. I'M HAPPY OUT HERE, YOU KNOW, AND I HAVE PLENTY OF FRIENDS.
RIGHT, WAFOU!?
WAFOU!

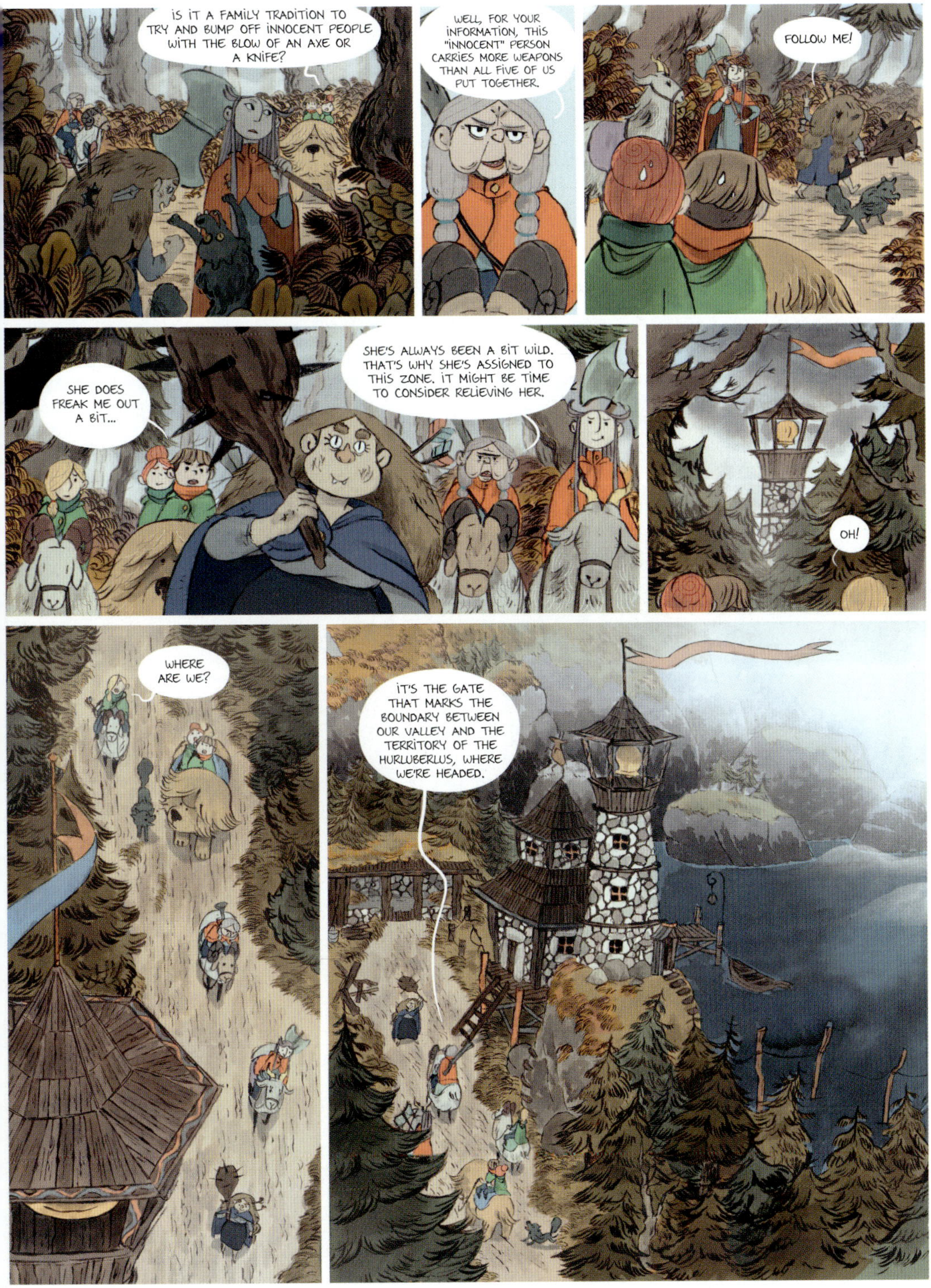
IS IT A FAMILY TRADITION TO TRY AND BUMP OFF INNOCENT PEOPLE WITH THE BLOW OF AN AXE OR A KNIFE?
WELL, FOR YOUR INFORMATION, THIS "INNOCENT" PERSON CARRIES MORE WEAPONS THAN ALL FIVE OF US PUT TOGETHER.
FOLLOW ME!
SHE DOES FREAK ME OUT A BIT...
SHE'S ALWAYS BEEN A BIT WILD. THAT'S WHY SHE'S ASSIGNED TO THIS ZONE. IT MIGHT BE TIME TO CONSIDER RELIEVING HER.
OH!
WHERE ARE WE?
IT'S THE GATE THAT MARKS THE BOUNDARY BETWEEN OUR VALLEY AND THE TERRITORY OF THE HURLUBERLUS, WHERE WE'RE HEADED.

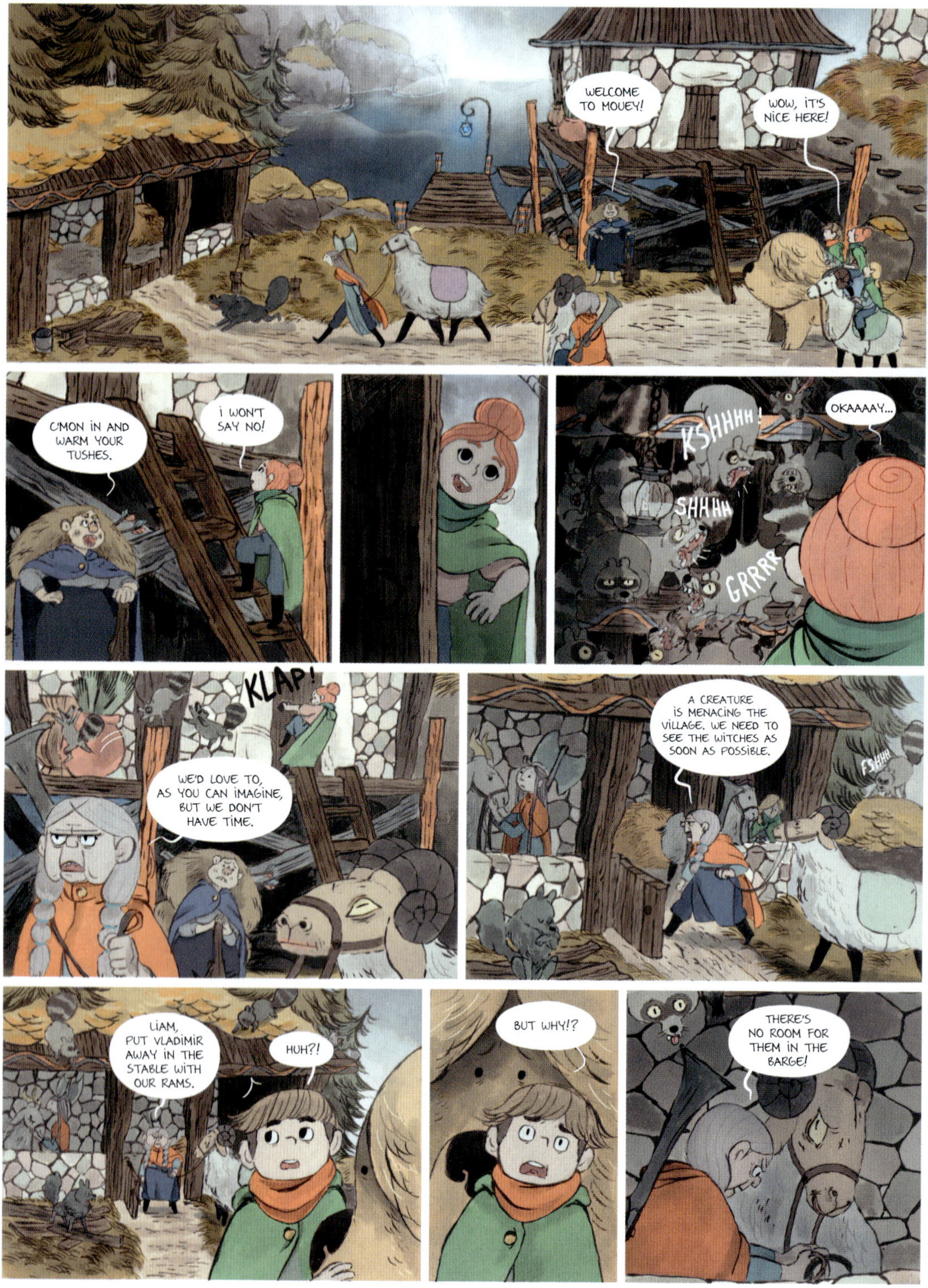
WELCOME TO MOUEY!
WOW, IT'S NICE HERE!
C'MON IN AND WARM YOUR TUSHES.
I WON'T SAY NO!
KSHHHH!
SHHHH
GRRRR
OKAAAAY...
KLAP!
WE'D LOVE TO, AS YOU CAN IMAGINE, BUT WE DON'T HAVE TIME.
A CREATURE IS MENACING THE VILLAGE. WE NEED TO SEE THE WITCHES AS SOON AS POSSIBLE.
FSHHH
LIAM, PUT VLADIMIR AWAY IN THE STABLE WITH OUR RAMS.
HUH?!
BUT WHY!?
THERE'S NO ROOM FOR THEM IN THE BARGE!

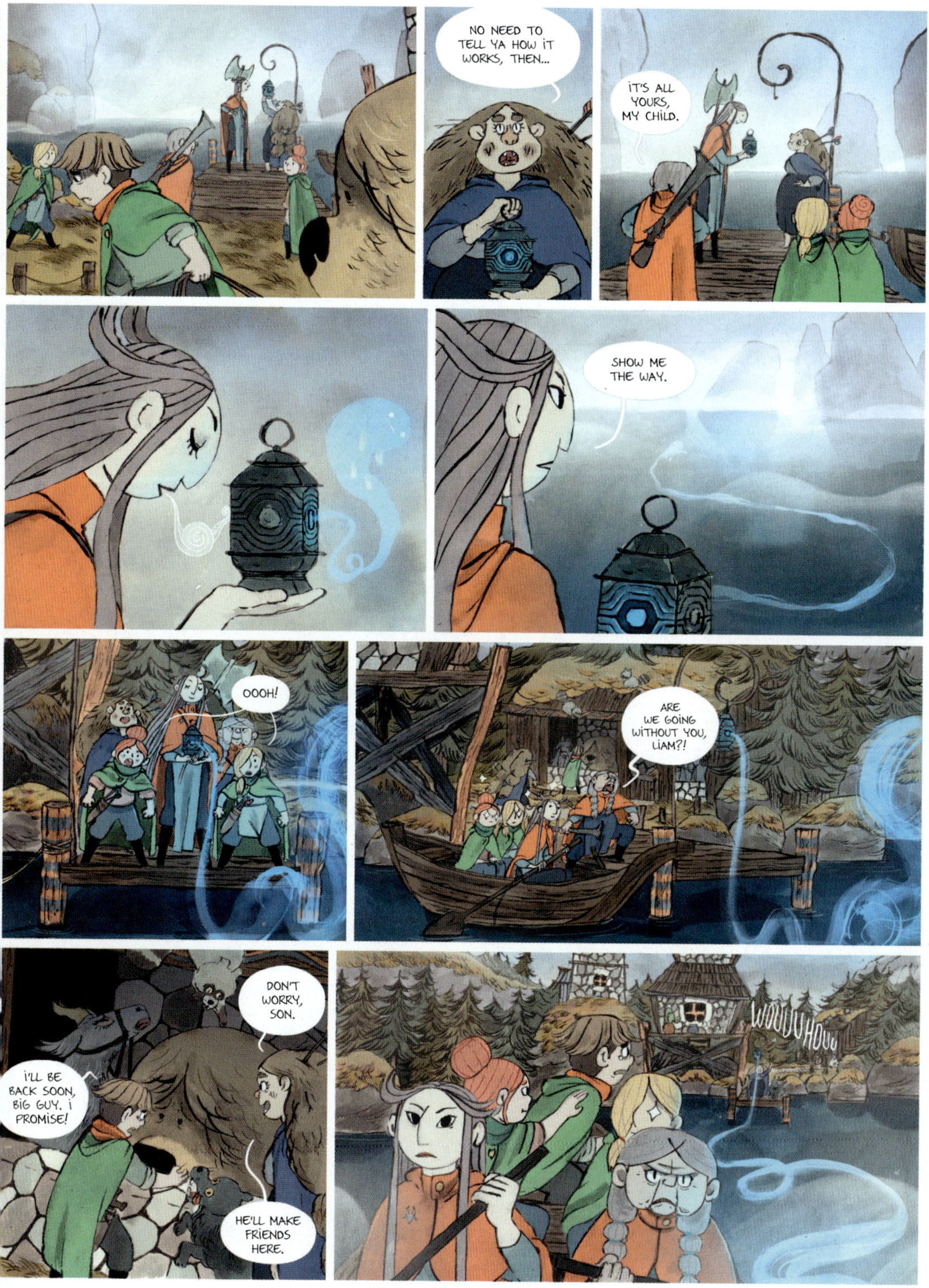
NO NEED TO TELL YA HOW IT WORKS, THEN...
IT'S ALL YOURS, MY CHILD.
SHOW ME THE WAY.
OOOH!
ARE WE GOING WITHOUT YOU, LIAM?!
DON'T WORRY, SON.
I'LL BE BACK SOON, BIG GUY. I PROMISE!
HE'LL MAKE FRIENDS HERE.
WOUUUHOUU

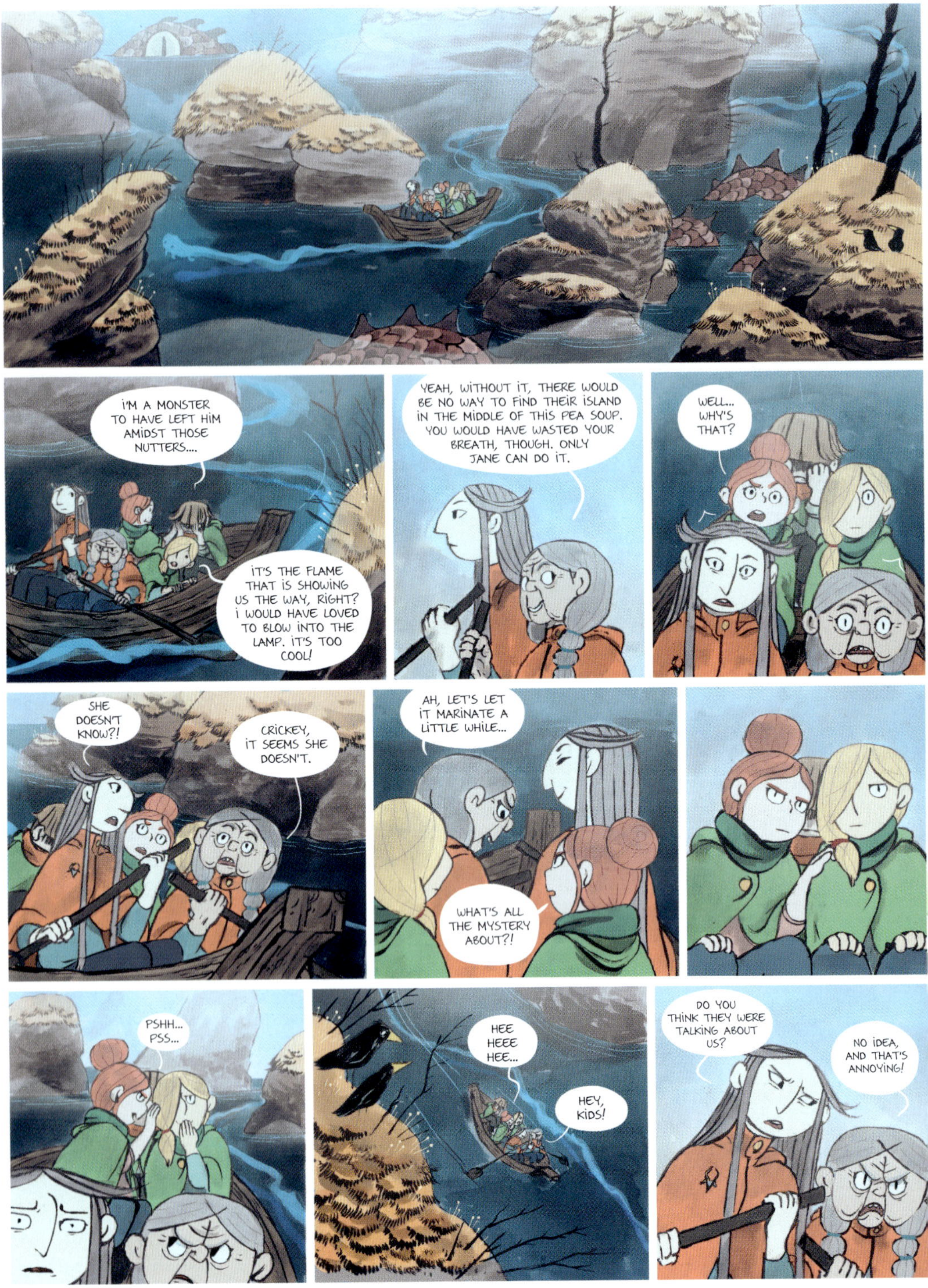
I'M A MONSTER TO HAVE LEFT HIM AMIDST THOSE NUTTERS....
IT'S THE FLAME THAT IS SHOWING US THE WAY, RIGHT? I WOULD HAVE LOVED TO BLOW INTO THE LAMP. IT'S TOO COOL!
YEAH, WITHOUT IT, THERE WOULD BE NO WAY TO FIND THEIR ISLAND IN THE MIDDLE OF THIS PEA SOUP. YOU WOULD HAVE WASTED YOUR BREATH, THOUGH. ONLY JANE CAN DO IT.
WELL... WHY'S THAT?
SHE DOESN'T KNOW?!
CRICKEY, IT SEEMS SHE DOESN'T.
AH, LET'S LET IT MARINATE A LITTLE WHILE...
WHAT'S ALL THE MYSTERY ABOUT?!
PSHH... PSS...
HEE HEEE HEE...
HEY, KIDS!
DO YOU THINK THEY WERE TALKING ABOUT US?
NO IDEA, AND THAT'S ANNOYING!

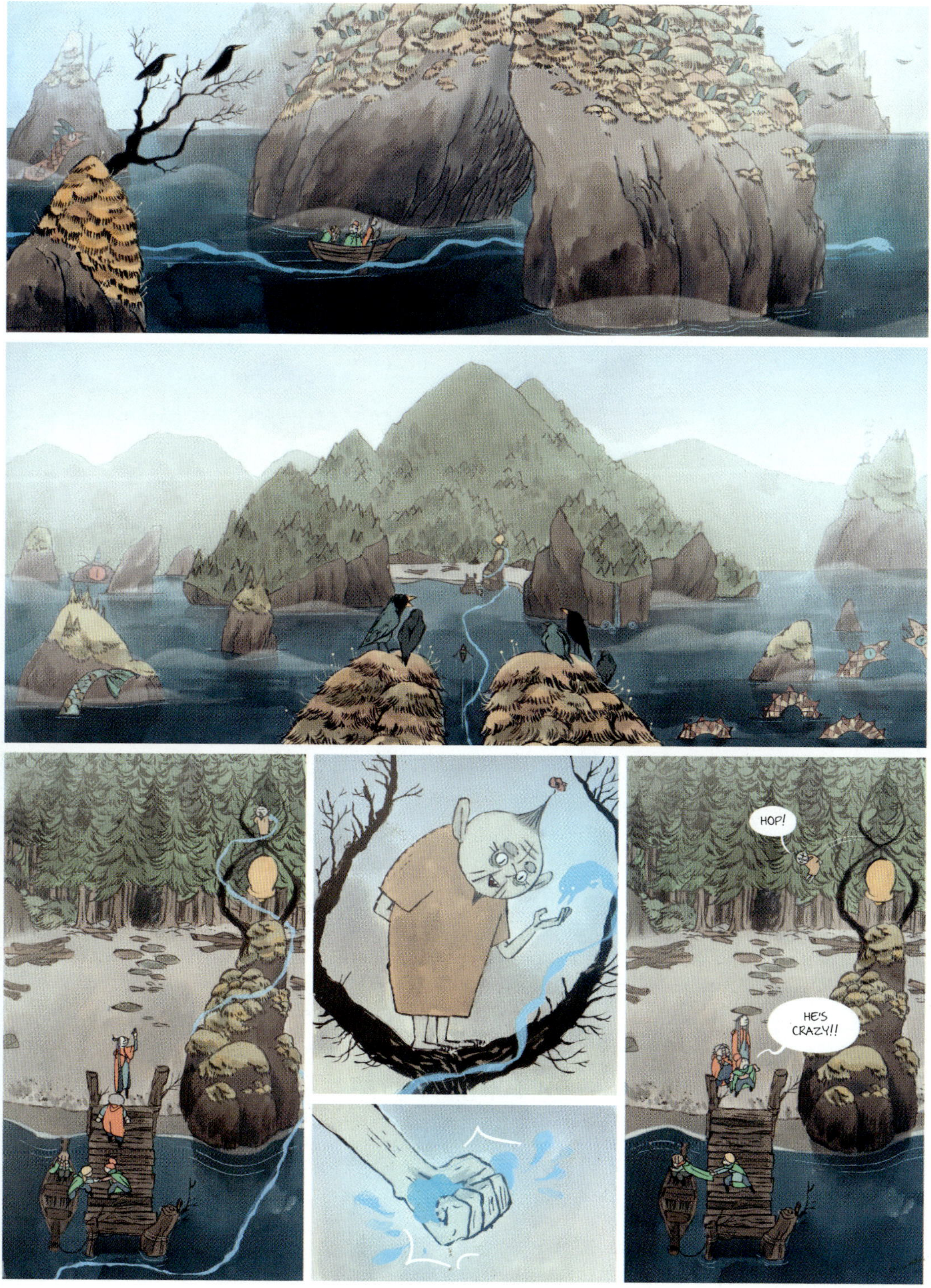
HOP!
HE'S CRAZY!!

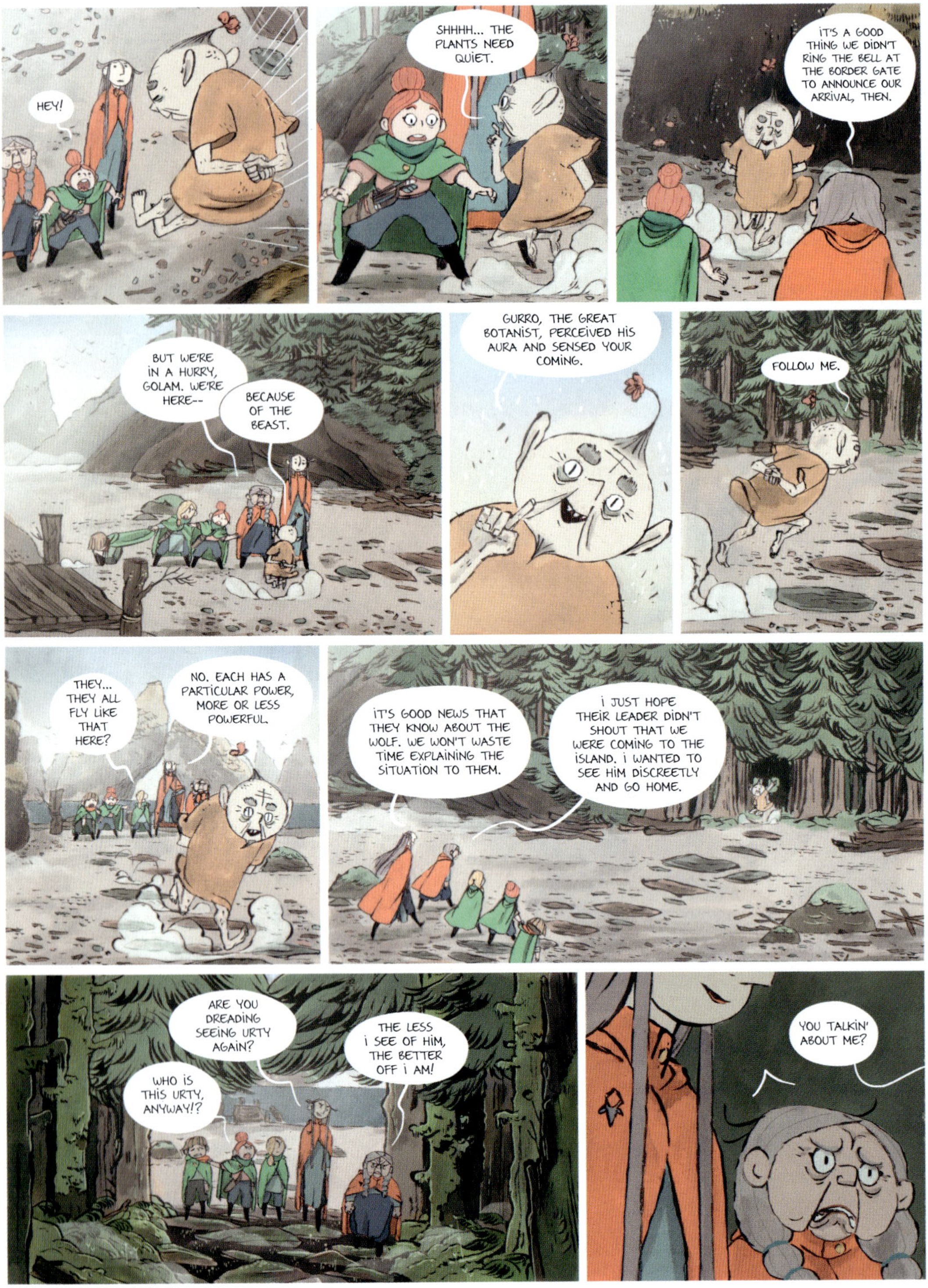
HEY!
SHHHH... THE PLANTS NEED QUIET.
IT'S A GOOD THING WE DIDN'T RING THE BELL AT THE BORDER GATE TO ANNOUNCE OUR ARRIVAL, THEN.
BUT WE'RE IN A HURRY, GOLAM. WE'RE HERE--
BECAUSE OF THE BEAST.
GURRO, THE GREAT BOTANIST, PERCEIVED HIS AURA AND SENSED YOUR COMING.
FOLLOW ME.
THEY... THEY ALL FLY LIKE THAT HERE?
NO. EACH HAS A PARTICULAR POWER, MORE OR LESS POWERFUL.
IT'S GOOD NEWS THAT THEY KNOW ABOUT THE WOLF. WE WON'T WASTE TIME EXPLAINING THE SITUATION TO THEM.
I JUST HOPE THEIR LEADER DIDN'T SHOUT THAT WE WERE COMING TO THE ISLAND. I WANTED TO SEE HIM DISCREETLY AND GO HOME.
ARE YOU DREADING SEEING URTY AGAIN?
WHO IS THIS URTY, ANYWAY!?
THE LESS I SEE OF HIM, THE BETTER OFF I AM!
YOU TALKIN' ABOUT ME?

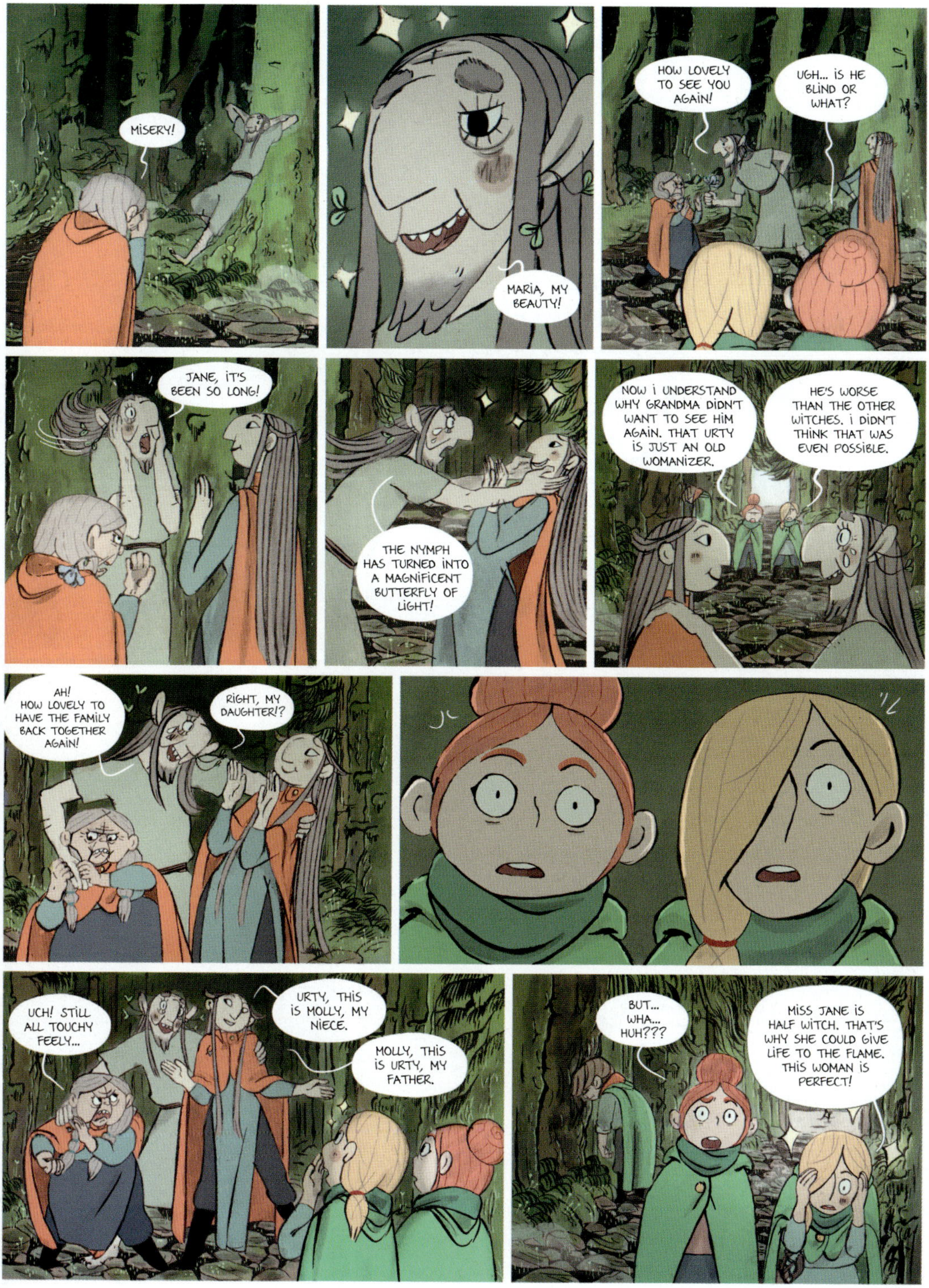
MISERY!
MARIA, MY BEAUTY!
HOW LOVELY TO SEE YOU AGAIN!
UGH... IS HE BLIND OR WHAT?
JANE, IT'S BEEN SO LONG!
THE NYMPH HAS TURNED INTO A MAGNIFICENT BUTTERFLY OF LIGHT!
NOW I UNDERSTAND WHY GRANDMA DIDN'T WANT TO SEE HIM AGAIN. THAT URTY IS JUST AN OLD WOMANIZER.
HE'S WORSE THAN THE OTHER WITCHES. I DIDN'T THINK THAT WAS EVEN POSSIBLE.
AH! HOW LOVELY TO HAVE THE FAMILY BACK TOGETHER AGAIN!
RIGHT, MY DAUGHTER!?
UCH! STILL ALL TOUCHY FEELY...
URTY, THIS IS MOLLY, MY NIECE.
MOLLY, THIS IS URTY, MY FATHER.
BUT... WHA... HUH???
MISS JANE IS HALF WITCH. THAT'S WHY SHE COULD GIVE LIFE TO THE FLAME. THIS WOMAN IS PERFECT!

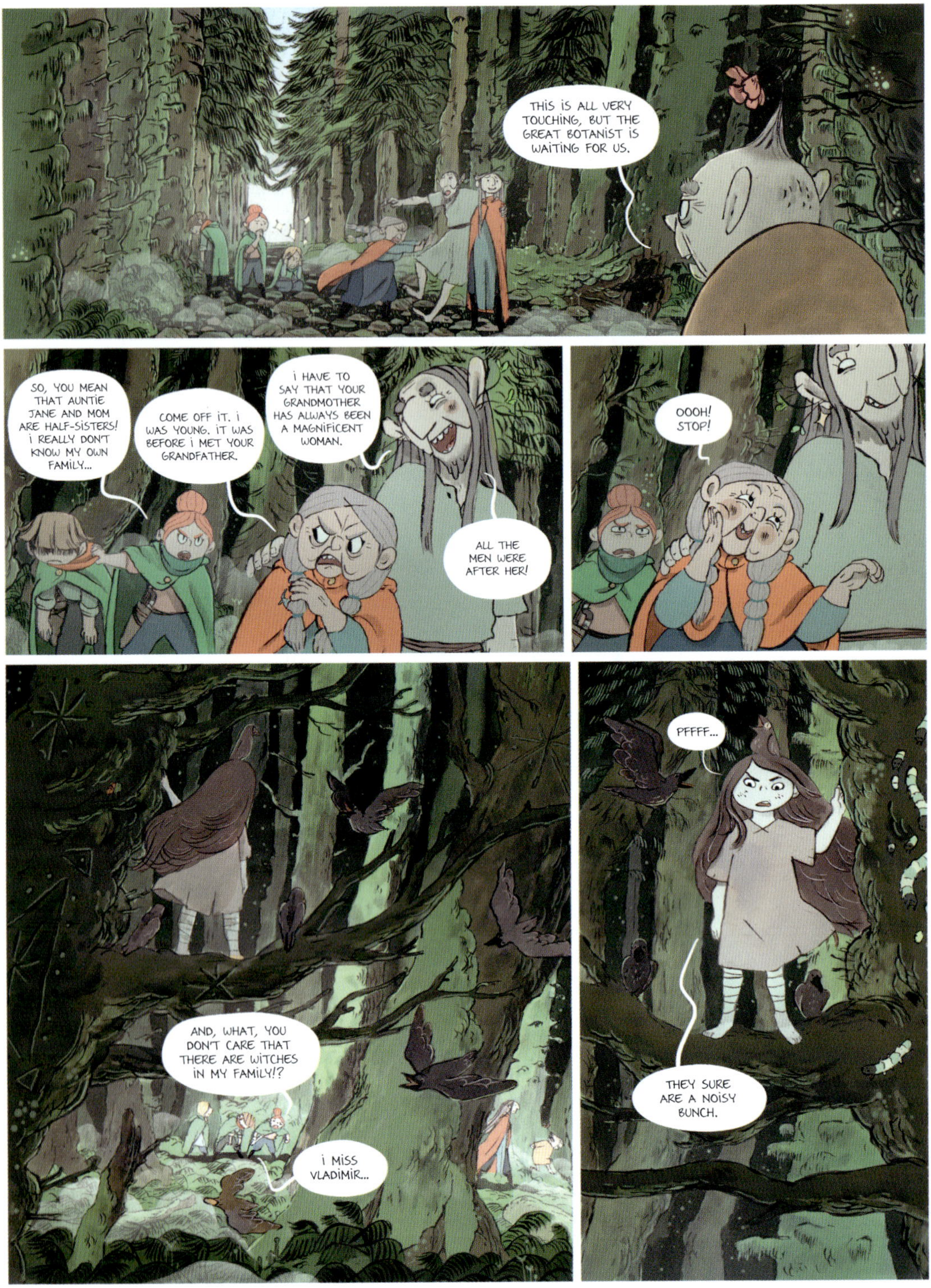
THIS IS ALL VERY TOUCHING, BUT THE GREAT BOTANIST IS WAITING FOR US.
SO, YOU MEAN THAT AUNTIE JANE AND MOM ARE HALF-SISTERS! I REALLY DON'T KNOW MY OWN FAMILY...
COME OFF IT. I WAS YOUNG. IT WAS BEFORE I MET YOUR GRANDFATHER.
I HAVE TO SAY THAT YOUR GRANDMOTHER HAS ALWAYS BEEN A MAGNIFICENT WOMAN.
ALL THE MEN WERE AFTER HER!
OOOH! STOP!
AND, WHAT, YOU DON'T CARE THAT THERE ARE WITCHES IN MY FAMILY!?
I MISS VLADIMIR...
PFFFF...
THEY SURE ARE A NOISY BUNCH.

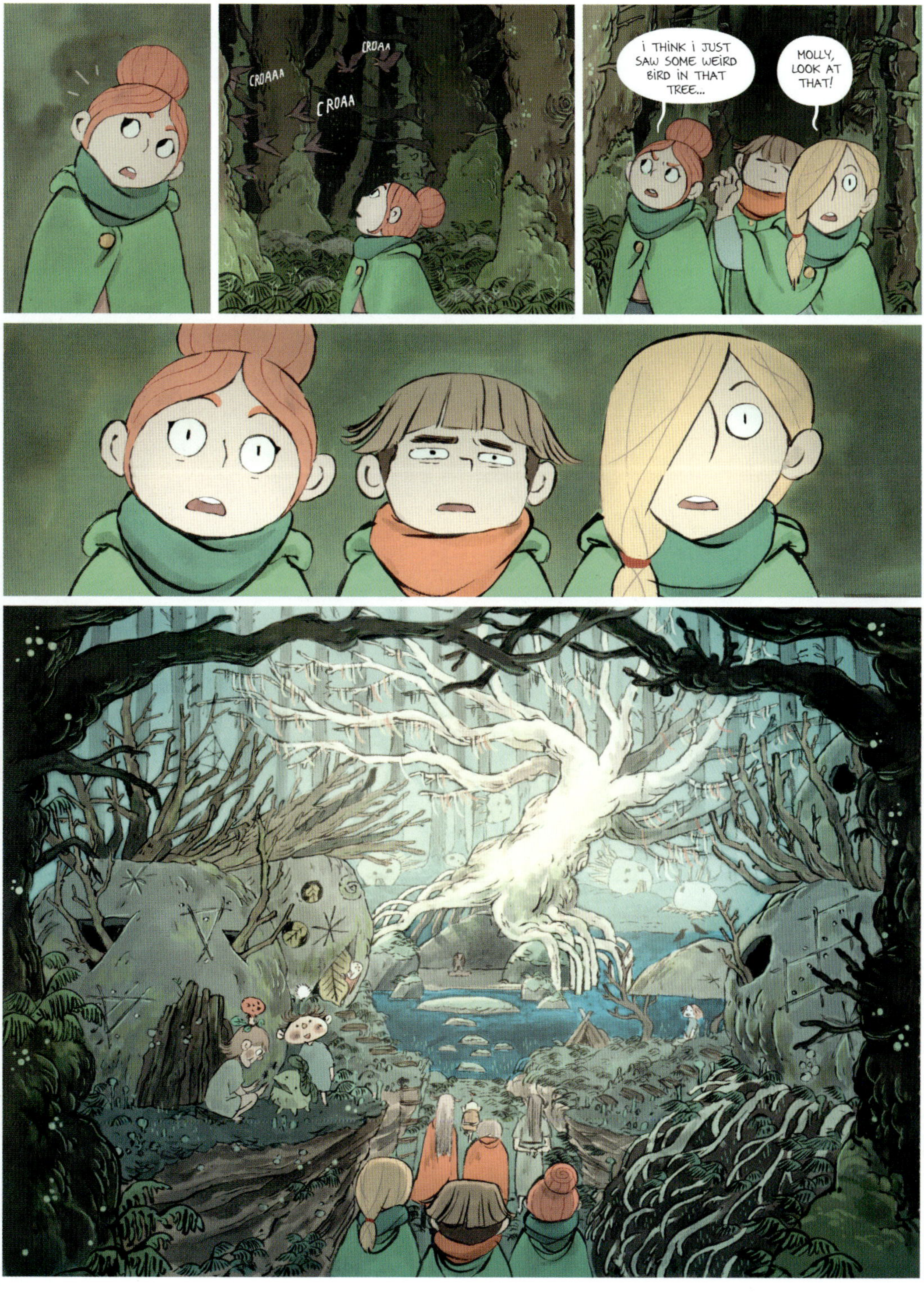

CROAAA
CROAA
CROAA
I THINK I JUST SAW SOME WEIRD BIRD IN THAT TREE...
MOLLY, LOOK AT THAT!

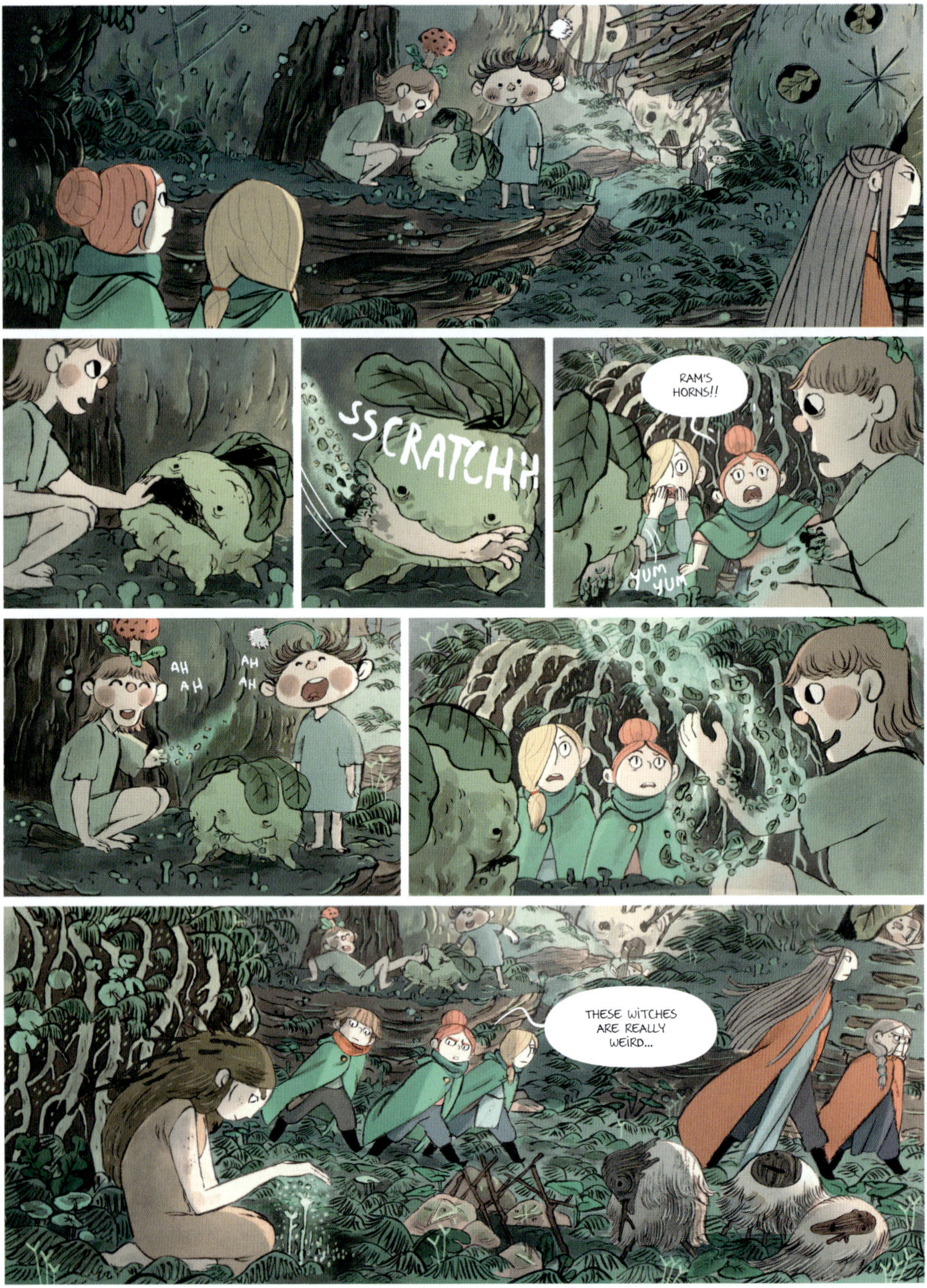
SSCRATCH!!
RAM'S HORNS!!
YUM YUM
AH AH
AH AH
THESE WITCHES ARE REALLY WEIRD...

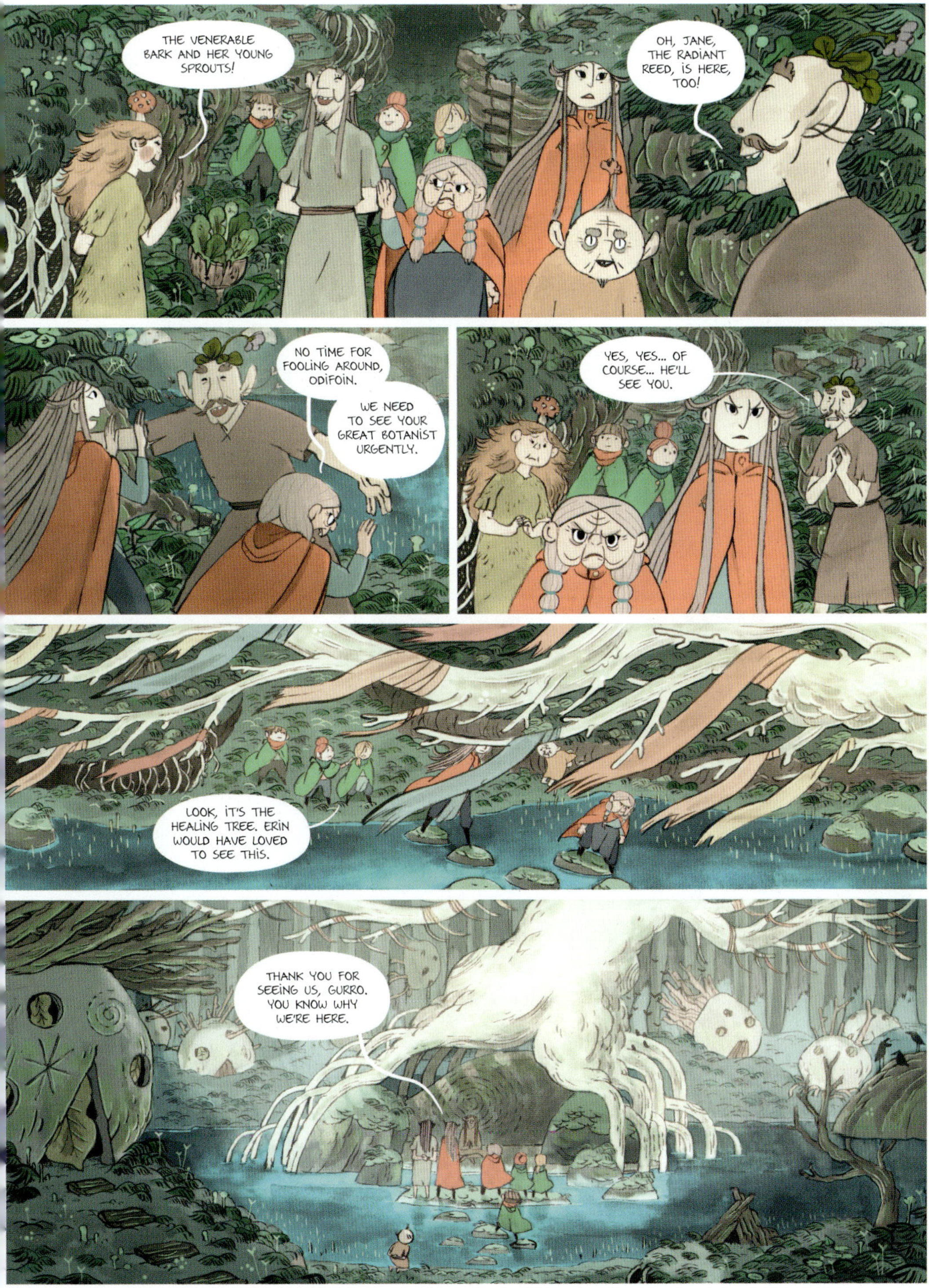
THE VENERABLE BARK AND HER YOUNG SPROUTS!
OH, JANE, THE RADIANT REED, IS HERE, TOO!
NO TIME FOR FOOLING AROUND, ODIFOIN.
WE NEED TO SEE YOUR GREAT BOTANIST URGENTLY.
YES, YES... OF COURSE... HE'LL SEE YOU.
LOOK, IT'S THE HEALING TREE. ERIN WOULD HAVE LOVED TO SEE THIS.
THANK YOU FOR SEEING US, GURRO. YOU KNOW WHY WE'RE HERE.

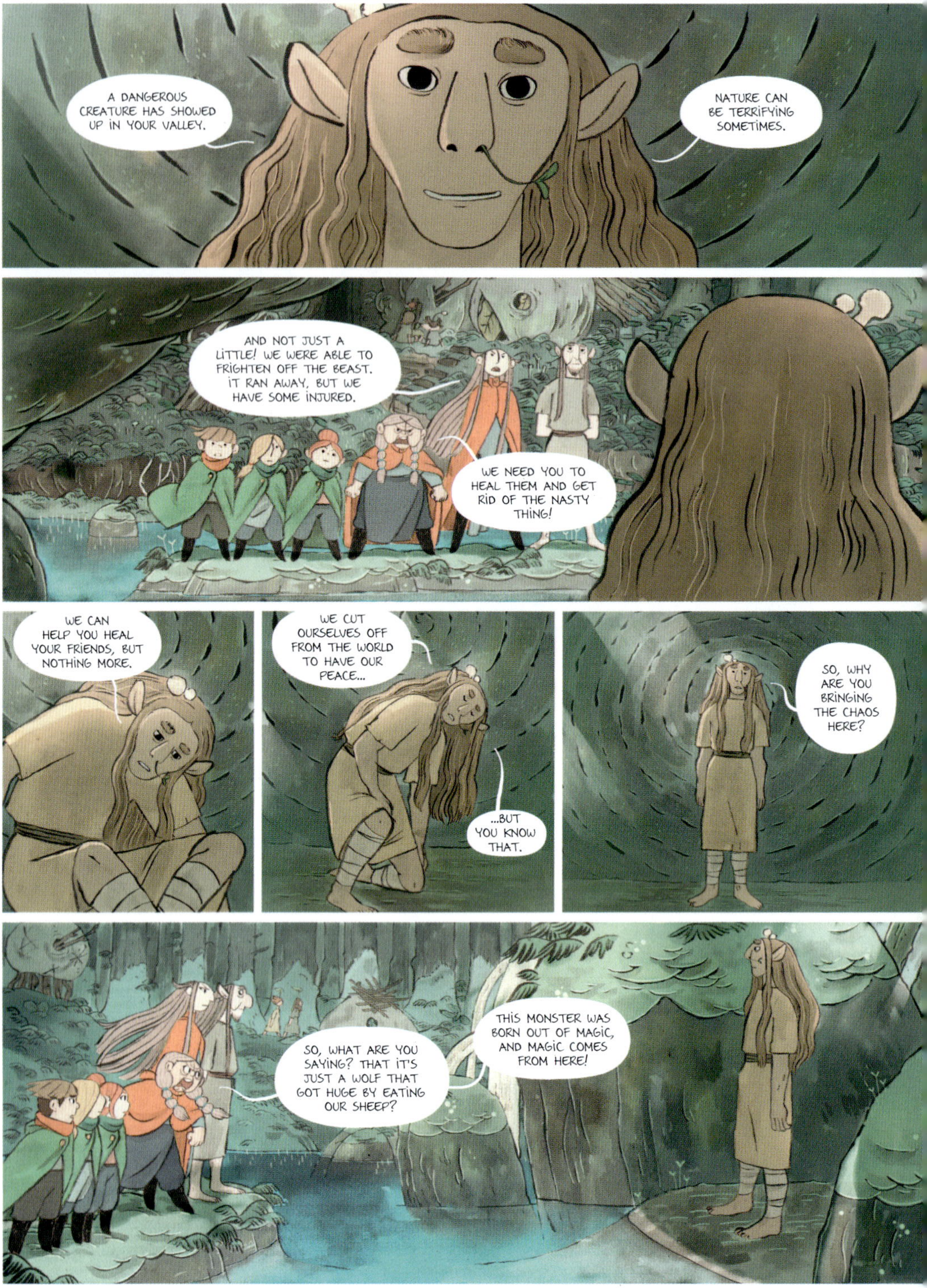

A DANGEROUS CREATURE HAS SHOWED UP IN YOUR VALLEY.
NATURE CAN BE TERRIFYING SOMETIMES.
AND NOT JUST A LITTLE! WE WERE ABLE TO FRIGHTEN OFF THE BEAST. IT RAN AWAY, BUT WE HAVE SOME INJURED.
WE NEED YOU TO HEAL THEM AND GET RID OF THE NASTY THING!
WE CAN HELP YOU HEAL YOUR FRIENDS, BUT NOTHING MORE.
WE CUT OURSELVES OFF FROM THE WORLD TO HAVE OUR PEACE...
...BUT YOU KNOW THAT.
SO, WHY ARE YOU BRINGING THE CHAOS HERE?
THIS MONSTER WAS BORN OUT OF MAGIC, AND MAGIC COMES FROM HERE!
SO, WHAT ARE YOU SAYING? THAT IT'S JUST A WOLF THAT GOT HUGE BY EATING OUR SHEEP?

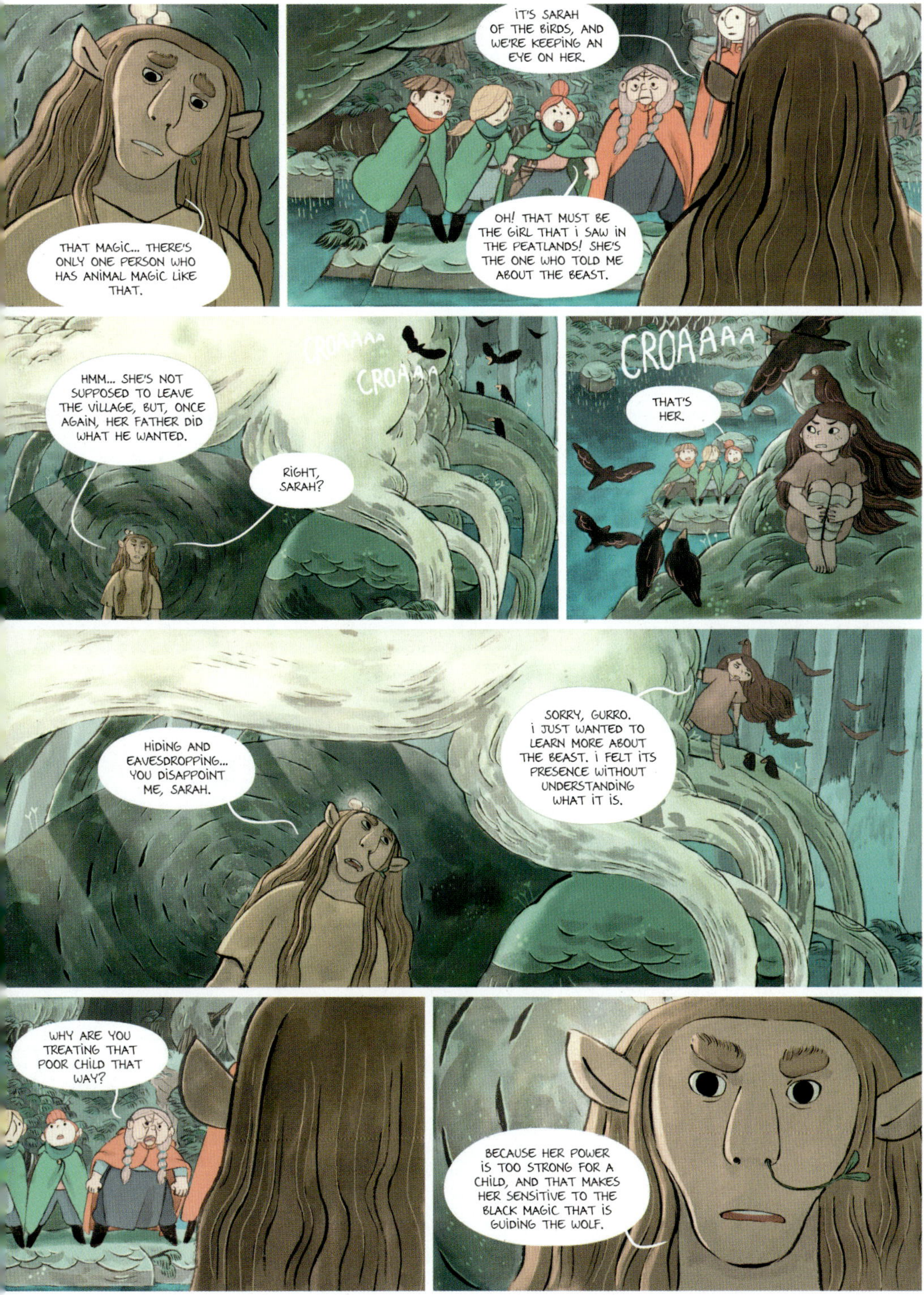
THAT MAGIC... THERE'S ONLY ONE PERSON WHO HAS ANIMAL MAGIC LIKE THAT.
IT'S SARAH OF THE BIRDS, AND WE'RE KEEPING AN EYE ON HER.
OH! THAT MUST BE THE GIRL THAT I SAW IN THE PEATLANDS! SHE'S THE ONE WHO TOLD ME ABOUT THE BEAST.
CROAAAA
CROAAAA
HMM... SHE'S NOT SUPPOSED TO LEAVE THE VILLAGE, BUT, ONCE AGAIN, HER FATHER DID WHAT HE WANTED.
RIGHT, SARAH?
CROAAAAA
THAT'S HER.
HIDING AND EAVESDROPPING... YOU DISAPPOINT ME, SARAH.
SORRY, GURRO. I JUST WANTED TO LEARN MORE ABOUT THE BEAST. I FELT ITS PRESENCE WITHOUT UNDERSTANDING WHAT IT IS.
WHY ARE YOU TREATING THAT POOR CHILD THAT WAY?
BECAUSE HER POWER IS TOO STRONG FOR A CHILD, AND THAT MAKES HER SENSITIVE TO THE BLACK MAGIC THAT IS GUIDING THE WOLF.

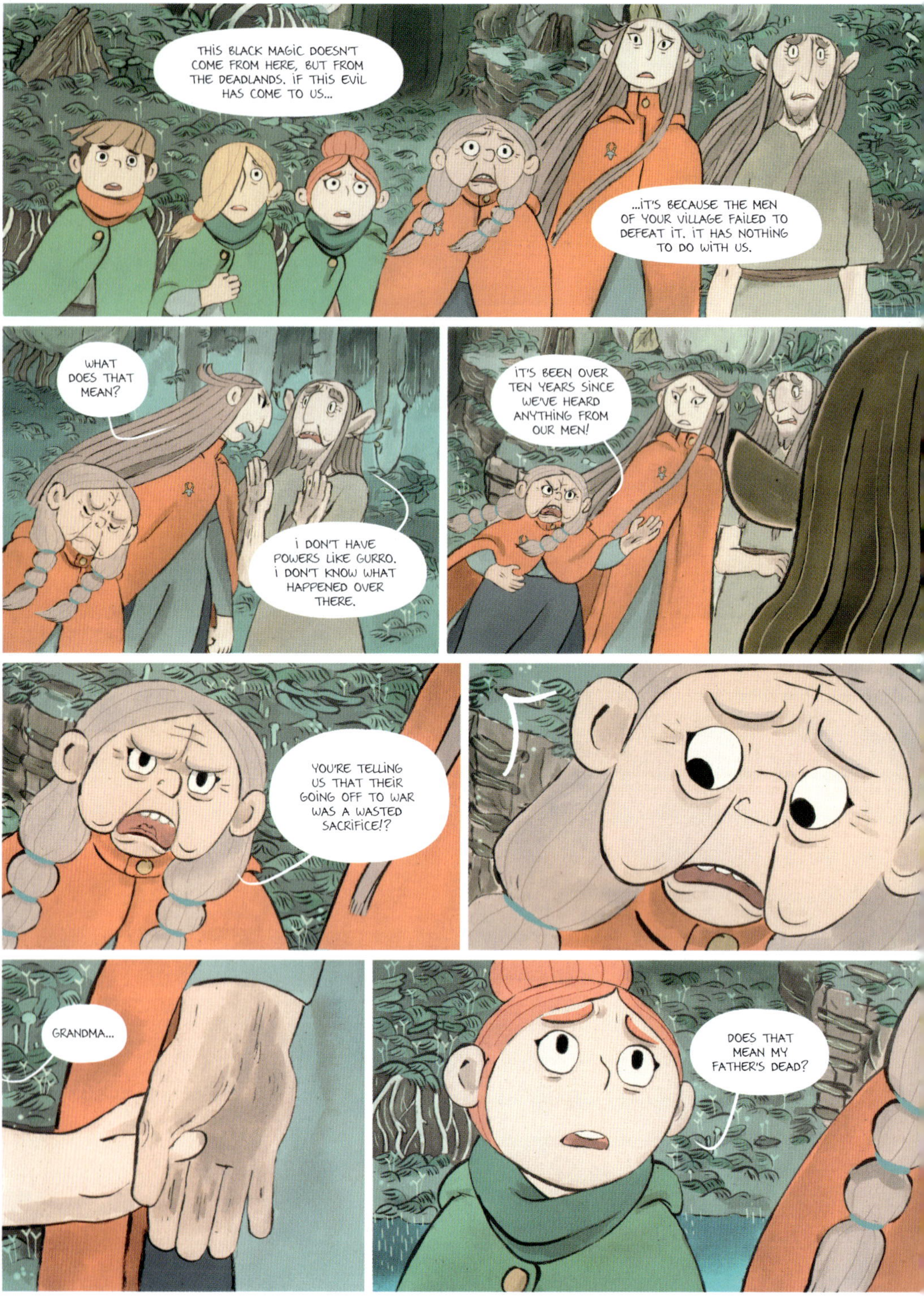
THIS BLACK MAGIC DOESN'T COME FROM HERE, BUT FROM THE DEADLANDS. IF THIS EVIL HAS COME TO US...
...IT'S BECAUSE THE MEN OF YOUR VILLAGE FAILED TO DEFEAT IT. IT HAS NOTHING TO DO WITH US.
WHAT DOES THAT MEAN?
I DON'T HAVE POWERS LIKE GURRO. I DON'T KNOW WHAT HAPPENED OVER THERE.
IT'S BEEN OVER TEN YEARS SINCE WE'VE HEARD ANYTHING FROM OUR MEN!
YOU'RE TELLING US THAT THEIR GOING OFF TO WAR WAS A WASTED SACRIFICE!?
GRANDMA...
DOES THAT MEAN MY FATHER'S DEAD?

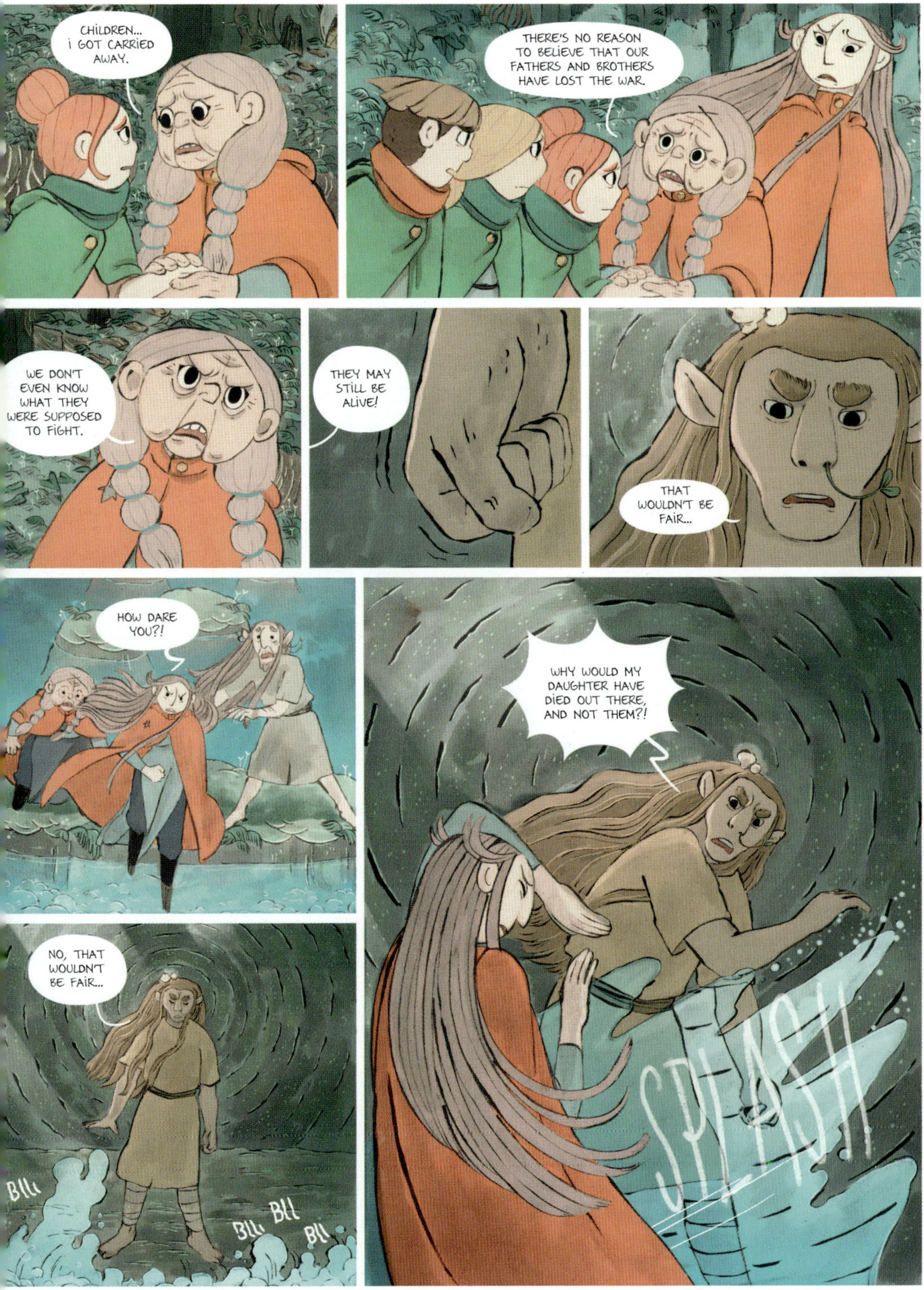
CHILDREN... I GOT CARRIED AWAY.
THERE'S NO REASON TO BELIEVE THAT OUR FATHERS AND BROTHERS HAVE LOST THE WAR.
WE DON'T EVEN KNOW WHAT THEY WERE SUPPOSED TO FIGHT.
THEY MAY STILL BE ALIVE!
THAT WOULDN'T BE FAIR...
HOW DARE YOU?!
NO, THAT WOULDN'T BE FAIR...
BLL
BLL BLL
BLL
WHY WOULD MY DAUGHTER HAVE DIED OUT THERE, AND NOT THEM?!
SPLASH

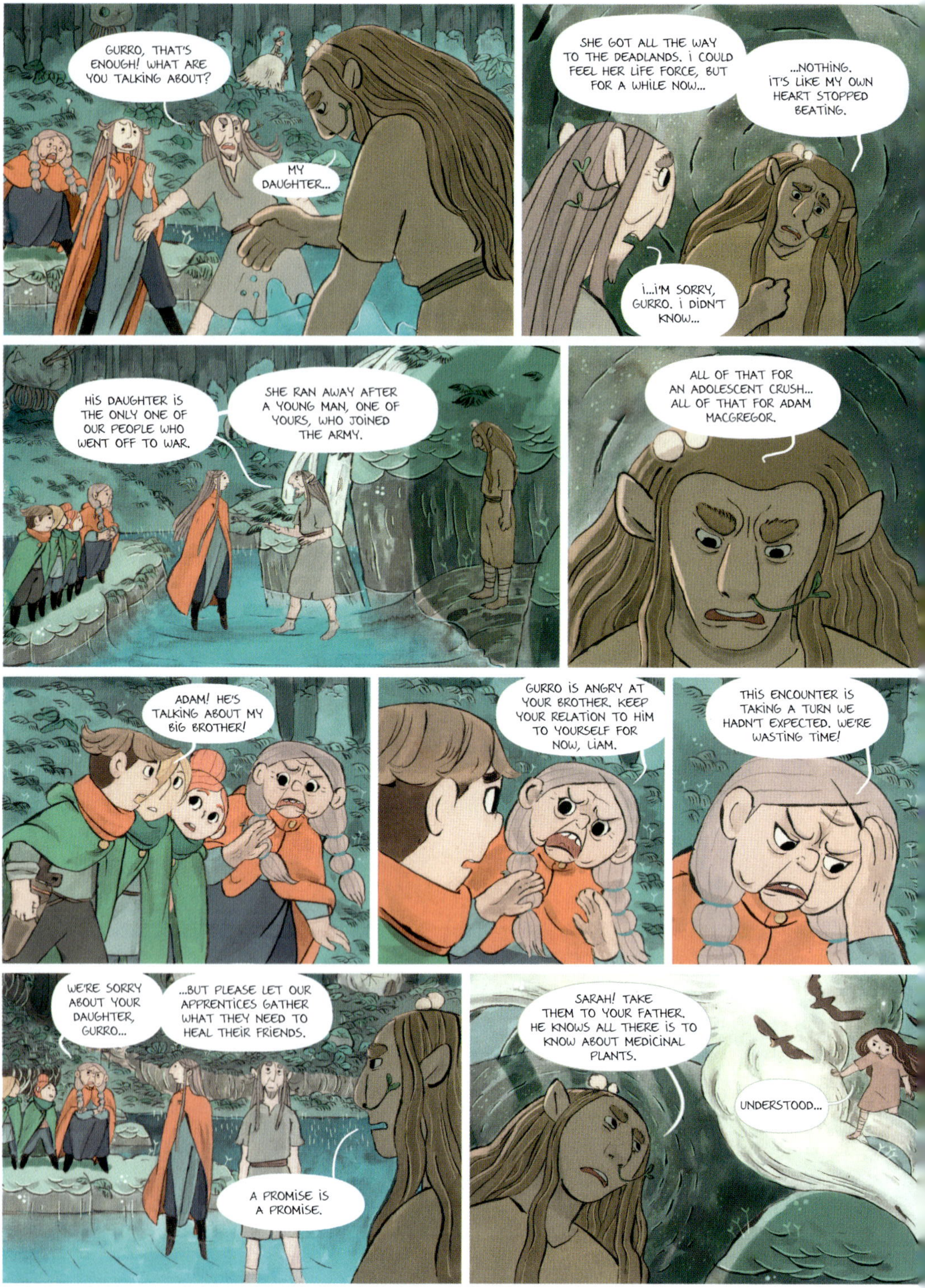
GURRO, THAT'S ENOUGH! WHAT ARE YOU TALKING ABOUT?
MY DAUGHTER...
SHE GOT ALL THE WAY TO THE DEADLANDS. I COULD FEEL HER LIFE FORCE, BUT FOR A WHILE NOW...
...NOTHING. IT'S LIKE MY OWN HEART STOPPED BEATING.
I...I'M SORRY, GURRO. I DIDN'T KNOW...
HIS DAUGHTER IS THE ONLY ONE OF OUR PEOPLE WHO WENT OFF TO WAR.
SHE RAN AWAY AFTER A YOUNG MAN, ONE OF YOURS, WHO JOINED THE ARMY.
ALL OF THAT FOR AN ADOLESCENT CRUSH... ALL OF THAT FOR ADAM MACGREGOR.
ADAM! HE'S TALKING ABOUT MY BIG BROTHER!
GURRO IS ANGRY AT YOUR BROTHER. KEEP YOUR RELATION TO HIM TO YOURSELF FOR NOW, LIAM.
THIS ENCOUNTER IS TAKING A TURN WE HADN'T EXPECTED. WE'RE WASTING TIME!
WE'RE SORRY ABOUT YOUR DAUGHTER, GURRO...
...BUT PLEASE LET OUR APPRENTICES GATHER WHAT THEY NEED TO HEAL THEIR FRIENDS.
A PROMISE IS A PROMISE.
SARAH! TAKE THEM TO YOUR FATHER. HE KNOWS ALL THERE IS TO KNOW ABOUT MEDICINAL PLANTS.
UNDERSTOOD...

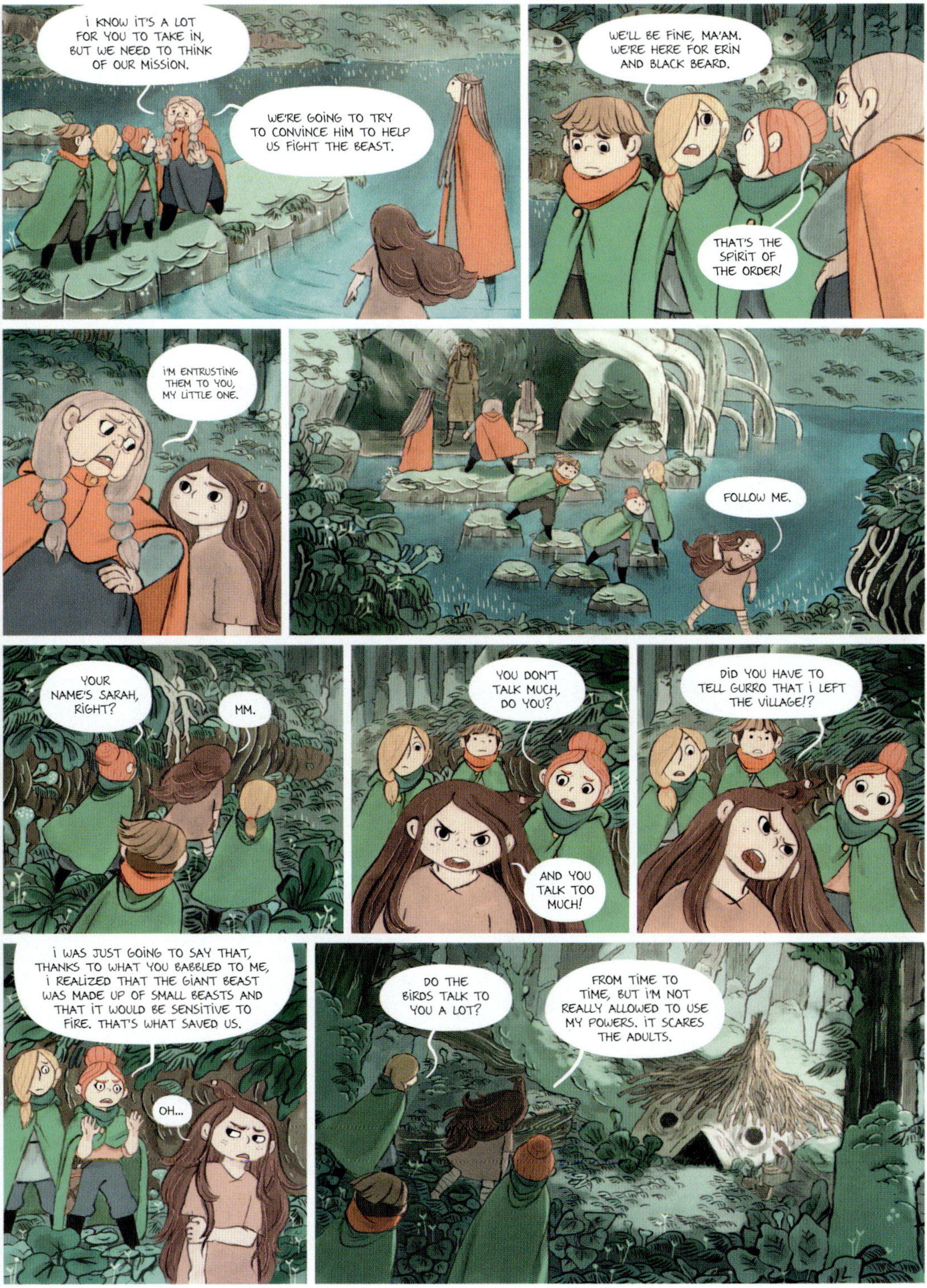
I KNOW IT'S A LOT FOR YOU TO TAKE IN, BUT WE NEED TO THINK OF OUR MISSION.
WE'RE GOING TO TRY TO CONVINCE HIM TO HELP US FIGHT THE BEAST.
WE'LL BE FINE, MA'AM. WE'RE HERE FOR ERIN AND BLACK BEARD.
THAT'S THE SPIRIT OF THE ORDER!
I'M ENTRUSTING THEM TO YOU, MY LITTLE ONE.
FOLLOW ME.
YOUR NAME'S SARAH, RIGHT?
MM.
YOU DON'T TALK MUCH, DO YOU?
AND YOU TALK TOO MUCH!
DID YOU HAVE TO TELL GURRO THAT I LEFT THE VILLAGE!?
I WAS JUST GOING TO SAY THAT, THANKS TO WHAT YOU BABBLED TO ME, I REALIZED THAT THE GIANT BEAST WAS MADE UP OF SMALL BEASTS AND THAT IT WOULD BE SENSITIVE TO FIRE. THAT'S WHAT SAVED US.
OH...
DO THE BIRDS TALK TO YOU A LOT?
FROM TIME TO TIME, BUT I'M NOT REALLY ALLOWED TO USE MY POWERS. IT SCARES THE ADULTS.

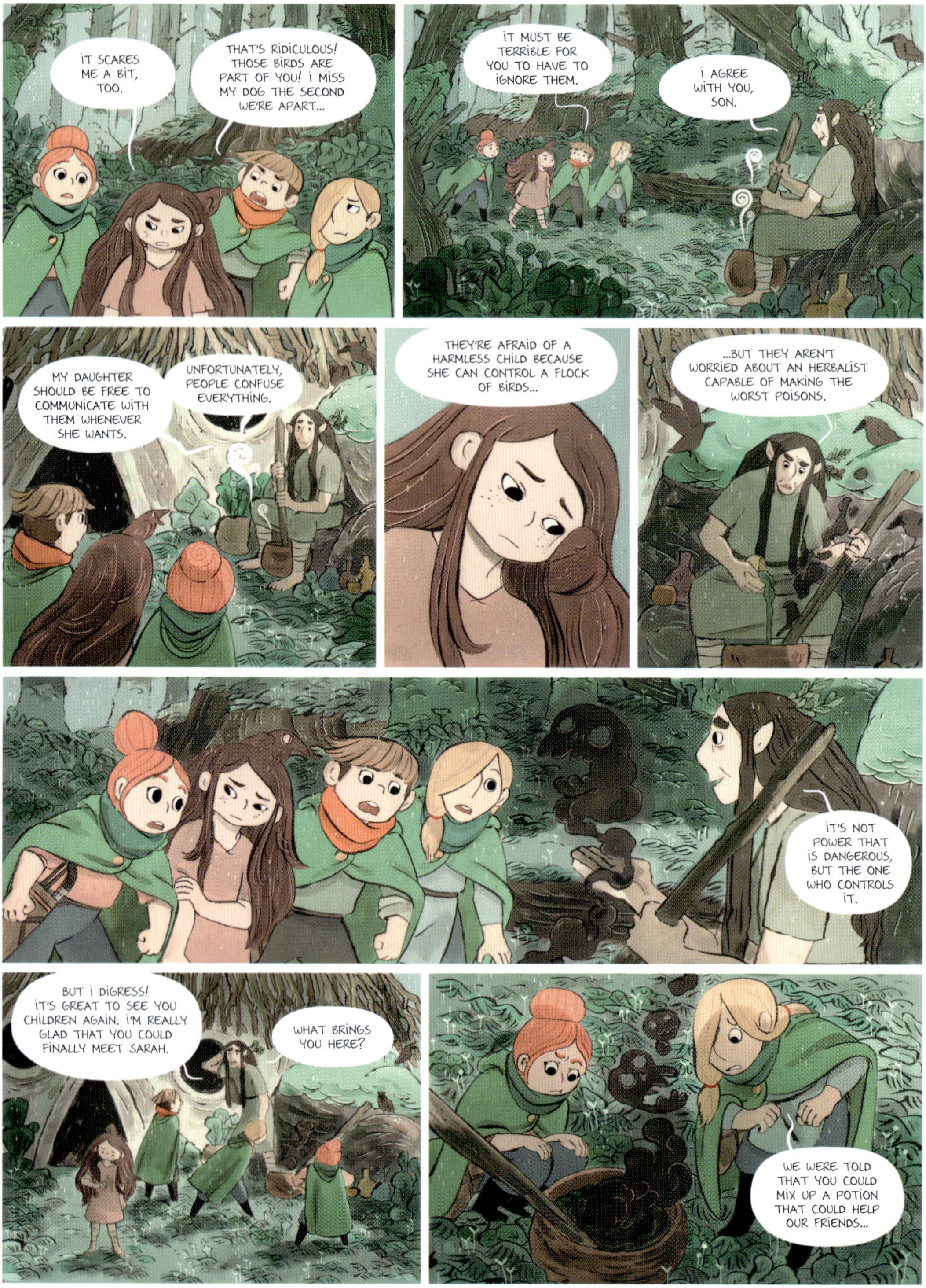
IT SCARES ME A BIT, TOO.
THAT'S RIDICULOUS! THOSE BIRDS ARE PART OF YOU! I MISS MY DOG THE SECOND WE'RE APART...
IT MUST BE TERRIBLE FOR YOU TO HAVE TO IGNORE THEM.
I AGREE WITH YOU, SON.
MY DAUGHTER SHOULD BE FREE TO COMMUNICATE WITH THEM WHENEVER SHE WANTS.
UNFORTUNATELY, PEOPLE CONFUSE EVERYTHING.
THEY'RE AFRAID OF A HARMLESS CHILD BECAUSE SHE CAN CONTROL A FLOCK OF BIRDS...
...BUT THEY AREN'T WORRIED ABOUT AN HERBALIST CAPABLE OF MAKING THE WORST POISONS.
IT'S NOT POWER THAT IS DANGEROUS, BUT THE ONE WHO CONTROLS IT.
BUT I DIGRESS! IT'S GREAT TO SEE YOU CHILDREN AGAIN. I'M REALLY GLAD THAT YOU COULD FINALLY MEET SARAH.
WHAT BRINGS YOU HERE?
WE WERE TOLD THAT YOU COULD MIX UP A POTION THAT COULD HELP OUR FRIENDS...

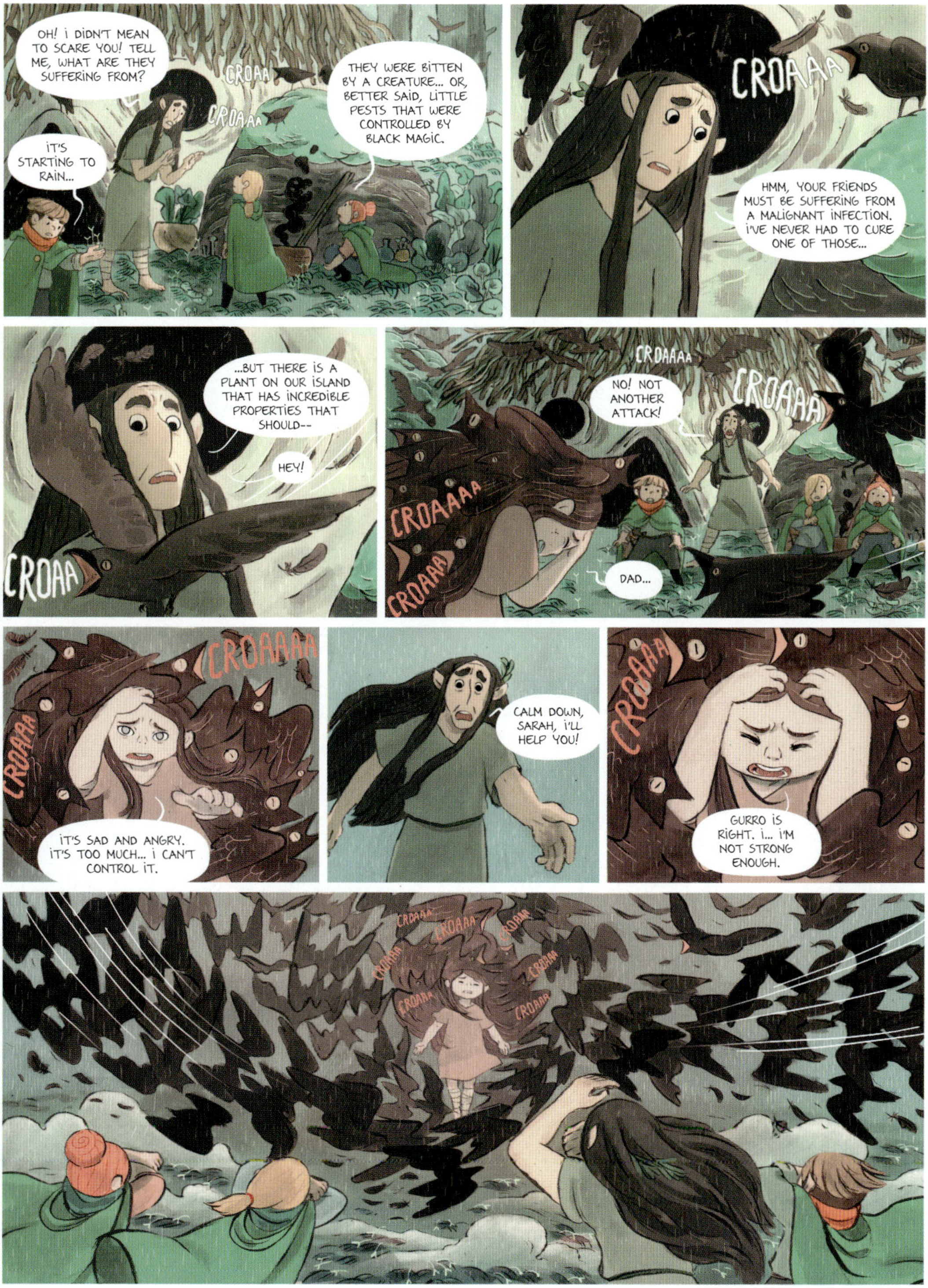
OH! I DIDN'T MEAN TO SCARE YOU! TELL ME, WHAT ARE THEY SUFFERING FROM?
CROAA
CROAAA
IT'S STARTING TO RAIN...
THEY WERE BITTEN BY A CREATURE... OR, BETTER SAID, LITTLE PESTS THAT WERE CONTROLLED BY BLACK MAGIC.
CROAAA
HMM, YOUR FRIENDS MUST BE SUFFERING FROM A MALIGNANT INFECTION. I'VE NEVER HAD TO CURE ONE OF THOSE...
...BUT THERE IS A PLANT ON OUR ISLAND THAT HAS INCREDIBLE PROPERTIES THAT SHOULD--
HEY!
CROAA
CROAAAA
NO! NOT ANOTHER ATTACK!
CROAAA
CROAAAA
CROAAA
DAD...
CROAAAA
CROAAA
IT'S SAD AND ANGRY. IT'S TOO MUCH... I CAN'T CONTROL IT.
CALM DOWN, SARAH, I'LL HELP YOU!
CROAAAA
GURRO IS RIGHT. I... I'M NOT STRONG ENOUGH.

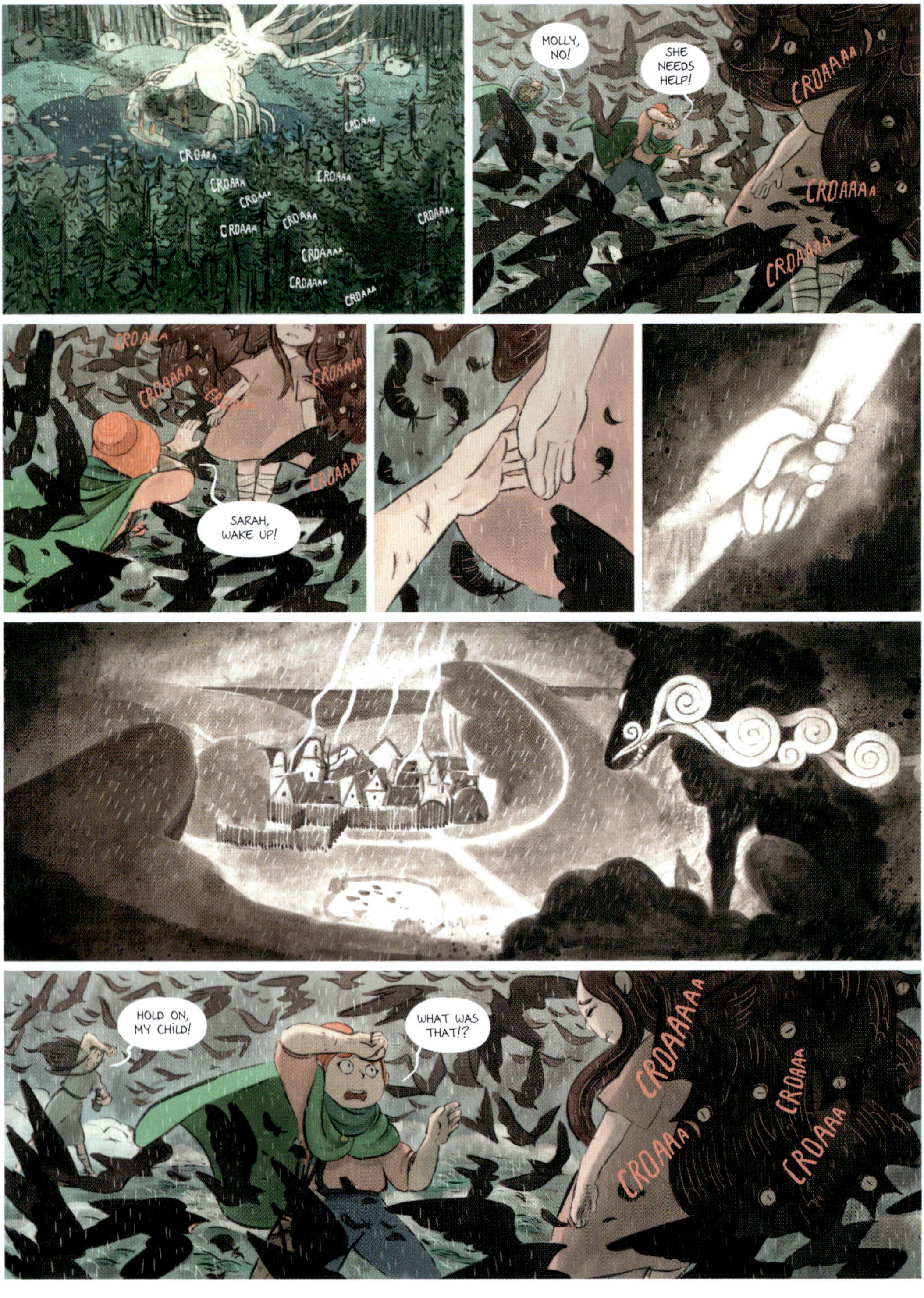
CROAAA
CROAAA
CROAAA
CROAAA
CROAAA
CROAAA
CROAAA
CROAAAA
CROAAAA
CROAAAA
CROAAA
MOLLY, NO!
SHE NEEDS HELP!
CROAAAA
CROAAAA
CROAAAA
CROAAAA
CROAAAA
CROAAAA
CROAAAA
SARAH, WAKE UP!
HOLD ON, MY CHILD!
WHAT WAS THAT!?
CROAAAAA
CROAAA
CROAAA
CROAAA

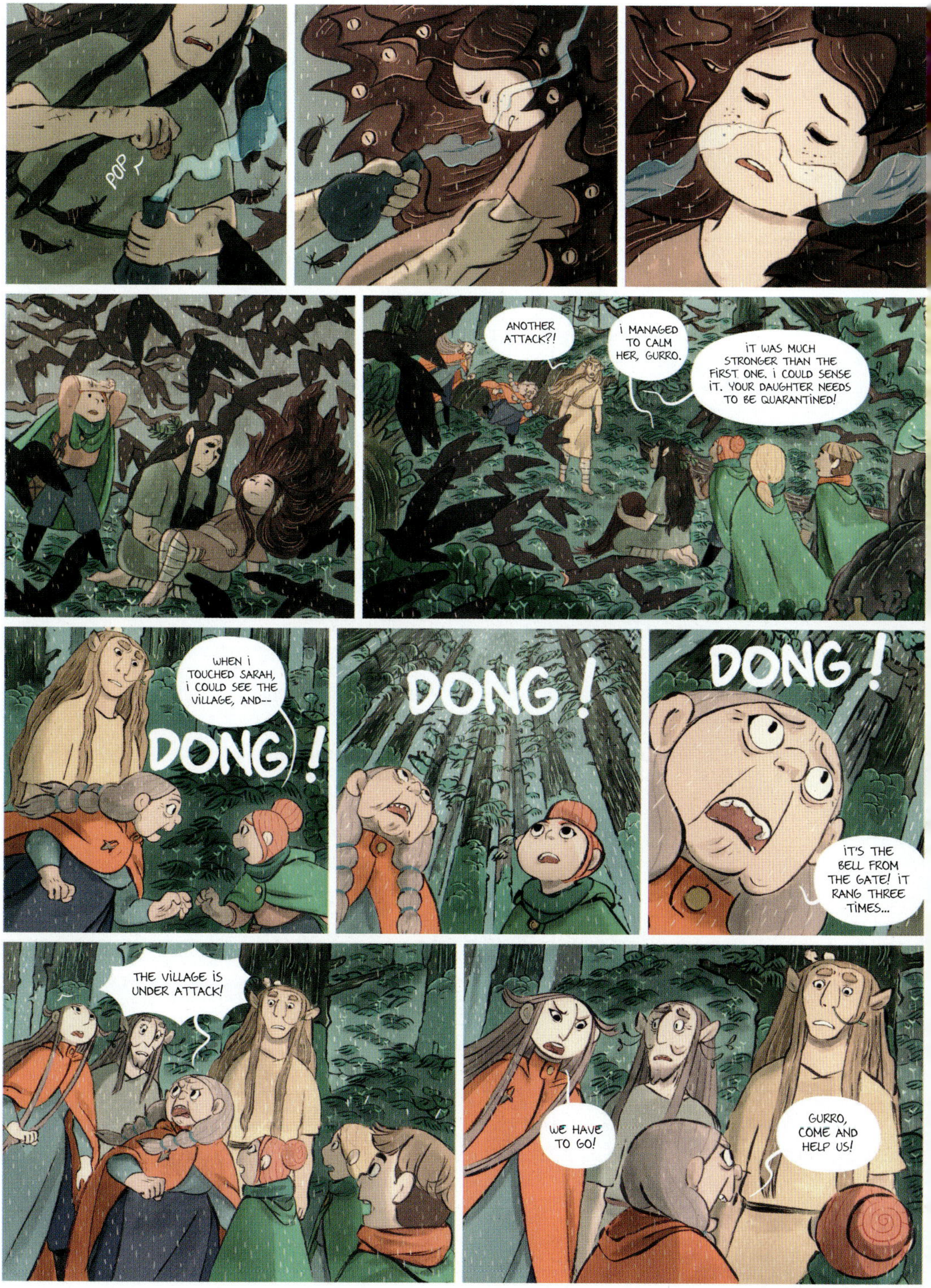
POP
ANOTHER ATTACK?!
I MANAGED TO CALM HER, GURRO.
IT WAS MUCH STRONGER THAN THE FIRST ONE. I COULD SENSE IT. YOUR DAUGHTER NEEDS TO BE QUARANTINED!
WHEN I TOUCHED SARAH, I COULD SEE THE VILLAGE, AND--
DONG!
DONG!
DONG!
IT'S THE BELL FROM THE GATE! IT RANG THREE TIMES...
THE VILLAGE IS UNDER ATTACK!
WE HAVE TO GO!
GURRO, COME AND HELP US!

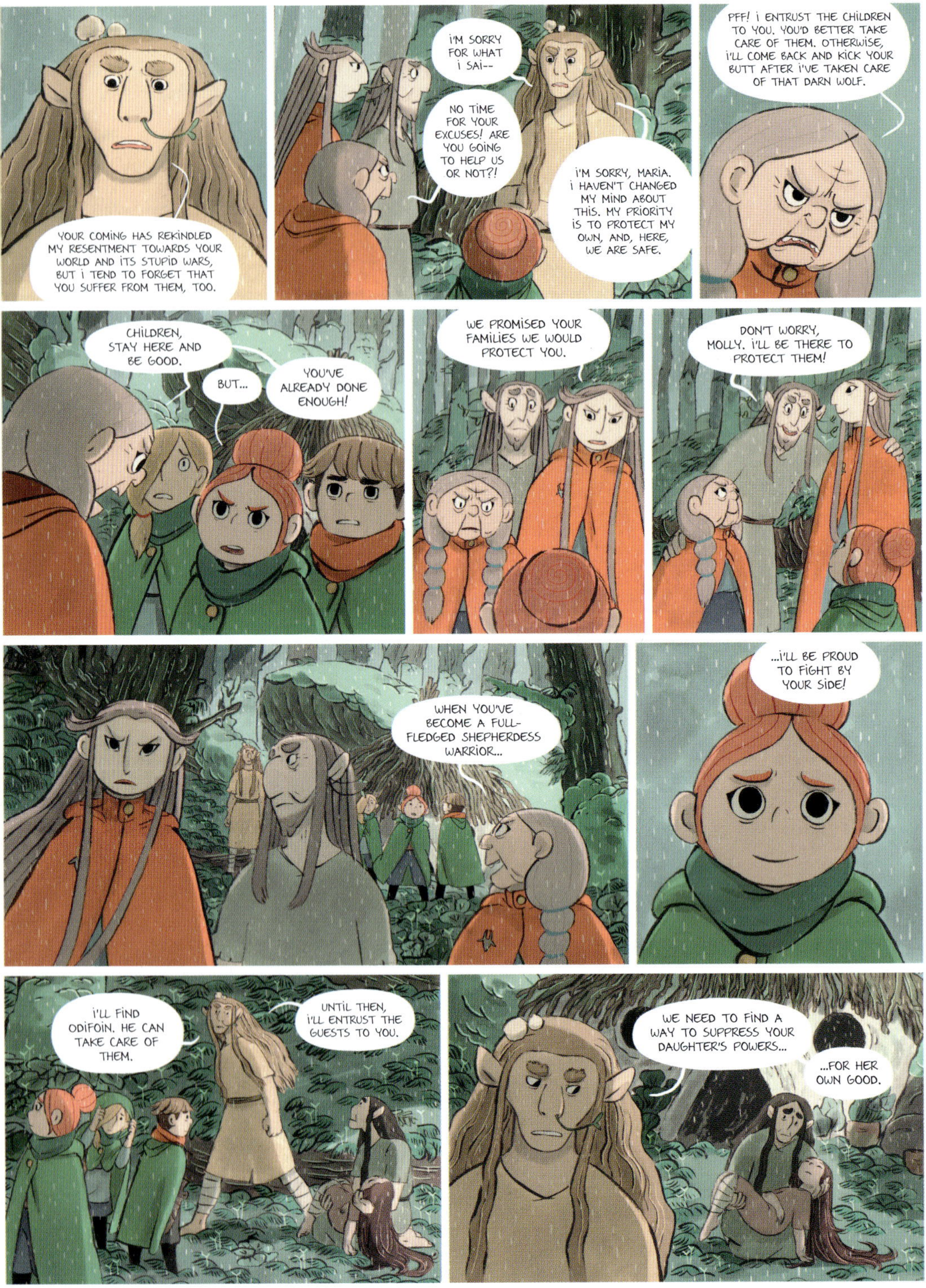
YOUR COMING HAS REKINDLED MY RESENTMENT TOWARDS YOUR WORLD AND ITS STUPID WARS, BUT I TEND TO FORGET THAT YOU SUFFER FROM THEM, TOO.
I'M SORRY FOR WHAT I SAI--
NO TIME FOR YOUR EXCUSES! ARE YOU GOING TO HELP US OR NOT?!
I'M SORRY, MARIA. I HAVEN'T CHANGED MY MIND ABOUT THIS. MY PRIORITY IS TO PROTECT MY OWN, AND, HERE, WE ARE SAFE.
PFF! I ENTRUST THE CHILDREN TO YOU. YOU'D BETTER TAKE CARE OF THEM. OTHERWISE, I'LL COME BACK AND KICK YOUR BUTT AFTER I'VE TAKEN CARE OF THAT DARN WOLF.
CHILDREN, STAY HERE AND BE GOOD.
BUT...
YOU'VE ALREADY DONE ENOUGH!
WE PROMISED YOUR FAMILIES WE WOULD PROTECT YOU.
DON'T WORRY, MOLLY. I'LL BE THERE TO PROTECT THEM!
WHEN YOU'VE BECOME A FULL-FLEDGED SHEPHERDESS WARRIOR...
...I'LL BE PROUD TO FIGHT BY YOUR SIDE!
I'LL FIND ODIFOIN. HE CAN TAKE CARE OF THEM.
UNTIL THEN, I'LL ENTRUST THE GUESTS TO YOU.
WE NEED TO FIND A WAY TO SUPPRESS YOUR DAUGHTER'S POWERS...
...FOR HER OWN GOOD.

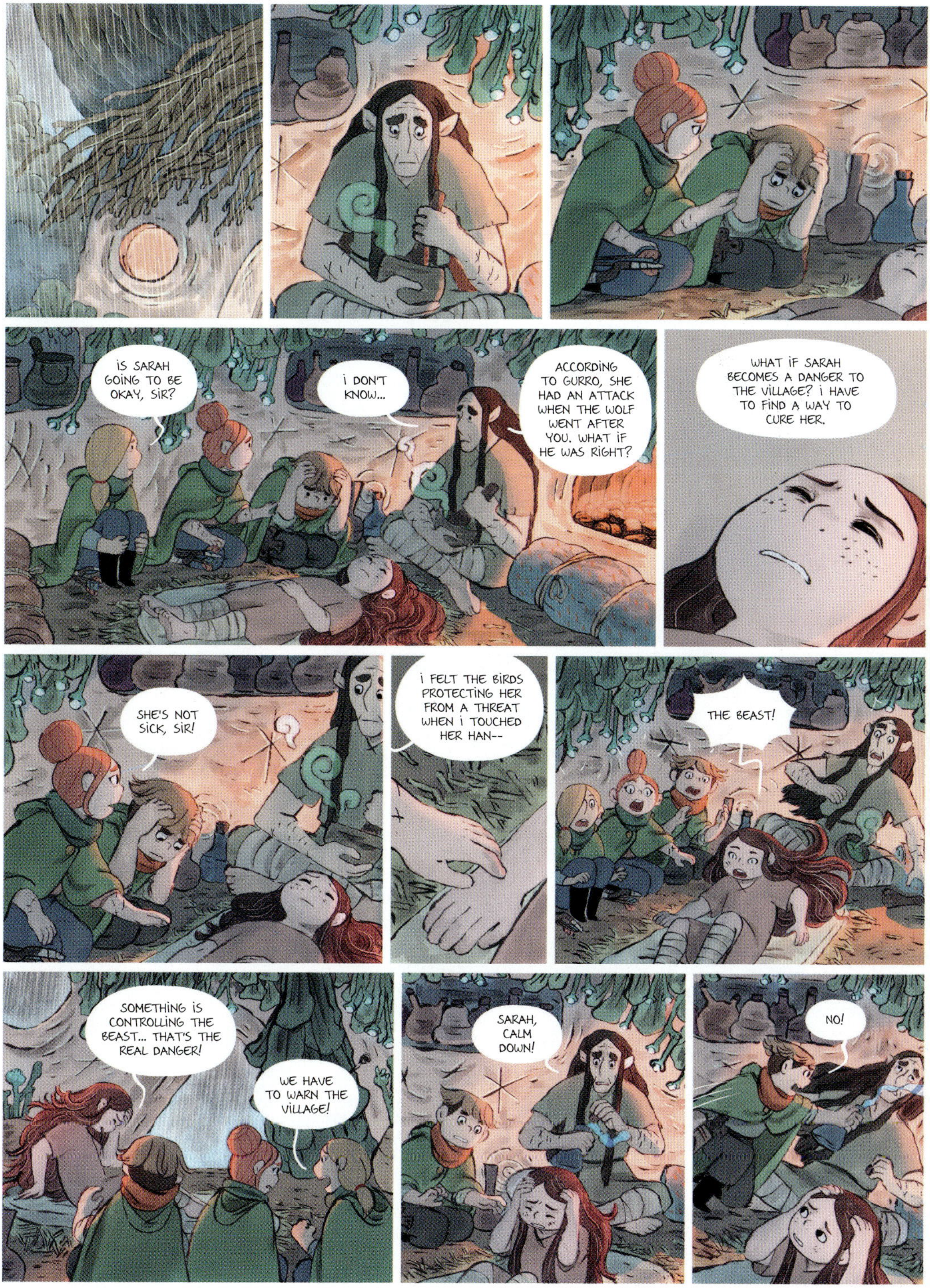
IS SARAH GOING TO BE OKAY, SIR?
I DON'T KNOW...
ACCORDING TO GURRO, SHE HAD AN ATTACK WHEN THE WOLF WENT AFTER YOU. WHAT IF HE WAS RIGHT?
WHAT IF SARAH BECOMES A DANGER TO THE VILLAGE? I HAVE TO FIND A WAY TO CURE HER.
SHE'S NOT SICK, SIR!
I FELT THE BIRDS PROTECTING HER FROM A THREAT WHEN I TOUCHED HER HAN--
THE BEAST!
SOMETHING IS CONTROLLING THE BEAST... THAT'S THE REAL DANGER!
WE HAVE TO WARN THE VILLAGE!
SARAH, CALM DOWN!
NO!

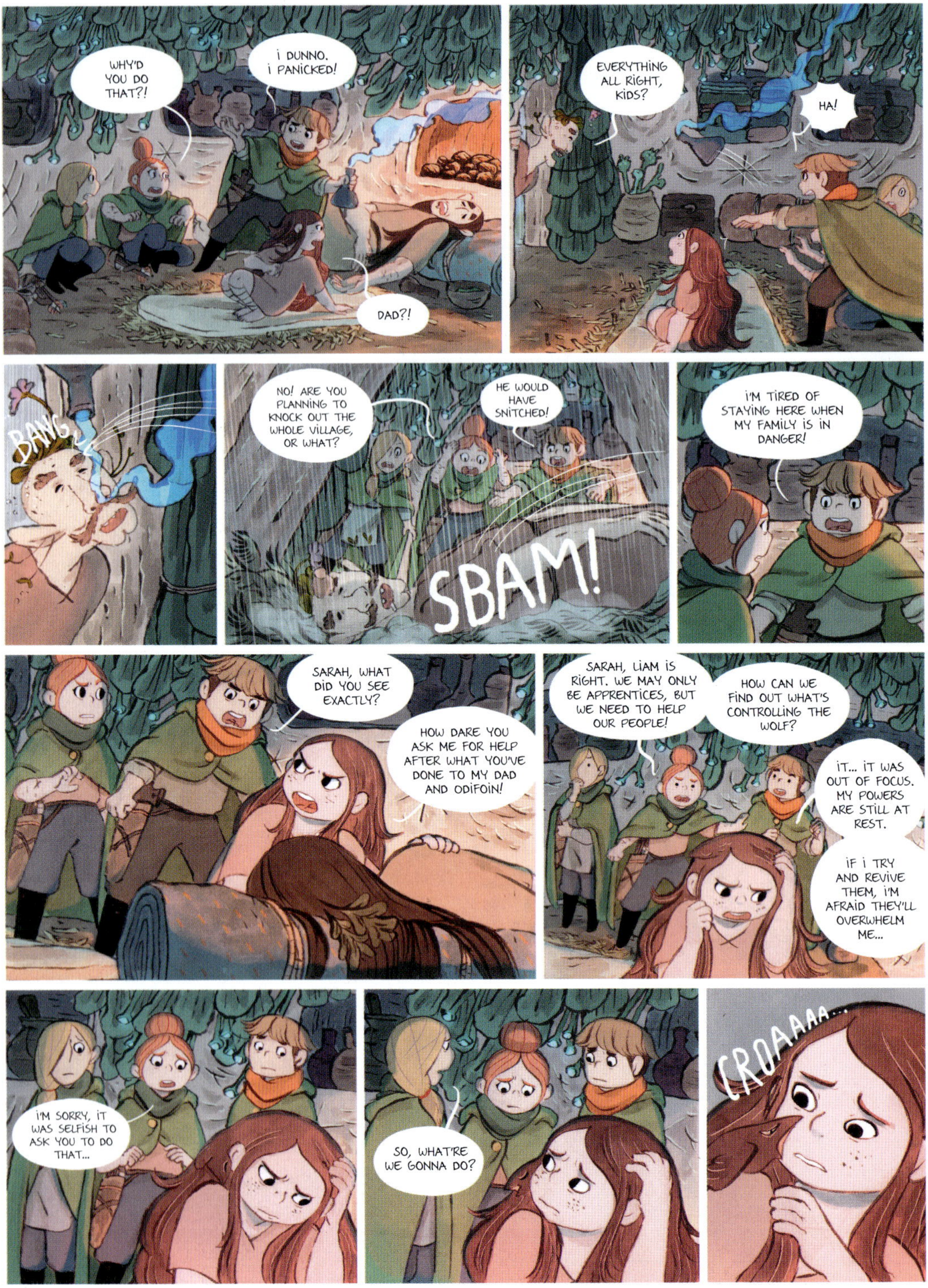
WHY'D YOU DO THAT?!
I DUNNO. I PANICKED!
DAD?!
EVERYTHING ALL RIGHT, KIDS?
HA!
BANG
NO! ARE YOU PLANNING TO KNOCK OUT THE WHOLE VILLAGE, OR WHAT?
HE WOULD HAVE SNITCHED!
SBAM!
I'M TIRED OF STAYING HERE WHEN MY FAMILY IS IN DANGER!
SARAH, WHAT DID YOU SEE EXACTLY?
HOW DARE YOU ASK ME FOR HELP AFTER WHAT YOU'VE DONE TO MY DAD AND ODIFOIN!
SARAH, LIAM IS RIGHT. WE MAY ONLY BE APPRENTICES, BUT WE NEED TO HELP OUR PEOPLE!
HOW CAN WE FIND OUT WHAT'S CONTROLLING THE WOLF?
IT... IT WAS OUT OF FOCUS. MY POWERS ARE STILL AT REST.
IF I TRY AND REVIVE THEM, I'M AFRAID THEY'LL OVERWHELM ME...
I'M SORRY, IT WAS SELFISH TO ASK YOU TO DO THAT...
SO, WHAT'RE WE GONNA DO?
CROAAAA...

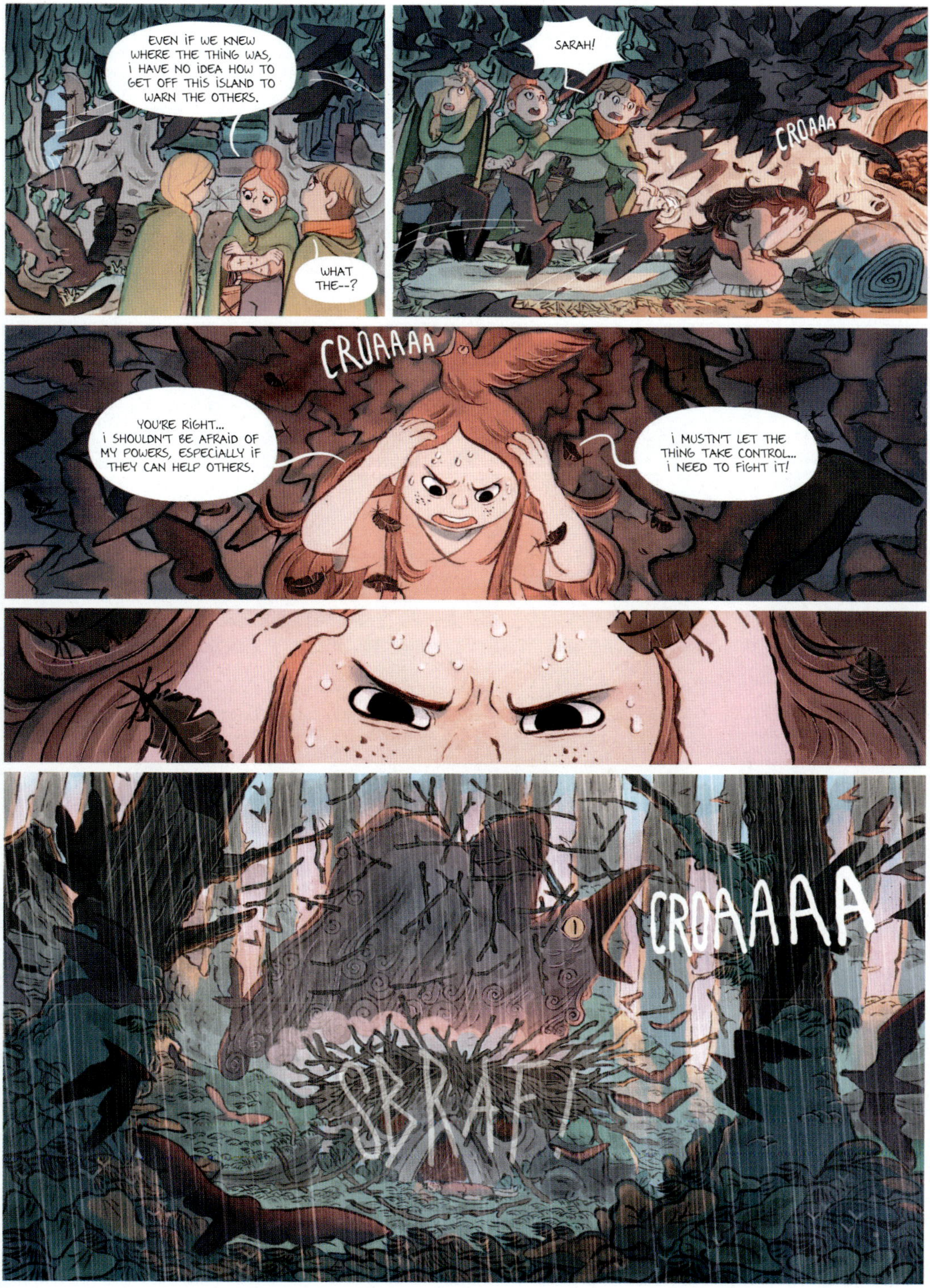
EVEN IF WE KNEW WHERE THE THING WAS, I HAVE NO IDEA HOW TO GET OFF THIS ISLAND TO WARN THE OTHERS.
WHAT THE--?
SARAH!
CROAAA
CROAAAA
YOU'RE RIGHT... I SHOULDN'T BE AFRAID OF MY POWERS, ESPECIALLY IF THEY CAN HELP OTHERS.
I MUSTN'T LET THE THING TAKE CONTROL... I NEED TO FIGHT IT!
CROAAAA
SBRAF!

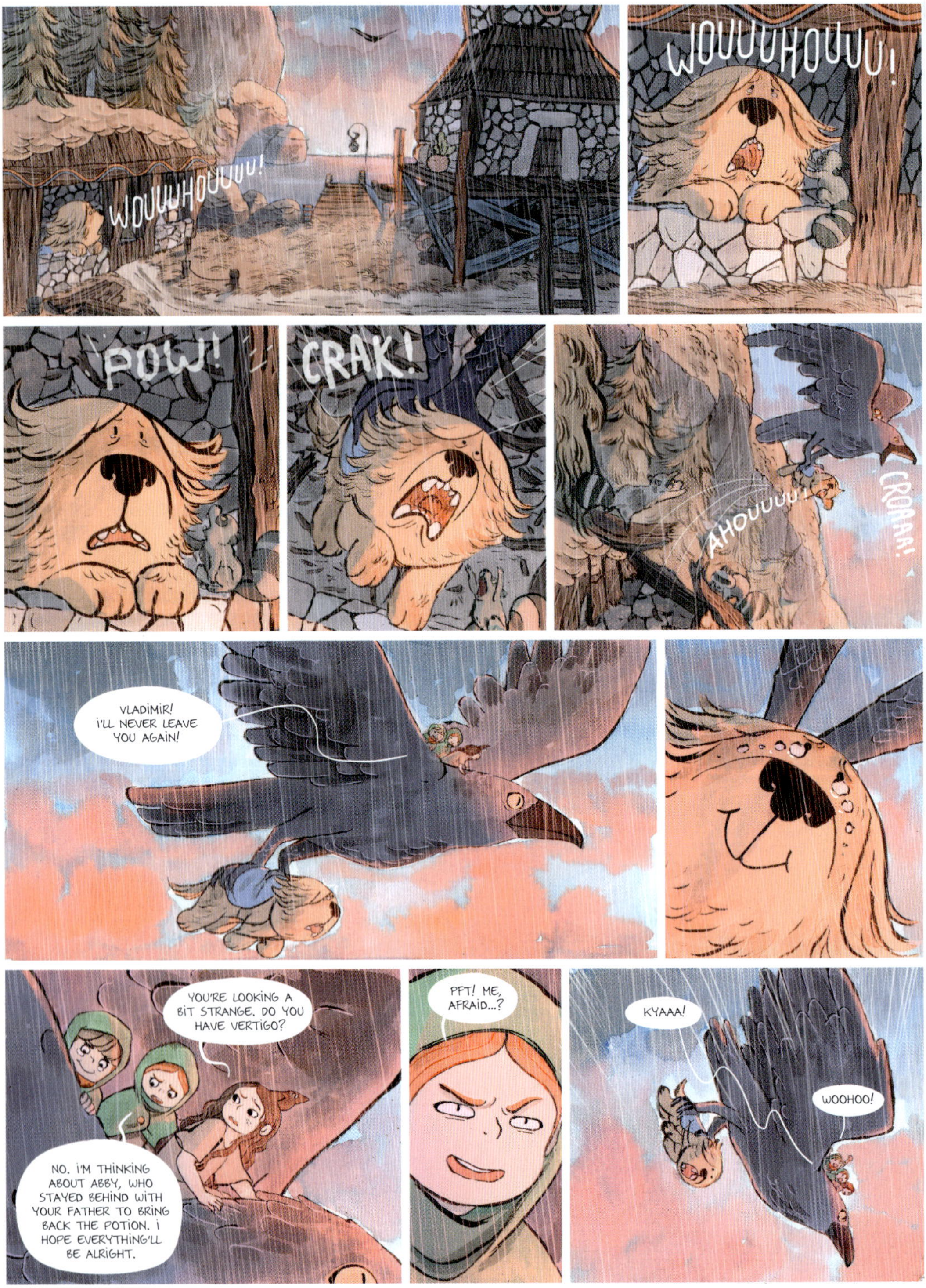
WOUUUHOUUUU!
WOUUUHOUUUU!
POW!
CRAK!
AHOUUUU!
CROAAA!
VLADIMIR! I'LL NEVER LEAVE YOU AGAIN!
YOU'RE LOOKING A BIT STRANGE. DO YOU HAVE VERTIGO?
NO. I'M THINKING ABOUT ABBY, WHO STAYED BEHIND WITH YOUR FATHER TO BRING BACK THE POTION. I HOPE EVERYTHING'LL BE ALRIGHT.
PFT! ME, AFRAID...?
KYAAA!
WOOHOO!

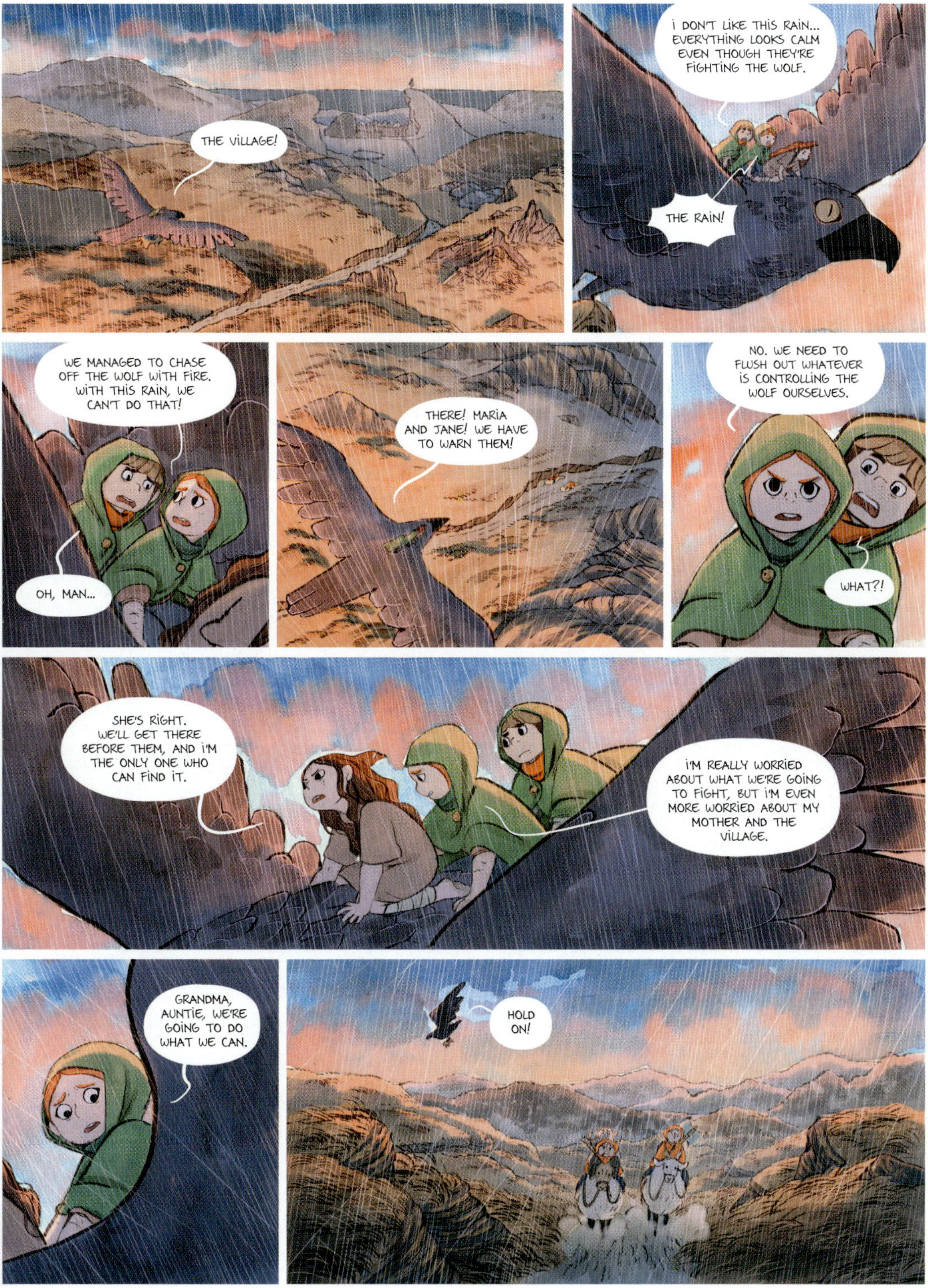
THE VILLAGE!
I DON'T LIKE THIS RAIN... EVERYTHING LOOKS CALM EVEN THOUGH THEY'RE FIGHTING THE WOLF.
THE RAIN!
WE MANAGED TO CHASE OFF THE WOLF WITH FIRE. WITH THIS RAIN, WE CAN'T DO THAT!
OH, MAN...
THERE! MARIA AND JANE! WE HAVE TO WARN THEM!
NO. WE NEED TO FLUSH OUT WHATEVER IS CONTROLLING THE WOLF OURSELVES.
WHAT?!
SHE'S RIGHT. WE'LL GET THERE BEFORE THEM, AND I'M THE ONLY ONE WHO CAN FIND IT.
I'M REALLY WORRIED ABOUT WHAT WE'RE GOING TO FIGHT, BUT I'M EVEN MORE WORRIED ABOUT MY MOTHER AND THE VILLAGE.
GRANDMA, AUNTIE, WE'RE GOING TO DO WHAT WE CAN.
HOLD ON!

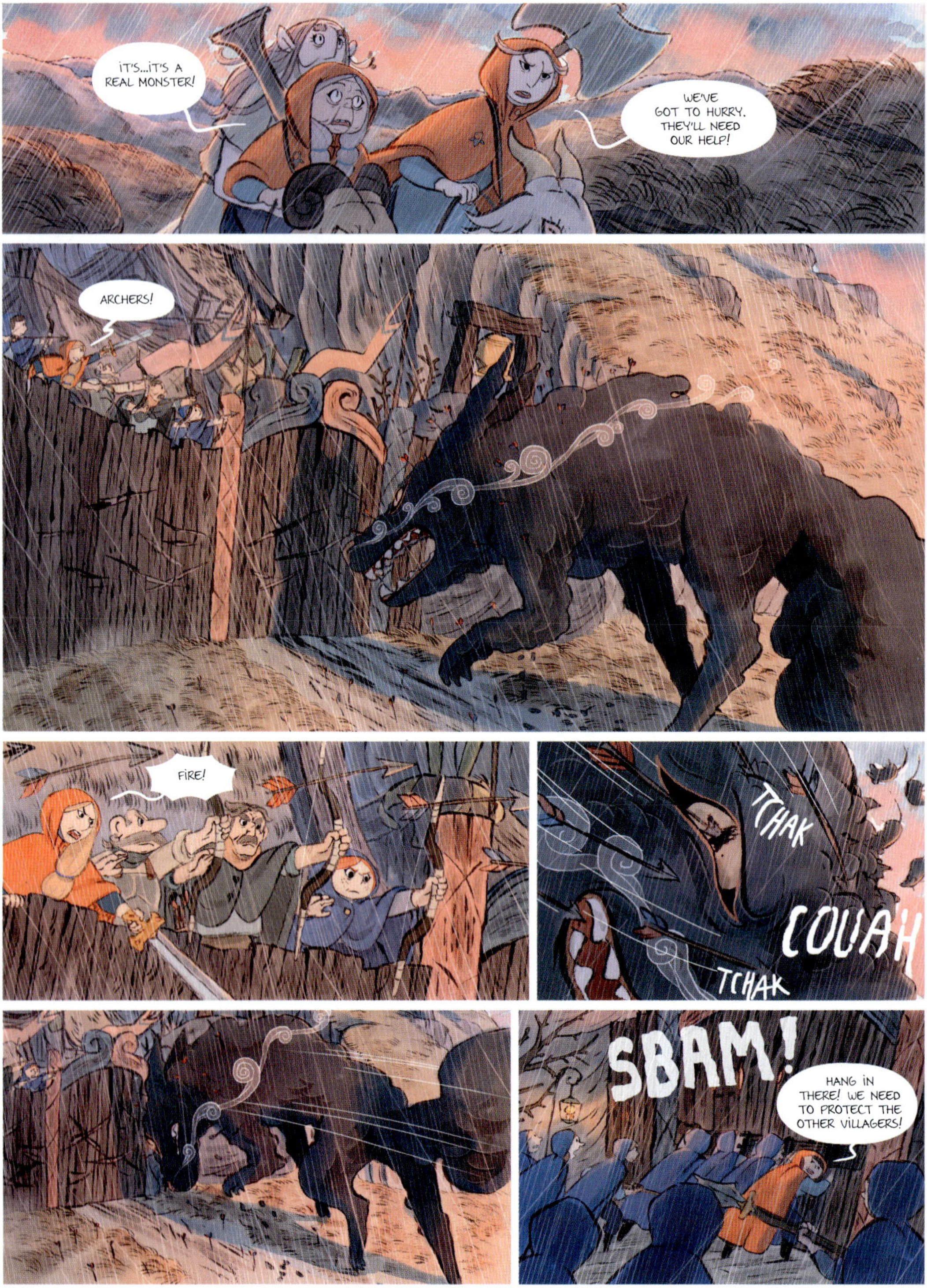
IT'S...IT'S A REAL MONSTER!
WE'VE GOT TO HURRY. THEY'LL NEED OUR HELP!
ARCHERS!
FIRE!
TCHAK
COUAH
TCHAK
SBAM!
HANG IN THERE! WE NEED TO PROTECT THE OTHER VILLAGERS!

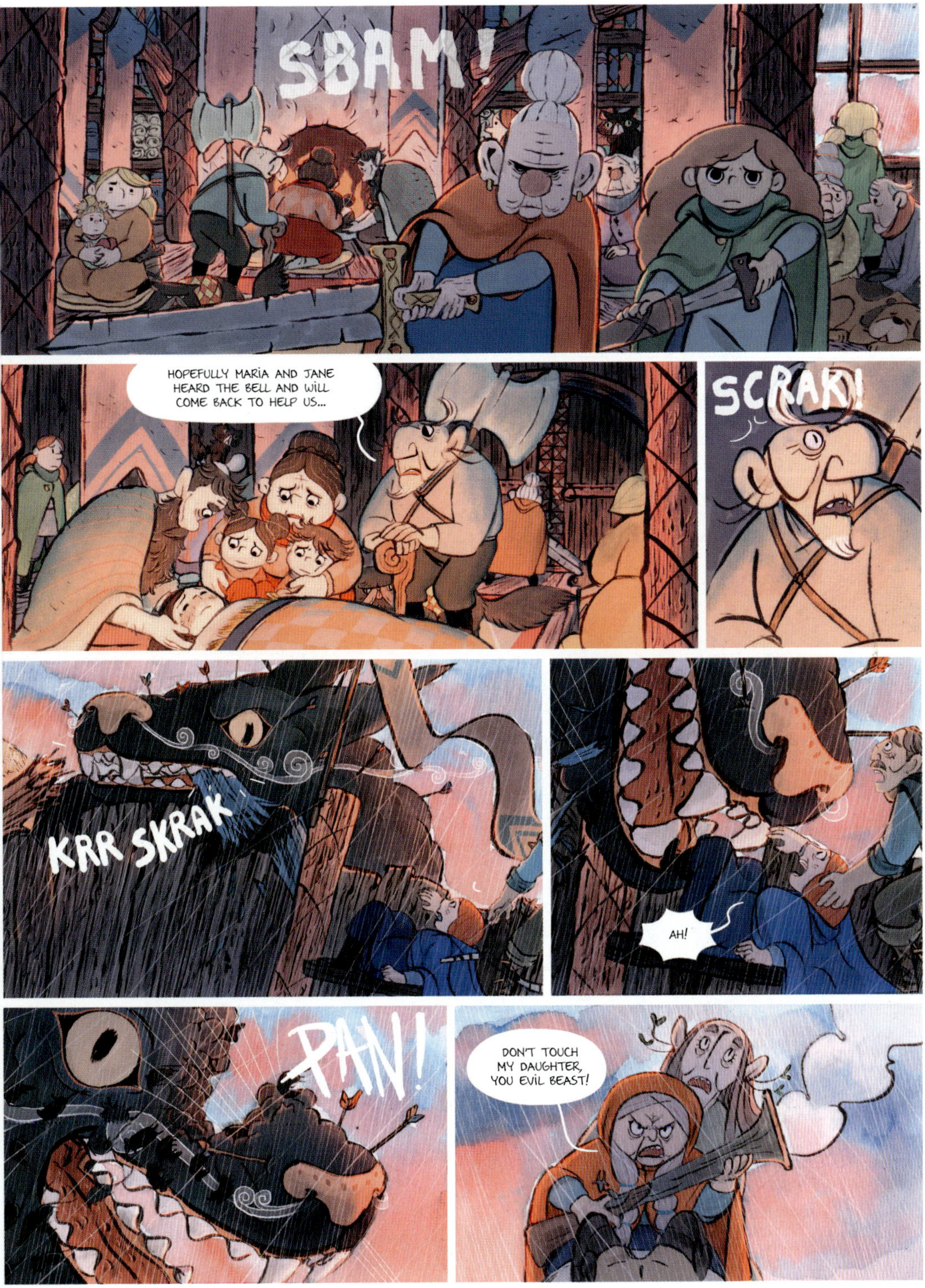
SBAM!
HOPEFULLY MARIA AND JANE HEARD THE BELL AND WILL COME BACK TO HELP US...
SCRAK!
KRR SKRAK
AH!
PAN!
DON'T TOUCH MY DAUGHTER, YOU EVIL BEAST!

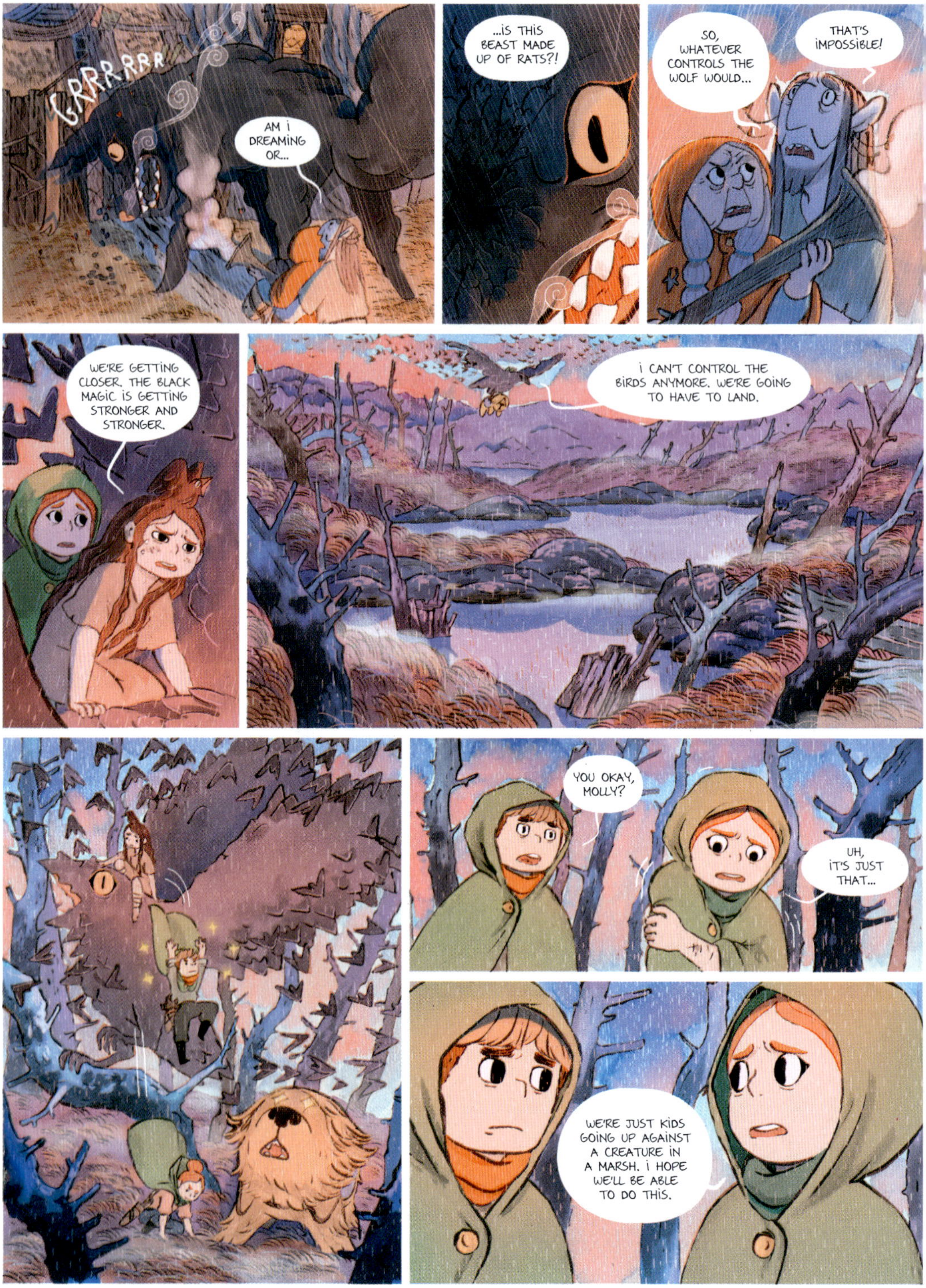
GRRRRRR
AM I DREAMING OR...
...IS THIS BEAST MADE UP OF RATS?!
SO, WHATEVER CONTROLS THE WOLF WOULD...
THAT'S IMPOSSIBLE!
WE'RE GETTING CLOSER. THE BLACK MAGIC IS GETTING STRONGER AND STRONGER.
I CAN'T CONTROL THE BIRDS ANYMORE. WE'RE GOING TO HAVE TO LAND.
YOU OKAY, MOLLY?
UH, IT'S JUST THAT...
WE'RE JUST KIDS GOING UP AGAINST A CREATURE IN A MARSH. I HOPE WE'LL BE ABLE TO DO THIS.

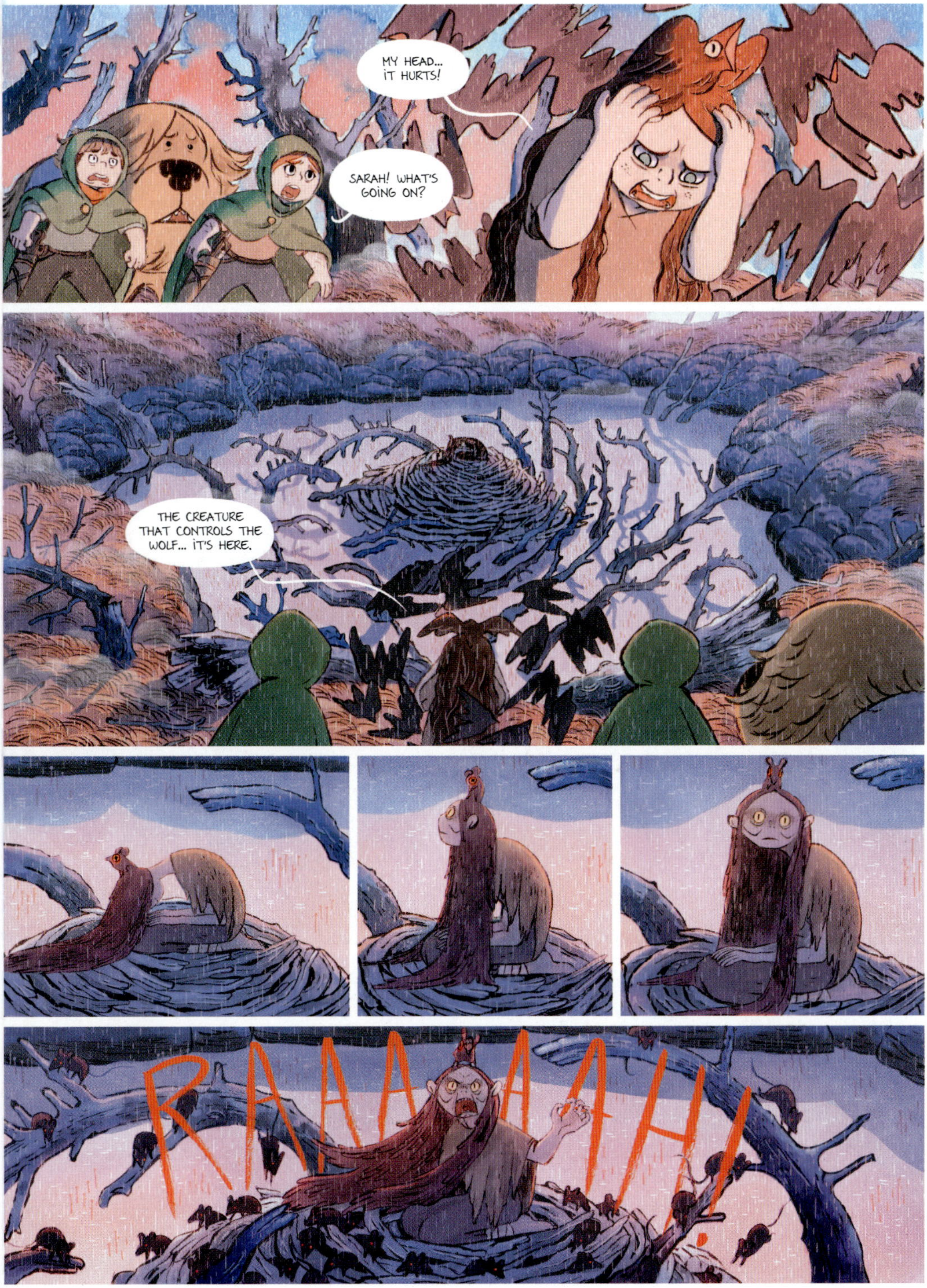
MY HEAD... IT HURTS!
SARAH! WHAT'S GOING ON?
THE CREATURE THAT CONTROLS THE WOLF... IT'S HERE.
RAAAAAH!

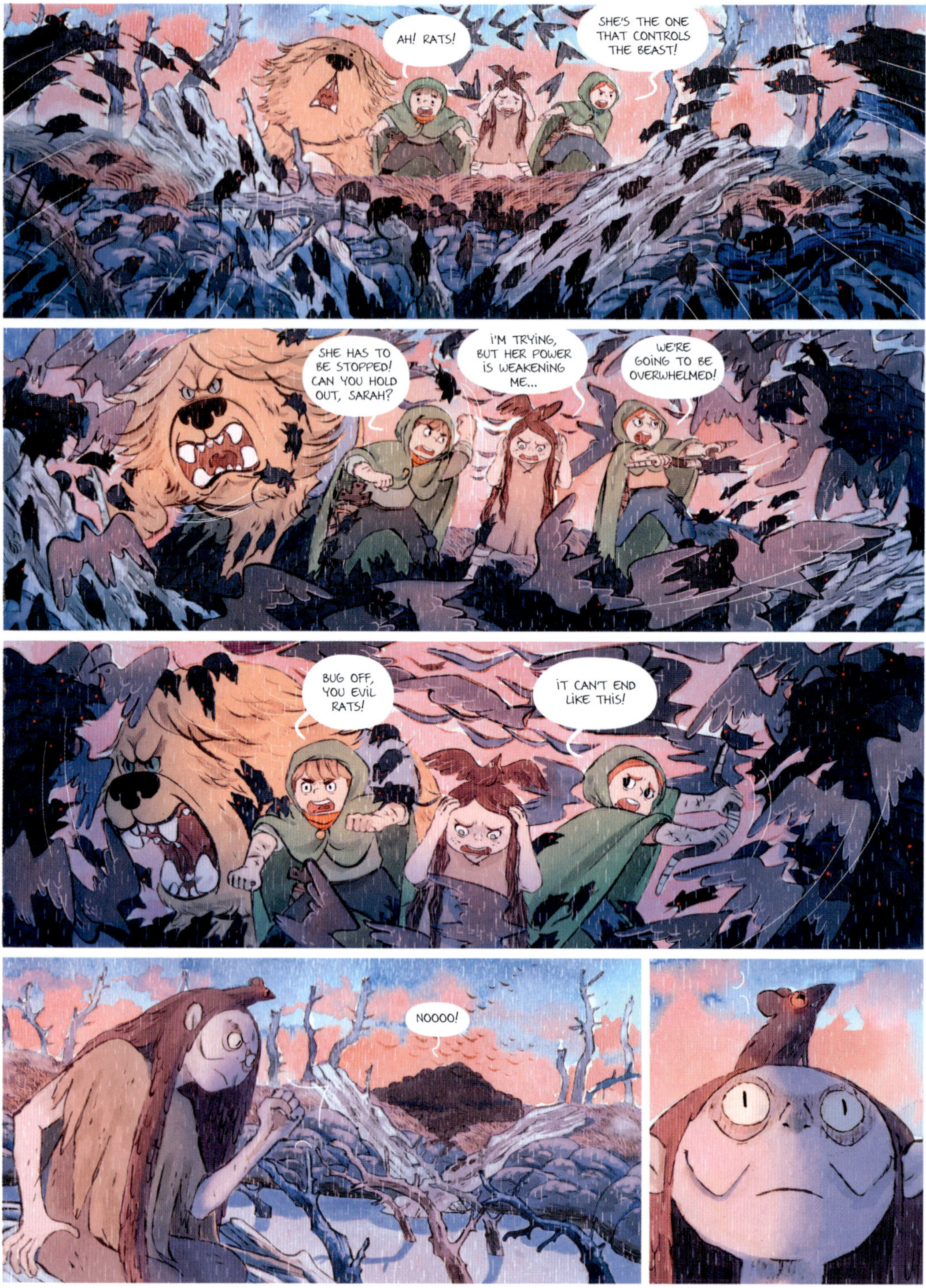
AH! RATS!
SHE'S THE ONE THAT CONTROLS THE BEAST!
SHE HAS TO BE STOPPED! CAN YOU HOLD OUT, SARAH?
I'M TRYING, BUT HER POWER IS WEAKENING ME...
WE'RE GOING TO BE OVERWHELMED!
BUG OFF, YOU EVIL RATS!
IT CAN'T END LIKE THIS!
NOOOO!

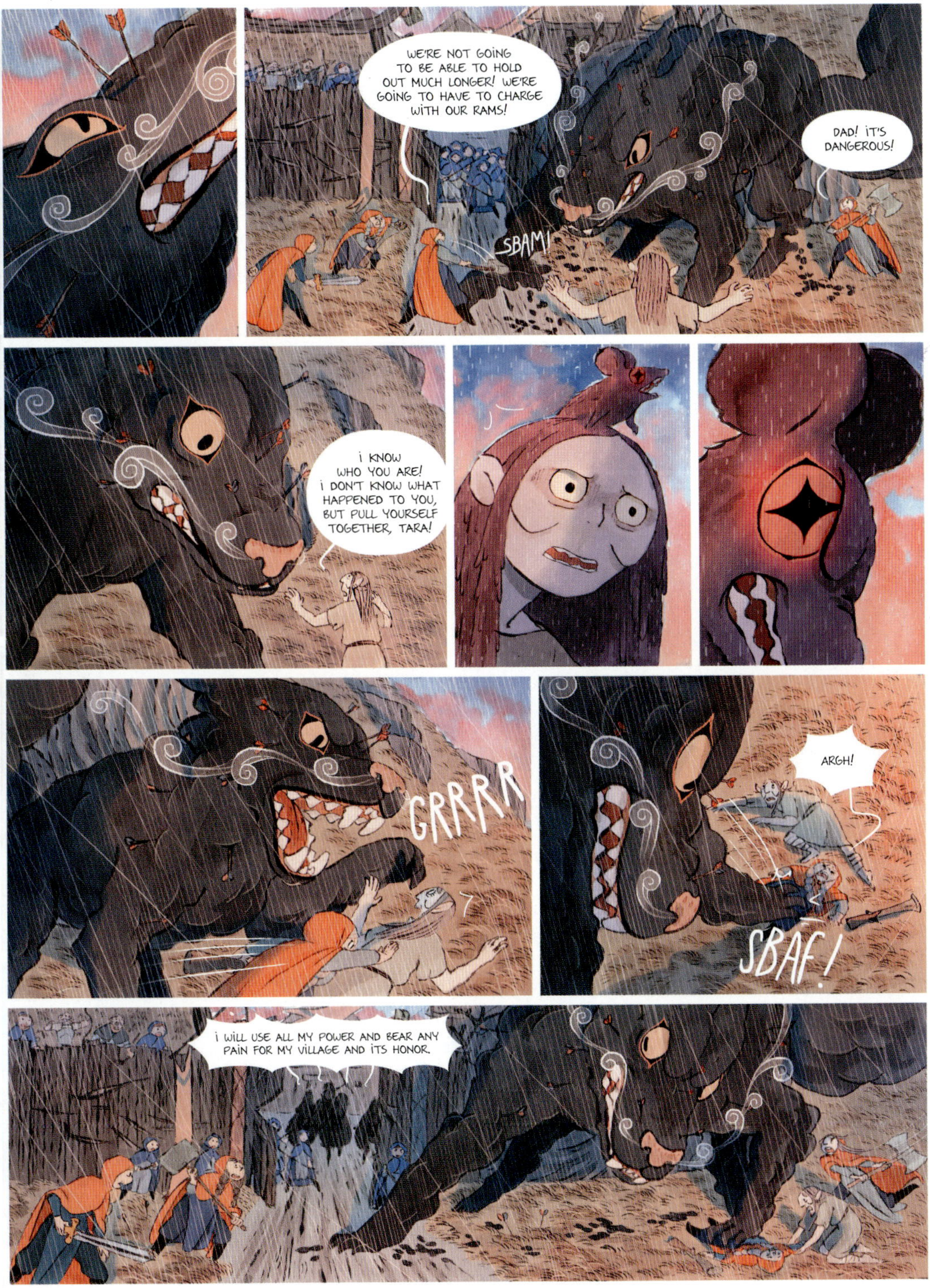
WE'RE NOT GOING TO BE ABLE TO HOLD OUT MUCH LONGER! WE'RE GOING TO HAVE TO CHARGE WITH OUR RAMS!
SBAM!
DAD! IT'S DANGEROUS!
I KNOW WHO YOU ARE! I DON'T KNOW WHAT HAPPENED TO YOU, BUT PULL YOURSELF TOGETHER, TARA!
GRRRR
ARGH!
SBAF!
I WILL USE ALL MY POWER AND BEAR ANY PAIN FOR MY VILLAGE AND ITS HONOR.

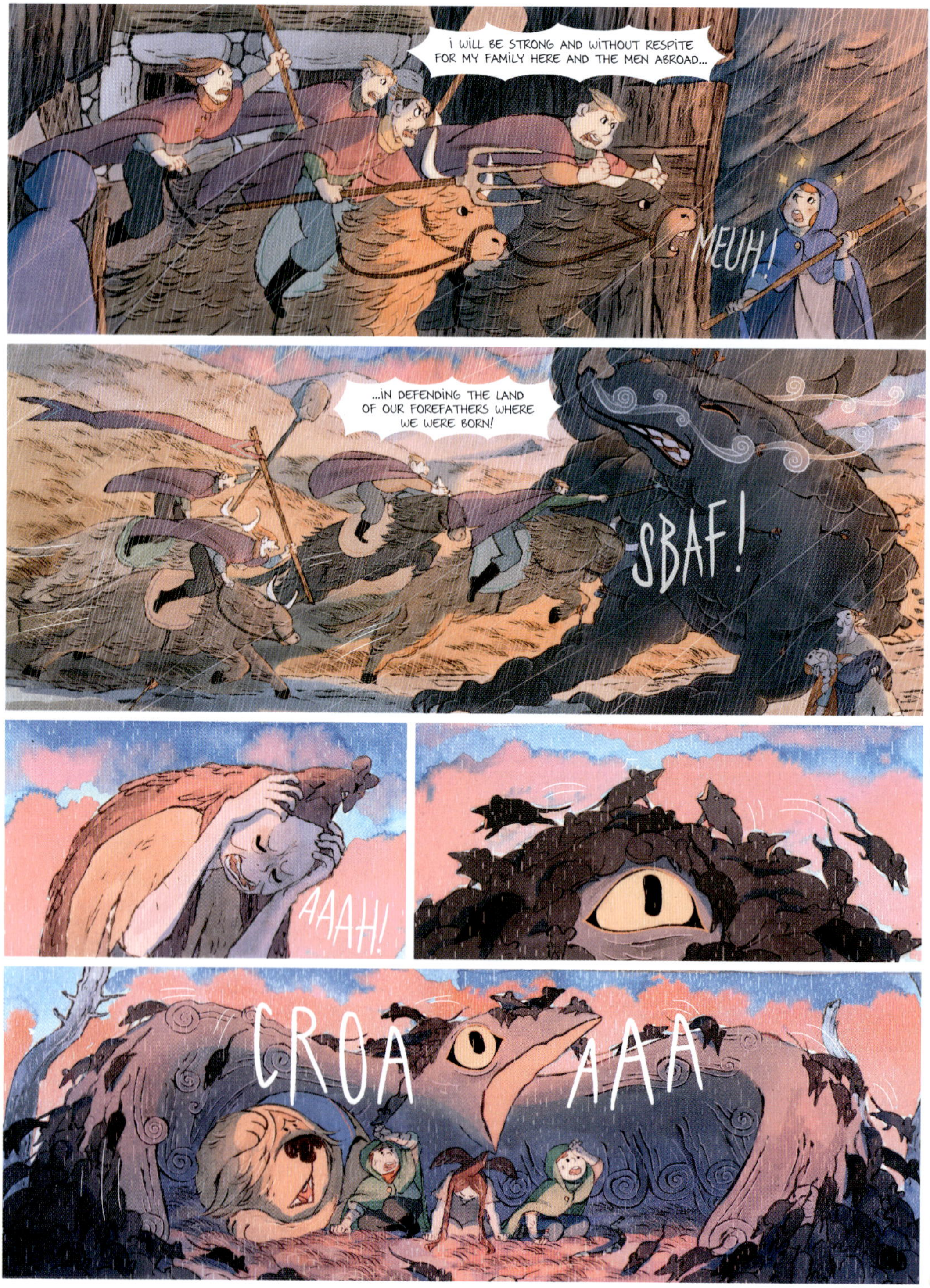
I WILL BE STRONG AND WITHOUT RESPITE FOR MY FAMILY HERE AND THE MEN ABROAD...
MEUH!
...IN DEFENDING THE LAND OF OUR FOREFATHERS WHERE WE WERE BORN!
SBAF!
AAAH!
CROA AAA

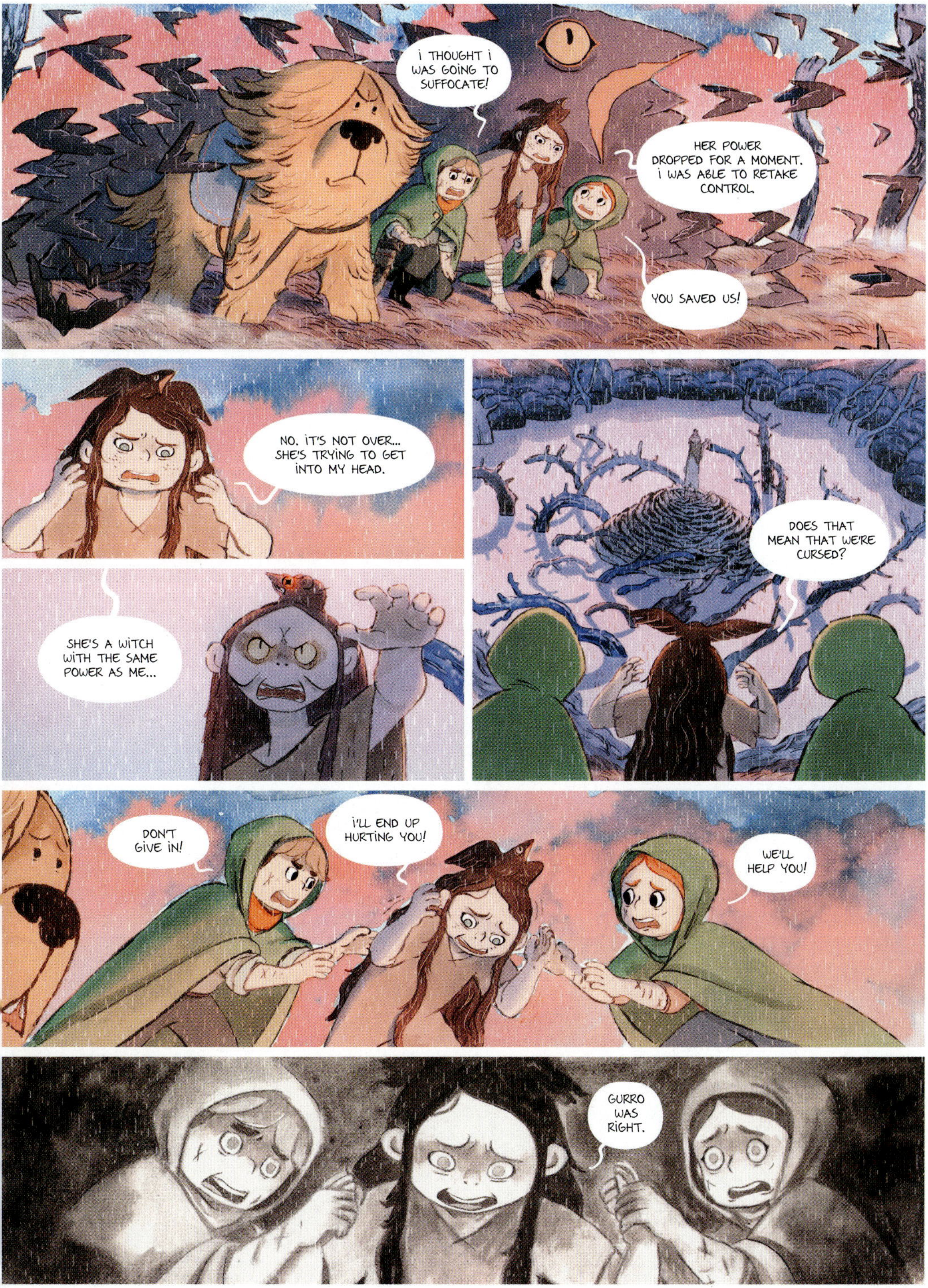
I THOUGHT I WAS GOING TO SUFFOCATE!
HER POWER DROPPED FOR A MOMENT. I WAS ABLE TO RETAKE CONTROL.
YOU SAVED US!
NO. IT'S NOT OVER... SHE'S TRYING TO GET INTO MY HEAD.
SHE'S A WITCH WITH THE SAME POWER AS ME...
DOES THAT MEAN THAT WE'RE CURSED?
DON'T GIVE IN!
I'LL END UP HURTING YOU!
WE'LL HELP YOU!
GURRO WAS RIGHT.

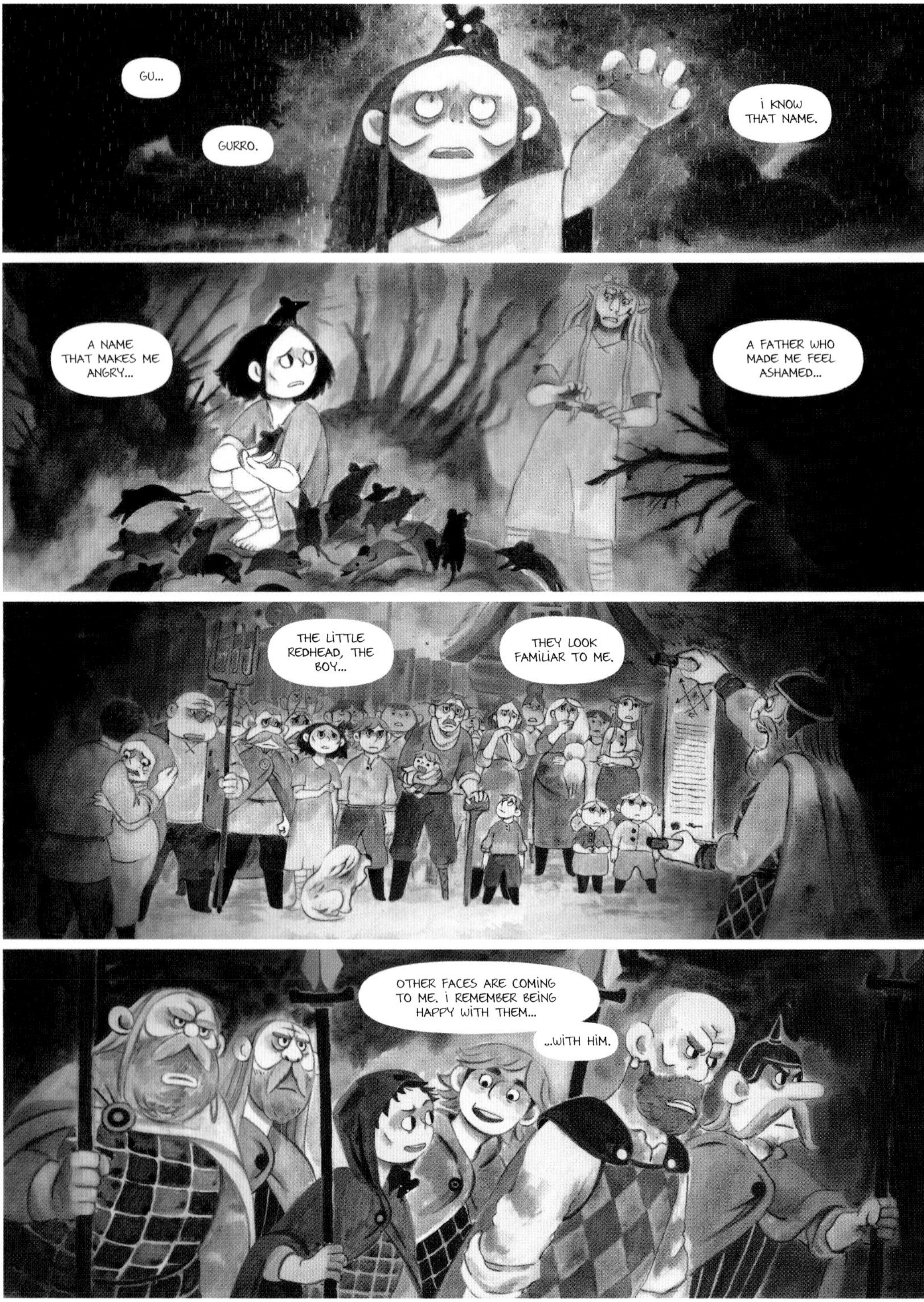
GU...
GURRO.
I KNOW THAT NAME.
A NAME THAT MAKES ME ANGRY...
A FATHER WHO MADE ME FEEL ASHAMED...
THE LITTLE REDHEAD, THE BOY...
THEY LOOK FAMILIAR TO ME.
OTHER FACES ARE COMING TO ME. I REMEMBER BEING HAPPY WITH THEM...
...WITH HIM.

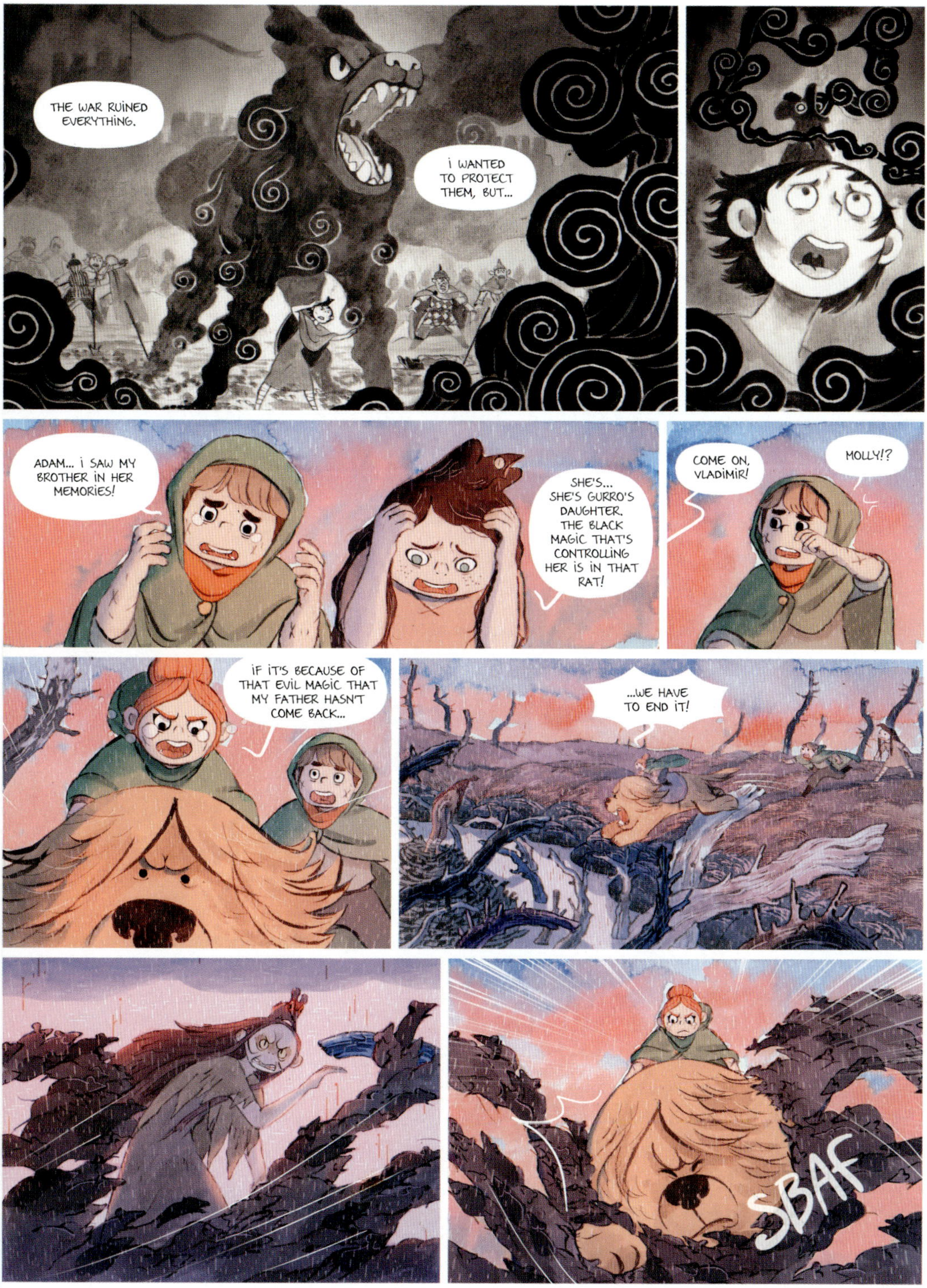
THE WAR RUINED EVERYTHING.
I WANTED TO PROTECT THEM, BUT...
ADAM... I SAW MY BROTHER IN HER MEMORIES!
SHE'S... SHE'S GURRO'S DAUGHTER. THE BLACK MAGIC THAT'S CONTROLLING HER IS IN THAT RAT!
COME ON, VLADIMIR!
MOLLY!?
IF IT'S BECAUSE OF THAT EVIL MAGIC THAT MY FATHER HASN'T COME BACK...
...WE HAVE TO END IT!
SBAF

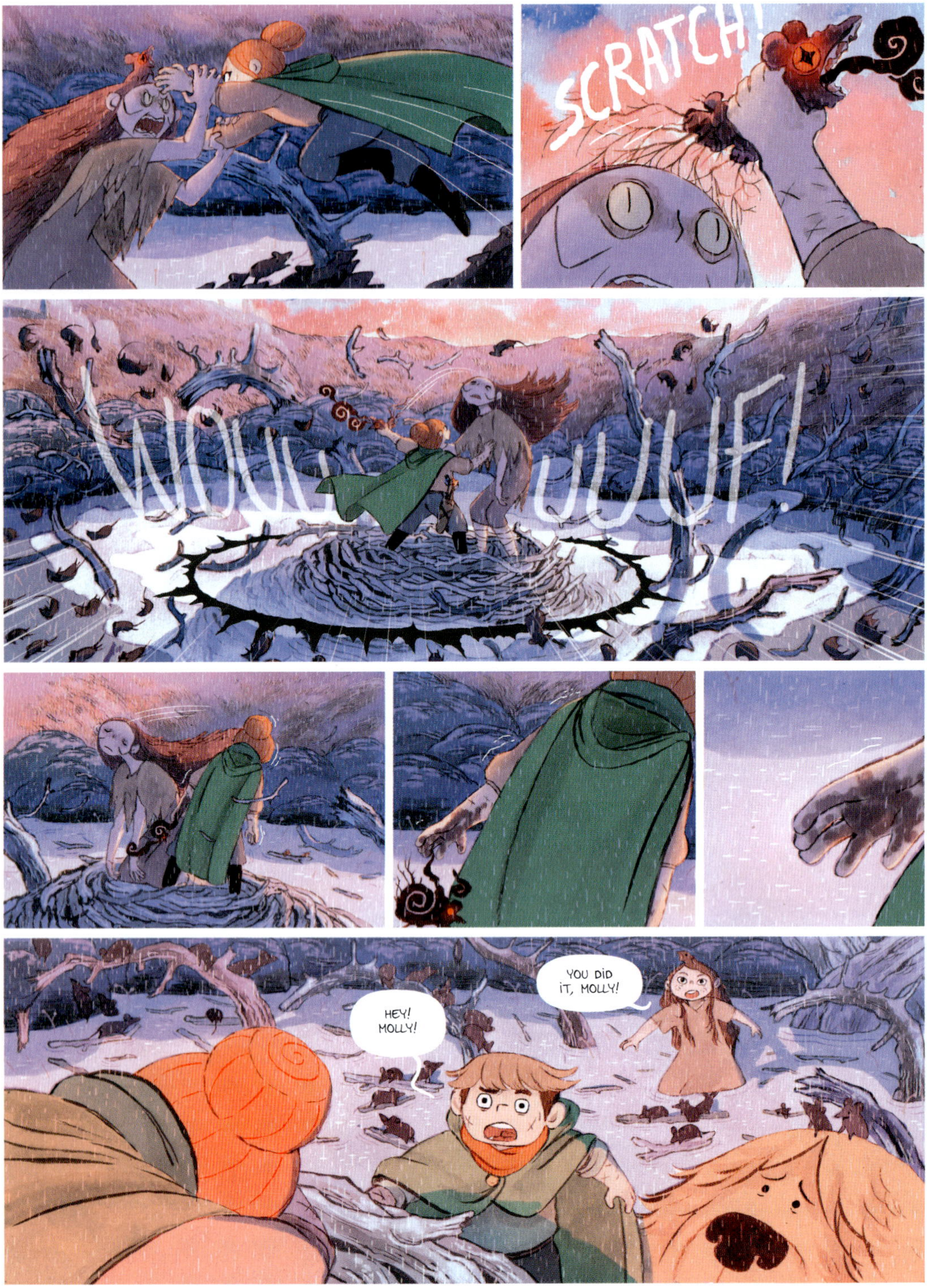
SCRATCH!
WOOUUUUUF!
HEY! MOLLY!
YOU DID IT, MOLLY!

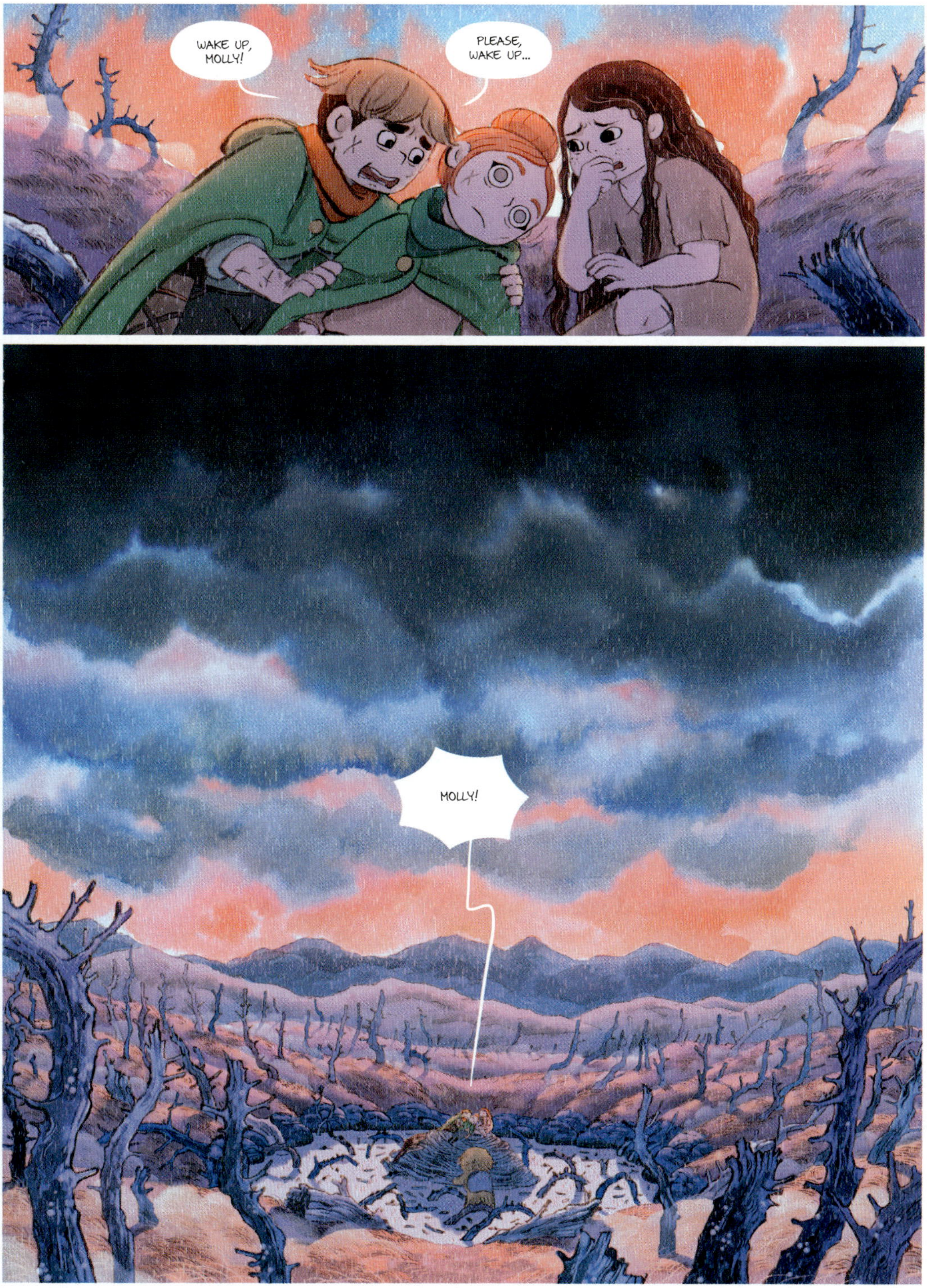
WAKE UP, MOLLY!
PLEASE, WAKE UP...
MOLLY!

TO BE CONTINUED...

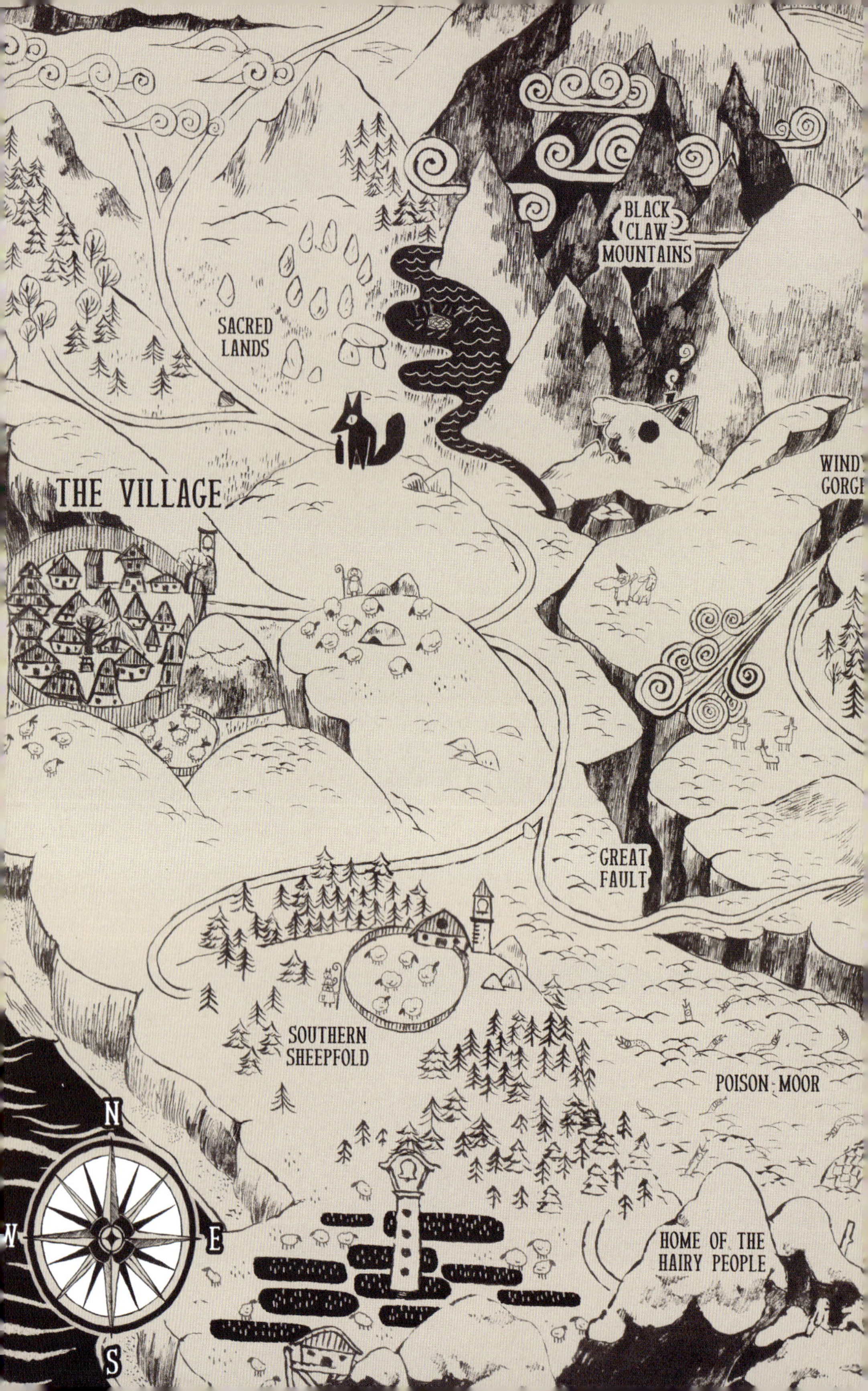

BLACK CLAW MOUNTAINS
SACRED LANDS
THE VILLAGE
WIND GORGE
GREAT FAULT
SOUTHERN SHEEPFOLD
POISON MOOR
HOME OF THE HAIRY PEOPLE
N
W
E
S

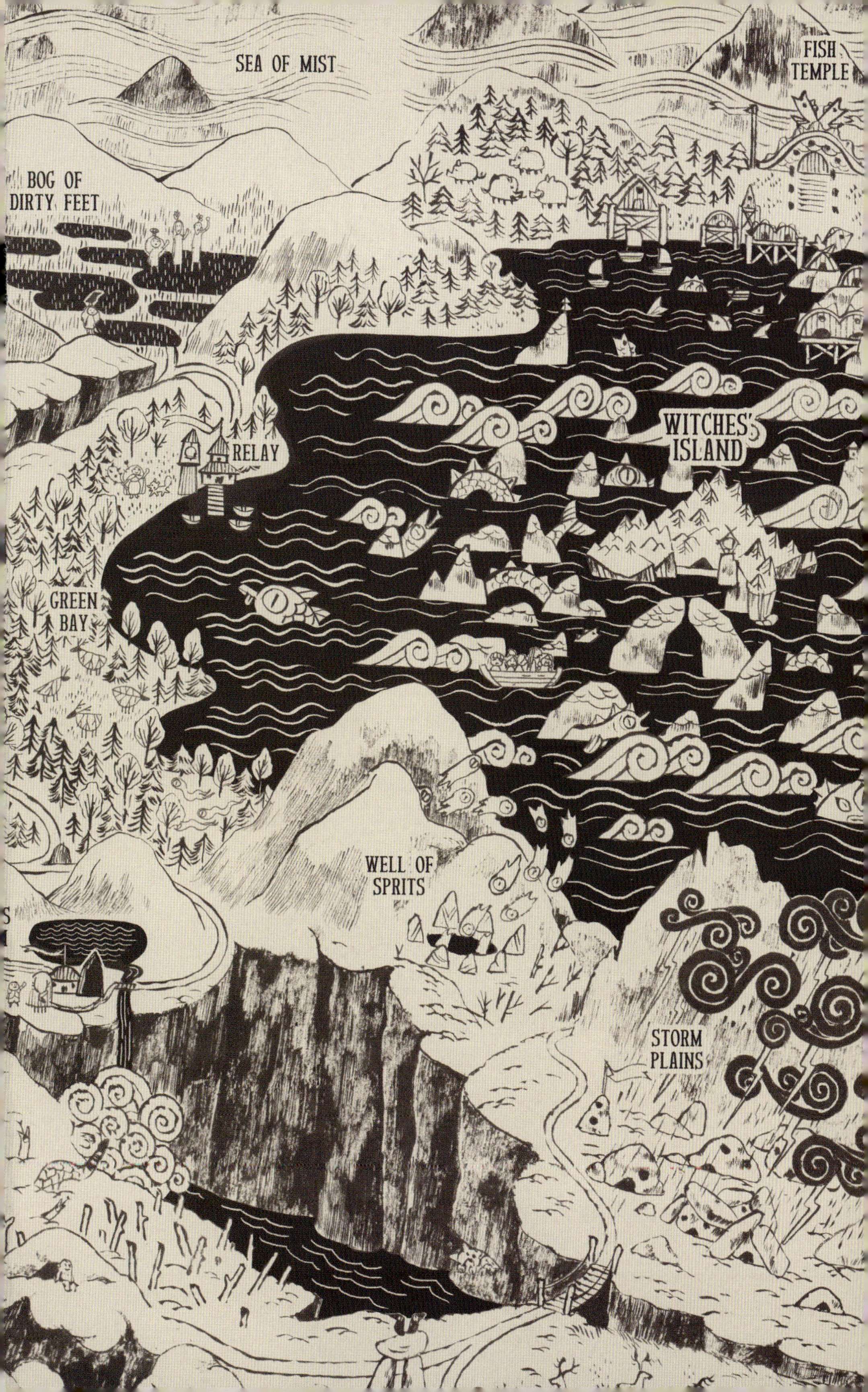
SEA OF MIST
FISH TEMPLE
BOG OF DIRTY FEET
RELAY
WITCHES' ISLAND
GREEN BAY
WELL OF SPRITS
STORM PLAINS

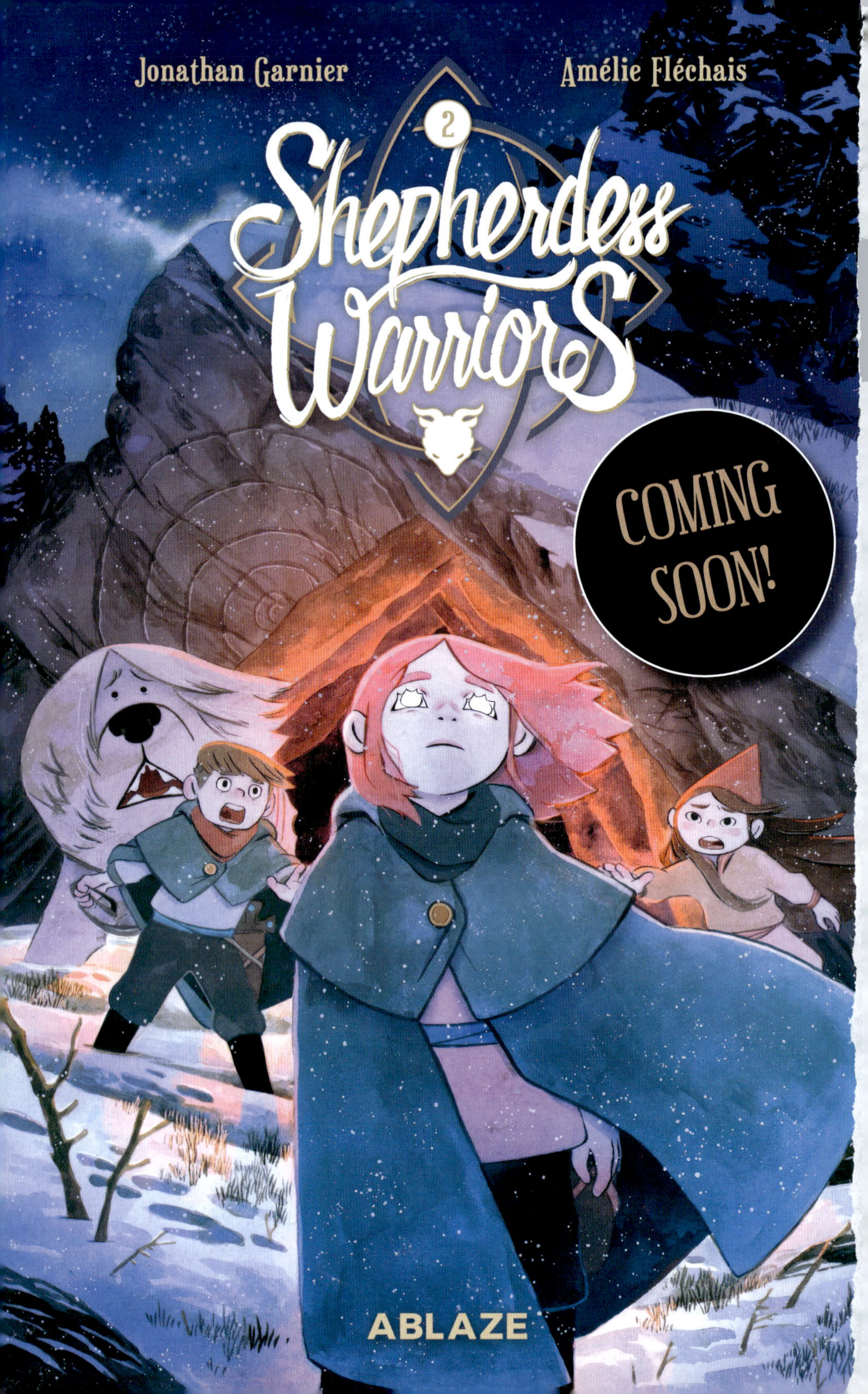
Jonathan Garnier
Amélie Fléchais
2
Shepherdess Warriors
COMING SOON!
ABLAZE

Contemporary Pragmatism

Edited by

John R. Shook &
Paulo Ghiraldelli, Jr.

Volume 2
Number 1
June 2005

Rodopi

AMSTERDAM - NEW YORK, NY 2005

The paper on which this book is printed meets the requirements of "ISO 9706:1994, Information and documentation - Paper for documents - Requirements for permanence".

ISSN: 1572-3429
ISBN: 90-420-1707-4
©Editions Rodopi B.V., Amsterdam - New York, NY 2005
Printed in The Netherlands

Contemporary Pragmatism

Volume 2 Number 1   June 2005

Contents

Symposium on Richard Rorty

Kai Nielsen
Pragmatism as Atheoreticism: Richard Rorty   1

Chandra Kumar
*Foucault and Rorty on Truth and Ideology: A Pragmatist View
from the Left*   35

Chase B. Wrenn
Pragmatism, Inquiry, and Truth   95

Christopher Voparil
On the Idea of Philosophy as Bildungsroman: *Rorty and his Critics*   115

Articles

Eugene Halton
Peircean Animism and the End of Civilization   135

David Boersema
Eco on Names and Reference   167

Sarah M. McGough
*Pragmatism and Poststructuralism: Cultivating Political
Agency in Schools*   185

Book Reviews

Mary Magada-Ward
Review of Sharyn Clough, *Beyond Epistemology: A Pragmatist Approach
to Feminist Science Studies*   203

Jacoby Adeshei Carter
Review of Hugh P. McDonald, *John Dewey and Environmental Philosophy*   208

Contemporary Pragmatism
Vol. 2, No. 1 (June 2005), 1–33

Editions Rodopi
© 2005

Pragmatism as Atheoreticism: Richard Rorty

Kai Nielsen

This essay offers an account of Rorty's version of pragmatism after the so-called linguistic turn, including his attack on epistemology and metaphysics, his metaphilosophy, his theory of morality, and his political philosophy. Woven into this account of Rorty are some of the most important criticisms made of Rorty, and considerations about how Rorty has responded or could have responded.

Richard Rorty is a controversial figure in contemporary philosophy. The very mention of his name in a respectful tone gets some philosophers hot under the collar and from others a prompt dismissal. Others, including some very important others, take him very seriously indeed. Among them some think his views are largely on the mark and importantly creative and innovative (e.g., Donald Davidson and Michael Williams) while others take him equally seriously but think his views are deeply and importantly flawed (e.g., Bernard Williams and Charles Taylor). I am, to show my colors, largely of the Donald Davidson-Michael Williams persuasion. I, like them, think Rorty is one of the most important philosophical figures of our time. While like them I have criticized and recorded my reservations about Rorty's work (Nielsen 1991; Nielsen 1996, 385–423; Nielsen 1999; and Nielsen 2003, 191–223), I continue to think he has clearly articulated some very important things in the way they should be articulated. Indeed I would conjecture (always a chancy matter concerning such things) that, like Ludwig Wittgenstein, John Rawls, Jürgen Habermas, W. V. Quine, and Davidson, Rorty will be studied in the next century and will not, like many others of current fame, become the Herbert Spencers of our time.

In accordance with such convictions, I shall here give an account of his version of pragmatism after the so-called linguistic turn, his attack on epistemology and metaphysics, his metaphilosophy and his accounts of morality and political philosophy. I will weave into my account what I take to be some of the most important criticisms that have been made of Rorty and consider some of the ways Rorty has responded or could have responded. As I have indicated above, I have in the past criticized Rorty but here I (for the most part) want to

bring out what he is up to, the power of it and some of why he has the stature I
have attributed to him. Rorty would scoff at being called a systematic philosopher but, as with Quine and Davidson, if one reads him attentively and in
detail it will become apparent how the various parts of his account fall into a
coherent and interrelated whole yielding an understanding and a vision that
gives us a remarkable take on what philosophy has been, is now and could,
with luck, become. I will try to provide a sense of something of that.

1. Pragmatism as Anti-Representationalism

Rorty, in a manner very unlike Wittgenstein's, is lavish with his isms. He
typically characterizes the stance he takes in terms of some ism or other
(though typically a negative one): anti-representationalism, anti-epistemology,
anti-essentialism, anti-metaethics, anti-ethical theory, anti-authoritarianism,
anti-grand social theory, anti-metaphysics, anti-Philosophy-philosophy and the
like. This could be summed up in what I think is a pervasive attitude, indeed a
deeply held conviction, of Rorty's, namely his *anti-theoreticism: his deep
distrust of theory.* This runs through all the topics he discusses, from
metaphilosophy to epistemology and metaphysics, to ethics and politics. The
pervasiveness and the rationale for this shall be a *leitmotif* of this essay.

One thing should be immediately recognized as problematic: the very
idea of anti-Philosophy-philosophy. That proves, some of his critics will say,
that Rorty wants to see the *end of philosophy* and indeed that he is being
frivolous about and dismissive of philosophy. Rorty rejects that characterization and one can see why from a characterization he makes in *The
Consequences of Pragmatism* (Rorty 1982, xiv–xvii). Rorty remarks that
"'philosophy' can mean simply what Sellars calls 'an attempt to see how
things, in the broadest possible sense of the term, hang together, in the broadest
possible sense of the term'." Rorty goes on to say (1) that "no one would be
dubious about philosophy taken in this sense" and (2) that this activity covers
many people, including many intellectuals, who would not normally be
thought to be philosophers and *may* exclude some professional people, able in
their own way, who are traditionally classified as philosophers, e.g., Alonzo
Church or Richmond H. Thomason. (Tolstoy or George Elliot, however, on the
above characterization, are philosophers and, as Rorty says, "Henry Adams
more of a philosopher than Frege.")

Rorty goes on to say, I repeat, "No one would be dubious about philosophy taken in this sense." But many would be dubious, and with good reason,
about *Philosophy*, which is something more specialized, where '*Philosophy*' is
taken to mean "following Plato and Kant's lead in asking questions about the
nature of certain normative notions (e.g., 'truth', 'rationality', 'goodness') in
the hope of better obeying such norms."[1] So *Philosophy* is an affair of the

*P*hilosophic Tradition while *p*hilosophy is something quite common and pervasive among reflective people and has nothing necessarily to do with any professional discipline or activity. "Pragmatists," Rorty adds, "are saying that the best hope for *p*hilosophy is not to practice *P*hilosophy. They think it will not help to say something true to think about Truth, nor will it help to act well to think about Goodness, nor will it help to be rational to think about Rationality" (Rorty 1982, xv).

Some might think that this is not only to be anti-theoretical but that it is also to be crudely Luddite. But we must remember that when Rorty is talking about Truth, Goodness and Rationality, he is taking them to be proper names of objects — goals or standards — objects of ultimate concern. He takes them to be interlocked Platonic notions. He has a long and careful elucidation of such notions and particularly of the whole Cartesian and Kantian traditions whose usefulness, and even their very intelligibility, he puts in question (Conant 1994, xxvii–xxxiii).[2]

The claim that there is nothing dubious or problematical about *p*hilosophy in contrast to *P*hilosophy, however, can be challenged by noting that philosophers like Wittgenstein would find both *p*hilosophy and *P*hilosophy problematic. Seeing how things hang together, especially in the broadest possible sense of the term, is no easy or unproblematic feat. It is not altogether clear what it would be like to do this or what our criteria for success here would be. To weave and unweave the web of our beliefs until we gain an understanding of the 'scheme of things entire' may be such an utterly hapless task — as hapless as *P*hilosophy — that it is better not to try to engage in it. Indeed we may only have an inchoate sense of what we are after.

However, on the contrary *p*hilosophy is not nearly as problematic as *P*hilosophy. We have some sense of what it would be like to forge a belief pattern that would cohere and not just be a mere jumble. Full and complete coherence is another thing. We have no idea what that is. But we have an idea how to get our affairs in order and we have some idea how people in Europe or North America, for example, should live. Not a precise idea, of course, but some, albeit contestable, idea that could be developed and articulated with persuasiveness and care. And when I said that philosophers like Quine, Davidson, and Rorty have accounts of philosophy that hang together, you understood something of what to expect in reading their accounts to either confirm or disconfirm what I said. We have, in fine, some coherent sense of how to do *p*hilosophy, but no coherent sense of how either intelligibly or usefully to do *P*hilosophy. The pragmatist realizes that she can best do *p*hilosophy by being anti-*P*hilosophical. She wants to bring an end to *P*hilosophy but not to *p*hilosophy. By doing *p*hilosophy she can perhaps gain something of a sense of things, make some sense of our world, some sense of the problems of human beings and how not to distract ourselves with the pseudo-problems of *Philosophy*: asking and giving fallibilistically, fully aware of our finitude, and without the 'ambition of transcendence', something of what a just society or even a world would be and something of how ways a life could be fulfilling. To translate into the concrete, as Rorty does in doing philosophy we can, for example, come to see how things under Bush-Blair are going very badly for democracy (Rorty 2004, 10–11). In seeking these things pragmatists do not expect a perfect fit, but they are not satisfied with just a jumble of beliefs either. They seek to give some coherence to their beliefs and some sense of what is important and what is not. Pragmatists, classical and neo, care about these things and believe that Platonic-like reflections on Reason, the Truth, and Justice will do nothing to yield enlightenment. Indeed these Platonic undertakings will just serve to impede our understanding of what Rorty's anti-theoreticism comes to or of how to make some sense of our lives or some sense of how things should be ordered in our world.

Rorty characterizes pragmatism as anti-representationalism (Rorty 1990; Rorty 1996, 635–37). This is a view which meshes nicely with *p*hilosophy and is a major tool in the setting aside of *Philosophy*, particularly in its Cartesian and Kantian forms. It is also a major tool in his attack on foundationalism, the conception of mind as a mirror of nature (a key notion in representational theories of knowledge), his rejection of correspondence theories of truth, his setting aside of epistemology and his rejection of the conception of knowledge as accurate representation depending on an *a priori* knowledge of mind as something inner that each of us has a direct and privileged access to and which affords *P*hilosophy with a foundational knowledge of 'ultimate reality', a grasp of 'the unconditional' and criteria of 'unconditional validity'.

As Rorty puts it in the very first page of *Philosophy and the Mirror of Nature*, "Philosophy as a discipline ... sees itself as the attempt to underwrite or debunk claims to knowledge made by science, morality, art or religion. It purports to do this on the basis of its special understanding of the nature of knowledge and of mind. Philosophy can be foundational in respect to the rest of culture because culture is the assemblage of claims to knowledge and philosophy adjudicates such claims" (Rorty 1979, 3). *Philosophers can come to know something, this traditional claim of *Philosophy* contends, that no one else can know so well. *Philosophy*, as Kant contended, is "a tribunal of pure reason, upholding or denying the claims of the rest of culture" (Rorty 1979, 4). It can do this in studying persons as knowers of the activity of representation. This will enable us, the claim goes, to see how knowledge is possible, how a knowledge is possible which consists in accurate representation of what is outside of the mind. To "understand the possibility and the nature of knowledge is to understand the way in which the mind is able to construct such representations" (Rorty 1979, 3).

On this traditional conception of *Philosophy* its core concern is to yield a general representation of reality. It will be a theory which will divide up culture into areas that "represent reality well, those which represent it less well, and those which do not represent it at all" (despite their pretense of doing so) (Rorty 1979, 3). Perhaps physics, sociology and theology would count as examples of each. The expectation that this traditional foundationalist conception of *Philosophy* gave expression to was that it was here where *Philosophy* enabled us to "touch bottom": where one found the convictions which permitted one to explain and justify one's activity *as* an intellectual and thus to discover the significance of one's life" (Rorty 1979, 4).

The long and complicated narrative — though a narrative packed with arguments — that is *Philosophy and the Mirror of Nature* documents such a conception of *Philosophy*. It does so first for Descartes' conception of mind pointing out how this came to seem compelling, shows why after all it wasn't, shows how foundational epistemology grew out of it in Locke's account which in turn led to Kant's synthesis responding to difficulties in Locke, how *Philosophy* came in the early twentieth century to then be transformed into foundational analytic philosophy and in turn how this was finally rather decisively undermined by the logical behaviorism of Sellars and Quine with Sellars displaying of the myth of the given and with Quine's attack on the claim to have *a priori* knowledge and to be able to demarcate the analytic and the empirical. This, together with the work of the latter Wittgenstein, undermined foundationalism and the claim to a distinctive role for *Philosophy* rooted in epistemology or conceptual analysis.

Rorty then goes on to consider the attempt to articulate a 'naturalistic epistemology' and then to articulate, criticize and set aside the attempt to articulate a philosophy of language with a theory of reference à la Saul Kripke, David Lewis and Hartley Field which, resisting the holism of Quine and Davidson, would (if successful) yield a metaphysical realism or a 'scientific realism' that appeals fundamentally to physics and takes physics at face value. Physics, as David Lewis claims, "professes to discover the elite properties" where 'elite properties' means the ones whose "boundaries are established by objective sameness and difference in nature" (David Lewis 1984, 226, quoted by Rorty 1991, 7). These 'elite properties' show how nature is carved at the joints yielding the one true objective description of the world. It yields (*pace* Putnam) an account of reference which is not 'made true' by our referential *intentions* (Lewis 1984, 227–28, italics mine). We have here the return of metaphysics in the form of a robust realism attuned, so it is claimed, to a scientific mindset.

I doubt very much if *physics* professes to discover such elite properties. Rather it is some *Philosophers* such as David Lewis who make such claims and that it is not a doctrine of physics that physicists have or even seek, namely a set of concepts that enable us to 'carve nature at the joints'. This is a meta-physical metaphor that some metaphysically inclined philosophers with the ambition of transcendence wish to attribute to physics. Indeed it may even be a metaphysical doctrine that some physicists nearing retirement seek to arti-culate. But it is hardly a part of physics itself. But be that as it may, Rorty responds to Lewis's scientific realism in the following way. He remarks that anti-representationalists "see no sense in which physics is more independent of our human peculiarities" than morality, social anthropology, literary criticism or a host of other practices — various areas of culture answering to different human needs and interests — viewing things from often different perspectives and with various interests in mind. We have, Rorty goes on to claim, no coherent conception of a language-independent determinate reality, no con-ception of how words relate to non-words such that the words picture them, no conception of how sentences correspond to facts (sentence shaped bits of the world) such that these true sentences picture them or, our intentions aside, no sense of how we can get an accurate representation of how things are in the world independent of a particular language or scheme of representation or a set of optional practices. We have no understanding of what it would mean to stand outside any language — any language at all — and just compare our language with the world to see how it maps it or mirrors it.

There is, no doubt, with many *P*hilosophers and theologians, an 'ambition of transcendence' but, *pace* Thomas Nagel or Stanley Cavell, we only have with such talk a blur of words and inchoate feelings without the slightest idea what it would be for us to achieve or in any way even to gesture at transcendence or in any way (*pace* Habermas and Karl-Otto Apel) to gain some 'universal validity' floating free of the contingencies of time and place and the imprint of what just happens to be our acculturation.

We understand how one cobbling together of beliefs may be more coherent than another. But this inescapably is just from where we stand, given our own take on things. But we have no idea what it would be like to gain a context-free coherence which just yields a cluster of beliefs or considered convictions that are justified *period*. Justification is always with reference to a given audience, with given interests at a particular time and place. Truth is usually time-independent but justification never is. We can sensibly aim at getting what for a time and place is the best justified cluster of coherently hanging together beliefs that careful inquiry can then attain, that at the time are best *taken* to be true, but they always might at some later time be reasonably taken to be false. We cannot simply by fiat or any other way rule this out. If we say we want beliefs or convictions that are not only the ones that at a given time are the most reasonable and reasonably taken to be true, but as well *just are true full stop*, then we are asking, not for a ton of bricks, but for the tone of bricks. If our aim is to obtain beliefs which just are true and known timelessly to be true, we have just another incoherent ambition of transcendence. There is no way to escape our finitude. No representationalist account or for that matter anti-representationalist account is going to give us such a skyhook for all times and climes: show us how our propositions (or sentences if you will) correspond to the way the world is — the way the world just is in itself. The ambition of transcendence is something we should resolutely set aside.

Anti-representationalism, to summarize, is an account "which does not view knowledge as a matter of getting reality right, but rather as a matter of acquiring habits of action for coping with reality" (Rorty 1991, 1). Anti-representationalists reject the very idea that beliefs can represent reality; they are neither realists nor anti-realists. Truth, they claim, is not an *explanatory* property. The correct but platitudinous "'P' is true if and only if P' does not claim that 'P' corresponds to or represents anything. Anti-representationalists reject the whole realist/anti-realist problematic, denying that the very idea "notion of 'representation' or that of 'fact of the matter' has any useful role in *philosophy*" (Rorty 1991, 2).

Rorty is not denying that there are links between our language and the rest of the world, but these links are *causal* not *epistemological*. We cannot avoid being in touch with the world. We have no idea of what it would be not to be in touch with it. As one macro-object we are constantly impinged on by other macro-objects both animate and non-animate. We causally speaking bang around like billiard balls colliding with each other.

Our languages, as much as our bodies, are shaped by our environment. Our languages could no more be 'out of touch' with our environment (grandiosely the world) than our bodies could. But we speak here of causal contact and not of representation. The fitting is a coping with our environment not a fitting by accurate representation. Rorty is thoroughly Darwinian. That is, like all the other pragmatists, Rorty takes Darwin seriously and tailors his account to fit and build on Darwin.

However, as Rorty asserts again and again in *Philosophy and the Mirror of Nature, causation is one thing and justification is another.* Like Davidson he thinks that only a belief can justify another belief. Justification comes through gaining a coherent pattern of beliefs. We, in weaving and unweaving our web of beliefs, justify them; and in doing this we justify one belief in terms of others. We seek, for a time, and for certain purposes, to get the most coherent pattern of beliefs we can forge. But all this justification is time and place and interest dependent. We never escape fallibilism and historicism. In pushing justification as far as it can go, we seek, for a time, the widest and most coherent cluster of beliefs we can muster, but each time for a particular purpose or set of purposes. We do not understand (perhaps *pace* Sellars) what it would be like to get the most coherent set of beliefs *period*.

We also need for justification to obtain to have an intersubjective consensus concerning this. It is these two things — having something that is intersubjective and having a consensus — which will give us the only viable conception of objectivity that we can have. Anything more is just *objectification* which gives us the usual Platonistic illusion. We have a fallibilistic, coherentist method of justifying beliefs replacing epistemology; we have as well a coherentist model of justification replacing a deductivist one. Anti-representationalism, at least Rorty style, is holistic, logical behaviorism, perspectival, anti-essentialist (nominalist), historicist, and fallibilist.

Critics have repeatedly attacked, with varying degrees of subtlety, this view as relativistic and/or irrationalist (e.g. Putnam 1990, 18–24; Kolakowski 1996, 52–57 and 67–76; and Bloom, 1987), decreasing in subtlety as we go from the first to the third. Rorty has repeatedly brushed these criticisms aside (Rorty 1991, 21–34, 203–10; Rorty 1996, 24–29, 31–51; and Rorty 1998a, 43–62).

A relativistic view is, as Rorty characterizes it, "the view that every belief on a certain topic, or perhaps about *any* topic is as good as every other" (Rorty 1982, 166). And an irrationalist is someone who says you can say anything or hold anything on any topic or issue you like whether you have any reasons for it or not if you feel like saying it or holding it. You should live by your gut feelings whatever they are no matter whether you have reasons for them or not. Rorty says that both these views are absurd views that practically no one holds. Certainly, as we already have seen, he does not hold them. He seeks to justify beliefs by getting them into coherent patterns and he attends to reasons for beliefs and against them and plainly regards these things as reasonable things to do. He does not think, however, that one can attain an ahistorical Archimedian point, that one can free oneself completely from one's acculturation and that one can escape ethnocentrism, not in the anthropologist's sense that we must think that what our culture thinks is so or right is so or right and that the beliefs of other cultures, where they differ from ours, must be wrong. That is that our tribe has the right way of viewing things and the other tribes, where they differ from us, are mistaken. But he was using 'ethnocentrism' to connote an inescapable condition — roughly synonymous with 'human finitude' *and* as loyalty to a liberal tolerant sociopolitical culture that prides itself as being open to other cultures and other points of view where these cultures are themselves tolerant (Rorty 1991, 15). In short, not being ethnocentric in the anthropologist's sense. But 'ethnocentric' in Rorty's sense of the unblinking acceptance of our finitude as inescapable and with it the recognition that we cannot stand utterly free from our culture and our place in history. But loyalty to such a liberal culture, as everyone knows, is not something that is universal. There are, of course, people, including intellectuals, as Rorty stresses elsewhere, who are not liberals: Nietzsche and Loyola, for example, and he could have added, to get a little more contemporary, Karl Schmidt (Rorty 1991, 179–84). We can call them mad if we like but that is just to hit them over the head with a conception of 'rational' from liberal culture — a conception which they do not share. Nor is it to refute them with arguments or to show our views to be in any way superior. Rorty takes this impasse or deadlock to be inescapable. Where our reflective equilibria are challenged, and for the fallibilist the most cherished practices in accordance with which she lives are challenged, there is, Rorty claims, nothing more non-circular that can be said. To try to push such questions so far is itself the irrational attempt by Platonic types — irrational because unintelligible — to seek to ground our practices, not just on other practices, but on something external to *all* other practices. Unless we believe that our belief-systems are like axiomatic systems — something they are not — there are no first principles that we *must* just start with and not question.

When many philosophers claim that Rorty is a relativist or irrationalist they are really accusing him of historicism and a practice-oriented philosophy. To that he will willingly plead guilty. But this is not relativism or irrationalism, but a claim that there is no absolute or ahistorical conception of justification that yields unconditionality. But this is not at all to claim that anything goes or that any belief is as good as any other. It is just to reject Absolutism and Platonism and it is anything but evident that Rorty is mistaken here.

Charges of his being caught in self-referential paradoxes or performative self-contradictions here rather naturally hove into sight. And they again have been pushed against Rorty's account. He responds, like Wittgenstein, that he has no *P*hilosophical views to set against representationalism, foundationalism, theories of truth, metaphysics, Platonic conceptions of the Good and the like. He is not claiming to have gotten things right. He is not a systematic philosopher with *P*hilosophical views on things, but he is, like Wittgenstein, Heidegger and Dewey, an edifying *p*hilosopher whose aim is to edify, that is to help his "readers, or society as a whole, break free from outworn vocabularies and attitudes, rather than to provide 'grounding' for the institutions and customs of the present" (Rorty 1979, 366–7). (This is not to say he is not a systematic philosopher in the sense mentioned earlier.)

Yet Rorty also refers to himself as an anti-representationalist, an anti-foundationist, an anti-essentialist. This seems to put him in a self-referential paradox. However, by using antis here he may be indicating he is rejecting views without asserting or assuming alternative views. Yet he also calls himself a pragmatist, a historicist, a nominalist, and a holist. There he seems to be asserting positive views, but then he seems at least to be unsaying what he says when he says he is setting out no philosophical views. But here his distinction between *P*hilosophy and *p*hilosophy frees him from self contradiction and from self-referential paradox. What Rorty is rejecting is

Philosophy — grand metaphysical, epistemological, or ethical theories — by claiming they are either useless or incoherent. But he is not doing it by making a Philosophical claim himself but by making a claim in philosophy which is for him the unproblematic hum-drum attempt to try to see how things hang together. In attacking these Platonic-Kantian conceptions and replacing them with his own non-Philosophical conceptions he is further showing how our concepts in practice hang together. He is being anti-Philosophical in being philosophical where Philosophy and philosophy refer to quite different activities. He would be in self contradiction if he claimed to be an anti-Philosophical Philosopher, but not by being an anti-Philosophical philosopher. Such a philosopher need not be setting one metaphysics against another or one epistemology against another. He just adds additional antis to his list and does that from a non-Philosophical point of view. He is not caught up in the Philosophical tradition anymore than Wittgenstein and Dewey were. Nor need he be authoritarian in espousing anti-authoritarianism. Rorty puts the matter rather differently himself in *Philosophy and the Mirror of Nature*, but in a way that is compatible with my more direct and less puzzling way in which I untangled him from a putative referential self-contradiction (Rorty 1979, 370–72).

I turn now to a very perceptive criticism of Rorty's account which I think actually comes to a *friendly amendment* which considerably strengthens Rorty's own account. It is an account given by Michael Williams (Williams 2003). Williams remarks, "Rorty betrays an attraction to views that are seriously in tension with the pragmatism he officially espouses" (Williams 2003, 62). Williams explains what is at issue and then proceeds to show why Rorty in line with his overall views shouldn't be attracted to such views.

Rorty, as we have seen, generally takes a fallibilist and historicist stance. Many beliefs vary extensively over time and place; even our firmest considered judgments, as Rawls acknowledges, are at least in principle revisable; there is no ahistorical standard, no universal criteria of validity or soundness of judgment to which we can appeal to assess whole belief-systems or forms of life or of what we take to be our most important and crucial commitments in some *final and unassailable* way. This is fallibilism and it comes to much the same thing as *mild* skepticism — Hume's 'mitigated skepticism'. It is the view, as Williams puts it, "that nothing is absolutely certain, that (given enough stage-setting) anything is revisable; that even the most deeply entrenched views can be revised or abandoned" (Williams 2003, 76). Williams goes on to characterize this mild or mitigated skepticism as fallibilism (Williams 2003, 76). *Radical* skepticism, he observes, is a much more severe form of skepticism. It holds "not just that nothing is absolutely certain: rather, with respect to a given subject matter, there is not the slightest reason for believing one thing rather than another" (Williams 2003, 76). But

Rorty, Williams acknowledges, sees the absurdity of this *radical* skepticism just as he does of relativism. He takes it as plainly so "that no one finds every view on any topic of importance equally appealing" (Williams 2003, 76).[3] No one, Rorty realizes, is either a *radical* skeptic or a relativist and there are good Davidsonian reasons (which Rorty accepts) for denying that anyone can be and that not because they take the views of common sense as practically authoritative (Williams 2003, 78). Whatever a person's belief about common sense, there are logical reasons for saying it is incoherent to be a *radical* skeptic. Belief must precede doubt and make doubt possible. Fallibilism teaches us that (1) we can doubt anything but not everything at once and (2) that we cannot even doubt unless we already believe some things. Universal Cartesian doubt is impossible, indeed conceptually incoherent. It is not enough to doubt to say 'I doubt'.

Indeed Peirce, Wittgenstein, and Davidson are very likely right that massive agreement is a precondition of meaningful disagreement. Williams remarks, correctly, that "the distinction between fallibilism and *radical* skepticism [and relativism] is crucially important for a philosopher like Rorty. This is because, while fallibilism is an essential part of pragmatism, *radical* skepticism is rooted in the very epistemological ideas that pragmatists reject (Williams 2003, 76, italics mine). Rorty generally sees this — for example in *Philosophy and the Mirror of Nature* and in *The Consequences of Pragmatism* — but he at times forgets it in *Contingency, Irony and Solidarity*. The culprits here are his talk of 'ultimate commitments', and 'final vocabularies' and his conception of irony. Rorty holds, in *Contingency, Irony and Solidarity*, that everyone subscribes to some ultimate set of commitments which they articulate in for them in some, what they take to be, 'final vocabulary'. Rorty puts it thus:

> All human beings carry about a set of words which they employ to justify their actions, their beliefs and their lives.... I shall call these words a person's 'final vocabulary'. It is 'final' in the sense that if doubt is cast on the worth of these words, their user has no noncircular argumentative recourse. Those words are as far as he can go with language; beyond them there is only helpless passivity or a resort to force (Rorty 1989, 73).

Pragmatists (including Rorty) should have no truck with '*final* vocabularies', '*ultimate* commitments', 'sets of *ultimate* commitments' or even of an ironist *as* someone who "has radical doubts about her final vocabulary", and with these radical, and continuing doubts, becomes a *radical* skeptic. This sounds more like existentialism or logical positivism where decision and commitment are king and is arbitrary. But a fallibilist (which is what a good pragmatist is, and Rorty usually is) and a logical holist are not like that, they have no final vocabulary. They will, as everyone will, carry about a set of words which they will employ to justify their actions, beliefs, and their lives. *At a given time* their spade *may* be turned, but later they may come to view things differently. For a fallibilist this can go on indefinitely. There is no point at which she *must* stop with some ultimate commitment and say 'Here I stand. I can do no other.' We do not have to go into circular arguments and, even if we do, if the circle is big enough, as Quine noted, no harm will be done. Faced with an argument or a rejection of what she (the fallibilist) says she just keeps the conversation going. She may be in what at least is an apparent head-on conflict and not know on a given occasion what to say. But there is no 'last word' or ultimate commitments functioning like axioms or ultimate postulates which for each person is her 'ultimate vocabulary' which can in no way be challenged and from which everything follows. That such, or indeed anything, is a 'last word' is not at all the fallibilist and holist picture. Williams well says, in good pragmatist fashion, "all we ever do is reweave the web of belief as best we know how in the light of whatever considerations we deem to be relevant.... Nothing is immune to revision" (Williams 2003, 78). We, of course, get tired, impatient, bored, or sometimes do not know what further to say. But we, or others later, may always pick up the conversation. There is no point at which it *must* halt: where the *final* word has been said. Williams remarks, "As a pragmatist, Rorty should have no truck with the language of 'finality'" (Williams 2003, 78). There are to be sure situations which can "arise that reveal differences of opinion that are deep and apparently irresolvable" (Williams 2003, 78). Williams remarks concerning this, in closing his essay, are very perceptive and I quote them in full.

> But the sort of holist Rorty generally claims to be should treat such irresolvability as always relative to our current argumentative resources, which are in constant flux. If we see no way to resolve a dispute maybe we should look for one. We may find one or we may not. It depends on ingenuity and luck. But whether a dispute can be resolved (or creatively transcended) is a thoroughly contingent affair. It offers no reason to think that there is a theoretically interesting, epistemically based partition of our commitments into those that involve elements of a final vocabulary and those that do not. For a holist, there is no such thing as a commitment that is ultimate in the sense that it *can* only be defended in a circular way, for there is no way of saying once and for all what our dialectical resources may turn out to comprise. Recognizing the contingency of our dialectical situation is the antidote to the virus of finality and thus the cure for the skeptical diseases it induces. Contingency is the friend of fallibilism but the sworn enemy of skepticism: that is of

irony. As we have seen this is Rorty's own insight. That he loses track of it is the most ironic result of all (Williams 2003, 79).

As I said at the beginning of my discussion of Williams, I take his criticisms to amount to a friendly amendment of Rorty's thought. I think it strengthens Rorty's account and takes out an important tension from his account. Sticking with fallibilism while eschewing radical skepticism brings out Rorty's better pragmatist self.

I want now in closing this section to remind us of some of the things that Rorty has achieved. When reflected on they should be seen to be really radical and innovative. He has given us a rationale for the setting aside of epistemology and the philosophy of mind. He has told a story of the development of modern philosophy from Cartesianism, to Locke, to Kant's transcendentalism synthesizing Cartesian rationalism with Lockean empiricism. And then he has trenchantly criticized Kantian transcendentalism. He has also shown us how neo-Kantianism finally transformed itself into the foundationalism of logical empiricism with *language* replacing *mind* as the key philosophical category. He then went on to depict how the holism and logical behaviorism of Wittgenstein, Quine, Sellars and Davidson radically transformed analytic philosophy and, in reality if not intent, brought about its demise except as a certain style of writing. With this, Rorty has it, we move from systematic philosophy aspiring to be a scientific discipline to edifying or therapeutic philosophy without such disciplinary or scientistic applications or rationale. This transformation from *P*hilosophy to *p*hilosophy: from a *discipline* which would, being the 'guardian of rationality', *ground* all knowledge in all areas of culture, to an *activity* which aids individuals or society as a whole to "break free from outworn vocabularies and attitudes" and to see a little better how things hang together and with this to somewhat more adequately make sense of their lives, eschewing the search for something unconditional and thus unattainable and perhaps even incoherent: some skyhook which provides "a 'grounding' for the intuitions and customs of the present"(Rorty 1979, 12; Rorty 1982, xiv). This plainly is a de-scientization and de-professionalization of philosophy, but it is a de-theoreticization of it as well. The novelist becomes closer to the *p*hilosopher than the physicist. The philosopher's very self-image changes. I will in the next section turn to Rorty's discussion of morality and his take on what moral philosophy should be like and in the section following that, to his discussion of politics and his thinking about society and social life. We should also note that talk of morality and normative politics is very much intertwined for him. We will see the great sea change from logical empiricism (from around 1940–1960) where the only legitimate ethical theory could be meta-ethics and the only legitimate *philosophical* treatment of political theory or politics could be 'meta-politics'.

2. Morality and Moral Philosophy

Rorty consistently with the increasingly greater influence of John Dewey on his thinking has turned more and more to writing and thinking, sometimes in concrete ways, about morality, society and politics while continuing his long term interest — some would say obsession — with metaphilosophy.

Rorty in these domains, as elsewhere, is determinately anti-theoretical. Meta-ethics, the tradition of moral theory, the epistemology of ethics and foundational moral theory yield, he has it, nothing of significance. There are the great dead philosophers of the Tradition, many of whom have carefully reflected on morality and politics and there are, as roughly our contemporaries, astute moral and moral and political philosophers such as John Dewey, John Rawls, Thomas Scanlon, and Jürgen Habermas, but their accounts (Dewey's less so than the others) are still, as Rorty sees it, importantly, including deeply methodologically, flawed. Moreover, Rorty also has it, we neither learn anything from them that we in non-philosophical ways did not know already nor rationally guarantee this knowledge in some securer way by studying such theories. We learn more about what it is to live a good life and what a good society would be like from reading good novelists, say George Elliot or Leo Tolstoy, or perceptive journalists of integrity, than we learn from philosophers. Philosophy with its over-systemization, claims to be yielding universal know-ledge and claims that unconditional validity is something to be had in moral theory. But this, Rorty claims, leads us down the garden path (Rorty 2000, 56–61). There is no unconditional validity in moral theory or anywhere else.

How then does Rorty approach such matters? Well he practices Wittgensteinian therapeutic philosophy *and* he gives us historical narratives of how and why we got into the various pickles we got into. What we are left with is to do some Augean stable cleaning and to do what he calls (misleadingly, I believe, to people who have not read Kierkegaard) 'edifying philosophy'. He offers a broadly Humean-Deweyian alternative to the claims of reason of the rationalist tradition. (He does this prominently in Rorty 1998a, 53–55, 167–85, 202–227; Rorty 1998b, 45–58; Rorty 1999, xvi–xxxii, 72–90; and Rorty 2000, 1–30 and 56–64.)

I shall first focus on his "Ethics Without Principles" (Rorty 1999, 72–90) because in it he marshals together succinctly and clearly his central claims about morality. Here he makes plain how pragmatists — he has principally in mind himself and Dewey — want to get rid of the notion so prominent in Kant of unconditional moral obligation (Rorty 1999, 83). Moreover, pragmatists do not believe in *unconditional* human rights. We do not have rights (*pace* Ronald Dworkin) that just trump other considerations *in all situations*: that give us something that can never rightly be overridden. Rorty's account of morality, by contrast, is thoroughly historicist, anti-essentialist, and contextual, rejecting all claims to substantive universal moral principles or claims to unconditionality.

Rorty takes, as does Dewey, Darwin seriously, arguing that we differ from other animals simply in the complexity of our behavior though of course part of that behavior consists in the unique ability to speak. Following up on that "pragmatists ... treat inquiry — in both physics and ethics — as the search for adjustment, and in particular for that sort of adjustment to our fellow humans which we call 'the search for acceptable justification and eventual agreement'" (Rorty 1999, 72). We should call this 'inquiry' and not call it, as it has been traditionally called, 'being on the quest for truth'. This does not mean we cannot say, as good disquotationalists, that moral utterances in the indicative mode can be said to be true or false (Rorty 1998a, 19–42). But there is no goal of inquiry or deliberation that gains truth though there is a goal that consists in getting the best justified beliefs that we can get and this is so as much for ethics as for physics (Rorty 1999, 72–90). We act to cope with ourselves, with others and with our environment. That rather than representation is what goes on. That fits perfectly with Darwin and a Deweyian form of naturalism where *objectivity* comes to *intersubjectivity* and where we get a holism and a logical behaviorism. Moreover, unlike an anti-realism in ethics or a non-cognitivism or an error theory, on this pragmatist account, moral judgments are just as embedded in the world as biological ones or the claims of physics. We, as we have noted, are always in *causal* contact with the world. We could not fail to be and as far as justificatory contact goes both the claims of science and the claims of morality are justified in a basically similar coherentist way. Moreover, since pragmatism is anti-essentialist, moral values have not intrinsic versus extrinsic features. Everything for an anti-essentialist is relational through and through, so we cannot have a Platonic world with a contrast between appearance and reality or an empirical realm and a *noumenal* realm (the latter, for Kant, being the proper realm of morality) (Rorty 1999). There is no way to ask, as the radical skeptic wishes, 'Is our knowledge of things adequate to the way things really are?' Instead pragmatists ask: Are our ways of describing things, of relating them to other things, such as to make them fulfill our needs more adequately then our prior ways of describing things and responding to them? Or can we do better? Can our future be made better than the past? This can be a question of morality as well as in physics. We get no morality/science divide, and no is/ought divide. Values and facts, in a means-end continuum, are always scrambled together and they cannot be unscrambled.

We are not going to get the Kantian and even Wittgensteinian distinction between categorical imperatives and hypothetical ones (Wittgenstein 1993, 37–44). We are not going to get the unconditionally claimed by both Kant and Wittgenstein because, given anti-essentialism, nothing could be unrelated and not causally dependent on other things. But all the ways things are related to each other are through and through contingent.

We get prudential matters, Rorty argues, somewhat misleadingly using 'prudential', when we have customs or habits, routine matters, where various such practices are simply routinely a matter of doing the thing done; doing, as Rorty puts it, what comes naturally, e.g. looking after one's children or normally telling what one sincerely believes to be the truth. By contrast morality and law arise, he has it, when we can no longer rely on habit or custom. We are in such a situation when a person's needs begin to "clash with those of her family, or her family's with those of the neighbor's, or when economic strains begins to put her community into warring classes, or when the community must come to terms with an alien community." We will have to move from the routine of the doing of the thing done to deliberation, to figuring out (if we can) what is to be done. And there moral issues arise. As Dewey puts it, "Right is only an abstract name for the multitude of concrete demands in action which others impress upon us, and of which we are obliged, if we would live, to take some account." However, it is important to recognize that this distinction between custom (the routine) and morality (the non-routine) is a distinction of degree not of kind. For Kant (and for Wittgenstein as well) such a pragmatist conception of morality is a denigration of morality. It doesn't catch the categoricalness of morality, the demandingness of the ought. It merely talks about people's adjusting their needs to others' needs and deliberating on how to do this when doing so is not something that is obvious and routine. But Rorty thinks this is all we can reasonably expect to get. Moreover, it suffices. Belief in categoricalness is illusory and unnecessary.

Rorty, while recognizing important differences between Hume and Dewey, thinks that over morality they are both playing on the same side of the street, particularly if we have in mind the Hume of Annette Baier's *A Progress of Sentiments*. Hume, Dewey, and Baier, Rorty argues, together contrast well with Kant and such Kantian philosophers as Apel and Habermas. Kant makes a sharp distinction between reason and sentiment. And Kant took the essence of reason to be "complete universality (and hence necessity and immutability..." (Rorty 1999, 75). Thus for him and for Kantians generally they are on the reason side of the so-called reason/sentiment split; Hume, Baier, Dewey and Rorty himself come down on the sentiment side. Baier praises Hume for "his willingness to take sentiment, and indeed sentimentality, as central to the moral conscience" and for "de-intellectualizing and de-sanctifying moral endeavor ... presenting it as the human equivalent of various social controls in animal or insect populations" (quote by Rorty 1999, 76). Kant, by contrast, as with Plato before him, sought to escape contingency by seeking in the *noumenal* realm immutable moral truth. Kant, without being able, except terminologically, to get out from under Plato, had, as we have seen, a conception of the essence of reason as complete universality and with it necessity and immutability, seeking to ascertain what is to be done from the very idea of *universalizability:* something which yields only formal formulae, e.g. "If X is good for B in situation Y it must also be good for anyone relevantly like B in the same or relevantly similar situations." If I say this is a good apple I cannot consistently deny that an apple exactly like that apple is also a good apple. But such things remain hypothetical and do not determine anything *substantive.* So much for the categorical imperative — the vaunted foundation of morals; Rorty remarks, "All that the categorical imperative does, Dewey said, is to commend 'the habit of asking how we should be willing to be treated in a similar case'" (Rorty 1999, 75).

Hume, by contrast, and Rorty believes rightly, and with a sense of realism, believes that what is key to moral understanding is human sentiment and particularly sympathy. The thing to do is see how morality is rooted in our emotional life and with that de-intellectualizing and de-sanctifying moral endeavor: pulling it down from its reified Platonic and Kantian heaven. Hume, Dewey and Rorty distrust the notion of moral obligation and with Baier would take appropriate *trust* to be the central moral notion. Rorty is attuned to Baier's claim that the "villain is the rationalist, law-fixated tradition in moral philosophy" — a tradition, Rorty claims, "which assumes that 'behind every moral intuition lies a universal rule'" (Rorty 1999, 76). But that is just our old friend *universalizability* again. Rorty goes on to add that the "tradition assumes that Hume's attempt to think of moral progress as progress of sentiments fails to account for our feeling for moral obligation.... [But] there is nothing to account for; moral obligation does not have a nature, or a source, different from tradition, habit and custom. Morality is simply a new and controversial custom" (Rorty 1999, 76). It is a new practice, which with us children of the Enlightenment and modernity, seeks to widen our sympathies and loyalties to the whole human race (Rorty 1998b, 45–58). But, with his thorough anti-essentialism and historicism, Rorty sees nothing in our human natures or in our reason that, apart from a particular acculturation, imperatively drives us this way. Hume's 'natural sympathies' are simply sympathies arising from and structured by a certain sort of acculturation. Rorty takes human nature to be malleable all the way down. It is just a contingent fact about some of us that we have such sympathies. When this phenomena is thoroughly secularized and naturalized and with this de-mythologized and sentimentalized we get a Kantian/Habermasian universalism *so transformed.* Still a Humean universalization of the sentiment of sympathy may not obtain. There is nothing about us that will make it the case that such Humean sentiments will obtain. Cosmopolitan liberals will *hope* that such sentiments will become very widespread. But that is a hope not a warranted belief that it is likely to obtain.

Rorty's account here is often just rejected out of hand. Thomas Nagel (Nagel 1998, 3), for example, says of Rorty's "Human Rights, Rationality and Sentimentality" that it is perfectly awful (Rorty 1998a, 167–85). Philosophers such as Bernard Williams, Ernest Gellner, and David Lewis find Rorty's account, to put it mildly, deeply flawed. And philosophers, in some ways similar to Rorty, such as Hilary Putnam, Stanley Cavell, James Conant, and Jürgen Habermas, find it relativistic, subjectivistic, debilitatingly skeptical and some even find it, in effect, nihilistic. Rorty has been at pains to patiently reply. A core response is his distinguishing *ethnocentrism* (our finitude, our being without an Archimedian point, our not getting a point of view outside of our practices and language-games to assess them) *from relativism*. He remarks ".. there is no truth in relativism, but this much truth in ethnocentrism: we cannot justify our beliefs (in physics, ethics, or any other area) to everybody, but only to those whose beliefs overlap ours to some appropriate extent" (Rorty 1991, 30). This is the core to Rorty's response to such criticisms. He thinks that the attempted escape from ethnocentricity (as he characterizes it) is like trying to escape our finitude and to see things somehow *sub specie aeternitatis*. But that is like trying to molt out of our skins.

Yet most philosophers throughout the history of philosophy have been trying to do this. Is this all dross and illusion, however psychologically understandable? Rorty thinks that it is. His most famous (infamous?) making of a case for it occurs in what some think are a chilling few pages in his "Hilary Putnam and the Relativist Menace" (Rorty 1998a, 50–55).

There I think Rorty well brings out what is at issue and why it is so important. He begins with the familiar and widely accepted distinction between truth and justification. Justification, as we have seen, is time and place dependent but truth is not. For something to be warrantedly assertable it is no more than for us to be able to figure out whether a person or persons is (are) in a good position, given her or their interests and values, and "those of [her or] their peers, to assert some statement p." This is why Rorty asserts, rather disconcertingly to some philosophers, that he "views warrant as a *sociological matter, to be ascertained by observing the reception of a person's statement by his peers*" (Rorty 1998a, 50, italics mine). This just seems to delete the normative and to geld warranted assertability. But Rorty presses us to say what more could be meant by warrant, given the inescapability of ethnocentrism. How could we, he presses us, get a "non-sociological sort of justification...?"

Putnam sees it as *a reductio* of such a conception that Rorty holds no appeal can be made to a 'fact of the matter' "to adjudicate between the possible world in which the Nazis win out, inhabited by people for whom the Nazis' racism seems common sense and our egalitarian tolerance crazy, and the possible world in which we win out and the Nazis' racism seems crazy" (Rorty 1998a, 51).

Rorty claims there is no fact of the matter that would settle that dispute. To believe the contrary, he argues, rests on taking "truth as idealized acceptability." But that claim, besides being false, can mean no more than 'rational acceptability to an ideal community'. That is all 'idealized rational acceptability' can mean. Moreover, since no such community "is going to have a God's eye view, this ideal community cannot be anything more than *us* as we should like to be" (Rorty 1998a, 52). Moreover, he challenges us to say what the 'us' can mean here except "us educated, sophisticated, tolerant liberals, the people who are willing to hear the other side, to think out all the implications, and so on" (Rorty 1998a, 52). In short, the sort of persons that both Putnam and he would like to be at their best. Rorty remarks, "Identifying 'idealized rational acceptability' with 'acceptability to *us* at our best' is just what I had in mind when I said pragmatists should be enthnocentrists rather than relativists" (Rorty 1998a, 52).

But when 'being warranted' can mean no more than being 'rationally acceptable' this will always invite the question 'To whom?' That question will always lead back, Rorty claims, "to the answer '*us*' at our best. So all a fact of the matter whether p is a warranted assertion can mean is a fact of the matter about our ability to feel solidarity with a community that views p as warranted" (Rorty 1998a, 53).

Putnam rejoins to this, but in a possible world in which the Nazis win "Rorty himself would not feel solidarity with the culture that results." Rorty in turn remarks, "But neither would Putnam, nor the rest of 'us' just described. The presence or absence of such a sense of solidarity is [says Rorty], on my view, the heart of the matter" (Rorty 1998a, 53). Then he gives what has been felt to be his really repugnant case.

> Part of the force of the Darwinian picture I am suggesting is that the spirit of Sartre's famous remarks about a Nazi victory was right, though the letter is a bit off. Sartre said:
>
> > Tomorrow, after my death, some men may decide to establish Fascism, and the others may be so cowardly or slack as to let them do so. If so Fascism will then be the truth of man, and so much the worse for us." (From Jean-Paul Sartre, "Existentialism is a Human-ism" from Walter Kaufmann, ed., *Existentialism From Dostoevsky to Sartre*, New York: American Library, 1975, p. 358).
>
> Sartre should not have said that Fascism will be "the truth of man." There is no such thing. What he should have said is that the truth (about certain very important matter, like whom one can kill when) might be forgotten, become invisible, get lost — and so much the worse of *us*. 'Us' here does not mean 'us humans' for Nazis are humans too. It means something like 'us tolerant wet liberals'. So much the worse for

truth too? What does that question mean? I take the force of the antiabsolutism embodied [in the above text] is that it doesn't mean *anything* — that we cannot find a purpose for this additional comment. When we go so do our norms and standards of rational assertability. Does truth go too? Truth neither comes nor goes. That is not because it enjoys an atemporal existence, but because 'truth' in this context is just the reification of an approbative adjective, an adjective whose use is mastered once we grasp, as Putnam puts it, that a statement is true of a situation just in case it would be correct to use the words of which the statement consists in that way in describing the situation.' Correct by whose standards? Ours. Who else's? The Nazis'? (Rorty 1998a, 53–54).

This puts forcefully why many people have thought Rorty's views relativistic, subjectivistic or nihilistic. It should be seen, we now see, as ethnocentric, but ethnocentric or relativistic or subjective, it would still mean for groups who forms of life greatly differ, e.g. the Nazis and us, the Azande and us, Fundamentalists and us, or the Fundamentalists of our culture and other Fundamentalists, that there would be no way, without asserting some particular ethnos, of saying which of these opposing belief systems are right and which are wrong or more nearly one or the other. We *seem* here just stuck with our own beliefs or belief-systems. This ethnocentrism is what many have thought of as relativism because for a person encultured in one way there is no transcending his or her way, where the enculturation of the conflicting groups is very different, to allow him or her to decide on any other belief-system than his or her own. For there to be an alternative and thus a way of arguing, deliberating, or conversing our way into making something like a gestalt-switch in our beliefs, the people opposing us must be "language users whom we can recognize as better versions of ourselves." But we liberals and the Nazis regard each other as mad, not as people we can converse with. We are simply abusive to each other (and by our own lights rightly), but then there is (or at least seems to be) no way of reasoning or talking it out so as to come to agreement or at least to *agree* to disagree. There seems to be either avoidance or fighting and where avoidance is impossible one group will use its force to make the other group submit. Power, brute power, calls the tune.

That is what it in fact came to. And we non-Nazis are grateful that the outcome was as it was given what the Nazis had become. Is there any good reason to think it *must* come to that? For it not to come to that or its opposite exercise of brute power, it must be the case that there is an overlap between their beliefs and ours to some *appropriate* extent.[4] Is that the case between us and the Nazis? The mutual characterizing of the other as mad strongly suggests there is not. Moreover, we liberals have the gut feeling that even the very idea of talking it out with the Nazis is obscene. The very idea is abhorrent to us and the reasons are obvious. But also plainly the feeling is mutual.

However, suppose counterfactually the situation is such that somehow it is impossible to fight or more realistically that in the fighting we come to a stalemate of exhaustion where we realize that neither of us can win and that there is no rational alternative to talking. Is there nothing we could say to each other? Remember the Nazis were part of a wider civilization — they did not come down from Saturn — and many were highly educated both in the sciences and the humanities and that the Nazi regime was the successor to the liberal culture of Weimar. Is there no overlap of beliefs to a sufficiently appropriate extent to make conversing and persuasion possible? A crucial sticking point with us liberals (or socialists) is their racism. But for those Nazis at least who are educated, couldn't we point out (now assuming we have to talk seriously and not blow smoke in each other's eyes) that there is no such thing as 'the Jewish race' or the 'Aryan race'? What they thought in the case of the Jews was a race was an ethnic group with a distinctive religion. And the so-called 'Aryan race' was neither a race nor an ethnic group. Jews, whatever the image the Nazis have of them, belong to the same racial group with the same evolutionary history as non-Jews. An informed Nazi and a sophisticated Nazi must have known that or could in reality (if he is not too blocked) be taught that. Many Nazi intellectuals would have been so warped that they would not hear it or were afraid to hear it. But it is possible and indeed probable to believe that a sophisticated Nazi could reply "Of course there is no Jewish race. That is just ideology to build on the Christian anti-Semitic prejudices of the masses to insure than they will be with us in creating a *Juden-Frei* world." To the question, "Why do you want to exterminate them?" the sophisticated Nazi responds "Yes, if that it is a necessary preliminary to our forging of a pagan Nordic civilization that will be free of such abhorrent things as Judaism and Christianity." He goes on to add that after they have done with the Jews, and when the time is ripe, though in some other way, *given their numbers* and the need for our utopia to keep some mass of people, we should abolish Christianity and reeducate — that is, reprogram — Christians and eradicate those we cannot. But given their numbers reeducating them is desirable. "If they were a small group," says ours sophisticated Nazi, "it would be perhaps simpler and more effective just to eradicate them." But the central point is that only by acting in one or another of these ways can we build our Nordic pagan utopia. But, it should be responded, if the situation somehow requires further argument, even here it is possible to argue, though how we would do it is somewhat less obvious. We do not have here something which is 'essentially contested' or 'incommensurable' for nothing is. But we also sense that there is something phony and disgusting about engaging in argument here. We liberals know that we are not going to go over to the Nazi side. No matter how the argument goes here we will stand pat. Moreover, the very idea of arguing with such people with those views seems to us revolting. Does this somehow throw a monkey wrench into the discussion?

Some more theoretical considerations should back up the case that there is always room, no matter how difficult or how unwanted, for conversation and argument to go on, we are saddled with fallibilism not radical skepticism, relativism or decisionism and that that makes the difference. These considerations are from the very notions that Rorty has taken from Davidson on communication, the rejection of the scheme/content distinction and his argument for the incoherence of incommensurability. Rorty, abandoning his earlier belief in incommensurability, and with his acceptance of Davidson's account as the best game in town, gives reasons for our being assured that between people there must always be a large overlap of beliefs always making conversation possible.[5] Liberals and Nazis do not inhabit 'different worlds', have such different belief systems that it makes talk and possible agreement between them impossible. Neither, when they must talk, and talk sincerely, can they come away from that conversation quite the same as before it. And the same obtains for us. No matter how abhorrent Nazism is, we liberals, can find some wiggle room for talk if we will or if our circumstances are such that we must. We are never in the position, *theoretically speaking*, where we must just say 'Here I stand. I can do no other; my spade is turned.' To think otherwise is a common error of existentialism and non-cognitivist decisionism: the common error of Sartre and Reichenbach. There never is a last word between us and the Nazis such that we just have to decide without any reason what is to be done. But I do not speak of necessarily having decisive reasons. Moreover, that many can be expected to ignore them does not gainsay what I have just been saying. That sometimes people will just fail to take into consideration what is plainly before them does not show that they do not have reason to assent to those reasons. Given that I want to be healthy and want to live a long time means that I have reason to exercise whether I acknowledge it or act on it or not.

This brings us back to Michael Williams's friendly amendment of Rorty's account — an amendment that I argued Rorty should adopt to make his account more consistent and more persuasive. The same should be said for moral beliefs as was said about non-moral beliefs. There is no room for *radical* skepticism in the domain of morals either. It is not, from a justificatory point of view, how we just happen to feel, rooted in what turns out (causally speaking) to be the most embedded aspects of our acculturation that is crucially relevant concerning issues of what is to be done.[6] And a recognition of this is not to abandon Rorty's Darwinian perspective. Radical skepticism over morals is as much an enemy of pragmatism as is such skepticism over scientific and 'epistemological' inquiries. Fallibilism, an integral part of pragmatism, is what we need, not radical skepticism over morality. We can, and should, make appeals to a de-mythologized conception of reasonableness, something roughly after the fashion of Rawls or Scanlon, and do that without making a split between reason and sentiment and without being captured by the rationalism of Reason of either Plato or Kant or of the latter's contemporary, more or less, followers. We can speak of reasonableness without rationalism or universal validity and still keep the emotional roots of our moral lives (a gesture here in the direction of Hume). Remember there is no *last* word so that we must just rely on our commitment.

3. Politics and Political Thought

As we shall see, Rorty's account of politics and political thought fits hand and glove with what he says about morality. In fact, and more broadly, in spite of, or perhaps because of, Rorty's eschewing of *P*hilosophy for *p*hilosophy his account of morals and politics is remarkably well meshed, fitting in exemplary fashion Sellars's conception of *p*hilosophy as the attempt to see how things hang together in the broadest sense of the term. With Rorty's anti-*P*hilosophy *p*hilosophy and his anti-theoretical views concerning what he said about epistemology, it came as no surprise what he said about morality. The same thing follows for politics: what he says about it is prefigured in what he says about morality and epistemology; that is, it is easy to predict over general matters what he will say about politics and political thought from his views which we have already discussed. His anti-representationalism, his anti-essentialism, his holism, logical behaviorism, his historicism, his finitism are consistently applied in all domains of his thought and action yielding a coherently articulated pragmatism (though a pragmatism rather different from any of the classical pragmatisms). This goes as well for what I have called his anti-*P*hilosophy *p*hilosophy and his anti-theoreticism.

   With no more prolegomena, I shall now turn to his views on politics and political thought building on what he has said about morality and moral thought. Rorty is a passionate and committed — his ironism notwithstanding — social democratic liberal (Rorty 1998c). But consistent with his views on philosophy, it is a liberalism without foundations or some other kind of grounding — Kantian or utilitarian or in critical theory.

   Some philosophers, such as Rawls and Scanlon, give an *articulation* of liberalism — they clarify the ways it hangs together and has a rationale — but they cannot, Rorty has it, give, nor can anyone else, a grounding or philosophical justification (particularly 'an ultimate' justification) of liberalism or any other political or social orientation. All they can do, and not only them, is play vocabularies (clusters of beliefs) off one against another and suggest, concerning the old vocabularies, that we might try some other way of viewing things for we might like it better: it might more adequately meet our needs. It might open up some new things for us (Rorty 1998a, 202–27). This is sure to make many philosophers unhappy. As we have seen in discussing his anti-foundationalism, anti-essentialism, historicism, and more generally his anti-*Philosophy philosophy*, there are metaphysicians who will have strong desires for more, but, if Rorty is on the mark, they can't coherently get it (which means they can't get it). Rorty rejects a transcendental deduction of liberalism and reads Rawls as doing the same and thus rejects Habermas's attempt to do so as well as Kant's (Rorty 1991, 189; Rorty 2000, 56–64).

How can he (if he can) do that? He does it by putting *politics first and philosophy afterwards*; he does it by putting concrete political policies — specific suggestions and plans for what is to be done before principles; he proceeds by self-consciously starting from where we are in the life-world before theorizing about this life-world. As Rawls starts with considered judgments and seeks to forge them into a wide and general reflective equilibrium (a consistent, coherent and perspicuous account of them) so, Rorty has it, we in the liberal democracies should start our political thinking with our distinctive rather specific moral and political beliefs (protection of civil liberties, the importance of equality, avoidance of unnecessary suffering, universities where freedom of speech is respected and free discussion is encouraged, a country where genuinely free elections obtain with universal suffrage, where the rule of law is respected, where the right to immigrate and emigrate is honored, and the like) and then construct political principles to help further explicate and render coherent the rationale of these practices so that these specific political beliefs that are part of our political culture are not seen to be just a jumble and a mess, yet where the concrete practices structure the principles we have and where *sometimes* the principles alter some of the practices or support new ones. But it is crucially mainly a bottoms up approach, though it remains an education in the coherence of considered convictions. Philosophy grounds nothing, but it can, with luck and energy, reorder more perspicuously what we have and suggest, *starting* by our own lights — whatever other light could we have? — new and inventive ways of doing things and seeing ourselves. Rorty rightly points to feminism as instancing something that has done this for us (Rorty 1998a, 202–27). Moreover, political thinking and responding has sometimes enlivened us to new utopian futures. But the principles and the philosophical articulations and indeed idealizations are always parasitical on the practices, though out of the smithy of them new practices will sometimes emerge and many practices will change sometimes suggested by the principles we have or the new philosophic conceptions we with ingenuity create or come to entertain.

Still it is democracy before philosophy. The tail never wags the dog. *Philosophy* only articulates, perspicuously displays, suggests; it does not ground politics or even adjudicate political issues. It is in our specific concretely articulated and practically articulated proposals and actions where it is determined what is to be done sometimes with an ancillary helping hand from theory. *Praxis*, to use the jargon, rules the day.

But that is not the way the cultural left in Europe and North America sees it. *Philosophy*, often arcane *Philosophy*, is the thing for that left in Europe and in North America. *Philosophy*, the obscurer the better, is somehow taken as an indispensable backup for left politics. Rorty remarks, "Philosophy is 'in' on the left in a way in which it was 'out' during the period of 1920–1960 — the period in which American social democrats nodded briefly and respectfully in Dewey's direction and then got down to the details of reform and reeducation" (Rorty 1987, 510). Then he adds in a footnote, "This treatment was one Dewey himself welcomed. Dewey thought of himself as freeing us up for practice, not as providing theoretical foundations for practice" (Rorty 1987, 511). And this is exactly the way Rorty thinks of his own practice. And this fits well in all domains with how he proceeds and conceptualizes himself as proceeding in philosophy. *Philosophy* drops out and *p*hilosophy remains though never as "the question of Reason" (whatever that means).

Let me close with two supplements to the above remarks about Rorty and politics. One has to do with the depth and consistency of Rorty's anti-theoreticism and the other comes back again to his ethnocentrism (his conception that there is no escaping our finitude and his rejection of the ambition of transcendence). Both have in this context to do with his differences with his fellow pragmatist Richard Bernstein, but they apply equally as well to his differences with Jürgen Habermas.

Turning to his anti-theoreticism first. Rorty remarks in his "Thugs and Theorists":

> My basic disagreement with Bernstein, as far as I can see, is about the utility of theory (and, in particular, of those parts of theory usually labelled "philosophy") in thinking about the present political situation, as opposed to its utility in imagining a liberal utopia. I am near the Bell end of the spectrum, in the sense that I cannot find much use for philosophy in formulating means to the ends that we social democrats share, nor in describing either our enemies or the present danger. Its main use lies, I suspect, in thinking through our utopian visions. Bernstein and Habermas are somewhere in the middle of this spectrum (though still well within the range I intended to cover with the term "we"). They are both concerned to develop large-scale analyses of the "political meaning" of contemporary phenomena. In particular, as philosophers, they are concerned to relate philosophical doctrines and vocabularies (e.g., what Habermas calls "the philosophical discourse of modernism") to politics (Rorty 1987, 569).

Rorty thinks this useless. We, for the reasons we have discussed, never gain an intelligible or useful Archimedian point which transcends our practices and enables us to both stand inside and outside our language-games. We never get a skyhook that enables us to recognize how things just are in themselves apart from the various descriptions of them such that we could critique them and adjudicate them. This is a *P*hilosophical ambition that cannot be met.

Secondly, large scale analysis of the 'political meaning' of contemporary phenomena is pointless. Such theoreticians desire to practice *Ideologiekritik* and to provide a philosophical account of the nature and goal of this practice (Rorty 1986, 569). Rorty thinks whatever usefulness it may have had in the past this unmasking of bourgeois ideology has "long been overworked and has turned into self-parody" such as "exposing the imperialistic presuppositions of Marvel Comics or campaigning against the prevalence of 'binary oppositions'" (Rorty 1987, 569–70). Rorty adds, "This belief has helped produce the idiot jargon that Frederick Crews has recently satirized as 'Leftspeak' — a dreadful, pompous, useless, mishmash of Marx, Adorno, Derrida, Foucault and Lacan. It has resulted in articles that offer unmaskings of the presuppositions of darker unmaskings of still earlier unmaskings" (Rorty 1987, 570). It has diverted energies away from the left which should fasten concretely on investigating what is to be done. What are our options available within the system or about it, if the system is what we on the left think it is, how to overthrow it, about what could replace the system if it were overthrown and about how to attain something approximating equality both domestically and globally? I share Rorty's views about this 'funny book Marxism' and *much*, though not all, of what he says about *ideologiekritik*. Moreover, we do not need any more meta-narratives. The cultural left has gotten over-theoretical, over-philosophical (Rorty 1987, 570). And over-philosophical in a very bad way.

However, as I have argued elsewhere, Rorty makes three related mistakes here (Nielsen 2003, 191–223). He (1) identifies the current First World left with the *cultural* left; (2) he identifies systematic theorizing on the left with grand *philosophical* theory; and (3) he does not pay attention to the *Ideologiekritik* of Marx and Engels (say, in the *Germany Ideology*), to Gramsci, Georg Lukacs, Lucien Goldmann, or Noam Chomsky. Ideology is still with us. The so-called end of ideology itself turned out to be an ideology and Noam Chomsky, for example, has done a pretty good job of critiquing it (Bell 1961; Aiken 1969; Aiken and Bell 1969). If ideology is still with us (as it is), and pervasively working its pernicious effects, why is critique of it now pointless and overworked?

To go to (1), Rorty utterly ignores the phenomenon of so-called analytical Marxism. Here we have a form of Marxism, not obscure and pompous like Marxism is in Althusser or Balibar, but clear and forceful in both de-mystifying Marx and Marxism and in developing systematic clearly articulated social theory and normative political argument. If Rorty likes and appropriates aspects of the work of Rawls and Scanlon (as he does) why doesn't he like and appropriate aspects of the work of G. A. Cohen and Andrew Levine? There is in analytical Marxism careful work by the cooperative efforts of political scientists, economists, sociologists and philosophers. It still *might* be over-theoretical, but at least it is not obscurantist. Such theoretical things may be impossible, á la Rush Rhees and Peter Winch, to do in the social sciences but the burden of proof, given the impressive work mentioned above, is with Rorty. He should not assume they are giving us obscure meta-narratives. Unless and until he shows that they are doing something neither useful nor plausible, his critique of left wing thought is wide of the mark.

Remember that this large scale theorizing is not philosophical but social scientific. G. A. Cohen's account and defense of historical materialism was not an account of a grand teleological narrative, but an explication and defense of an empirical theory of epochal social change, confirmable and infirmable, though *perhaps* disconfirmed. Nothing turns on these theoreticians calling themselves analytical Marxists. (Not all of them do.) It turns on rather the careful empirically and conceptually responsible stream of thought that characterizes their work. Perhaps after Quine we should call no philosophers or anyone else analytical or just take that appellation to connote a style of writing. But until Rorty gives us good reasons for setting such political and social theorizing aside his repudiation of neither Marxism nor socialism (which need not be identified with Marxism), on the one hand, nor large scale empirical theorizing on the other will have much credibility. Remember Weber and Durkheim without being socialists did large-scale theorizing and it is anything but evident that their work is all dross. Moreover, we must not take their theorizing to be *P*hilosophical theorizing or the writing of grand meta-narratives. Metaphysics, epistemology, meta-ethics and systematic moral theory are one thing. Rorty arguable is right about them. But systematic social science is another. But I don't deny that over-theorization is an issue here. It is salutory to remember Stuart Hampshire's quip: the difference between anthropology and sociology is that you learn something from the first and you don't from the second. Still there is no closure here and Rorty should not write as if there were. Remember that Noam Chomsky, a thorough anti-theoretician about *social* theory, does ideology critique superbly and it is not on Marvel Comics.

I want now to turn to the second issue, namely our old friend relativism and ethnocentrism again. I harp on this for it is concerning this issue that Rorty has been repeatedly criticized and concerning which he sometimes has been taken to be evasive. Here the criticism by Richard Bernstein is important to note (Bernstein 1992, 278–82). Bernstein argues that Rorty has not been successful in setting aside or evading relativism. And instead of fallibilism (which is compatible with non-relativism and the full acceptance of our contingency) Rorty with his 'Here I stand. I can do no other.' ends up not with fallibilism but a *fideist Absolutism* (Bernstein 1992, 278). We can always, Rorty claims, redescribe a belief to make it look either better or worse. There is no such thing as *the correct description* of a belief. Partisan universal claims made within a given vocabulary will be accepted if we find the vocabulary attractive. "In the final analysis, Rorty has little more to say than that he will or will not find a vocabulary attractive.... For all questions concerning the adoption or rejection of a vocabulary boil down to whether we have a pro or anti attitude toward it. Whatever our attitude, it is just the contingent effect of historical contingencies. Debates about our basic values and norms are not rational. They are only rhetorical strategies for getting others to adopt our attitudes" (Bernstein 1992, 278). This is a fideistic absolutism for it finally comes to the proclamation 'Here I stand (and I hope you will also stand here).' Bernstein then says:

> his type of fideism makes one question just how successful Rorty is in outflanking and evading the charge of relativism. There are silly versions of relativism where one maintains that any belief is just as good or true as any other. It would be unfair to accuse Rorty of advocating such a vulgar relativism, for he does try to show why his vocabulary is a more attractive redescription. Nevertheless, it isn't clear why in his liberal utopia one would no longer feel the force of the relativist objection. Presumably this is because the liberal ironist has abandoned the distinction between relative and absolute validity. She knows that no final vocabulary can be grounded in something more fundamental, that anything can be made to look good or bad by redescription, that there are no constraints on the invention of new vocabularies. The ironist wants to drop the term "relativism" but contrary to what Rorty says — she doesn't get rid of a nagging problem; she merely renames it "contingency" (Bernstein 1992, 279).

Whether we speak of 'relativism' or 'contingency', still on Rorty's account anything can be made to look good or bad if one is clever and imaginative enough. "There is never a non-trivial *reason* for favoring one vocabulary rather than another" (Bernstein 1992, 280). There are skeptical doubts here, but they are what Peirce in attacking Cartesianism called paper doubts. Rorty never really doubts his commitment to liberal democracy. Bernstein remarks:

The primary reason why Rorty never "seriously" questions his liberal convictions is that his entire project depends upon defending "the fundamental premise ... that a belief can still regulate action, can still be thought worth dying for, among people who are quite aware that this belief is caused by nothing deeper than a contingent historical circumstance" (p. 189). Without this "fundamental premise" his entire project falls apart (Bernstein 1992, 280).

But this claim of Rorty's, which is also a famous claim of Isaiah Berlin's, is, I say, quite reasonable. If there is no *alternative* to contingency, as there isn't, there isn't a reason to get upset about contingency: we just have to live in a world without God, Reason, the Absolute, or Universality. Beckett is right: we are on earth, there is no cure for it. It is irrational to wish for what can't be had and it is silly to ask 'Why not be irrational?'. It is like asking 'Why not be cruel?'. Bernstein realizes that Rorty's fundamental premise can be given a reasonable reading, namely "the reasonable thesis that once we give up foundationalism or claims to absolute validity then we must recognize that all our beliefs are always open to criticism and revision. Nevertheless, aware of our own fallibility, we can be passionately committed to the beliefs that regulate our actions" (Bernstein 1992, 280).

The fallibilist, as we have seen, is neither a radical skeptic nor a subjectivist. She does not say that if she finds something attractive or has a pro-attitude toward it then it is acceptable. This is, as Bernstein says, a rejection of fallibilism and so it is. The fallibilist *au contraire* doesn't give up the distinction between good and bad reasons, although she will contextualize them and historicize them and recognize they can be contested. But this is fallibilism not radical skepticism. We are back to what we saw Michael Williams noting, namely that in *Contingency, Irony and Solidarity* Rorty slides away from fallibilism, which is generally his stance, into a *radical* skepticism and thus in effect rejects fallibilism, a sworn enemy of skepticism. The fallibilist position, as we have known it since Peirce, has neither relativist nor subjectivist implications. The fallibilist recognizes, as Bernstein remarks, that the distinction between good and bad reasons is context-dependent and always contestable. When challenged about her fundamental beliefs, the fallibilist is open to considering whether she should modify or abandon them. The fallibilist is open to what Habermas calls the "force of the better argument and recognizes that there can always be disputes about what counts as the better argument" (Bernstein 1992, 281). This historicist fallibilism is, to repeat, not a relativism, not a subjectivism and not a radical scepticism.

But Bernstein points out, as did Michael Williams, that the Rorty of *Contingency, Irony and Solidarity* is not a fallibilist but with his ironist a radical skeptic: things boil down to just having pro and con attitudes. As

Bernstein puts it, with Rorty's ironist "there is not basis for making a distinction between *rational* persuasion and other forms of persuasion. This distinction is completely relative to the vocabulary we adopt. And since there is no reason for adopting a given vocabulary, we are licensed to count as 'rational persuasion' whatever 'looks good' to us" (Bernstein 1992, 281).

Rorty should heed his better pragmatist self and stick with what is his pragmatism. Something that is an integral part of his thought except for the lapse into radical skepticism in *Contingency, Irony and Solidarity*. He should jettison talk of irony, of a final vocabulary and of continuous and persistently occurring doubts about what is not intelligible anyway and certainly do not comport with pragmatism, namely 'a final vocabulary'. Here he is too much like a man in Hume's philosopher's closet. He should stick with fallibilism, historicism, finitism and the unflinching recognition of our contingency. But with that, though not with radical skepticism, we still can give good and bad reasons and get them into wide reflective equilibrium. There is no need to be a Dostoevskian underground man.

NOTES

1. Where I italicize and capitalize *P*hilosophy I am speaking of the meta-physical-epistemological position of the Tradition which Rorty repudiates and claims should be set aside. When I use *p*hilosophy with a little 'p' and italicized I am speaking of the Sellarian thing that Rorty thinks is both unproblematic and a valuable thing to do. Where neither the 'p' in philosophy nor Philosophy is italicized I am being neutral concerning which (if either) is to be claimed. In spite of the harshness of his dismissal of *P*hilosophy, Rorty is not saying the great dead philosophers, who were usually both (I add) *P*hilosophers and *p*hilosophers, should not be read and studied. Of course they should, Rorty like any sensible and reflective person regards them as an indispensable and precious part of our cultural heritage. I should add that Sellars, his characterization of *p*hilosophy notwithstanding, actually did, and very extensively, *P*hilosophy.

2. James Conant (1994) in an insightful discussion raises questions as to whether it is uselessness or unintelligibility that is centrally at issue. It looks like it can't be both for to discover that something is useless would seem at least to presuppose that it is intelligible. In his earlier writings Rorty stressed unintelligibility; in his later writings he stresses lack of usefulness. Conant makes it evident that there is something to be sorted out here.

3. We get a self-referential paradox when we get something which is at least supposedly self-refuting. That is either (1) the sentence is shown to be false in the very fact of its being said, e.g., 'There are no words in this sentence' or (2) liar-type paradoxes, e.g. 'This sentence is false' which must be false if it is true and true if it is false. Sometimes self-reference, as Simon Blackburn has pointed out, is benign as in the sentence "All English sentences should have a verb." It happily includes itself in the domain of sentences it is talking about. The difficulty lies in forming a condition that

only excludes pathological self-reference and in determining what *pathological* self-reference is.

4. There will, of course, be disputes over what counts as 'appropriate' here.

5. One might briefly put it this way: (1) if communication is to be possible there must be an overlap of beliefs; (2) communication is actual so therefore it is possible; (3) there therefore must be some overlap of beliefs. Perhaps premise (1) is challengeable by saying for communication to be possible only *some understanding* is necessary not some overlap of beliefs. But could we have any understanding without an overlap of beliefs? Perhaps but hardly likely.

6. Rorty repeatedly insists in *Philosophy and the Mirror of Nature* on the importance of distinguishing questions of causal explanation from questions of justification. See Rorty 1979, 210, 229, 254–56, 361, 375, 388.

REFERENCES

Aiken, Henry David. (1968) "The Revolt Against Ideology," in *The End of Ideology Debate*, ed. Chaim Waxman (New York: Clarion Books), pp. 229–58.

Bell, Daniel. (1960) *The End of Ideology* (New York: The Free Press).

Bell, Daniel, and Aiken, Henry David. (1968) "Ideology — A Debate," in *The End of Ideology Debate*, ed. Chaim Waxman (New York: Clarion Books), pp. 259–80.

Bernstein, Richard. (1992) *The New Constellation* (Cambridge, MA: MIT Press).

Bloom, Allan. (1987) *The Closing of the American Mind* (New York: Simon and Schuster).

Conant, James. (1994) "Introduction," in *Words and Life* by Hilary Putnam (Cambridge, MA: Harvard University Press), pp. xi–xxvi.

Kolakoswki, Leszek. (1996) "A Remark on Rorty" and "A Remark on our Relative Relativism," in *The State of Philosophy*, ed. Józef Niznik and John Sanders (London: Praeger), pp. 52–57, 67–76.

Lewis, David. (1984): "Putnam's Paradox," *Australasian Journal of Philosophy* 62, pp. 221–236.

Nagel, Thomas. (1998) "Go with the Flow," *Times Literary Supplement* (28 August), pp. 3–4.

Nielsen, Kai. (1991) *After the Demise of the Tradition: Rorty, Critical Theory and the Fate of Philosophy* (Boulder, CO: Westview Press).

————. (1996) *Naturalism Without Foundations* (Amherst, NY: Prometheus Books).

———. (1999) "Taking Rorty Seriously," *Dialogue* 37, pp. 503–18.

———. (2002) *Globalization and Justice* (Amherst, NY: Humanity Books).

Putnam, Hilary. (1990) *Realism with a Human Face* (Cambridge, MA: Harvard University Press).

Rorty, Richard. (1979) *Philosophy and the Mirror of Nature* (Princeton, NJ: Princeton University Press).

———. (1982) *Consequences of Pragmatism* (Minneapolis: University of Minnesota Press).

———. (1987) "Thugs and Theorists," *Political Theory* 15, pp. 564–80.

———. (1990) "Pragmatism as Anti-Representationalism," in *Pragmatism: From Peirce to Davidson* by John P. Murphy (Boulder, CO: Westview Press), pp. 1–6.

———. (1991) *Objectivity, Relativism and Truth* (Cambridge, UK: Cambridge University Press).

———. (1996) "Pragmatism," in *Routledge Encyclopedia of Philosophy*, ed. Edward Craig (London: Routledge), vol. 7, pp. 632–640.

———. (1998a) *Truth and Progress* (Cambridge, UK: Cambridge University Press).

———. (1998b) "Justice as a Larger Loyalty," in *Cosmopolitics*, ed. Pheng Cheah and Bruce Robbins (Minneapolis: University of Minnesota Press), pp. 45–58.

———. (1998c) *Against Bosses, Against Oligarchies: A Conversation with Richard Rorty* (Charlottesville, VA: Prickly Pear Pamphlets).

———. (1999) *Philosopy and Social Hope* (London: Penguin).

———. (2000) "Universality and Truth" and "Response to Habermas," in *Rorty and His Critics*, ed. Robert Brandon (Malden, MA: Blackwell), pp. 1–30, 56–69.

———. (2004) "Post Democracy," *London Review of Books* 26 (April), pp. 10–11.

Williams, Michael. (2003) "Rorty on Knowledge and Truth," in *Richard Rorty*, ed. Charles Guignon and David Hiley (Cambridge, UK: Cambridge University Press), pp. 61–80.

Wittgenstein, Ludwig. (1993) *Philosophical Occasions, 1912–1951*, ed. James Klogge and Alfred Nordman (Indianapolis: Hackett).

Kai Nielsen
Adjunct Professor of Philosophy
Philosophy Department
Concordia University
1455 Maisonneuve Blvd. West
Montreal, Quebec H3G 1M8
Canada

Contemporary Pragmatism
Vol. 2, No. 1 (June 2005), 35–93

Editions Rodopi
© 2005

Foucault and Rorty on Truth and Ideology: A Pragmatist View from the Left

Chandra Kumar

An anti-representationalist view of language and a deflationary view of truth, key themes in contemporary pragmatism and especially Richard Rorty, do not undermine the notion, in critical theory, of ideology as 'false consciousness'. Both Foucault and Marx were opposed to what Marxists call historical idealism and so they should be seen as objecting to forms of ideology-critique that do not sufficiently avoid such an 'Hegelian' perspective. Foucault's general views on the relations between truth and power can plausibly be construed in a way that makes them compatible with a Marxian critical theory.

1. Introduction

Critical theory since Marx has emphasised the role of illusion in the perpetuation of oppression. Oppression-sustaining illusions are the trademark of the ideological. In the critical theorist's sense of 'ideology', ideology distorts and does so in ways that are functional for a social order that is marked by systematic oppression and exploitation. Critical theorists, like proponents of any theory in any domain, believe they can offer a less distorted perspective on certain matters; they claim to have a less falsifying account of the world — specifically, the social and political world — than what is given in the more dominant or 'hegemonic' ideologies. They view the critique of ideology as being instrumental to enlightenment, a secular kind of enlightenment, and to the liberation of human beings from modern structures of power and illegitimate authority. For a sample of work on critical theory see Guess (1985), Roderick (1986), McCarthy (1978), Benhabib (1986), and Held (1980).

More or less reflectively, many people today maintain a sceptical attitude towards this tradition. Critical theory has itself been subject to criticism, scorn, and ridicule. Michel Foucault was no exception to this sceptical 'postmodern' mood (as it is sometimes called) even though Foucault arguably neither was nor viewed himself as being a postmodernist.[1] Foucault was sceptical of Enlightenment conceptions of a *general* emancipation. His interest in the relations between knowledge and power did not translate into speculations about an ideal society: a society in which the reign of mystifying ideologies will be overcome. His work as a critical intellectual was distant from such utopian endeavours, in this respect very different from that of Jürgen Habermas, the most widely read and discussed contemporary critical theorist.[2]

In his 'Two Lectures' Foucault expressed scepticism about the critique of ideology partly on the grounds that power in modern society has much less to do with ideology than critical theorists assume. Instead of focusing on the role of ideological belief-systems in the manner of critical theorists, Foucault wanted to examine the (more or less) coercive *practices* and subtle *techniques* by which people are subjected and subject themselves to discipline; practices and techniques that, in Foucault's view, have been closely linked to the development of the human and social sciences. The way that modern relations of power and authority have developed and been sustained, Foucault believed, is not primarily through the inculcation of ideological distortions or 'false consciousness' but, more decisively, through "the production of effective instruments for the formation and accumulation of knowledge — methods of observation, procedures for investigation and research, apparatuses of control" (Foucault 1980, 102). Foucault stressed these developments and the fact that 'apparatuses of control' and surveillance and the social practices and disciplines linked with them have commonly been overlooked, even by Marxist and other critical theorists who explain the reproduction of oppression in terms of mass 'ideological mystification' or 'false consciousness'.

This Foucauldian objection to ideology-critique is the topic of section two. There I argue that Foucault's position, though different from Marx's in subtle ways, is actually consonant with Marx's (and Engels') core criticism, in *The German Ideology*, of what has come to be known as historical idealism. Like Marx, Foucault resisted the tendency to discuss prevailing ideas and ways of thinking as if these had magically sprung from some ahistorical heaven; and like Marx, he eschewed the sort of narrative in which ideologies play a dominant or starring role in the historical process. Yet these warnings about *certain forms* of critique should not be seen as vitiating the idea of critical theory in general or the critique of ideology in particular. This, at any rate, is something I try to make clear and persuasive in what follows.

But that is not all Foucault said about ideology. In one of his well-known interviews ('Truth and Power') Foucault maintained that "the notion of ideology" as it has been used by Marxists and others on the Left, is problematic because ideology always stands in virtual opposition to something else which is supposed to count as truth. Now I believe that the problem does not consist in drawing the line between that in a discourse which falls under the category of scientificity or truth, and that which comes under some other category, but in seeing historically how effects of truth are produced within discourses which in themselves are neither true nor false. (Foucault 2000, 119)

Here Foucault was voicing opposition to a particular tradition of ideology-critique. For purposes of this discussion, I will call Foucault's objection his 'truth objection to ideology-critique'.

Before elaborating on this, it is worth noting that Foucault had other, related objections to ideology-critique. He also objected on the grounds that "the concept of ideology refers, I think necessarily, to something of the order of a subject" and that, in the case of Marxism, "ideology stands in a secondary position relative to something which functions as its infrastructure, as its material/economic determinant, etc." (Foucault 2000, 119). I have elsewhere argued (Kumar 2003) against the first type of objection: against the view that critical theory necessarily presupposes a problematic philosophical theory of the self or human nature or 'subject' — such as Kantian conceptions of a transcendental subject or Rousseauian conceptions of human nature. The second objection is less elaborated in Foucault's work than the first. Foucault was opposed to economic determinism in Marxian theory. For the most part I avoid this issue here. While I try to show that Foucault can be interpreted as being opposed to the same sort of thing, historical idealism, that Marx and Engels objected to in *The German Ideology*, I do not deny that one can consistently reject both historical idealism *and* the Marxian idea that the economic system is, causally speaking, the most important factor in our explanations of ideology and other social phenomena. I think this is exactly what Foucault did. For him there were important social phenomena including "psychiatric internment, the mental normalisation of individuals, and penal institutions" that "have no doubt a fairly limited importance if one is only looking for their economic significance" but are "undoubtedly essential to the general functioning of the wheels of power" (Foucault 2000, 117). This suggests that power, for Foucault, was a more important category than the economic. There are issues that need careful consideration in this context, for example, the question whether Marxian theory, charitably understood, is actually rival or complementary to Foucault's genealogical analyses. These issues deserve separate treatment; here I simply wish to stress that Foucault's aversion to a Marxian historical materialist perspective does not make Foucault an historical idealist.

My focus will be more on Foucault's 'truth objection' than on his objections to Marx's so-called economic determinism. Foucault's truth-objection was linked to his understanding of modern 'disciplinary power' and 'normalisation' and the connections these have to the production of knowledge. In one of his provocative claims regarding truth and power, Foucault asserted that "[t]he problem is not changing people's consciousness — or what's in their heads — but the political, economic, institutional regime of the production of truth" (2000, 133). Foucault's central argument here, it would seem, is that even truth, or what is taken as truth, as produced in various disciplines deemed scientific, often works in the service of power. I do not think this insight provides a telling objection to all critical conceptions of ideology but only to those that draw a hard and fast line between science and truth on one side and ideology on the other. Critical theory, Marxian or otherwise, need not do so; or so I will argue. But Foucault's truth objection may be viewed, not only as a critique of such *scientistic* conceptions of ideology but also of certain problematic conceptions of and stances toward truth. What is less clear is whether those conceptions, problematic as they seem to be, are inseparably entangled with the 'notion of ideology' as deployed by critical theory.

Related to much talk of truth and its assumed liberating potential is a kind of picture of the relation between humans and the rest of the world: a *representationalist* picture, according to which truth is what emerges or becomes present when our beliefs, our minds, our sentences and our language-games, theories or world-views, accurately represent what the world is 'really' like apart from all of our discursive practices, our values, needs and interests, our conceptual and theoretical assumptions and beliefs. The assumption is that there is an intrinsic nature of reality, that 'in the final analysis' the trail of the human is not over all, that truth is what we get when we are properly disposed towards or properly represent this nonhuman, nonlinguistic reality. (Note that this picture becomes less plausible if we are thinking of social realities, for there the observer is more obviously also a participant-observer.) The critique of this representationalist image, especially as it has been articulated by contemporary pragmatists, seems to create problems for those who wish to contrast 'the way things are in themselves' with 'the way things are ideologically represented by (or to) us'.

Moreover, certain developments in philosophical thinking about truth *seem* to have made it more difficult for social critics to refer to their opponents' views as ideological while viewing their own as non-ideological or at least less ideological. One of these developments is the rise of postmodernism in our intellectual life over the past thirty years. 'Postmodernism' is not a term I will try to define. But in its apparent opposition to all forms of rationalism, particularly those most clearly stemming from the Enlightenment, postmodern thought is sceptical of 'truth-talk' (a phrase from the pragmatist philosopher, Robert Brandom) or at least certain kinds of truth-talk. Postmodernism may now be on the decline but whether or not this is so, perhaps scepticism is in order, at least towards *certain conceptions* of truth. Perhaps some truth-talk, in particular the sort of truth-talk that has prevailed in philosophical and theological discourse through the ages, *should* be dropped. Interestingly the movement against *such* truth-talk is alive and well in analytical philosophy as well. The idea of truth has steadily been 'deflated' and the movement towards a deflationary view of truth can be seen in the context of a broader dissatisfaction with representationalism.[3]

Representationalism, though not invented by Descartes, is a central doctrine of Cartesian thought. Descartes split the world into two substances (Mind and Matter) and a broad swathe of post-Cartesian English philosophy revolves around the issue of the relations between them; specifically, the questions whether and how the mind (or language) can be seen to accurately represent what is really 'out there' beyond the mind (beyond language). The foil for such endeavours is usually the epistemological sceptic, the one who denies that we can ever possess genuine knowledge of the world 'as it really is' apart from how we humans think about it. This sort of modern sceptic makes the most of the metaphysical divide assumed by representationalism, denying that we can know that we have successfully, representationally, forged a bond between the human and nonhuman worlds.[4] Representationalism is the general framework within which both sceptical and non-sceptical 'realist' and 'anti-realist' philosophers have their disputes. The framework is nicely depicted by Bjørn Ramberg in a discussion of two prominent anti-representationalists, Richard Rorty and Donald Davidson. Ramberg characterises representationalism as a view of the world, implicit in much analytical philosophy (but not only analytical philosophy) that rests on "two problem-defining assumptions":

> The first is the Kantian idea that knowledge, or thinking generally, must be understood in terms of some relation between what the world offers up to the thinker, on one side, and on the other the active subjective capacities by which the thinker structures for cognitive use what the world thus provides. [Note that Kant's idea is a variation on a Cartesian theme.] The second is the Platonic conviction that there must be some particular form of description of things, which, by virtue of its ability to accurately map, reflect, or otherwise latch on to just those kinds through which the world presents itself to would-be knowers, is the form in which any literally true — or cognitively significant, or ontologically ingenuous — statement must be couched. Together, these comprise what Rorty calls representationalism. (Ramberg 2001, 351)

I will argue that even with a deflationary view of truth (which will be elaborated in section four) and even with an acceptance of anti-representationalism — the denial or the putting aside of the two 'problem-defining assumptions' mentioned by Ramberg — there remains a non-misleading way to think of the contrast, in critical theory, between truth and ideology, or better, between ideological and non-ideological consciousness. To put it another way: One can be as thoroughly anti-representationalist as a Richard Rorty or a Michel Foucault and yet, contrary to both, still reasonably cling to a critical sense of 'ideology', a sense in which to be under the sway of ideology is, in part, to be under the spell of a specific kind of delusion or illusion.[5] Anti-representationalism and the deflation of 'truth' do not undermine the critique of distorting or mystifying ideologies. If representationalism is as incoherent or problematic as contemporary pragmatists such as Rorty, Ramberg, Kai Nielsen, Michael Williams, and Hilary Putnam (who calls it metaphysical realism rather than 'representationalism') believe, this would not establish that the 'notion of ideology' in critical theory is also so deeply problematic. (I will go along with Nielsen, Ramberg, and Putnam; unlike Rorty, they do not think we would do better to forget ideology once we accept pragmatism into our hearts. For a sample of anti-representationalist writings, see Rorty (1983), Ramberg (1993), Putnam (2001), Nielsen (1991), and Williams (1995). Again, note that Putnam does not disavow all notions of representing but he is, in effect, anti-representionalist in the same sense as the others.)

So I claim it is important to stick with a notion of ideology as 'false consciousness', suitably demystified of both representationalist and rationalist assumptions. Foucault's truth objection, construed as a kind of historicised anti-representationalist critique, works against a *certain* notion of ideology, a scientistic one, but not against all critical notions. In making this case, I also contend that Foucault's general ideas on the connections between truth and power are not only compatible with a form of Marxian critical theory, they actually make more sense than they otherwise would when placed within (or at least alongside) the latter.

2. Foucault and Marx against historical idealism

In an interesting discussion of Foucault's views on power and politics, Nancy Fraser made the following comment which is, I think, illuminating in a way that she did not intend: "Foucault's genealogy of modern power establishes that power touches people's lives more fundamentally through their social practices than through their beliefs" and this "suffices to rule out political orientations aimed primarily at the demystification of ideologically distorted belief systems" (Fraser 1989, 18). Fraser's implied contrast between practices and beliefs is odd; for what practice is not belief-laden, what social practice can be understood without understanding something of the beliefs, assumptions and attitudes of the participants in the practice? Nevertheless, there is a more charitable way of understanding Fraser (and Foucault) in this context; but this interpretation would situate Foucault more in the tradition of Marxian thought than Foucault sometimes seemed willing to countenance.

Let me explain. Fraser's suggestive comment is similar to Marx's and Engels' criticisms, in *The German Ideology*, of what is sometimes called 'historical idealism'. They accused the "German ideologists," most of them followers of Hegel or strongly influenced by his philosophy of history, of interpreting and explaining social and historical change in terms of an autonomous world of ideas, theories, or world-views, rather than placing the latter in the context of more 'material' developments in social and economic institutions and practices. One of the problems with the German ideology, Marx and Engels argued, was the tendency to discuss historical change as if it had "taken place in the realm of pure thought" (Marx and Engels 1985, 39). The Young Hegelians, they wrote, "consider conceptions, thoughts, ideas, in fact all the products of consciousness, to which they attribute an independent existence, as the real chains of men (just as the Old Hegelians declared them the true bonds of human society)." The Young Hegelians thought we could look to the 'products of consciousness' to discover both the fundamental causes of and constraints on the forms of human relations and human activity that prevail in different historical periods. They implied that the critique of this free-floating consciousness was the most crucial factor in bringing about substantial improvements in social and cultural life.

Marx and Engels believed that the Young Hegelians were, in effect, practicing a conservative or at least very limited form of critique. These critics were only fighting against certain interpretations or phrases and forgetting "that to these phrases they themselves are only opposing other phrases, and that they are in no way combating the real existing world when they are merely combating the phrases of this world." The suggestion is not that 'phrases' and 'interpretations' are not part of the 'real existing world'. In context, 'real existing world' means something like 'the historical world of socio-economic institutions and practices within which theories, language and thought are embedded and from which ideologies emerge'. This interpretation squares with their scathing remark that "[i]t has not occurred to any one of these philosophers to inquire into the connection of German philosophy with German reality, the relation of their criticism to their own material surroundings" (Marx and Engels 1985, 41).[6] 'Reality' qualified by 'German' suggests a social, political, economic reality, not Reality *simpliciter*; and as Nielsen, Michael Williams, and Rorty suggest, it is less than clear that we even know what we are talking about when we refer to 'reality-in-general' or reality 'as-it- is-in-itself'. (See section four for further discussion of this.)

Similarly, Foucault believed that ideas, theories, world-views, moral codes and ways of thinking and 'problematising' generally, are historically conditioned by, and have no meaning apart from, an historical background of social practices, traditions, customs, institutions, all pervaded by relations of control, domination, power and resistance — a background of 'material practices', so to speak. Like Marx and Engels, he believed that an effective form of critique would not simply criticise the 'products of consciousness' but would also view 'consciousness' as a product. (This is a key feature of genealogy in Foucault's work.) Foucault wished to historicise these 'products of consciousness' in a particular way, to view them against a background of social power, to examine how they emerged from coercive social practices or how they have functioned to preserve or to challenge social and political hierarchies and other relations of power.

It is noteworthy that in criticising forms of historical idealism, Marx and Engels were not suggesting that there *were* no dominant ideologies, world-views or theories, nor were they suggesting that it was futile or pointless to expose them to rational criticism. It is reasonable to suppose that, on the contrary, they regarded the idealism of the 'German ideology' as playing a role in a culturally dominant ideology and that they were exposing it to rational criticism. In claiming that social change (or the lack of social change) is not traceable to a "realm of pure thought," they were not suggesting that modern life was devoid of "ideologically distorted belief-systems" if this means "belief-systems which, partly through distortion and falsehood, *contribute* to or *reinforce* existing or developing structures of power and authority." They devoted much of their lives to exposing and criticising what they regarded as pro-capitalist ideologies that in important ways distort our understandings of social and political life. They would not have denied that capitalism is sustained as a social form with the help of a dominant ideology or ideologies (in the sense specified).[7] Their point was that the critique of such belief-systems probably would be feckless and have conservative effects so long as these critiques remained safely in the "realm of pure thought"; remained, that is, trapped in a discourse or vocabulary that treats history as if it were primarily the manifestation of a more basic intellectual process (a world of ideas); and so long as intellectuals refused to inquire into the connections which their ideas, principles and theories have to social and economic realities. If my reading of Fraser's reading (quoted above) of Foucault is accepted, then it makes sense to think that Foucault and Marx did not differ *in this respect*; that is, both repudiated what Marxists call historical idealism. Many historians and social scientists, even if they are not Marxian, are now suspicious of historical idealism, though they tend not to acknowledge the Marxian pedigree of their suspicions and tend to be suspicious of Marx's historical materialism as well, in effect saying "a plague on both your houses." (For clear, though sometimes conflicting versions of historical materialism coming from the 'school' of Marxism known as 'Analytical Marxism', see Cohen (1978, 1988); Miller (1984); Nielsen (1989); and Levine, Sober, and Wright (1995).)

The differences between Marx and Foucault have more to do with what replaces historical idealism. While Marxists have emphasised the development of modes of production (the forces and relations of production) as the crucial determinants of ideology and of social and historical change, Foucault emphasised strategies and techniques of social control and, to a lesser extent, strategies and techniques of resistance. Nevertheless, neither Marx's base/superstructure model of society nor Foucault's power model establish that the critique of ideology is an incoherent or unworthy practice.[8] Even if prevailing ideologies are rooted in economic relations of production and the conflicts arising from these, as Marxians say, this does not imply that it is pointless or futile to criticise those ideologies; at most, it implies that such critiques would be even more cogent when ideology is understood and depicted in a broader 'material' context, that is, when it is adequately historicised and linked to prevailing socio-economic structures — when Feuerbach is supplemented by Marx. (Note that this has nothing to do with a view to which some Marxists such as Engels have been prone, namely *metaphysical* materialism, the view that all reality is ultimately only matter. On decoupling Marxian theory from materialist metaphysics, see Norman (1989, 59–80)). Similar things can be said of Foucault's quasi-materialist objection to ideology-critique. Perhaps the critical intellectuals *should* put greater emphasis on material practices and techniques of control other than the ideological or 'purely' ideological — 'panoptical' techniques for monitoring employees and isolating them from each other, for example. Moreover, one should not simply assume without argument that masses of people are ideologically deluded to act in ways supportive of their own oppression. These points should be acknowledged but taken as friendly advice rather than as undermining ideology-critique. They do not establish the futility or pointlessness of the latter; they imply only that such critiques should be more consciously integrated with analyses of material practices and techniques of social and political control and resistance and that one should try to provide good reasons, preferably embedded in plausible historical narratives, for the claim that ideology (as a form of 'false consciousness') does significantly contribute to maintaining oppression.

Foucault's more influential scepticism towards critical theory with ideology-critique at its core, has more to do with what I have called the 'truth-objection'. It is here that Foucault seems to join forces with Rorty in order to move social criticism away from the tradition of grand critical theory; but in particular, away from the idea of exposing the irrationalities and distortions of dominant ideologies (or 'false consciousness').

3. 'Truth', 'freedom' and 'power' as interlocked notions: Taylor on Foucault

In thinking about the truth/ideology contrast that seems to underpin the idea of ideology as false consciousness, it may be useful first to address a common sort of criticism of Foucault that was raised in the 1980s. Philosophers such as Charles Taylor and a number of others commented on Foucault's apparent self-contradictions and 'normative confusions' (Taylor 1986, 69–102; see, as well, Fraser, who wrote of Foucault's 'empirical insights and normative confusions' (1989, 17–68), Habermas (1987, 238–93; 1986, 103–8) and Walzer (1988, 191–209).) Some of Foucault's statements provoked worries about his apparent moral and cultural relativism, his fatalism or even nihilism. The following passage, for example, worried Taylor (and others as well):

> The important thing here ... is that truth isn't outside power or lacking in power; contrary to a myth whose history and functions would repay further study, truth isn't the reward of free spirits, the child of protracted solitude, nor the privilege of those who have succeeded in liberating themselves. Truth is a thing of this world: it is produced only by virtue of multiple forms of constraint. And it induces regular effects of power. Each society has its own regime of truth, its 'general politics' of truth: that is, the types of discourse which it accepts and makes function as true; the mechanisms and instances that enable one to distinguish true and false statements; the means by which each is sanctioned; the techniques and procedures accorded value in the acquisition of truth; the status of those who are charged with saying what counts as true. (Foucault 2000, 131)

Taylor was troubled by these and similar general remarks in Foucault's writings and interviews about the links between truth and power. He was also troubled by the *apparent* fact that Foucault's "analyses seem to bring *evils* to light; and yet he wants to distance himself from the suggestion which would seem inescapably to follow, that the negation or overcoming of these evils promotes a good" (Taylor 1986, 69). Taylor characterised Foucault's position as follows:

There is no truth which can be espoused, defended, rescued against systems of power. On the contrary, each such system defines its own variant of truth. And there is no escape from power into freedom, for such systems of power are co-extensive with human society. We can only step from one to another. (Taylor 1986, 70)[9]

According to Taylor, Foucault was mistaken about the interrelations between truth, power and freedom, indeed about the concepts of 'truth', 'power' (or 'domination') and 'freedom'.

Taylor maintained that Foucault was caught in a self-defeating relativism, using these concepts in ways that amount to abusing them. How, Taylor wondered, could Foucault have made such claims about the inseparability of truth and power while, without contradiction, believing his genealogies were in any meaningful sense *critical* of 'truth regimes'? Foucault did not think that his historical analyses of modern power were morally or politically neutral. They were, at least, meant to make us think twice about some of our norms and practices, to show that what looks like progress and freedom was, or is, at least in some significant respects neither progress nor freedom. But given (what Taylor regards as) Foucault's relativist ways of speaking about truth, freedom and power, what good reasons could he have had for making these claims? On what non-arbitrary basis could one take the side of 'subjugated knowledges' in opposition to dominant paradigms of knowledge? On what non-mythical, non-question-begging, non-arbitrary basis could Foucault have criticised the 'disciplinary society' or the 'society of normalisation'? If there is no escape from power into freedom, no truth outside power (if 'truth is already power'), what rational moral justification is there or could there be for resisting and trying to change or to overthrow an existing system of power? (But then couldn't we also ask: What justification is there or could there be for *not* resisting, for acquiescing in the *status quo*?) Taylor suggested that Foucault was confused on these matters and he tried to give a diagnosis of this confusion in the context of Foucault's *Discipline and Punish* and *History of Sexuality. Volume One.*

Taylor and several other commentators have insinuated that in *Discipline and Punish* the emergence and development of modern 'humanitarian' forms of punishment is depicted as if these were, at best, morally on a par with prior forms of punishment in which torture and public executions were regular, ritualised practices. More generally, some of Foucault's interpreters and critics have remarked on his apparent unwillingness sufficiently to acknowledge moral progress in the emergence and development of modern institutions, practices and norms. Clifford Geertz made the strong claim that Foucault gave us "a kind of Whig history in reverse   a history, in spite of itself, of the Rise of Unfreedom" (Geertz 1978, 6; cited by Hoy 1986, 11). That seems to imply that in Foucault's genealogies modern societies are depicted as actually regressing, in terms of freedom, from pre-modern societies. Whatever the most plausible interpretation of Foucault may be,[10] readers of Foucault can accept Taylor's suggestion that Foucault's impatience with modernist claims about progress was, for the most part, rooted in his "concrete reading of this 'humanitarian-ism', which [he saw] as a growing system of control" (Taylor 1986, 80).

Again, Foucault's accounts of modern techniques of control and disci-pline were not value-free or politically neutral. He would have been the first to acknowledge this: he made no pretensions to being neutral in the sense of not taking sides in social and political conflicts; he evinced no longing for transcendence, that is for 'rising above' any historically specific social and political concerns in his work. In fact he was suspicious of the assumption that this could be done in the social and human sciences. And in Foucault's 1971 Dutch television discussion with Noam Chomsky (it wasn't much of a debate) he said, in no uncertain terms, that

> one of the tasks that seems immediate and urgent to me, over and above anything else, is this: that we [in our intellectual work] should indicate and show up, even where they are hidden, all the relationships of political power which actually control the social body and oppress or repress it. (Foucault 1974, 171)

Foucault was active in political struggles; the struggles of prisoners, for example. Evidently he did not suspend his moral convictions and his concern for certain marginalised groups (but not only for them) when he wrote about the development of modern conceptions and techniques of punishment, norms of sexual health or sanity, and modern forms of 'governmentality' generally. He knew that these values and concerns led him to ask certain questions, pose certain problems, pursue certain lines of inquiry and to be more interested in or sympathetic with certain interpretations of events rather than others (Bernstein 1992, 142–71). He may not have been an advocate of critical *theory*, including Marxian theories, or interested in doing moral *philosophy*, but he was doing work and saw himself as doing work that was informed by certain moral convictions; work that was both empirically-oriented and critical of certain tendencies (critical of certain social practices and ways of thinking) character-istic of modern (Western) societies.

Yet in Foucault's genealogies the values tend to be implicit and he typically refused, even when pressed, to defend his views by appealing to or articulating a moral or normative theory, framework or perspective; more precisely, he refused to yield to the Platonistic urge to ground values he plainly shared (such as autonomy) either in something nonhuman (God's will, laws of nature, the intrinsic nature of reality) or in the 'intrinsically human' or, like Habermas, in the 'universal presuppositions of communicative action'.[11] Foucault did not try to depict an ideal society, particularly when this is conceived as a society that promotes the realisation or fulfilment of a hitherto repressed human nature. (His main point of contention with Chomsky was on this very question; that is, the question whether there is any point or value in trying to give an account of a possible future, better social order in which human nature might be freely expressed or fulfilled.) All the same, Foucault was not an amoralist or politically neutral in his writing about modern power (if that is even possible); though he was no doubt elusively hard to categorise politically.

In Taylor's judgment, the unarticulated moral perspective behind Foucault's critical accounts of modern power (of the 'carceral society', the 'disciplinary society', the 'society of normalisation'), a perspective that would make sense of these critical histories as coherent forms of critique, could have been "something akin to the Schillerian/Critical Theory notion that modern discipline has repressed our own natures and constituted systems of domination of man by man." However, as noted above, this 'Schillerian/Critical Theory' perspective with its appeal to an ideal of liberation of human nature, was repudiated by Foucault. It was repudiated by him partly because, as Taylor put it, "the ideology of expressive liberation, particularly in connection with sexual life, is [for Foucault] itself just a strategy of power." But if the ideology of expressive liberation is itself a strategy of power (not an unnatural reading of Foucault's *History of Sexuality, Volume One*), then Foucault's critique of this ideology then seems to imply or to presuppose "some idea of a liberation, but not via the correct or authentic expression of our natures." Instead, it would be "a liberation from the whole ideology of such expression, and hence from the mechanisms of control which use this ideology." Moreover, "[i]t would be a liberation which was helped by our unmasking falsehood; a liberation aided by the truth" (Taylor 1986, 80).

But Foucault refused to adopt such a stance, according to Taylor. 'Unmasking falsehood', 'liberation aided by the truth': these phrases suggest the notion that Foucault was giving us a critique of ideology. Yet Foucault seems not only not to have seen it this way but to have been ironically dismissive of the idea. Recall one aspect of the truth objection: Foucault believed that theorists who claim to be unmasking ideology tend, unhelpfully, to conceive of truth and science in opposition to false, ideological consciousness. Troubled by Foucault's reluctance to view himself as standing up for truth against power, Taylor's core response was to argue that Foucualt's critical accounts of systems of control, like all critical theory, presuppose the notions of truth and freedom in such a way that truth is opposed to power and ideology and some idea of freedom is at least implicitly appealed to as a critical standard to evaluate (or even recognize) relations of power and domination. And he claimed that this is just a matter of using the relevant words in a coherent way, in a way that does not reduce to confused nonsense and that preserves the critical intent behind much of Foucault's political writing.

Taylor remarked, correctly, that any form of domination, even if it is partly self-imposed, is possible only if there is "a background of desires, interests, purposes" that people have and if "it makes a dent in these, if it frustrates them, prevents them from fulfilment, or perhaps even from formu-lation," diminishing freedom in these ways (Taylor 1986, 91). Foucault's genealogies can be critical only if power and domination can be counterposed to truth and freedom. This is the core of Taylor's argument:

> ... 'power' belongs in a semantic field from which 'truth' and 'freedom' cannot be excluded. Because it is linked with the notion of the imposi-tion on our significant desires/purposes, it cannot be separated from the notion of some relative lifting of this restraint, from an unimpeded [or less impeded] fulfilment of these desires/purposes. But this is just what is involved in a notion of freedom ... power, in [Foucault's] sense, *does not make sense* [as a critically useful category] without at least the idea of liberation. (Taylor 1986, 91–2)

And the truth, Taylor wrote, "is on the side of the lifting of impositions, of what we have just called liberation.... To speak of power, and to want to deny a place to 'liberation' and 'truth', as well as the link between them, is to speak incoherently" (Taylor 1986, 93). This is how 'truth' fits into the picture:

> 'Power' in the way Foucault sees it, closely linked to 'domination', does not require a clearly demarcated perpetrator, but it requires a victim. It cannot be a 'victimless crime', so to speak. Perhaps the victims also exercise it, also victimise others. But power needs targets. Something must be being imposed on someone, if there is to be domination. *Perhaps that person is also helping to impose it on himself, but then there must be an element of fraud, illusion, false pretences involved in this. Otherwise, it is not clear that the imposition is in any sense an exercise of domination.* (Taylor 1986, 91; emphasis added)

In regard to the (relatively unimportant) question of Foucault interpreta-tion, I am inclined to the view that Foucault cannot plausibly be construed as denying Taylor's main points and that Taylor's (rather conceptual) argument does not address Foucault's deeper critique of modern power. For example, the fact that Foucault's critical histories of modern practices and norms seem to presuppose an idea of freedom does not establish the plausibility of the Enlightenment ideal of a *general* emancipation. The differences here between Foucault and more utopian thinkers such as Marx and Habermas are not merely conceptual (or even moral) but rooted in differing assessments of historical feasibility and of what is the most useful theoretical or interpretive framework for understanding and coping with power and oppression in the modern world.

Even so, it may be worth remembering Taylor's general point about Foucault's critical histories. There are two features of these histories that make them *critical* analyses of modern social life: (1) they unmask illusions that people have about themselves and their social practices, in part by showing that these practices are, despite appearances, feeding some system or 'network' of social coercion or control; and relatedly (2) they show, or at least suggest, how these systems of control work to frustrate or prevent the fulfilment or satisfaction of some 'significant' desires, purposes, needs or interests, not only directly or 'negatively' through repression but also (in Foucault's historical narratives) "by inducing in us a certain self-understanding, an identity" which, characteristically, locks us into power relations though not only as passive victims but often as agents and victimisers as well. What Taylor suggests is that (1) and (2) presuppose or rely upon (a) a distinction between true and false beliefs about ourselves and our social practices, as well as (b) some minimal idea of liberation, the idea that Foucault's 'power/knowledge' regimes, if they exist, make us (or many of us) less free or less autonomous than we could be in other social contexts.[12]

In effect, Taylor's response to the truth objection (to his understanding of it) is to remind us that critical language-games such as Foucault's cannot coherently disavow a concern for truth or a valuing of truth. This would be a sensible response, provided that by 'truth' one meant, simply and redundantly, 'truths as opposed to or as distinct from falsehoods', provided that truth is not held out as a goal of inquiry above and beyond the goal of justifying our beliefs as best we can in our circumstances, and provided that a concern for truth is not confused with a concern for Truth.[13]

4. Anti-representationalism and the deflation of truth

To explain and elaborate on the preceding section's conclusion, I will begin by referring to one of the classical pragmatists, John Dewey. Dewey wrote that "the profuseness of attestations to supreme devotion to truth on the part of philosophy is matter to arouse suspicion." Such attestations, he claimed, have "usually been a preliminary to the claim [that philosophy can be, or tell us about] a peculiar organ of access to highest and ultimate truth" (Dewey 1958,

410; citation from Davidson 1990, 279). Foucault was no less suspicious than Dewey of such (rather boastful) philosophical claims about or relating to truth. He certainly did not believe that there was a special realm of philosophical truth or that philosophy as a particular discipline had unique access to the nature of truth, let alone to 'highest and ultimate truth', whatever that may be. Foucault and Dewey, both anti-essentialists, did not leave much room for the idea that truth even has an essence or nature. (Of course, the classical pragmatists, including Dewey, did have theories of truth and this is a key difference between them and contemporary pragmatists such as Rorty and Nielsen; the latter reject classical pragmatist theories of truth and retain the anti-representationalism and anti-essentialism).

However, it is not clear why *such* truth-talk, *such* assumptions about truth and philosophy, are necessary or even helpful for understanding the distinction between true and false beliefs (or sentences, utterances, propositions). Much of our speech and communication, not only those instances in which ideology is being criticised, seems to rely on and take for granted this distinction. Manifestly frustrated with Foucault's provocative claims about truth and power, Michael Walzer correctly (though condescendingly) observed that Foucault, like anyone else, used declarative sentences; he made assertions of which it makes sense to say that they are or were either true or false or probably true or probably false; and he implied and assumed things that are or were either true or false or probably true or probably false (Walzer 1988). But this can be understood as just another way of saying, trivially, that Foucault was linguistically competent; the ability to wield a true/false distinction can be understood simply as being part of what makes communication possible (Ramberg 2001; Davidson 1990). We all know how to operate with the ordinary concept of truth, how to draw a true/false distinction, even if we have no idea what the supposed essence or nature of Truth may be.

Perhaps more interestingly, Foucault, unlike some of his less careful admirers, was *not* sceptical in any sort of Cartesian or relativistic way about claims to scientific knowledge: he suggested that he wanted to resist 'scientism', which he construed as "a dogmatic belief in the value of scientific knowledge," but that he was not concerned to argue for "a sceptical or relativistic refusal of all verified truth" (1982, 212). Whatever the significant differences are between Taylor and Foucault in this context, they, like everyone else, both make use of a true/false distinction and both would in circumstances of actual inquiry prefer to believe truths rather than falsehoods in their domains of inquiry.

The trouble begins when, reflecting on what we seek when we seek truth, we interpret truth in representationalist terms; as Wittgenstein might say, when we bring in a certain, superfluous metaphysical picture.[14]

What anti-representationalists find most objectionable is precisely the metaphysical baggage that tends to be attached to our truth-talk: the idea that truth is a relation of representation or correspondence between mind (or language) and the world, that truth is the crucial relation or property that keeps us solidly grounded in the world, keeps us from losing touch with it or being alienated from it, and that truth is the primary goal of inquiry, a goal that surpasses the 'mere' justification of our views to other people and to ourselves. These ideas (among others), the argument goes, are excisable from our understanding of truth; the claim is that it is an illusion, or at any rate unhelpful and problematic to think that representations (in our heads or in our language in the form of statements or propositions) may somehow 'connect' us to reality. We are already in constant *causal* contact with the world beyond our bodies; there is nothing beyond this that connects us to, or that ensures our bond with, the nonhuman world. From this perspective, human interaction with the nonhuman is of a piece with the interaction of nonhuman animals with their environments; we humans just cope with our environments in different, often more complex ways involving language but like the other animals, we are fully part of the spatio-temporal universe and like them, we struggle to cope with and adapt ourselves to our environments. Sticking with this naturalistic Darwinian conception of ourselves (while resisting the temptation to depict characteristic-ally human attributes as somehow ennabling us to transcend our socio-cultural contexts, the contingency of our lot, or our finitude), Rorty and Nielsen recommend that we see our various, frequently overlapping 'vocabularies' or 'language-games' as being no more (or no less) than different ways of adapting to and coping with our environments and our lives; they should not be viewed as being, in addition, different ways of representing what reality is like apart from human needs and ways of interpreting and describing (Rorty 2000; Nielsen 1996, 2001).

Pragmatists do not deny that we can make true statements about things that exist independently of our minds. They are not like Bishop Berkeley, as they do not think that to be is to be perceived, but they reject the notion that we can match bits of our languages to bits of the non-linguistic world so that we can be sure that just those bits of language (perhaps along with a few other bits with the same meaning) accurately represent or mirror the world. Such a view of language mirroring reality seems to rest on the idea that we can transcend the vicissitudes of language in order to see, finally free from our historically specific enculturation, which beliefs or sentences or propositions correspond to what the world is really like in itself, what it would be like anyway, apart from our modes of description and categorisation. But this idea of mirroring the wordless essence of things is just what pragmatists suggest we can do well without.

Given this understanding, both Rorty and Nielsen still maintain that we can go on as usual drawing a true/false distinction (it is useful after all), trying to be truthful and honest in pursuit of our various projects, but they equally stress that we can do this without any commitment to representationalism or to any philosophical *theory* about the nature of Truth.

Two contemporary 'truth' deflationists, Paul Horwich and Michael Williams, argue in their different ways that philosophy should give up the search for a robust theory of Truth; they try to provide support for Rorty's contention that "truth is not the sort of thing one should expect to have a philosophically interesting theory about"; as well as the contention that it will not help in justifying one's beliefs to know the essence of Truth (Rorty 1982, xiii, xv).

Williams stresses the deflationary character of Alfred Tarski's 'disquotational' account of the truth predicate. Tarski's general formula is that "p is true in L [a particular 'natural' language] if and only if P" — "'Snow is white' is true (in English) if and only if snow is white," and so on. Williams thinks that this schema captures something about the ordinary concept of truth, about the meaning of the predicate 'is true', even if it seems not to tell us anything new or exciting. But it gives us a way of looking at our use of the adjective 'true'. He claims that "[p]erhaps in conjunction with some additional conventions to cover cases like 'Everything he told you was true, where 'true' is used in connection with statements not directly quoted, it fixes the extension of the truth predicate for language L." He argues that this tells us "all, or just about all, we need to know about truth"; though he adds that, in addition to using it for verbal convenience, we use the word 'true' as a normative compliment or to indicate agreement (Williams 1986, 223–41). English speakers also use the word 'true' in other ways that have been of little interest to epistemologists in the analytical tradition. For example, we might speak of a 'true work of art'. Here 'true' means something like 'genuine', a kind of normative compliment.

Horwich in a similar vein says that when it comes to the question of the meaning of 'truth', "just about the only uncontroversial fact to be found in this domain" is "that the proposition that snow is white is true if and only if snow is white, the proposition that tachyons exist is true if and only if tachyons exist, and so on" (Horwich 1990, 127). Horwich generalises this 'uncontroversial fact' with the "equivalence schema":

"the proposition *u (that p)* is true if and only if *p*"

Like Williams, Horwich argues that this minimal understanding of the concept of truth, an understanding that merely gives a formal, general schema that can be concretised with the insertion of particular assertions or propositions in place of *p*, is all we need; that is, it is all we need in order to understand the predicate 'is true' (Horwich 1999a, p. 20). Horwich and Tarski provide formal accounts which, though perhaps not complete accounts of truth (though what a 'complete account' could be is not clear), are accounts of how, typically, we use the word 'true' or the predicate 'is true'. In speaking of the concern for truth, then, the only sense of 'true' that we need, according to deflationism, is the sense that is conveyed by our acceptance of typical instances of the equivalence schema — our disposition to accept non-paradoxical sentences like 'It is true that snow is white if and only if snow is white.'

Deflationism is not a form of 'reductionism' with respect to truth. Our willingness to settle for disquotationalism (i.e., the schema "'p' is true in L if and only p") plus comments on the performative use of 'true' — where it functions as a way of endorsing, commending, indicating agreement or cautioning us that even our best justified beliefs may be found not to be justified by a future community — does not commit us to viewing truth as being semantically reducible to some more basic notion of justification or anything else. Truth remains a primitive, indefinable notion. And in saying that some beliefs of ours, though justified may not after all be true, we are in fact reminding ourselves of our fallibility. This cautionary role of the concept of truth, for Rorty, is its most important function. Truth in its cautionary use helps us to preserve a sense of our fallibility because it reminds us that "[b]elief is as intrinsically disputable as it is intrinsically veridical" (Rorty 2001b, 375). The important point here is that in saying "X is perfectly justified but may not be true," we should not be taken to imply either (a) that X though justified may not after all accurately represent reality as it is in itself (as the correspondence theory would have it) or (b) that X though currently justified may not be justified at the ideal end of inquiry (as a Piercean 'epistemic' theory would have it). Recall that, on the disquotational view, 'X is true' does not say or mean 'X is assertable' or 'X is assertable by the norms of my culture' or 'X is what will be agreed to at the ideal end of inquiry'. These are not, on disquotational views, equivalent expressions. 'X is true' just says (and means) whatever X says, so that, typically, 'X is true' is rightly assertable whenever X is.

Significantly, there is no attempt on deflationary views to explain or account for the relation between our representations of the world and the world — through some causal theory of reference, for example. For the deflationist (or as Horwich would say, minimalist) but not for correspondence theorists, there is no general problem about how our beliefs 'hook up with' or 'map onto' an 'external' reality.

Though Davidson rejected deflationism and minimalism on the grounds that these views do not tell us all that we need or want to know about truth, the minimalist conception does square with with Davidson's view that there is no sense to the idea "of an uninterpreted reality, something outside all schemes and science" to which our sentences, theories or conceptual schemes correspond or fail to correspond (Davidson 1985, 198). In this context Davidson was using the word 'uninterpreted' in a broad sense: anything that involves language is interpreted. But though Davidson was using 'uninterpreted' in this broad way, it was appropriate to do so in the context of his discussion of the representational-ist 'scheme-content' dualism. In this broad sense of 'uninterpreted', even planets, mountains, rivers and trees are not part of an uninterpreted reality; we use language and concepts just in identifying anything as planets, mountains, rivers and trees and in so doing we presuppose an indefinite number of things — just think of what is involved, how much we presuppose and commit ourselves to just in speaking of the planets (Putnam 1983, 1985). We could say that before the planet Pluto was discovered it *was* an uninterpreted reality, since nobody knew about it and we humans did not bring it into being by discovering it or beginning to describe it. In saying this we would be saying what the pragmatist considers truistic and trivial — as distinct from a deep metaphysical insight. The pragmatist, by rejecting the correspondence theory with its inherent representationalism, does not commit to a kind of metaphysical idealism. That Pluto exists independently of people, that it existed before it was discovered by people, that its existence is *causally* independent of human existence and human inquiry, these things no one can reasonably deny. Pluto would exist even if people did not exist. But how can we (anti-representationalists) say this? If we take seriously Davidson's critique of the dualism of conceptual scheme and uninterpreted, undifferentiated content, how can we then say that Pluto, as a distinct entity of the sort we call a planet, existed before humans began to conceptualise it and talk about it? Wouldn't that commit us to saying that Pluto is part of the world as it really is, as it is apart from our take on it, our ways of talking about planets?

The right anti-representationalist answer will seem question-begging to 'realists': namely, that according to *our* norms for describing planets we cannot rightly say that Pluto would cease to exist when humans cease to exist or that it came into being when we categorised it as the ninth furthest planet from the sun in our solar system. Our norms for planet-description include the idea that the existence of the planets is causally independent of human activities. If someone were sincerely to state that Pluto literally came into being when someone spotted it, this person would not be using the word 'Pluto' in the way it is normally used. (See Rorty's argument in his 'Response to Ramberg', 2001b, 374.) In speaking of Pluto (normally) we are speaking the language of planet-description but this, pragmatists insist, is not Nature's language; we are not describing things just the way the world compels us to describe them or representing a part of the world as it intrinsically, essentially is apart from our linguistic and social practices. Anti-representationalists such as Rorty and Davidson deny that this idea of representing the way things really are can be cashed out in a non-question-begging way.

For anti-representationalists, then, what needs to be dropped from our understanding of truth is the idea that the truth of our beliefs can be analysed, explained or accounted for in terms of the relations between our beliefs (or statements, propositions, etc.) and an uninterpreted reality (in the broad sense of 'uninterpreted'). For as soon as we specify a part of the world to which our sentences or theories correspond, we defeat the purpose of talk of truth-as-correspondence. In specifying or identifying non-linguistic entities we are already presupposing a language, norms of description, explanation and so on. We are not attaining some vantage point 'beyond' language and then comparing or matching parts of that language with parts of the non-linguistic world; such 'transcendence', again, is an illusion. But the representationalist idea of truth-as-correspondence was supposed to highlight the tight connection (or 'isomorphism') between true beliefs or sentences and non-linguistic reality, between our knowledge of reality and reality itself. Rorty, sympathetic to Michael Williams's scepticism towards epistemological scepticism, puts the anti-representationalist point this way:

> Williams has pointed out that epistemology, the idea of a philosophical account of something called 'human knowledge', and scepticism, the idea that human beings are incapable of knowledge, go hand-in-hand. As long as you talk about knowledge of snow, or the Trinity, or positrons, it is hard to be either an epistemologist or a sceptic, for you have to respect the norms built into discourse about these various things. Only when you start talking about Our Knowledge of Reality as such, a topic concerning which there are no norms, can you become either. 'Reality' and 'Our Knowledge of Reality' are alternative names for the normless. That is why metaphysics and epistemology go together like ham and eggs. (Rorty 2001b, 375–6)

Referring to John McDowell's attempt to rescue the idea of inquiry being somehow 'answerable to the world', Rorty makes a similar point forcefully and provocatively, relating it to the pervasive sense of alienation that he finds in philosophy from Plato to contemporary thinking about truth, reference and meaning:

> We shall fear that the world is on the verge of absconding as long as we think that causal connection with the world is not a tight enough way of bonding with it.... One should just cling to the thought that what Kant

calls our 'empirical' self — the only one we have — is the causal
product of the 'empirical' world, the only one there is.... [John
McDowell, in his *Mind and World*, keeps alive] the pathos of possible
distance from the world. He does this when he insists ... that merely
causal relations with the world do not suffice. This claim keeps alive the
pathetic Kantian question about the 'transcendental status' of the world.
(Rorty 2001c, 124)

Although my aim here is not to provide decisive arguments for anti-
representationalism and deflationary views of truth, I do wish to stress the
distinctiveness of these views and to draw attention to some of their
implications (and non-implications). So I wish to stress, with Horwich, that
"[t]he deflationary attitude toward truth ... is a reaction against the natural and
widespread idea that the property of truth has some sort of underlying nature
and that our problem as philosophers is to say what that nature is, to analyse
truth either conceptually or substantively, to specify, at least roughly, the
conditions necessary and sufficient for something to be true" (Horwich 1999a,
239). Williams, likewise, stresses that the importance of the deflationary view is
not that it offers new insights into the nature of truth but that "it challenges us to
say why we need any theory of truth along anything like traditional lines"
(1986, 223).[15] Correspondence theorists point to problems with coherence
theories of truth and other epistemic theories, while coherence theorists attack
the idea of correspondence. One of the virtues of minimalist or deflationary
views, according to Williams, is that the deflationist "is committed neither to
fleshing out the idea of truth as correspondence nor to showing that truth is at
bottom some kind of epistemic notion" (such as ideal rational acceptability or
coherence). The deflationist "has doubts about both projects: about their
feasibility and, above all, about their point" (Williams 1986, 226).
      As to feasibility, the deflationist doubts that truth can be defined in terms
of ideal justification or verification conditions, in terms of what it is good to
believe or in terms of a relation between language (or mind) and the world that
is specifiable independently of the relation between some beliefs and other
beliefs. She also doubts that there is anything like a 'property' common to all
true sentences — moral, aesthetic, mathematical, scientific, commonsensical
and other types of sentences which can be true or false — other than their being
amenable to being plugged into Horwich's equivalence schema (or into Tarski's
disquotational schema).
      Both Rorty and Nielsen maintain that once we abandon representational-
ism, we can accept that all kinds of sentences from many kinds of vocabularies
(not just those of the 'hard sciences') can have truth-values, be true or false.
Without the idea of the intrinsic nature of reality there is little sense or point in

singling out some types (say, the sentences of physics) as giving us 'real, substantial truth' whereas other types (say, moral judgments) are somehow second-rate truths, not really mapping onto the world as do the sentences of the physical sciences. For the deflationist, truths are truths and none of our beliefs, judgments or sentences 'map onto the world'; inasmuch as she is an anti-representationalist she will avoid making invidious distinctions between forms of inquiry on the basis that some of these more accurately represent the intrinsic nature of reality than others. She will give up all such talk and talk instead about acquiring justified beliefs about things like snow or US foreign policy or unicorns or planets; it is all about providing more or less coherent accounts of *specific* things or domains, not of Reality or the World.

Being concerned with truth in a particular context of inquiry (say, in the context of sociological inquiry into the functioning of the modern state) should be distinguished from being concerned with Truth in philosophy. In philosophy, Truth ('truth itself') has been an object of reflection and inquiry; the adjective 'true' has been nominalised. The deflationists and anti-representationalists are reacting against what they perceive to be the 'inflated' conceptions of truth that have preoccupied philosophers or been implicit in their philosophising. In the history of western philosophy, they think, truth has been treated as if it were more than just a matter of verbal convenience, cautionary, a normative compliment or a way of indicating agreement (as in 'Yes, that's true'). Rorty repeatedly suggests that Truth in philosophy (and in the broader culture) often functions as a virtual secular substitute for God, as a quasi-divine relation between humans and an unchanging or constantly changing reality, a relation that transcends historical and cultural contexts; or again, one that facilitates our separating the wheat from the chaff in our discourse by distinguishing the genuinely truth-tracking, world-depicting vocabularies (typically, those of the 'hard sciences') from the less truth-tracking or purely non-cognitive vocabularies (typically, those of the 'soft sciences' and the humanities). Truth, in this replacement-for-God role, not only in western philosophy and culture, has been treated as an object of ultimate concern whose essence philosophers (or some other reflective, diligent inquirers) are specially trained or positioned to reveal or discover. (But even if it is not thought to be an object of ultimate concern, thinking of truth as an object or property or as having a nature is problematic. The grammatical similarity between the predicate 'is true' and, for example, the predicate 'is magnetic', may have encouraged the bad idea that we may have a useful theory of truth just as we have a useful theory of magnetism.)

What the pragmatist anti-representationalist refuses, then, is not the pursuit of justified beliefs in this or that domain of inquiry but i) a certain interpretation of what we are doing when we say we are pursuing truth and ii) the urge — the Platonistic urge — to grasp the nature of Truth itself, to provide a general informative theory of Truth that would explain, for example, what all true sentences (sentences in mathematics, aesthetics, morality, physics, biology, history and so on) have in common that 'makes' them true and distinguishes them from the false ones.

I have discussed the second point in the context of anti-representationalism and the questionable ideas of the 'intrinsic nature of reality' or 'how things are in themselves'. On the first point, Rorty insists that the distinction between truth and justification is not as interesting as philosophers have made it out to be. (See Rorty's review of Habermas's *Truth and Justification*, 2003.) As we have seen, it makes linguistic sense to say that even the most adequately justified belief may be false and so the true/false couplet is not equivalent in meaning to the justified/unjustified couplet. This counts against attempts to provide necessary and sufficient conditions for truth in terms of ideal justification and related 'epistemic' notions; and, as mentioned above, it points to what Rorty regards as the most useful function served by the ordinary concept of truth — it cautions us not to view ourselves as infallible, reminding us that even our best justified beliefs may turn out not to seem justified to a future community, one that is a better version of ourselves (Rorty 1998, pp. 43–63) . Rorty's point, however, is that even though truth is a primitive, indefinable notion, irreducible to justification, the only way we have of ascertaining whether an inquirer is pursuing truth is by ascertaining whether they are pursuing justification. Another way of putting this is to say that a concern for truth, in practice, is indistinguishable from a concern for justification.

What do we mean when we say that one should pursue truth or show a concern for truth in one's inquiries? Do we mean anything coherent at all? Perhaps we do, but there may be no non-circular way to show this; there may be no getting behind our use of phrases such as 'pursue truth' or 'concern for truth' to some essential property that indicates the presence of truth. When we speak without irony of the concern for truth, it seems we run together the concepts of truth and (ideal) justification; it seems we mean 'concern for justification' but we call it 'concern for truth'. On the one hand, justification and truth are not equivalent in meaning, the latter irreducible to the former in ordinary usage, particularly our cautionary use of 'true'; on the other hand, if we do not take to heart Rorty's point about the concern for truth being nothing more, in practice, than the concern for justification, then we run the risk of returning to representationalism with all its problems. This is the move, the positing of truth as a goal of inquiry above and beyond justification, that leads us down the garden path (Rorty 1998, 19–42).

What is involved in inquiry? First, to state the obvious, in any domain of inquiry the inquirers typically will aim to contribute to knowledge of that part of the world into which they are inquiring. They will, at least, be interested in distinguishing justified from unjustified views in their domains of inquiry. But they will also, in showing a concern for truth, try to present their views in ways that are not significantly misleading, that take into account at least some relevant opposing views, that do not ignore relevant and available evidence, and that do not depend on an unwillingness to question their own assumptions, methods, premises, and so on (or an unwillingness to have them questioned). Perhaps most inquirers assume that the most warranted beliefs or theories in their domains of inquiry are the beliefs or theories most likely to be true (or approximately true). Then we can say, innocuously enough, that they will aim for truth; but in coming to see what this comes to, eschewing representationalist accounts of truth, we see that it means that they will use methods which they believe are best suited, in particular contexts of inquiry, to yielding rationally justified beliefs, beliefs which have the 'force of the better argument' (as Habermas puts it) on their side.[16] There will be good reasons for adopting these beliefs, holding them true (or at least justified) though we may caution ourselves that they may not, even if justified, be true; and the gloss Rorty puts on this, again, is that they may not seem justified to a future community. In pursuing truth, then, the standards and criteria used will be those assumed most likely to yield justified beliefs in particular contexts of inquiry. We can (and do) call this sort of thing aiming for truth, but we could just as well — and more literally — call it aiming for the best justified beliefs we can attain regarding some problem/s in specific domains of inquiry.

Note that this idea of aiming for truth (that is, trying to form justified beliefs) is compatible with the idea of using torture in certain situations to find out the truth. The idea of 'truth at all costs' thus should raise an eyebrow. And before waxing lyrical about the intrinsic value of truth (as has often been done in the history of truth-talk) one should consider Somerset Maugham's remark, written in the context of a discussion of philosophers' quarrels about the meaning of 'truth', that "a bridge that joined two great cities would be more important than a bridge that led from one barren field to another"; some truths are more important, more worth uttering, less trivial, or misleading or counter-productive than others (Maugham 2001). This commonsensical recognition fits with the pragmatist critique of philosophical discourse about intrinsic value; if there are many situations in which it would be cruel to assert what we regard as true (such as 'I find you ugly') or it would be counterproductive (such as 'You would understand my meaning if you were less selfish'), why say truth is intrinsically valuable? If there are such recurring situations in which it would not be a good thing to be truthful why not content ourselves with the idea that a concern for truth (i.e., for acquiring and putting forth justified beliefs) will in many (or most) cases be instrumentally valuable, helping us to achieve greater happiness, freedom, and democracy, for example? Isn't that good enough?

In speaking of the concern for truth, then, we should say that such a concern, if it is anything coherent, involves trying to arrive at the most coherent and plausible justified position currently achievable and treating contrary views with reasonable open-mindedness. Is there something more metaphysical to the concern for truth? If so, that metaphysical turn is not necessary for making sense of it.

Keeping in mind Horwich and Williams and their deflationary accounts of the meaning of 'truth', the pursuit of truth can be understood as the pursuit of justification without thereby equating truth and justification. Truth remains a primitive notion, unanalysable in terms of something allegedly more basic: in terms of ideal justification, what is good to believe, what would be verified in ideal conditions, what would be consented to in ideal conditions and so on. Again, for the deflationist anti-representationalist, truth is truth and there is not much more, after all, to be said about the nature of truth.

It should be clear that a concern for truth, *so conceived*, is distinct from a concern to analyse or uncover the meaning or essence or nature of Truth. It is distinct from a concern for 'truth itself' in that sense. Truth itself is not the object of our investigations, if 'truth itself' is thought to refer to a theoretically significant property common to all true sentences or theories, a property, like magnetism, which might play a causal role so that it could even, perhaps, explain the success of our methods or theories.[17]

Bernard Williams, in his *Truth and Truthfulness: An Essay in Genealogy* (2002), expresses discomfort with the idea that the pursuit of justified beliefs in some domain is in practice the same as the pursuit of truth in that domain; that aiming for truth is not a separate thing from aiming for justification — though, again, truth in its ordinary sense is not *semantically* reducible to justification. Williams thinks that we need to have some criteria for distinguishing the good from the bad methods of justifying beliefs, the truth-tracking methods from the distorting methods and he thinks that pragmatism falls short here. But consider Rorty's response to Williams on this point:

> ... the only answer the pragmatist can give [to "the question of how we tell methods of acquiring truth from other methods of producing consensus"] is that the procedures we use for justifying beliefs to one another are among the things that we try to justify to one another. We used to think that Scripture was a good way of settling astronomical questions, and pontifical pronouncements a good way of resolving moral dilemmas, but we argued ourselves out of both convictions. But suppose we now ask: were the arguments we offered for changing our approach to these matters good arguments, or were they just a form of brainwashing [or ideology]? At this point, pragmatists think, our spade is

turned. For we have, as Williams himself says ... no way to compare our representations as a whole with the way things are in themselves....

[In claiming that metaphysics and epistemology can show us which procedures are truth-acquiring and which not] Williams would seem to be claiming that these metaphysicians and epistemologists stand on neutral ground when deciding between various ways of reaching agreement. They can stand outside history, look with an impartial eye at the Reformation, the Scientific Revolution and the Enlightenment, and then, by applying their own special, specifically philosophical, truth-acquiring methods, underwrite our belief that Europe's chances of acquiring truth were increased by those events. They can do all this, presumably, without falling back into what Williams scorns as 'the rationalistic theory of rationality'....

As far as I can see, Williams's [argument] stands or falls with the claim that analytic philosophers really can do the wonderful things he tells us they can — that they are ... independent experts whose endorsement of our present ways of justifying beliefs is based on a superior knowledge of what it is for various propositions to be true. Williams would have had a hard time convincing Nietzsche, Dewey or the later Wittgenstein that they had any such knowledge. (Rorty 2002)

Consider Rorty's claim that because pragmatists cannot make sense of representationalism and the correspondence theory of truth — the idea that truth is a matter of correspondence between representations and the way things are in themselves apart from any representations — they cannot say, in any non-circular way, why the arguments for, say, discarding Aristotelian physics in favour of more modern assumptions about the physical world, are justified.

Rorty is suggesting, again, that we cannot attain some vantage point outside our whole web of beliefs, attitudes and preferences and then compare this web to something called 'the way things are' or 'the intrinsic nature of reality'. Science no more than religion or poetry can do *that*. But this does not imply that we cannot have better or worse arguments for this or that opinion; Rorty surely cannot be denying or committed to denying this truism. To do so would be to move too quickly from "There is no point of view beyond language (beyond historically specific linguistic practices) from which to compare our language to non-linguistic reality" to "There is no point of view from which reasonably to criticise some of our current practices and ways of speaking."

The important Rortyan point is that 'better' and 'reasonable' should be glossed as "better or more reasonable according to the standards of this or that community — perhaps extending, in some cases, to all or most of humanity." There is, for anti-representationalists (and to use sexual metaphors) no getting beneath, behind or on top of our talk about the world to the world-as-it-is-in-itself, there in its naked, uninterpreted reality. There are only more or less justified, more or less coherent views, theories, perspectives, and it is in these terms that we must distinguish more or less distorting, more or less ideological perspectives.

In *Philosophy and Social Hope* (2000, p. 20) Rorty concedes that we can make "local" and "contextual" distinctions between "ideological education" and "non-ideological education." Typically he is suspicious of such talk, implying that when critical theorist's theorise about ideology they are opposing ideology to reality-as-it-is-in-itself or to universal validity.

Foucault, like Rorty, was an anti-representationalist and, like Rorty, he raised doubts about ideology-critique insofar as its proponents, Marxian or otherwise, assumed a notion of truth as accurate representation of the intrinsic nature of things — including the intrinsic nature of 'man'. But we have seen that the idea of pursuing truth in a particular domain of inquiry can be disentangled from representationalism if we blur the distinction between aiming for truth and aiming for ideal justification — ideal by the lights of some present community — without thereby *defining* truth in terms of justification. By focusing attention on practices of justification we can come to see that there is no need finally to appeal to a nonhuman authority (the World or How Things Are In Themselves) to ground our beliefs.

By jettisoning the image of language magically representing non-linguistic chunks of reality, we also drop the Platonistic idea of, to quote Ramberg again, "a particular form of description of things, which, by virtue of its ability to accurately map, reflect, or otherwise latch on to just those kinds through which the world presents itself to would-be knowers, is the form in which any literally true — or cognitively significant, or ontologically ingenuous — statement must be couched" (Ramberg 2001, 351). But neither move prevents us from speaking of more or less coherent or justified, more or less distorting or ideological perspectives.

That we do not have a globally encompassing super-perspective beyond all particular perspectives does not entail that we do not (or cannot) have more or less rational perspectives on our social and political lives and on how they might be made better. 'Rationality' and 'reasonableness' may not be names for a faculty or capacity that facilitates the sort of 'transcendence' or 'grounded-ness' that have been the promise of various strands in our metaphysical and epistemological traditions in philosophy and theology, but we may nevertheless be able to come to more or less coherent and reasonable views on things. We need simply to remain contextualist about everything, including our notions of 'reasonableness', 'rationality' and 'ideology'.

5. Foucault's 'truth-objection' to ideology-critique

Foucault's 'truth objection' to ideology-critique, however, was not simply a philosophical questioning of assumptions about truth. Here is a further statement of that objection in another of Foucault's interviews:

> Philosophers or even, more generally, intellectuals justify and mark out their identity by trying to establish an almost uncrossable line between the domain of knowledge, seen as that of truth and freedom, and the domain of the exercise of power. What struck me, in observing the human sciences, was that the development of all these branches of knowledge can in no way be dissociated from the exercise of power. Of course, you will always find psychological or sociological theories that are independent of power. But, generally speaking, the fact that societies can become the object of scientific observation, that human behaviour became, from a certain point on, a problem to be analysed and resolved, all that is bound up, I believe, with mechanisms of power — which, at a given moment, indeed, analysed that object (society, man, etc.) and presented it as a problem to be resolved. So the birth of the human sciences goes hand in hand with the installation of new mechanisms of power. (1990, 106)

In a similar spirit, Barry Allen (one of Foucault's sympathetic commentators and a fine Foucault scholar) gives this answer to Nietzsche's question 'What good is truth?':

> In itself, truth is neither good nor wicked.... Considered in abstraction from *what* truth is in question, *for whom* it is passing true and to *what effect*, truth 'itself' has no more value than coins apart from their circulation. It should be no more surprising that truth can be used badly or be a source of disorder or political control than to hear the same said of money. The question 'What good is truth?' can and must therefore be divided into many smaller, local questions, and these questions touch directly upon those who (to recall [C. Wright] Mills's description) 'professionally create, destroy, elaborate ... symbols'. (1991, 439)

Allen presents these claims in the context of a discussion of Foucault's contention, against those who would contrast truth and science to ideology and power, that "[t]he political question ... is not error, illusion, alienated consciousness or ideology; it is truth itself" (Foucault 2000, 133).

How is one to interpret Foucault (and Allen) and the idea that the political question is 'truth itself' rather than 'error, illusion, alienated consciousness'? There seems to be something right in what Foucault and Allen are gesturing at, yet it is not clear why it should be viewed as a critique of ideology-critique rather than as being itself another instance of ideology-critique. We must keep in mind here that Foucault was not using the word 'truth' in any ordinary sense. He stipulated that in this context 'truth' means "not 'the ensemble of truths to be discovered and accepted' but, rather, 'the ensemble of rules according to which the true and the false are separated and specific effects of power attached to the true'" (2000, 132). Foucault was well aware that in the various human and social sciences, research is pursued which does in fact produce knowledge of societies and human behaviour. Evidently there is some concern for truth (in the sense specified in section four) in these disciplines and these disciplines, undeniably, have expanded our repertoire of truths or at least justified beliefs, in various domains of inquiry. There is more knowledge now than there was before 'society' and 'man' became 'problem-atised' and made into objects of scientific theory and analysis. There has, in fact, been an explosion of knowledge in modern times and there is a constant demand for more of it — for more truth. Moreover, this has occurred under the banner of science and the human and social sciences have in fact strived, not without success, to be more or less scientific: there has been, though of course not invariably or comprehensively, a concern for empirical evidence and for formulating hypotheses which can be verified or (more or less) confirmed or disconfirmed by seeing how well they, in comparison to rival hypotheses, square with or account for the publicly available evidence — evidence which disputants can in appropriate circumstances of inquiry recognise to be evidence. There has in this way and to this extent been a concern for truth, for finding out more truths about society and human behaviour, and the discourses embodying this concern have been more or less scientific, more or less reliant on concepts and sentences with (what are widely agreed to be) empirical referents and more or less linked to (what are widely agreed to be) empirical (though theory-laden) research programs.

However, contrary to the assumptions of some Marxian and other leftist writers (though not of Marx himself) truth and science are not necessarily or inherently opposed to or independent of power.[18] As Allen correctly remarks, "truth [even truth or justified belief in science] can and regularly does serve this function [i.e., supports some structure of power]" and he adds, "[o]ne might even guess that an asymmetry of power may be all the more stable without the liability of a lie" (1991, 438). But if this is the case, then the notion of ideology as 'false consciousness' is misleading. That notion has too often been set out in ways that suggest that there is a hard and fast line between truth and science, on the one hand, and ideology on the other; but we know that science can also contribute to sustaining oppressive and exploitative social relations. Discourses (or, using Rorty's terminology, vocabularies) should be seen as webs of interrelated statements and judgments embedded in social practices and as being geared towards human (sometimes political) purposes; the image of the disinterested pursuit of knowledge should be taken with a grain of salt. Since purposes are not the sorts of things that are true or false (though there may be good or bad purposes) perhaps it does make sense to say that discourses as a whole are 'neither true nor false'. (But why can discourses not be regarded as more or less distorting or falsifying, more or less coherent or ideological, particularly if one of our purposes is to come to a more comprehensive reflective understanding of a particular domain of social reality — for example, US foreign policy?) At any rate, the important question is not "How does such and such a disourse falsify our understanding and, by doing so, contribute to sustaining domination or oppression?" The more pertinent question is "Whose truth, which rationality, are we implicitly supporting with our research in this or that domain of inquiry?" or "Whose interests are we serving by contributing to or working within the parameters of this rather than that research program, this rather than that paradigm of what counts as knowledge or of what counts as a problem to be solved?"

However, construed as above, Foucault's criticism only seems effective against conceptions of ideology that draw a *hard and fast* line between truth and science, on the one hand, and power and ideology on the other. But there are better conceptions of ideology than that from which critical theory can draw. There is in fact another notion of ideology implicit in leftist usage and in critical theory, one that combines what Geuss calls the 'functional' and 'epistemic' conceptions of ideology, as follows: an ideology, in a pejorative sense of 'ideology', is a web or cluster of (interrelated) beliefs and norms which tend to circulate and function in society in ways that serve *primarily* the needs and interests of some dominant social group or class; and part of what makes it possible for the ideology to so function is that it gives people a distorted understanding of their social world in certain crucial ways.[19] This conception of ideology is *not* committed to denying the justifiability or truth of most or even many of the beliefs of those who are under the sway of an ideology; nor is it committed to denying many or even most of the beliefs that are part of the ideology.[20] However, 'ideology' in this sense does signify that there are widely shared, socially and morally significant, unjustified beliefs, beliefs that give us a distorted understanding of things.

Given this conception of ideology or false consciousness, it is possible to expand on Taylor's claim (against what he regards as Foucault's position) that a concern for truth — as distinct from a concern for Truth — will be opposed and antagonistic to power and ideology. With these qualifications: a concern for truth will be antagonistic to power *in certain persistent social contexts, given some plausible assumptions about what people are like in those contexts and given some plausible views about social and political history.* We should not try, in Cartesian fashion, to suspend all our beliefs, including more or less theory-laden beliefs about the social world and human behaviour. How do we demonstrate the value of truth independently of all we take to be true? There is no way to do so. Instead, we are forced to argue that *some* of what we hold true is worth stressing and that so stressing it will be of value. Relating this to truth and ideology, the point to be argued is that in certain social and historical contexts and in certain domains of inquiry and reflection, a concern for truth will inherently be opposed and antagonistic to power and ideology. This is, in fact, not very different from saying that in some important social and historical contexts and in certain domains of inquiry and reflection, distorting or falsifying ideologies are likely to be prevalent, false consciousness will reign.

6. False-consciousness in history

In this section the reader is invited to assess the plausibility of some broad empirical generalisations about ideology in human societies. These general claims, if plausible, should be sufficient to defeat or at least deflate Foucault's (and Rorty's) scepticism regarding the notion of 'ideology' or 'false consciousness'. I will elaborate certain Marxian claims about ideology in class societies, particularly capitalist societies; but it is the functional/epistemic conception of ideology that is at issue, not the 'ideology as opposed to science' conception that Foucault seems to have attributed to Marxian and other critical theorists.

On the functional/epistemic conception of ideology, we are ideologically mystified to the extent that we are under the sway of misleading, distorting, or otherwise illusory beliefs and theories which tend to encourage or promote dispositions and attitudes that contribute in a systematic way to sustaining relations of unequal power in which some people dominate or oppress others. That is an elaboration of a conception of 'false consciousness' or 'ideological mystification' as these phrases have been used by Marxian (and sometimes Feminist) critical theorists — though it is not the strictly Leninist conception of ideology as a class-serving form of consciousness.[21]

For Foucault, one of the effects of the 'power/knowledge regimes', insofar as these regimes create or perpetuate forms of domination, is to undermine the freedom or autonomy of people by depoliticising them or politicising them in ways that support rather than challenge existing or developing structures of power (see Minson 1985). As Taylor pointed out, this form of 'manufacturing of consent', so to speak, relies on distortion and/or deception (including self-deception). It relies on the widespread acceptance of some morally and politically significant beliefs that mislead, distort, and give us a false sense of what is happening around and to us; it can only be sustained if people are, to some extent, deceived about the 'grid' of power relations in which they are enmeshed, unaware or only dimly aware of the processes undermining their freedom. This insufficient awareness — insufficient from the point of view of those who value freedom — is something that Foucault's genealogies attempt to counter, making us more aware, dispelling some illusions. One such illusion is that we are acting freely so long as we are not being prevented from doing what we want to do by the state authorities; the illusion is to think that the only form of power that impinges on our freedom can be that power which emanates from the state (or a ruling class) and is exercised in a repressive, top-down manner. This is an illusion, according to Foucault, because often our very desires and aspirations are the product of subtle or not-so-subtle manipulation and other sorts of coercion in more local settings, and power is productive as well as repressive, it does not always work by 'saying no' — in Foucault's more colourful language, our self-conceptions are in many ways the products of "a multiplicity of organisms, forces, energies, materials, desires, thoughts, etc." and a "result of the effects of power" though not only the power of the state or a dominant social class (1980, 97–8). At the same time, Foucault maintained, these 'local' exercises of power tend to have 'global' effects: they have been functional for the state's control over our lives and for the continuing stabilisation and strengthening of the evolving (capitalist) economic relations. Foucault was, in this instance, engaging in a kind of ideology-critique: he was critically exposing a pervasive bit of 'false consciousness', in a non-idiosyncratic, philosophically unencumbered sense of 'false consciousness' or 'ideological mystification' (philosophically unencumbered inasmuch as no theory of Truth is involved or presupposed[22]).

Nevertheless, the point worth stressing here, regardless of questions of Foucault interpretation, is that there are true beliefs and there are false beliefs (or, if you prefer, more or less justified, more or less distorting beliefs) and that oppressive institutions and practices are sustained *at least partly* because people are badly mistaken about what they are, how they function and what negative effects they have on the possibilities for human emancipation. If, over considerable stretches of time, these culturally pervasive beliefs and the norms associated with them are not publicly scrutinised and challenged to any significant extent, this will tend to have a stabilising effect on relations of oppression and exploitation, or what comes to virtually the same thing, an anti-destabilising effect. Such stabilising beliefs are, in that way, part and parcel of the history of domination and exploitation. This history does not reflect what Habermas calls a 'democratic will-formation'. Slavery, patriarchy, class domination, racial and ethnic domination, imperialism and many other salient features of human history, do not issue from a consensus rooted in free and open discussions in which the force of the better argument prevailed or from anything like that. Yet these forms of domination have never been sustained long without surrounding themselves with a halo of morality; although they have not been products of rational persuasion in an 'ideal speech situation', they have been rationalised as being good, just, humane, natural, proper, the expression of God's will, the best of all possible or feasible worlds, and so on. On the other hand, people have throughout history questioned and resisted these forms of domination, seeing (to some extent) their accompanying halos of morality as deceptive bits of justifying rhetoric nicely moulded to suit the needs of power.

Foucault was right to stress that in ordinary social life asymmetrical power relations are pervasive; but it is also right to say, as Marvin Harris put it, that "[t]hese inequalities are as much disguised, mystified, and lied about as old age and death" (1989, 6). Harris in his anthropological studies has made clear how many of the forms of domination and oppression mentioned in the preceding paragraph have been bolstered by myths about human beings, human societies, nature, God, the cosmos, history and countless less general false beliefs and views about specific events and actions. Even if one agrees (as Harris does) with Marx's suspicions about historical idealism and so does not treat ideas, world-views and all the 'products of consciousness' as if these were the most basic 'independent variables' in social explanation, it is not un-reasonable to believe that falsifying or mythical forms of consciousness have throughout history played a significant role in persuading (or duping) people into perpetuating hierarchical social relations; relations they would be (or would have been) more likely to resist if they were not (had not been) under the sway of these myths; relations which, at the same time, many people have questioned and resisted and do question and resist, unpersuaded by the halo of system-sustaining ideology surrounding them.

Consider a non-contemporary example of ideology. In societies highly dependent upon slave production (such as Ancient Greece) slaves were con-ceived in the dominant culture in a way that would 'justify' or rationalise the institution of slavery.[23] Aristotle contributed to such a culture, for example, when he argued that "it is by nature that some men are slaves but others are freemen" and that therefore "it is just and to the benefit of the former to serve the latter" (1986, 553). For Aristotle, a genuine slave was not a slave by mere law or custom backed by force (though he tended to be that too) but was "by his nature not his own but belong[ed] to another." Naturally it was both for his own good and the good of "the whole" (that is, the type of social order Aristotle preferred) that he was like "a thing possessed," "an instrument which, existing separately, can be used [by the 'freeman'] for action" (1986, 551). And there was also little doubt in Aristotle's mind or in the dominant culture generally, that "the male is by nature superior to the female" and that therefore it is better for "the male to rule and the female to be ruled" (1986, 551). (For a detailed account of Aristotle's views and assumptions about women, see Susan Moller Okin, (1979).)

The point here is not to moralise about Aristotle the person or even about Ancient Greek culture but to draw attention to what were, at the time, some culturally pervasive ways of understanding the social world. Aristotle was part of a culture (a culture to which he contributed) in which social and political inequality were taken for granted as being part of the natural order of things. As Engels (with slight exaggeration) remarked:

> Among the Greeks and Romans the inequalities of men were of much greater importance than their equality in any respect. It would necessarily have seemed insanity to the ancients that Greeks and barbarians, freemen and slaves, citizens and peregrines, should have a claim to equal political status. (Engels 1976, 128)[24]

The key points are that these ancient 'world-views' likely (a) functioned to prop up Ancient Greek forms of class domination and patriarchy and (b) included some false beliefs and assumptions, beliefs which were crucial *at the time*, for these normative conceptions of society and social order to be persuasive enough to serve the interests they did. They included, for example, convenient beliefs about women and slaves possessing certain traits 'by nature' which made them suitable for occupying subordinate positions in society; beliefs which, from our twenty-first century relatively educated point of view, we tend to regard as being false. There is no escaping the taking of a position here and we can only do this by our own lights; to speak pejoratively of ancient Greek ideology is, at least implicitly, to judge that oppression-sustaining illusions played an important role in ancient Greece. Again, there is no philosophical high-road here; we need to take 'first-order' empirical and normative positions about actual societies and this holds as much for those who deny that 'ideology' is a useful notion as for those who speak of the ideological mystification of social relations.

Moving ahead to modernity, Marx compared the situation of workers in capitalist society to the situation of slaves in slave societies in terms of the potential significance of a certain "advance in awareness":

> [Labour's] recognition of the product as its own, and the judgment that its separation from the conditions of its realisation [that is, its sytematic

subordination to the demands of capital accumulation] is improper —
forcibly imposed — is an enormous advance in awareness, itself the
product of the mode of production resting on capital, and as much the
knell to its doom as, with the slave's awareness that he *cannot be the
property of another*, with his consciousness of himself as a person, the
existence of slavery becomes a merely artificial, vegetative existence,
and ceases to be able to prevail as the basis of production. (1978, 254)

When enough slaves begin to view themselves more as persons and less
as the property of persons, Marx seems to have been suggesting, slave-based
socio-economic orders are then doomed to give way (sooner or later) to some
other form of social life. And when the working classes in a capitalist world
begin to view their systematic subordination to the demands of capital
accumulation, their extreme lack of control over the conditions of work, the
determination of their fate by a more or less fiercely competitive labour market,
and the private, individual control over the fruits of their social labour, as
wrong, as basically exploitative and coercive, as being contrary to their own
good and, I would add, as *changeable* to something more democratic, this
growing social- and self-awareness, Marx was suggesting, sounds the death-
knell for the capitalist system. (This is not incompatible with the Marxian claim
that such psychological shifts will only become effective levers for social
transformation under certain material conditions.)

For those who wish to see democracy expanded to include some form of
economic and workplace democracy, these are rather hopeful ideas — ideas
that have nothing to do with the form of authoritarian rule that existed in the
Soviet Union and other so-called 'Communist' countries. But Marx and many
Marxists have underestimated the staying power of capitalism. In a discussion
of 'what keeps capitalism going', Michael Lebowitz characterises capitalism (in
a Marxian way) as follows:

Capitalism is a relationship in which the separation of working people
from the means of work and the organisation of the economy by those
who *own* those means of work has as its result that, in order to survive,
people must engage in a transaction — they must sell their ability to
work to those owners. But, the characteristic of capitalism is not *simply*
that the mass of people must be wage-laborers. It is also that those who
are purchasing that capacity to perform labor have one thing and only
one thing that interests them [*qua* capitalist] — profits (and more
profits); that is to say, the purchasers of labor-power are capitalists, and
their goal is to make their capital grow. (Lebowitz 2004)

This (rather authoritarian) relation between capital and labour, combined with market exchange of the products of labour, forms the core of the type of economic system that now unequivocally predominates globally. But capitalism is a system, a way of life, that has not only developed the forces of production like no other system of production and distribution in history (as its defenders and critics alike observe), it has also developed the forces of destruction and the technologies of political and social control like no other system in history (though the Soviet Union, which was not capitalist, tried and apparently failed to keep up). At this point in history (the early twenty-first century) the leader in terms of forces of destruction and technologies of control is, of course, the US. In military and economic terms the US is indeed the most powerful, and therefore the most dangerous, empire in the history of the world. The forces of destruction and technologies of control at its disposal, apparently at the disposal of a ruling class, or a section of the ruling class, that seeks unrivalled global domination, make it so (Chossudovsky 2002; Mahajan 2002). These technologies for killing and controlling are used for many purposes. Marxists specialise in detecting how they are used to preserve or to expand capitalist class rule, both globally and domestically. No one can reasonably be confident today that broad social struggle will overcome these increasingly destructive or sophisticated methods of control and repression. The weapons of mass destruction and the immense powers of surveillance and propaganda at the behest of the wealthy and powerful today is mind-boggling and can be, frankly, depressing to contemplate.

Nevertheless, the technologies of control and destruction have been developed, it would seem, partially to counteract what Marx called 'advances in awareness' (Schweickart 2003). As societies have become more democratic — at least paying lip service to democratic ideals and ideals of freedom and equality — dominant classes and elites have struggled to keep democracy at bay, using all manner of techniques of repression, diversion, and control, not only in their own societies but, due to the expansionist nature of capitalism, in other societies as well when the populations of those societies resist the subjection of their countries to foreign economic interests. The 'advances in awareness' to which Marx referred are not small, minor advances but 'enormous' ones because they are changes in belief which have potentially significant effects on whole ways of life and they are morally progressive changes, contributing to the ability of the slaves and the workers to conceive of and act more effectively toward their own greater freedom (as well as a more general human freedom). But such changes of world-view typically come not just from the questioning of a few core general beliefs (such as the belief that some people are 'by nature' slaves) but from the critical questioning of a whole cluster of interconnected beliefs, more or less concrete (such as beliefs about particular masters and particular slaves). 'Advances in awareness' involve the reorganisation of beliefs to some extent: discarding some beliefs and attitudes as a result of increased awareness through reflection and experience while adopting others that one previously thought false or at least did not hold true; and generally, such a moral-political reorientation would involve changes in stress so that certain beliefs once downplayed are now emphasised and vice versa, all as part of a more coherent re-ordering of the 'products of consciousness' than what had previously been attained. Whether or not such advances in awareness, such re-weaving of one's moral and political outlook, sound the death-knell of a whole mode of production, the idea that they help prepare the way for advances in freedom should hardly be surprising. It would be more surprising if they had no impact whatsoever, even if the impact in a short-term perspective is mainly to bring forth increased repression from the powers-that-be.

When Marxists criticise what they see as bourgeois or capitalist ideology, typically they criticise not only general assumptions about current social hierarchies but also particular capitalist class-serving or class-biased beliefs about particular events, actions, policies, individuals or groups. This is what the Marxian political scientist and activist Michael Parenti is doing when he depicts the political and ideological climate in the US in the 1980s and 90s:

> One can see instances of false consciousness all about us. There are people with legitimate grievances as employees, taxpayers, and consumers who direct their wrath against welfare mothers but not against corporate welfarism, against the inner city poor not the outer city rich, against human services that are needed by the community rather than regressive tax systems that favor the affluent. They support defense budgets that fatten the militarists and their corporate contractors and dislike those who protest the pollution more than they dislike the polluters.
>
> In their confusion they are ably assisted by conservative commentators and hate-talk mongers who provide ready-made explanations for their real problems, who attack victims instead of victimisers, denouncing feminists and minorities rather than sexists and racists, denouncing the poor rather than the rapacious corporate rich who create poverty. So the poor are defined as "the poverty problem." The effects of the problem are taken as the problem itself. The victims of the problem are seen as the cause, while the perpetrators are depicted as innocent or even beneficial.
>
> Does false consciousness exist? It certainly does and in mass marketed quantities. It is the mainstay of the conservative reactionism of

the 1980s and 1990s. Without it, those at the top, who profess a devotion to our interests while serving themselves, would be in serious trouble indeed. (Parenti 1996, 213–4)

Note that this was written before the 9/11 atrocities in the US. From a socialist, liberal egalitarian or even old-fashioned conservative perspective, matters have become worse and more intense since then. While not denying Parenti's claims I would add that such distortions, if that is what they are, cannot plausibly be explained just in terms of the imposition of ideas by ruling classes and other dominant groups.

To see this, consider the hypothesis that whenever and wherever there is systemic social hierarchy and domination and there is no broad social upheaval on the horizon, it is likely that throughout the society there will be widely shared false beliefs and assumptions which are important elements of justifications for the *status quo*. This is likely, given some plausible assumptions about what people are like in such persistent social contexts. One plausible assumption is that oppressed people, especially when they are living in desperate, even hopeless conditions, gravitate towards world-views that give them some hope; this makes them more open to the influence of consoling myths, particularly religious myths. Religion, Marx claimed, is not only the "opium of the people," it is also "the sigh of the oppressed creature, the heart of a heartless world," and "the spirit of spiritless conditions" (1975, 175). Marx held that religious consciousness, though an illusory form of consciousness which usually functions to legitimise an hierarchical social order, is not simply imposed on oppressed people by the ruling classes. Rather, the oppressed themselves participate in constructing their religious world-views (including such consoling beliefs as the belief in a better afterlife) in large measure as a response to their harsh, alienating conditions of life; it gives people hope and a sense of meaning in their lives even when they have resigned themselves to an earthly life of toil, hardship and suffering. But — so as not to beg questions — whether or not one views religious forms of consciousness as being basically illusory, one can reasonably suppose that illusory beliefs and the practices associated with them have played an important role in social history. Even if one denies that religious consciousness is illusory, resting on false or incoherent views, one can hardly reasonably deny that throughout history widespread illusions have *contributed* to holding people back from acting to move their social world in a more egalitarian or at least less undemocratic direction.

Yet it is understandable that not all oppressed people want to dedicate themselves to forming justified beliefs about the social order that oppresses them. As William Shaw remarks in a discussion of Marxian views on ideology, "it is not easy to live with" the idea "that the social order is fundamentally and arbitrarily exploitative and that one and one's family are condemned to a life of toil on behalf of a class that can claim no justification for its privileges." Shaw continues:

> Few, if any, subaltern classes have found themselves able to live with an unvarnished picture of their social predicament. They have, instead, constructed interpretations of reality that make it easier to bear, and in this respect they are far from being passive victims of ideas imposed upon them by their rulers. (Shaw 1989, 440)

Yet this is not to say that the persistence of system-supporting ideologies is merely the result of psychological weakness on the part of the 'subaltern classes'. In a context in which no fundamental social change is possible (which is usually the case) the acceptance of a mystifying, ruler-supporting ideology may be in the subjects' best interests — it may even be a matter of survival. For example, in India members of impoverished castes have sometimes ardently supported the caste system with all its accompanying mythology — what we moderns would regard as mythology. But it has been in their interests to do so since "access to such menial jobs as construction worker, toddy-wine maker, coir maker, and so forth depends on caste identity validated by obedience to caste rules" and "if one fails to maintain membership in good standing one loses the opportunity to obtain work even of the most menial kind, and plunges still further into misery" (Harris 1980, 62). In general, people's belief-systems tend to adapt to what they must do to make a living and, as Shaw suggests, this may make it too burdensome and painful to have 'an unvarnished picture of their social predicament'. Truth can be intolerable.

But that can only be part of the story that accounts for the prevalence and persistence of ruler-supporting, distorting ideologies. Not all exploited and oppressed people accept the myths that justify the social order. And there is always, as Foucault stressed, resistance and recalcitrance. To understand why the views of these resisters and dissenters tend not to become culturally dominant, we must also look at the rulers and dominant elites. In this context, a relevant observation is that those who dominate and live in comfort and luxury do not, generally, want to see themselves as merely being the lucky beneficiaries of hierarchical social arrangements. It is more realistic to believe that they want to see themselves in a better light than that; they worry about their self-image. Because they typically do not wish to view themselves as exploiters, merely lucky to occupy their socially privileged positions of power and influence, they will be prone to creating self-flattering 'final vocabularies' (stories about themselves to which they cling) and to convincing themselves and others how deserving they are of all the powers and privileges which they actually enjoy at the expense of others — and not only those others who do most of the work.[25] (The feudal doctrine of noble blood is an example, as is the bourgeois belief that what is good for big business is typically good for most people.) This need to see themselves as morally good, inherently noble, as benevolent, as being entitled to what they have, as beneficial to the world and so on, sometimes overwhelms their concern for truth, when the two things conflict. Also, as Shaw remarks, "rulers are like other people in generalising readily and falsely from their own situation, in having difficulty in understanding interactions from the perspective of others, and in failing to picture accurately and vividly the circumstances governing the lives of those outside their circle" (1989, 439). Typically these tendencies will lead members of dominant groups to avoid being too honest about the 'ignoble origins' of their position in society — origins in imperialistic plunder, for example — and even about how this position is maintained; their concern for truth is not likely to manifest itself in these areas.

However, as a corrective to the above claims about the avoidance of truth on the part of the dominant, we should also realise that not everyone among the powerful and privileged will be so evasive and they may have no qualms about maintaining their position. They will have some concern for truth in regard to how things work in the social world simply because this will be instrumental to maintaining (or expanding) their power and privilege; and they will realise or at least have some general sense that it is crucial, for the system of power and privilege to be sustained, that the exploited and oppressed do not become too critical of the social order and do not view themselves as being in a common predicament in relation to it. Wealthy and powerful people, or some of them, if they are at all clear-headed, know very well that social protest, rebellion and revolt are not good for their own interests in maintaining their wealth and power. Some will see the importance, when there are opportunities for broader segments of the population to become better informed about their political and social environments, that the great mass of people do not come to an articulate understanding of such things. It is important, to maintain any power structure and system of privilege, that certain things are not open to consistent public scrutiny: if they were, it might be too hard to maintain the system of privilege.

The above claims are, of course, controversial. But it is worth asking whether they are justifiable, whether they are warranted by the evidence of history that has been accumulated. But a Marxian cannot be satisfied with a merely psychological description of rulers and ruled, oppressors and oppressed. (For a critique of such 'psycho-political' approaches see Parenti 1999). In this context, what they would add is the non-psychological point that dominant social classes and elites have, *because of their economic dominance*, disproportionate control over what Marx called the 'the means of mental production'; control over means of economic production leads, directly or indirectly, to control over the means of mental production. These include "the major institutions that educate and indoctrinate young people, acquire and transfer knowledge, and articulate and mould popular opinion, as well as the physical resources those institutions utilise" (Shaw 1989, 433). Shaw presents some general hypotheses, rooted in the Marxian tradition, on how the ideas of the economically dominant class become the ruling ideas. I quote him at length:

> Economic dominance often leads to control of the means of mental production simply because their ownership can be a source of profit, and the economically dominant are in a position to acquire such assets. This will not be the case in pre-capitalist societies...because of the restricted role of the market and because of their less developed means of mental production. In those societies, literacy and formal education are limited; only classes or groups with sufficient leisure are in a position to occupy themselves, actively and self-consciously, with the development, elaboration, and communication of ideas in a systematic way. Because material circumstances sharply restrict the number of knowledge workers, economic dominance thus results in a predominantly ruling-class involvement with the means of mental production...
>
> In some modes of production, like advanced capitalism, the ruling class will have a strong economic interest in promoting (certain types of) education and research. And in all societies, ruling classes will have an interest in guaranteeing that the ideas that dominate popular consciousness are, *at a minimum*, compatible with continuation of the existing order... [emphasis added]
>
> Neither the ruling class nor its state need actively manage the means of mental production or involve itself intimately in the world of ideas. The crucial point is only that a ruling class will not tolerate the spread of ideas that would subvert the legitimacy of its rule ... throughout history the governing classes and their institutions have employed coercion against ideas judged hostile or potentially subversive. No fancy mechanism is required to explain this fact. Perceived self-interest along with an all-too-common human dislike of, and lack of tolerance for, alien thoughts and alternative outlooks will suffice. Nor is the underlying principle mistaken: ideas can be dangerous. (1989, 434–5)

Because of effective elite or ruling class control of the major means of mental production (or what some critical theorists have called the 'consciousness industry') the ideas that become culturally dominant, even if they are not conscious bits of propaganda for the existing order or for the defense of particular interests within that order, will tend to reflect the social outlook of members of the ruling class. This is just a side-effect of their direct or indirect control over the 'means of mental production'. As a result the dominant ideas, however diverse they may be, will tend to be constrained by assumptions about the naturalness or goodness of the existing order. Again, in the dominant culture the concern for truth is not likely to surface to any great extent in those areas where it might lead to a persistent questioning of those assumptions; the pursuit of justified beliefs in these areas will, in the mainstream culture, be truncated by the way the controllers of the major means of mental production consciously or unwittingly discourage such endeavours. Although it has never been the case that the subordinate classes have been entirely controlled in their thinking by the dominant classes, it has always been the case that their social outlooks have been developed from a disadvantaged position (due, in part, to their lack of effective control over the major means of mental production). This has made it harder for them to escape the distortions of dominant ideologies.

In contemporary industrial societies, particularly those which dominate on the world stage, it is especially important that capitalism itself, with its class divisions, not be critically discussed in the public sphere to any significant extent. This puts sharp constraints on critical discussion: when critical questions about specific events, policies or actions, might justifiably or reasonably lead to further critical questions about the broader system in which these events, policies or actions occur (or even about the regime responsible for them), then even the more specific, concrete discussions tend to be affected.

This is especially evident in official discourse on international politics. Consider, for example, the way the recent bombing of Yugoslavia was justified as being a 'humanitarian' intervention and the way attention was focused on how horrible the Serbian leader Milosevic had been toward the Kosovar Albanians. Attention was focused on his 'ethnic cleansing' (which increased exponentially after the bombing started, though the refugees from Kosovo were not only Albanian but included many Serbs as well as other groups in Kosovo, fleeing not only Serbian forces but also the Albanian terrorist, narco-trafficking Kosovo Liberation Army as well as NATO bombs). This was the way the bombing was justified to the vast majority of people in the United States and throughout the West. In the presentation of this event to the public, few questions were raised that might lead to a broader, critical understanding of the situation. Simple questions were avoided: questions such as 'Why is Yugoslavia getting this treatment but not Turkey or Indonesia?' If humanitarian considerations were the underlying motive of Western bombing of cities, why has there been no bombing of Ankara or Jakarta, since these regimes have done at least as much if not more harm than than the Milosevic regime?[26]

    To answer these questions, we would have to examine the nature of
Western interests in former Yugoslavia, Turkey and Indonesia. What made the
Milosevic regime different? Perhaps, to offer a suggestion, the Milosevic
regime, however brutal, was more reluctant to put the country under the jurisdiction of Western corporate and banking interests. The regimes of Bosnia-
Herzegovina and Croatia have also been brutally repressive, but they had
opened up their economies to the IMF and the World Bank to a far greater
extent.[27] Turkey has played a significant role in suppressing democratic forces
including Kurdish independence movements in the Middle East — with
particular ferocity during the 1990s. Why was the Iraqi leader Saddam Hussein
vilified for brutal repression of Kurds while Turkey has been supported in
almost every conceivable way? And if the first war against Iraq (1991) was a
matter of protecting the sanctity of borders as enshrined by international law,
why did the media presentations fail to recall the US invasion of Panama less
than two years earlier? Did they forget? Have they, more recently, simply
forgotten the role of the US, Saudi Arabia and Pakistan (the latter two under the
US's tutelage) in creating, training, arming and funding the terrorist group
known as Al-Qaeda? These three countries are plainly just as guilty as
Afghanistan for 'harbouring' terrorists. Why did the media presentations not
critically question the very idea of bombing Afghanistan, particularly in light of
the fact that not one of the suicide hijackers who attacked the US in 2001 was
actually Afghani? Or in light of the complete illegality of the war (as with the
recent bombing, invasion and occupation of Iraq)? Or in light of the fact that
Afghanistan had been ravaged by years of warfare beginning in 1979, with the
two superpowers (at the time) destroying much of the country? When the US
and England imposed devastating sanctions on Iraq (leading to more than a
million deaths, mostly of children) because of Iraq's possession of 'weapons of
mass destruction', why (as Edward Herman asks) did the mainstream culture
not even speak of the fact that something akin to genocide was going on
(Herman 2004)? And what about Indonesia? What made General Suharto's
Indonesian regime (with a horrific record of brutal massacres dating back to
1965) more worthy of Western support and aid than Nicaragua in the 1980s
under the Sandinistas? Was General Suharto more democratic or peace-loving
or rights-respecting than Daniel Ortega, then leader of the Sandinistas? Or was
he merely friendlier to US corporate interests? The questions mount. Above all,
why is it that the dominant culture never questions the right of Western powers
to make these decisions about everyone else? Why should the dominance of the
Western states be so accepted as if it were a law of nature? Do these states have
an admirable record of peaceful international diplomacy? Do they promote
freedom and democracy (or environmental safety) in the world?

These are just some examples in the sphere of international politics of reasonable questions about specific events or policies that might lead to a broader, more critical understanding of the global situation and of the way the global capitalist economy has been evolving and how it is being managed and policed. All of the facts mentioned or alluded to in the two preceding paragraphs are publicly available. Many of them are facts that have been reported in mainstream newspapers — though usually the questions are not asked in the way I have asked them. If these questions were actually pursued with even a modicum of rigour and intelligence in mainstream media and education, perhaps capitalism would not look like the benign modernising, civilising force it is made out to be in official ideology, to understate it. But this would run contrary to the interests of our rulers. Because they have disproportionate influence on cultural life, the culturally *dominant* norms of political correctness (which tend not to be recognised as such) permit discussion only within a narrow range, reflecting the outlook and interests of the powerful and privileged, just as in Aristotle's day. This narrowing of perspective and discussion (a narrowing of the field of possible statements, of the bounds of the thinkable) makes perfect sense, however, from the point of view of system stability. A population with a much broader perspective, a willingness to ask certain questions about the structure of our societies, about the dominant institutions, the dominant culture and so on, plainly would be a real threat to those who most benefit from the existing institutions. Ruling elites and ruling classes do not want to encourage *that* sort of critical questioning, *that* sort of concern for truth. In the most crucial cases, power does not want the truth to be spoken to or about it.

I submit that these claims (controversial though they may be) square with Foucault's suggestion that where there *is* plenty of institutional support for the pursuit of truth in the human or social sciences, the 'disciplines' are not 'independent of power'. They are often part of networks of social control and the knowledge that is accumulated is pursued within a framework that excludes critical questions about the functioning of the major political, economic and social institutions. The *production* of knowledge is often premised on the *suppression* of the concern for truth on key matters relevant to the promotion of human freedom. For this reason, I would suggest that Foucault's critique becomes even more cogent when it is at least combined with a more explicitly Marxian critical theory perspective.

7. Conclusion

If the broadly empirical claims in this essay (particularly those made in the section six) are for the most part plausible, there is some basis for the old

Gospel saying about the truth making us free; it has a rational kernel to it. But the important questions here are more empirical than philosophical. Even if I have not been convincing in my empirical claims, at least one can see that the question whether we should continue to speak of ideology in a pejorative sense depends very much on one's empirical (though not value-free) judgments about social history and modern society. Moreover, the idea of liberation through truth should not be seen as being some sort of conceptual (or any other kind of) necessity, but as an empirical generalisation. Coming to a more coherent or impartial understanding of the social world and of the possibilities for change, may not always be a step towards greater freedom. After all, history is not merely or even primarily an intellectual process. Nevertheless, I have tried to show, in an admittedly general way, that a concern for truth in certain areas would work against the interests of the powerful and that, potentially, it would be useful to those who are oppressed by them. Again, there is no good way of showing this without making substantive claims about society and human behaviour; and there is no interesting way of doing that without using or presupposing some theory, some conceptual framework or other. What should be asked, in this context, is whether that dependence on particular theories and substantive views has led me to falsify history or to misrepresent or ignore crucial or relevant evidence. (I did not say 'misrepresent the intrinsic nature of reality'.) Have I put forth claims about ideology, power or the concern for truth, that crucially rely on false assumptions? Are these claims themselves not true or improbable or misleading in some important way? And is there a non-Marxian theoretical (or non-theoretical) way of looking at social history and contemporary society that conflicts with a Marxian perspective and that could give us a more coherent account of ideology or an account that would show why there is no need, after all, to speak of ideology? Those are the key questions.

Commenting on Terry Eagleton's defence of a conception of ideology as false consciousness, Rorty remarks:

> So when Eagleton says all women ought to become feminists because 'an unmystified understanding of their oppressed social condition would logically lead them in that direction', we anti-representationalists construe him as saying 'Those non-feminist women will get more of what we think they ought to want if they become feminists'. (1992, 41–42)

I think Rorty is only partly right about how 'we anti-representationalists' should or could construe Eagleton's claim. He is right to suggest that the phrase 'an unmystified understanding of their oppressed social condition' should not be construed as 'the one true account of social reality'. He is also right to suggest that 'non-feminist women' should not be argued into feminism by trying to convince them that they are being untrue to their intrinsic nature as human beings or that they have failed to grasp '*the* correct way of seeing or understanding social reality as it is in itself, as it is apart from any discourse, interpretation or perspective'. Instead, 'we anti-representationalists' should openly say that we think freedom is good (while being clear about what we mean by 'freedom') and that there would be much more freedom for many more people in the sort of non-patriarchal world that feminists want — and, I would add, the sort of democratic world that socialists want. *If* that is what Rorty is suggesting as a corrective to (his construal of) Eagleton's 'realist' account of ideology, it seems to me right, so far as it goes.

At the same time, 'we anti-representationalists' can also construe Eagleton's claim as follows: we can say that it is better to have a wider range of justified beliefs about how and why women are oppressed, how and why their freedom is unnecessarily inhibited or curtailed and about how the situation might be changed, than is typically put forth or assumed in the mainstream cultures of modern societies; that there are many unjustified and/or misleading beliefs and assumptions in our culture that tend to be encouraged by the dominant, culture-producing institutions; and that feminists have, collectively, drawn our attention to some of these beliefs and assumptions and have thereby given us a less mystified, if not entirely unmystified, understanding of our lives in modern, sexist society. The gaining of a truer, less distorting perspective or, as Nielsen puts it, a "more extensively truth-bearing system of thought," is valuable insofar as (a) we value not being deluded about the barriers to freedom and (b) we value freedom (Nielsen 1989, 112).[28]

Since Rorty plainly shares these values and since the notion of ideology put forth here seems to be a useful way of categorising certain tendencies in social and cultural life that systematically frustrate the full flowering of human freedom, it is not clear why Rorty should dismiss that notion as he does. Anti-representationalism does not imply or entail that it makes no sense to speak of mystifying or distorting ideologies; that, at any rate, is one of the main arguments of this paper. But Rorty does not think that pragmatism or anti-representationalism *alone* are sufficient to show the uselessness or incoherence of ideology-critique. His disparagement of such conceptions of ideology has more to do with his belief that they do not give us a useful way of categorising things, based on Rorty's own assessments of the historical evidence and of how modern capitalism works, the historical feasibility of socialism and, most conspicuously in Rorty's writing, the political culture of the US and the role of the US in the world.[29] But typically Rorty focuses on the representationalism of writers such as Eagleton (or the 'transcendentalism' of writers such as Habermas). Again, if my claims about the social world in the preceding section are somewhat plausible, then the functional/epistemic conception of 'ideological mystification' or 'false consciousness' as I have construed it remains a useful (and not too technical) conception for those who wish to understand the (social) world and to act more effectively to improve it. Minimally, I claim that philosophers' and other intellectuals' misgivings about Truth and about 'the notion of ideology' or 'false consciousness', may be relevant when it comes to criticising various forms of Enlightenment rationalism and, more broadly, Platonism in our various discursive projects, but they do not provide sufficient reason for viewing ideology-critique as being conceptually, morally or empirically inadequate, misleading or otherwise problematic in its very conception.

NOTES

1. Amy Allen (2003) presents a compelling case for not lumping Foucault in with other so-called 'counter-Enlightenment' or 'postmodern' thinkers. She argues that the Foucault/Habermas debate that raged in the recent past is better understood as a debate about two ways of practicing Enlightenment criticism than as a conflict between an Enlightenment project (Habermas) and a postmodern or counter-Enlightenment project (Foucault).

2. But see footnote 1. See also, for some of Habermas' relevant writings, his *Knowledge and Human Interests* (1971); *Communication and the Evolution of Society* (1979); and *The Philosophical Discourse of Modernity* (1987).

3. For a sample of analytical writing on deflationary or minimalist conceptions of truth, see Simon Blackburn and Keith Simmons (1999), as well as Paul Horwich (1990).

4. I say 'modern' sceptic because Michael Williams (2001) makes a strong case for distinguishing modern from ancient scepticism.

5. See especially Raymond Geuss's account of ideology in (1985).

6. Note that 'material surroundings', for Marx and Engels, includes the natural environment as well as social and economic institutions. One writer who brings out the importance of ecological constraints on human social organisation and ideology (far more thoroughly than Marx and Engels were in a position to do) is the late Marvin Harris, a quasi-Marxian anthropologist who has left a great legacy of non-pedantically-written books and articles on 'cultural materialism' with numerous instances of its application. See Harris (1980) for his most sustained attempt to defend his 'materialist' theory against various theoretical rivals in both the social sciences and 'popular culture'. For a critical (though sympathetic) evaluation of Harris's work see Sanderson (2002).

7. The view that there is a dominant ideology is criticised by Nicholas Abercrombie et al. (1980). But then see Terry Eagleton's critical discussion of this book (1991, pp. 35f). For a Marxian story about how the 'dull compulsion of the economic', habit, and certain features of everyday life in class society, contribute to the formation of distorting ideologies, see Mills (1989, pp. 421–45), and Shaw (1989). Rosen (2000, p. 396) distinguishes the idea of a "dominant ideology" from the idea that there is a pervasive "absence of consciousness of shared interests"; he is less sceptical of the latter. But proponents of ideology-critique may rejoin that ideology is part of the

explanation for why there is a broad lack of social and class solidarity among the nonruling classes. If the hegemonic ideas were more socialist and less bourgeois than they are, for example, perhaps there would be a more widespread 'consciousness of shared interests.' Rosen is unhappy with what he calls 'the theory of ideology' on the grounds that it assumes an unjustified functional explanation of ideology. This issue of functional explanation is, I think, interesting, but to assess the claim that there is a dominant ideology or ideologies in modern society it is not necessary to settle it. What we need to do first is to look at the empirically-oriented studies that have been produced on this topic, such as Chomsky and Herman (1988), Chomsky (1989), Parenti (1992) and (1993), McChesney (2004), and many others. I think these studies thoroughly establish that there is indeed something like a dominant (class-serving) ideology that is put forth mainly (but not only) by the various mass media institutions in the wealthiest modern societies. Though the focus of these authors is on ideology in the United States, they are all quick to point out that US ideology goes wherever the US goes (more precisely, wherever US-based corporations go) and that in other capitalist countries, while the mechanisms of ideological control may be more (or less) subtle they nevertheless work in similar ways to legitimise forms of class domination. These authors focus on class domination but they do not mean to suggest (not at all) that dominant ideologies are only class ideologies — they would not deny that unjustified patriarchal and racist norms and beliefs are also part of the dominant cultures of our modern world.

8. It is true that Foucault, in the 1980s towards the end of his life, began to distance himself from the idea that all his work was about power — instead it was about the history of the modern 'subject'. What I am referring to here is Foucault's work in the *Discipline and Punish* period of the 1970s and including Foucault's *History of Sexuality, Volume One*. During this period it would have made sense to speak of Foucault's 'power model of society'. Moreover, the history of the 'constitution of subjects' was always, for Foucualt, linked to the history of modern forms of power. That connection gave the Nietzschean bite to Foucault's work.

9. Taylor's version of Foucault, it seems to me, is more relativist and fatalist and more easily lends itself to nihilist attitudes than do the words of Foucault himself. But before considering a different (and more charitable) way of interpreting Foucault, I will present Taylor's argument in order to assemble some reminders on issues relating to the critique of ideology; perhaps this could serve as an antidote to a version of relativism which is, though confused, often expressed.

10. Indirectly, Allen (2003) shows how implausible the strong Geertzian interpretation of Foucault is.

11. For a pragmatist critique of Habermas on this point, see Richard Rorty (2001a).

12. In (2003) I argue that Foucault should be understood as appealing to a particular ideal of autonomy, one that is common to liberal and socialist traditions.

13. Rorty thinks Taylor has a more inflated conception of truth; see Rorty's critique of Taylor (1998, pp. 84–97).

14. See Ludwig Wittgenstein (1976).

15. It is not even clear why we need a theory of truth along non-traditional lines such as those adumbrated by Davidson (1990). Rorty has tried to deflate this aspect of Davidson's work. Rorty asks: "Why is your new theory not an instance of changing the

subject rather than a theory of truth?" and "If you now say truth is not something to be pursued, but that it is what is preserved in valid inference, why should we think that you are talking about the same notion of truth that has been in our philosophical tradition since Plato?" and further, "If the concept of truth comes in a package with the concepts of belief, meaning, rationality, intention, and so on, and all these are necessary to explain linguistic behaviour, why call it a theory of truth? Why is it any more a theory of truth than of meaning, belief, or behaviour generally?" (2001d). Nevertheless, even if, contrary to Rorty, Davidson's model of triangulation can be said to help us model something like the 'structure and content of truth', it remains unclear what such a theory would be good for. Would it help us to discern what is ideological or distorting in our discourse? Does ideology-critique presuppose or imply any theory of truth? Does such a theory provide us a better grounding or justification for our practices and views of morality, politics, art, science or religion? There is certainly room for scepticism here.

16. We may acknowledge this point while also acknowledging that there is not likely to be a purely philosophical or non-contextual way to specify the appropriate norms and standards of justification for all domains of inquiry and reflection. It is possible to share Habermas' commitment to free discussion among democratic citizens while suppressing the urge — if it is there — for transcendence or for the 'unconditional' or noncontextual. On the topic of Habermas's theory of truth and justification I have found useful a rough draft of an article by Kai Nielsen, "Habermas and the Ambition of Transcendence" as well as Rorty (2001a).

17. Williams, in the course of defending a minimalist conception of truth, provides a strong argument — one which, I believe, has yet to be given a convincing rebuttal — against Richard Boyd and others who think that truth plays some explanatory or causal role and therefore that truth itself must be a substantial property which we might have an interesting theory about:

> What does it come to to say that the success of our methods is explained by the truth of our theories? Simply this: that the methods we use to investigate elementary particles work as well as they do because the world is made of such particles behaving more or less the way we think they do; that the methods we use to investigate the transmission of inherited traits work as well as they do because heredity is controlled by genes in more or less the way we think it is; that the methods we use...etc. To spell out the explanation we should have to assert, in a qualified way, all the theories we currently accept, or all those belonging to 'mature' sciences. But the predicate 'true' saves us the trouble, for we can compress this tedious rehearsal of current views into a single sentence and say 'Our methods work because the theories that inform them are approximately true.' However, no difference has been shown between explaining the success of our methods in terms of the truth of our theories and simply explaining it in terms of the theories themselves. So, even if we concede that scientific realism has genuine explanatory power [though it is not clear what that means here], we are no nearer to establishing the need for a substantial notion of truth. (Williams 1986, 230)

18. A key target of these Foucauldian claims seems to be the French Marxian philosopher, Louis Althusser (see 1971, 11–67, 127–88). If so, I think that is a slightly uncharitable reading of Althusser. But historically, it has been the case that some

Marxist and other leftist writers (and activists) have too easily and without qualification contrasted truth and science to ideology (in a pejorative sense); but so too have non-Marxists and anti-Marxists such as Karl Popper. In Althusser's case, however, science is distinguished even from what Geuss calls 'ideology in a positive sense', for he regarded socialist ideology, to which he adhered, as being in a different realm from science. This is decidedly not a view shared by Marx.

19. For Geuss's (more nuanced) account of the functional and epistemic conceptions see (1985, 12–19).

20. Joseph Heath (2000) suggests that only by interpreting people uncharitably can we come up with the idea that ideology plays a role in maintaining oppressive systems. He finds it off-putting, elitist, and unDavidsonian of critical theorists to insinuate that they may know something about the oppression of 'ordinary' people that the people themselves do not know (or do not know as well or as thoroughly) and he suggests that the reproduction of oppression can be explained through an analysis of the 'coordination problems' of the oppressed and exploited rather than by attributing to them irrational beliefs expressive of a distorting ideology. I have insufficient space to argue against Heath on this point but it is worth pointing out here that (1) there is no reason in principle why people who study social theory and history cannot come to know more than those who do not put as much time and energy into these subject matters, as is the case with any subject matter; (2) that this fact does not entail that those who through careful inquiry have come to know more will become elitist, paternalistic vanguards imposing a top-down discipline on the less knowledgeable; (3) Davidson only said *most* of our beliefs must be true; if attributing false beliefs on *certain* matters helps us to gain a more coherent explanatory-interpretive-descriptive account of someone's behaviour then on Davidson's account of interpretation that is precisely what we must do; and (4) Heath provides no reason for the idea that we must choose between explaining the persistence of oppressive situations in terms of coordination problems and explaining them in terms of ideology; he does not tell us why these two things cannot, or do not, work in tandem — with ideology playing a larger role in some cases and free-rider problems doing so in other cases.

21. For Marxists and Leninists, 'ideology' is not necessarily a pejorative term denoting an inherently falsifying and/or morally objectionable perspective (see Mills 1985; McCarney 1980; and Nielsen 1989). Nevertheless, any critical theory, Marxian or Feminist or whatever, is likely to employ a conception of 'false consciousness' or 'ideological mystification' as I have specified it, as when Marxists speak in derogatory terms of 'bourgeois ideology' and feminists of 'patriarchal ideology'. These pejorative ways of speaking of ideology are what critics such as Foucault, Rorty and many postmodernists find problematic.

22. And no theory of the Subject need be presupposed either; see my (2003).

23. For an account of the development of slavery from a non-dominant to a dominant mode of production in the Greek and Roman Empires, see Lekas (1988) and de Ste. Croix (1981). These authors maintain that class struggle in the ancient Greek world was less overt between slaves and masters than between the poorer sections of the citizenry and the richer sections; but there was nevertheless sporadic slave resistance, though more so during the reign of Rome than that of Greece.

24. We can add 'men and women' to Engels' list. One example of this attitude towards equality and inequality is Plutarch's statement: "[The equality] the many aim at is the greatest of all injustices and God has removed it out of the world as being unattainable; but he protects and maintains the distribution of things according to merit" (cited in Lekas 1988, 251).

25. My use of the phrase 'final vocabularies' is an adaptation from Rorty that does not precisely fit the way he used the phrase. See Nielsen's essay in this journal for a critical discussion of Rorty's usage.

26. For a thorough account of the breakup of Yugoslavia up to and including the US-led NATO bombing campaign, see Parenti (2000).

27. See Chossudovsky (1998); but see also several (well-researched) articles in *Covert Action Quarterly* no. 68 (Fall-Winter 1999), as well as the previous two or three issues of that journal.

28. Nielsen could just as well have written of a "more extensively *justified* system of thought" so as to avoid connotations of truth being a substantial thing or property that is attached to systems of thought. Having discussed this matter with him, I am sure that now he would prefer to phrase things in terms of systems of thought being more or less coherent, more or less justified, more or less ideological, though he still could speak of such systems being more or less 'truth-bearing', given his deflationist conception of truth.

29. In Rorty (2000, p. 129), he chastises what he and Allan Bloom call "the Nietzscheanized left" for telling us that the US "is rotten to the core — that it is a racist, sexist, imperialist society, one which can't be trusted an inch, one whose every utterance must be ruthlessly deconstructed." But it is not only the 'postmodern (Nietzscheanized) left' that holds these views. The non-postmodern, socialist left does as well (Noam Chomsky, for example), and even liberals and conservatives all over the planet are coming to see the US as a very racist, sexist, and imperialist society, though of course not the only one. Of course that is not all the US is, but it is these things, is it not? What is Rorty saying, that the US is *not* imperialist, that it is *not* a racist or sexist society, that the plutocrats running the show *should* be trusted? Or that these problems, to the extent they exist, are just aberrations and not systematic, not rooted in the way the institutions are structured? Which is the more justified view, Chomsky's or Rorty's? One needn't be an Enlightenment rationalist, as Chomsky is, to affirm that Chomsky's version of US history and politics is more coherent and plausible than Rorty's or, say, Michael Walzer's. And if Chomsky's is the better justified view, better by our own lights in terms of standards not alien to Rorty or Walzer, then it seems that it would be foolish to drop the notion of ideology from our vocabulary. *Manufacturing Consent* is all about the production and dissemination of ideology, for example, and it does not rely on any philosophical notions of truth, rationality, or goodness.

REFERENCES

Abercrombie, Nicholas, Stephen Hill, and Bryan S. Turner. (1980) *The Dominant Ideology Thesis* (London: Allen & Unwin).

Allen, Amy. (2003) "Foucault and Enlightenment: A Critical Reappraisal," *Constellations* 10, pp. 180–198.

Allen, Barry. (1991) "Government in Foucault," *Canadian Journal of Philosophy* 21, pp. 321–440.

Althusser, Louis. (1971) *Lenin and Philosophy and Other Essays* (New York: Monthly Review Press).

Aristotle. (1986) *Aristotle. Selected Works*, ed. H. G. Apostle and L. P. Gerson (Grinell, IA: Peripatetic Press).

Benhabib, Seyla. (1986) *Critique, Norm and Utopia* (New York: Columbia University Press).

Bernstein, Richard. (1992) "Foucault: Critique as Philosophic Ethos," in *The New Constellation: The Ethical-Political Horizons of Modernity/Postmodernity* (Cambridge, MA: MIT Press), pp. 142–171.

Blackburn, Simon, and Keith Simmons, eds. (1999) *Truth* (New York: Oxford University Press).

Chomsky, Noam. (1989) *Necessary Illusions: Thought Control in Democratic Societies* (Toronto: CBC Enterprises).

Chomsky, Noam, and Edward S. Herman. (1988) *Manufacturing Consent: The Political Economy of the Mass Media* (New York: Pantheon Books).

Chossudovsky, Michel. (1998) *The Globalisation of Poverty: Impacts of IMF and World Bank Reforms* (Halifax, Nova Scotia: Fernwood Books), pp. 243–260.

———. (2002) *War and Globalisation* (Oakland, CA: Global Outlook Publishing).

Cohen, G. A. (1978) *Karl Marx's Theory of History* (Princeton, NJ: Princeton University Press).

———. (1988) *History, Labour and Freedom* (Oxford: Clarendon Press).

Davidson, Donald. (1985) "On the Very Idea of a Conceptual Scheme," in *Inquiries into Truth and Interpretation* (Oxford: Clarendon Press), pp. 183–198.

———. (1990) "The Structure and Content of Truth," *Journal of Philosophy* 87, pp. 279–328.

de Ste. Croix, G. E. M. (1981) *The Class Struggle in the Ancient Greek World* (London: Duckworth).

Dewey, John. (1958) *Experience and Nature* (New York: Dover).

Eagleton, Terry. (1991) *Ideology: An Introduction* (London: Verso Press).

Engels, Friedrich. (1976) *Anti-Dühring* (Moscow: International Publishers).

Foucault, Michel, and Noam Chomsky. (1974) "Human Nature: Justice versus Power," in *Reflexive Water: The Basic Concerns of Mankind*, ed. Fon Elders (Amsterdam: Souvenir Press), pp. 135–197.

Foucault, Michel. (1980) "Two Lectures," in *Power/Knowledge: Selected Interviews and Other Writings, 1972–77*, ed. Colin Gordon (New York: Pantheon Books), pp. 78–108.

———. (1982) "Afterword: 'The Subject and Power'," in *Beyond Structuralism and Hermeneutics*, 2nd edn, ed. Hubert L. Dreyfuss and Paul Rabinow (Chicago: University of Chicago Press), pp. 208–252.

———. (1990) *Politics, Philosophy, Culture: Interviews and Other Writings 1977–84*, ed. L. D. Kritzman (London and New York: Routledge).

———. (2000) "Truth and Power," in *Michel Foucault. Power. Essential Works of Foucault, 1954–1984, Volume 3*, ed. James D. Faubion (Toronto: Penguin), pp. 111–133.

Fraser, Nancy. (1989) *Unruly Practices: Power, Discourse and Gender in Contemporary Social Theory* (Minneapolis: University of Minnesota Press).

Geertz, Clifford. (1978) "Stir Crazy," *New York Review of Books* (26 January), pp. 3–4, 6.

Geuss, Raymond. (1985) *The Idea of a Critical Theory. Habermas and the Frankfurt School* (Cambridge, UK: Cambridge University Press).

Habermas, Jürgen. (1971) *Knowledge and Human Interests*, trans. J. J. Shapiro (Basingstoke, UK: Heinemann Educational Publishers).

———. (1979) *Communication and the Evolution of Society*, trans. Thomas McCarthy (Boston: Beacon Press).

———. (1986) "Taking Aim at the Heart of the Present," in *Foucault: A Critical Reader*, ed. David Couzens Hoy (Oxford: Blackwell), pp. 103–108.

———. (1987) *The Philosophical Discourse of Modernity* (Cambridge, Mass: MIT Press).

Harris, Marvin. (1980) *Cultural Materialism: The Struggle for a Science of Culture* (New York: Vintage Books).

―――. (1989) *Cows, Pigs, Wars and Witches* (New York: Vintage Books).

Heath, Joseph. (2000) "Ideology, Irrationality and Collectively Self-Defeating Behavior," *Constellations* 7, pp. 363–371.

Held, David. (1980) *An Introduction to Critical Theory* (Berkeley: University of California Press).

Herman, Edward S. (2004) "The Cruise Missile Left (Part 5): Samantha Power and the Genocide Gambit," *Znet Commentary* online at http://www.zmag.org/content/ showarticle.cfm?SectionID=21&ItemID=5538.

Horwich, Paul. (1990) *Truth* (Oxford: Oxford University Press).

―――. (1999a) "The Minimalist Conception of Truth," in *Truth*, ed. Simon Blackburn and Keith Simmons (New York: Oxford University Press), pp. 239–263.

―――. (1999b) "Davidson on Deflationism," in *Donald Davidson: Truth, Meaning and Knowledge*, ed. Urszula M. Zeglen (London and New York: Routledge), pp. 20–24.

Hoy, David Couzens. (1986) "Introduction," *Foucault: A Critical Reader*, ed. David Couzens Hoy (Oxford: Blackwell), pp. 1–25.

Kumar, Chandra. (2003) "Progress, Freedom, Human Nature and Critical Theory," *Imprints: A Journal of Analytical Socialism* 7, pp. 106–130.

Lebowitz, Michael A. (2004) "What Keeps Capitalism Going?" *Monthly Review* 56 (2), online at http://www.monthlyreview.org/0604lebowitz.htm

Lekas, Padelis. (1988) *Marx on Classical Antiquity. Problems of Historical Methodology* (New York: St. Martin's Press), pp. 53–129.

Levine, Andrew, Elliot Sober, and Erik Olin Wright. (1995) *Reconstructing Marxism* (London: Verso Press).

Mahajan, Rahul. (2002) *The New Crusade: America's War on Terrorism* (New York: Monthly Review Press).

Marx, Karl. (1975) *Contribution to the Critique of Hegel's Philosophy of Right*, in *Collected Works* (New York: International Publishers).

―――. (1978) *Grundrisse*, in *The Marx-Engels Reader*, 2nd edn, ed. Robert Tucker (New York: W.W. Norton).

Marx, Karl, and Frederick Engels. (1985) *The German Ideology*, ed. C. J. Arthur (Moscow: International Publishers).

Maugham, Somerset. (2001) *The Summing Up* (New York: Vintage Books).

McCarney, Joe. (1980) *The Real World of Ideology* (Atlantic Highlands, NJ: Humanities Press).

McCarthy, Thomas. (1978) *The Critical Theory of Jürgen Habermas* (Cambridge, MA: MIT Press).

McChesney, Robert W. (2004) *The Problem of the Media: U.S. Communication Politics in the 21st Century* (New York: Monthly Review Press).

Miller, Richard. (1984) *Analyzing Marx: Morality, Power and History*. Princeton, NJ: Princeton University Press.

Mills, Charles W. (1985) "'Ideology' in Marx and Engels," *Philosophical Forum* 16, pp. 327–346.

———. (1989) "Determination and Consciousness in Marx," *Canadian Journal of Philosophy* 19, pp. 421–445.

Minson, Jeffrey. (1985) *Genealogies of Morals: Nietzsche, Foucault, Donzelot and the Eccentricity of Ethics* (New York: St. Martin's Press).

Nielsen, Kai. (1989) *Marxism and the Moral Point of View* (Boulder, CO: Westview Press).

———. (1991) *After the Demise of the Tradition: Rorty, Critical Theory and the Fate of Philosophy* (Boulder, CO: Westview Press).

———. (1996) *Naturalism Without Foundations* (Amherst, NY: Prometheus Books).

———. (2001) *Naturalism and Religion* (Amherst, NY: Prometheus Books).

Norman, Richard. "What is Living and What is Dead in Marxism?" *Canadian Journal of Philosophy* suppl. 15, pp. 59–80.

Okin, Susan Moller. (1979) *Women in Western Political Thought* (Princeton, NJ: Princeton University Press).

Parenti, Michael. (1992) *Make-Believe Media: The Politics of Entertainment* (New York: St. Martins Press).

———. (1993) *Inventing Reality: The Politics of News Media* (New York: St. Martins Press).

———. (1996) *Dirty Truths* (San Fransisco: City Lights Books).

———. (1999) "Against Psychopolitics," in *History as Mystery* (San Fransisco: City Lights Books), pp. 241–265.

———. (2000) *To Kill a Nation: The Attack on Yugoslavia* (London: Verso Press).

Putnam, Hilary. (1983) "Why There Isn't a Ready-Made World," in *Realism and Reason* (Cambridge, MA: MIT Press), pp. 205–229.

———. (1985) "After Empiricism," in *Post-Analytic Philosophy*, eds. John Rajchman and Cornel West (New York: Columbia University Press), pp. 20–31.

———. (2001) *The Threefold Cord: Mind, Body and World* (New York: Columbia University Press).

Ramberg, Bjørn. (1993) "Strategies for Radical Rorty (... *'but is it progress?'*)," *Canadian Journal of Philosophy* suppl. 19, pp. 223–246.

———. (2001) "Post-Ontological Philosophy of Mind: Rorty versus Davidson," in *Rorty and His Critics*, ed. Robert B. Brandom (Oxford: Blackwell), pp. 351–369.

Roderick, Rick. (1986) *Habermas and the Foundations of Critical Theory* (London: Macmillan).

Rorty, Richard. (1983) *Consequences of Pragmatism* (Minneapolis: University of Minnesota Press).

———. (1992) "We Anti-Representationalists," *Radical Philosophy* 60 (Spring), pp. 40–44.

———. (1998) *Truth and Progress* (Cambridge, UK: Cambridge University Press).

———. (2000). *Philosophy and Social Hope* (New York: Penguin).

———. (2001a) "Universality and Truth," in *Rorty and His Critics*, ed. Robert B. Brandom (Oxford: Blackwell), pp. 1–30.

———. (2001b) "Response to Ramberg," in *Rorty and His Critics*, ed. Robert B. Brandom (Oxford: Blackwell), pp. 370–377.

———. (2001c) "Response to McDowell," in *Rorty and His Critics*, ed. Robert B. Brandom (Oxford: Blackwell), pp. 123–128.

————. (2001d) "Response to Davidson," in *Rorty and His Critics*, ed. Robert B. Brandom (Oxford: Blackwell), pp. 74–80.

————. (2002) "To the Sunlit Uplands," *London Review of Books* 24 (31 October), p. 31.

————. (2003) "Review of *Truth and Justification* by Jurgen Habermas," *Notre Dame Philosophical Reviews* online at http://www.ndpr.icaap.org/content/archives/2003/12/rorty-habermas2.html

Rosen, Michael. (2000) "*On Voluntary Servitude* and the Theory of Ideology," *Constellations* 7, pp. 393–407.

Sanderson, Stephen K. (2002) "Marvin Harris, Meet Charles Darwin: A Critical Evaluation and Theoretical Extension of Cultural Materialism," presented at the annual meeting of the American Anthropological Association, New Orleans, November 2002. Online at http://www.chss.iup.edu/sociology/Faculty/Sanderson%20Articles/Harris-Meet-Darwin.htm.

Shaw, William H. (1989) "Ruling Ideas," *Canadian Journal of Philosophy* suppl. 15, pp. 425–448.

Schweickart, David. (2003) "Does Historical Materialism Imply Socialism?" Paper delivered at Conference in Honour of Kai Nielsen, Concordia University, Montréal, Québec.

Taylor, Charles. (1986) "Foucault on Freedom and Truth," in *Foucault: A Critical Reader*, ed. David Couzens Hoy (Oxford: Blackwell), pp. 69–102.

Walzer, Michael. (1988) "The Lonely Politics of Michel Foucault," in *The Company of Critics. Social Criticism and Political Commitment in the Twentieth Century* (New York: Basic Books), pp. 191–209.

Williams, Bernard. (2002) *Truth and Truthfulness: An Essay in Genealogy* (Princeton, NJ: Princeton University Press).

Williams, Michael. (1986) "Do We (Epistemologists) Need a Theory of Truth?" *Philosophical Topics* 14, pp. 223–241.

————. (1996) *Unnatural Doubts: Epistemological Realism and the Basis for Scepticism* (Princeton, NJ: Princeton University Press).

————. (2001) "Epistemology and the Mirror of Nature," in *Rorty and His Critics*, ed. Robert B. Brandom (Oxford: Blackwell), pp. 191–212.

Wittgenstein, Ludwig. (1976) *Philosophical Investigations*, trans. G. E. M. Anscombe (Oxford: Blackwell).

Chandra Kumar
Lecturer
School of Politics
University of Kwazulu-Natal
MTBORO7
Howard College Campus
Durban 4041
South Africa

Contemporary Pragmatism
Vol. 2, No. 1 (June 2005), 95–113

Editions Rodopi
© 2005

Pragmatism, Truth, and Inquiry

Chase B. Wrenn

This article considers whether pragmatists who embrace minimalism about truth can consistently hold that truth is a goal of inquiry. Richard Rorty has argued that they cannot, because there is no practical difference between pursuing minimalist truth and pursuing well-justified belief. I argue that there are practical differences between pursuing truth and justification, and that pragmatic minimalists can and probably should embrace truth as a goal of inquiry.

1. Introduction

Charles S. Peirce once defined pragmatism as the

> opinion that metaphysics is to be largely cleared up by the application of the following maxim for attaining clearness of apprehension: 'Consider what effects that might conceivably have practical bearings we conceive the object of our conception to have. Then, our conception of these effects is the whole of our conception of the object.' (1982a, 48)

More succinctly, Richard Rorty has described the position in this way:

> Pragmatists think that if something makes no difference to practice, it should make no difference to philosophy. (1998, 19)

In thinking about truth, pragmatists will thus ask what practical difference we conceive the truth of a proposition to make. Some pragmatists have thought they could define truth, as "what it works to believe" or "the good in the way of belief," for example, but Rorty has a different view. Consider the proposition that snow is white. Though it makes a practical difference whether snow is white or not, Rorty thinks it makes no further difference whether the proposition has the property of truth. That is, the truth of the proposition makes no difference that snow's being white does not already make. When we think of the practical difference we conceive truth itself to make, Rorty thinks we will find none. If he is right, pragmatists should probably not consider truth to be a philosophically important property of propositions.

Not only pragmatists have taken the view that truth is not a property or, at least, not a philosophically important one. Versions of this view have been known as "disquotationalism," "deflationism," and "minimalism." Characteristically, the minimalist denies that a claim such as "'Snow is white' is true" ascribes the property of truth to the proposition that snow is white. Rather, it just ascribes the property of whiteness to snow. There is, for the minimalist, no such property as truth to ascribe.

The minimalist view of truth may conflict with the common intuition that truth is a goal of inquiry. After all, it is hard to see how inquiry could aim at truth if truth is not an interesting, metaphysically substantial property of beliefs. My aim here is to show that pragmatic minimalists can consistently consider truth a goal of inquiry, and that they probably should do so.

As a foil to my position, I will consider Richard Rorty's argument for the opposite conclusion. Rorty adds to pragmatism and minimalism a relativistic view of epistemic justification. On that view, a belief is justified to an audience just in case it satisfies their standards of acceptable belief (which I will call their *epistemic standards*). He thinks it then follows that there is no practical difference between pursuing the truth and trying to be persuasive; and, since minimalism tells us there is no such thing as truth toward which inquiry could aim, he concludes that there is no interesting sense in which truth is a goal of inquiry. I outline Rorty's view and his argument in section two, and in sections three and four I argue that there *are* practical differences between pursuing the truth and pursuing audience-relative epistemic justification. This makes room for pragmatic minimalists who accept relativism about justification to consider truth a goal of inquiry. In section five, I extend my argument to apply if epistemic justification is not relative to an audience. Though in that case there may be no practical difference between pursuing justification and pursuing truth, there are still good reasons for pragmatic minimalists to consider truth a goal of inquiry. I make some concluding remarks in section six.

A cautionary note before going further: I do not launch a general criticism of Rorty's alleged "relativism" or "antirealism," nor do I attack pragmatism (in general or as Rorty conceives it) below. My concern is the compatibility of philosophical pragmatism, minimalism about truth, and the view that truth is a goal of inquiry. Rorty thinks they are mutually inconsistent, and I disagree. I take pragmatism and minimalism as common ground between Rorty and me, and I show how to make room for truth as a goal within that context. Discharging that task, of course, will also require some discussion of why Rorty is mistaken in thinking it impossible.

2. Rorty's Argument

Rorty's argument against truth as a goal of inquiry turns on three assumptions. The first two I will not question in this paper: pragmatism and minimalism. The third assumption is Rorty's audience-relative conception of epistemic justification. I will grant that assumption until section five. This section sketches both Rorty's minimalism and his view of epistemic justification, and it shows how he uses them against the claim that truth is a goal of inquiry.

Minimalism contrasts with two other common philosophical approaches to truth. The first is *representationalism*, typified by "correspondence" theories of truth. On a representationalist account, there is more to the truth of 'Snow is white' than just snow's being white. In addition, there is a relation of "correspondence" or "accurate representation" between the proposition that snow is white and the world. The job of a theory of truth, on this view, is to give a philosophical explanation of what the correspondence relation comes to.

The second contrasting approach is *epistemicism*. This is the view that truth is somehow reducible to epistemic justification. For example, an epistemicist might claim that a proposition is true just in case it is believed with justification, or it could be, or it would be by an ideal inquirer. The details of these theories often depend on an underlying theory of epistemic justification. For example, coherence theories of truth often rely on the view that a belief is justified just in case it coheres with a comprehensive system of beliefs. The so-called "pragmatic" theory of truth presupposes that a belief is justified whenever it is effective or beneficial for one to adopt it. We should keep in mind that *pragmatism* is not equivalent to the pragmatic theory of truth. Rorty, for example, has flirted with pragmatic theories of truth, but his considered view is that that is a mistake.

Along with many other philosophers, Rorty is a minimalist about truth. Minimalists deny that there is any interesting relation of "correspondence" or "accurate representation" in virtue of which true propositions are true. They also deny that truth is a property reducible to epistemic justification. In short, they deny that truth is a property at all. For 'Snow is white' to be true, on this view, is no more and no less than for snow to be white. According to minimalism, the word 'true' no more identifies an interesting property than the word 'nothing' identifies an interesting because un-thing-like thing. We understand the conceptual system behind our uses of 'nothing' by understanding the logic of the word. Similarly, minimalists believe that one can understand everything there is to understand about truth by understanding the uses of the word 'true'. Ordinarily, they also believe that the most important aspect of our uses of 'true' is given by a version of Tarski's Convention T: The proposition that p is true if and only if p.

Rorty's own version of minimalism acknowledges only three important uses of 'true'. These are:

(a) an endorsing use

(b) a cautionary use, in such remarks as "Your belief that S is perfectly justified, but perhaps not true" — reminding ourselves that justification is relative to, and no better than, the beliefs cited as grounds for S, and that such justification is no guarantee that things will go well if we take S as a 'rule of action' (Peirce's definition of belief)

(c) a disquotational use: to say metalinguistic things of the form "'S' is true iff——.' (Rorty 1991, 128)

To understand these uses of 'true', Rorty thinks it is unnecessary to say anything with metaphysical bite, especially anything that involves treating truth as a real property exemplified by some propositions and not others. In the endorsing use of 'true', use (a), one might say something like 'It is true that snow is white' or 'What Grandma told you about saving money is true'. The function of 'true' here is just to mark one's endorsement of the claim or claims it modifies. One might as well have said simply 'Snow is white' or repeated what Grandma told you about saving money. It is useful to have a predicate like this in a language, especially when one wishes to make blanket endorse- ments of sets of claims too large to assert individually. For example, we do not have time for me to repeat everything Grandma told you about saving money. Nevertheless, we do have time for me to say that it was all true.

This naturally brings us to the disquotational use of 'true', use (c). Here the predicate is a logical operator for bringing sentences (or classes of them) up from an object language into a metalanguage. This too can be useful. For example, I am unable use the language of number theory to state every theorem of number theory, for there are infinitely many theorems and I have only finite time. I could achieve the same effect, though, by using the truth predicate in a metalanguage and saying something like 'All the theorems of number theory are true'. As W. V. Quine puts the point, "The logician talks of sentences only as a means of achieving generality along a dimension he cannot sweep out by quantifying over objects. The truth predicate then preserves his contact with the world, where his heart is." (1970, 35) One might wonder, then, just how the endorsing and disquotational uses of 'true' differ.

Rorty is little help in answering that question; I have been unable to find a place where he discusses it. At risk of putting words into his mouth, then, let me make the following suggestion. The endorsing use of 'true' is a species of the disquotational use, but the disquotational use is broader. Whenever one uses 'true' to talk simultaneously of sentences and the world, or to talk about the logical relationships among sentences, the use is disquotational. Sometimes this commits a speaker to the claims 'true' modifies. When it does, 'true' has an endorsing use. When it does not, as in the following examples, the use of 'true' is disquotational but not endorsing:

It's going to be a lean winter if Madame Seesalot's predictions are true.

'Snow is white' is true if and only if snow is white.

Frank's stories could be true, but I doubt his life has been that interesting.

The cautionary use of 'true' requires delicate handling. Considering it could easily lead one to a more substantive view of truth than minimalism allows. *Why*, one might ask, do some of our beliefs hold up longer and work for us better than others? *Why*, one might go on, do we need to be reminded that even our most justified beliefs may not pan out in the long run? A natural answer is this:

Some of our beliefs serve us better than others *because they are true*. They accurately represent reality independent of our minds. Our most justified beliefs, however, are never guaranteed to be true in this sense. So, we need to remind ourselves occasionally that our justified beliefs might turn out not to be apt rules for action, for they may not correspond to the way things really are.

This answer leads to representationalism, and it gets there by treating truth as a property with explanatory power. In Rorty's view, no appeal to truth is able to produce a real explanation. He writes:

[It] would be a mistake to think of 'true' as having an explanatory use on the basis of such examples as 'He found the correct house because his belief about its location was true' and 'Priestley failed to understand the nature of oxygen because his beliefs about the nature of combustion were false'. The quoted sentences are not explanations but promissory notes for explanations. To get them cashed, to get real explanations, we need to say things like 'He found the correct house because he believed that it was located at ...' or 'Priestley failed because he thought that phlogiston ...'. The explanation of success and failure is given by the details of about what was true or what was false, not by the truth or falsity itself — just as the explanation of the praiseworthiness of an action is not 'it was the right thing to do' but the details of the circumstances in which it was done. (1991, 140)

We do not need to construe cautionary uses of 'true' as warnings about the possibility of inaccurate representation. Instead, Rorty considers them reminders that:

justification is relative to an audience and that we can never exclude the possibility that some better audience might exist, or come to exist, to whom a belief that is justifiable to us would not be justifiable. But, as Putnam's "naturalistic fallacy" argument shows, there can be no such thing as an "ideal audience" before which justification would be sufficient to ensure truth. For any audience, one can imagine a better-informed audience and also a more imaginative one — an audience that has thought up hitherto-undreamt-of alternatives to the proposed belief. (1998, 22)

Here Rorty invokes relativism about epistemic justification but the invocation is not essential to his main point, which is only that justification is always fallible. No matter how well justified one of our beliefs might seem to us today, something could could force us to give it up tomorrow. The claim that p is true simply does not follow from the claim that someone is well justified in believing that p. For Rorty, cautionary uses of 'true' are reminders that truth is *not* epistemic, not reminders that it *is* representational.

In at least one place, Rorty insists that the disquotational use of 'true' does not account for its cautionary use (1998, 60), but that is somewhat misleading. The point of the cautionary use of 'true' is that we should not close the book on p once and for all just because our belief that p passes muster with our present epistemic standards. We, our standards, or our information might improve in such a way that we feel compelled to replace our belief that p with the belief that Not-p. What matters here is less the possibility of better audiences than the present audience's fallibility, which 'true' highlights in its cautionary use. Despite what Rorty says, then, we could assimilate the cautionary use of 'true' to the disquotational use after all. "S's belief that p is justified but perhaps not true" would then amount to "S's belief that p is justified, but maybe Not-p anyway." The latter claim would do what Rorty intends the cautionary use of 'true' to do; it would remind us that the standards that make for S's justification in believing that p are not enough to guarantee that p.

Though it is not essential to his explication of the cautionary use of 'true', Rorty's relativism about justification does figure in his rejection of truth as a goal of inquiry. That relativism amounts to the following analysis of justification:

For any S who believes that p and any audience A, S's belief that p is justified to A if and only if it satisfies A's epistemic standards

where an audience's "epistemic standards" are its standards of acceptable belief. There is no such thing on this view as justification apart from justification relative to an audience and its standards. If there is any such thing as epistemic justification full stop, then, it is justification relative *us* and what *we* take our best epistemic standards to be. For Rorty, "justification is relative to an audience" (1998, 22), and it has a lot to do with how convincing a case one could make to an audience for believing as one does.

Given pragmatism, minimalism, and the audience-relativity of epistemic justification, Rorty acknowledges only a trivial sense in which truth can be a goal of inquiry. That is the sense of 'goal' in which a person has whatever goals she thinks she has. For example, an ancient archer might think she is trying both to hit bull's-eyes and to please the goddess Diana. In the trivial sense, this archer has two separate goals. However, as there is no such goddess as Diana and no such thing as pleasing her, there is no nontrivial sense in which this archer is trying to do any more than to hit bull's-eyes. If we say truth is a goal of inquiry, Rorty thinks, we might mean only that inquirers often think they are trying to get beliefs that are not only justified but true. In the trivial sense of 'goal', we would be right, but we would also be saying nothing about the nature or aims of inquiry. We would only be describing the state of mind of certain inquirers who, in Rorty's view, are making a mistake analogous to the Dianic archer's (1998, 29).

Rorty's case for this view begins with pragmatism. The only way we can try to get true beliefs, Rorty thinks, is by trying to get beliefs that accord well with our epistemic standards. This indicates that there is no difference in practice between aiming for truth and aiming for increased epistemic justification; whatever you *think* your goals are, you will *do* exactly the same things. As a pragmatist, Rorty is suspicious of positing two distinct goals when there is no difference between their pursuits.

By itself, this is not enough to undermine the view that truth is a goal of inquiry over and above mere epistemic justification. Consider our archer again, but now suppose Diana does exist and we mortals can please her only by hitting bull's-eyes. In this case, hitting bull's-eyes and pleasing Diana *are* two different things, even though we can do the latter only by doing the former.

There would still be no practical difference between trying to please Diana and trying to hit bull's-eyes, but religious archers *would* be trying to bring about two separate states of affairs. One involves the relative positions of arrows and targets, and the other involves Diana's mood.

Here is where minimalism comes into the argument. According to minimalism, there is no such thing as "truth" for us to seek in inquiry, just as there is no such goddess as Diana for us to please in archery. It would therefore be a mistake to consider the justification of our beliefs to be a property making it more likely that they have the additional property of being true. Instead, Rorty thinks we must fall back on the audience-relative conception of epistemic justification.

In inquiry, then, our aim is to get beliefs that are justified in the sense that they satisfy our community's epistemic standards. There is no practical difference between doing this and trying to get true beliefs, and there is no property of truth over and above justification at which we could aim. Except in the trivial sense, then, Rorty concludes that truth is not a real goal of inquiry.

3. One Practical Difference Between Pursuing Truth and Pursuing Justification

The non-existence of truth as a possible goal over and above epistemic justification would not entail the reducibility of truth to justification. It would mean only that we *can* aim for justification, for there is such a property our beliefs could have, but we *cannot* aim for truth because (a) there is no such property and (b) there is no practical difference between what we call "pursuing the truth" and trying to get beliefs that are justified in Rorty's sense of the word.

Rorty's case, it should be clear, depends on there being no practical difference between pursuing the truth and pursuing epistemic justification relative to one's community. He arrives at this claim by considering what one does in making assessments of truth and justification. As he puts it, "assessment of justification and assessment of truth are, when the question is about what I should believe now, the same activity" (1998, 22). If they should turn out to be *different* activities, though, we could make sense of inquiry as the pursuit of truth rather than just an effort to be as persuasive as one can be. In this section and the following one, I will argue that there *are* practical differences between pursuing truth and pursuing justification relative to an audience.

Rorty bases his identification of assessing truth with assessing justification on the first-person case, "when the question is what I should believe now." I think he is wrong about this case, but it will be helpful to begin with a case of a different sort. Suppose Marge makes one of the following claims:

(1) Homer believes that Bart has been arrested.
(2) Homer's belief that Bart has been arrested is justified.
(3) Homer's belief that Bart has been arrested is true.

It makes a practical difference which assertion Marge makes. If she asserts (1), she attributes a belief to Homer but commits herself no further. She could be entitled to attribute that belief whether or not she agrees with Homer and whether or not she approves of his grounds for believing as he does.

Marge's commitments in asserting (2) are more complicated. First, asserting (2) would commit her to everything asserting (1) would, for all Homer's *justified* beliefs are Homer's beliefs. Furthermore, in keeping with the Rortyan conception of justification we are assuming until section five, asserting (2) would commit Marge to considering Homer's so believing to be acceptable by the lights of whatever audience is relevant in the context. In the simplest case, Marge is a member of that audience and she endorses its standards. Consequently, asserting (2) would conditionally commit Marge to agreeing with Homer. Unless she has relevant, outweighing evidence Homer lacks, she is acknowledging that the standards she endorses commend agreement with Homer to her.

Asserting (3) would involve Marge in commitments orthogonal to those of asserting (2). Where (2) carries a *conditional* commitment to agree with Homer, (3) carries an *unconditional* one. Marge is never entitled to call Homer's belief true while disagreeing with him. Yet there is a normative element present in (2) that is absent in (3). Marge can legitimately call Homer's belief true without taking *any* particular position on its standing vis-à-vis any epistemic standards. For example, she might agree with Homer that Bart has been arrested, while insisting that his belief is unjustified because it is based on hallucinations induced by a Guatemalan insanity pepper.

These are practical differences between merely attributing a belief to someone, calling the belief justified, and calling it true. Appreciating those differences can help us to see how assessing justification and assessing truth differ in third-person cases. To assess the justification of someone else's belief is to decide what stance to take toward a claim like (2). On the Rortyan conception of justification, this means deciding whether the belief satisfies a community's epistemic standards. To assess the *truth* of someone's belief is to decide what stance to take toward a claim like (3). It is a matter of seeing whether things are as this person says they are; given she believes that p, it is a matter of finding out whether p or Not-p.

For example, if Marge were assessing Homer's belief's justification, she would be concerned with some questions about *Homer*. Why does he think Bart has been arrested? Are his reasons the kind we would ordinarily accept or find convincing? Has he ignored any relevant evidence available to him? When she finally decides whether to consider the belief justified or not, she will not necessarily have come to *any* particular views about Bart. On the other hand, in assessing Homer's belief's truth, Marge is mainly concerned with just one question: Has Bart been arrested? This is a question about Bart, and Marge is interested in the grounds of Homer's belief only as a possible source of information about what has happened to Bart.

The question of Homer's belief's justification is a question about Homer and not Bart. The question of its truth is a question about Bart and not Homer. Insofar as these are different questions, looking for answers to them are different activities. Their outcomes are independent in the sense that all the logical possibilities are open: Marge might find Homer's belief justified and true, justified and untrue, unjustified and true, or unjustified and untrue. At least in third-person cases, assessing justification and assessing truth are *not* the same activity.

But maybe we have moved too fast. One might object that the activities I have associated with assessing the truth of someone else's beliefs bear no practical difference to those associated with assessing the *justification* of one's own beliefs. That is, one might contend that I decide whether *your* beliefs are true by considering whether *I* am justified in agreeing with you. If so, then all I have really shown so far is that third-person assessments of justification differ from first-person assessments of justification. Furthermore, the first-person case seems far more relevant to the question whether truth can be one's goal in inquiry. To deal with this objection fully, we need to consider the first-person case in more detail.

4. Truth and First-person Justification

I am still assuming relativism about epistemic justification. I discharge that assumption in section five. To see the practical difference between concern for truth and concern for audience-relative first-person justification, we can start by considering some points made by a pair of Rorty's pragmatist forebears: Charles S. Peirce and John Dewey.

Both Peirce and Dewey were interested in distinguishing better from worse forms of inquiry. Peirce conceives of inquiry as a struggle to move from the "uneasy and dissatisfied" state of doubt to the more settled state of belief, in which one can act confidently. In "The Fixation of Belief," he considers four ways of making that move: the method of tenacity (i.e., sticking to one's doxastic guns come what may), the method of authority (i.e., believing what the powerful tell one to believe), the a priori method of "what is agreeable to reason," and the scientific method. He finds that only the last method is correct, for he thinks it is the only one with mechanisms built in to make sure that the world as we experience it has a say in both what we believe and how we form our beliefs (Peirce 1982b, 75).

Dewey defines inquiry as "the controlled or directed transformation of an indeterminate situation into one that is so determinate in its constituent distinctions and relations as to convert the elements of the original situation into a unified whole" (Dewey 1982, 319–20). Like Peirce, he thinks of inquiry as a response to a certain kind of predicament, in which one does not know what to *do* because one does not know what to *think*. Also, for Dewey, not just any response to such a predicament will do. "Men think in ways they should not," he writes, "when they follow methods of inquiry that experience of past inquiries shows are not competent to reach the intended end of the inquiries in question" (1982, 318–9). Just as Peirce believes our inquiries should tune our beliefs to the world as we experience it, Dewey believes that the world as we have it through experience of past inquiries should inform our conduct in future inquiries.

For both Peirce and Dewey, maintaining contact with the world as we experience it requires us to take a critical and fallibilistic stance toward *both* our beliefs *and* our methods of acquiring them. It is not enough, in their view, simply to apply heuristics or existing community standards blindly, nor is it correct to form one's beliefs haphazardly without applying any particular standards or strategies. Inquirers should be willing to ask two different kinds of questions. The first asks whether candidate beliefs satisfy existing epistemic standards. The second asks whether beliefs that accord with those standards tend to hold up over time, as we accumulate more experience.

Now let us consider an inquiry whose topic is Bart's alleged arrest. Rorty would say there is no practical difference between trying to decide whether it is true that Bart has been arrested and trying to decide whether I would be justified in believing he has been. Furthermore, on the audience-relative conception of justification, to decide whether I am justified in thinking Bart has been arrested is to decide whether I would satisfy my community's standards if I believed he had been. Notice that the question of those standards' adequacy does not arise if I am interested in justification alone. That question is simply irrelevant to whether my belief would satisfy the standards. Just as the question of Homer's belief's justification was about Homer but not Bart, the question of *my own* audience-relative justification is about *me* but not Bart. If all I want is a justified belief, then all I'm interested in doing is what would enable me to get away with believing what I come to believe and, perhaps, to convince others in my community. I am indifferent to whether I come to believe that Bart has been arrested only if he has been.

Now imagine that I am interested in more than just the Rortyan justification of my belief; I am interested in its truth. That is, I want to believe that
Bart has been arrested if and only if Bart *has* been arrested. In these circumstances, I want more than just to get a belief my peers will find convincing. My
getting away with thinking Bart has been arrested is not necessarily any
indication that he has been. I want to form my belief in such a way that it is
unlikely to be overturned by future experience. At the very least, that means
avoiding methods of inquiry I have found to be unreliable, and it may also
involve *using* methods I have found to be reliable in the past.

The practical difference between judging one's own justification and
judging the truth of one's beliefs, then, consists in one's preparedness to take a
critical stance towards one's epistemic standards. For my beliefs to be justified,
in Rorty's audience-relative way, they need only to satisfy my community's
epistemic standards. Assessing my own belief's justification, then, is a simple
matter of applying the standards, *and it does not require evaluating their
adequacy or reliability.* Now, it may be that I can judge the truth of my beliefs
only by applying epistemic standards (for example, by judging the quality of
my evidence for believing one way or another), but assessing the truth of my
beliefs goes beyond the *mere* application of those standards. It also includes a
concern for their adequacy. If Peirce and Dewey are right, this means that
inquiry at its best does include a concern for truth over and above a concern for
Rortyan justification. At its best, that is, inquiry aims at truth.

On the account I am suggesting, then, one's goal is truth when one's
goal is to believe that *p* only if *p*, and one's goal is justification when one's
goal is to believe that *p* only if doing so would satisfy one's community's
epistemic standards. The practical difference between these two states is that, in
the former case but not necessarily the latter, one's attitude towards one's
community's standards is critical and fallibilistic.

Note that distinguishing the assessment of justification from the assessment of truth requires us to sacrifice neither minimalism nor pragmatism. This
is because neither minimalism nor pragmatism conflicts with the view that
epistemic standards can be more or less adequate. For example, minimalists can
say that standards are adequate insofar as they tend to give the nod to true (and
not false) beliefs, where 'true' is used disquotationally. Good standards to
apply in deciding whether Bart has been arrested, on such a view, are those
whose satisfaction makes it likely that, if I believe Bart has been arrested, then
he has been. Pragmatists need only add that we can tell whether our standards
are adequate in this sense only by seeing how well beliefs that accord with them
hold up in the face of future experience.

Rorty has his own view of what makes epistemic standards better or
worse. We can ask not only what our epistemic standards *are*, but what they

would be if we were at our reflective best, that is, if we were the "educated, sophisticated, tolerant, wet liberals" (1998, 52) we strive to be. He maintains that this is the only sense to be made of the idea of "better standards," once we have given up the representationalist view of truth. Consequently, Rorty might concede that there is a practical difference between pursuing truth and *unreflectively* pursuing audience-relative epistemic justification, but he could go on to claim that there is not a practical difference between pursuing truth and pursuing justification relative to our best standards. But, he might go on, since there is no such property as truth and there is such a property as justification relative to those standards, there is no goal of truth.

This objection abandons the audience-relative conception of justification in favor of an ethnocentric conception. On such a view, to be *really* justified is not just to satisfy an audience's epistemic standards, but to satisfy *our best* standards, which are the standards we think we would embrace if we were at what we conceive to be our best. Because the objection gives up relativism about justification, I will not answer it in this section, where my aim has been to show there is a practical difference between pursuing truth and pursuing audience-relative epistemic justification. Next, I consider whether a non-relativistic account of justification leaves room for truth as a goal of inquiry.

5. Extending the Argument

My argument above depends on Rorty's relativistic conception of epistemic justification. Given pragmatism, minimalism, and that view, there are practical differences between trying to get true beliefs and trying only to get justified beliefs. On Rorty's grounds, then, pragmatists can and probably should count truth among the goals of inquiry. Though all pragmatic minimalists will agree with Rorty that what makes no difference to practice should make no difference to philosophy, not all will agree with his relativism about justification. Even Rorty himself often seems to favor the "ethnocentric" view. We should there-fore consider whether there is sense to be made of truth as a goal of inquiry on a non-relativistic construal of epistemic justification. I argue in this section that there is.

The argument here differs from that of section four. I do not argue that there is a practical difference between pursuing non-relativistic justification and pursuing truth. Rather, I will be arguing that the conjunction of pragmatism, minimalism, and non-relativism about epistemic justification actually *implies* that truth is a goal of inquiry. Given non-relativism about justification, it would be inconsistent for the pragmatic minimalist to follow Rorty's lead and deny that truth is a goal of inquiry.

There are two forms of non-relativism to take into account. Both forms construe epistemic justification as more than just satisfying an audience's epistemic standards. Instead, they treat justification as a matter of conformity with *adequate* epistemic standards, and a belief is more justified the more adequate the standards. In keeping with pragmatism and minimalism, though, we cannot construe adequacy here in terms of a tendency to produce "accurate representations." That would be to fall back into the representationalist picture of truth as correspondence to the mind-independent world, and the pragmatic minimalist rejects that picture. There are two forms of non-relativism that avoid this picture, however.

The first such form is Rorty's ethnocentric conception of justification. On this conception, for standards to be better or worse is for them to be better or worse by *our best lights*, that is, by what we take to be our own best judgment. The relevant "we," says Rorty, comprises "us educated, sophisticated, tolerant, wet liberals, the people who are always willing to hear the other side, to think out all the implications, and so on — the sort of people, in short, whom Putnam and I hope, at our best, to be" (1998, 52). Needless to say, Rorty denies epistemic justification in this sense is sufficient for truth.

A second form of non-relativism draws heavily on the disquotational use of the word 'true'. One can say that epistemic standards are adequate to the extent that they tend to give the nod to true beliefs, but 'true' is here being used disquotationally. Adequacy on this conception is not a matter of promoting accurate representation in the metaphysically robust sense of representationalism. It is just a matter of having a tendency to approve the belief that *p* only if *p*.

Given pragmatism, these two non-relativistic conceptions come to the same thing; there is no practical difference between them. The only way to tell whether a set of standards is adequate in the ethnocentric sense is to see whether it tends to approve beliefs that hold up under scrutiny as we improve ourselves epistemically, by becoming better informed and more imaginative. That, however, is no different from our only way of telling whether a set of standards tends to approve true beliefs. All we can do is see whether the beliefs the standards approve tend to hold up even as we become more imaginative and better informed, i.e., whether they hold up in the face of future experience.

I say more about well-informed, imaginative audiences below. For now, though, let us take non-relativism about epistemic justification to be the view that epistemic justification derives from the satisfaction of adequate epistemic standards, and let us take standards to be adequate to the extent that they tend to promote beliefs that hold up under the scrutiny as we become more imaginative and better-informed.

Now let us try to imagine inquiry not aimed at truth. To keep things con-crete, let the subject of our inquiry be the question whether protons are larger than electrons. For pragmatists, the *meaning* of the claim "Protons are larger than electrons" consists of the practical difference it would make for protons to be larger than electrons. For minimalists, the *truth* of the claim simply consists in protons' *being* larger than electrons. By minimalism, our inquiry un-concerned with truth is unconcerned with whether protons are larger than electrons. By pragmatism, this means our inquiry is unconcerned with whether the practical consequences of protons' being larger than electrons obtain.

An imaginative audience is one that can see the practical differences it would make for protons to be larger, smaller, or the same size as electrons. They can imagine in detail how things would seem or what experience would be like in each case. An audience is well-informed to the extent that it is aware of how things *do* seem or of what experience *is* like. The more imaginative and well-informed an audience is, the better they can tell whether things *do* seem as they *would* seem if protons were larger than electrons. Our inquiry un-concerned with truth, then, is also unconcerned with producing beliefs that will hold up under the scrutiny of well-informed, imaginative audiences. This is because it is unconcerned with whether protons are larger than electrons, and for protons to be larger than electrons is for the practical consequences of 'Protons are larger than electrons' to obtain. By our non-relativism about epistemic justification, it follows that the inquiry is unconcerned with *justifica-tion* as well. Pragmatic minimalists who are not relativists about justification cannot consistently maintain that inquiry aims at justification but not truth.

But, one might object, doesn't this argument trade on the fact that there is no practical difference between pursuing non-relativistic justification and pursuing truth? And wasn't that supposed to be a reason to *deny* that truth is a goal of inquiry? Wouldn't we do just as well to say only that inquiry aims at producing more or better non-relativistically justified beliefs, without mention-ing truth at all?

My argument may take advantage of the sameness in practice between pursuing non-relativistically justified beliefs and pursuing true beliefs, but I do not think this is a reason to deny that truth is a goal of inquiry. The argument shows that truth must be a goal of inquiry if non-relativistic justification is. It would be inconsistent for pragmatic minimalists to deny that. The force of the objection, then, must be that there are overriding reasons not to *say* that truth is a goal of inquiry, even though that is a consequence of minimalist pragmatism. At one point, Rorty seems to argue that there are such overriding reasons. He thinks the old-fashioned and highfalutin rhetoric of truth is inferior to his own newfangled rhetoric of "solidarity" and "intersubjective, unforced agreement" because the former invites representationalism and bad metaphysics. He writes,

Some pragmatists might see no reason why they too should not say, ringingly, robustly, and commonsensically, that the goal of inquiry is *truth*. But they cannot say this without misleading the public. For when they go on to add that they are, of course, not saying that the goal of inquiry is correspondence to the intrinsic nature of things, the common sense of the vulgar will feel betrayed. For "truth" sounds like the name of a goal only if it is thought to name a *fixed* goal — that is, if progress toward truth is explicated by reference to a metaphysical picture, that of getting closer to what Bernard Williams calls "what is there anyway." Without that picture, to say that truth is our goal is merely to say something like: we hope to justify our beliefs to as many and as large audiences as possible. But to say that is to offer only an ever-retreating goal, one that fades forever and forever when we move. It is not what common sense would call a goal. (1998, 39)

This line of argument strikes me as very bad. For one thing, giving up the metaphysics of representationalist truth does *not* force pragmatic minimalists to construe aiming at truth only as hoping to justify our beliefs to lots of people. Rather, they can say quite simply that we aim for truth when we try, for any *p*, to believe that *p* if and only if *p*. As pragmatists, they would then add that the best symptom of *p* is that it seems to be the case to those in a position to tell both how things do seem and how they would seem if *p*. There is no spooky metaphysics here.

Another problem is Rorty's claim that pragmatists who call truth a goal of inquiry will mislead the public. As philosophers interested in being clear, we might want to avoid saying misleading things. By the same token, though, we should acknowledge the important difference between *invitation* and *implication*. It might *invite* bad metaphysics to call truth a goal of inquiry, but it *implies* neither representationalism nor any substantive metaphysical theses. Pragmatic minimalists should not be afraid to say that truth is a goal of inquiry, especially if that is consequence of their view. If "the common sense of the vulgar will feel betrayed," then too bad for the vulgar. Pragmatists should respond to their feelings of betrayal by saying what they mean when they call truth a goal of inquiry and by arguing for their preferred views of justification, truth, and inquiry. They should not try to conceal the consequences of their views just because they might be hard to explain.

My point here is just that dropping relativism about justification does not force us to stop considering truth a goal of inquiry. To the contrary, a non-relativist conception of justification consistent with pragmatism and minimalism is *inconsistent* with the claim that truth is *not* a goal of inquiry.

Another possible objection, though, is that the case has been overstated. The argument I have offered supports the conclusion that truth is a goal of inquiry if non-relativistic justification is, but I have not yet argued for the antecedent. Rorty might thus deny that non-relativistic justification is properly considered a goal. He might say such justification, like truth, is "an ever retreating goal" we can never know we have attained. Thus, he could go on, it is better to maintain that *neither* truth nor non-relativistic justification is a goal of inquiry.

The objection depends on the claims (a) that non-relativistic justification is epistemically isolated in the sense that we can never know we have attained it and (b) that it is a mistake to construe an epistemically isolated state as a goal. Both claims are too dubious to accept.

Consider (a). Why should we think non-relativistic justification is epistemically isolated? Presumably, this is because we can never be infallibly certain a belief will hold up under the scrutiny of audiences better informed and more imaginative than we are. That is no strike against non-relativistic justification, though. We can never be infallibly certain we have attained *any* goal, but surely there are some goals we can know we have attained. Non-relativistic justification appears to be no more epistemically isolated than anything else. When a belief holds up under the scrutiny of more imaginative, better informed audiences, we have evidence it is non-relativistically justified. When it does not, we have evidence it is not. As with any goal, knowing we have attained this one is primarily a matter of, first, attaining it and, second, having good evidence we have attained it. There is no reason to think either is impossible.

Even if non-relativistic justification were epistemically isolated, however, it would not follow that it cannot be a goal. For different reasons, dying for one's country and proving $\pi = 3$ are epistemically isolated, but they are possible goals. More to the point, perhaps, it might be impossible for me to know I have designed the most efficient refrigerator possible, but that could still be my goal. Having the goal would motivate me to keep trying out new ideas in hopes of improving my designs. It keeps my mind open to the possibility that there are possible improvements no one has thought up yet. Similarly, the aim of non-relativistic justification can motivate a person to keep trying to improve her beliefs and to keep subjecting them to the scrutiny of better and more imaginative audiences. All that really follows from the epistemic isolation of a goal is that we might keep aiming for it after we have already (but unknowingly) achieved it. In the case of non-relativistic justification, that just means keeping a critical and open mind even if one's beliefs are bound to hold up under the scrutiny of better audiences. Its putative epistemic isolation is no good reason to deny non-relativistic justification's status as a goal.

6. Conclusion

By design, minimalism is an approach to truth with few consequences of meta-physical or epistemological interest. Surely the claim that truth is not a goal of inquiry is epistemologically interesting, so minimalists should hope they are not committed to it. Some minimalists may want to go even further. They may want to claim that the question whether truth is a goal of inquiry is *independent* of their theory of truth. That is, they may want to say that their theory is compatible with either accepting or rejecting truth as a goal of inquiry.

I have not argued that minimalism by itself is committed to treating truth as a goal of inquiry. Instead of considering minimalism in isolation, I have considered it in conjunction with pragmatism. This conjunction of views leads Rorty to reject truth as a goal of inquiry. Minimalism forces him to deny that inquiry aims at producing beliefs with the property of being true, and he sees no practical difference between what we call pursuing the truth and our efforts to be as convincing as possible. He thinks his pragmatism then forces him to deny that truth is a goal.

But Rorty is mistaken. There *are* practical differences between pursuing the truth and simply trying to be convincing. In third-person cases of belief evaluation, we can aptly describe the difference by saying that the question whether *S*'s belief that *p* is justified is a question about *S*, but the question whether it is true is equivalent to the question whether *p*. In the first-person case, the difference comes down to one's attitude toward the standards and methods used in forming one's beliefs. When one's aim is truth, over and above convincingness or audience-relative justification, one is willing to view one's standards critically and fallibilistically.

If we think of justification non-relativistically, there may indeed be no practical difference between pursuing truth and pursuing justification. Yet if that difference does disappear, it is not a reason for pragmatic minimalists to deny that truth is a goal of inquiry. If anything, it is a reason for them to explain why we do not need to consider truth a metaphysically substantive property to pursue it, and why pursuing truth might be a good idea anyway. Whether justification is relative to an audience or not, pragmatic minimalists can and probably should count truth a goal of inquiry.

REFERENCES

Dewey, John. (1982) "The Pattern of Inquiry," in *Pragmatism: The Classic Writings*, ed. H. S. Thayer (Indianapolis: Hackett), pp. 316–334.

Peirce, Charles S. (1982a) "Definition and Description of Pragmatism," in *Pragmatism: The Classic Writings*, ed. H. S. Thayer (Indianapolis: Hackett), pp. 48–60.

————. (1982b) "The Fixation of Belief," in *Pragmatism: The Classic Writings*, ed. H. S. Thayer (Indianapolis: Hackett), pp. 61–78.

Quine, W. V. (1970) *The Philosophy of Logic* (Englewood Cliffs, NJ: Prentice-Hall).

Rorty, Richard. (1991) *Objectivity, Relativism, and Truth* (Cambridge, UK: Cambridge University Press).

————. (1998) *Truth and Progress* (Cambridge, UK: Cambridge University Press).

Chase B. Wrenn
Assistant Professor of Philosophy
Philosophy Department
University of Alabama
Tuscaloosa, AL 35487-0218
United States

Contemporary Pragmatism
Vol. 2, No. 1 (June 2005), 115–133

Editions Rodopi
© 2005

On the Idea of Philosophy as *Bildungsroman*: Rorty and his Critics

Christopher Voparil

The appearance of several new works and a multivolume critical anthology devoted to Richard Rorty casts in bold relief the surprising lack of sympathetic interpretations his work has generated over the past few decades. After examining the complex nature of the critical reaction to Rorty, this essay reviews two new introductions to his thought that attempt to approach him in a spirit of hermeneutic charity. I argue that Rorty's somewhat neglected idea of treating philosophy as a *Bildungsroman* may shed some light on the problem of how to read Rorty usefully.

To include Richard Rorty alongside Michel Foucault and Jacques Derrida as the most widely read philosophers of the late twentieth century no longer seems a stretch. Few living intellectuals can match Rorty's interdisciplinary breadth of influence. Rorty criticism has gone beyond a cottage industry: Richard Rumana's (now three year-old) annotated bibliography of the secondary literature on Rorty boasts over 1200 entries, some 80 representatives of which have been republished by Sage in a four-volume collection devoted to Rorty's work, edited by Alan Malachowski. New books and anthologies on Rorty now proliferate faster than one can keep track, much less fully digest; in addition to their edited works, Rumana and Malachowski have each authored monographs of their own.[1]

Despite the added clarity and perspective these new works provide, there remain a number of unexplained complexities connected with the broader reception of Rorty's work. Most significant here is how precious few of the hundreds, nearly thousands, of writings on Rorty portray him in a positive or sympathetic light. Drawing on two new treatments of Rorty by Rumana and Malachowski, my central claim in this essay is that the small minority of positive treatments of Rorty are best understood as instances of treating philosophy as an edifying *Bildungsroman*, an idea developed, albeit sporadically and insufficiently, in Rorty's thought itself. Drawing an intimate link between philosophy and the selfhood of its practitioners, the idea of philosophy as

Bildungsroman coheres with the pragmatist framework of Rorty's thought more generally and rests on the historicist and antitranscendentalist assumption that philosophers or the words they use are not "authorities on something other than themselves," nor are they "closer to how things are in themselves." They are only, as Rorty puts it, "closer to *us*," the culturally-constituted individuals who employ them.[2]

1. The Puzzle of the Rorty Phenomenon

Oddly, for all his omnipresence and international renown — *Contingency, Irony, and Solidarity,* for instance, has been published in twenty-two languages — there are no Rortyan schools of thought, and no cadre of Rortyan "followers" scampering to churn out Rortyan tracts and fulfill the promise of his project. Unlike Foucault and Derrida, one would be hard pressed to locate a single thinker claiming to be a Rortyan. Yet there is no doubt that Rorty's work, with its sheer erudition, clarity, and characteristic wit, has proved highly engaging and enlightening to many over the past three decades. For one, it is now commonplace to cite Rorty as single-handedly responsible for the recent resurgence of the tradition of American pragmatism. But Rorty's influence has long transcended the discipline of philosophy; true to his Deweyan heritage, he is quite adept at writing for wider audiences. A *New York Times* book review recently referred to him as the American philosopher most talked-about outside of philosophy departments, and Harold Bloom famously dubbed him "the most interesting philosopher in the world."[3] Add to this that Rorty himself is a consummate collaborator, enthusiastically promoting the work of others and always willing to generate responses to responses to foster vigorous ongoing debates, and the surprising lack of converts to Rortyanism becomes even more perplexing.[4]

These new works reveal a second peculiarity about the Rortyan secondary literature — namely, that so much of it is unambiguously hostile. Indeed, the greatest as yet unsolved puzzle surrounding the Rorty phenomenon may very well be the question of why so much of the secondary literature is negative or hyper-critical in nature. In the introduction to his bibliography, Rumana notes that of the 1200 plus entries, "only a small percentage are friendly to Rorty," and enumerates the two articles and three books, including his own, that are on the whole positive. Several more books and articles are "respectful," he continues, and one is "descriptive and noncommittal." Rumana perorates, "Nearly all the rest are negative reactions to his work" (ix).

Even Rorty's most sympathetic readers seem at a loss to explain why so little of the voluminous secondary literature is positive. Acutely aware of this oddity, Rumana begins his introduction to the massive bibliography with the quip, "If one is known by the enemies one makes, then Richard Rorty is, indeed, a well-known man." Although he provides a useful categorization of the "three areas that generate most of the vitriol," Rumana confesses he is ultimately "not sure how to explain the many negative reactions to Rorty" (xi).

Malachowski's insightful introduction to Rorty's *oeuvre*, published since Rumana compiled his massive bibliography, would also be included on the short list of Rorty-friendly works.[5] In a somewhat anomalous practice for an introductory treatment, Malachowski sees fit to devote an entire chapter and the bulk of a second to discussion of Rorty's critics. While Malachowski provides chapter and verse evidence of how often the shots of Rorty's critics miss their mark and is quite good at elucidating the unique nature of much Rorty criticism, including the often encountered "sheer complacency" and "self-satisfied failure to rise to [Rorty's] challenge," in the end he is unable to offer much more than the general conclusion that Rorty has been deeply and profoundly misunderstood by many of his critics. Obviously frustrated by such reactions, Malachowski is reduced to flinging offhanded jabs himself: "Perhaps the conclusion we should draw from Rorty's critics' proven inability to articulate the clear and conclusive refutation of his views that should be so easily forthcoming if he is so obviously wrong is that *they* are wrong" (*RR* 168).

This brings us to a third curiosity. One thing that both Rumana's bibliography and Malachowski's 4-volume anthology affirm, despite the penchant for glancing blows, is the richness of the vast secondary literature on Rorty. As Rumana puts it in his bibliography, "It seems a lot of people from a wide variety of disciplines and perspectives have something to say about him" (ix). This is not an insignificant point. Rorty clearly has impacted an astonishingly wide array of disciplines. In his final chapter Malachowski outlines the extent to which Rorty's work is debated in disciplines like legal studies, international relations, feminist studies, literary theory, and even business ethics. Besides the fact that, as one reviewer put it, "there must be something to be said for anyone who attracts widespread hostility," there is a larger, more profound point to be made here — actually, two.

Even if many of the uncharitable takes on Rorty can be explained, as Malachowski holds, by "shallow, inadequate readings of Rorty's texts," Rorty's uncanny ability to stimulate people into having something to say, at least on a Deweyan pedagogical paradigm, is an achievement of the highest order. Put another way, even when "shallow and inadequate" as an accurate representation of his position, the critical reactions to Rorty's work remain marked by an imaginative richness and originality of perspective that few other thinkers inspire. After all, who could have predicted that Rorty would have an influence on legal studies or business ethics?

The second point concerns the flipside of the overwhelmingly negative character of the Rorty literature: the small minority of positive accounts. These sympathetic readings may prove more telling than the entire lot of hyper-critical commentary. What is noteworthy about the few positive assessments of Rorty's approach is that they are not gestures of philosophical affiliation, at least not primarily so. And virtually no one can be found defending Rorty's "creative misreadings" of James or Dewey, or his interpretations of Kant or Hegel. Likewise, Rorty's method of "redescription" is not exactly an embrace-able approach, at least not for dyed-in-the-wool philosophers. So what is it exactly that Rorty's sympathizers are affirming?

Although more explicit in Malachowski's work because of his self-consciously introspective preface, both Malachowski and Rumana allude to feeling a unique sort of personal gratitude to Rorty. Not so much a debt to Rorty the man, though his widely recognized collegiality does inspire this. Interestingly, it is more of a debt to Rorty's work, the kind of deep, un-repayable debt eloquently described by Emerson in his essay on "Friendship" as that owed those "who carry out the world for me to new and noble depths, and enlarge the meaning of all my thoughts."[6] That is, the kind of debt that accompanies provocations to individual growth, and a debt that makes mani-fest the Rortyan idea of philosophy as an edifying *Bildungsroman*. I will return to this claim more specifically below.

2. Fresh Perspectives on Rorty

The appearance of these new works is a boon to philosophers and students of philosophy alike. Achieving a mastery of the vast secondary literature on Rorty has long ceased to be humanly possible. Rumana's annotations, along with his useful thematic cross-referencing, offer the kind of critical roadmap that will prove an invaluable resource both for established scholars and curious neo-phytes in the years to come. Multivolume compilations like Malachowski's that bring together from varied and obscure sources some three and half decades of scholarship are undoubtedly essential. As with his previous edited collection, *Reading Rorty*, which in my view remains the best one-volume collection on Rorty, at least on his work up to the late 1980s, Malachowski succeeds in amassing a vibrant "combination of fresh talent and old hands."[7] Organized chronologically as well as thematically, the collection will be especially useful for scholars of Rorty, particularly for the section on reactions to Rorty's pre-*Philosophy and the Mirror of Nature* [hereafter *PMN*] work from his peers at the time. Every period in Rorty's development, as well as virtually every facet of this thought, are well-represented from perspectives both within and outside philosophy proper. "Classic" essays on Rorty by Hilary Putnam, Donald Davidson, Daniel Dennett, and Richard Bernstein are here, as well as important recent writings, by Keith Topper, Ruth Anna Putnam, and numerous others.[8] As Bernstein notes in his brief foreword to

Rumana's bibliography, the collections have a value that transcends Rorty: they also serve as aids "for understanding the philosophical and intellectual issues that have preoccupied thinkers for the past several decades."

For those still trying to make sense of Rorty, we have the individually authored works by Rumana and Malachowski. Rumana's *On Rorty* is most accessible (and probably the briefest) work to appear on Rorty to date. Despite being fraught with an inexcusable number of typographical errors (in a work that is 90 pages I noticed eight, without looking systematically, including "Immedicay" and "Inentionality" [*sic*] in bold type on facing pages), his discussions of four major themes in Rorty's thought yield a lucid, fresh perspective that achieves an enormous amount of breadth and depth for its brief compass. Malachowski's *Richard Rorty* is a work of greater scope and ambition. Although classed as an "introduction," it is first-rate piece of scholarship that traces the development of Rorty's ideas from his early essays through his well-known works, with an eye to liberating Rorty from persistent misrepresentations of his views. Like Rumana's, the book succeeds where the vast majority of Rorty commentators fail: in providing a "useful" reading of Rorty. In what follows, I argue that this achievement is the result of a fundamental shift in their respective conceptions of philosophy and its purpose brought about by their engagement with Rorty's writing, and exemplifying the idea of approaching philosophy as an edifying *Bildungsroman.*

Part of the Wadsworth Philosophers Series designed for "both philosophy students and general readers" and boasting over 100 works on "major philosophers throughout history," Rumana's *On Rorty* provides a brief, accessible introduction that, as Rumana puts it in the preface, gives "some sense of what the hoopla is about," while doing justice to the complexity of Rorty's thought. Organized thematically around very general but classic philosophical topics, like "The Mind and Human Nature" and "The Self and Morality," Rumana adopts the novel approach of beginning each chapter with a stage-setting device that briefly revisits a major figure in the philosophical tradition — Plato, Descartes, Kant, Aquinas — before considering Rorty's arguments. As anyone who has ever taught Rorty to undergraduates knows, his writings contain an enormous amount of name-dropping and presume a familiarity with the philosophical tradition and its major themes and problems not easily procured. It is often difficult to discuss Rorty without reference to a mountain of philosophical and historical baggage that demands as much attention as Rorty's thought itself. Rumana has found a useful way to provide readers with enough historical context and background to appreciate Rorty's significance and intent, yet avoids saddling them with so much of it that they sink before getting to Rorty.

The opening chapter of Rumana's *On Rorty*, "What is Philosophy?", for instance, nicely conveys to those outside the discipline what it meant for a philosophical insider like Rorty who "knows where all the philosophical skeletons are buried" to launch the kind of wide-ranging critique of traditional philosophy that he did in 1979 with *PMN*, while President of the American Philosophical Association no less.

Part of Rumana's explanatory success owes to his attention to how fundamentally Rorty views philosophy as "a game played with language," where the pictures and metaphors that grip us are not only expressive rather than descriptive, but arbitrary. Appreciating this insight yields a clearer understanding of Rorty's wholesale rejections of timeless philosophical premises. As Rumana puts it, "since language is a messy affair, there is no way to find an origin in thought or in experience by which to construct a vocabulary adequate to something like the real world." Though complicated by the embrace of pragmatism that follows Rorty's linguistic turn, he establishes how Rorty's view of "the ubiquity of language" has profound implications for epistemology, ontology, realism, idealism, and for truth itself, understood as a correspondence between our concepts and an independent reality. Once one makes the linguistic turn and holds that "where there are no sentences there is no truth," philosophy loses its fundamental foothold in the external world (*OR* 11–15).

This focus on language also allows Rumana to put Rorty's somewhat bewildering turn to "redescription" in its proper context. Dispelling the view of *PMN* as an expression of "a one time 'true believer' who has lost his faith," Rumana traces the origins of Rorty's view of language to several essays that appeared in 1961, when Rorty first takes the stance that "since any metaphysical, epistemological, or axiological argument can be defeated by redefinition, nothing remains to make a virtue of necessity and to study this process of definition itself."[9] In his more recent work Rorty refers to this endeavor as "redescription," and embraces it as a characterization of his own "method." Rumana nicely fleshes out what this making "a virtue of necessity" involves by linking it to the importance of "dialogue" for Rorty: "Dialogue for Rorty becomes an end in itself. There is no attempt to have the final word on what is real since this would end the dialogue; keeping the dialogue going itself is the purpose" (*OR* 10).

Rumana dubs this overall philosophical orientation "the romantic conversational approach to philosophy," calling attention to a strand of Rorty's thought that remains underappreciated. Rather than adopt an "argumentative discourse," Rorty prefers to "tell stories about individuals and their culture" (*OR* 15). Going so far as calling Rorty "a proponent of Romantic Individualism," Rumana's reading foregrounds the poetic foundations of Rorty's post-Philosophical, with a capital "P," culture and highlights the centrality of "moral storytelling" for Rorty. The chapter in which Rumana develops this perspective, entitled "The Self and Morality," is the book's strongest and most ambitious. Beginning with a discussion of Kantian morality, he situates Rorty's stance by contrasting it with the Enlightenment assumption that "its views truly reflected essential human qualities"; for Rorty, the Enlightenment is simply "one of the many stories that western culture has told about itself" (*OR* 41, 53–54). The virtue of Rumana's account in this chapter, where in good Rortyan fashion he forges a creative alignment between Freud's new metaphor of the mind and Joyce's *Ulysses,* is that he underscores the moral framework that grounds Rorty's practice of redescription, largely via a discussion of Rorty's important and somewhat neglected essays on Freud.[10] The value of Freud from Rorty's point of view, Rumana rightly contends, is that he offers "a new set of psychic metaphors for creating one's own life story" (*OR* 56).

An important piece of the argument is the link between Rorty's "stories" and the idea of a *Bildungsroman.* Drawing on the earlier essay, "Philosophy as a Kind of Writing," penned at the time Rorty was working on *PMN* and just before his first essay on Freud, Rumana conveys the moral or ethical context in which Rorty understands stories or "self-descriptions." Rather than thinking about "right and wrong" in terms of a "common moral consciousness [that] contains certain intuitions concerning equality, fairness, human dignity, and the like, which need to be made explicit through the formation of principles," Rorty suggests an alternative: "the longer men or cultures live, the more *phronesis* they may, with luck, acquire — the more sensitivity to others, the more delicate a typology for describing their fellows and themselves."

Since the Romantics, Rorty continues, "the poets, the novelists, and the ideologues" rather than the philosophers have been the most help in this effort. More specifically,

> Since the *Phenomenology of Spirit* taught us to see not only the history of philosophy, but that of Europe, as portions of a *Bildungsroman*, we have not striven for moral knowledge as a kind of *episteme.* Rather, we have seen Europe's self-descriptions, and our own self-descriptions, not as ordered to subject matter, but as designs in a tapestry which they will still be weaving after we, and Europe die.[11]

As Rumana argues, the key here is understanding how for Rorty "the aesthetics of metaphorical descriptions is an important element in ethics" (*OR* 55).

Ultimately, for Rorty developing this kind of "moral sensitivity" entails, as he has argued more recently, the cultivation of a kind of sentimental or sympathetic imagination that, alas, "genres such as ethnography, the journalist's report, the comic book, the docudrama, and, especially, the novel" are better suited to then philosophy.[12]

3. Rorty and *Bildung*

The fresh, sympathetic hermeneutic shared by both Rumana and Malachowski, to whom we will turn in a moment, seems rooted in a similar experience at once philosophical and personal. It relates to the idea of *Bildung* or edification, and echoes an experience Rorty himself describes in his quasi-autobiographical essay, "Trotsky and the Wild Orchids."[13] In the introduction to his bibliography, Rumana recounts the history of his own engagement with Rorty's work. At a time when "confronted with all the different schools and methodologies concerning first principles, one confronts an abyss where reason and thought breaks down; there is really no way to resolve fundamental issues." Rather than adopt a transcendental response to this crisis, Rumana resolved to "adopt an ironic attitude and learn to read philosophy in another way" — one that "clicked" with his reading of Rorty — "for its style and as a genre." In other words, to read the genre of philosophy "as an edifying *bildungsroman*" (*OR* xiii).

Malachowski's *Richard Rorty* opens with a highly personal preface that recalls Rorty's own account of his unprecedented turn to autobiography: "Perhaps this bit of autobiography will make clear that, even if my views about the relation of philosophy and politics are odd, they were not adopted for frivolous reasons."[14] Malachowski's preface similarly seeks to account for the origins of his philosophical position through a personal narrative, which turns out to have the same moral as Rorty's. As Malachowski puts it, we should "stop trying to beat private aesthetic delights into social shape, into consistently worthy public projects." The equivalent of Rorty's socially useless love for wild orchids here is the poems of Ezra Pound. The preface tells how Malachowski comes to the realization, arrived at via the inspiration of Rorty, that certain "areas of culture" should be pursued "for personal insight and pleasure," and thereby abandons the search for "a rational explanation of the accidental nature of [his] seemingly profound experiences with Pound's poetry" (*RR* xii).

The idea of a *Bildungsroman* is associated with the literary tradition inaugurated by Goethe's *Wilhelm Meister's Apprenticeship*. Typically translated as a "novel of education" or "novel of formation," the word derives its meaning from the "self-culture" or "self-formation" implied by *Bildung*. Such novels trace the moral, psychological, and social development of a young character who journeys from youthful provinciality and innocence to a more complex social and personal maturity borne of conflict, growth, and, above all, newfound self-knowledge. But at the moral core of the *Bildungsroman* is the assumption, however faint and quixotic, that such tales might lead the reader to greater self-development as well.

Rorty's philosophical *oeuvre* has functioned as a sort of *Bildungsroman* in this latter sense for a number of his more sympathetic readers. It is a sense of indebtedness for spurring this self-development that best accounts for their support of his work, rather than philosophical affiliation as such.

Although never fully developed or expounded upon at any length, the idea of philosophy as *Bildung* or edification has been a recurring motif in Rorty's work over the past 25 years, surfacing without warning at critical junctures and fading from view for years at a time. The concept of *Bildung* first appears in the final chapter of *PMN*, entitled "Philosophy without Mirrors." Opening in a cautionary tone, after 350 pages of rigorous assault on modern philosophy's unnecessary baggage, Rorty reflects that the road ahead of philosophy, in the wake of the critique of foundational epistemology, is largely uncharted. It is difficult, he concedes, to imagine what "philosophy without epistemology" would look like. The tentative route he vaguely gestures toward centers on displacing the acquisition of knowledge as the highest goal of thinking. In its place, he suggests, following Hans-Georg Gadamer, that we substitute the idea of "*Bildung*" or self-formation. But citing this term as "too foreign" and the word "education" as "too flat," he drops *Bildung* and adopts "edification" as the moniker for this new genre of philosophizing, the project of "finding new, better, more interesting, more fruitful ways of speaking."[15]

Rorty goes on to sketch two modes of edification. The first consists of the hermeneutic activity of "making connections" between different cultures — between ours and more exotic ones — or different historical periods or different vocabularies. Borrowing a phrase from Michael Oakeshott, Rorty dubs this "philosophy as 'the conversation of mankind.'" The second mode consists in the "poetic" activity of "thinking up such new aims, new words, or new disciplines." In both cases, the aim of edifying discourse is to "take us out of our old selves," as a way to "aid us in becoming new beings." Edification is discussed as a contrasting form of philosophizing to the "systematic" mode, and gets subsumed under the conception of "therapeutic" philosophy Rorty attributes to Wittgenstein, Heidegger, and Dewey. These three are "therapeutic rather than constructive, edifying rather than systematic" because their "aim is to edify — to help their readers, or society as a whole, break free from outworn vocabularies and attitudes, rather than to provide 'grounding' for the intuitions and customs of the present." Although highly suggestive, the relevance of *Bildung* here seems limited to the first sense, understood negatively as a wedge in Rorty's anti-representationalist project.[16]

In *Contingency, Irony, and Solidarity* [hereafter *CIS*], the second sense of *Bildung* as the "poetic" activity of creating new metaphors and self-understandings figures more prominently. Because of how Rorty's shift from reasons and rational argument to new images and metaphors privileges the imagination, it is the "strong poets" who become the primary engines of social change. Rather than an anomaly, this shift is best seen as a continuation of the fundamental insight that guides *PMN*, namely that "It is pictures rather than propositions, metaphors rather than statements, which determine most of our philosophical convictions." This same insight and its link to *Bildung* have re-emerged in Rorty's more recent work, but now with a more explicitly political dimension; for instance, in the essay "American National Pride," where the theme of replacing knowledge as the goal of thinking takes center stage.[17]

As Malachowski points out, there is nothing in this conception of philosophy as edification or *Bildung* that gives philosophy a distinctive role or that "prevents philosophy from being swallowed up by those areas of culture, such as literature, where practitioners are more accustomed to letting ambitions and self-deception follow the lead of the imagination rather than reason" (*RR* 60). Such a fate of course does not worry Rorty; his work since *CIS* can be read as an embrace of this very outcome. Yet in *CIS,* where, as Malachowski suggests, Rorty is still paving the way for post-epistemological philosophy and not yet practicing it himself, the notion of *Bildungsroman* receives a more explicitly philosophical gloss in the quintessentially Rortyan attempt to read Heidegger through Proust in the chapter called "Self-Creation and Affiliation: Proust, Nietzsche, and Heidegger." If Heidegger's account of Being can be divorced from the "metaphysical urge" that led him to seek some "affiliation with a superior power" and to take "his own idiosyncratic spiritual situation for the essence of what it was to be a human being," he can seen as doing the same thing as Proust — namely, "attempting autonomy." In other words, "trying to get out from under inherited contingencies and make his own contingencies, get out from under an old final vocabulary and fashion one which will be all his own."[18]

Like Proust, Rorty argues, Heidegger was engaged in an attempt "to create a new self by writing a bildungsroman about [his] old self." Here Rorty offers his best description of what it would mean to approach philosophy as a *Bildungsroman*: "Think of Heidegger as doing the sort of thing for 'Being's poem' which a critic might try to do for 'poetry in English'." He continues,

> Such a critic writes a bildungsroman about how English poetry came to be what it now is. Heidegger is writing a bildungsroman about, in his phrase, "what Being is." He tries to identify the philosophers, and the words, which have been decisive for getting Europe to the point where it is now. He wants to give us a genealogy of final vocabularies which will show us why we are currently using the final vocabulary we are by telling a story about the theorists (Heraclitus, Aristotle, Descartes, and so on), whom we have to go through rather than around. But the criterion of choice of figures to discuss, and of elementary words to isolate, is not that the philosophers or the words are authorities on

something other than themselves — on, for instance, Being. They are not revealers of anything except us — us twentieth-century ironists. They reveal us because they *made* us. "The most elementary words in which Dasein expresses itself" are not "most elemental" in the sense that they are closer to how things are in themselves, but only in the sense that they are closer to *us*.

In the end, what did Heidegger in from this perspective is that, unlike Proust, "who succeeded because he had no public ambitions," Heidegger "thought he knew some words which had, or should have had, resonance for *everybody* in modern Europe."[19]

The upshot of all this, and the thing that is most relevant to the issue of Rorty and his critics, is how, given this conception of philosophy, we should read Heidegger. Rorty's take on what it would mean to approach Heidegger's philosophy as a *Bildungsroman* could just as easily apply to Rorty himself, and account for the positive reception of Rorty by his select group of salutary commentators: "Reading Heidegger has become one of the experiences with which we have come to terms, to redescribe and make mesh with the rest of our experiences, in order to succeed in our own projects of self-creation."[20] Like the *Bildungsroman* more generally, what is revealed in our engagement with it has more to do with ourselves than with the truth or reality it reveals. The same can be said for the positive interpreters of Rorty's work. How we approach Rorty, or any other philosopher, as Heidegger well knew, is more a function of ourselves than the words contained therein. Although perhaps not appropriate for all thinkers, reading philosophy as a *Bildungsroman* has enabled a small minority of Rorty's readers to not only take something away from it, but to take it to heart.

4. Reading Rorty Usefully

To return to Malachowski, the upshot of this new approach to Rorty for his book, he tells us, is that he gives up on "the search for the 'real Rorty', the one that could be deduced from the sum of all the authors he had read, the one that could be called up squarely before the tribunal of the tradition he attacked" (*RR* xii–xiii). Although he does not mention it here, Malachowski is author of an essay on Rorty written a decade and a half ago (and included in the new multivolume collection) that takes this very tack and chides Rorty for his "errors of judgment" in both underestimating how much philosophy still needs epistemology, and overestimating "the creative autonomy of language."[21] Giving up on the real Rorty has not meant dropping Rorty altogether; on the contrary, Malachowski tells us he "continued to take his increasingly large body of work seriously, if in a lighter spirit" (*RR* xiii). Like Rumana's move to start reading philosophy in a different way, approaching Rorty in a Rorty-like lighter spirit yields a very different perspective for Malachowski; the current book, he informs us, is the product of this shift.

One way of putting this difference is to describe it as making the usefulness of an interpretation the key consideration, rather than its accuracy. The abandonment of traditional philosophy's claim to representational accuracy has been a hallmark of Rorty's pragmatist stance since *PMN*. Malachowski, it seems, has warmed to this shift since his earlier essay and even come to embrace it, stating that his book "does not even attempt to portray the 'real Rorty.'" Instead, the book's claim to interpretive authority rests on "how 'useful' the resulting portrait of Rorty is." But this begs the question, "Useful for what?" Here Malachowski offers three clearly defined criteria. His interpretation is useful to the extent that it: "facilitates appreciation of what Rorty is trying to achieve"; "encourages exploration of important issues raised by Rorty's key writings"; and "clears the path to a proper consideration as to how socially and intellectually useful Rorty's main themes are." In short, usefulness for Malachowski in this context seems to reside in counteracting the prevailing "hyper-critical" approaches to Rorty where "Rorty's ideas are knocked to the ground *before* they have been given a chance to demonstrate whether they can fly" (*RR* 3–7).

Indeed, Malachowski's introduction reads like a brief for what one may call the principle of hermeneutic charity. Approaching Rorty charitably means, "first to take him at his own word and then try to maximize the coherence of the results." A good methodology in general, perhaps. But it is particularly needful here: first, because of the rather obvious "*premature* lack of sympathy" Rorty seems to engender, and second, because such a "sympathetically agnostic" attitude is required to appreciate the "Gestalt-switch" Rorty's radically novel picture of philosophy entails (*RR* 3).

I think Malachowski succeeds in the terms of his own criteria, and succeeds superbly. Malachowski is a discerning reader of Rorty. His discussions of Rorty's major works and their relation to his broader *oeuvre* are thoughtful and revealing; the chapter on *CIS*, perhaps Rorty's most opaque and arguably most crucial work, is particularly good. Many will find his account of "redescriptive philosophy" in the final chapter helpful. His style is vibrant and readable, and his pages abound with fresh metaphors: "unlike [Ezra] Pound, Rorty is no Humpty Dumpty figure"; "The impression of effortlessness [in Rorty's ability to refashion other philosophers' positions] is a function of Rorty's unique skills — a sort of philosophical 'Dean Martin effect'" (*RR* xiii, 182). Yet this book is much more than the best general introduction to Rorty that I have seen, and it surely is that. It stands as an exemplar of how to read a thinker usefully.

Despite his earnest efforts not to peg the "real Rorty," in Malachowski's repeated claims that many of Rorty's critics have misunderstood his work, accuracy of interpretation seems to displace the standard of usefulness, or at least suggest the possibility that representationalism cannot be jettisoned altogether. This is not to dispute Malachowski's claim that Rorty is "more influential than understood." Clearly there are critics given to dismissing Rorty out of hand who fail to fully engage the complexity of his stance. Yet even though Malachowski makes a compelling case for how it is possible to continue to talk of "errors of interpretation ... without committing ourselves to further talk about what his work 'really signifies,'" this tends to obscure the fact that some simply see Rorty's work as irrelevant to their purposes.[22]

Nevertheless, Malachowski is on to something when he asks, "Why, if Rorty's views are so *clearly* wrong, are his philosophical critics so quick to reach for their rhetorical guns?" (*RR* 139). In the chapter Malachowski devotes to Rorty's critics he limits himself to critics from within philosophy proper, since they seem to be the ones who most acutely perceive Rorty as a threat. Critiques by Simon Blackburn, Alasdair MacIntyre, Thomas Nagel, John Searle, and Bernard Williams, whom Malachowski credits with, unlike many of his philosophical brethren, "tak[ing] the trouble to try to get inside Rorty's philosophical skin," are given a thoughtful hearing (*RR* 160). Here Malachowski's discussions are nuanced and revealing, each one illuminating another aspect of Rorty's stance that, like a kind of philosophical hologram, seems to disappear in each new attempt to pin down and dismiss him. Malachowski succeeds in illustrating what he dubs the "communications gap" — the degree of "incommensurability" or "mismatch" — that exists between Rorty's writings and the critical barbs of his critics. What irks him most and leaves him downright dumbfounded are the instances where critics attempt to refute Rorty merely by reasserting claims he has explicitly questioned, inexplicably ignoring the entire thrust of his argument: "Rorty's critics continue vilifying their own empty, enraged hands, not realizing that he has long since slipped their grasp" (*RR* 163). Malachowski is ultimately at a loss to adequately account for this, and he is forced to conclude:

> Perhaps the conclusion we should draw from Rorty's critics' proven inability to articulate the clear and conclusive refutation of his views that should be so easily forthcoming if he is so obviously wrong is that *they* are wrong. Perhaps that is the solution to our puzzle. Perhaps our earlier talk of a 'mismatch' that prevents a conclusive verdict on the state of play regarding Rorty and his critics was just too kind. (*RR* 168)

There may be another way to understand this situation, one that is illuminated by Malachowski's own account and that relates to the idea of philosophy as *Bildungsroman*. In his introduction Malachowski describes what he calls an "unwillingness, or perhaps inability, to take his staunch refusal to propound substantive claims seriously" on the part of Rorty's critics (*RR* 19). Rather than substantive claims to truth, knowledge, or rationality, he argues that Rorty's claims serve a different function:

> They are not designed to instill a fresh set of beliefs derived from literal content of the statements they encapsulate, but rather to *prod* us, by way of 'edification' (Rorty's term for the "project of finding new, better, more fruitful ways of speaking") into exploring fresh ways of describing things. (*RR* 19)

Malachowski continues on to claim that one of the main aims of his book is "to show that Rorty's views, and hence his 'position-free position', are 'edifyingly' presented 'to achieve an effect', that they should not be 'tastelessly' interpreted as further, if oblique and controversial, contributions to philosophy's age-old quest for the final, truthful picture of reality."[23]
       Like the romantic *Bildungsroman*, part of the function of Rorty's edifying discourse is not only for us to reexamine our philosophical assumptions, but, much more fundamentally, "to take us out of our old selves by the power of strangeness, to aid us in becoming new beings."[24] His opposition of "the desire for edification" to "the desire for truth" in *PMN*, and in *CIS* of the "ironist" to the "metaphysician," is meant to prompt us to ask, following Nietzsche, "What is it in us that wants truth?" and to disabuse us of whatever this something is.
       To return to Rorty's critics, perhaps some are "inclined to foist false claims on Rorty" and "so often content themselves with simply *reasserting* claims he has long questioned," as Malachowski claims, simply because these philosophers either do not want or are not ready to become "new beings" (*RR* 139). As a result, the dismissive, ill-supported criticisms of Rorty that seem to have little connection with his actual views, along with what Malachowski rightly describes as the "unconscious inverted principle of charity" that goes along with them, may be more usefully understood as a function of their attachment to their old selves than as confused or deficient efforts to get Rorty right. Conversely, we have the sympathetic attempts by Rumana and Malachowski to do justice to a rich body of work by those who have already, thanks to Rorty, found their new selves.
       Yet the sympathetic attitude characteristic of these approaches to Rorty does not mean they are uncritical. Because his book grows out of the need to counteract certain misleading readings of Rorty, Malachowski's tone on the whole is much more expository than critical. However, he does raise the interesting possibility that Rorty's approach may be "motivationally inadequate" in

that "once his pragmatist advice [is] heeded, there would be little incentive to create and explore new thoughts" (*RR* xv). In his final chapter, Rumana recounts how Rorty's embrace of ethnocentrism and the impossibility of a noncircular justification of our culture's practices have gone hand in hand with a supreme confidence that simply pointing out "the practical advantages of liberal institutions" will be enough to justify it to "representatives of other cultures."[25] He makes a persuasive case that such proclamations amount to "preaching to the converted," arguing that "Only where someone already comes from a culture that has a rich enough vocabulary of democratic values will the appeal to those values make sense" (*OR* 81–82). This becomes a potentially serious issue when one recalls that the ethical base of "we-intentions" that provides the social glue of Rorty's liberal democracy, as well as Rorty's conception of justice as a "larger loyalty," which is premised upon the (successful) extension of a feeling of loyalty or solidarity to distant and different others, rests on the assumption that democratic values will essentially sell themselves.

Rorty's response to such shortcomings is, as one would assume, not a return to rationality or foundations or any other ahistorical or decontextualized universality that will accomplish the work of social cohesion automatically. Instead, for Rorty it is a matter of cultivating the sympathetic imagination through "sentimental education" and, again, an emphasis on moral storytelling — specifically, "sad, sentimental stories."[26] Yet Rumana articulates a compelling critique of Rorty's claim that we divide ourselves into ironical self-redescribers in private and solidaristic bearers of sentimental fellow-feeling in public. Rumana avers this misgiving without disagreeing with the basic premise of Rorty's antifoundationalist solidarity that "there is no inferential connection between the disappearance of the transcendental subject — of 'man' as something having a nature which society can ... understand — and the disappearance of human solidarity."[27] Rumana's point is that "there is also no inferential connection between the loss of transcendental subject and a gain in solidarity" either. This strikes me as a point where Rorty is particularly vulnerable, and Rumana rightly "sees no reason to give Rorty the benefit of the doubt" (*RR* 85).

5. Revisiting Rorty

If Malachowski is right that "Rorty has helped do for philosophy what he contends Freud did for the Nietzschean conception of self-creation: democratize it," that such an endeavor is greeted more by angered dismissal than sympathetic embrace should be of no surprise, particularly when emanating from those who once believed philosophy to be the master discipline. As these works clearly demonstrate, others unburdened by such weighty responsibilities can read Rorty differently, and get something quite valuable as a result, even if that something, in the end, may no longer qualify as properly 'philosophical'. As Malachowski describes it, Rorty's writing "lifted" him out of his "parochial environment ... poetry, literature and indeed the arts in general became much more alive" for him (*RR* 183, xi–xii).

The idea of reading philosophy as a *Bildungsroman* certainly requires greater articulation and development; I have only been suggestive here. But whatever its philosophical underpinnings and merits, or lack thereof, an attitude that permits reactions like Malachowski's and allows us to experience the edifying force of inspiration, may not be such a bad thing for all of us, philosophers and nonphilosophers alike. With this in mind, perhaps for many of us Rorty's work may warrant a second look.

NOTES

1. The new works discussed in this essay are: Alan Malachowski, ed., *Richard Rorty*, 4 vols. (London: Sage Publications, 2002); Malachowski, *Richard Rorty* (Princeton, NJ: Princeton University Press, 2002); Richard Rumana, ed., *Richard Rorty: An Annotated Bibliography of Secondary Literature* (Amsterdam: Rodopi, 2002); and Rumana, *On Rorty* (Belmont, CA: Wadsworth, 2000). References in the text refer to the individually authored work by Malachowski as *RR* and by Rumana as *OR*. In addition, the last few years alone have seen a steady flow of other edited volumes devoted to Rorty, including Charles Guignon and David Hiley, eds., *Richard Rorty* (Cambridge, UK: Cambridge University Press, 2003); Matthew Festenstein and Simon Thompson, eds., *Richard Rorty: Critical Dialogues* (Cambridge, UK: Polity Press, 2002); and John Pettegrew, ed., *A Pragmatist's Progress* (Lanham, MD: Rowman and Littlefield, 2000); not to mention re-issues of older collections, like Malachowski's *Reading Rorty: Critical Responses to Philosophy and the Mirror of Nature (and Beyond)* (Oxford: Blackwell, 1990; 2002).

2. *Philosophy and the Mirror of Nature* (Princeton, NJ: Princeton University Press, 1979), p. 359.

3. Anthony Gottlieb, "The Most-Talked About Philosopher," a review of *Objectivism, Relativity, and Truth*, *New York Times* (2 June 1991), sect. 7, p. 30. On Rorty's role in the pragmatist revival, see for example Morris Dickstein, ed., *The Revival of Pragmatism: New Essays on Social Thought, Law, and Culture* (Chapel Hill, NC: Duke University Press, 1998), introduction.

4. Besides Donald Davidson and Harold Bloom, Rorty has promoted the work of lesser-known figures like Brazilian philosopher Roberto Mangabeira Unger and Argentine jurist Eduardo Rabossi. See *Essays on Heidegger and Others: Philosophical Papers, vol. 2* (Cambridge, UK: Cambridge University Press, 1991) and *Truth and Progress: Philosophical Papers, vol. 3* (Cambridge, UK: Cambridge University Press, 1998), respectively. For some examples of Rorty dutifully responding to each of his critics, see Herman J. Saatkamp, Jr., ed., *Rorty and Pragmatism: The Philosopher Responds to his Critics* (Nashville, TN: Vanderbilt University Press, 1995); Robert

Brandom, ed., *Rorty and His Critics* (Oxford: Blackwell, 2000); and Matthew Festenstein and Simon Thompson, eds., *Richard Rorty: Critical Dialogues.* In all of these collections, amazingly, Rorty has written an individual response to each essay.

5. In the spirit of full disclosure, I must confess that my own work on Rorty though not uncritical falls into this category as well. Approaching Rorty in a spirit of hermeneutic charity that takes his claims seriously, I argue that Rorty can be read as writing a form of political theory. See Christopher Voparil, "The Problem with Getting It Right: Richard Rorty and the Politics of Antirepresentationalism," *Philosophy and Social Criticism* 30 (2004), pp. 221–246; and *Politics and Vision in the Thought of Richard Rorty* (Lanham, MD: Rowman and Littlefeld, forthcoming). Like Rumana and Malachowski, who confesses to being lifted from his "parochial intellectual environment" by Rorty's "breathtakingly wide" interests, I too found my world expanding as a result of my contact with Rorty's writing.

6. Ralph Waldo Emerson, "Friendship," in *Essays: First and Second Series* (New York: Vintage Books, 1990), p. 113.

7. See *Reading Rorty: Critical Responses to Philosophy and the Mirror of Nature (and Beyond).* My only regret is that the nearly $1000 price tag on the new collection with keep smaller libraries from acquiring it, as was the case my own institution.

8. Lamenting the absence of one's personal favorites is never completely fair, but I was surprised not to see any of the reviews or essays on Rorty by Alasdair MacIntyre or Jürgen Habermas. My short list of omitted favorites would include: Richard Shusterman, "Pragmatism and Liberalism Between Dewey and Rorty," *Political Theory* 22 (1994), pp. 391–413; Cornel West, "The Politics of American Neo-Pragmatism," in *Post-Analytic Philosophy*, ed. John Rajchman and Cornel West (New York: Columbia University Press, 1985), pp. 259–275; and Sheldon Wolin, "Democracy in the Discourse of Postmodernism," *Social Research* 57 (1990), pp. 5–30. In fairness to Malachowski, these and a number of other memorable essays not focused exclusively on Rorty may have been excluded for that reason; including less well-known pieces that are not readily available elsewhere also seems to have been part of Malachowski's approach. Only three of the twenty essays included in his other edited work, *Reading Rorty*, are here, making that volume still a "must have."

9. Rorty, "Recent Metaphilosophy," *Review of Metaphysics* 15 (1961), pp. 299–318, quoted in Rumana, *OR*, p. 10. The reference to Rorty as a "true believer" is from Richard Bernstein, *The New Constellation: The Ethical/Political Horizons of Modernity/Postmodernity* (Cambridge, MA: MIT Press, 1991), p. 251. If Rorty ever was a true believer, and I tend to think he wasn't, it came very early and did not last. In the introduction to *Richard Rorty: An Annotated Bibliography of Secondary Literature*, Rumana mentions the conclusion he came to in his dissertation, which compared the early Rorty to his later works. Although he started in search of any "radical conversions," he found that "If there was any change in his thinking about philosophy, it came as an undergraduate. What I discovered was that from 1956 to the present his thinking has developed but there was no significant break" (xiii).

10. See "Freud and Moral Reflection," in *Essays on Heidegger and Others*; and "Freud, Morality, and Hermeneutics," *New Literary History* 12 (1980), pp. 177–185.

11. Rorty, "Philosophy as a Kind of Writing: An Essay on Derrida," in *Consequences of Pragmatism* (Minneapolis: University of Minneapolis Press, 1982), p. 91, and quoted in part in Rumana, *OR*, p. 54.

12. Rorty, *Contingency, Irony, and Solidarity* (Cambridge, UK: Cambridge University Press, 1989), p. xvi.

13. See "Trotsky and the Wild Orchids," in Rorty, *Philosophy and Social Hope* (New York: Penguin Books, 1999), pp. 3–22. As Rorty describes it, "The more philosophers I read, the clearer it seemed that each of them could carry their views back to first principles which were incompatible with the first principles of their opponents, and that none of them ever got to that fabled place 'beyond hypotheses'. There seemed to be nothing like a neutral standpoint from which these alternative first principles could be evaluated. But if there were no such standpoint, then the whole idea of 'rational certainty', and the whole Socratic-Platonic idea of replacing passion by reason, seemed not to make much sense.... As far as I could see, philosophical talent was largely a matter of proliferating as many distinctions as were needed to wriggle out of a dialectical corner. More generally, it was a matter, when trapped in such a corner, of redescribing the intellectual terrain in such a way that the terms used by one's opponent would seem irrelevant, or question-begging, or jejune" (10). Interestingly, *PMN* opens with a similar sentiment: "Almost as soon as I began to study philosophy, I was impressed by the way in which philosophical problems appeared, disappeared, or changed shape as the result of new assumptions or vocabularies" (xiii).

14. "Trotsky and the Wild Orchids," p. 5.

15. *Philosophy and the Mirror of Nature*, pp. 359–60.

16. Ibid, pp. 360, 5, 11–12. See also statements like, "In this attitude, getting the facts right is merely propaedeutic to finding a new and more interesting way of expressing ourselves, and thus of coping with the world" (359); and "To see keeping a conversation going as a sufficient aim of philosophy, to see wisdom as consisting in the ability to sustain a conversation, is to see human beings as generators of new descriptions rather than beings we hope to be able to describe accurately" (378).

17. Ibid, p. 12. See Rorty, *Achieving Our Country: Leftist Thought in Twentieth-Century America* (Cambridge, MA: Harvard University Press, 1998), pp. 3–38. As the title to Rorty's most recent collection of essays suggests, it is now "Social Hope" rather than *Bildung* that is heralded as the successor to knowledge in post-epistemological philosophy.

18. *Contingency, Irony, and Solidarity,* pp. 103, 110, 97.

19. Ibid, pp. 117–9.

20. Ibid, p. 118.

21. See Malachowski, "Deep Epistemology Without Foundations," in Malachowski, *Reading Rorty*, pp. 138–55.

22. Malachowski rightly makes the case for pragmatic criteria: "errors can be identified relative to a variety of practical considerations extraneous to conceptions of 'the real meaning' of an author's words. These include the goals and purposes of reading the relevant texts" (*RR*, p. 5).

23. *RR*, p. 22. Single quotation marks are a reference to a long passage of Rorty's quoted by Malachowski on p. 20. For the original, see *Philosophy and the Mirror of Nature*, pp. 371–2.

24. *Philosophy and the Mirror of Nature*, p. 360.

25. See Rorty, "On Ethnocentrism: A Reply to Clifford Geertz," in *Objectivity, Relativism, and Truth: Philosophical Papers, vol. 1* (Cambridge, UK: Cambridge University Press, 1991), p. 209, quoted in Rumana, *RR*, p. 81.

26. On this point see Rorty, "Human Rights, Rationality, and Sentimentality," in *Truth and Progress*, pp. 167–85.

27. *Contingency, Irony, and Solidarity*, p. 68, quoted in Rumana, *RR*, p. 85.

Christopher Voparil
Assistant Professor of Humanities
College of Arts and Sciences
Lynn University
3601 North Military Trail
Boca Raton, Florida 33431
United States

Contemporary Pragmatism
Vol. 2, No. 1 (June 2005), 135–166

Editions Rodopi
© 2005

Peircean Animism and the End of Civilization

Eugene Halton

Charles Peirce claimed that logically "every true universal, every continuum, is a living and conscious being." Such a claim is precisely what hunter-gatherers believe: a world-view depicted as animism. Suppose animism represents a sophisticated world-view, ineradicably embodied in our physical bodies, and that Peirce's philosophy points toward a new kind of civilization, inclusive of what I term *animate mind*. We are wired to marvel in nature, and this reverencing attunement does not require a concept of God. Marveling in nature proves to be not only a motive source of human evolution, but key to continued development.

> "Our intelligence cannot wall itself up alive, like a pupa in its chrysalis. It must at any cost keep on speaking terms with the universe that engendered it."
>
> William James[1]

1. Of Evolutionary Love and Devolutionary Hate

Charles Peirce opens his 1893 essay "Evolutionary Love" with the sentence: "Philosophy, when just escaping from its golden pupa-skin, mythology, proclaimed the great evolutionary agency of the universe to be Love." Now this is the common understanding of philosophy as a transformation of the wisdom of mythology into a more self-conscious endeavor. It is a statement that I suspect Peirce scholars take at face value, ignoring its Hegelian implication that the earlier stage is *aufgehoben*, "overcome," and now a discarded husk of history. Mythologists might think otherwise. What if the statement is true, but in a regressive sense? What if philosophy was born as caterpillar, not butterfly?

Why is it that the progress of the modern west and its philosophy involved an inversion of that first insight of philosophy, seeing the great evolutionary agency of the universe to be Hate, that Hobbesian state of nature, that "warre of every one against every one," that Darwinian "struggle for existence?" How did that living Evolutionary Love come to be seen as unreal, as that nominalistic fiction that, as Peirce put it, almost drove John Stuart Mill mad? How did it become unreal and replaced by dead mechanistic Hate? Was it progress, as commonly assumed, or regress?

I claim that the progress in the development of consciousness alluded to by Peirce and taken more broadly as historical development, was a progress in precision embedded within a regression of consciousness. The free butterfly of winged thought awoke in its bed, like Kafka's Gregor Samsa, to find itself transformed into a caterpillar. It dreamed of transforming itself back into a butterfly, but that dream, which is called history, was a lie that it told itself, because it neglected the golden pupa-skin necessary to the transformation, the golden pupa-skin that remained ingredient in its very body. That golden pupa-skin was not simply "mythology," but a consciousness that I will call *animate mind*.

Perhaps Socrates is that philosophical Gregor Samsa, his brooding, breathing, bodily-aware warrior and stone-cutting self transforming into the critical thinker whose muse shows him the negative, the doubting consciousness. Socrates is that pivot of critical consciousness who yet learns from Diotima, as Plato tells us in *The Symposium*, that love is the child of poverty and plenty, and philosophy is the loving pursuit of wisdom.

The course of Charles Peirce's philosophical development is the story that begins with the modern caterpillar rediscovering its golden pupa-skin and ends with the butterfly of animate mind recovered, but now transformed from its regressive descent. I wish to show that Peirce's religious writings and late philosophy coalesce with ideas of religious animism, and that these ideas have profound import for contemporary life, delineating a new philosophical anthropology in pragmatic perspective. Suppose animism, far from being a belief of "primitives" and an opinion of the obscurantist founder of semeiotic, represents a sophisticated world-view, one literally and ineradicably embodied in our physical bodies, and that Peirce's philosophy points toward a new kind of civilization, inclusive of animism.

I claim that the modern way of seeing things, the nominalistic myth of the machine that has dominated the modern outlook, is suicidal, and needs to be supplanted by one that rediscovers the living nature of the universe — the inner subjectivity of nature, and general relation as a reality. I mean by this also that the continued growth of science itself will involve coming to terms with mind-like or soul-like qualities in nature and not solely in us. Such a view will be semeiotic realism, in Peirce's terms, reconnecting us as children of the earth attuned to that larger community of interpretation which is the community of life on which we depend.

The history of religion is a subarea of history in general. Peirce sees history as one of what he termed "idioscopic" or special sciences, and as a branch of "psychognosy." But there is another view of history, given by Paul Shepard:

history is a lie. Perhaps I am wrong, but I suspect that most of you are living in that lie, the lie of history. This matrix involves beliefs that civilization represents progress over pre-agricultural ways of hunter-gatherers, that this progress shows itself in the Greco-Judaic-Christian roots of the West, that this progress achieves new footing in the rise of the modern scientific world-view, that civilization is itself that process whose chief end has been the progressive development of reasonableness.

This sounds pretty good. But let's suppose another story. Suppose that civilization represents a regressive de-maturing of consciousness. And suppose that modern life represents a mechanical infantilization of consciousness, and that modern nominalistic civilization can be taken as a regressive "primitivism," one itself built on the very foundations of civilization itself.

2. A Neglected Argument for the Unreality of God

> With the Indians it is different. There is strictly no god. The Indian does not consider himself as created, and therefore external to God, or the creature of God. To the Indian there is no conception of a defined God. Creation is a great flood, forever flowing, in lovely and terrible waves. In everything, the shimmer of creation, and never the finality of the created. Never the distinction between God and God's creation, or between Spirit and Matter. Everything, everything is the wonderful shimmer of creation.... — D. H. Lawrence[2]

I would like to outline a neglected argument for the unreality of the concept of God. My argument by no means rejects Peirce's well-known essay, "A Neglected Argument for the Reality of God." Rather, I am in complete agreement with his conclusion, as I hope you will see.

Let me begin with one of Peirce's definitions of God: "If a pragmaticist is asked what he means by the word 'God,' he can only say that ... if contemplation and study of the physico-psychical universe can imbue a man with principles of conduct analogous to the influence of a great man's works or conversation, then that analogue of a mind — for it is impossible to say that *any* human attribute is *literally* applicable — is what he means by 'God'..." Peirce's view here suffers from anthropomorphism, though he admits this himself. But he goes on:

> Now such being the pragmaticist's answer to the question what he means by the word "God," the question whether there really *is* such a being is the question whether all physical science is merely the figment — the arbitrary figment — of the students of nature, and further whether the *one* lesson the Gautama Boodha, Confucius, Socrates, and all who from any point of view

have had their ways of conduct determined by meditation upon the physico-psychical universe, be only their arbitrary notion or be the Truth behind the appearances which the frivolous man does not think of; and whether the superhuman courage which such contemplation has conferred upon priests who go to pass their lives with lepers and refuse all offers of rescue is silly fanaticism, the passion of a baby, or whether it is a strength derived from the power of truth. Now the only guide to the answer to this question lies in the power of the passion of love which more or less overmasters every agnostic scientist and everybody who seriously and deeply considers the universe. But whatever there may be of *argument* in all this is as nothing, the merest nothing, in comparison to its force as an appeal to one's own instinct, which is to argument what substance is to shadow, what bed-rock is to the built foundations of a cathedral.[3]

That same instinct to which Peirce appeals in his neglected argument is also the basis for his claim for a third form of logical inference, which he termed abductive inference, a largely unconscious and instinctive but valid mode of inference. Without abductive inference, science would be impossible in Peirce's view. Abductive inference, or the human capacity for making good guesses or hypotheses, is an extrarational form of inference. It is what we call "intuition" in everyday language, inferring even though one may not yet have the reason why. And it is an irreducible modality of logical inference, along with deductive and inductive inference.

Peirce claimed that through abductive inference, new information validly enters into scientific reasoning. Without it, as in Popper's view that hypothesis is not itself logical, a lucky but not logical guess, science is reduced to a calculating machine or knowledge system operating solely through deductive and inductive inferences; with it, science is a life, rooted in the desire to learn. Knowledge, in Peirce's view of science, is not the big thing it is for many other theories of science. Rather, it is the desire to learn, rooted in inquiry.

Peirce's appeals to instinct have troubled philosophers, especially those who believe that all human beliefs are social constructions, including human nature. Yet I claim that the evolutionary record reveals that human nature results from a fascinating bio-social process of development that required the exercise of one's instinctive inferencing, which remains embedded in the human body today, though repressed by the rational-mechanical outlook of modern consciousness.

We need to look to the conditions of hunter-gatherer life for the most direct picture of how a human propensity for abductive inferencing evolved, a better view, in my opinion, than that afforded by machine models of human consciousness. I am also claiming that the historical conception of God itself marks the moment of human alienation from participation in the conditions through which human abductive inference evolved. Pygmies in Africa, who with Australian aboriginals constitute the oldest continuous culture on earth, going back 40,000 to 50,000 or more years, do not use a "concept" of God, despite their deep religiousness and highly sophisticated forms of intuitive awareness. The closest they come to it, perhaps, is with the idea of "mother forest," which is not a concept but a palpable and variescent presence. The question is what is meant by the concept of God, and whether conceptual intelligence is the proper "center of gravity" for such a question.

I once attended a Pueblo corn dance with Alfonso Ortiz, an anthropologist and a Pueblo. He told me, "White people think we pray to make it rain, but that's not it. The rain does its part, and we must do ours." This is non-causal reasoning, participation consciousness.

As Lévy-Bruhl put it, using the unfortunate term "prelogical," "The prelogical mind does not objectify nature thus [by logical classification].... It lives it rather, by feeling itself participate in it, and feeling these participations everywhere; and it interprets this complexity of participations by social forms."[4] When one considers oneself participating in creation, as hunter-gatherers and the later Peirce did, creation's continuous beginning remains a palpable presence, not a remote abstraction. Only one need not consider such participation as prelogical, as Lévy-Bruhl did, but as the bodily-felt source of abductive inference. Being "participate in it" is literally the center of gravity of animate mind.

In another key definition, Peirce says: "'Do you believe this Supreme Being to have been the creator of the universe?' Not so much *to have been* as to be now creating the universe..."[5] Now this definition of God as Creator creating seems to me to signal a break with the foundational God story of the Judeo-Christian-Islamic "World" religion.

Though Peirce was a practicing Christian, and though his religious writings can be read as a defense of Christianity, I claim that his philosophical ideas go further, toward animism, as when he says that "...every true universal, every continuum, is a living and conscious being."[6] This is a semeiotic radicalism that causes even some Peirceans to shy away. Elsewhere Peirce says, "When we gaze upon the multifariousness of nature we are looking straight into the face of a living spontaneity. A day's ramble in the country ought to bring that home to us."[7]

Peirce's understanding of signs allows intelligence its full embodiment in the body and out of the body: "The psychologists undertake to locate various mental powers in the brain; and above all consider it as quite certain that the faculty of language resides in a certain lobe; but I believe it comes decidedly nearer the truth (though not really true) that language resides in the tongue. In my opinion, it is much more true that the thoughts of a living writer are in any printed copy of his book than that they are in his brain."[8] If a living writer's thoughts are more in his book than in his brain, can we not say by analogy that the Creator is to be found in each act of creation rather than in something apart?

There is no spectator God, apart, isolate from Creation. That God is an unreal social construction, mirror of the advent of civilization, when humanity separated itself from the primordial matrix of variescent life as the original Other in which it participated, an act that could be called de-animalization, for animals are largely the first other of the mind's eye, as Paul Shepard has noted. With agriculture and civilization humankind began to behold itself as Other, narcissistically projecting its alienation from original participation to separate spectator in its mirror world of the community of gods. And the community of gods eventually gave way through "focal vision" to Jewish monotheism, a further rationalization and alienation from variescent earth.

Christianity is an anthropocentric religion, seeing divinity incarnated in a single human being, a divine representative, a focal point. From a historical perspective, Jesus was an aspect of a collective incarnation, the birth of a new order of being, which Karl Jaspers termed the *axial age*. Buddha, Socrates, and Jesus were births, among others, of social transformation described by Jaspers and Lewis Mumford, an age which bodied forth the power of the person — as against the civilizational structures with their centralized armies, bureaucracies, and writing. Writers recorded their living acts, and we know them from these records. But what about those who did not have an enlightened and literate Plato? To what extent were Buddha and Jesus re-eruptions of ancient shamanic awareness into civilizational structure, but now axialized? If we consider, even partially, what the unrecorded shamans lived from, the Plato-less shamans, we might be able to see to what extent civilization has been a march of progress one step forward, two steps backward.

Consider that fusion of Jewish monotheism, which deserted myth and the cycles of life for otherworldly transcendence and for history, with Greek idealism. In Paul Shepard's words:

> Is *mythos* really more immature than *logos*? Is there not some doubt that a rationally ordered system, regardless of how supremely logical...is the end of wisdom?
>
> ... The Greek ideal of youthfulness and intellectual skepticism are celebrated roots of Western consciousness, but their price is high. The destruction of living myth was undertaken in Hellenistic times with the best intentions.... But the new logic could not provide a world of purpose, lively with spiritual activity, its ceremonial celebrations deserving of deep fidelity; it was not an alternative to a mythic, ritual foundation for passage-making in the life stages of the individual.

With the translation of the Old Testament from Hebrew to Greek to create the Septuagint Bible and the interaction of Jewish and Greek cultures beginning in the third century B.C., two roots of the modern West were joined, sharing goals of spiritual and intellectual abstraction and asceticism.[9]

Greek idealizing met with Jewish rationalizing monotheism and its conception of desert as empty, as "tohu bohu" rather than living habitat. Out of this turn from mythology to logos, philosophy emerged backwards, as it were, from its golden pupa-skin, a caterpillar in the contraction of consciousness.

The "religions of the book," so crucial to the development of modern consciousness, are hooked on the horns of Plato's dilemma: Can one communicate in writing the living spontaneity of life that so moved Socrates that he refused to inscribe it? Or Jesus? Or Mohammed? Or Buddha? Or Anonymous? Socrates said that the only true writing is face-to-face, soul-to-soul, "graven in the soul" (we know this because Plato wrote it down: the contradiction of the wound that heals). In other words, the only true writing is with *living text*, treated as living communication. Socrates's point was that fixing thought to script is a retreat from living thinking, as Joseph Ransdell has reminded me. Hence elocution by rhetoricians, by the sophists, using the art of memory (memorizing speeches by using public symbols in the place of the speech) is false, despite its Olympic-like performative appeal, in not being fully alive to the moment. And hence the "religions of the book," by analogy, are false in their fixing of the ongoing creation of all things to ideal histories inscribed in "sacred" texts, fixed to past places and special people.

Music, when once played, as Eric Dolphy noted, is gone, in the air. Books are but leaves, meant to hold beauties and truths. But as leaves fall and are reborn, so are books mere stopping places of the living quick of creation. The book is but a congealed form of conduct, a temporary resting place of ideas. It was never meant to be a terminus and it is a vast mistake as a basis for consciousness. To live "by the book" is to be a mere recipe, cut from the chorus of creation. Consider the text when it is most alive, say, in Shakespeare. The words breathe off the page, awaiting incarnation in action. They are there to be breathed, voiced, enacted anew.

The axial religions tend to claim that one needs the "gyroscope" of another, of a Holy One-for-All, to find one's way to the Creator. This is a bottleneck view of divinity. But the pre-civilizational peoples were aware of something more, something simple that became lost as common practice, something preserved in mysticism, in my opinion, but as "secret," more complicated and cryptic. They were aware that what we term "religion" is the living effort to connect to and participate in the all-surrounding life of ongoing creation, which touches all things, including us.

What is more primitive: the view that all things are living signs, to whom it is our highest duty to attune our biologically neotenous selves to the wisdom they hold for us, or that all matter is ultimately mechanism, and we ourselves but spawning machines — Cartesian water-statues, neural-net computers? Our foraging ancestors lived in an animate universe, perfused with living signs. We proud moderns live in a dead universe, a tick-tock universe to which life is ultimately reducible. We live in the ghost in the machine legacy of nominalism; they lived in a fantastic realism. They, and the other aboriginal peoples, indeed lived in a paradise, eating far better and working far less than their civilizational counterparts, as the anthropological and archaeological evidence indicates.[10]

The pygmies have sacreds and secrets, localized in streams and stones and plants and animals, in living mother forest, and when things go wrong, she has fallen asleep, and they awaken her through ritual and song: divinity as a forest of symbols, as heaven on earth. The Judeo-Christian-Islamic "World" religion, by contrast, says that heaven is a place to go to and that it is not to be found on earth. Though humankind originated in paradise, in the Garden of Eden, it was expelled for acquiring knowledge of good and evil, perhaps an accurate metaphor for the radically changed way of life brought about by agriculturally-based civilization.

Civilization changed bodies, but by and large for the worse: it caused people to become 4 to 6 inches shorter on average (which only was offset in the last 100 or so years in industrial countries), to suffer increase in diseases, to reduce spacing between childbirths, affecting the crucial early mother-infant interactions, to radically increase amount of work time, to devastate the landscape (as the "fertile crescent" remains devastated even today). It even changed dominant blood types. Biology is not limited to genetics, and even there, agricultural peoples exploded populations of bioregions with their frequencies.

The book of Genesis maintains that a man was created by God from the earth, that a woman was created from the body of a man, and that both partook of the forbidden tree of knowledge of good and evil. Seduced by the serpent, the woman, Eve, in turn seduced the man, Adam, to eat the forbidden fruit. Patriarchal monotheism viewed the animal other and the woman as causes for separation from participation in paradise, in effect, it devalued the animality of humankind. These carnal seduc-tions doomed humankind henceforth to exile from its true home, Eden, the bountiful garden of paradise.

Wandering humankind would work and struggle its entire life, cut off from its direct connection to the Creator. Life became an ideal struggle, especially in the Christian-Islamic traditions, to gain re-admittance to paradise — but only for the afterlife. And only through the ways Jesus and Mohammed independently offered.

The gulf between humankind and paradise grew. Though expelled from Eden for eating of the tree of knowledge, it was now knowledge, that is, the belief in the teachings of Jesus or Mohammed, which paradoxically would provide re-entry to heaven's fruits. Only by following the way of another could one follow the way for oneself, and only by dying could one find "eternal life." Death marked the way to re-connect to the Creator; heaven became a disembodied afterlife, disconnected from living being, from mortal existence.

In the idealization of life a schism exists between material and spiritual being. Life on earth is but a wandering from humanity's true home, the dematerialized perfection of ethereal paradise. In heaven, to put it in earthy terms, shit does not happen. Or so the story goes. But what if the story is a vast fabrication that the Judeo-Christian-Islamic religion tells itself? A fabrication connected to its conception of the Creator as radically separate from its creation? What if life itself is paradise, is heaven on earth? What if life itself is the living duality of flesh and spirit, of carnal semeiosis? What if life itself is the dreaming into being of creation itself?

3. Sink or Swim?

Latin *mergere*: dip, plunge, sink

The gospel of Christ says that progress comes from every individual merging his individuality in sympathy with his neighbors. On the other side, the conviction of the nineteenth century is that progress takes place by virtue of every individual's striving for himself with all his might and trampling his neighbor under foot whenever he gets a chance to do so. This may accurately be called the Gospel of Greed. — Charles Peirce[11]

Understanding Peirce's ideas involves understanding his rejection of nominalism as a basis of the modern mind — in effect, a rejection of modern mind itself, though growing out of it. In "Evolutionary Love" he criticized Darwinism as over-expanding the place of competition to produce the anti-social Gospel of Greed philosophy. He also argued against egoism, or rugged individualism, as denying the social nature of reality, and juxtaposed the Christian view, cited above, as exemplifying "evolutionary love."

In "Evolutionary Love" Peirce claimed that Darwin's theory is evolution by Firstness, a crucial yet incomplete view. Peirce attempted to incorporate it into a three-modality approach inclusive of Secondness and Thirdness, using Clarence King's catastrophe theory — sudden shifts of population — as evolution by Secondness, and what he termed *agapasm*, or evolutionary love, as evolution by Thirdness.

He framed his argument for evolution by Thirdness through habit as a kind of Lamarckian evolution:

Habit is mere inertia, a resting on one's oars, not a propulsion. Now it is energetic projaculation (lucky there is such a word, or this untried hand might have been put to inventing one) by which in the typical instances of Lamarckian evolution the new elements of form are first created. Habit, however, forces them to take practical shapes, compatible with the structures they affect, and, in the form of heredity and otherwise, gradually replaces the spontaneous energy that sustains them. Thus, habit plays a double part; it serves to establish the new features, and also to bring them into harmony with the general morphology and function of the animals and plants to which they belong. But if the reader will now kindly give himself the trouble of turning back a page or two, he will see that this account of Lamarckian evolution coincides with the general description of the action of love, to which, I suppose, he yielded his assent.[12]

Hence Thirdness, as semeiosis, general relation, habit-making and taking, is the stuff of evolutionary love. Mind is Thirdness, which may involve brain, though not reducible to it. Peirce took the position that the human brain is an adaptation to mind, considered as Thirdness, not the reverse, and that there is a "reasonableness energizing in the universe."[13]

I do not disagree with the idea of evolutionary love, only with the idea of "merging his individuality in sympathy with his neighbors," as Peirce expresses it. It depends on how he means "merging." It seems to me to undervalue the place of spontaneous, bodying forth social soul as the real source of individuality, not reducible to "egoism." The Christian outlook would also view this merging process as mediated by Christ, viewed as a divine human of a different order from the rest of the community: in effect, one specially designated individual who retains individuality as something more than a "neighbor."

My criticism of Peirce's statement, more succinctly, is that I think one should *live* one's individuality, one's spontaneous being, "in sympathy with one's neighbors" rather than "merge" it away. Perhaps the difference seems trivial; perhaps it is, depending on just what Peirce meant by "merging." But in my opinion it makes a profound difference. Elsewhere Peirce too easily describes the individual self as something that is nothing in the larger scheme of things. Take his statement from 1891: "Everybody will admit a personal self exists in the same sense in which a snark exists; that is, there is a phenomenon to which that name is given. It is an illusory phenomenon; but still it is a phenomenon. It is not quite *purely* illusory, but only *mainly* so. It is true, for instance, that men are *selfish*, that is, that they are really deluded into supposing themselves to have some isolated existence; and in so far, they *have* it. To deny the reality of the personality is not anti-spiritualistic; it is only anti-nominalistic."[14]

Denying the reality of personality seems to me to be nominalistic, if one accepts that being a person involves the bodying forth of one's qualitatively unique being. That is why I prefer *to live my individuality in sympathy* rather than *merge* it. The fallacy is to assume that one must merge one's individuality in order to realize sympathy with one's neighbors. Yet we are already "in the swim," immersed in the social, in and through our very individuality, our spontaneous being (as, metaphorically speaking, sperm and eggs are well aware from the start).

Consider too Peirce's statement: "... the supreme commandment of the Buddhisto-christian religion is, to generalize, to complete the whole system even until continuity results and the distinct individuals weld together. Thus it is, that while reasoning and the science of reasoning strenuously proclaim the subordination of reasoning to sentiment, the very supreme commandment of sentiment is that man should generalize, or what the logic of relatives shows to be the same thing, should become welded into the universal continuum, which is what true reasoning consists in..."[15]

Peirce's idea of a "buddhisto-christian religion" is striking, and I speculate that it would be atheistic, would be a form of religious atheism. More to the point, however, is that the welding approach seems problematic. What would a stone-cutter, say a Socrates or Jesus, considered in their day jobs as cutters and hence sensitive to the qualities of each stone joined in an edifice, say to the jolly welder of all things? After all, Jesus said, "Show me the stone that the builders rejected: that is the keystone" (Gospel of Thomas, 66), suggesting that each individual matters in the continuum of being. Does welding allow joining, genuinely continuous yet involving the variescence of that joined? Or does this view see the forest but not the trees?

Each and every being involves a bubbling forth of an unfathomable individuality which is a real element of creation, not to be "merged" away. To merge away one's individuality is ideal love, the Christ's mistake: the idealized-passion of the Christ, merging with the all. To *live* one's spontaneous being in sympathy with one's neighbors in life, human and non-human, marks a key difference. For we are wired to marvel in nature.

In my opinion D. H. Lawrence punctured the human pretension "to be any bursting Infinite, or swollen One Identity," the pretension of the king-god through possession, or of the victim-god, through identification of will and consciousness with all things.

The way of Alexander, of Power and dominion over things, results in materialism. But Lawrence understood more deeply than Peirce, it seems to me, that the way of Christianity, of merging with all things, also results ultimately, however unintended, in materialism: unattainable idealized love eventually gives way to its opposite, materialized hate. Humankind must live with ideals, but can never live by them, for to do so is to live from mental consciousness rather than from the fullness of being. This is precisely analogous to Peirce's criticisms of attempts to make science practical as undervaluing the place of mature sentiment as a better guide to everyday life.

I additionally argue that the cultural nominalism that marks the consciousness of the modern era, of the "flesh and blood" of the average modern mind, as Peirce put it, embodies the destructive trajectory of mentalized consciousness. Somewhere along the line that idealized love grown out of Judeao-Greco-Christian roots transformed itself into the mechanical world-picture, with its "philosophy of greed." Idealized love gave way to devolutionary hate.

It is said that love conquers all, that Christianity is a religion of love, and that such love begets progress. Yet consider idealized love, that bitter fruit of Christianity which withers sensuous presence in the Name of the Ideal. What growth does it lead to? To the growth of the imperialist West? To the growth of Hobbesworld, wherein all that is natural is imbued with competitive Hate? Where Love is merely a fiction?

Why did philosophy emerge out of a sense of love as the great evolutionary agency of the universe, as Peirce put it, and yet "grow" to a view that competitive invidious advantage — or anti-love — is the sole evolutionary agency, and that general relation is unreal? Is this progress, or is it possible that "devolutionary" better describes this undevelopment? I view the spirit of modern life as one whose end is devolutionary hate, murderously-suicidal hate, and that end as the legacy of the idealization of life.

Lawrence punctures the bubble of pretension of identifying with "swollen One Identity," through a victim-god savior or a king-god of worldly power, by recognizing the necessity to live from the minute particulars, not from abstractions. Lawrence: "Every single living creature is a single creative unit, a unique, incommutable self. Primarily, in its own spontaneous reality, it knows no law. It is a law unto itself. Secondarily, in its material reality, it submits to all the laws of the material universe. But the primal, spontaneous self in any creature has ascendance, truly, over the material laws of the universe; it uses these laws and converts them in the mystery of creation." Lawrence's philosophy of living spontaneity is of a piece with Peirce's outlook on this one point — despite Peirce's antipathy to the "literary" mind — each allowing qualitative uniqueness. Yet Peirce would merge it away, if I understand him correctly, as though it were a community of theoretical inquiry rather than an incommutable element of the vital community.

Melville saw this problem clearly in *Moby Dick*, where Ishmael experiences the epiphany of the continuity of humankind and life while squeezing spermaceti with his shipmates, shattering his Isolatoism, biblically embedded in his very name: "...let us squeeze hands all round; let us all squeeze ourselves into each other; let us squeeze ourselves universally into the very milk and sperm of kindness."

It is said of Ishmael in Genesis 16:12, "He shall be a wild man; his hand shall be against every man, and every man's hand against him." Yet he rejoins the community of humankind through friendship with Polynesian hunter-gatherer harpooner Queequeg, literally joining hands with shipmates in the inexpressible milk and sperm of human kindness, the vat of spermicetti taken from the whale's head, whiteness of communion. And after the catastrophe, he emerges from the death-void, bouyed by Queequeg's casket, itself birthed from "the button-like black bubble at the axis of that slowly wheeling circle," the death-abyss of the sunk world-ship.

Yet Ishmael's experience of merging with the All was not enough. For his grasp of the social nature of reality required his concrete relations with the individual others in his life. He continues: "Would that I could keep squeezing that sperm for ever! For now, since by many prolonged, repeated experiences, I have perceived that man must eventually lower, or at least shift, his conceit of attainable felicity, not placing it anywhere in the intellect or fancy; but in the wife, the heart, the bed, the table, the saddle, the fireside, the country; now that I have perceived all this, I am ready to squeeze case eternally...."

The idealization of the passions seems to me to be a key issue in considering modern consciousness, one dealt with by the deepest critics of modern life, a community that would include William Blake, Herman Melville, Fyodor Dostoyevsky, Nietzsche, Lawrence, and Milan Kundera, among others. The modern error, as I see it, is rooted in a longer idealizing tradition of the West: in the monotheizing of Judaism, in the idealizing forms of Plato (even though he himself shows the problem through Socrates), in the resulting fusion of the Judeo-Christian-Islamic religion: passions by the book.

Sentimentalizing the passions — what Kundera calls "*homo sentimentalis*" in his novel *Immortality* — means treating the passions as an ideal, a value. To see its terrible aspect, consider Captain Ahab when he emerges on deck in *Moby Dick*, avatar of rational madness:

> But as the mind does not exist unless leagued with the soul, therefore it must have been that, in Ahab's case, yielding up all his thoughts and fancies to his own supreme purpose; that purpose, by its own sheer inveteracy of will, forced itself against gods and devils into a kind of self-assumed, independent being of its own. (chap. 44)

In Ahab one sees the ultimate trajectory of idealized love. Melville is saying that despite the monomaniacal madness of the Isolato consciousness, of its isolation from and attempt to possess the world community of life and the world community of humankind (and we might say its mad quest for oil!), despite its endgame of murderous suicide, that it too weeps the same salt water tears as the rest of humanity. The Isolato consciousness must die; it is foredoomed. We are its endgame.

When philosophy emerged from mythology, it proclaimed the great evolutionary agency of the universe to be Love. When modern materialism emerged from post-Medieval Christendom, it proclaimed the great evolutionary agency of the universe to be self-maximizing Hate, Hobbes's perpetual war, a veritable hand of Ishmael, raised against all others.

As the great rational-mechanical machine of modernity perfected itself, in our time, it sought to possess the "phantom of life" itself, as Melville called the great white whale. Captain Ahab: "All my means are sane, my motive and my object mad."

Captain Ahab: "To the last I grapple with thee; from hell's heart I stab at thee; for hate's sake I spit my last breath at thee! Ye damned whale!"

Ahab hurls his harpoon for hate's sake, and, entangled in it, merges in antipathy with the object of his quest, the great white whale, the "phantom of life" itself. Pure subject meets pure object, devoid of soul, of community, of love, in a fusion of the would-be power-god and victim-god "holding the bubble of the all" in ultimate realization of devolutionary hate: murderous suicide.

Modern consciousness, believing itself freed from fate, from nature, from any limitations whatsoever, seals its fate in the very act of so thinking. Ahab's quest, the legacy of Ockham, culminates in its total self-undoing. Instead of freedom, the mad quest to arrive at a thing-in-itself, stripped of mediation, results in Ahab, pure Cartesian-Kantian subject, bound to the "pure object," Moby Dick, by his umbilicus of Hate, the line of his own flame-baptized harpoon. His final attainment of unity with the Phantom of Life itself is his own murderous suicide.

Modern nominalism would treat triadic mediation as a fiction, yet mediation is the very reality without which the via moderna leads to one destination and one destination only and once for all time: Death, murderous suicide, the final toll of the fiction of nominalism.

In Ahab's end the eviction of purport from the modern world-view is revealed as a tragic flaw, for indeed, the nominalistic mechanical world-picture is a false Idol, which retains a crypto-religious telos: the perfection of that human self-alienation that began with agricultural civilizing, with the very invention of the concept of God. God was not banished by modern materialism, quite the contrary. Secretly, though visibly, the concept of God is perfected *sub-rosa* through it. I am speaking, of course, about the one, true God of our time, to whom all here, myself included, are fated to pay obeisance to, namely: *Deus ex Machina*.

From Lawrence's view — which I think offers an interesting perspective on Peirce's — both the way of the king-god and that of the victim-god would hold the bubble of the All in their hands, while ignoring the lesson of their fingers, the last lesson, as Lawrence puts it: "The last lesson? — Ah, the lesson of his own fingers: himself: the identity; little, but real. Better, far better, to be oneself than to be any bursting Infinite, or swollen One Identity."

The lesson of one's own fingers, I would agree, holds far more than all the gaseous galaxies, spinning by rules according to the great modern timepiece, far more than saviors and prophets and kings, bottlenecking our awareness, even more than Peirce's "supreme commandment." If the deepest purpose in life is nothing less than to become the ongoing creation of the universe in the myriad ways of one's life, then, it seems to me, one does this best not by identifying with the All through a savior or prophet or swollen ideal of a God or gods — even that of science, but by attuning to and laboring well the minute particulars in the path of one's life. From this living from one's "little, but real" identity bubbling into being and doing, flows Peirce's "universal continuum," it seems to me, as motive source and consequence rather than abstract focal point of conduct. This, to my understanding, is what is meant by the Native American idea "to walk in beauty" and by Peirce's understanding of the aesthetic basis of conduct, of Beauty as the intrinsically admirable.

We are wired to marvel in nature, and this reverencing attunement does not require a concept of God. Quite the reverse. The development of concepts of God, especially with the rise of agriculturally-based civilizations, represent the development of human alienation from what could be called the divine presence of the living universe. That is, the concept of God is the peeling away from direct, felt participation in the creation of the universe, from participation in the Creator, considered as felt presence rather than concept.

If, as Peirce claimed, religion is poetry completed, then marveling in nature, without and within, is the completion of religion. The religions of the book are rooted in an alienated conception of nature (and landscape), as though the living desert, in particular, could be "tohu bohu," and as though a particular human and written history could provide a better basis for belief than marveling in nature, without and within.

Such anthropocentrism is inadequate as a basis for religion in the long run, in my opinion. Worse, in the disconnect from animate mind, from hunter-gatherer consciousness as participatory inquisitive awareness of the living land, the civilized religions, particularly those of the book, by and large embarked on a regressive bottlenecking of consciousness, a kind of devolutionary infantiliza-tion at odds with our human neotenic nature.

The king-god and the victim-god scenarios that mark the Judaeo-Christian-Muslim tradition and its civilizational origins converge today in the literal perfection of the *deus ex machina*, grand electro-inquisitor, the avatar of devolutionary hate. It will not save us from the fate of the global house of cards we are perfecting, quite the opposite: it is turning the biosphere into it.

We are participant in creation all the time, not mere spectators occasionally merging into it — that would assume our individuality to be a separate existence rather than as continuous with the bubbling into being. Our individuality, the living quick as Lawrence puts it, is itself a reality of the universe actively pouring forth creation.

In Peirce's terminology, I am viewing the question from the Firstness of it, and from the viewpoint of practice. From that point of view, Peirce's scientists are merging away at the all of truth, in theory, as well they should. But from the perspective of practice, science is in our time a frail little child's boat, and that merging is a kind of sub-human activity, insufficient for full-bodied practical life, as Peirce saw so well. As science grows to maturity, it realizes that its ultimate port is Beauty, which involves Goodness and Truth. And in Beauty each and every being is, in its individuality — not apart from it — participant in ongoing creation.

4. Children of the Earth

One of these days, perhaps, there will come a writer of opinions less humdrum than those of Dr. (Alfred Russel) Wallace, and less in awe of the learned and official world ... who will argue, like a new Bernard Mandeville, that man is but a degenerate monkey, with a paranoic talent for self-satisfaction, no matter what scrapes he may get himself into, calling them 'civilization', and who, in place of the unerring instincts of other races, has an unhappy faculty for occupying himself with words and abstractions, and for going wrong in a hundred ways before he is driven, willy-nilly, into the right one. Dr. Wallace would condemn such an extravagant paradoxer.

— Charles Peirce[16]

I propose that the universe is a vast cosmic fantasia, dreaming into being, which we perceive as the Spirit-That-Moves-In-And-Through-All-Things. And I claim that we do truly perceive this in our bodily being, that our bodily being is an incarnation of this cosmic fantasia, dreaming into being. Humans are Pleistocene de-matured primates, whose de-maturity shows itself in adaptability and reliance on cultural learning. In fact humans may be excessively and dangerously adaptable.

Suppose us to be that "degenerate monkey," whose instincts are more plastic than those of other animals. I take this to mean that the native American expression for humans as "children of the earth" is literally true, in an evolutionary sense, and that to be human means to be more dependent on the inpouring signs from all-surrounding life, indeed, to find our maturity in attuning ourselves to what David Abram, in defining animism, has happily called the relation of the human to the-greater-than-human.

Consider Peirce's example of how rational mind, being newer and progressive, is also more infantile than instinctive mind:

I doubt very much whether the Instinctive mind could ever develop into a Rational mind. I should expect the reverse process sooner. The Rational mind is the Progressive mind, and as such, by its very capacity for growth, seems more infantile than the Instinctive mind. Still, it would seem that Progressive minds must have, in some mysterious way, probably by arrested development, grown from Instinctive minds; and they are certainly enormously higher. The Deity of the Théodicée of Leibniz is as high an Instinctive mind as can well be imagined; but it impresses a scientific reader as distinctly inferior to the human mind. It reminds one of the views of the Greeks that Infinitude is a defect; for although Leibniz imagines that he is making the Divine Mind infinite, by making its knowledge Perfect and Complete, he fails to see that in thus refusing it the powers of thought and the possibility of improvement he is in fact taking away something far higher than knowledge. It is the human mind that is infinite. One of the most remarkable distinctions between the Instinctive mind of animals and the Rational mind of man is that animals rarely make mistakes, while the human mind almost invariably blunders at first, and repeatedly, where it is really exercised in the manner that is distinctive of it. If you look upon this as a defect, you ought to find an Instinctive mind higher than a Rational one, and probably, if you cross-examine yourself, you will find you do. The greatness of the human mind lies in its ability to discover truth notwithstanding its not having Instincts strong enough to exempt it from error. This is the marvel and admirable in it; and this essentially supposes a generous portion of the capacity for blundering....

The conception of the Rational Mind as an Unmatured Instinctive Mind which takes another development precisely because of its childlike character is confirmed, not only by the prolonged childhood of men, but also by the fact that all systems of rational performances have had instinct for their first germ. Not only has instinct been the first germ, but every step in the development of those systems of performances comes from instinct. It is precisely because this Instinct is a weak, uncertain Instinct that it becomes infinitely plastic, and never reaches an ultimate state beyond which it cannot progress. Uncertain tendencies, unstable states of equilibrium are conditions sine qua non for the manifestation of Mind.[17]

To say that Rational mind is an immature, "more infantile" capacity than Instinctive mind suggests to me that a rational civilization, far from being enlightened — or simply mature, is more likely to be infantile: subject to the unbearable enlightenment of being. By contrast, our hunter-gatherer, neotenized bodies evolved to find their maturity as "children of the earth" omnivorously attending to the signs of surrounding life, to the instinctive intelligence of the environment, and nurturing their "degenerate monkey" nature by cultivating the twenty year course of prolonged development in appropriate care and ritual.

The human brain evolved through foragers who practiced subtle attunement to surrounding life as their way of life. Sensing the forest of symbols and savannah of signs was what literally grew Big Brain, and perhaps eventually gave it its linguistic syntax; and to "read" and ruminate upon prey and food and all the omens of life involved a dramatic participation in the entrancement that is life. To hunt and gather involves both hyper-attuning activity as well as meditative quieting of the body, especially if you don't want to be some other predator's prey. This is by no means "primitive."

It is primarily the living Others, especially the animal and plant Others, who guided us to the discovery of the symbol, as we hunted, gathered, tracked, danced, dreamed, played, revered, ruminated over and became them, incorporating them into our emergent souls (and stomachs!) and finding resonance with them in the mammalian and reptilian parts of our brains. Their intelligible grammars became the basis of human language, in my view.

Imagine that you could be profoundly aware in detail of events a couple of kilometers away in a natural setting, by listening to the ripples of non-human calls signifying a disturbance. Imagine being profoundly aware in detail of everything about a creature, non-human or human: its bodily state, including functioning of its internal organs, its emotional state, even its intentions, by reading the over 5,000 potential signs found in its tracks. These are but two real "primitive skills" wherein close attunement to grammars of nature provide highly sophisticated practices with articulated "grammars" to be internalized, and practical wisdom to be generalized in ritual life. These are the living things of which symbols were originally made, in my view.

In *The Tender Carnivore and the Sacred Game* Shepard argues that the traditional hunter-gatherer hunter is the one who most reveres animals, and that we remain inescapably entwined in "the sacred game," a play on prey and the ritual play of the hunt.[18] Animals nourish us in ways deeper than material food, they nourish our souls and are a primary means through which we became human. Perhaps that is why 30 to 40 percent of characters in young children's dreams are animals. Interestingly, hunter-gatherers continue populating about 30 percent of the characters of their dreams with animals, where the number drops to 6 percent for men and 4 percent for women in American society, suggesting another indicator of anthropocentric consciousness.[19]

Consider anthropologist Richard Nelson's statement: "I believe the expert Inupiaq hunter possesses as much knowledge as a highly trained scientist in our own society, although the information may be of a different sort. Volumes could be written on the behavior, ecology, and utilization of Arctic animals — polar bear, walrus, bowhead whale, beluga, bearded seal, ringed seal, caribou, musk ox, and others — based entirely on Eskimo knowledge.... A Koyukon elder, who took it upon himself to be my teacher, was fond of telling me: Each animal knows way more than you do.... This statement epitomizes relationships to the natural world among many Native American people. And it goes far in explaining the diversity and fecundity of life on our continent when the first sailing ship approached these shores."[20]

From this view, which gives greater weight to instinctive intelligence, we are not superior to animals, but must attune ourselves to their instinctive intelligence to find our own maturity as genetically de-matured apes. Again, from one of Richard Nelson's Koyukan teachers: "The bear can outmind you." And respectful attunement is due not only to the animals, but also the plant beings and landscape. From this perspective, it is a human conceit to deny the sacredness of all life forms, whose deaths give us life. To communion-practicing Christians, the sacred game is narrowed to eating the Christ divinity figure — sacred game awareness is narrowed to the sacrificial consciousness of agricultural civilization — but to hunter-gatherers all eating is holy communion. Our brains remain the living manifestation of the fantastic reality that was the world of the foragers — human and prehuman, for we carry the achievements of the mammals and even their reptilian ancestors in us, in the limbic system and brain stem. All this becomes particularly evident in hypnotic phenomena, it seems to me, and also in dreaming.[21]

Hence full awareness of human instinctive intelligence involves the broader living community of instinctive reasonableness. Without that attunement, the ongoing observation of nature, mind contracts to mirroring its immature self, signified in its abstracted concept of God.

When philosophy escaped "from its golden pupa-skin, mythology, [and] proclaimed the great evolutionary agency of the universe to be Love," it was in the process of idealizing love, of creating an abstracted understanding of love that was a contraction of consciousness. That idealization found its abstracted underside in the modern era, which proclaimed the great evolutionary agency of the universe to be Hate, that great ticking clock of loveless mechanism.

Peirce's philosophy of consciousness reveals parallels in many ways closer to that of hunter-gatherers than to that of the civilized scientist or philosopher of the modern era. I view it as an element of a final participation consciousness in the making, from a most unlikely source: a physicist-mathematician-logician-scientist.

We are neotenic or newborn-like creatures, literally "children of the earth," in our very physiology. Peirce's discussion of humankind as a "degenerate monkey, with a paranoic talent for self-satisfaction," whose rationality is an immature capacity, suggests that there was a maturity in hunter-gatherer consciousness which consisted in acknowledging the immaturity of the human ego and rationality, and in seeing the need to attune ourselves to the greater environmental intelligence.

The "agricultural revolution" of 10,000 to 12,000 years ago on which cities are based never ended, nor did the expulsion from Eden, which we act out today. Civilization marches onward, devouring the earth in its unlimited population and power expansion.

Civilization, or city-fication, not only introduced many positive fruits, but also introduced an anthropocentric consciousness that marked a radical departure from the animate mind of the hunter-gatherer, a consciousness unhinged from its relation to the greater surrounding world of life. It created new forms: of social inequality, mass-killing warfare, shorter, nutritionally debased people, kingship, "world religions" with religious dependence focused on prophets, and a sense that human power could expand without limit. Human power pretty much has, until our time, when it bumped into the limits of organic life brought about through consequences of human overpopulation, environmental degradation, and "the Gospel of Greed."

In short, civilization was the creation of what Lewis Mumford termed a *Megamachine*. As Mumford expressed it in his book, *The Myth of the Machine*:

> Conceptually the instruments of mechanization five thousand years ago were already detached from other human functions and purposes than the constant increase of order, power, predictability, and, above all, control. With this proto-scientific ideology went a corresponding regimentation and degradation of once-autonomous human activities: 'mass culture' and mass control' made their first appearance. With mordant symbolism, the ultimate products of the megamachine in Egypt were colossal tombs, inhabited by mummified corpses; while later in Assyria, as repeatedly in every other expanding empire, the chief testimony to its technical efficiency was a waste of destroyed villages and cities, and poisoned soils: the prototype of similar 'civilized' atrocities today. As for the Egyptian pyramids, what are they but the precise static equivalents of our own space rockets? Both devices for securing, at an extravagant cost, a passage to Heaven for the favored few.[22]

What if civilization, as megamachine, systematically distorted the process of human development, *replacing neoteny with deliberate infantilization*?

5. Infantilization

The first fruit of the scientific spirit must have been a Theology, and some confused Cosmogony; for it is man's way to attack the most difficult questions first, and attempt detailed answers to them. What the first religion was like one would give something to know. To tell us would be a suitable task for a Shakespeare and a Browning, in collaboration with a Darwin, a Spencer, and a Hegel. — Charles Peirce[23]

Civilization can be considered as a rational-historical process of progressive infantilization. Domestication involved generalizing neoteny out to the edible environment, through breeding de-matured grasses and animals, co-dependent on human cultivation, and separation from wildness through encapsulation within the "caretaking" institutions of the village. The facts that time between childbirths contracted greatly, average nutrition deteriorated, leisure time drastically reduced, and an anthropocentric consciousness emerged all suggest radical changes to the ways children became socialized.[24]

Individual awareness was relieved by specialized institutions, so that one person could attend to more specialized functions, but this benefit can also be viewed as a form of awareness deprivation, of de-attuning to the general living habitat. When we separated ourselves from direct participatory musement with the wild plants and animals, when we settled into domestication and civilization and walled ourselves into the city, we began to mirror ourselves as Other and to lose the wild plants and animals as other. We began to lose the community of instinctive intelligence that was our passage to maturity.

Modern mechanical civilization can be viewed as devolving yet further, toward a total fetalized environment perhaps best symbolized by the earth-escaping, encapsulated astronaut. Consciousness becomes a ghost in the womb of the machine, a virtual astronaut escaping the earth, attached through institutional umbilicals to the machine, as though that matrix were not itself a social construction. The rational-mechanical system of modern life is indeed a social construction, the projection of a schizoid, fetalizing consciousness which has lost touch with creation. Imagine a diagram of concentric circles, depicting what I am calling the contraction of consciousness. The outer one is Animate Mind, the middle one is Anthropocentric Mind, and the inner one is Mechanicocentric Mind.

The direct perception of the Creator is diminished in the contraction from animate mind. For animate mind, attuned to and involved in surrounding life, perceives through the instinctive intelligence of its living environment as well as its own instinctive intelligence. Our neotenous nature not only involves, but in my view *requires* abductive attunement, whose original object are wild animals and plants and the general signs of life, as Shepard has pointed out — as one expression of our instinctive intelligence.

Though we humans are domesticators of the earth, we yet retain wild bodies, and, in my opinion, wild needs. If one would like to tap into one's wild heritage today, one could eat Paleolithic instead of the Neolithic diet which is the basis of modern eating. The Paleolithic or hunter-gatherer diet is what shaped the development of the human body, and the popular Atkins and South Beach diets of today seem to me to be diminished variations of it. Eating Paleolithic typically involves a wide range of greens, fruits, nuts, berries, legumes, roots, and about 30 percent protein, derived mainly from lean meat, and no domesticated grains or refined sugars.

Or try seeing from peripheral vision instead of focus vision — put your hands out to the sides and wiggle fingers, then move hands back while viewing both left and right until you reach your limit of visual range. Then do this vertically. Then see in "wide-angle" vision. You will feel as though you are in the picture rather than a spectator of it. Movement is easier to detect in natural surroundings. You will also have improved night vision. In my opinion, even something as simple as seeing the world most of the time through wide-angle vision marks a radical shift in consciousness. Reliance on focalized vision in cityscape and especially in literacy seems to me one physiological correlate of the "spectator consciousness," displaced from participation in being.

As William Blake put it, "He who sees the Infinite in all things sees God. He who sees the ratio only sees himself." With the increased rationalism of anthropocentric, and especially mechanicocentric mind, we close the doors of perception to narrow chinks, losing that circumambient perception that is the natural legacy of our hunter-gatherer bodies. From this perspective, religion cannot develop separated from an ongoing attunement to nature in the long run. Instead, it becomes infantilized, as the Judeo-Christian-Islamic tradition illustrates, in my opinion. The living spontaneity of creation is abstracted to a distant father-figure who created the universe in a foundational past and who is reachable through the institutional filter of the "world religion" and its special inter-mediaries. From my perspective, Peirce offers the possibility of a genuine reconnection of religion to the attunement to nature and of science to living spirit in his philosophies of science and religion.

Cities mark the de-attuning to nature and the turn toward power-centered human social organizations. Modernity marks the mythic idealization of the machine, furthering its separation from the reality of life, from outpouring, over-flowing, exuberant, variescent life, as that which comprises the body of concrete reasonableness. I earlier termed this "progression" a contraction of consciousness. Another way of putting it is that it is a process of *Infantilization*, a systematic reversal of the requirements of our neotenic species to attune itself to the greater surrounding environmental intelligence of concrete reasonableness. And unless we can undergo a radical re-attunement fairly quickly, it will spell death for global civilization. The past 10,000 to 12,000 years have been a diminution of conscious-ness into ever-increasing "mind-forg'd manacles" of civilized life. But those 10,000 to 12,000 years are but a veneer on our hunter-gatherer bodies, which indeed are truly "the stuff of which dreams are made," but real dreams. Our continued attempt to live on that veneer is murderously suicidal.

We are living in the endgame of the idealizing consciousness, by which I mean that the expansion of rational-mechanical civilization, brought about through the contraction of consciousness, has reached a dangerous and terminal crisis in relation to the outer resources of the earth and the inner resources of humanity. Without a thoroughgoing transformation of global civilization, it is likely to self-destruct within a couple of decades.

To return to my earlier thesis: the concept of God is the moment of human alienation from the divine presence of the living universe, from the cosmic fantasia of life. In this perspective the universe is an act of self-creation and self-renewal, and the purport of life is not simply to reproduce genes and species, but to further living reasonableness. Material evolution is more than a Darwinian Gospel of Greed, it also involves genuine social relation as a dynamic, what Peirce termed evolutionary love. Material evolution is in this sense involved in general evolution, in the development of real generals. Therefore all life arrives in potential, if it is not destroyed first or if it does not destroy itself, at the developmental point where it begins to take control of its destiny.

To take one example, consider the idea, associated with Teilhard de Chardin but also developed earlier by Vladimir Vernadsky, that evolution is in the process of building a life-saving "noosphere" (like the atmosphere, stratosphere, etc.), a planetary film of intelligence, in which "life's domain" would be ruled by reason. Chardin thought that the liberation of rational mind would free the body and soul as well, producing a universal, nature-mastering intelligence in harmony with Christian ideals. But he was ruinously naive, in my opinion. Perhaps those Christian ideals are as well; life cannot be lived by ideals for long, as ideals need to be lived by life, and tempered by life. What could be worse than the perfection of the rule of rationalized reason over life's domain, as though "life's domain" is not reasonable in itself!

The ethereal "noosphere" of mind is indeed a globalizing power today, but not in the buoyant way that they conceived it; a noose-sphere would be more accurate. A planetary film of intelligence is precisely what we already have been installing: a vast, rational-mechanical, anti-body system whose ultimate goal is to eradicate fully incarnate human being and variescent life. This is the legacy of modern nominalism and its ethereal ghost in the machine. It severs spirit from living embodiment, and mind from earth.

Ockham's philosophy of nominalism attempted to slice the throat of the living, general nature of things, splitting them into individual particulars and conventions, which stood for or "named" the particulars, but were in themselves unreal. In order to perfect that project — the "modern road" or *via moderna* as Ockham's nominalism was called — the philosophical basis for modernity, eventually one comes to the point where, as a living, general thing, one must slice one's own throat: Ockham's razor as Ahab's end. That, as I see it, is where the *via moderna* has taken us.[25]

Each and every day the throat of nature is being sliced globally, not only the outer devastation of forests and species and air and sea and climate, but the inner nature of humanity as well, unable to stand the nominalistic ideology that all that can be loved is a fiction, that only anti-social hate is a reality of nature, and that nature is a kind of machine. To dramatize it further: humankind, the greatest killer of the biosphere, is itself an endangered species, endangered not only by the outer consequences of global Power culture on the life of the earth, but also by its "deforestation" of its inner life. We are the legacy of the Sumerian Gilgamesh, who would "ascend to the heavens" through power, who would kill the forest spirit Humbaba and "cut down the Cedar," who would defy and defame the gods, who would "establish fame for eternity," who would nevertheless die.

For the first time since civilizational being developed, we have reached the limits of civilization, globally. Thin-blooded scientific-technical civilization cannot match the thick-blooded fountain of life as a basis for living unless it gives up its enlightenment pretensions, and the unbearable enlightenment of being which they have already produced. We need to conceive a new civilizational structure that can, for the first time, incorporate limits in alignment with nature, globally. Why do people naively assume that the same modern, rational human consciousness — and its science and technology and economics — which produced the dying global sewer we are increasingly living in, is alone capable of reversing the deadly forces it released? As though, for example, simply increasing agricultural productivity on the same amount of land won't also continue to increase population somewhere?

Until contemporary science-techno-culture can put "mater" back in "materialism," and can rediscover that indeed the universe is a perfusion of living signs, not a dead tick-tock machine, we will live out this murderous-suicidal endgame of nominalism, increasingly removed from self-originated experience by a veil of machines. That is, of course, the secret teleology of anti-teleological modern clock culture.

6. Animate Mind and Newton's Sleep

> I turn my eyes to the schools and universities of Europe
> And there behold the Loom of Locke, whose Woof rages dire,
> Wash'd by the Water-wheels of Newton: black the cloth
> In heavy wreaths folds over every nation: cruel works
> Of many Wheels I view, wheel without wheel, with cogs tyrannic
> Moving by compulsion each other, not as those in Eden, which,
> Wheel within wheel, in freedom revolve in harmony and peace.
> — William Blake, from *Jerusalem*

Participation consciousness was sacrificed in the long road of civilization and modern life, sacrificed for the development of critical reason, of abstract thought. The modern age has had as its task the perfection of this process. That perfection is now in its endgame, and we have utterly divorced ourselves from creation in the growth of spectatorial "camera-consciousness," as Owen Barfield put it.[26]

Nominalism and clocks arose in the fourteenth century. Over the next few centuries the normal mechanical world-view mythically projected clock-culture onto the universe and made it the basis of science, and Peirce's philosophy involves a rejection of its nominalistic premises. Peirce sees the universe as in a process of genuine creation, in which life and intelligence are real emergent properties of that universe, not freakish accidents.[27]

Peirce's outlook shows the possibility for a new civilizational framework, involving a broadened conception of science which finds no contradictions between its investigations and the soul of the Creator. What if reverence is not something God or the gods "want," but is simply the tone of participating in creation? For hundreds of millennia our ancestors attuned themselves through passionate awareness to the circumambient voices and visions of life. We evolved that instinctive reverence that is the basis of Peirce's Neglected Argument. Tracking, foraging, hunting and gathering, and the clan-based rites accompanying these practices were all passages in the pursuit of wisdom. All of these practices proclaimed the great evolutionary agency of the universe to be love, and it is to these practices and the bodies they produced, that philosophy owes its origins — and perhaps a clue to its destiny.

In viewing musement as the opening through which the God idea plays forth, Peirce found a way out of the contest between doubt and belief that characterizes modern culture.[28] Modern consciousness can be characterized as involving a negation of the traditional world-view of the West, and as the age of rational-mechanical consciousness. Aristotle was not only overturned by Galileo, but one sees perhaps more obviously in the doubting, nominalistic spirit of Thomas Hobbes the need of the age to "just say no" to received beliefs.

Consciousness has not "expanded" in a "progress" of history; quite the contrary, it has contracted. Modern science, despite its precision and seeming enlargement of our understanding of the universe, represents the contracted, nominalistic view, denying the reality of generals. Evolution is not devoid of general reasonableness, as though it were only a competitive calculus machine. That Darwinian model of evolution is fundamentally flawed, taking one modality of general evolution as the whole picture, as Peirce argued. As such, it is part of the matrix of modern mind, contracted to precision in understanding those aspects of things which conform to the requirements of the megamachine.

The ongoing creation of the universe, a crucial idea in Peirce, is not allow-ed in Darwinism, because there is no CREATION, in the genuine sense of this word, no spontaneous intelligence as ingredient in the development of the living universe. In the Darwinian view, change is through chance adaptive variations, and reasonableness itself is an "adaptive" strategy humans evolved. Darwinians combine justified fear of religious fundamentalism by so-called "creation science" believers, who are Christian ideologues seeking biblical legitimation, with a dogmatic phobia of the possibility of Thirdness as operative in evolution (to use Peircean shorthand). Neither the Darwinian side nor the "creation science" side allow for creation in Peirce's sense, though a thorough-going "intelligent design" argument — perhaps more of a Gaia perspective — should at least be open to it.

The Darwinian/Hobbesean account of nature is an aspect of "single vision, and Newton's sleep!" as William Blake termed it. Consider William Blake's painting of Newton, which depicts him as supple, leaning over with compass, figuring out the ratio of things. That rational "ratio" of Newton's genius may be true in its precision, but it is still "the spectre of reason," a secondary emanation of the Poetic Imagination, blind to awareness of circumambient life, a fundamentally incomplete, abstracted vision of the universe. It is also an accurate, literal depic-tion of the "focus vision" of the civilized peoples, fallen from the wide-angle perception of circumambient life, of what Ortega y Gassett called the "universal attention" of the hunter, who is aware that seeing from the full range of visual field allows greater sensing of movement and better night vision.

The romantic movement was, in my opinion, the instinctive life's attempt to survive in the face of infantilizing rationality. The twentieth-century was an incarnation of precise, accurate, infantilism, as far as thought was concerned: Intellectual Kaliyuga. Isaac Newton's world-machine, in which, despite Einstein, we still live, represents an unloved child. Newton was himself an incarnation of intellectual Kaliyuga: he was born "posthumously," meaning that his father died before his birth, and his mother remarried soon after and infant Isaac was jettison-ed to maids and servants; unfathered, unmothered, uncared for. Newton strikes me as a brilliant incarnation of the schizoid personality, who found relief through shaping a precise abstract world in which emotion and empathy are unreal, in which mechanism is all: our tick-tock world. In my view this scientific mega-machine needs to grow up, and to do so will involve beginning with triadic semeiosis, which involves the dyadicism of mechanism but is not reducible to it. Our projection of our humanity into the infant-machine consciousness, far from excluding telos, embodies the crypto-teleology of suicide.

Consider, by contrast to his painting of Newton, how Blake's image of God enclosed in a sphere is one of the Poetic Imagination as primary, and the hand of God, reaching out from the sphere in an inverted "V" is the "compass" of the ratio, correctly proportioned as secondary emanation. Something like this is how our very bodies are made, attuned as hunter-gatherers over hundreds of millennia in reverence to all-surrounding life. We are competitive creatures, to be sure, but competitive in the sacred game of life, ritual predators and game, gatherers of plants and mates and songs, ever-attuning in awareness and Poetic Imagination, while evolving our symbol-using forebrain.

In opening the door of musement, Peirce allowed that *il lume naturale* its valid place in human consciousness, one virtually denied by critical so-called Enlightenment. More, he re-opened the door of inner vision that the contraction of consciousness, originally brought about through domesticating civilization, had progressively closed. For modern mechanico-centric nominal mind is nothing less than the infantilization of human reason: the Endarklement.

The conditions for what Peirce termed *Musement*, the play of mind, might be at odds with that greater requirement for work first introduced with agricultural civilization, and re-sharpened in the culture of rationalized capitalism. Consider that the average workweek for hunter-gatherers was about 17 hours, far less than the average required by agriculturally-based societies. Hunter-gatherer working conditions seem ripe for the play of musement, and indeed, the descriptions of participation consciousness one reads in ethnographies suggest to me that musement is a more valued practice for this way of life. Not musement on neglected arguments for the reality of God, which would seem beside the point I suspect, but musements and ruminations on the animal others, on the various omens of life, on the all-surrounding presence of the Creator, manifest in the minute particulars of variescent life. To be a hunter-gatherer is to be a sophisticated naturalist, expert in plant life and animal ethology, the sophisticated art and science of tracking, and numerous other "occupations."

There are innumerable ways in which contemporary life could be informed by prehistoric life. Indeed, if history is, as Lewis Mumford put it, a "fibrous structure," being informed by whatever might be valuable is preferable to a Hegelian-style jettisoning of the past. Re-animating contemporary life is no impossible return to a golden age. In fact, "primitive skills" of hunting, gathering, tracking are already informing contemporary life, ranging from the pharmaceutical industry to US special forces.

Contemporary culture has much to learn from such "simple" ways of being. Turning to a "simple" way of being may be preferable to the complex primitivism that marks the being of our time. Consider, for example, the tactile and empathic devotion typical of hunter-gatherers toward their young in comparison with typical child-rearing attitudes in megatechnic America.

The end of human development is not to see through the design of things, as perfected critical consciousness, and it is certainly not to preside over it like a God, like the spectator God concepts spawned by the Judeo-Greco-Christian-Islamic tradition. For what could be worse than the "degenerate monkey, with a paranoic talent for self-satisfaction," as Peirce depicted homo sapiens sapiens, whose rationality is an immature capacity, presuming to preside over the design of life — and from intellect of all things! — as though intellect is the basis of reasonableness, and as though life in itself lacks reasonableness. In my view, the goal of human development is to become the design, designing, to become participant in the self-designing design. In this sense intellect's purport would be to become instinct with life. As William Blake said, "Imagination is spiritual sensation" and "energy is eternal delight" and "Energy is the only life and is from the body" and "We are put on earth for a little space that we may learn to bear the beams of love."

Poetic Imagination, spontaneous creative soul, is a real aspect of evolution not reducible to the machine-matrix of modern mind. But the modern mind is typically disabled by cultural nominalism, unable to see how those mind capacities of humans and of life more generally are realities that are outside its ghost-in-the-machine rules.

Peirce is the philosopher who first identified both the pervasiveness and falsity of nominalism, against which he posed his triadic, semeiotic realism. I take his critique of the philosophy of nominalism to apply to the broader culture of modern life as well, as cultural nominalism. A central feature of cultural nominalism is modern science. Although a critic of nominalism, Peirce also championed modern science and its genuine achievements, while yet arguing in different ways that it would outgrow its false nominalistic premises.

In describing science Peirce says, "by science we all habitually mean a living and growing body of truth."[29] And his view of the end of science is: "The only end of science, as such, is to learn the lesson that the universe has to teach it. In induction it simply surrenders itself to the force of facts. But it finds, at once, — I am partially inverting the historical order, in order to state the process in its logical order, — it finds I say that this is not enough. It is driven in desperation to call upon its inward sympathy with nature, its instinct for aid, just as we find Galileo at the dawn of modern science making his appeal to *il lume naturale....* The value of *facts* to *it*, lies only in this, that they belong to Nature; and Nature is something great, and beautiful, and sacred, and eternal, and real, — the object of its worship and its aspiration. It therefore takes an entirely different attitude toward facts from that which Practice takes."[30] Here one sees the breadth of Peirce's understanding of science, and a view of its relation to Nature strikingly similar to that of the religious views of hunter-gatherers. Still, William Blake gives a quite different view worth considering, saying,

> *Art is the Tree of Life...*
> *Science is the Tree of Death.*

Despite Peirce's allowance of abductive inference and his critique of nominalism, his idea of completely unfettered inquiry, remote from "vitally important topics," seems to me problematic. Science and its practical sibling technology are and have been involved in capitalism from early on. Peirce saw capitalism as a "Philosophy of Greed," but idealized science such that he ignored its actual involvement not only in capitalism, but in the building of the mega-machine of modern life, which is the purport of nominalism. His views may be accurate for a long run, but thanks to science and its wedding to technology, consummated perhaps in the Manhattan Project, humanity and earthly, variescent life may not be around for a long run.

Normal science, along with normal technology, normal economics, and the whole normal modern world-view, as practiced thus far, are proving to be "precise mechanisms" of death. Further, they are involved in the crypto-teleology of cultural nominalism, namely the unacknowledged goal of replacing those organs by which life comes to awareness with mechanisms of the megamachine, to the point of ultimately replacing life itself: a world of smart bombs and insensate people, of unlimited consumptive possessiveness, even unto the soul of creation.

When Peirce claimed "Do not block the road of inquiry" as prime directive for science, he little knew how twisted this maxim would become in the twentieth-century, when its variants would be used as excuses to open Pandora's box over and over. Even inquiries whose validity rests in an indefinite future must be based in a precarious present whose prime directive is to give reasonableness to the future. When inquiry violates that directive, must it not be blocked simply to allow its own life to continue into the indefinite future?

When Peirce argued that science is too "thin" for the practice of life, that it was in a state of relative immaturity, and that theory should be kept separate from practice, he acknowledged that scientists represent specialized inquirers, but another implication of his argument is that scientists are a form of immature human being, qua scientists. In my opinion this is a clear argument against techno-cracy, and implies that fallibilism requires science to reconcile inquiry to the conditions of life and its possible limits, those conditions representing mature reasonableness relative to immature science. It means that scientific inquiry, as attunement to the living signs of nature, must respect its own immaturity relative to those signs, especially in the age of the infantilized megamachine, and allow those signs their weight in policy decisions and the ethics of research. Not blocking the road of inquiry does not mean that inquirers are justified in speeding down the road at breakneck speed, willy nilly, unnecessarily risking their lives and the community of life.

The unlimited community of inquirers must, in my opinion, acknowledge its responsibilities to its incarnate body. And in this portion of the universe, its incarnate body is the living earth. A genuine citizen of the unlimited community of inquiry would feel in his or her gut that responsibility to cultivate life, to participate in the creation of the universe by cultivating fellow species toward their own continued wild evolution: look what happened to that ape who became human in two million years, thanks to the community of mature, instinctive life to which it attuned itself.

What is two million years in the unlimited community of inquiry? The unlimited community of inquiry, in short, must be a good citizen in the unlimited community of life, or what's a living universe for? The unlimited community of inquirers is not limited to those human interpreters of the future, for we should allow the full weight of those previous insights into the nature of things into the community as well, inclusive of instinctive intelligence, human and animal, into that "generalized other" within, through which we think in dialogue.

Should we discover and institutionalize the means to rebuild science and transform the dynamics of civilization, animating life toward inquisitive aware-ness, it will involve, in my opinion, arriving eventually at creatures aware that truth is the breath of the Creator on creation, and that the further creation and pursuit of truth, goodness and beauty involves an attunement to all-surrounding life, not an isolation from it. It will again be able to proclaim, even in its science, that the great evolutionary agency of the universe is Love.

It will become instinct with life, a paradoxical critical instinct. It will realize that truth ultimately becomes beauty, as life already is aware in its own being. But guess what, dear reader, that is precisely the path humans were on, before our tilling of the soil and civilizing removed us from participation with the living earth to becoming spectators of life, from being children of the earth to becoming that form of infantilized dominion whose master symbols are "civilization" and "God."

The time has come to escape from this degenerate, leaden primitivism that is modern civilized consciousness, and to revive the broadened awareness of animate mind. That mind lives as a reality embodied in the human, Pleistocene body-mind, though repressed by the machine of modernity. And that mind is the one Peirce was led to in his lifelong development, in which, at the end of the *via moderna*, he found the means to re-open philosophy to its golden legacy.

NOTES

1. William James, "The Compounding of Consciousness," in *The Writings of William James*, ed. John J. McDermott (Chicago: University of Chicago Press, 1977), p. 556.

2. D. H. Lawrence, "Indians and Entertainment," in *Mornings in Mexico* (Salt Lake City: Gibbs M. Smith, 1982), p. 116 (first published in *New York Times*, 26 October 1924).

3. Charles S. Peirce, *The Collected Papers of Charles Sanders Peirce*, ed. Charles Hartshorne, Paul Weiss, and Arthur Burks (Cambridge, MA: Harvard University Press,

1931–58), vol. 6, para. 502–3. Hereafter citations from *Collected Papers* are noted by volume and paragraph number, for example, *CP* 6.502–3.

4. Lucian Lêvy-Bruhl, *How Natives Think* (London: George Allen and Unwin, 1926), pp. 129–30.

5. *CP* 6.505.

6. Peirce, "Detached Ideas Continued and the Dispute Between Nominalists and Realists (439)," in *The New Elements of Mathematics by Charles Peirce, vol. 6: Mathematical Philosophy*, ed. Carolyn Eisele (Atlantic Highlands, NJ: Humanities Press, 1976), p. 345. Hereafter cited as *New Elements*.

7. *CP* 6.553

8. *CP* 7.364.

9. Paul Shepard, *Nature and Madness* (Athens: University of Georgia Press, 1982), pp. 78, 80.

10. S. Boyd Eaton, Marjorie Shostack, and Melvin Konner, *The Paleolithic Prescription* (New York: Harper and Row, 1988). Marshall Sahlins, "The Original Affluent Society," in *Stone-Age Economics* (Chicago: Aldine, 1973), pp. 1–39.

11. *CP* 6.294.

12. *CP* 6.300.

13. Eugene Halton, *Bereft of Reason* (Chicago: University of Chicago Press, 1995).

14. *CP* 8.83.

15. *CP* 1.673.

16. *Charles Sanders Peirce: Contributions to The Nation, Part Three: 1901–1908*, ed. Kenneth Laine Ketner and James Edward Cook (Lubbock: Texas Tech University, 1979), pp. 17–18.

17. *CP* 7.380–1.

18. Paul Shepard, *The Tender Carnivore and the Sacred Game* (Athens, GA: University of Georgia Press, 1998).

19. G. W. Domhoff, *Finding Meaning in Dreams: A Quantitative Approach* (New York: Plenum, 1996).

20. Richard Nelson, "Searching for the Lost Arrow: Physical and Spiritual Ecology in the Hunter's World," in *The Biophilia Hypothesis*, ed. S. R. Kellert and E. O. Wilson (Washington, DC: Island Press, 1993). Tom Brown, Jr., *The Science and Art of Tracking* (New York: Berkley Pub. Group, 1999).

21. Eugene Halton, "The Reality of Dreaming," *Theory, Culture, and Society* 9 (1992), pp. 119–39. Halton, "The Living Gesture and the Signifying Moment," *Symbolic Interaction* 27 (2004), pp. 89–113.

22. Lewis Mumford, *The Myth of the Machine, vol. 1: Technics and Human Development* (New York: Harcourt, Brace, Jovanovich, 1967), p. 12.

23. *CP* 7.384

24. Donald Henry, *From Foraging to Agriculture: The Levant and the End of the Ice Age* (Philadelphia: University of Pennsylvania Press, 1989).

25. Eugene Rochberg-Halton, *Meaning and Modernity* (Chicago: University of Chicago Press, 1986).

26. Owen Barfield, *The Rediscovery of Meaning, and Other Essays* (Middletown, CT: Wesleyan University Press, 1973).

27. Peirce claimed that there is "a reasonableness energizing into being" in the universe, framing it in terms of Thirdness as habit-taking. His view is that habit-taking arose out of primordial chance, as he stated in 1898: "But in this endless haphazard shindy between generalization and chance this generalization happens to come about, namely a limited but still a general tendency toward the formation of habits, toward repeating reactions that had already taken place under like circumstances ... although this was doubtless smashed like the others billions upon billions of times, to use a hyperbole of stating matters infinitely weaker than I really mean, yet still, it was often springing from its ashes, and on the whole was tiring out the lawlessness, until at length, — of course after an infinite lapse of time subsequent to the first moment, although infinitely long ago, there came to be a decided and so to say a sensible degree of tendency in nature to take habits.... The acquiring [of] a habit is nothing but an objective generalization taking place in time. It is the fundamental logical law in course of realization." Peirce, "Abstracts of Eight Lectures," in *New Elements*, p. 141.

28. Peirce also addressed this problem in his philosophy of "critical common-sensism." How to reconcile that critical consciousness, based on the capacity of rational doubting, with belief in a meaningful universe, was the problem that haunted two of Peirce's literary contemporaries, Herman Melville and Fyodor Dostoyevsky. These two novelists saw through the problem of the modern age, and proposed a means out of it, with perspicacity surpassing that of Peirce, in my opinion; although Peirce's chief concern was developing a logic of the long run.

29. *CP* 6.428.

30. Peirce, *The Essential Peirce, vol. 2* (Bloomington: Indiana University Press, 1998), pp. 54–55.

Eugene Halton
Professor of Sociology and American Studies
Department of Sociology
810 Flanner Hall
University of Notre Dame
South Bend, Indiana, 46556
United States

Contemporary Pragmatism
Vol. 2, No. 1 (June 2005), 167–184

Editions Rodopi
© 2005

Eco on Names and Reference

David Boersema

This article provides an overall explication of the work of Umberto Eco as it relates to philosophy of language, in particular to the issues of reference and proper names. Drawing on the works of earlier pragmatists, especially Peirce, and drawing on Eco's own work in semiotics, I argue that Eco offers telling criticisms of and corrections to the standard treatments of reference and names.

Known outside of academia primarily as the author of best-selling "intellectual" novels such as *The Name of the Rose* and *Foucault's Pendulum*, and known inside of academia primarily as the author of important works in semiotics such as *The Open Work* and *A Theory of Semiotics*, Umberto Eco has for decades addressed issues of reference and names and has done so from a perspective explicitly indebted to pragmatism generally and Charles Peirce particularly. Drawing heavily, though not uncritically, on Peirce's semiotic writings, Eco has recently enunciated his notion of "contractual realism"; a notion, he says, that is consistent with his previous attempts "to elaborate a theory of content featuring a blend of semantics and pragmatics" (2000, 5).

A summary statement of this contractualist position involves four components: (1) referring is an action that speakers perform on the basis of a negotiation, (2) in principle the act of reference effected by using a term might have nothing to do with the knowledge of the meaning of the term or even with the existence of the referent, with which it has no causal relationship, (3) nevertheless, there is no designation definable as rigid that does not rest on an initial description ("label"), albeit a highly generic one, and (4) therefore, even apparent cases of absolutely rigid designation constitute the start of the referential contract, or the auroral moment of the relation, but never the final moment (2000, 295-96).

What are Eco's reasons for maintaining these claims? Before directly answering this question, a brief summary of the standard accounts of reference and names, the descriptivist view and the causal view, is provided in the first section.

1. Descriptivist and causal views of reference and names

We use names to refer to objects in the world, but how does this happen? When we say that Aristotle was a Greek philosopher, how does the name "Aristotle" refer to a uniquely particular individual? Or, to put the question another way, in virtue of what does the name "Aristotle" (successfully) refer to, or pick out, the person Aristotle? One answer is that the name refers to the object because we associate certain descriptions with the name, descriptions that in fact pick out or identity the object. The descriptive content uniquely picks out, or determines, what object the name refers to. So, when a speaker claims that Aristotle was a Greek philosopher, that speaker refers to Aristotle by (the use of) the name "Aristotle" because the speaker has some descriptions associated with the name, for example, "the most famous student of Plato," or "the teacher of Alexander the Great," or "the author of the *Nichomachean Ethics*," etc. This view is called the Descriptivist account because names refer to objects in virtue of the descriptions that speakers associate with the names. Names refer to objects basically because, and only because, speakers use names to refer to objects.

Philosophically, this Descriptivist account was motivated by Gottlob Frege and Bertrand Russell. Frege noted that there is a difference between the claims that (1) "The Morning Star is the Morning Star" and (2) "The Morning Star is the Evening Star." Sentence (1) is an example of the form a = a and it is true independent of any astronomical information we might have, whereas Sentence (2) is of the form a = b and we had to discover that it was true. But if "The Morning Star" and "The Evening Star" are just two names for the same object, the planet Venus, why would there be any difference between these sentences? Since both names refer to the same object, it seems that both sentences are simply saying that Venus is Venus. Frege concluded that names have both a reference and a sense (or meaning). So, the reference of "The Morning Star" is the same as for "The Evening Star," namely, Venus. But the sense of "The Morning Star" is something like "the particularly bright celestial object that is at such-and-such a place in the morning sky" while the sense of "The Evening Star" is something like "the particularly bright celestial object that is at such-and-such a place in the evening sky." While the reference is the same, the senses are different. The sense provides the descriptive content for the name.

This Descriptivist account also explained, for Frege, why sentences with nonreferring names, such as "Sherlock Holmes," can still be meaningful and can be true or false. That is, we take the sentence (3) "Sherlock Holmes was British" to be true but sentence (4) "Sherlock Holmes was American" to be false. But since there is no Sherlock Holmes (that is, "Sherlock Holmes" is nonreferring), then how can this be? For Frege, it is because the name

"Sherlock Holmes" has a sense even if it has no reference, and the sense is provided by some description or other.

Bertrand Russell, among others, questioned the notion of senses, but nevertheless he, too, argued that the nature and function of names are accounted for via descriptions associated with those names. For Russell, ordinary proper names are "really usually descriptions" and "the thought in the mind of the person using a proper name correctly can generally only be expressed explicitly if we replace the proper name by a description" (1912, 54). The descriptions might vary from time to time or from speaker to speaker. One speaker might associate "the most famous student of Plato" with the name "Aristotle" while another speaker might associate "the teacher of Alexander the Great" with the same name. This variance-of-descriptions was later emphasized by John Searle. As Searle put it,

> Suppose we ask the users of the name "Aristotle" to state what they regard as certain essential and established facts about him. Their answers would constitute a set of identifying descriptions, and I wish to argue that though no single one of them is analytically true of Aristotle, their disjunction is. Put it this way: suppose we have independent means of identifying an object, what then are the conditions under which I could say of the object, "This is Aristotle?" I wish to claim that the conditions, the descriptive power of the statement, is that a sufficient but so far unspecified number of these statements (or descriptions) are true of the object. In short, if none of the identifying descriptions believed to be true of some object by the users of the name of that object proved to be true of some independently located object, then the object could not be identical with the bearer of the name. It is a necessary condition for an object to be Aristotle that it satisfy at least some of these descriptions. (1969, 169)

The Descriptivist account has been criticized on various counts. Saul Kripke, in his book *Naming and Necessity*, raised several objections that many philosophers of language found sufficient to refute descriptivism. Underlying the objections was Kripke's insistence that what a name refers to might not at all be what a speaker using the name refers to; there is a difference between semantic reference and speaker reference. For Kripke, the name "Aristotle" designates a particular individual even if a speaker uses the name "Aristotle" to designate some other individual (perhaps because the speaker is confused about who Aristotle was). So, it might well be that none of the descriptions that a speaker associates with a given name in fact uniquely pick out the object whose name it is. The flip side of this objection is that it might turn out that some other object in fact fits those descriptions. Even in such a case, says Kripke, the name would not necessarily refer to that object. So, if it turned out to be the case that all of the things a speaker associates with Aristotle really aren't true of Aristotle, but — unbeknownst to the speaker — turned out to be true of someone else (say, Plato), it would still be the case that the name "Aristotle" refers to Aristotle and not to Plato. For Kripke, a name is not simply a designator, but it is a *rigid designator*; that is, it refers to the same object in all scenarios in which it refers to anyone at all.

Having analyzed the cluster theory of reference and having found it "wrong from the fundamentals," Kripke proposes to present a "better picture" of how reference takes place. In general, he says, our reference depends not just on what we think ourselves, but on other people in the community, the history of how the name reached one, and things like that. It is by following such a history that one gets to the reference. This better picture, which Kripke says is not a *theory*, has nonetheless served as the nascence and kernel of what has come to be called the casual theory of reference. Kripke gives a "rough statement" of such a theory:

> A rough statement of a theory might be the following: An initial baptism takes place. Here the object may be named by ostension, or the reference of the name may be fixed by a description. When the name is 'passed from link to link', the receiver of the name must, I think, intend when he learns it to use it with the same reference as the man from whom he heard it. (1980, 96)

The sense in which this is a *causal* theory of reference is that the passage of a name from link to link is said to secure a causal connection between the name of an object and the object. The initial baptismal act of naming the object (by ostension, perhaps) establishes the causal connection in the first place. Later uses of the name must be connected to the object in some sort of causal chain stretching back to the original naming act. As noted above, Kripke does not explicitly propose a theory of reference. However, others (such as Michael Devitt) have attempted to forge a fuller causal account of reference based on Kripke's picture. According to Devitt:

> The central idea of a causal theory of names is that our present uses of a name, say 'Aristotle', designate the famous Greek philosoher Aristotle, *not* in virtue of the various things we (rightly) believe true of him, but in virtue of a causal network stretching back from our uses to the first uses of the name to designate Aristotle. It is in this way that our present uses of the name "borrow their reference" from earlier uses. It is this social mechanism that enables us all to designate the same thing by a name. (1981, 25)

This simple statement of a causal theory indicates what Devitt takes to be the basic elements of the theory. Reference, or designation, is explained in terms of *d-chains* (short for "designating chains"). There are three types of links in a d-chain: (1) groundings, which link the chain to an object, (2) abilities to designate, and (3) communication situations in which abilities are passed on or reinforced (i.e., reference borrowing).

In a grounding, for Devitt, a person perceives an object (preferably face to face), correctly believing it to be an object of a certain very general category. The grounding consists in the person coming to have "grounding thoughts" about that object as a result of the act of perceiving the object. A grounding thought about an object includes a mental representation of that object brought about by an act of perception. The name, having been grounded, can now be used by speakers to refer to the object because a causal link has been established between the initial use of the name and the object, and a causal link can be established between later uses of the name and the initial use. For instance, having named his cat "Nana," a speaker could then exercise his new ability to refer to Nana by saying, for example, "Nana is hungry." He could speak to his friends about Nana, thus enabling them in turn to refer to Nana. These friends (and their uses of the name "Nana") are causally linked to Nana by perceiving (hearing) the speaker's utterances in which reference to Nana is made. Since to perceive is to be causally affected, they are now causally linked in a sense to Nana. These friends now have the ability to refer to Nana because of this causal linkage.

With this summary survey of the standard views of reference and names in mind, Eco's position can be explicated.

2. Interpretation and unlimited semiosis

From his earlier writings (e.g. 1979, 11) to his later works (e.g. 1995, 12), Eco has indicated an affinity to speech act theory. In particular, he has noted (2000, 280 and 1990, 208) an acceptance of P. F. Strawson's (1950) proposal that referring is not something an expression does but something someone can use an expression to do. Speakers, not expressions, refer. Citing Strawson, Eco remarks that giving the meaning of an expression is to give general directions for its use to refer to particular objects or persons and giving the meaning of a sentence (rather than of an expression) is to give general directions for its use in making true or false assertions.

Eco's emphasis on the "doings" of language, including referring expressions, is reminiscent not only of William James's notion of "workings" and of John Dewey's notion of "living behaviors," but also of Charles Peirce's view that referring expressions are signs, involving both interpretation and unlimited semiosis, both aspects of language and reference that Eco repeatedly stresses.

These stresses have evolved over time, however. Though sometimes misunderstood as propounding an idealist, or a there-is-nothing-beyond-the-text, view, some of Eco's early writings on semiosis sounded just that way:

> Therefore the process of unlimited semiosis shows us how signification, by means of continual shiftings which refer a sign back to another sing or string of signs, circumscribes *cultural units* in an asymptotic fashion, without even allowing one to touch them directly, though making them accessible through other units. Thus one is never obliged to replace a cultural unit by means of something which is not a semiotic entity, and no cultural unit has to be explained by some platonic, psychic or objectal entity. Semiosis explains itself by itself: this continual circularity is the normal condition of signification and even allows communicational processes to use signs in order to mention things and states of the world. (1979, 198)

What Eco means by "unlimited semiosis" is drawn from Peirce's conception of a sign, or something that represents something to someone. Every sign involves an object (or thing represented), a sign (or that which does the representing), and an interpretant (or that by which the sign represents). An interpretant is not an interpreter (such as a person) and Peirce was purposefully omitting from a sign's conception that it must be intentionally emitted or artificially produced. Rather, an interpretant is that which guarantees the validity of the sign. With respect to the issue of unlimited semiosis, the point, for Eco, is that an interpretant is another representation. As he notes, "in order to establish what an interpretant is, it is necessary to name it by another sign and so on. At this point there begins a process of *unlimited semiosis*" (1976, 68). Interpetants can be varied: an (apparently) equivalent sign-vehicle in another semiotic system (e.g., a drawing of a dog to correspond to the word "dog"); an index directed to a single object (e.g., pointing); an emotive association which acquires the value of an established connotation (e.g., dog signifying fidelity), among others.

While Eco is insistent that "interpretation is indefinite" (1992, 32), he is equally insistent that "there are somewhere criteria for limiting interpretation" (1992, 40). As he phrases it, there is not only the intention of authors and audiences, but also of texts themselves. One example (among a number that he gives) of the limits of interpretation and of the constraints of a text is the following story, taken from John Wilkins's 1641 work, *Mercury; or, the Secret and Swift Messenger*:

> How strange a thing this Art of Writing did seem at its first Invention, we may guess by the late discovered Americans, who were amazed to

see Men converse with Books, and could scarce make themselves believe that a Paper could speak....

There is a pretty Relation to this Purpose, concerning an Indian Slave; who being sent by his Master with a Basket of Figs and a Letter, did by the Way eat up a great Part of his Carriage, conveying the Remainder unto the Person to whom he was directed; who when he had read the Letter, and not finding the Quantity of Figs answerable to what was spoken of, he accuses the Slave of eating them, telling him what the Letter said against him. But the Indian (notwithstanding this Proof) did confidently abjure the Fact, cursing the Paper, as being a false and lying Witness.

After this, being sent again with the like Carriage, and a Letter expressing the just Number of Figs, that were to be delivered, he did again, according to his former Practice, devour a great Part of them by the Way; but before he meddled with any, (to prevent all following Accusations) he first took the Letter, and hid that under a great Stone, assuring himself, that if it did not see him eating the Figs, it could never tell of him; but being now more strongly accused than before, he confesses the Fault, admiring the Divinity of the Paper, and for the future does promise his best Fidelity in every Employment.

Of course, says Eco, we could interpret this story in many ways, but it cannot be interpreted to mean anything whatsoever. If there is something to be interpreted, says Eco, the interpretation must speak of something that must be found somewhere, and in some way respected. Maintaining his commitment to the pragmatics of a speech act approach, Eco avoids saying that a given interpretation is false (though he does not deny this), but minimally points out that some interpretations are infelicitous. Even though there is a difference, for Eco, between interpreting a text and using a text, what and how a text (or, noted earlier, an expression) signifies has to do with what we do with it. This involves two related elements: purpose and coherence.

Citing Peirce again, that "the idea of meaning is such as to involve some reference to a purpose," Eco stresses that purpose connects interpretation and semiosis generally to something outside of language. Above I remarked that, by advocating unlimited semiosis, Eco had been misread as holding some form of idealism. Here he makes it clear that this is not his position. Speaking of purpose and interpretation, he claims: "Maybe it has nothing to do with a transcendental subject, but it has to do with referents, with the external world, and links the idea of interpretation to the idea of interpreting according to a given meaning" (1990, 38). Purpose, as related to interpretation, involves aspects of a text are or can be pertinent to a coherent interpretation. On (at least) one interpretation of the fig story above, figs are in themselves not particularly relevant; the story could have mentioned apples. On (at least) one other interpretation, figs are particularly relevant, as they carry certain connotations (say, biblical). What determines the relevant aspects of what is important for interpretation is not given in isolation, but (1) is a matter of "checking upon the text as a coherent whole" (1992, 65). As will be seen below, this becomes especially important for the issue of reference because Eco rejects the notion that expressions or sentences are taken in isolation.

3. Reference and names

In his essay "On Truth: A Fiction" (1988, 41–59) Eco remarks that "...in order to use a sentence referentially you must grasp its meaning, and in the process of grasping the meaning of *it eats meat* the use of *it* depends on a previous interpretation, not necessarily on a referent" (1988, 52). Likewise, in *The Open Work*, he states, "A sentence such as 'That man comes from Paris', uttered in front of Napoleon during his exile on Saint Helena, must have awakened in him a variety of emotions such as we could not even imagine. In other words, each addressee will automatically complicate — that is to say, personalize — his or her understanding of a strictly referential proposition with a variety of conceptual or emotional references culled from his or her previous experience" (1989, 30). For the present, the point of these remarks is, as was noted above, that Eco rejects the notion that expressions or sentences are taken in isolation. This is not merely the claim that what a speaker refers to is contextualized, but what an expression or term refers to is contextualized. This is not to deny any distinction between speaker reference and semantic reference, but it is to insist that both are a matter of interpretation, interpretation that is ineliminably social: "Every attempt to establish what the referent of a sign is forces us to define the referent in terms of an abstract entity which moreover is only a cultural convention" (1976, 66). By insisting on the "cultural convention" nature of reference, and of signs generally, Eco — once again — is not advocating an idealist position, but rather the contractualist position identified earlier. Of particular concern here is how this contractualist position elucidates reference and names. Two aspects of these issues have been especially highlighted in his writings, his take on rigid designators and his take on haecceities.

For quite some time, Eco has expressed reluctant "acceptance" of the notion of rigid designation. In *Semantics and the Philosophy of Language* (1984), he claimed that this notion, which he associates with both Kripke and Putnam, works not simply because there was an introductory event for the designator (e.g., a baptismal event), but "the encyclopedic set of more or less definite descriptions I was able to provide" (1984, 75). Not only is interpretation inextricable at the baptismal event, but also it is so throughout the intermediary links of speakers using the designator. It is the encyclopedic descriptions, not the baptismal events followed by causal chains of usages, that allow reference to occur, for Eco. He offers several arguments, or at least scenarios, to support this view. One, science fiction, example is the following: In order to avoid future world wars, the United Nations decides to establish a Peace Corps of ISC (Inter-Species Clones). These clones, being independent of national and ethnic heritage, would be fair and unbiased with respect to any conflicts. The UN Assembly, simply to come to some agreement, must speak about this new "natural kind" prior to them existing, indeed in order to make them exist. Eco claims that it is clear that, what would be christened as an ISC would not be some original "thing" but an encyclopedic description of such a thing. Eco takes this science fiction example to show that it is evident that

> ...we use linguistic expressions or other semiotic means to name "things" first met by our ancestors, but it is also evident that we frequently use linguistic expressions to describe and to call into life "things" that will exist only after and because of the utterance of our expressions. In these cases, at least, we are making recourse more to stereotypes and encyclopedic representations than to rigid designators. (1984, 76).

One can object that Eco has missed an important point of the causal view, namely that how the reference is fixed is unimportant. The point is that, once fixed, the designator is rigid; it always picks out the same thing in any possible world in which it picks out anything at all. However, Eco thinks the attempt to separate out any purely semantic features of reference from pragmatic ones will not work. Insofar, he says, that the view of rigid designation proffers that names are directly linked to the essence of what they designate, and insofar as this view takes such an essence as a solid core of ontological properties "that survive any counterfactual menace" (1990, 209), it seems adamantly to exclude any kind of contextual knowledge. Such exclusion, for Eco, is illusory at best. As he puts it, in order to use the designator properly, a cultural chain is needed, a chain of *word-of-mouth information*. The only way to make this view understandable, or at least coherent, is to take the pragmatic dimension for granted, as it is what survives the process of transmission across usages that constitutes the identifiable essence of what is designated. For Eco,

> The causal theory of proper names could only work if one (i) takes for granted that it is possible to teach and to learn the name of an object x by direct ostension and (ii) the ostension takes place in face of an object that is able to survive its namer.... But what happens when one names a human individual, let us say, Parmenides? The causal chain is broken when Parmenides dies. From this point on, the speaker w telling the hearer y something about Parmenides must introduce into the picture

some definite descriptions.... The speaker y must learn to use the name *Parmenides* according to the set of contextual instructions provided by w and is obliged to resort to contextual elements every time he wants to ascertain whether the name is used in the right sense: *Paremenides? Do you mean the philosopher?* It is true that the instructions provided by w "causes" the competence of y, but from this point of view every theory of language is a causal one.... It is exactly such a form of nonphysical and indirect causality that calls for a pragmatic explanation of the process. (1990, 209–10)

Reiterating that reference (i.e., referential usages) not be taken in isolation, Eco claims that designators, including names and definite descriptions, have the function of providing speakers and hearers with elements necessary for identification of a given thing. This identification is a process, one that is not only distinct from the presupposition of existence, but is dependent on pragmatic phenomena of cooperation and negotiation.

In his more semiological mode of addressing this point, Eco claims, "The problem of proper names is similar to the problem of iconic signs, which are commonly supposed to refer to someone without there being a precise code to establish who this person is (for example, images of people).... The expression /Napoleon/ denotes a cultural unit which is well defined and which finds a place in a semantic field of historical entities." (1976, 86–87) Eco's latest works, both fiction and nonfiction, reiterate this view, as, for example, in the following conversation from his latest novel, *Baudolino*:

> "Tell me one thing at least," [Baudolino] interrupted her. "You are the hypatias, in the name of Hypatia: this I can understand. But what is your name?"
> "Hypatia."
> "No, I mean you — yourself — what are you called? To distinguish you from other hypatia... I'm asking: what do your companions call you?"
> "Hypatia."
> "But this evening you will go back to the place where all of you live, and you will meet one hypatia before the others. How will you greet her?"
> "I will wish her a happy evening. That's what we do."
> "Yes, but if I go back to Pndapetzim, and I see, for example, a eunuch, he will say to me: Happy evening, O Baudolino. You will say: Happy evening, O ... What?"
> "If you like, I will say: Happy evening, Hypatia."
> "So all of you then are called Hypatia."

"Naturally. All hypatias are called Hypatia, no one is different than the others, otherwise she wouldn't be a hypatia."

"But if one hypatia or another is looking for you, just now when you are absent, and asks another hypatia if she has seen that hypatia who goes around with a unicorn named Acacious, how would she say it?"

"Just as you did. She is looking for the hypatia who goes around with a unicorn named Acacious." (2002, 421–2)

Carrying the semiological mode further, Eco (1984) considers whether a mirror image is, or at least functions like, a proper name or rigid designator:

In an extreme attempt to find one more relation between mirror images and words, we might compare mirror images to proper names.... [But] there is a difference between a mirror image and a proper name, in that a mirror image is an *absolute proper name* as it is an absolute icon. In other words, the semiotic dream of proper names being immediately linked to their referent ... arises from a sort of *catoptric nostalgia*.... Such catoptric apparatus would be a rigid-designation apparatus. There is no linguistic contrivance which would provide the same guarantee, not even a proper name, because in this event two conditions of absolutely rigid designation would be missing: (1) the original object might well not exist at the moment and also might never have existed; (2) there would be no guarantee that the name corresponds to that object alone and to no other having similar characteristics.

We therefore come to discover that the semantics of rigid designation is in the end a (pseudo-) semantics of the mirror image and that no linguistic term can be a rigid designator (just as there is no absolute icon). If it cannot be absolute, any rigid designator other than a mirror image, any rigid designator whose rigidity may be undermined in different ways and under different conditions, becomes a *soft or slack designator*. As absolutely rigid designators, mirror images alone cannot be questioned by counterfactuals. In fact, I could never ask myself (without violating the pragmatic principles regulating any relation with mirrors): "If the object whose image I am perceiving had properties other than those of the image I perceive, would it still be the same object?" But this guarantee is provided precisely by the threshold-phenomenon a mirror is. The theory of rigid designation falls a victim of the magic of mirrors. (1984, 211–3)

Given the distortions of "fun house" mirrors, I would add that one could indeed ask oneself whether the object whose image one is perceiving would be the same object if it had properties other than those presently perceived!

It has been remarked that Eco has expressed a reluctant acceptance of rigid designation. The sense of acceptance has to do with the fact that Eco acknowledges that at some level there can be acts of reference that do not presuppose an understanding of the meaning of the terms used for referring (i.e., that we can use designators simply to designate, without knowing the meaning of the term or whether the referent even exists). Nevertheless, acts of referring involve an inherent semiological element of trust and reveal an ambiguity in the notion of rigid designation. The ambiguity is this: on the one hand, we are supposed to assume that the referent causes the "appropriateness" of the reference, while, on the other hand, we are to assume that the receiver of the name must intend to use it with the same reference as the person from whom the receiver learned it. This is not, says Eco, the same thing. The second assumption relates to what Eco means by speaking of the element of trust. In mundane communicative interaction, we accept a great number of references on trust. For example, if someone tells us that he must take urgent leave of absence because Virginia is ill, we accept that "Virginia" refers to someone who is in some way dependent upon the speaker for Virginia's well-being. "We collaborate in the act of reference, even when we know nothing of the referent and even when we do not know the meaning of the term used by the speaker." (2000, 292)

Among the aspects of this communicative trust is the feature of names that they cannot be merely denotative. If proper names did not have content (i.e., if they were not to some extent connotative), not only could we not use antonomasias, such as "The Voice" for Frank Sinatra, but also we could not use individual names as the sum of properties, such as "He is a real Rambo." The point here for Eco is that designators, including names, have descriptive content, not merely accidently, but inherently. This content is linked to the contractual, social nature of names and of reference generally. Rigid designation might have an introductory function, to get the contract started, so to speak, but it does only that. Names then take on a social life of their own.

A second concern that Eco raises about the causal view of names, besides general concerns about rigid designation, is the nature of the underlying commitment to haecceities. While acknowledging that a commitment to the "thisness" of some individual does not constitute a commitment to any necessary essence of that individual (at least, essence in terms of properties), Eco still requires that there be some principle of individuation in order for haecceity — and, for that matter, the notion of rigid designation — to make sense. But it is just this notion of a principle of individuation that is very much a matter of negotiation within the contractual theory of meaning. As Eco phrases it, "the attribution of identity (or authenticity) depends on different parameters, negotiable or negotiated from one time to the next" (2000, 323). In supporting this claim, he provides some examples, such as:

1. The abbey of Saint Guinness was built in the twelfth century. Scrupulous abbots had it restored day by day, replacing stones and fixtures as they fell victim to wear and tear, and so from the point of view of materials the abbey we see today no longer has anything to do with the original (i.e., there are no original parts remaining). From the point of view of architectonic design it is the same one. If we favor the criterion of identity of form over identity of materials, and moreover, if we introduce the criterion of homolocality (the modern abbey stands in exactly the same place as did the original), from a tourist's point of view, we are led to say that this is the same abbey.

2. Citizen Kane, who dreams of building the perfect residence, finds it in Europe in the abbey of Cognac, which has remained intact since the time of its construction. He buys it, has it dismantled, with the stones numbered before having it shipped back to Xanadu, and then reconstructed. Is this the same abbey? To Kane, yes, as his criterion is identity of materials (and perhaps form). But if the appropriate criterion (i.e., principle of individuation) is homolocality, then no.

The point, of course, is that there is a pragmatics of individuation and of haecceities, so to insist, as Kripke does, that we can make sense of rigid designators outside of the social, contractual nature of reference and names, is simply mistaken.[1]

4. Inference and evidence

In a discussion of Peirce on concepts and sensations, Eco says that "to name is always to make a hypothesis" (2000, 62). In addition, Eco claims that "inferential processes (mainly under the form of Peircean *abduction*) stand at the basis of every semiotic phenomenon" (1984, 8). These remarks point to a crucial feature of Eco's conception of interpretation being at the core of reference and names. To see this, Peirce's notion of abduction (which he also at times calls "hypothesis") first needs to be explained.[2]

Peirce distinguished three types of inference: deduction, induction, and abduction. He distinguishes them using what he calls a Rule, a Case, and a Result. Peirce illustrates these notions with an example of white beans selected from a bag of beans. A deductive inference is characterized as follows:

Rule: All the beans from this bag are white.
Case: These beans are from this bag.
    Therefore:
Result: These beans are white.

An inductive inference is characterized differently:

> Case: These beans are from this bag.
> Result: These beans are white.
>   Therefore (probably):
> Rule: All the beans from this bag are white.

Finally, an abductive inference has the form:

> Rule: All the beans from this bag are white.
> Result: These beans are white.
>   Therefore (probably):
> Case: These beans are from this bag.

How this relates to reference and names is that the interpretation of signs is inescapably abductive. Eco draws an example from Augustine, pointing out the limitations and underlying presuppositions about ostension. Here Augustine asks Adeodatus how he would explain the meaning of the expression "to walk." Adeodatus states that he would simply start walking (with, we imagine, some sort of verbal clue such as "it's to do this!"). But what would he do to explain the expression if he were already walking, ask Augustine (i.e., if the action and "do this" didn't work). Adeodatus exclaims that he would just walk faster. Augustine, of course, notes that this would not distinguish "to walk" from "to hurry up," noting that ostensive signs do not provide or clarify meaning by means of simply induction. Eco insists that a frame of reference is necessary, a metalinguistic (or, rather, a metasemiotic) rule expressed in some way prescribing what rule should be used in order to understand ostension. But at this point we have already arrived at the mechanism of abduction. Only via hypothesizing Adeodatus's behavior (Result) as a Case of a Rule will any sense be made. "Abduction," Eco states, "is, therefore, the tentative and hazardous tracing of a system of signification rules which will allow the sign to acquire its meaning." (1984, 40)

Names, of course, are a species of signs. Another example illustrates how this conception of abductive inference directly connects to reference and names. It is taken from Voltaire's *Zadig* and involves the character Zadig making reference to a dog and a horse he had never encountered. One day while walking near a wood, Zadig is approached by the Queen's Chief Eunuch who asks if Zadig has seen the Queen's dog. Though he hadn't, he replied that the dog was actually a bitch, a very small spaniel that had recently had puppies, that its left forefoot was lame and it had very long ears. Just at that moment, the Master of the King's Hounds came by and asked Zadig if he had seen the king's horse pass by. Though he hadn't, he replied that the horse was the best galloper in the stable, it was fifteen hands high, with a very small hoof; as well, its tail was three-and-one-half feel long, the studs on its bit were of 23 carat gold and its shoes of eleven scruple silver. The Chief Eunuch and the Master of the King's Hounds are astonished that Zadig could know these things about the animals, not having seen them. (Indeed, they did not believe he hadn't seen them.) Zadig then explained how he inferred these properties of the animals. For example, he saw animal tracks on the sand and judged them (based on past experience) to be dog prints; the sand was always less hollowed by one paw than by the other three; the marks of horse-shoes were all perfectly equally spaced; from the marks his hoofs made on certain pebbles he knew (based on past experience) the horse had been shod with eleven scruple silver; etc. Using certain designators as identity operators in the context of his discussions (e.g., *she* had recently had puppies, *its* tail was a certain length, *the* dog, etc.), Zadig engaged in abductive reasoning while making reference to the unseen animals. In Eco's "retelling" of this incident, as he incorporates it in his *The Name of the Rose*, Brother William (i.e., Zadig) even correctly uses the horse's name, Brunellus, though no name had been uttered in his presence. The point here is that Zadig is able to refer based on his abductive inferences of semiological information.

Closely connected to this feature of naming as hypothesis is the in-eliminability of evidence in relation to reference. Zadig's ability to refer to the dog and horse (and his ability qua Brother William to use "Brunellus" to refer to the king's horse) is dependent upon evidence culled, in this case, from non-linguistic signs. Clearly, what counts as evidence are signs carrying some recognized or enunciated similarity to other signs. Eco states three conditions on signs being so related: (1) it cannot be explained more economically, (2) it points to a single cause[3] (or very limited set), and (3) it fits in with other evidence. The importance here is not so much for "normal" cases of evidence, such as clues leading to inferences about a crime. Rather, the point about evidence relates to how even names can be used and understood, and that they are so used and understood only against a background of inference and interpretation.

Appealing to Putnam's notion of using expressions successfully as part of a community of speakers, and relying on the use in some sense that is determined by "expert" speakers, Eco gives the following example:

> For example, faced with the sentence *Napoleon was born in Cambridge*, convinced as I am that *my* Napoleon was born in Ajaccio, by no means do I agree to use the name according to the intentions of the Community, because, out of the principle of charity at least, I immediately suspect that the speaker intends to refer to *another* Napoleon. Therefore I do my best to check the appropriateness of the reference, trying to induce my

interlocutor to interpret the [nuclear content of the expression] that he makes correspond to the name *Napoleon*, to discover perhaps that his Napoleon is a used car salesman born in this century, and so I find myself faced with a banal case of homonymy. Or I realize that my interlocutor intends to refer to my Napoleon, and therefore intends to make a historical proposition that defies current encyclopedic notions (and therefore the Mind of the Community). In such a case I would proceed to ask him for convincing proof of his proposition. (2000, 300–301)

Just who has been referred to by the use of the name "Napoleon" here is in part a matter of interpretation and inference, with evidence playing an important role in the inference. On the relation between naming and evidence, Robert Steinman (1982) has shown that the causal chain connecting an object and an utterance of its name is not necessary and suggested a spectrum of cases that involve the relationship between naming and evidence. Steinman showed the causal chain to not be a necessary condition for reference to succeed with the following example. Suppose Bob is at a party and sees the wife of his friend Dave. During their conversation, Dave's wife informs Bob that Dave names all of his pets 'Sal'. She also tells Bob that, Dave being a one-pet-at-a-time man, there is never any confusion as to what he is referring to when he utters the name 'Sal'. (At any time, Dave has at most one pet and that pet's name is 'Sal'.) Several days later, Bob comes over to Dave's house and Dave shows Bob his new pet goldfish. Upon seeing the fish for the first time, Bob remarks, "Sal sure is a fine specimen!" In this case, Bob's utterance of the name is not causally connected to the object, even though he successfully referred to the object. The evidence that Bob has about the name of the object (Dave is a one-pet man, Dave names all of his pets 'Sal', Dave's wife is known to be a reliable person, who always tells the truth, etc.) is what made successful reference possible. And the larger point here with Eco is the inherent connection between names and our ability to refer (as well as their ability to refer), interpretation, and Eco's contractual view of reference.[4]

NOTES

1. In his earlier works, especially *The Role of the Reader*, Eco's account of haecceity and individuation is intimately tied up with a Peircean semiotic view. Here he claims that "this object is only such insofar as it is thought under a certain profile" (1979, 181). Being a sign, anything, including any "thisness," must involve an interpretation (or representamen) and that carries with it the unlimited semiosis noted above. This necessarily includes an element of habit, or law, required for the general applicability of the notion of "thisness" (e.g., "this" entails "not that").

2. Eco cites this example from Peirce on a number of occasions, such as (1976, 131), (1983, 203), (1990, 157).

3. Though Eco does not delve into the nature of cause, obviously, from a semio-logical point of view, whatever counts as a cause is some form of sign and one that presupposes an underlying abductive relation.

4. The connection to Wittgenstein, via Steinman here, is neither accidental nor incidental for Eco. In *Kant and the Platypus*, he makes an explicit connection to Wittgenstein by citing the latter's remarks that one must not confuse the meaning of a name with the bearer of a name (see Wittgenstein's *Philosophical Investigations*, section 40). Eco claims that "acts of reference are possible only insofar as we know the meaning of the terms used for referring" (2000, 288), suggesting a view that runs counter to Kripke's notion of rigid designation.

REFERENCES

Devitt, Michael. (1981). *Designation* (New York: Columbia University Press).

Eco, Umberto. (1976) *A Theory of Semiotics* (Bloomington: Indiana University Press).

———. (1979) *The Role of the Reader* (Bloomington: Indiana University Press).

———. (1983) *The Name of the Rose* (New York: Harcourt, Brace, Jovanovich).

———. (1984) *Semiotics and the Philosophy of Language* (Bloomington: Indiana University Press).

———. (1987) "Meaning and Denotation," *Synthese* 73, 549–568.

———. (1989) *The Open Work* (Cambridge, MA: Harvard University Press).

———. (1990) *The Limits of Interpretation* (Bloomington: Indiana University Press).

———. (1992) *Interpretation and Overinterpretation* (Cambridge: Cambridge University Press).

———. (1994) *Six Walks in the Fictional Woods* (Cambridge, MA: Harvard University Press, 1994.

———. (1995) *The Search for a Perfect Language* (Cambridge, MA: Blackwell).

———. (1998) *Serendipities* (New York: Columbia University Press).

———. (2000) *Kant and the Platypus* (New York: Harcourt Brace).

———. (2002) *Baudolino* (New York: Harcourt Brace).

Eco, Umberto, and Thomas A. Sebeok, eds. (1983) *The Sign of Three* (Bloomington: Indiana University Press).

Eco, Umberto, Marco Santambrogio, and Patrizia Violi, eds. (1988) *Meaning and Mental Representation* (Bloomington: Indiana University Press).

Frege, Gottlob. (1997) *The Frege Reader*, ed. Michael Beraney (Oxford: Blackwell).

Kripke, Saul. (1980) *Naming and Necessity* (Cambridge, MA: Harvard University Press).

Peirce, Charles S. (1931–35, 1958) *Collected Papers of Charles Sanders Peirce*, 8 vols., ed. Charles Hartshorne, Paul Weiss, and Arthur Burks (Cambridge, MA: Harvard University Press).

Putnam, Hilary. (1975) *Mind, Language and Reality* (Cambridge, MA: Cambridge University Press).

Russell, Bertrand. (1912) *The Problems of Philosophy* (London: Williams and Norgate).

Searle, John. (1969) *Speech Acts: An Essay in the Philosophy of Language* (Cambridge, UK: Cambridge University Press).

Strawson, Peter. (1950) "On Referring," *Mind* 59, 320–344.

Steinman, Robert. (1982) "Naming and Evidence," *Philosophical Studies* 41, 179–192.

Wittgenstein, Ludwig. (1953) *Philosophical Investigations*, trans. G. E. M. Anscombe (New York: Macmillan).

David Boersema
Professor of Philosophy
Department of Philosophy
Pacific University
Forest Grove, Oregon 97116
United States

Contemporary Pragmatism
Vol. 2, No. 1 (June 2005), 185–201

Editions Rodopi
© 2005

Pragmatism and Poststructuralism: Cultivating Political Agency in Schools

Sarah M. McGough

While the differences between pragmatist and poststructural views may often appear insurmountable, I argue here that putting the two in dialogue offers solutions to particular problems within each tradition, especially as they relate to agency. I describe John Dewey and Judith Butler's theories of agency and analyze the political acts and educational implications to which each account gives rise. I show how each theory rescues the other from pitfalls and, when read together, a more robust vision of agency and political change relative to education is formed. I conclude by depicting how this agency can be cultivated in classrooms.

The field of philosophy of education traces a strong legacy to the work of the American pragmatists. Their interest in knowledge through inquiry, the process of growth, and the flourishing of democracy have greatly impacted the ways educational theorists have depicted the process and goals of education. While not as obvious as in more overtly political philosophy, central to pragmatist theory has been an account of the human subject, its role as an agent, and its ability to effect political change. Recently, many philosophers of education have posed serious challenges to the underlying assumptions pragmatists hold regarding the nature of the student and the best approaches to living life well that schools foster. In particular, contemporary philosophers of education persuaded by the work of Michel Foucault and that of more recent poststructuralists, often struggle to make sense of agency, intention, and the role of the individual subject, especially in the context of social justice issues, identity, and education.

While the differences between pragmatist and poststructural views may at times appear insurmountable, I will argue here that putting the two in dialogue and artfully combining them offers solutions to particular problems within each tradition, especially as they relate to agency. When each is critically informed by the other, a fruitful way for understanding political change is revealed. Finally, this new sense of agency and political change gives rise to suggestions for implementation in a primary location of agency cultivations, schools.

Within this paper, I will describe two theories of agency offered by key figures within each tradition: John Dewey, who has offered the most comprehensive pragmatist understanding of agency, and Judith Butler, whose contemporary interpretation of agency is particularly intriguing. The theories show considerable similarity as well as important points of difference and the fruitfulness of reading them together has largely been overlooked. I will begin by delineating Butler's theory of agency, including the political acts to which such an account gives rise. Then, I will do the same for Dewey, highlighting the philosophers' points of contention and agreement along the way. Next, I will show how each theory rescues the other from certain pitfalls and, when combined, a more robust vision of agency and political change relative to education is formed. While I will allude to educational aspects of each theorist's account of agency as I go, the concluding section will draw out some educational implications in more detail.

1. Judith Butler, subjugation, and discursive agency

Understanding Butler's theory of agency entails first understanding her unique depiction of the process of becoming an embodied subject. Drawing on Foucault's theory of power as productive, Butler describes a process of discursive construction, where the circulating power of cultural norms and practices brings the subject into being and produces the effect of a bounded, identity-marked, material body. Through continual repetition of identity defining acts and being interpellated by others, a stable subject with an apparently coherent identity results. The subject is forced to continue the performance of such an identity in order to maintain its constitution as a viable being — to have a social position that is recognized and which affords the subject the ability to speak and be heard. This process of subjugation is not a single act or event, but rather a series of discursive reiterations that cite norms and cultural constraints. For Butler, performativity is the repetition of cultural norms and codes, the activity of which styles and constitutes us because it has the ability to produce what it names. The traits and identities imparted are then sustained through bodily comportment and the continued force of cultural structures. Traits that appear natural or as essences, like gender, come from without with such force and constancy that they appear as though internally sprung and their seeming naturalness goes largely unquestioned.

The subject is compelled to perform identity constraints and cite norms and it is in this regard that Butler breaks from her humanist forerunners, including the pragmatists. Working against the notion of a prediscursive agent who chooses to do a deed, Butler shows that the subject must performatively repeat these norms in order to maintain its status as a recognizable human. Importantly, however, Butler adds that this non-humanist subject is not entirely culturally determined and, even though constructed, the very circulations of power that constitute the subject render it capable of agency.[1] Butler, here, is also responding to her structuralist counterparts who also describe subject construction; because they posit that it is an event which happens once and for all, they deny the possibility of agency and radical change of cultural structures.

Because performativity is a compelled, ongoing process, a space for agency occurs in the way that one varies required repetition, resignifies language, or misappropriates the essentializing identity terms thrust upon one by others. When identity is understood as the signification of political signs, agency becomes resignification and variation of necessary repetition and is capable of revealing signification as never fully fixed or determined. The subject's exploitation of the unstable language which constitutes him or her is often spontaneous and unpredictable. It is spawned in minute instances of power redeployment, rather than transcendence, and is capable of producing significant effects over time insofar as it reveals the problematically constructed nature of identity-defined life and difficulties with the social institutions that support it. Performatives are provisionally successful not because they emit from a subject's intention, but rather because they bear a history of authority through their citations of established practices.[2] Butler's agent, then, wields neither sovereign power nor intention. Agency is an effect and redeployment of power rather than a property of a person.

Given Butler's account of the process of becoming an agent, certain exercises of agency as political protest and change follow. While keeping in mind that the success of political insurrection is always provisional according to Butler, subjugation and its inherent acts of violence and exclusion call for insurrection. When subjects are interpellated and forced to repeat cultural constraints, they continually define and reinforce a boundary of which types of life and living are acceptable and which are not. Thereby hierarchies of identity and living and, moreover for Butler, alterity, are established. While unspoken and largely unimaginable, a realm of exclusion is constructed and maintained as that opposed to which identity-based living is defined. Those who do not fulfill cultural standards (and here the language is tricky, for they cannot exist as linguistic subjects if they do not do so) or who fail to uphold viable interpellations are relegated to this realm of exclusion and are often kept there through violent acts. They are silenced and alternative ways of living and being are foreclosed.

Although we can never achieve total inclusivity of what counts as human (because categories always have boundaries), we can work toward producing resignifications that reveal exclusions and draw in those previously excluded. Butler urges us to work toward connections and against exclusions.

Democracy and associated ways of living become more radically inclusive for Butler when terms of exclusion (like 'queer') are affirmed by discursive outliers, enabling them to return to the realm of discussion. Additionally, agency can expose the failures of cultural norms to achieve their goals, including the normative aim of cohesive, unified identity. Drawing on Slavoj Žižek and Jacques Lacan, Butler argues that identity categories never achieve their intended unity. Rather, a space of indeterminacy is left open where subjects may ponder or display the ways in which they do not fit under certain identity labels. Symbolic law and norms may be called into question by failing to perform as a uniform subject or by revealing how the law has created more than it intended. Finally, subjects can show how striving for identity coherence requires that one continually distinguish oneself from the abject who has been excluded from one's identity category, thereby causing distance and dif- ferentiation, rather than connection between people.

Rather than perpetuating differentiation and exclusion via expanding the list of acceptable identity positions, identity categories should be corrupted or rendered ambiguous according to Butler. They should not, however, be pre- maturely denied or erased because they are necessary for cultural existence and the signification of certain states of living (such as 'woman' as subordination or a list of sexual attributes). Butler's agency appreciates the democratic political potential of these categories as open and contested and encourages subjects to invoke the categories, especially as terms of affiliation for political action, while simultaneously critiquing them. She aims for a "crossroads" connecting identity positions out of acknowledgment of their founding and perpetual acts of exclusion and she envisions this space as one of connection and resignification of identity terms.[3]

2. John Dewey, construction through transaction, and agency via habit

Like Butler, understanding agency entails understanding the making and activities of the subject for Dewey. More explicitly for Dewey, however, the subject he describes is often that of the child, the student. Subjectivity begins, at base, with the organism. Organisms are body-minds which form and are dynamically formed by transactions with the environment, including language and other organisms. Transaction is an ongoing process of exchange which brings the body into being. While Dewey at times appears to uphold a belief in the prediscursive materiality and substance metaphysics that Butler denies,[4] reading his account of transaction through a poststructural lens and with an emphasis on the process of transaction suggests that there is no organism or essence that exists prior to transaction. Rather, the transaction brings the organism into being. It shapes the body, behavior, and knowledge, producing a recognizable person. Transaction puts the process first, as opposed to interaction which privileges an already existent subject. Transaction assumes distinctions between organism and environment arise from this process, rather than predate it.[5] Finally, transaction is a continuous process that subjects must continue in order to maintain their status in the world as living, acting, efficacious beings. Like Butler's compelled discursive performativity, the subject actively and necessarily participates in the establishment and perpetuation of its existence.

For Dewey, a key player in transaction is impulse. Impulses are native bursts of energy, typically taking the form of demands for actions or objects that can bring about action. Impulses try to find opportunities where power can be enacted. Butler's more nuanced theory of power, via Foucault, proves useful here in rescuing Dewey from what, at times, appears to be a belief in the wielding of power from without. Impulses might more appropriately be understood as drawing out or directing power that is already circulating within the subject and redeploying it in terms of the constitutive power structures that enable being. This sense is clearly evident within Dewey's own words, "It is not so much a demand for power as search for an opportunity to use a power already existing."[6]

Impulse for Dewey can be explosive, intelligent, and gradually played out, or suppressed and tucked away. While Butler's more spontaneous sense of agency might be more aligned with explosive impulses, Dewey sides with impulses that are investigated and gradually played out. Dewey argues that rigid customs avoid and suppress impulses because they are seen as threatening. Opposingly, he insists that impulses can be taken up as fruitful agents of change. Because of this, he targets the classroom as a space for inquiring into one's impulses, their potential meaning, and how they might be constructively put to use. Dewey envisions impulses as a font of ingenuity and innovation and attempts to harness them through intelligent inquiry and specified purposes. Impulses strike out in new directions, but always with the goal of restoring unified action.

Butler, on the other hand, posits a bodily excess that is not pinned down by normative structures, interpellation, or current ways of understanding the world and can be used to work against the essentializing process of unification. To explain, Butler depicts the body as exceeding interpellation from others and the speech acts it issues itself.[7] This excess, with its newness and potential for change, shows considerable similarity to Dewey's impulse.[8] Problematically, both theorists pose an organic or bodily aspect of agency that is native or outside of language, aspects which seem to contradict their theories of subject construction and which are key to understanding agency and change. Neither offers a sufficient account of where impulses or bodily excess originate relative to cultural and linguistic constraints, leaving a flaw in their theories of agency.

While impulse for Dewey, and linguistic insurrection for Butler, occur at the level of the individual, Dewey's notion of agency moves to the level of the social through his discussion of habit and transaction. Habits organize impulses into predispositions in light of situations that necessarily include the environment and other people. Habits, unlike impulse, are acquired ways of being that are formed through interaction with social institutions and cultural norms, as well as the organizing force of intelligent inquiry. Taken together, habits render the body as a pattern of activities and behaviors. In Dewey's words, "All habits are demands for certain kinds of activity; and they constitute the self. In any intelligible sense of the word will they *are* will."[9] There is no complete person behind the habit, just as there is no doer behind the deed for Butler. We do not use habits at will because we do not preexist them. "The use itself *is* the habit, and 'we are the habit'." (Dewey 1922b, 21)[10]

Habits can be routine and mechanical skills or adeptness that enable people to operate in the world with ease. Habits often appear as corporeal: as bodily comportment, appearance, and gesture. More significant for Dewey is an understanding of habit as a predisposition to act or a sensitivity to ways of being, rather than an inclination to repeat identical acts or content precisely. The compulsive urge to act is propelled by desire. Habits give rise to desire and organize the body and environment in ways that allow desires to be pursued. The pursuit of desire is possible because habits carry out judgment and intelligence. They organize perceptions, form ideas and meaning, and incorporate and work with the environment to develop 'know-how' — knowledge of how to act in the world. Habits provide "working capacities" that enable the enactment of thoughts and desires.[11]

While perhaps most obviously calls to bodily action, habits are often linked to knowledge. Steven Fesmire clarifies, "Pragmatism views habit not in terms of a condition *reflex*, but in terms of intelligent reconstruction of problematic situations."[12] When formed tentatively as hypotheses in light of intelligent foresight into future, unpredictable, circumstances, habits can be flexible agents of change whose form emerges as situations unfold.[13] Or, in Dewey's words, "the intellectual element in a habit fixes the relation of the habit to varied and elastic use, and hence to continued growth."[14] In this way, habits, as intimately tied to intelligent reflection, are projective and sites of agency. They can be changed in ways that change the subject and, through transaction, can effect change in the world as well. The heart of agency lies in the process of acquiring new habits and changing old ones.

Even when revealed as oppressive or unjust, habits cannot be simply dropped at will. As for Butler, because the subject is constituted and enabled by cultural structures and norms, we should not try to overthrow habits entirely (as though we could be freed from them), but rather rework them in liberating ways. Indeed it is nonsensical to suppose the complete removal of habit.

Instead, Dewey proposes the replacement of old habits by those that are more intelligent and just. Ideally because habits are "adjustments *of* the environment, not merely *to* it," adopting new habits can change the environmental pheno-mena which produced the problematic old habit.[15]

Intriguingly, given the common understanding of habit as ongoing repetition, Dewey argues that habits must not necessarily be repeated. He claims, "Repetition is in no sense the essence of habit. Tendency to repeat acts is an incident of many habits but not of all."[16] Given transaction, repetition only happens after a habit is formed if the environment stays the same and the continued action proves fruitful. Clearly we have seen through Butler that many habits must be repeated, especially those which culturally position the subject and are necessary for continued recognition. Resonating with Butler's claims about the necessity of repetition but the possibility of variation on repetition, Dewey contends that subjects are bound to repeat, but not particular things or reflections of a stagnant world. Rather, they show a proclivity; what and how they repeat may vary. Differing from Butler, however, Dewey's variations on repetition are often provoked by change in the environment or unsatisfactory states. The acquisition of a new habit, for Dewey, also tends to arise more slowly out of the old than does Butler's more spontaneous account of linguistic breaks.

Agency is enhanced for Dewey through the process of intelligent reflection. This is a process of inquiry whereby subjects discover problems with old habits, predict the types of activities that future states of affairs will demand, and then craft and adopt new habitual alternatives. Instances of conflict, impasse, and frustration often develop into problematic situations which call otherwise unconscious habits into view and the search for a new way to act begins. Deliberation involves figuring out what combinations of habits and impulses would likely produce desired activities and consequences. This entails foresight into the future, but Dewey cautions that we cannot fully predict the future, nor should we, for habits should ultimately be concerned with remedying the present situation. The inquiry is not carried out narrowly within the confines of the individual mind, but in the actual transaction between organism and environment occurring at that moment. It involves experimenting with new ways of being and trying them out in concert with the environment.

The experimental nature and plasticity of habit suggests that Dewey should be interpreted as understanding habits themselves as flexible — as being held tentatively, as subject to change, and as not fully determined by normative ways of being. They offer a sense of continuity, where new activity is not simple repetition, nor is it a radical break from the past, but is capable of effecting change both within the individual subject and the surrounding world. They are central to Dewey's notion of growth, but growth without teleology; a key educational ideal and motivation for change lacking in Butler's more undirected notion of variation on performativity. Growth describes how continuous experiences can develop physical, intellectual, and moral capacities — actualizing them and helping them to inform one another so that they continue in a chain (though not necessarily linearly) that enables one to live satisfactorily. Growth expresses the movement invoked by experience which compounds upon itself and freedom depends on the continued development and growth of experience.[17] Insofar as Dewey conceives of freedom as the ability to change oneself, to frame purposes in the world, and to enact environmental change, flexible habits are central to achieving this goal.

Agency is enhanced and educational goals are achieved through practicing the process of changing and developing new habits. For Dewey, this activity is well suited for the classroom. Educational situations can be constructed that raise student awareness of their habits and the ways in which their habits might be implicated in problems, including tendencies to disconnect from students different from oneself, rigidity in traversing a changing world, and failures to communicate with others. Teachers can aid students in the process of intelligent reflection and attune them to their actions and corresponding consequences. Within classrooms, students can engage in activities that link people, like work and civics, thereby helping students to understand the ways their activities effect others, their potential for agency, and their ability to produce political change.

3. Reading Dewey and Butler Together

Both Butler and Dewey offer useful and provocative notions of agency. Both, however, have shortcomings and inconsistencies. This section investigates some of those problems and considers how, when read together, each theory may help rescue the other from certain pitfalls. I will conclude the section by showing how these concerns and possible solutions might help craft a more robust vision of agency.

First, Dewey, despite upholding habits as changeable, at times poses a problematic core of habits that abides. This core provides one the identity and sense of self he believes is necessary for enacting positive freedom (as the ability to frame purposes relative to one's capacities) and is a critical facet of deliberation. For Dewey, identities teach us about ourselves and options available to us. Framing and enacting aims requires a strong, coherent sense of self. Indeed, he calls for learning situations that target our identities and further their expression.[18] While Dewey allows that even this core is a contingent cultural product that may be changed over time, he seems to cherish it in ways that I believe overlook how that core may be complicit in oppressive acts toward others or in stagnant notions of one's self or one's identity group.

Butler provocatively asks, "To what extent is 'identity' a normative ideal rather than a descriptive feature of experience?"[19] As described earlier, Butler reveals the constraining and essentializing ways in which subjects are pressured to fulfill identities — an activity for Butler which is, and should be, doomed to fail. Moreover, in order to enhance agency, Butler insists that we need to forego our efforts to maintain stable categories of self-identity and be willing to be interpellated within and outside of the categories in which we envision ourselves so that we may subversively misrecognize and misrepresent them. Hence Butler presents identity construction as a political process and identity as a political effect, thereby offering up new matter for political change and complicating Dewey's goal of individual identity development. She locates a fruitful future in relinquishing coherence. This suggestion is well-aligned with the notion of agency as power redeployment which does not require internal coherence to be achieved. In this way, she urges Dewey to go one step farther in his support of elastic habits — to trace them all the way down to reveal that fundamental defining identities are not necessary.

Secondly, Butler's criticisms of Pierre Bourdieu's habitus can inform Dewey's notion of habit spelled out here. Habitus and Dewey's habits bear significant resemblance, but differ considerably given Dewey's depiction of transaction. Butler argues that Bourdieu focuses too much on how the habitus is formed, rather than how it or the environment can be changed.[20] She charges him with a more structuralist reading of social institutions as determining the construction of the subject once and for all, therefore eliminating a space for agency and significant change.[21] While Dewey's habits are also largely constructed by present cultural forces, they are not determined. Rather, transaction is a continuous process of subject formation, undergoing continual change. It is not prompted by a stimulus, but rather is always actively engaging with the world around it and the subject's present habits. The process extends in both directions; as the subject is formed and changed, alteration of exterior conditions occurs. Moreover, change of the environment can be specifically targeted when change of habit occurs at the level of intelligent reflection, taking environmental problems into consideration.

Butler contends that in the moments when Bourdieu does describe change of habitus, such change is motivated by environmental necessity. In many instances, change of habit for Dewey is also provoked by changes in the world that demand the subject's adaptation in order to maintain stability. Butler argues that it may never appear necessary to alter certain systems of oppression or hierarchy, thus leaving stagnant and unjust habits in tact. Butler claims that iterability is not narrowly sparked by environmental necessity or the desire for balance. Rather, it typically occurs spontaneously or with the movement of language itself. I largely agree with Butler's criticism that change should not be simply sparked by environmental conditions, but I also think nearly the same critique could be leveled at Butler.[22] It is not clear in her account why subjects would be motivated to change the discursive power structures that constitute them, particularly if they maintain a space of privilege for that subject. Because of these concerns, dealing with unjust habits and systems of oppression is a problem of education. Within schools teachers can craft situations that reveal problems such as white privilege that might otherwise go unnoted or unchallenged by students. Those teachers can also cultivate a standard of assessing equality and identity issues as students judge the success of their actions, thereby highlighting moments and issues in need of alteration and provoking students to engage them. Change of habit, of the performance of identity, and of the social institutions that support them is thus neither the result of environmental necessity nor linguistic happenstance.

Butler is correct, however, in drawing attention to the play and failures of language, for it is there that she identifies a key element missing from Dewey's account of agency and change. It is fair to say that Butler would also apply her criticism of Bourdieu's inability to recognize the break of language onto Dewey.[23] Dewey, too, does not see that the ordinary language that brings us into being can be ruptured by an unexpected, extraordinary speech act. Butler, drawing on Jacques Derrida, locates the power of speech in this break which forcefully interrupts linguistic tradition by introducing the unspeakable out of context, rather than in the linking of language to prior context, as is the case with Bourdieu. This break is able to contest the sedimented ordinary and is the back upon which agency rides. While Dewey certainly includes language within his more encompassing term 'environment', he underestimates its potential as a platform for agency and a more nuanced notion of agency must centrally draw upon this potential.

Problems arise, however, when the play of language seems to exclude an active agent and this is a fault of Butler's theory. As was described earlier, the subject must engage in citation to continue to exist and agency is located within moments of resignification — moments which often occur by chance. Veronica Vasterling has persuasively argued that because the reiteration takes place in the movement of language itself, agents really have limited intention over it.[24] She rightly contends that the resulting notion of agency in not very viable insofar as the subject is not much of an active participant in the shaping of its own existence, the content, and way it cites.[25] Butler fails to show how subjects can actively rework the circumstances in which they find themselves via iteration. A closer reading of Butler does reveal that just because we cannot ensure that our words will be received in the ways we intend, does not mean that we cannot act intentionally. Rather, we can try to steer resignification and the production of certain types of meaning, including the exposure of exclusion I described earlier. Vasterling astutely responds that this can be legitimate agency because it has initiative and intervention, but adds that it must be picked up by others to effect broad change. Dewey's transactional account, which poses a closer linking of people and educational situations where students work together to achieve desired ends, can provide the social aspects and provocation of initiative that makes the more active sense of agency Vasterling seeks complete.

Indeed habit, for Dewey, is inherently social. This differs considerably from Butler's more individualistic account of performativity and iterability. Butler theorizes the agency of the individual and, while accounting for others as the audience of performatives, does not theorize collective social action. For Dewey, habits are never divorced from associated living and with working toward improving life conditions with others. Dewey depicts freedom as intelligent use of habits and the impulses they organize, where intelligence is geared toward growth and social flourishing.[26] Political agency still begins with the individual, but is necessarily and intricately connected to others via transaction. Dewey's notion of political agency is inseparable from living the democratic life. Butler's portrait of linguistic construction, on the other hand, implicates other people, but does not extend back out in the other direction—to show how the political protests of the individual are connected to those of others or their well being.

Because bodily habit, via transaction, is always constituted by influences from without which interact with impulses and inquiry, then necessarily extends back outward to interact with the cultural environment, a stage is set for corporeal enactments that confound the structures that compel and constrain them and often do so publicly and alongside others. While also allowing a space for discursive acts of resistance, Dewey's habit pushes past Butler's adherence to linguistic insurrection and offers a way of understanding the concrete realities of living bodies, including the corporeal experiences of material inequalities and their potential for corporeal resistance. Though Butler asserts that language can have real effects on bodies, habits both display and protest those effects, thereby offering a more complete concept of agency.[27]

Two related critiques have been waged against Butler's oversight of the corporeal aspects of agency. Lois McNay argues that Butler doesn't give an account of the felt, lived experience of gender as performative. McNay claims that this makes Butler's notion of agency seem devoid of actual human experience and social/historical location.[28] Because habits are the most essential aspects of the everyday activities of each individual, they necessarily bear with them that individual's particularity, the conditions of his or her context, and his or her vested interest in the experience of gender and oppression. Nancy Fraser has also argued that Butler doesn't account for embodied intersubjectivity. I believe that when habits are understood in the context of everyday associated living with others, the goals of democracy, and the process of transaction, a more complete picture of embodied intersubjectivity appears.

Fraser has also criticized Butler on another issue, that of the criteria guiding the enactment of agency toward political change. Fraser faults Butler for valorizing resignification as being good simply by virtue of being change and not providing a criteria of what counts as good change.[29] Clearly neither agency nor the ability to resist ensure political effectiveness and Butler does not show us how to analyze the effects acts of resistance do have. Or, as Martha Nussbaum has argued, Butler doesn't differentiate good subversions that confront problems with identity and bad subversions that work against justice.[30] Nussbaum faults Butler for not upholding a normative vision that can guide and access political change, and, while my earlier discussion does show that Butler's depiction of subjugation does point toward certain acts of exclusion revealing protest as important, I believe Fraser and Nussbaum are largely correct. When Dewey is read in contrast to Butler, pragmatism can offer a justification for which reworkings of habit and which instances of political change are good, while still recognizing, as Butler warns, that these criteria themselves are already wrapped up in power. While Dewey would dissuade holding a comprehensive portrait of the good life for the future, the pragmatist notions of truth and flourishing can provide judgment on the goodness and effectiveness of acts, as well as point toward directions for future change. Moreover, when these pragmatist principles are seated within the political ideals of democracy, criteria of equality, justice, and associated living may be drawn upon. While Nussbaum thinks that norms like equality need to be fully articulated, a Deweyan reading of coordinated habit would suggest that these visions do not have to be fully articulated, but rather if their elements are experienced at the level of satisfactory embodied living, they will be sought and maintained.

A ground level criteria that Dewey would uphold is that of constructive communication. As opposed to Butler's linguistic disjoint, which certainly can be fruitful in itself, flexible habits seek to lead us to successful interaction, including communication. Butler's variations on repetition, however, reach a moment of impasse where a problem with the world has been revealed but not resolved. Restored communication for Dewey, is restored coordinated action: action that can work to improve the well being of all parties involved and therefore extends political agency to the acts of a group. Communication is not only a criteria of successful acts of political agency, but is also a tool for fostering them. Insofar as changing one's self relies on or is aided by the observations of others who communicate problems they notice with that person's habits back to him or her, political change becomes a more social process, a process of communication and education. Teachers and students can engage in these types of discussions by acutely watching the habitual activity of other students and sharing their remarks on problems or injustices that those habits present so that they become material for inquiry and change.

When read together, Dewey and Butler's theories of agency show valuable points of overlap and supplement one another in areas of weakness. Both locate agency within the process of subject construction and offer similar accounts of how it is carried out through performativity and habit. Combining Butler's sophisticated account of power, appreciation for linguistic insubordination, and focus on problems of identity coherence, with Dewey's embodied notion of habits, the ongoing process of transaction, and pragmatist and democratic criteria for political effectiveness, offers a more robust notion of political agency which I sum up under the Deweyan inspired name of flexible habits. Flexible habits entail a propensity for change and a sensitivity to resistance that supports and invites acts of corporeal and linguistic insubordination. They target and cultivate a likelihood and a possibility that seems to occur most often unpredictably for Butler. And while still retaining the potential for signifying in unexpected ways and with unintended effects, the process of inquiry and the role of the classroom can make political acts more intelligent, with effects that are seen, foreseen, and experienced. Thereby a more just motivation for and assessment of political agency and activity is offered. More than just a chance resignification, flexible habits entail an active confrontation with the symbolic realm, where conflicts among values and the failures of ideals are targeted and exposed through an intelligent, educational process.

4. Educational implications

The notion of agency emerging here, as informed by both Dewey and Butler, suggests an element of skill in traversing problems well. That skill is the intelligent enactment of flexible habits, including the use of and response to speech. As a skill, it is an ability that can, and perhaps should, be cultivated in the chief social institution of skill building, schools. Without making the effects of political agency through mass teaching clichés or commodities,[31] developing flexible habits can provide resources for countering social problems. Dewey thought democratic action required having certain tools, tools developed through education. Flexible habits provide these tools of democratic agency.

As a skill or tool, agency via flexible habits is something that is reflected upon and intentionally used. In light of my comments earlier, these elements seem to contradict performativity and iterability as described by Butler, especially given that Butler doesn't allow self-reflexivity because one cannot get outside of power to reflect.[32] Following Butler's critic, Veronica Vasterling, I believe political change can still happen in the way Butler describes and yet agents can be reflective and intentional where this sense of intention is not a humanist notion of having complete control over the world.[33] Moreover, their political effectiveness is most likely strengthened by these intelligent activities. Schools could well be tasked with cultivating and refining reflection primarily within the context of problematic situations and reworking habits. Students can learn how to reflect within and because of power and they can learn how their reflections upon their activities helps insure that change is positive.[34] They could also overtly discuss systems of oppression, constraints of identity, and the status of democratic living in order to guide student intention and goals.

Classrooms can provide a space which supports and is sensitive to acts of subversion — a space where alternatives ways of being are tested out and where political change is collectively forged. Such a space would make resistance conceivable, possible, and meaningful. Indeed, such an institutional and social space would bring attention to flexible habits, for otherwise they might go unnoted. It could draw attention to their significance and ways in which others might respond to and join in with the changing habits of an individual student. Not only might teachers unite the acts of their individual students, but they might teach students about and unite them with larger social efforts for change, thereby revealing to students the power of social collaboration and the far reaching effects of individual agency. Robert Westbrook, drawing on Dewey's own words, described this well in terms of Dewey's conception of politics as organized intelligence which analyzes social ends and works to secure them:

> Political activity in a democracy was in the broadest sense an educational enterprise, but this function did not rule out the exercise of power. True education was not 'a cloistered withdrawal from the scene of action,' for 'there is no education when ideas and knowledge are not translated into emotion, interest, and volitions. There must be constant accompanying organization and direction or organized action and practical work. 'Ideas' must be linked to the practical situation, however, hurly-burly that is.[35]

Within each classroom, students can be guided through the process of inquiry, both at the level of reflection and action. They can learn to investigate their subject positions and how they are implicated in the oppression of others or themselves. Through the teaching of history and language arts, students can learn about discursive and material traditions of violence and exclusion. They can learn about the force of injury that certain words and interpellations bear when cited in specific contexts and they can learn how to work against those or rework those terms in ways that become affirmative. More just and positive events of history can teach students "to appreciate the values of social life" and give them motivation to promote it in the present.[36] These types of teachings can raise student moral commitment to injustice such that, as Barbara

Applebaum has suggested, when privileged students learn of their complicity in injustice they are more likely to be less comfortable with their privileged positions and change themselves. Of course, teachers must be careful not to romantically uphold the ideal of an individual "hero" student who can stand outside of the situation and work against injustice.[37] Such voluntaristic activity would overlook Butler's account of subjugation and each individual's ongoing acts of complicity, if not outright injustice, therein. Students cannot choose to abandon their identities, but can invoke their agency to craft subversions of them and to replace elements of their privilege related habits with those that are more just or which disrupt the traditional category they represented. Crossroads between students can be forged during such activity.

Within schools, flexible habits can be targeted in ways that display the ambiguity and arbitrariness of identity. Insofar as apparently natural and fixed identity markers, such as gender and race, are actually habitual, flexible habits, as the ability to vary and resignify even these markers, can reveal that identity is never fully determined and is subject to cultural construction. Communication, as a means and goal of changing habit, can assist students in making sense of and acting on this revealed fact. Teachers can help students understand themselves and envision their future relative to shifting identities that are open to critique.

Within her discussions of performativity and political agency, Butler almost never discusses the role of schools in enhancing agency or being a space where it plays out. And, while Dewey does initially attribute significant influence of schools on developing agency, particularly in the context of cultivating democratic citizens, over time he grew less confident that schools could be the chief location of building political agency and democracy.[38] However, given the notion of agency constructed here from both philosophers, schools can be key places where students develop political agency and enact it in pursuit of social goals and justice.

NOTES

1. Judith Butler, *Bodies that Matter: On the Discursive Limits of 'Sex'* (New York: Routledge, 1993), p. x.

2. Ibid., p. 226–7.

3. Ibid., p. 116.

4. Particularly within Dewey's discussion of existence versus essence, where the former are the metaphysically given. For more, see Jim Garrison, "What a Long Strange Trip Its Been, or, The Metaphysics of Presence: Derrida and Dewey on Human Development," *Philosophy of Education Society Yearbook* (2000), pp. 1–10, p. 4.

5. Gert Biesta and Nicholas C. Burbules, *Pragmatism and Educational Research* (Lanham, MD: Rowman and Littlefield, 2003), p. 26.

6. John Dewey, *Human Nature and Conduct* (Mineola, NY: Dover Publications, 2002), p. 141. All following references to this work refer to this publication, with one noted exception.

7. Judith Butler, *Excitable Speech: A Politics of the Performative* (New York: Routledge, 1997), p. 155.

8. Shannon Sullivan also notes similarities between impulse and bodily excess. Impulse, according to Sullivan, can't be the bodily excess because it can't meaningfully be separated from habit (using Dewey's scheme). I disagree. Impulse can be related to and not yet fully pinned down as habit, thereby serving as a firepoker to urge habits to organize or enact in new ways. Just because habit and impulse can't be fully separated doesn't mean impulse can't act as excess in certain moments. Rightly, however, Sullivan warns that this excess should not be viewed as outside of social performatives and habits, for this denies the transactional account of the subject's active remaking of itself. See *Living Across and Through Skins: Transactional Bodies, Pragmatism, and Feminism* (Bloomington: Indiana University Press, 2001), pp. 101–3.

9. Dewey, *Human Nature and Conduct*, in *The Middle Works of John Dewey*, vol. 14, ed. Jo Ann Boydston (Carbondale: Southern Illinois University Press, 1983), p. 21.

10. Biesta and Burbules, *Pragmatism and Educational Research*, p. 38.

11. Dewey, *Human Nature and Conduct*, p. 25.

12. Steven A. Fesmire, "Educating the Moral Artist: Dramatic Rehearsal in Moral Education," *Studies in Philosophy and Education* 13 (1995), p. 216.

13. Charlene Haddock Seigfried, *Pragmatism and Feminism* (Chicago: University of Chicago Press, 1996), p. 246. See also Dewey, *Democracy and Education* (New York: Macmillan, 1916), pp. 339–40.

14. Dewey, *Democracy and Education*, p. 48.

15. Dewey, *Human Nature and Conduct*, p. 52.

16. Ibid., p. 42.

17. John Dewey, *Experience and Education* (West Lafayette, IN: Kappa Delta Pi, 1938 [1998]), pp. 28, 40.

18. John Dewey, *Outlines of a Critical Theory of Ethics*, in *The Early Works of John Dewey*, vol. 3, ed. Jo Ann Boydston (Carbondale: Southern Illinois University Press, 1969), p. 305.

19. Judith Butler, *Gender Trouble* (New York: Routledge, 1990), p. 16.

20. Butler, *Excitable Speech*, pp. 155–6.

21. Butler, *Bodies that Matter*, p. 9.

22. Veronica Vasterling has issued such a critique in "Butler's Sophisticated Constructivism: A Critical Assessment," *Hypatia* 14 (1999), pp. 17–38, at p. 31.

23. Butler, *Excitable Speech*, p. 142.

24. Vasterling, "Butler's Sophisticated Constructivism," p. 28.

25. Ibid.

26. Dewey, *Human Nature and Conduct*, p. 166.

27. Butler, *Gender Trouble*, p. 148.

28. Lois McNay, "Subject, Psyche, and Agency: The Work of Judith Butler," *Theory, Culture & Society* 16 (1999), pp. 175–193, at p. 178.

29. Fraser in *Feminist Contentions*, ed. Seyla Benhabib, Judith Butler, Drucilla Cornell, and Nancy Fraser (New York: Routledge, 1995), p. 215.

30. Martha C. Nussbaum, "The Professor of Parody," *The New Republic* 220 (22 February 1999), pp. 37–45.

31. Butler warns against this in *Gender Trouble*, p. xxi.

32. It may even be the case in a strict reading, like that taken by Seyla Benhabib, that Butler's subject is so implicated in the language that constitutes him or her that s/he cannot reflect upon or change it. See Benhabib in *Feminist Contentions*, ed. Seyla Benhabib, Judith Butler, Drucilla Cornell, and Nancy Fraser (New York: Routledge, 1995).

33. Vasterling, "Butler's Sophisticated Constructivism," p. 26.

34. Barbara Applebaum also gets at this in "Social Justice Education, Moral Agency, and the Subject of Resistance," *Educational Theory* 54 (2004), pp. 59–72.

35. Robert Westbrook, *John Dewey and American Democracy* (Ithaca, NY: Cornell University Press, 1991), pp. 442–3, quoting from Dewey, "Is There Hope for Politics?" in *The Later Works of John Dewey*, vol. 6, ed. Jo Ann Boydston (Carbondale: Southern Illinois University Press, 1931), p. 188.

36. Dewey, *Democracy and Education*, pp. 215–6.

37. Applebaum, "Social Justice Education, Moral Agency, and the Subject of Resistance," pp. 68–70.

38. Westbrook, *John Dewey and American Democracy*, p. 508.

Sarah M. McGough
Doctoral Candidate
Educational Policy Studies and Gender and Women's Studies
University of Illinois
Champaign, Illinois 61820
United States

Contemporary Pragmatism
Vol. 2, No. 1 (June 2005), 203–210

Editions Rodopi
© 2005

Book Reviews

Sharyn Clough. *Beyond Epistemology: A Pragmatist Approach to Feminist Science Studies*. Lanham, MD: Rowman and Littlefield, 2003. Pp. viii + 167 pp. Cloth ISBN 0-7425-1464-1. Paper ISBN 0-7425-1465-X.

In this wide-ranging, forthright, and thought-provoking work, Sharyn Clough urges feminist science scholars to dispense with global epistemological projects and to return to "the empirical and fallibilistic assignment of warrant to individual theories." (16) On my view, the chief support for Clough's proposal is to be found in her last chapter, "A Pragmatist Case Study: Back to the Theory of Evolution." It is here that she presents a compelling sketch of the kind of "internal" criticism (120) that she is advocating. Accordingly, I would like to begin the body of this review by exploring her concluding analyses of biological function and the "pragmatist prescription" (143) that she derives from them.

Clough's discussion in this final chapter revolves around Margie Profet's controversial theory of menstruation. In contrast to the traditional view, which emphasizes menstruation's role in preparing the female reproductive tract for the implantation of a newly fertilized egg, Profet argues that menstruation is best understood as itself a naturally selected system that serves to defend against sperm-borne pathogens. On Clough's gloss, Profet's achievement is to have "described the function of menstruation in a way that newly synthesizes a variety of immunological and physiological research previously thought to be unrelated." (139)

In a manner reminiscent of Evelyn Fox Keller's treatment of Barbara McClintock's discovery of transposition, Clough is principally concerned to explain "why Profet's arguments for menstruation sound so revolutionary and why her work has largely been ignored in the scientific literature." (140) She begins by presenting an elegant and succinct account of what is involved in giving a biological mechanism a functional analysis, emphasizing that "to ascribe functional status to a mechanism is always relative to a number of pragmatic, or second-order, considerations about the systems within which that mechanism is situated." (132) Invoking Derek Turner's suggestion that functional ascriptions require the availability of familiar functional analogues,

Clough claims that "it is likely that human interests and cultural context will (and have) influenced what sort of analogues are available and salient." (133)

In its widest implications, this recognition of the influence of human interests suggests to Clough the need to undertake what she calls a "genealogical account" (136) of etiological explanations. To facilitate such an undertaking, she appeals to Nelson Goodman's analysis of confirmation, which she summarizes in the following way: "We decide that a theory or hypothesis is confirmed by its positive instances if the theory contains categories or predicates that our linguistic *practices* have allowed us to habitually 'project.' Projectible predicates, or hypotheses containing those predicates, are those that have been 'entrenched,' through practice or habit, in language use." (122–3) With specific respect to the neglect of Profet's theory in the scientific literature, Clough argues that this can be explained by the fact that Profet's theory lacks two of the three levels of entrenchment "required to get a functional account projected and subsequently tested." (144) That is, because sustained research interest in the defensive capabilities of the female reproductive tract is lacking, hypotheses concerning menstruation's role in thwarting sperm-borne pathogens are not yet "projectible." For Clough, understanding why this is the case is *the* obligation of the feminist science scholar. In her words, "Examinations of the historical context of particular sorts of masculine bias in biology and physiology (as elsewhere) might help answer how the pregnancy predicate came to be of interest – that is, how it came to be entrenched in physiology and biology – while the sperm-borne pathogen-defense predicate did not." (146)

This, then, is Clough's chief constructive recommendation for future feminist science scholarship: Narrow critical focus to how and why certain predicates have become entrenched in particular research programs. It is her conviction that doing so will allow feminist science scholars to stake a viable middle ground between a naïve, "objectivist," trust in "a correspondence relation between any given knowledge claim and the features of the world described by that claim" (8) and radical skepticism: "we'd be in pretty good shape to criticize the objectivist claim that certain biological systems, and functions within those systems, are 'naturally given.' At the same time we would be able to avoid the skepticism of the view that sexist scientists just 'make up' functions, or that our feminist prescriptions are merely relative to our feminist politics and/or free from evidential constraints." (146) For Clough, this is because this kind of "contrite fallibilism" (123) — and the holism that she maintains it implies — permits both confidence in the assumption that "most of the categories that we habitually project must successfully refer" (123) and warrant for a "flexible and dynamic" approach to these categories: "the categories can be refined, we can rethink their range of application, and over time, when necessary, we can discard them." (124) In concert with the narrowing of critical focus, such flexibility, Clough insists, will also allow feminist science scholars to escape "the problems of abstraction and the overgeneralizations that often inform our categories of analysis." (25) (She is particularly concerned with "references to science as if it were a monolithic, homogenous institution" (26) and generalizations about women and men that "often ignore important distinctions among women and among men." (27))

Because I regard it as the strength of her book, I have so far focused on the constructive recommendations that Clough makes. Indeed, my hope is that Clough herself will undertake a full-fledged genealogical analysis of the projectibility of the "pregnancy predicate" in future work. I turn now to her criticisms of what she calls the "epistemological" emphasis of much current feminist science scholarship. I am much less persuaded by this aspect of her project. This is largely because I have reservations about her appeal to the work of Donald Davidson, an appeal that motivates and shapes her critique. These misgivings are threefold. First, I think that it is a mistake to accept uncritically Davidson's account of the scheme/content distinction. Second, I think that this uncritical acceptance leads Clough to make procrustean readings of the work of Helen Longino and Lynn Hankinson Nelson. Third, I think that Davidsonian semantics gives us an unworkable theory of metaphor. This last is immediately troubling because Clough herself endorses research in the cognitive sciences on the nature of mental representation. (12) I regard exploration into the operations of what George Lakoff and Mark Johnson have called "conceptual" metaphor to be some of the most promising of this research. In the remainder of this review, I will set forth each of these reservations.

What sparks Clough's appeal to Davidson's work is her animating conviction that "It is no longer clear that a philosophical examination of truth, evidence, and/or method helps us identify and address those scientific practices that systematically disadvantage already marginalized peoples." (2) Her suspicion of the efficacy of such philosophical examination derives from her conception of the aim of epistemology as the solution to, or removal of, the worry that "our beliefs about the world may be just as they are, and yet the world — and so the truth about the world — may be very different." (10) On her view, then, epistemology is the project of "designing criteria for discriminating between competing knowledge claims" (7), criteria, moreover, that "must be independent from questions of gathering new evidence, as the nature of evidence is itself the issue of concern." (11) Understood in this way, the epistemological impulse is thus directed against the threat of conceptual relativism (what Clough calls global skepticism). As such, epistemologists must assume a meaningful distinction between scheme and content, which Clough, following Davidson, describes in the following way: "The objects in our physical environment are said to be sensed (this is the sense data or content) and then screened through our subjective perceptual frameworks (the filtering scheme of our political values, worldview, and/or language)." (12)

Davidson maintains that the scheme/content distinction is untenable and that the idea of rival or alternative conceptual schemes is nonsensical. As Ron Bombardi delineates Davidson's position, "the focus of his argument is not on the idea of incommensurable theories *per se*. Rather it is on the claim that two or more theories can be both competitors *and* fail to share a common referential apparatus, a common conceptual scheme." (1988, 69) According to Bombardi, Davidson's argument proceeds as follows: "Davidson first proposes that we 'accept the doctrine that associates having a language with having a conceptual scheme.' Secondly, he suggests that we 'say that two people have different conceptual schemes if they speak languages that fail of inter-translatability.' Finally, he offers to demonstrate, apriori, that in fact there never can be grounds for concluding that two people speak nonintertranslatable languages." (Ibid.) The gist of Davidson's demonstration of this last is his insistence that, unless we can translate a great deal of another's utterances, we have no right to assume that she is even speaking a language. As Clough notes in her discussion of Davidson's conceit of the "radical" interpreter, "Davidson's claim amounts to the point that for interpretation to begin, the radical interpreter must initially assume that the same relationship between truth and belief holds between those she is interpreting as it does for herself." (118) But, as Bombardi points out, Davidson's argument only establishes the following: "The warrant offered in support of this premise [that there can never be grounds for supposing that two people speak languages that fail of *inter*-translatability], however, allows the speaker *S* of *L* to determine that *S'* speaks *L'* provided only that *S can translate what S' says into L*. Nothing in this subargument requires that *S'* be able to translate utterances from *L* into *L'*." (1988, 70) That is, Davidson's argument hinges upon the unsubstantiated assumption that translatability is necessarily a symmetrical relation. In Bombardi's words, "Unless it is buttressed by this assumption, Davidson's criterion of languagehood is insufficient to warrant any wholesale rejection of relativism." (1988, 71) Most importantly, there *are* cases of asymmetric translation; for example, though we can translate the Roman numeral system into the Arabic one, "a systematic sort of nontranslatability will encumber all Arabic-to-Roman translation manuals because zero makes possible the number line and with it a conception of number that is entirely foreign to the Latin language" (1988, 72). It follows that Davidson's attempted dissolution of conceptual relativism fails. And, if so, there is thus still a need for what Clough characterizes as the (feminist) "specification of normative criteria — either apriori or through a naturalized, scientific account of human cognition — that would indicate truth, least partiality, or maximal objectivity." (9)

I turn now to a related concern. Clough's allegiance to the Davidsonian claim that all epistemological projects must assume a problematic scheme/ content distinction results in her presenting highly skewed readings of Helen Longino and Lynn Hankinson Nelson's work. In particular, I think that Clough's parsing of Longino's central conception of background beliefs as gendered "filters" (12) is simply wrong. For Longino, a background belief is one element in "a picture of scientific inquiry in which models and theories are adapted/legitimated through critical processes involving the dynamic interplay of observational and experimental data and background assumptions." (1990, 13) This is because background beliefs concern "regularities discovered, believed, or assumed to hold." (1990, 45) In this way, they are what allow us to take a given state of affairs as evidence for a particular hypothesis. To be sure, some of our background beliefs concern the issue of gender — for example, our association of femininity with passivity and masculinity with activity — but not all of them do. Instead, "the background belief is an enabling condition of the reasoning process in much the same way that environmental and other conditions enable the occurrence of causal interactions." (1990, 44) Likewise, I think that Clough's attempts to distinguish her constructive project from Nelson's radicalized feminist empiricism turn on a too hasty endorsement of Davidson's controversial interpretation of Quine's holism as incomplete. That is, Clough follows Davidson in charging Quine with "making the questionable assumption that there is a meaningful epistemological distinction between unanalyzed sensory cues and one's worldview or analysis of those cues." (36) On my reading of Quine's work, however, his notions of stimulus meaning and observation sentence are unpacked in terms of speakers' behavior (especially assent) and so are much closer to Davidson's own conception of occasion sentences. Clough's recommendations are much closer to Nelson's (radicalized Quinean) position than she realizes.

Lastly, and more briefly, I question the utility of Davidsonian semantics for science criticism because I think that the view of metaphor derived from his semantics offers no resources for addressing the constitutive role of metaphor in scientific inference. (Following the lead of philosophers of science as otherwise diverse as Kuhn, Hesse, Harding, and Keller, I regard this as a pressing task for science criticism.) As is well known, Davidson's view of meaning is extensionalist or truth-conditional. On Clough's gloss, "in the simplest cases of beliefs — that is, those expressed in occasion sentences — the events and objects that cause those beliefs (the *extension* of those beliefs) also determine their contents or meaning (the *intension* of those beliefs." (107) What this implies is that all metaphors, for Davidson, mean only what the sentence used to express them means in its literal sense. Consequently, most metaphorical utterances are (literally) false. Nonetheless, Davidson claims that metaphors function to (somehow) direct our attention to neglected features of our environment. (1978, 441, 444) As Mark Johnson puts it, "On Davidson's view a metaphorical utterance is essentially a stick (consisting of a literal sentence) that one uses to hit another person, so that they will see or notice something. Davidson has *no account whatever* of how it is that the literal sentence used is in any way connected up with what the hearer comes to notice." (1987, 72)

My objective in this review has been two-pronged: (1) to laud Clough's constructive recommendations for future feminist science scholarship, especially her arguments for the value of narrowing critical focus and for flexibility in the categories of our analysis, and (2) to question the merit of her (Davidsonian inspired) criticisms of feminist epistemological projects. Yet, regardless of my reservations about the critical aspect of her project, I nonetheless have found engaging with Clough's arguments to be very stimulating.

REFERENCES

Bombardi, Ron. (1988) "Davidson in Flatland." *Australasion Journal of Philosophy* 66, 66–74.

Davidson, Donald. (1978) "What Metaphors Mean," repr. in *The Philosophy of Language*, 4th edn., ed. A. P. Martinich (New York: Oxford University Press, 2001), pp. 435–446.

Johnson, Mark. (1987) *The Body in the Mind* (Chicago: University of Chicago Press).

Longino, Helen. (1990) *Science as Social Knowledge* (Princeton, NJ: Princeton University Press).

Mary Magada-Ward
Middle Tennessee State University

Hugh P. McDonald. *John Dewey and Environmental Philosophy.* Albany: State University of New York Press, 2004. Pp. xix + 227. Cloth ISBN 0-7914-5873-3. Paper ISBN 0-7914-5874-1.

There are two driving and related questions in environmental ethics which are sometimes made explicit, though the answers to each are very often assumed and hidden. First, what constitutes sufficient environmental protection? Second, what features must an environmental ethic include or exclude if it is to afford sufficient environmental protection? It is a commonly held position among environmental philosophers that pragmatism in general, and the philosophy of John Dewey in particular, fails to answer either of these questions satisfactorily. Hugh P. McDonald endeavors to show in *John Dewey and Environmental Philosophy* that the philosophy of Dewey can with very little alteration be made into a sound environmental ethic. McDonald argues that Dewey "reconstructs" rather than rejects the notion of intrinsic value in nature, and that his moral holism provides a nonanthropocentric justification for an environmental ethic insofar as human beings are in nature and depend for their very existence upon the environment they are obligated to care for it, and to so care for its sake, not the advantage of so caring to them.

McDonald devotes the first chapter "Environmental Ethics and Intrinsic Value," to a presentation and analysis of the concept of intrinsic value in the work of some leading environmental philosophers, namely, Tom Regan, J. Baird Callicott, and Holmes Rolston, III. Though the connection with the rest of the book is not immediately clear, McDonald manages to give a thorough, though at times repetitive, presentation of some intricate and frequently obscure philosophical positions. McDonald is never explicit about his answer to the two questions stated above. In answer to the second question, like many environmental philosophers, he assumes that a notion of intrinsic value and nonanthropocentrism are necessary conditions for an adequate environmental ethic, ands so throughout the book he reads Dewey in this way. As regards intrinsic value, McDonald argues in the third chapter "Dewey's Instrumentalism," that Dewey does not reject the notion of intrinsic value; rather, Dewey's task is one of "... refining rather than abandoning the notion. Dewey does not deny the relation; on the contrary he incorporates it after critically qualifying it, that is, he transforms it." (91) McDonald argues that value is an intrinsic quality of actions and things on Dewey's view. The objective features of either a course of action or those of a thing acted upon are inherent in those things as its bearer "... [t]his is because the quality must be a quality of something *as* a quality." (96)

Dewey's reconstruction of intrinsic value is far from what is meant by many of the environmental philosophers who employ the concept. Intrinsic value in the hands of Regan, Callicott, and Rolston alike is the ready-made possession of either individual organisms, wholes, such as species and ecosystems or both individual organisms and wholes. Dewey argues against the idea that intrinsic value is an end "in itself" which is final or complete. On Dewey's account, ends can be separated neither from means, nor from future ends, in relation to which they will become means. Dewey understands all ends as either requiring continuous activity or as serving a double function as both an end to present activity and means to still further activity. The difficulties associated with reading Dewey as an advocate of intrinsic value theories could have been avoided by McDonald if not for his failure to recognize his presuppositions about the correct answers to the questions I posed at the beginning. McDonald assumes that any environmental ethic which does not include a notion of intrinsic value cannot afford adequate environmental protection. His task then becomes one of making Dewey's philosophy appear to have this presumably indispensable feature of an environmental ethic, even though the similarities of Dewey's conception to that of say Regan, Callicott, or Rolston are in name only.

This is not the only case of McDonald failing to recognize common presuppositions and subsequently missing the opportunity to make a creative and imaginative contribution to the field. He treats nonanthropocentrism as an essential feature of a viable environmental ethic. Rather than challenging this presupposition, McDonald seems to accept it. He frequently attempts to portray Dewey's thought as nonanthropocentric, but such a reading of Dewey is incorrect. On McDonald's reading of Dewey, the good of individual organisms is subordinated to the good of the species as a whole. He writes: "[t]he value of individuals of a species could be treated as morally considerable but not obligatory. (134) He further argues that if some number of individuals need be sacrificed to promote the good of the species those individuals ought to be sacrificed. If in fact Dewey's ethics is nonanthropocentric, then the same must be true in the case of human beings. That is, if the health of the human species requires the sacrifice of individual members, those members ought to be sacrificed. But Dewey certainly would not endorse such a view with regard to human beings as is evidenced by his article entitled "The Ethics of Animal Experimentation" (1926) in which he advocates the use of animals in scientific and medical experimentation, but not the use of human beings. Dewey then, or McDonald on his behalf, is hard pressed to offer a justification for why such treatment is acceptable in the case of nonhuman animals, but impermissible with regard to human beings, which does not privilege the human species over nonhuman species. If he cannot, then he must give up the claim that Dewey's ethic is nonanthropocentric. This difficulty arises because McDonald bought into a presupposition prevalent in much of the contemporary work done in environmental philosophy, namely, the belief that it is not possible to construct an anthropocentric environmental ethic which will provide sufficient environmental protection.

Aside from the questionable attribution of intrinsic value and nonanthropocentrism to Dewey's philosophy as an environmental ethic, McDonald's book is an important catalyst to a continued examination of pragmatism, and Dewey in particular, in environmental ethics.

Jacoby Adeshei Carter
Purdue University